BUZZ BOOKS 2016
FALL/WINTER

BUZZ BOOKS 2016
FALL/WINTER

EXCLUSIVE EXCERPTS FROM 40 TOP NEW TITLES

Publishers Lunch

INGRAM

CREDITS

Publishers Lunch has been the "daily essential read" for the book publishing business for sixteen years, and is the largest-circulation news communication in the world for publishing professionals. Publishers Marketplace is the web site associated with Publishers Lunch, providing round-the-clock news and analysis, deal reports, job listings, and many unique databases and tools that help publishing professionals find critical information, connect with each other, and do business better electronically.

Bookateria, is a giant online book discovery store driven by an "industry insider's" view. Our focus is books making news and building buzz, as we tap into our comprehensive coverage of the books and authors that booksellers, editors, agents, rights-buyers, reviewers and others are talking about. Our own staff catalogs "buzz books" that the industry is touting as new discoveries of note, and some of the other featured Bookateria lists draw on recommendations from a variety of booksellers and bellwether award nominations to connect avid readers everywhere to great reads.

Publishers Lunch
2 Park Place, #4
Bronxville, NY 10708
Information@publishersmarketplace.com
www.publishersmarketplace.com

Michael Cader, Founder

Robin Dellabough, Projects Director

Michael Macrone, Chief Technology Officer

Sarah Weinman, Senior Editor

Kathy Smith, Editor

Cover design by Charles Kreloff

Distribution and printing by Ingram

Typesetting by Julie Ink

Ebook development by Brady Type

buzz.publishersmarketplace.com

Thanks to our publishing partner:

Ingram Content Group is the world's largest and most trusted distributor of physical and digital content. Our mission is helping content reach its destination. Thousands of publishers, retailers, libraries, and educators worldwide use our products and services to realize the full business potential of books, regardless of format. Ingram has earned its lead position and reputation by offering excellent service and building innovative, integrated print and digital distribution solutions. Our customers have access to best-of-class digital, audio, print, print on demand, inventory management, wholesale and full-service distribution programs.

CONTENTS

INTRODUCTION	11
THE FALL/WINTER 2016 PUBLISHING PREVIEW	12
BUZZ BOOKS AUTHORS APPEARING AT BOOKEXPO AMERICA	25
EXCERPTS BY PUBLISHER	26
ABOUT NETGALLEY	28

PART ONE: FICTION

Christina Baker Kline CHRISTINA'S WORLD (William Morrow)	31
Marie Benedict THE OTHER EINSTEIN (Sourcebooks Landmark)	41
T.C. Boyle THE TERRANAUTS (Ecco)	59
Suzanne Chazin NO WITNESS BUT THE MOON (Kensington)	85
Sonali Dev A CHANGE OF HEART (Kensington)	103
Andrew Gross THE ONE MAN (Minotaur Books)	117
Patrick Hoffman EVERY MAN A MENACE (Atlantic Monthly Press)	137
Pam Jenoff THE ORPHAN'S TALE (Mira Books)	149
Paulette Jiles NEWS OF THE WORLD (William Morrow)	161
Shari Lapena THE COUPLE NEXT DOOR (Pamela Dorman Books)	173
Margot Livesey MERCURY (Harper)	193
Rae Meadows I WILL SEND RAIN (Henry Holt)	219
Ann Patchett COMMONWEALTH (Harper)	231

Steven Price
BY GASLIGHT (Farrar, Straus and Giroux) — 261

Shanthi Sekaran
LUCKY BOY (Putnam) — 277

Maria Semple
TODAY WILL BE DIFFERENT (Little, Brown and Company) — 299

Marisa Silver
LITTLE NOTHING (Blue Rider Press) — 311

Amor Towles
A GENTLEMAN IN MOSCOW (Viking) — 331

PART TWO: DEBUT FICTION

Brit Bennett
THE MOTHERS (Riverhead Books) — 343

Jade Chang
THE WANGS VS. THE WORLD (Houghton Mifflin Harcourt) — 361

Emily Fridlund
HISTORY OF WOLVES (Atlantic Monthly Press) — 371

Stephanie Gangi
THE NEXT (St. Martin's Press) — 381

Nathan Hill
THE NIX (Alfred A. Knopf) — 401

Tasha Kavanagh
THINGS WE HAVE IN COMMON (Mira Books) — 423

Affinity Konar
MISCHLING (Lee Boudreaux Books) — 433

Forrest Leo
THE GENTLEMAN (Penguin Press) — 449

Elan Mastai
ALL OUR WRONG TODAYS (Dutton) — 461

Teresa Messineo
THE FIRE BY NIGHT (William Morrow) — 475

Meg Little Reilly
WE ARE UNPREPARED (Mira Books) — 497

Helen Sedgwick
THE COMET SEEKERS (Harper) — 517

Anna Snoekstra
ONLY DAUGHTER (Mira Books) — 531

PART THREE: NONFICTION

Lauren Collins
WHEN IN FRENCH (Penguin Press)   547

Elizabeth Lesser
MARROW (Harper Wave)   571

Beth Macy
TRUEVINE (Little, Brown and Company)   589

Sharon Moalem
THE DNA RESTART (Rodale)   607

Anne Sebba
LES PARISIENNES:
HOW THE WOMEN OF PARIS LIVED, LOVED,
AND DIED UNDER NAZI OCCUPATION (St. Martin's Press)   637

Margot Lee Shetterly
HIDDEN FIGURES (William Morrow)   647

Karen Stabiner
GENERATION CHEF (Avery)   661

iO Tillett-Wright
DARLING DAYS (Ecco)   677

Mara Wilson
WHERE AM I NOW? (Penguin Books)   701

Copyright   725

INTRODUCTION

For book lovers there is almost nothing better than getting your hands on an early look at the next big thing from favorite authors and hot new discoveries. This latest collection of *Buzz Books* gives you 40 chances to find your own great reads.

From beloved, bestselling authors, we have pre-publication samples of new work from Ann Patchett (*Commonwealth*), Andrew Gross (*The One Man*), T.C. Boyle (*The Terranauts*), Marisa Silver (*Little Nothing*) and others—plus the highly anticipated "next book" from Amor Towles following *Rules of Civility*, Maria Semple following *Where'd You Go, Bernadette*, and Christina Baker Kline following *Orphan Train*.

This new edition features thirteen big debuts, including the highly-touted *The Mothers* by Britt Bennett; *The Nix* by Nathan Hill; and *All Our Wrong Todays* by Elan Mastai; plus first novels of distinction from Jade Chang, Emily Fridlund, Stephanie Gangi, Affinity Konar, Forrest Leo, and Shanti Sekharan.

In nonfiction, there are early looks at world-renowned neurogeneticist Dr. Sharon Moalem's *The DNA Restart*, a regimen for a diet and lifestyle matched to your genetic make-up; Margot Shetterly's *Hidden Figures*, the untold true story of the African-American female mathematicians at NASA who provided the calculations that helped fuel some of America's greatest achievements in space; and iO Tillett-Wright's *Darling Days*, a coming of age memoir, at the intersection of punk, poverty, heroin, and art on New York's Lower East Side.

Regular readers know that each *Buzz Books* collection features early looks at titles that will go on to top the bestseller lists and critics' "best of the year" lists. And our comprehensive seasonal preview starts the book off with a curated overview of hundreds of notable books on the way later this year.

While *Buzz Books* feels like your own secret door inside book publishing, these collections are meant to be shared, so spread your enthusiasm and "to be read" lists online. For still more great previews, check out our separate *Buzz Books 2016: Young Adult Fall/Winter*. And if you're a fan of romance, we have exciting news: look for our very first *Buzz Books 2016: Romance* this July.

Visit buzz.publishersmarketplace.com for complete download links, lists and more.

Michael Cader
May 2016

THE FALL/WINTER 2016 PUBLISHING PREVIEW

It's another exciting season of new books ahead. Readers will find their way to many of the books previewed here and others yet to be discovered. To help you sift through the many thousands of fall and winter titles, we've selected what we think are among the most noteworthy literary, commercial, and breakout titles for adults, separated into five key categories.

You'll be able to sample many of the highlighted titles right now in *Buzz Books 2016: Fall/Winter*; they are noted with an asterisk. And please note: because we prepare this preview many months in advance, titles, content, and publication dates are all subject to change.

FICTION

Publishers normally save their most prominent literary titles for the fall, and this season is not lacking in notable names, with new books from Zadie Smith, Jonathan Safran Foer, Colson Whitehead, Ann Patchett and Michael Chabon, as well as sophomore efforts from Amor Towles, and more. Look out, too, for emerging voices such as such as Marcy Dermansky, Alexandra Kleeman, Rae Meadows, and Kathleen Collins.

The Notables

Margaret Atwood, *The Hag-Seed* (Hogarth, October)—the latest Hogarth Shakespeare installment

*T.C. Boyle, *The Terranauts* (Ecco, November)

Anne Carson, *Float* (Knopf, October)—stories and more from the renowned poet

Michael Chabon, *Moonglow* (Harper, November)

E.L. Doctorow, *Collected Stories* (Random House, November)—posthumous collection from the award-winning novelist

Emma Donoghue, *The Wonder* (Little, Brown, October)

Jonathan Safran Foer, *Here I Am* (FSG, September)—his first novel in 11 years, a mix of family and global drama

Alice Hoffman, *Faithful* (S&S, November)

Ha Jin, *The Boat Rocker* (Pantheon, October)

Jonathan Lethem, *A Gambler's Anatomy* (Doubleday, October)

Javier Marias, *Thus Bad Begins* (Knopf, November)

*Ann Patchett, *Commonwealth* (Harper, October)

Francine Prose, *Mister Monkey* (Harper, October)

Ron Rash, *The Risen* (Ecco, September)

*Maria Semple, *Today Will Be Different* (Little, Brown, October)—new from the author of *Where'd You Go, Bernadette*

Zadie Smith, *Swing Time* (Penguin Press, November)

Rose Tremain, *The Gustav Sonata* (Norton, October)

Colson Whitehead, *The Underground Railroad* (Doubleday, September)

Highly Anticipated

Aravind Adiga, *Selection Day* (Scribner, January)

Laura Dave, *Hello Sunshine* (S&S, January)

Marcy Dermansky, *The Red Car* (Liveright, October)—new from the author of *Bad Marie*

Louise Doughty, *Black Water* (Sarah Crichton Books, September)

Ward Just, *The Eastern Shore* (HMH, October)

*Christina Baker Kline, *Christina's World* (William Morrow, February) –about the iconic Andrew Wyeth painting "Christina's World" from a *New York Times* bestselling novelist

Herman Koch, *Dear Mr. M* (Hogarth, September)

James Lasdun, *The Fall Guy* (Norton, October)

*Margot Livesey, *Mercury* (Harper, September)

Richard Mason, *Who Killed Piet Barol?* (Knopf, January)

Eimear McBride, *The Lesser Bohemians* (Hogarth, September)—the sophomore effort from the author of *A Girl is a Half-Formed Thing*

Jonathan Rabb, *Among the Living* (Other Press October)

*Marisa Silver, *Little Nothing* (Blue Rider, September)

Steve Stern, *The Pinch* (Graywolf, September)

*Amor Towles, *A Gentleman in Moscow* (Viking, October)

Nell Zink, *Nicotine* (Ecco, October)

Nell Zink, *Private Novelist: Fiction* (Ecco, October)

Emerging Voices

Matt Bell, *A Tree or a Person or a Wall* (Soho, September)

Kathleen Collins, *Whatever Happened to Interracial Love?* (Ecco, December)

Peter Ho Davies, *Tell It Slant* (HMH, September)

Alexandra Kleeman, *Intimations: Stories* (Harper, September)

Andrew Krivak, *The Signal Flame* (Scribner, January)

Joe McGinniss, Jr., *Carousel Court* (S&S, September)

Graham Moore, *The Last Days of Night* (S&S, September)—from the Oscar-winning screenwriter and author

*Rae Meadows, *I Will Send Rain* (Holt, August)

*Steven Price, *By Gaslight* (FSG, October)

David Szalay, *All That Man Is* (Graywolf, October)

Juan Gabriel Vasquez, *Reputations* (Riverhead)—new from the author of *The Sound of Things Falling*

Teddy Wayne, *Loner* (S&S, September)

And Also

Charles Burns, *Last Look* (Pantheon, October)—his latest graphic novel

Alan Moore, *Jerusalem* (Liveright, September)—a new literary work from the notable comics artist and graphic novelist

DEBUT FICTION

Fall and winter are generally designated for major literary titles, but there's still plenty of room for new authors. We expect great things from debuts by Brit Bennett, Nathan Hill, Emily Fridlund, and Jade Chang, and to hear similar plaudits about new works by Emma Flint, Elan Mastai, Affinity Konar, and many more listed below.

*Brit Bennett, *The Mothers* (Riverhead, October)

*Jade Chang, *The Wangs Vs. the World* (HMH, October)

Sarah Domet, *The Guineveres* (Flatiron, October)

Kathleen Donohoe, *Ashes of Fiery Winter* (HMH, August)

Melanie Finn, *The Gloaming* (Two Dollar Radio, September)—debut from a journalist and filmmaker

Emma Flint, *Little Deaths* (Hachette Books, January)—fictionalized version of the Alice Crimmins case

*Emily Fridlund, *History of Wolves* (Grove/Atlantic, September)

*Stephanie Gangi, *The Next* (St. Martin's, October)

Jane Harper, *The Dry* (Flatiron, September)—highly touted debut from Australia

*Nathan Hill, *The Nix* (Knopf, September)

Joe Ide, *IQ* (Mulholland, October)—debut thriller

*Affinity Konar, *Mischling* (Lee Boudreaux Books, September)

*Forrest Leo, *The Gentleman* (Penguin Press, August)

Kelly Luce, *Pull Me Under* (FSG, November)

*Elan Mastai, *All Our Wrong Todays* (Dutton, January)

Amy Poeppel, *Small Admissions* (Atria, January)—debut expanded from award-winning play

Emily Robbins, *A Word for Love* (Riverhead, January)

Adelia Saunders, *Indelible* (Bloomsbury, January)

*Shanthi Sekharan, *Lucky Boy* (Putnam, October)

Kea Wilson, *We Eat Our Own* (Scribner, August)

COMMERCIAL FICTION

Our sampler alone is full of great commercial titles from Paulette Jiles, Andrew Gross, and Shari Lapena. Keep an eye out in particular for the newest suspense novel by Tana French; Thomas Mullen's thriller series kickoff, set in 1948 Atlanta; and much more.

Jeffrey Archer, *This Was a Man* (St. Martin's, November)

David Baldacci, *No Man's Land* (Grand Central, November)

*Marie Benedict, *The Other Einstein* (Sourcebooks, September)

Benjamin Black, *Golden Lane* (Holt, November)—the newest crime novel from John Banville's alter ego

Lee Child, *Night School* (Delacorte, November)

Harlan Coben, *Home* (Dutton, September)

Michael Connelly, *The Wrong Side of Goodbye* (Little, Brown, November)

Patricia Cornwell, *Chaos* (William Morrow, November)

Nick Cutter, *Little Heaven* (Gallery, January)

Janet Evanovich, *Turbo Twenty-Three* (Ballantine, November)

Tana French, *The Trespasser* (Viking, October)

Mark Frost, *The Secret History of Twin Peaks* (Flatiron, October)—tie-in to the new series, 25 years later

John Grisham, *The Whistler* (Doubleday, October)—the newest best-selling legal thriller

Jessica Grose, *Soulmates* (William Morrow, September)

*Andrew Gross, *The One Man* (Minotaur, August)

Sophie Hannah, *The Closed Casket: The New Hercule Poirot Novel* (William Morrow, September)

Charlaine Harris, *All the Little Liars* (Minotaur, October)

Mette Ivie Harrison, *For Time and All Enemies* (Soho, January)

Rob Hart, *South Village* (Polis, October)

Carl Hiassen, *Razor Girl* (Knopf, September)

Elin Hilderbrand, *Winter Storms* (Little, Brown, October)

Amanda Hocking, *Freeks* (St. Martin's, January)

Chris Holm, *Red Right Hand* (Mulholland, September)

*Paulette Jiles, *News of the World* (William Morrow, November)

Erika Johansen, *The Fate of the Tearling* (Harper, November)

Faye Kellerman, *Killing Season* (William Morrow, November)

*Shari Lapena, *The Couple Next Door* (Pamela Dorman Books, August)

Greer McAllister, *The Girl in Disguise* (Sourcebooks Landmark, March)

Jennifer McVeigh, *As Darkness Falls* (Putnam, January)

Derek B. Miller, *The Girl in Green* (HMH, January)

Jojo Moyes, *Paris for One and Other Stories* (Pamela Dorman Books, September)

Thomas Mullen, *Darktown* (37INK, September)

Stuart Neville, *So Say the Fallen* (Soho, September)

Carol O'Connell, *Blind Sight* (Putnam, September)—the next Mallory novel

Carolyn Parkhurst, *Harmony* (Pamela Dorman Books, August)

James Patterson, *Cross the Line* (Little, Brown, October)

Louise Penny, *A Great Reckoning* (Minotaur, August)

Jodi Picoult, *Small Great Things* (Ballantine, October)

Douglas Preston and Lincoln Child, *The Obsidian Chamber* (Grand Central, November)

Ransom Riggs, *Tales of the Particular* (Putnam, October)

John Sandford, *Escape Clause* (Putnam, October)

Karin Slaughter, *The Kept Woman* (William Morrow, September)

Martin Cruz Smith, *The Girl From Venice* (S&S, November)

Amy Stewart, *Lady Cop Makes Trouble* (HMH, Septemsber)

Anna Todd, *Nothing Less* (Gallery, December)

NONFICTION

Start your conversations in the fall and winter with new books by Thomas Friedman, Barton Gellman, Jessica Bennett, Nicholas Carr, Amy Schumer and many more across an array of nonfiction categories. And with the presidential election imminent, politics and current events are bursting with new titles.

Politics & Current Events

George Borjas, *We Wanted Workers* (Norton, October)—unraveling the American immigration narrative

Joe Conason, *Man of the World* (S&S, September)—another biography of Bill Clinton

Angela Davis, *Policing the Black Man* (Pantheon, January)

The Dalai Lama, Desmond Tutu, and Douglas Carlton Abrams, *The Book of Joy: Lasting Happiness in a Changing World* (Avery, October)

Bartow Elmore, *Citizen Coke* (Norton, December)—capitalism as seen through the prism of Coca-Cola

Thomas Friedman, *Thank You For Being Late* (FSG, November)—the latest book by the NYT columnist

Barton Gellman, *Dark Mirror* (Penguin Press, September)—on Edward Snowden and the surveillance state

Andrew Harding, *The Mayor of Mogadishu* (St. Martin's, November)

DJ Khaled, *The Keys: They Don't Want You to Read This Book* (Crown Archetype, September)

Wesley Lowery, *They Can't Kill Us All* (Little, Brown, November)—on the Black Lives Matter movement

Per Molander, *The Anatomy of Inequality* (Melville House, August)

Joshua Partlow, *A Kingdom of Their Own* (Knopf, October)—on the Karzai family and the ongoing Afghan war

David Wood, *What Have We Done* (Little, Brown, November)—on the moral quandary of endless wars

Lawrence Wright, *The Terror Years* (Knopf, August)—examining Al-Qaeda and the Islamic State

Gary Younge, *A Day in the Death of America* (Nation Books, October)—centers around a single day and the murders committed in that 24-hour period

Social Issues
Nicholson Baker, *Substitute* (Blue Rider, September)—the celebrated novelist goes back to school

Jessica Bennett, *Feminist Fight Club* (Harper, September)

Paul Bloom, *Against Empathy* (Ecco, December)—the case for rational compassion

*Lauren Collins, *When in French* (Penguin Press, September)—on the love of learning a new language

Sady Doyle, *Trainwreck* (Melville House, September)

Alexandra Horowitz, *Being a Dog* (Scribner, October)

Kat Kinsman, *Hi, Anxiety* (Dey Street, August)—on life with a very bad case of nerves

Cleve Jones, *When We Rise* (Hachette Books, October)—coming of age in San Francisco at the height of AIDS

*Anne Sebba, *Les Parisiennes* (St. Martin's, October)

Jonathan Starr, *It Takes a School* (Holt, September)—how a hedge fund manager started a school in Somaliland

Jeremiah Tower and Libby VanderPloeg, *Table Manners* (FSG, October)—how to behave in the modern world (and why you should bother)

Ruth Whippman, *America the Anxious* (St. Martin's, October)—how our pursuit of happiness leads to the exact opposite

Emily Witt, *Future Sex* (FSG, October)—on the contemporary climate of sex and more

Science & Technology
Jim Al-Khalili, *Aliens* (Picador, November)—leading scientists comment on the search for extraterrestrial life

Nicholas Carr, *Utopia is Creepy* (Norton, September)—new from the author of *The Shallows*

Paul Ford, *The Secret Lives of Web Pages* (FSG, January)

David France, *How to Survive a Plague* (Knopf, January)—the inside story of how citizens and science tamed AIDS

James Gleick, *Time Travel* (Pantheon, September)—a subversive exploration of this mind-bending topic

Tim Harford, *Messy* (Riverhead, October)—on the power of disorder to transform our lives

Joi Ito and Jeff Howe, *Whiplash* (Grand Central, September)—rules for surviving a faster future

Steven Johnson, *How We Got To Now, Book Two* (Riverhead, October)

Tracy Kidder, *A Truck Full of Money* (Random House, September)

Daniel Levitin, *A Field Guide to Lies* (Dutton, September)

Mike Massimino, *Spaceman* (Crown Archetype, October)—reflections from a former astronaut

Cathy O'Neil, *Weapons of Math Destruction* (Crown, September)—how big data increases inequality and threatens democracy

Lesa Cline-Ransome and James Ransome, *Germs* (Holt, January)

Geno Segre, *The Pope of Physics* (Holt, November)—on Enrico Fermi and the birth of the atomic age

Caitlin Shetterly, *Modified* (Putnam, September)—on the dangers of GMOs to food, land, and future

*Margot Lee Shetterly, *Hidden Figures* (William Morrow, December)—the story of the African-American women who helped win the space race

Daniel Siegel, *Mind* (Norton, November)—a journey to the heart of being human

Dava Sobel, *The Glass Universe* (Viking, November)—on a little-known group of women who made important contributions to astronomy

Sylvia Tara, *The Secret Life of Fat* (Norton, December)

Tim Wu, *The Attention Merchants* (Knopf, October)

History and Crime

Tyler Anbinder, *City of Dreams* (HMH, October)—400-year history of immigrant New York City

H.W. Brands, *The General vs. the President* (Doubleday, November)—on MacArthur and Roosevelt

Ethan Brown, *Murder in the Bayou* (Scribner, September)—a look at the "Jeff Davis 8" case

Margaret Creighton, *The Electrifying Fall of Rainbow City* (Norton, November)—murder at the 1901 World's Fair

Colin Dickey, *Ghostland* (Viking, October)—an American history of haunted places

Robert Gerwarth, *The Vanquished* (FSG, November)—why the first World War failed to end

Elizabeth Letts, *The Perfect Horse* (Ballantine, September)—the quest to rescue a horse kidnapped by Nazis

Joseph Llelyveld, *His Final Battle* (Knopf, September)—the last years of Franklin Delano Roosevelt

Andrew Lownie, *Stalin's Englishman* (St. Martin's, October)—on Guy Burgess and the Campbride spy ring

Beverly Lowry, *Who Killed These Girls?* (Knopf, October)—a look at the unsolved Yogurt Shop Murders

*Beth Macy, *Truevine* (Little, Brown, October)—a true story of the Jim Crow South

William Mann, *The Wars of the Roosevelts* (Harper, December)

Albert Marrin, *Uprooted* (Knopf, October)—the Japanese-American experience during World War II

Ben Mezrich, *The 37th Parallel* (Atria, September)—on "the secret truth" of America's UFO highway

Candice Millard, *Hero of the Empire* (Doubleday, September)—on the Boer War and the making of Winston Churchill

Craig Nelson, *Pearl Harbor: From Infamy to Greatness* (Scribner, October)

David Olshinsky, *Bellevue* (Doubleday, September)—Three centuries of stories about the infamous New York City hospital

Danny Orbach, *The Plots Against Hitler* (HMH, October)

Patrick Phillips, *Blood at the Root* (Norton, September)—on a previously little-known lynching

Joy Santlofer and Marion Nestle, *Food City* (Norton, September)—on four centuries of food-making in New York

Willard Sterne Randall, *1814: America Forged by Fire* (Liveright, September)

Heather Ann Thompson, *Blood in the Water* (Pantheon, August)—a history of the 1971 Attica prison uprising

Volker Ulhrich, *Hitler: Ascent, 1889-1939* (Knopf, September)

John Edgar Weideman, *The Louis Till File* (Scribner, November)—on Emmett Till and the dark past of his father, Louis

Ronald C. White Jr., *American Ulysses* (Random House, October)—a life of Ulysses S. Grant

Essays, Criticism, and More
Sophia Amoruso, *Nasty Galaxy* (Putnam, October)—from the NYT bestselling author of #GIRLBOSS

Luvvie Ajayi, *I'm Judging You* (Holt, September)—hilarious advice from the AwesomelyLuvvie.com blogger

Jodie Archer and Matthew L. Jockers, *The Bestseller Code* (St. Martin's, September)—on the anatomy of the bestselling novel

Dave Barry, *Best. State. Ever.* (Putnam, September)—the Florida columnist defends his home state

David Bianculli, *The Platinum Age of Television* (Doubleday, November)—on the evolution of what we watch

Belle Boggs, *The Art of Waiting* (Graywolf, September)—essays on fertility, medicine, and motherhood

Chloe Caldwell, *I'll Tell You in Person* (Coffee House/Emily Books, October)

Elena Ferrante, *Frantumiglia* (Europa, November)—essays and other writings from the bestselling author of the Neopolitan novels

Mark Greif, *Against Everything* (Pantheon, September)—essays from the n+1 founder

David Hajdu, *Love For Sale* (FSG, October)—on popular music in America

Fanny Howe, *The Needle's Eye* (Graywolf, November)—a meditation on time, violence, and chance

Siri Hustvedt, *A Woman Looking at Men Looking at Women* (S&S, December)

Abbi Jacobson, *Carry This Book* (Viking, October)—from the co-creator of the TV comedy "Broad City"

Tim Kreider, *I Wrote This Book Because I Love You* (S&S, January)

Daniel Menaker, *The African Svelte* (HMH, October)—on ingenious misspellings, with illustrations by Roz Chast and a foreword from Billy Collins

Caitlin Moran, *Moranifesto* (Harper, November)

Haruki Murakami, *Absolutely on Music* (Knopf, October)—conversations with conductor Seiji Ozawa

Okey Ndibe, *Never Look an American in the Eye* (Soho, October)—essays from the author of *Foreign Gods*

Nick Offerman, *Good Clean Fun* (Putnam, October)—essays and more from the co-star of *Parks & Recreation*

Benjamin Percy, *Thrill Me: Essays on Fiction* (Graywolf, October)

Jennifer Weiner, *It's All Material* (Atria, October)

Tom Wolfe, *The Kingdom of Speech* (Little, Brown, August)—notes on evolution and more

Biography & Memoir
Marina Abramovic, *Walk Through Walls* (Crown Archetype, October)—memoir from the provocative conceptual artist

Alex Beam, *The Feud* (Pantheon, December)—the end of the friendship between Edmund Wilson and Vladimir Nabokov

Leslie Bennetts, *Last Girl Before Freeway* (Little, Brown, December)—on the life of Joan Rivers

Carol Burnett, *In Such Good Company* (Crown Archetype, October)—memoir from the comedienne

Peter Ames Carlin, *Homeward Bound* (Holt, October)—a biography of Paul Simon

Tara Clancy, *The Clancys of Queens: A Memoir* (Crown, October)

Phil Collins, *Untitled Memoir* (Crown, October)

Blanche Wiesen Cook, *Eleanor Roosevelt, Vol. 3* (Viking, October)—a look at the years between 1939 and 1962

Jason Diamond, *Searching for John Hughes* (William Morrow, November)—learning about life from 1980s movies

Philip Eade, *Evelyn Waugh: A Life Revisited* (Holt, October)

Ruth Franklin, *Shirley Jackson: A Most Haunted Life* (Liveright, September)

Amy Gary, *In the Great Green Room* (Flatiron, January)—biography of children's author Margaret Wise Brown

A.A. Gill, *Pour Me: A Life* (Blue Rider, November)

Robert Gottlieb, *Avid Reader* (FSG, September)—long-awaited autobiography from the former editor at Knopf and *The New Yorker*

Tippi Hedren, *Tippi: A Memoir* (William Morrow, November)

Taraji P. Henson, *Around the Way Girl* (Atria, November)—from the co-star of *Empire*

Boris Johnson, *Shakespeare, The Riddle of Genius* (Riverhead, November)—biography of the bard from the mayor of London

Robert Kanigel, *Eyes on the Street* (Knopf, October)—a biography of urban planner Jane Jacobs

Kiese Laymon, *Heavy: An American Memoir* (Scribner, January)

John Le Carre, *The Pigeon Tunnel* (Viking, September)—memoir from the celebrated spy novelist

Shawn Levy, *Dolce Vita Confidential* (Norton, October)—on Fellini, Loren, and 1950s Rome

Megan Marshall, *Elizabeth Bishop: A Miracle for Breakfast* (HMH, February)

Jonathan Martin, *The Courage to Walk Away* (Atria, October)—memoir by the former NFL player who left football because of bullying

Joel McHale, *Thanks for the Money* (Putnam, November)—a parody of celeb memoirs

Richard Michelson and Edel Rodriguez, *Fascinating: The Life of Leonard Nimoy* (Knopf, September)

Willie Nelson, *Pretty Paper* (Blue Rider, November)

Mark Ribowsky, *Hank* (Liveright, November)—a new biography of country music star Hank Williams

Katey Sagal, *Grace Notes* (Gallery, October)

Amy Schumer, *The Girl with the Lower Back Tattoo* (Gallery, August)

Jean Kennedy Smith, *The Nine of Us* (Harper, October)—growing up as the youngest Kennedy daughter

Bruce Springsteen, *Born to Run* (S&S, September)

Elizabeth Vargas, *Between Breaths* (Grand Central, October)—a memoir of panic and addiction from the former morning show host

Robert Wagner (with Scott Eyman), *I Loved Her at the Movies* (Viking, November)—memoir from the actor on all the other actors he's known

Abby Wambach, *Forward: A Memoir* (Dey Street, December)—reflections from a legendary soccer player

*Mara Wilson, *Where Am I Now?* (Penguin, September)

*iO Tillett-Wright, *Darling Days: A Memoir* (Ecco, September)

And Finally
Allie Brosh, *Solutions and Other Problems* (Touchstone, October)—the follow-up to the massive bestseller *Hyperbole and a Half*

BUZZ BOOKS AUTHORS APPEARING AT BOOKEXPO AMERICA

Marie Benedict

Sonali Dev

Emily Fridlund

Nathan Hill

Affinity Konar

Beth Macy

Meg Little Reilly

Amor Towles

EXCERPTS BY PUBLISHER

GROVE ATLANTIC
Emily Fridlund *HISTORY OF WOLVES* (Atlantic Monthly Press)

Patrick Hoffman *EVERY MAN A MENACE* (Atlantic Monthly Press)

HACHETTE
Affinity Konar *MISCHLING* (Lee Boudreaux Books)

Beth Macy *TRUEVINE* (Little, Brown and Company)

Maria Semple *TODAY WILL BE DIFFERENT* (Little, Brown and Company)

HARLEQUIN
Pam Jenoff *THE ORPHAN'S TALE* (Mira Books)

Tasha Kavanagh *THINGS WE HAVE IN COMMON* (Mira Books)

Meg Little Reilly *WE ARE UNPREPARED* (Mira Books)

Anna Snoekstra *ONLY DAUGHTER* (Mira Books)

HARPERCOLLINS
Christina Baker Kline *CHRISTINA'S WORLD* (William Morrow)

T.C. Boyle *THE TERRANAUTS* (Ecco)

Paulette Jiles *NEWS OF THE WORLD* (William Morrow)

Elizabeth Lesser *MARROW* (Harper Wave)

Margot Livesey *MERCURY* (Harper)

Teresa Messineo *THE FIRE BY NIGHT* (William Morrow)

Ann Patchett *COMMONWEALTH* (Harper)

Helen Sedgwick *THE COMET SEEKERS* (Harper)

Margot Lee Shetterly *HIDDEN FIGURES* (William Morrow)

iO Tillett-Wright *DARLING DAYS* (Ecco)

HOUGHTON MIFFLIN HARCOURT
Jade Chang *THE WANGS VS. THE WORLD* (Houghton Mifflin Harcourt)

KENSINGTON
Suzanne Chazin *NO WITNESS BUT THE MOON* (Kensington)

Sonali Dev *A CHANGE OF HEART* (Kensington)

MACMILLAN
Stephanie Gangi *THE NEXT* (St. Martin's Press)

Andrew Gross *THE ONE MAN* (Minotaur Books)

Rae Meadows *I WILL SEND RAIN* (Henry Holt)

Steven Price *BY GASLIGHT* (Farrar, Straus and Giroux)

Anne Sebba *LES PARISIENNES: HOW THE WOMEN OF PARIS LIVED, LOVED, AND DIED UNDER NAZI OCCUPATION* (St. Martin's Press)

PENGUIN RANDOM HOUSE
Brit Bennett *THE MOTHERS* (Riverhead Books)

Lauren Collins *WHEN IN FRENCH* (Penguin Press)

Nathan Hill *THE NIX* (Alfred A. Knopf)

Shari Lapena *THE COUPLE NEXT DOOR* (Pamela Dorman Books)

Forrest Leo *THE GENTLEMAN* (Penguin Press)

Elan Mastai *ALL OUR WRONG TODAYS* (Dutton)

Shanthi Sekaran *LUCKY BOY* (Putnam)

Marisa Silver *LITTLE NOTHING* (Blue Rider Press)

Karen Stabiner *GENERATION CHEF* (Avery)

Amor Towles *A GENTLEMAN IN MOSCOW* (Viking)

Mara Wilson *WHERE AM I NOW?* (Penguin Books)

RODALE
Sharon Moalem *THE DNA RESTART* (Rodale)

SOURCEBOOKS
Marie Benedict *THE OTHER EINSTEIN* (Sourcebooks Landmark)

ABOUT NETGALLEY

At the end of some excerpts, you may find a link to read or request the full galley from NetGalley. NetGalley is a website where professional readers (reviewers, media, booksellers, librarians, educators and bloggers) can access digital galleys from over 300 participating publishers. NetGalley is completely free for professional readers, and there are over 300,000 already using the service. Digital galleys can be read on all major reading devices and tablets.

The galleys are protected files that cannot be shared, and you'll find specific instructions about how to access the files at the end of each excerpt. Find device-specific help in this FAQ.

Note: Publishers can choose how to provide access to the full galley, so you'll see two kinds of links here.

Most links are to REQUEST the title on NetGalley. Use your existing NetGalley account, or if you're new, you'll need to fill out a brief Bio about yourself so that the publisher knows a little more about your credentials (since these galleys are limited primarily to book trade professionals). Once the publisher approves your request, you can login and access the digital galley.

Or, you might see a NetGalley widget link. A widget is a pre-approved link to view the title. Click on the link to login or create a free NetGalley account and access the digital galley.

Questions? Email us at support@netgalley.com, or find @NetGalley on Twitter or Facebook. Happy reading!

PART ONE: FICTION

CHRISTINA'S WORLD

CHRISTINA BAKER KLINE

SUMMARY

From the author of the #1 *New York Times* bestseller *Orphan Train* comes a stunning and unforgettable novel about the mysterious and iconic Andrew Wyeth painting "Christina's World."

EXCERPT

Prologue

Later he told me he'd been afraid to show me the painting. He thought I wouldn't like the way he portrayed me: dragging myself across the field, fingers clutching dirt, my legs twisted behind. The arid moonscape of wheatgrass and timothy. That dilapidated house in the distance, looming up like a secret that won't stay hidden. Faraway windows, opaque and unreadable. Ruts in the spiky grass made by an invisible vehicle, leading nowhere. Dishwater sky.

He doesn't know me as well as he thinks he does.

People want to believe the painting, but all is not as it seems. He wasn't even in the field; he conjured it from a room in the house, an entirely different angle. He removed rocks and trees and outbuildings. The scale of the barn is wrong. And I am not that frail young thing, but a middle-aged spinster. It's not my body, really, and maybe not even my head.

Yes, the painting lies, but it tells a deeper truth. I've spent my life yearning toward that house, wanting to understand its secrets, paralyzed by its history. (There are many ways to be crippled, I've learned over the years, many forms of paralysis.) My ancestors fled to Maine from Salem, but like anyone who tries to run away from the past, they brought it with them. You can never escape the bonds of family history, no matter how far you travel. Something inexorable seeds itself in the place of your origin. And the skeleton of a house can carry in its bones the marrow of all that came before.

Who are you, Christina Olson? he asked me once.

Nobody had ever asked me that. I had to think about it for a while.

If you really want to know me, I said, we'll have to start with the witches. And then the drowned boys. The shells from distant lands, a whole room full of them. The Swedish sailor marooned in ice. I'll need to tell you about the underground tunnel that leads to Bird Cove, the false smiles of the Harvard man and the handwringing of those brilliant Boston doctors, the dory in the attic and the wheelchair in the sea.

And eventually—though neither of us knew it yet—we'd end up here, in this place, within and without the world of the painting.

By that time he would understand how to show what no one else could see.

Part One

Over the years, certain stories in the history of a family take hold. They're passed from generation to generation, gaining substance and meaning along the way. You have to learn to sift through them, separating fact from conjecture, the likely from the implausible.

Here is what I know: Sometimes the least believable stories are the true ones.

***

My mother drapes a wrung-out cloth across my forehead. Cold water trickles down my temple onto the pillow, and I turn my head to smear it off. I gaze up into her gray eyes, narrowed in concern, a vertical line between them. Small lines around her puckered lips. My brother Alvaro standing beside her, two years old, eyes wide and solemn.

She pours water from a white teapot into a glass. "Drink, Christina," she says.

"Smile at her, Katie," my grandmother Tryphena tells her. "Fear is a contagion." She leads Alvaro out of the room and my mother reaches for my hand, smiling with only her mouth.

It is 1896. I am three years old.

My bones ache. When I close my eyes I feel like I'm falling. It's not an altogether unpleasant sensation, like sinking into water. Colors behind my eyelids, purple and rust. My face so hot that my mother's hand on my cheek feels icy. I take a deep breath, inhaling the smells of wood smoke and baking bread, and I drift in the water, letting it carry me. My eyelids darken. The house creaks and shifts. Snoring in another room. The ache in my bones drives me back to the surface. When I open my eyes I can't see anything, but I can tell my mother is gone. I am floating again, but now I'm so cold it feels like I've never been warm. I'm trembling, my teeth chattering loudly in the quiet. I hear myself whimpering, and it's as if the sound is coming from someone else. I don't know how long I've been making this noise, but it makes me feel better, distraction from the pain.

The covers lift. My grandmother says, "There, Christina, hush. I'm here." She slides into bed beside me in her thick flannel nightgown and pulls me toward her. I settle into the curve of her legs, her bosom pillowy behind my head, her soft fleshy arm under my neck. She rubs my cold arms and I fall asleep in a warm cocoon smelling of talcum powder and linseed oil and baking soda.

***

Since I can remember, I've called my grandmother Mamey. It's the name of a tree that grows in the West Indies, where she went with my grandfather, Captain Sam, on one of their many excursions. The Mamey tree has a short, thick trunk and only a few large limbs and pointy green leaves, with white flowers at the ends of the branches, like hands. It blooms all year long, and its fruit ripens at different times. When my grandparents spent several months on the island of St. Lucia she made jam out of the fruit, which tastes like an overripe raspberry. "The riper it gets, the sweeter it gets. Like me," she said. "Don't call me granny. Mamey suits me just fine."

Sometimes I find her sitting alone, staring out the window in the Shell Room, our front parlor, where we display the treasures that six generations of sailors brought home in sea chests from their voyages around the world. I know she's pining for my grandfather, who died in this house a year before I was born. "It is a terrible thing to find the love of your life, Christina," she says. "You know too well what you're missing when it's gone."

"You have us," I say.

"Yes. But my heart aches for him."

She says, "I loved your grandfather more than all the shells in the Shell Room. More than all the blades of grass in the field."

***

My grandfather, like his father and grandfather before him, began his life on the sea as a cabin boy and became a ship captain. After marrying my grandmother he took her with him on his travels, transporting ice from Maine to the Philippines, Australia, Panama, the Virgin Islands, and filling the ship for the return trip with brandy, sugar, spices, and rum. Her stories of their exotic travels have become family legend. She traveled with him for decades, even bringing along their four children (three boys and a girl), until, at the height of the Civil War, he insisted they stay home. Confederate privateers were prowling up and down the East Coast like marauding pirates, and no ship was immune.

But my grandfather's caution could not keep his family safe: all three of his boys died young. One succumbed to scarlet fever; his four-year-old namesake, Sammy, drowned in a river one October when he was at sea. My grandmother could not bring herself to break the news until March. "Our beloved little boy is no more on earth," she wrote. "While I write, I'm almost blind with tears. No one saw him fall but the little boy who ran to tell his mother. The vital spark has fled. Dear husband, you can better imagine my grief than I can describe to you." Fourteen years later, their teenaged son, Alvaro, working as a seaman on a schooner off the coast of Cape Cod, was swept overboard in a storm. News of his death came by telegram, blunt and impersonal. His body was never found. Alvaro's sea chest arrived on Hathorn Point weeks later, its top intricately carved by his hand. My grandmother, disconsolate, spent hours tracing the outlines with her fingertips, damsels in hoopskirts with revealing decolletage.

***

My bedroom is still and bright. Light filters through the lace curtains Mamey crocheted, making intricate shapes on the floor. Dust mites float in slow motion. Stretching out in the bed, I lift my arms from under the sheet. No pain. I don't want to move my legs yet. I'm afraid to.

My brother Alvaro swings into the room, hanging onto the doorknob. He stares at me blankly, then shouts, to no one in particular, "Christie's awake!" He gives me a long steady look as he closes the door. I hear him clatter down the stairs, and then my mother's voice and my grandmother's, the clash of pots far away in the kitchen, and I drift back to sleep. Next thing I know, Al is shaking my shoulder with his spider-monkey hand, saying, "Wake up, lazy bones," and Mother, trundling through the door with her big pregnant belly, is setting a tray on the round oak table beside the bed. Oatmeal mush and toast and milk. My father a shadow behind her. For the first time in I don't know how long, I feel a pang that must be hunger.

Mother smiles a real smile as she props two pillows behind my head and helps me sit up. Spoons oatmeal into my mouth, waits for me to swallow between slurps. Al says, "Why're you feeding her, she's not a baby," and Mother tells him to hush, but she is laughing and crying at the same time, tears rolling down her cheeks, and has to stop for a moment to wipe her face with her apron.

"Why you crying, Mama?" Al asks.

"Because your sister is going to get well."

I remember her saying this, but it will be years before I understand what it means. It means my mother was afraid I might not get well. They were all afraid—all except Alvaro and me and the unborn baby, each of us busy growing and unaware of how bad things could get. But they knew. My grandmother, with her three dead children. My mother, the only one who survived, her childhood threaded with melancholy, who named her firstborn son after her brother who drowned in the pond. My father, who watched his baby brother die in his crib.

**

A day passes, another, a week. I am going to live, but something isn't right. Lying in the bed I feel like a rag wrung out and draped to dry. I can't sit up, can barely turn my head. I can't move my legs. My grandmother settles into a chair beside me with her crocheting, looking at me now and then over the top of her rimless spectacles.

"There, child. Rest is good. Baby steps."

"Christie's not a baby," Al says. He's lying on the floor pushing his green train engine. "She's bigger than me."

"Yes, she's a big girl. But she needs rest so she can get better."

"Rest is stupid," Al says. He wants me back to normal so we can race to the barn, play hide-and-seek among the hay bales, poke at the gopher holes with a long stick.

I agree. Rest is stupid. I am tired of this narrow bed, the slice of window above it. I want to be outside, running through the grass, climbing up and down the stairs. When I fall asleep I am careening down the hill, my arms outstretched and my strong legs pumping, grasses whipping against my calves, steady on toward the sea, closing my eyes and tilting my chin toward the sun, moving with ease, without pain, without falling. I wake in my bed to find the sheet damp with sweat.

"What's wrong with me? Why are my legs like this?" I ask my mother as she tucks a fresh sheet around me.

"You are as God made you."

"Why would he make me like this?"

Her eyelids flutter—not quite a flutter, but a startled blink and long shut eye that I've come to recognize: it's the expression she makes when she doesn't know what to say. "We have to trust in His plan."

My grandmother, crocheting in her chair, doesn't say anything. But when Mother goes downstairs with the dirty sheets, she says, "Life is one trial after another. You're just learning that earlier than most."

"But why am I the only one?"

She laughs. "Oh, child, you're not the only one." She tells me about a sailor in their crew with one leg who thumped around deck on a wooden dowel, another with a hunchback that made him scuttle like a crab, one born with six fingers on each hand. (How quickly that boy could tie knots!) One with a foot like a cabbage, one with scaly skin like a reptile, conjoined twins she once saw on the street … People have maladies of all kinds, she says, and if they have any sense they don't waste time whining about it. "We all have our burdens to bear," she says. "You know what yours is, now. That's good. You'll never be surprised by it."

Mamey tells me a story about when she and Captain Sam were shipwrecked in a storm, cast adrift on a precarious raft in the middle of the ocean, shivering and alone, with scant provisions. The sun set and rose, set and rose; their food and water dwindled. They despaired that they would never be rescued. She tore strips of clothing, tied them to an oar, and managed to prop this wretched flag upright. For weeks, they saw no one. They licked their salt-cracked lips and closed their sunburned lids, resigning themselves to their all-but-certain fates, blessed unconsciousness and death. And then, one evening near sundown, a speck on the horizon materialized into a ship heading directly toward them, drawn by the fluttering rags.

"The most important qualities a human can possess are an iron will and a persevering spirit," Mamey says. She says I inherited those qualities from her, and that in the same way she survived the shipwreck, when all hope was lost, and the deaths of her three boys, when she thought her heart might pulverize like a shell into sand, I will find a way to keep going, no matter what happens. Most people aren't as lucky as I am, she says, to come from such hardy stock.

***

"She was fine until the fever," Mother tells Dr. Heald as I sit on the examining table in his Cushing office. "Now she can barely walk."

He pokes and prods, draws blood, takes my temperature. "Let's see here," he says, grasping my legs. He probes my skin with his fingers, feeling his way down my legs to the bones in my feet. "Yes," he murmurs, "irregularities. Interesting." Grasping my ankles, he tells my mother, "It's hard to say. The feet are deformed. I suspect it's viral. I recommend braces. No guarantee they'll work, but probably worth a try."

My mother presses her lips together. "What's the alternative?"

Dr. Heald winces in an exaggerated way, as if this is as hard for him to say as it is for us to hear. "Well, that's the thing. I don't think there is one."

The braces Dr. Heald puts me in clamp my legs like a medieval torture device, tearing my skin into bloody strips and making me howl in pain. After a week of this, Mother brings me back to Dr. Heald and he removes them. My legs still bear the scars.

For the rest of my life, I will be wary of doctors. When Dr. Heald comes to the house to check on Mamey or Mother's pregnancy or Papa's cough, I make myself scarce, hiding in the attic, the barn, the four-hole privy attached to the shed.

***

On the linoleum floor of the kitchen I practice trying to walk in a straight line.

"One foot in front of the next, like a tightrope walker," my mother instructs, "along the seam."

It's hard to keep my balance; I can only walk on the outsides of my feet. If this really were a tightrope in the circus, Al points out, I would have fallen to my death a dozen times already.

"Steady, now," Mother says. "It's not a race."

"It is a race," Al says. On a parallel seam he steps lightly in a precise choreography of small stockinged feet, and within moments is at the end. He throws up his arms. "I win!"

I pretend to stumble, and as I fall I kick his legs out from under him and he lands hard on his tailbone. "Get out of her way, Alvaro," Mother scolds. Sprawling on the linoleum, he glowers at me. I glower back. Al is thin and strong, like a strip of steel or the trunk of a sapling. Why is he so sure-footed and quick? He is naughtier than I am, stealing eggs from the hens and attempting to ride the cows. I feel a pit of something hard and spiky in my stomach. Jealousy. Resentment. And something else: the unexpected pleasure of revenge.

I fall so often that Mother sews cotton pads for my elbows and knees. No matter how much I practice, I can't get my legs to move the way they should. But eventually they're strong enough that I can play hide-and-seek in the barn and chase chickens in the yard. Al doesn't care about my limp. He tugs at me to come with him, climb trees, ride Dandy the old brown mule, scrounge for firewood for a clambake. Mother's always scolding and shushing him to go away, give me peace, but Mamey is silent. She thinks it's good for me, I can tell.

You've just read an excerpt from Christina's World.

ABOUT THE AUTHOR

Christina Baker Kline is the author of five novels, including the #1 *New York Times* bestselling *Orphan Train*. Her other novels include *Bird in Hand, The Way Life Should Be, Desire Lines* and *Sweet Water*. Her essays, articles, and reviews have appeared in *The New York Times*, the *San Francisco Chronicle, Money, More,* and *Psychology Today*, among other places.

IMPRINT: William Morrow
PRINT ISBN: 9780062356260
PRINT PRICE: $26.99
EBOOK ISBN: 9780062356284
EBOOK PRICE: $21.99
PUBLICATION DATE: 2/14/17
PUBLICITY CONTACT: Kaitlyn Kennedy kaitlyn.kennedy@harpercollins.com
RIGHTS CONTACT: Juliette Shapland juliette.shapland@harpercollins.com
EDITOR: Katherine Nintzel
AGENT: Geri Thoma
AGENCY: Writers House
Territories sold:
HarperCollins Publishers, World Rights

THE OTHER EINSTEIN

a novel

"Fascinating and thoughtful"
— B. A. SHAPIRO, *New York Times* bestselling author of *The Art Forger* and *The Muralist*

MARIE BENEDICT

SUMMARY

What secrets may have lurked in the shadows of Albert Einstein's fame? His first wife, Mileva "Mitza" Marić, was more than the devoted mother of their three children—she was also a brilliant physicist in her own right, and her contributions to the special theory of relativity have been hotly debated for more than a century.

In 1896, the extraordinarily gifted Mileva is the only woman studying physics at an elite school in Zürich. There, she falls for charismatic fellow student Albert Einstein, who promises to treat her as an equal in both love and science. But as Albert's fame grows, so too does Mileva's worry that her light will be lost in her husband's shadow forever.

A literary historical in the tradition of *The Paris Wife* and *Mrs. Poe*, *The Other Einstein* reveals a complicated partnership that is as fascinating as it is troubling.

EXCERPT

Prologue
August 4, 1948
62 Huttenstrasse
Zürich, Switzerland

The end is near. I feel it approaching like a dark, seductive shadow that will extinguish my remaining light. In these last minutes, I look back.

How did I lose my way? How did I lose Lieserl?

The darkness quickens. In the few moments I have left, like a meticulous archeologist, I excavate the past for answers. I hope to learn, as I suggested long ago, if time is truly relative.

Mileva "Mitza" Marić Einstein

Part One

Every body continues at rest or in motion in a straight line at a constant velocity unless compelled to change by forces impressed upon it.

Sir Isaac Newton

Chapter One
Morning
October 20, 1896
Zürich, Switzerland

I smoothed the wrinkles on my freshly pressed white blouse, flattened the bow encircling my collar, and tucked back a stray hair into my tightly wound chignon. The humid walk through the foggy Zürich streets to the Swiss Federal Polytechnic campus played with my careful grooming. The stubborn refusal of my heavy, dark hair to stay fixed in place frustrated me. I wanted every detail of the day to be perfect.

Squaring my shoulders and willing myself to be just a little taller than my regrettably tiny frame, I placed my hand on the heavy brass handle to the classroom. Etched with a Greek key design worn down from the grip of generations of students, the knob dwarfed my small, almost childlike hand. I paused. *Turn the knob and push the door open*, I told myself. *You can do this. Crossing this threshold is nothing new. You have passed over the supposedly insurmountable divide between male and female in countless classrooms before. And always succeeded.*

Still, I hesitated. I knew all too well that, while the first step is the hardest, the second isn't much easier. In that moment, little more than a breath, I could almost hear Papa urging me on. "Be bold," Papa would whisper in our native, little-used Serbian tongue. "You are a *mudra glava*. A wise one. In your heart beats the blood of bandits, our brigand Slavic ancestors who used any means to get their due. Go get your due, Mitza. Go get your due."

I could never disappoint him.

I twisted the knob and swung the door wide open. Six faces stared back at me: five dark-suited students and one black-robed professor. Shock and some disdain registered on their pale faces. Nothing—not even rumors—had prepared these men for actually seeing a woman in their ranks. They almost looked silly with their eyes bulging and their jaws dropping, but I knew better than to laugh. I willed myself to pay their expressions no heed, to ignore the doughy faces of my fellow students, who were desperately trying to appear older than their eighteen years with their heavy waxed mustaches.

A determination to master physics and mathematics brought me to the Polytechnic, not a desire to make friends or please others. I reminded myself of this simple fact as I steeled myself to face my instructor.

Professor Heinrich Martin Weber and I looked at each other. Long-nosed, heavily browed, and meticulously bearded, the renowned physics professor's intimidating appearance matched his reputation.

I waited for him to speak. To do anything else would have been perceived as utter impertinence. I could not afford another such mark against my character, since my mere presence at the Polytechnic was considered impertinent by many. I walked a fine line between my insistence on this untrodden path and the conformity still demanded of me.

"You are?" he asked as if he weren't expecting me, as if he'd never heard of me.

"Miss Mileva Marić, sir." I prayed my voice didn't quaver.

Very slowly, Weber consulted his class list. Of course, he knew precisely who I was. Since he served as head of the physics and mathematics program, and given that only four women had ever been admitted, I had to petition him directly to enter the first year of the four-year program, known as Section Six. He had approved my entrance himself! The consultation of the class list was a blatant and calculating move, telegraphing his opinion of me to the rest of the class. It gave them license to follow suit.

"The Miss Marić from Serbia or some Austro-Hungarian country of that sort?" he asked without glancing up, as if there could possibly be another Miss Marić in Section Six, one who hailed from a more respectable location. By his query, Weber made his views on Slavic eastern European peoples perfectly clear—that we, as dark foreigners, were somehow inferior to the Germanic peoples of defiantly neutral Switzerland. It was yet another preconception I would have to disprove in order to succeed. As if being the only woman in Section Six—only the fifth to *ever* be admitted into the physics and mathematics program—wasn't enough.

"Yes, sir."

"You may take your seat," he finally said and gestured toward the empty chair. It was my luck that the only remaining seat was the farthest away from his podium. "We have already begun."

Begun? The class was not designated to start for another fifteen minutes. Were my classmates told something I wasn't? Had they conspired to meet early? I wanted to ask but didn't. Argument would only fuel the fires against me. Anyway, it didn't matter. I would simply arrive fifteen minutes earlier tomorrow. And earlier and earlier every morning if I needed to. I would not miss a single word of Weber's lectures. He was wrong if he thought an early start would deter me. I was my father's daughter.

Nodding at Weber, I stared at the long walk from the door to my chair and, out of habit, calculated the number of steps it would take me to cross the room. How best to manage the distance? With my first step, I tried to keep my gait steady and hide my limp, but the drag of my lame foot echoed through the classroom. On impulse, I decided not to mask it at all. I displayed plainly for all my colleagues to see the deformity that marked me since birth.

Clomp and drag. Over and over. Eighteen times until I reached my chair. *Here I am, gentlemen*, I felt like I was saying with each lug of my lame foot. *Take a gander; get it over with.*

Perspiring from the effort, I realized the classroom was completely silent. They were waiting for me to settle, and perhaps embarrassed by my limp or my sex or both, they kept their eyes averted.

All except one.

To my right, a young man with an unruly mop of dark brown curls stared at me. Uncharacteristically, I met his gaze. But even when I looked at him head-on, challenging him to mock me and my efforts, his half-lidded eyes did not look away. Instead, they crinkled at the corners as he smiled through the dark shadow cast by his mustache. A grin of great bemusement, even admiration.

Who did he think he was? What did he mean by that look?

I had no time to make sense of him as I sat down in my seat. Reaching into my bag, I withdrew paper, ink, and pen and readied for Weber's lecture. I would not let the bold, insouciant glance of a privileged classmate rattle me. I looked straight ahead at the instructor, still aware of my classmate's gaze upon me, but acted oblivious.

Weber, however, was not so single-minded. Or so forgiving. Staring at the young man, the professor cleared his throat, and when the young man still did not redirect his eyes toward the podium, he said, "I will have the attention of the entire classroom. This is your first and final warning, Mr. Einstein."

Chapter Two
Afternoon
October 20, 1896
Zürich, Switzerland

Entering the vestibule of the Engelbrecht Pension, I closed the door quietly behind me and handed my damp umbrella to the waiting maid. Laughter drifted into the entryway from the back parlor. I knew the girls were waiting for me there, but I didn't feel up to the well-intentioned interrogation just yet. I needed some time alone to think about my day, even if it was just a few minutes. Taking care to tread lightly, I started up the stairs to my room.

Creak. Damn that one loose step.

Charcoal-gray skirts swishing behind her, Helene emerged from the back parlor, a steaming cup of tea in her hand. "Mileva, we are waiting for you! Did you forget?" With her free hand, Helene took my hand in hers and pulled me to the back parlor, which we now referred to among ourselves as the gaming room. We felt entitled to name it, as no one used it but us.

I laughed. How would I have made it through these past months in Zürich without the girls? Milana, Ružica, and most of all Helene, a soul-sister of sorts with her sharp wit, kindly manner, and, oddly enough, a similar limp. Why had I waited even a day to let them into my life?

Several months ago, when Papa and I arrived in Zürich, I could not have imagined such friendships. A youth marked by friction from my classmates—alienation at best and mockery at worst—meant a life of solitude and scholarship for me. Or so I thought.

Stepping off the train after a jostling two-day journey from our home in Zagreb, Serbia, Papa and I were a bit wobbly. Smoke from the train billowed throughout Zürich's *Hauptbahnhof*, and I had to squint to make my way onto the platform. A satchel in each hand, one heavy with my favorite books, I teetered a bit as I wove through the crowded station, followed by Papa and a porter carrying our heavier bags. Papa rushed over to my side, trying to relieve me of one of my satchels.

"Papa, I can do it," I insisted as I tried to wriggle my hand out from under his grip. "You have bags of your own to carry and only two hands."

"Mitza, please let me help. I can handle another bag more easily than you." He chortled. "Not to mention that your mother would be horrified if I let you struggle through the Zürich train station."

Placing my bag down, I tried to extricate my hand from his. "Papa, I have to be able to do this alone. I'm going to be living in Zürich by myself after all."

He stared at me for a long moment, as if the reality of me living in Zürich without him just registered, as if we had not been working toward this goal since I was a little girl. Reluctantly, finger by finger, he released his hand. This was hard for him, I understood that. While I knew part of him relished my pursuit of a singular education, that my climb reminded him of his own hard-scrabble ascent from peasant to successful bureaucrat and landowner, I sometimes wondered whether he felt guilty and conflicted at propelling me along my own precarious journey. He'd focused on the prize of my university education for so long, I guessed that he hadn't actually envisioned saying good-bye and leaving me in this foreign place.

We exited the station and stepped into the busy evening streets of Zürich. Night was just beginning to fall, but the city wasn't dark. I caught Papa's eye, and we smiled at each other in amazement; we'd only ever seen a city lit by the usual dim, oil streetlamps. Electric lights illuminated the Zürich streets, and they were unexpectedly bright. In their glow, I could actually make out the finer details on the dresses of the ladies passing by us; their bustles were more elaborate than the restrained styles I'd seen in Zagreb.

The horses of a for-hire Clarence cab clopped down the cobblestones of the *Bahnhofstrasse* on which we stood, and Papa summoned it. As the driver dismounted to load our luggage onto the back of the carriage, I wrapped my shawl around me for warmth in the cool evening air. The night before I left, Mama gifted me with the rose-embroidered shawl, tears welling in the corners of her eyes but never falling. Only later did I understand that the shawl was like her farewell embrace, something I could keep with me, since she had to stay behind in Zagreb with my younger sister, Zorka, and my little brother, Miloš.

Interrupting my thoughts, the driver asked, "Are you here to see the sights?"

"No," Papa answered for me with only a slight accent. He'd always been proud of his grammatically flawless German, the language spoken by those in power in Austro-Hungary. It was the first step upon which he began his climb, he used to say as he badgered us into practicing it. Puffing up his chest a little, he said, "We are here to register my daughter for the university."

The driver's eyebrows raised in surprise, but he otherwise kept his reaction private. "University, eh? Then I'm guessing you'll want the Engelbrecht Pension or one of the other pensions of *Platenstrasse*," he said as he held the cab door open for us to enter.

Papa paused as he waited for me to settle in the carriage and then asked the driver, "How did you know our destination?"

"That's where I take many of the eastern European students to lodge."

Listening to Papa grunt in response as he slid into the cab alongside me, I realized that he didn't know how to read the driver's comment. Was it a slur about our eastern European heritage? We'd been told that, even though they adamantly maintained their independence and neutrality in the face of the relentless European empire building that surrounded them, the Swiss looked down upon those from the eastern reaches of the Austro-Hungarian Empire. And yet the Swiss were the most tolerant people in other ways; they had the most lenient university admissions for women, for example. It was a confusing contradiction.

Signaling to the horses, the driver cracked the whip in the air, and the carriage rumbled down the Zürich street at a steady clip. Straining to see through the mud-splattered window, I saw an electric tram whiz by the carriage.

"Did you see that, Papa?" I asked. I'd read about trams but never witnessed one firsthand. The sight exhilarated me; it served as tangible evidence that the city was forward-thinking, at least in transportation. I could only hope that the way its citizens treated female students was also advanced to match the rumors we'd heard.

"I didn't see it, but I heard it. And felt it," Papa answered calmly with a squeeze of my hand. I knew he was excited too but wanted to appear worldly. Especially after the driver's comment.

I turned back to the open window. Steep green mountains framed the city, and I swear I smelled evergreens in the air. Surely, the mountains were too distant to share the fragrance of their abundant trees. Whatever the source, the Zürich air was far fresher than that of Zagreb, ever redolent of horse dung and burning crops. Perhaps the scent came from the crisp air blowing off Lake Zürich, which bordered the southern side of the city.

In the distance, at what appeared to be the base of the mountains, I glimpsed pale yellow buildings, constructed in a neoclassical style, set against the backdrop of church spires. The buildings looked remarkably like the sketches of the Polytechnic that I'd seen in my application papers but vaster and more imposing than I'd imagined. The Polytechnic was a new sort of college dedicated to producing teachers and professors for various math or scientific disciplines, and it was one of the few universities in Europe to grant women degrees. Although I'd dreamed of little else for years, it was hard to fathom that, in a few months' time, I'd actually be in attendance there.

The Clarence cab lurched to a halt. The hatch door opened, and the driver announced our destination, "50 *Plattenstrasse*." Papa passed up some francs through the hatch, and the carriage door swung open.

As the driver unloaded our luggage, a servant from the Engelbrecht Pension hurried out the front door and down the entry steps to assist us with the smaller bags we were carrying by hand. From between the handsome columns framing the front door of the four-story brick town house, an attractive, well-dressed couple emerged.

"Mr. Marić?" the heavy-set, older gentleman called out.

"Yes, you must be Mr. Engelbrecht," my father answered with a short bow and an outstretched hand. As the men exchanged introductions, the spry Mrs. Engelbrecht scuttled down the stairs to usher me into the building.

Formalities dispensed with, the Engelbrechts invited Papa and me to share in the tea and cakes that had been laid out in our honor. As we followed the Engelbrechts from the entryway into the parlor, I saw Papa cast an approving glance over the crystal chandelier hanging in the front parlor and the matching wall sconces. I could almost hear him think, *This place is respectable enough for my Mitza.*

To me, the pension seemed antiseptic and overly formal compared to home; the smells of the woods and the dust and the spicy cooking of home had been scrubbed away. Although we Serbs aspired to the Germanic order adopted by the Swiss, I saw then that our attempts barely grazed the Swiss heights of cleaning perfection.

Over tea and cakes and pleasantries and under Papa's persistent questioning, the Engelbrechts explained the workings of their boardinghouse: the fixed schedule for meals, visitors, laundry, and room cleaning. Papa, the former military man, inquired about the security of the lodgers, and his shoulders softened with every favorable response and each assessment of the tufted blue fabric on the walls and the ornately carved chairs gathered around the wide marble fireplace. Still, his shoulders never fully slackened; Papa wanted a university education for me almost as much as I wanted it for myself, but the reality of farewell seemed harder for him than I'd ever imagined.

As I sipped my tea, I heard laughter. The laughter of girls.

Mrs. Engelbrecht noticed my reaction. "Ah, you hear our young ladies at a game of whist. May I introduce you to our other young lady boarders?"

Other lady boarders? I nodded, although I desperately wanted to shake my head no. My experiences with other young ladies generally ended poorly. Commonalities between myself and them were few at best. At worst, I had suffered meanness and degradation at the hands of my classmates, male and female, especially when they realized the scope of my ambitions.

Still, politeness demanded that we rise, and Mrs. Engelbrecht led us through the parlor into a smaller room, different from the parlor in its decor: brass chandelier and sconces instead of crystal, oaken panels instead of blue silken fabric on the walls, and a gaming table at its center. As we entered, I thought I heard the word *krpiti* and glanced over at Papa, who looked similarly surprised. It was a Serbian phrase we used when disappointed or losing, and I wondered who on earth would be using the word. Surely, we had misheard.

Around the table sat three girls, all about my age, with dark hair and thick brows not unlike my own. They were even dressed much the same, with stiff, white blouses topped with high lace collars and dark, simple skirts. Serious attire, not the frilly, fancifully decorated gowns of lemon yellow and frothy pink favored by many young women, including those I'd seen on the fashionable streets near the train station.

Looking up from their game, the girls quickly set their cards down and stood for the introduction. "Misses Ružica Dražić, Milana Bota, and Helene Kaufler, I would like you to meet our new boarder. This is Miss Mileva Marić."

As we curtsied to one another, Mrs. Engelbrecht continued, "Miss Marić is here to study mathematics and physics at the Swiss Federal Polytechnic. You will be in good company here, Miss Marić."

Mrs. Engelbrecht gestured first to a girl with wide cheekbones, a ready smile, and bronze eyes. She said, "Miss Dražić is here from Šabac to study political science at the University of Zurich."

Turning next to the girl with the darkest hair and heaviest brows, Mrs. Engelbrecht said, "This is Miss Bota. She left Kruševac behind to study psychology at the Polytechnic like yourself."

Placing her hand on the shoulder of the last girl, one with a halo of soft brown hair and kindly, grey-blue eyes framed by sloping eyebrows, Mrs. Engelbrecht said, "And this is our Miss Kaufler, who traveled all the way from Vienna for her history degree also at the Polytechnic."

I didn't know what to say. Fellow university students from eastern Austro-Hungarian provinces like my own? I had never dreamed that I wouldn't be unique. In Zagreb, every other girl near the age of twenty was married or readying for marriage by meeting suitable young men and practicing to run a household in their parents' home. Their educations stopped years before, if they ever went to formal schooling at all. I thought I'd always be the only eastern European female university student in a world of western men. Maybe the only girl at all.

Mrs. Engelbrecht looked at each of the girls and said, "We will leave you ladies to your whist while we finish our conversation. I hope that you will show Miss Marić around Zürich tomorrow?"

"Of course, Mrs. Engelbrecht," Miss Kaufler answered for all three girls with a warm smile. "Maybe Miss Marić will even join us in whist tomorrow evening. We could certainly use a fourth."

Miss Kaufler's smile seemed genuine, and I felt drawn to the cozy scene. Instinctively, I grinned back, but then I stopped. *Be careful*, I warned myself. *Remember the beastliness of other young ladies: the taunts, the name-calling, the kicks on the playground. The Polytechnic's mathematics and physics program lured you here, so you could follow the dream of becoming one of a very few female physics professors in Europe. You did not travel all this distance just to make a few friends, even if these girls are indeed what they seem.*

As we walked back to the front parlor, Papa linked his arm with mine and whispered, "They seem like remarkably nice girls, Mitza. They must be smart too, if they are here to study at university. It might be the right time to find a female companion or two, since we've finally met a few that might be your intellectual equals. Some lucky girl should get to share in all the little jokes you usually save for me."

His voice sounded oddly hopeful, as if he were actually eager for me to reach out to the girls we'd just met. What was Papa saying? I was confused. After so many years professing that friends did not matter, that a husband was not important, that our family and education alone counted, was he giving me some sort of test? I wanted to show him that the usual desires of a young woman—friends, husband, children—didn't matter to me, as always. I wanted to pass this strange examination with the highest honors, just as I had all others.

"Papa, I promise you I'm here to learn, not to make friends," I said with a definitive nod. I hoped this would reassure him that the fate he foretold for me—even wished for me—all those years ago had become my own embraced destiny.

But Papa wasn't elated with my answer. In fact, his face darkened, with sadness or anger I couldn't tell at first. Had I not been emphatic enough? Was his message truly changing because these girls were so different from all the others I'd known?

He was uncharacteristically quiet for a minute. Finally, with a despondent note in his voice, he said, "I had hoped you could have both."

In the weeks that followed Papa's departure, I avoided the girls, keeping to my books and my room. But the Engelbrechts' schedule meant that I dined with them daily, and courtesy required that I politely converse over breakfast and dinner. They constantly entreated me to join them in walks, lectures, café-house visits, theater, and concerts. They good-naturedly chided me for being too serious and too quiet and too studious, and they continued to invite me no matter how often I declined. The girls had persistence I'd never witnessed anywhere but within myself.

One early evening that summer, I was studying in my room in preparation for the courses beginning in October, as had become my custom. My special shawl was wrapped around my shoulders to ward off the chill endemic to the pension's bedrooms no matter how warm the weather. I was parsing through a text when I heard the girls downstairs begin to play a version of Bizet's *L'Arlésienne* Suite, fairly badly but with feeling. I knew the piece well; I used to perform it with my family. The familiar music made me feel melancholy, lonely instead of alone. Glancing over at my dusty tamburitza in the corner, I grabbed the little mandolin and walked downstairs. Standing in the entrance to the front parlor, I watched as the girls struggled with the piece.

As I leaned against the wall, tamburitza in hand, I suddenly felt foolish. Why should I expect them to accept me after I'd declined their invitations so frequently? I wanted to run back upstairs, but Helene noticed me and stopped playing.

With her characteristic warmth, she asked, "Will you join us, Miss

Marić?" She glanced at Ružica and Milana in mock exasperation. "You can see that we can use whatever musical assistance you can offer."

I said yes. Within days, the girls catapulted me into a life I'd never experienced before. A life with like-minded friends. Papa had been wrong, and so had I. Friends did matter. Friends like these anyway, ones who were fiercely intelligent and similarly ambitious, who suffered through the same sort of ridicule and condemnation and survived, smiling.

These friends didn't take away my resolve to succeed as I'd feared. They made me stronger.

***

Now, months later, I plopped down into the empty chair as Ružica poured me a cup of tea. The smell of lemon wafted toward me, and with a self-pleased grin, Milana slid over a plate of my favorite lemon-balm cake; the girls must have specially requested it for me from Mrs. Engelbrecht. A special gesture for a special day.

"Thank you."

We sipped tea and nibbled on the cake. The girls were unusually quiet, although I could see from their faces and the glances they shot one another that it was a hard-won restraint. They were waiting for me to speak first, to offer up more than an appreciation for the treats.

But Ružica, the most high-spirited, couldn't wait. She had the most abundant persistence and the least patience and simply burst with her question. "How was the infamous Professor Weber?" she asked, eyebrows knit in a comic interpretation of the instructor, well-known for his formidable classroom style and equally formidable brilliance.

"As billed," I answered with a sigh and another bite of cake; it was a glorious mix of sweet and savory. I wiped away a crumb from the side of my mouth and explained, "He insisted on consulting his roster before he let me sit in the classroom. As if he didn't know I was entering his program. He admitted me himself!"

The girls giggled knowingly.

"And then he made a dig about me coming from Serbia."

The girls stopped laughing. Ružica and Milana had experienced similar humiliations, having come from far reaches of the Austro-Hungarian Empire themselves. Even Helene, who hailed from the more acceptable region of Austria, had suffered her own degradations from her Polytechnic professors because she was Jewish.

"Sounds like my first day in Professor Herzog's class," Helene said, and we nodded. We had heard Helene's tale of mortification in excruciating detail. After noting aloud that Helene's surname sounded Jewish, Professor Herzog spent a substantial part of his first Italian history lecture focusing on the Venetian ghettos where Jews were forced to live from the sixteenth to eighteenth century. We didn't think the professor's emphasis was a coincidence.

"It isn't enough we are but a few women in an ocean of men. The professors have to manufacture other flaws and highlight other differences," Ružica said.

"How are the other students?" Milana asked in a clear attempt to change the subject.

"The usual," I answered. The girls groaned in solidarity.

"Self-important?" Milana asked.

"Check," I said.

"Heavily mustached?" Ružica suggested with a giggle.

"Check."

"Overly confident?" Helene proposed.

"Double check."

"Any overt hostility?" Helene ventured, her voice more solemn and cautious. She was very protective, a sort of mother hen for the group. Especially for me. Ever since I told them about what had happened to me on my first day at the upper school in Zagreb, the *Obergymnasium*, a story I'd shared with no one else, Helene was extra wary on my behalf. While none of the others had experienced such overt violence, they'd all felt the menace seething beneath the surface at one time or another.

"No, not yet anyway."

"That's good news," Ružica announced, ever optimistic. We accused her of fabricating silver linings in the blackest storms. She maintained that it was a necessary outlook for us and briskly recommended that we do the same.

"Sense any allies?" Milana tiptoed into more strategic territory. The physics curriculum required collaboration among the students on certain projects, and we had discussed strategies about this. What if no one was willing to partner with me?

"No," I answered automatically. But I paused, trying to follow Ružica's advice to think more optimistically. "Well, maybe. There was one student who smiled at me, maybe a little too long, but still, a genuine smile. No mockery. Einstein, I think is his name."

Helene's heavy eyebrows raised in concern. She was always on high alert for unwelcome romantic overtures. She believed them to be almost as much cause for concern as outright violence. Reaching for my hand, she warned, "Be careful."

I squeezed her hand back. "Don't worry, Helene. I'm always careful." When her expression failed to lighten, I teased, "Come on. You girls always accuse me of being *too* cautious, *too* private. Of only showing you three my true personality. Do you really think I wouldn't be careful with Mr. Einstein?"

Helene's worried look lifted, replaced by a smile.

I constantly astonished myself with these girls. Astonished that I had the words to express my long-buried stories. Astonished that I allowed them see who I really was. And astonished that I was accepted regardless.

You've just read an excerpt from The Other Einstein.

ABOUT THE AUTHOR

Marie Benedict is a lawyer with more than ten years' experience as a litigator at two of the country's premier law firms and for Fortune 500 companies. She is a magna cum laude graduate of Boston College with a focus in history and art history and a cum laude graduate of the Boston University School of Law. She lives in Pittsburgh with her family.

IMPRINT: Sourcebooks Landmark
PRINT ISBN: 9781492637257
PRINT PRICE: $25.99
EBOOK ISBN: 9781492637264
EBOOK PRICE: $25.99
PUBLICATION DATE: 10/1/16
PUBLICITY CONTACT: Lathea Williams lathea.williams@sourcebooks.com
RIGHTS CONTACT: Sara Hartman-Seeskin sara.hartman@sourcebooks.com
EDITOR: Shana Drehs
AGENT: Laura Dail
AGENCY: Laura Dail Literary Agency
TERRITORIES SOLD:
Brazil: Editora Gente
Czech Republic: Metafora
Germany: Kiepenheuer & Witsch
Greece: Ropi
Poland: Znak
Turkey: Kanes

PROMOTIONAL INFORMATION:
Major trade and consumer advertising; Galley mailings to booksellers and librarians; Featured author at Winter Institute, Book Expo America, ALA, and Indie regional shows; Major web promotions; Early NetGalley advertising; Book club marketing.

BOOKSELLER BLURBS:
"This is great historical fiction about the first wife of Albert Einstein, Mitza Maric, who was a brilliant physicist in her own right. Her relationship with Albert and her marriage reveal the difficulty for women during the early 20th century to have a career and how her own contributions to the field of developing science were stifled by her husband. A fascinating woman! This is a must read! Loved it!"—Stephanie Crowe, Page and Palette (Fairhope, AL)

NEW YORK TIMES
BESTSELLING AUTHOR OF
THE HARDER THEY COME

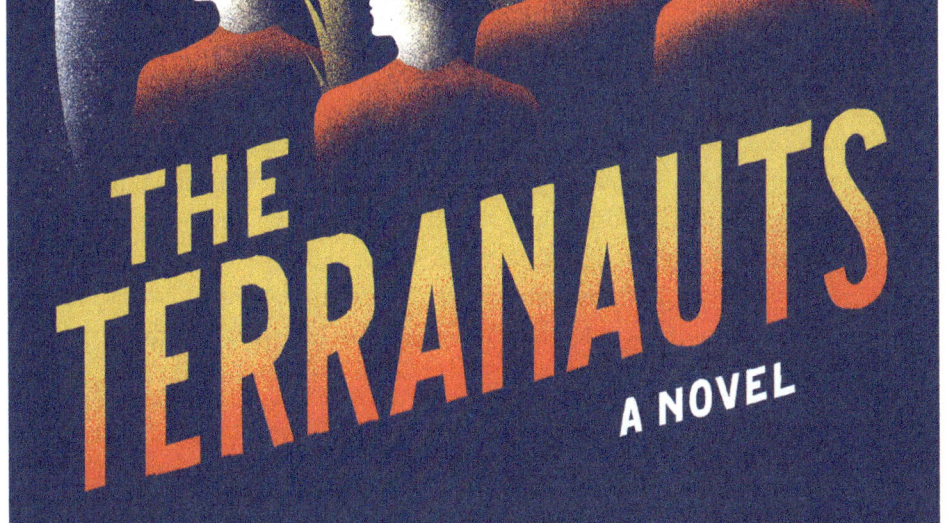

T.C. BOYLE

THE TERRANAUTS

A NOVEL

SUMMARY

From master storyteller T.C. Boyle, a hilarious, incisive deep-dive into human behavior through the eyes of eight young Terranauts, four men and four women voluntarily sealed inside a glass enclosure designed to serve as a prototype for a possible off-earth colony, who become entangled in much more than the game of survival.

EXCERPT

Part One
Pre-Closure

Chapter One
Dawn Chapman

We were discouraged from having pets—or, for that matter, husbands or even boyfriends, and the same went for the men, none of whom were married as far as anybody knew. I think Mission Control would have been happier if we didn't have parents or siblings either, but all of us did, with the exception of Ramsay, an only child whose parents had been killed in a head-on collision when he was in the fourth grade. I often wondered if that had been a factor in the selection process—in his favor, I mean—because it was apparent he was lacking in certain key areas and to my mind, at least on paper, he was the weakest link of the crew. But that wasn't for me to say—Mission Control had their own agenda and for all our second-guessing, we could only put our heads down and hope for the best. As you can imagine, we all sweated out the selection process—during the final months it seemed like we did nothing else—and though we were a team, though we pulled together and had been doing so through the past two years of training, the fact remained that of the sixteen candidates only eight would make the final cut. So here was the irony: while we exuded team spirit, we were competing to exude it, our every thought and move duly noted by Mission Control. What did Richard, our resident cynic, call it? A Miss America pageant without the Miss and without the America.

I don't recall the specific date now, and I should, I know I should, just to keep the record straight, but it was about a month before closure when we were called in for our final interviews. A month seems about right, time enough to spread the word and generate as much press as possible over the unveiling of the final eight—any earlier and we ran the risk of overkill, and of course Mission Control was sensitive about that because of what fell out with the first mission. So it would have been February. A February morning in the high desert, everything in bloom with the winter rains and the light spread like a soft film over the spine of the mountains. There would have been a faint sweetness to the air, a kind of dry rub of sage and burnt sugar, something to savor as I made my way over to the cafeteria for an early breakfast. I might have stopped to kick off my flip-flops and feel the cool granular earth between my toes or watch the leaf-cutter ants in their regimented march to and from the nest, both inside my body and out of it at the same time, a female hominid of breeding age bent over in the naturalist's trance and wondering if this earth, the old one, the original one, would still be her home in a month's time.

The fact was, I'd been up since four, unable to sleep, and I just wanted to be alone to get my thoughts together. Though I wasn't really hungry—my stomach gets fluttery when I'm keyed up—I forced myself to eat, pancakes, blueberry muffins, sourdough toast, as if I were carbo-loading for a marathon. I don't think I tasted any of it. And the coffee. I probably went through a whole cup, sip by sip, without even being conscious of it, and that was a habit I was trying to curtail because if I was selected—and I would be, I was sure of it, or that was what I told myself anyway—I'd have to train my system to do without. I hadn't brought a book, as I usually did, and though the morning's paper was there on the counter I never even glanced at it. I just focused on eating, fork to mouth, chew, swallow, repeat, pausing only to cut the pancakes into bite-sized squares and lift the coffee cup to my lips. The place was deserted but for a couple of people from the support staff gazing vacantly out the windows as if they weren't ready to face the day. Or maybe they were night shift, maybe that was it.

Somewhere in there, mercifully, my mind went blank and for maybe a split second I'd forgotten about what was hanging over us, but then I glanced up and there was Linda Ryu coming across the room to me, a cup of tea in one hand and a glazed donut in the other. You probably don't know this—most people don't—but Linda was my best friend on the extended crew and I can't really explain why, other than that we just happened to hit it off, right from day one. We were close in age—her thirty-two to my twenty-nine—but that didn't really explain anything since all the female candidates were more or less coevals, ranging from the youngest at twenty-six (Sally McNally, who didn't stand a chance) to forty (Gretchen Frost, who did, because she knew how to suck up to Mission Control and held a Ph.D. in rainforest ecology).

Anyway, before I could react, Linda was sliding into the seat across the table from me, gesturing with her donut and giving me a smile that was caught midway between commiseration and embarrassment. "Nervous?" she said, and let out a little laugh even as she squared her teeth and flaunted the donut. "I see you're carbo-loading. Me too," she said, and took a bite.

I tried to look noncommittal, as if I didn't know what she was talking about, but of course she could see right through me. We'd become as close as sisters these past two years, working side by side on the research vessel in the Caribbean, the ranch in the Australian outback and the test plots here on the E2 campus, but the only thing that mattered now was this: my interview was at 8:00, hers at 8:30. I gave her a tight smile. "I don't know what we've got to be nervous about—I mean, they've been testing us for over a year now. What's another interview?"

She nodded, not wanting to pursue the point. The buzz had gone round and we'd all absorbed it: this was *the* interview, the one that would say yea or nay, thumbs-up or thumbs-down. There was no disguising it. This was the moment we'd been waiting for through all the stacked-up days, weeks and months that seemed like they'd never end, and now that it was here it was nothing short of terrifying. I wanted to reach out to her and reassure her, hug her, but we'd already said everything there was to be said, teasing out the permutations of who was in and who was out a thousand times over, and all we'd done these past weeks was hug. I don't know how to explain it, but it was like a coldness came over me, the first stage of withdrawal. What I wanted, more than anything, was to get up and leave, and yet there she was, my best friend, and I saw in that moment how selfless she was, how much she was rooting for me—for us both, but for me above all, for my triumph if she should fail to make the grade, and I felt something give way inside me.

I knew better than anyone how devastated Linda would be if she didn't get in. On the surface, she had the sort of personality they were looking for—ebullient, energetic, calm in a crisis, the optimist who always managed to see her way through no matter how hopeless the situation might have looked—but she had a darker side no one suspected. She'd confided things to me, things that would have sent the wheels spinning at Mission Control if they ever got wind of them. It would be especially hard on her if she didn't make it, harder than on any of the others, but then I wondered if I wasn't projecting my own fears here—we all wanted this so desperately we couldn't begin to conceive of anything else. To make matters worse, Linda and I were essentially competing for the same position, the least technical aside from Communications Officer, which we both agreed Ramsay had just about locked up for himself because he was a politician and knew how to work not just both sides but the top, bottom and middle too.

I watched her face, the steady slow catch and release of her jaw muscles as she chewed.

"Stevie's a shoo-in, isn't she?" she said, her voice thickening in her throat.

I nodded. "I guess."

Linda had tried to make herself indispensable, the generalist of the group, looking to fit into one of the four slots that would most likely go to women. She put everything she had into it, not only with extra course work in closed-systems horticulture and ecosystems management, but especially in marine biology. She'd logged more hours underwater than anybody else during our dive sessions off Belize and she was a champion recruiter of invertebrates, and yet to my mind Stevie van Donk had the inside track on the marine ecosystems. For one thing, she had an advanced degree in the field, and for another, she looked great in a two-piece.

"She's such a bitch."

I had nothing to say to this, though I privately agreed. Still, bitch or no, Stevie was in.

It got worse yet: Diane Kesselring looked like a lock for Supervisor of

Field Crops, and Gretchen was first in line to oversee the wilderness biomes. What was left, when you conceded the Medical Officer, Director of Analytic Systems and Technosphere Supervisor—all male-oriented at this point—was really a caretaker position: MDA, Manager of Domestic Animals, the pygmy goats, Ossabaw Island pigs, Muscovy ducks and chickens that would provide the crew with essential fats and animal protein.

"Dawn, what's the matter?"

Linda leaned across the table and took hold of my hand, but I didn't respond. I couldn't. I was a mess. "You're not going to break down on me, are you? After all we've been through together? You're going to make it. I know it. If one person's going to make it, you are."

"But what about you? I mean, if I'm in—"

Her smile was the saddest thing, just a quiver of her lips. "We'll see."

She looked away. The room was empty now, the people at the far table either gone off to work or home to bed depending on their shift. My stomach felt bloated. I could feel the blue vein at my hairline pulsing the way it did when I was overwrought. Linda's parents had kept horses, as well as chickens and Vietnamese pot-bellied pigs on their property outside Sacramento, and she knew barnyard animals like a veterinarian—but she wasn't a veterinarian, only a B.S. in animal sciences, and forgive me for saying this, she was maybe a bit chunkier than the ideal and not really all that pretty, looking at it objectively, that is. Not that it should matter, but it did, of course it did. Mission Control was looking for the same thing NASA was, people who fit the "adventurer profile," with high motivation, high sociability and low susceptibility to depression, but all of us fit that description, at least the ones who'd made it this far (to what Richard called the "Sweet Sixteen," a sports reference I didn't get till someone explained it to me). Beyond that, beyond the factors they ticked off on the barrage of tests they'd subjected us to, from the Minnesota Multiphasic Personality Inventory Questionnaire to what they'd observed when we worked as a team under stress, I'd have been lying to myself if I didn't think they wanted a candidate who looked good, someone pretty, prettier than Linda anyway.

Am I out of line here? I don't know, but sometimes you do have to be objective, and when I looked at myself in the mirror—even without makeup—I saw someone who'd represent the Mission to the public better than Linda. I'm sorry. I've said it. But it's a fact.

"Yes," I said. "Yes. Yes. I'm praying you get in, I really am—as much as I'm praying for myself. More, even. Imagine the two of us in there, the two Musketeers, right?" I tried to smile, but I couldn't. I felt my eyes fill with tears. The thing was—and I'm ashamed to admit it—they weren't just for her.

Linda set down the donut and licked her fingertips one by one. It took an eternity. Then she lifted her face and I saw that her eyes were swimming too. "Hey," she said, sweeping the hair off her shoulder with a flip of her chin, "no worries. Whatever happens, there's always Mission Three."

***

We all essentially wore the same outfit to work, male and female alike—jeans, T-shirt and hiking boots, with a hooded sweatshirt for the cool of morning or the winter days when it could get surprisingly brisk—but on this particular morning I'd opted for a dress. Nothing too showy, just a pale-green tank dress I'd worn once or twice when a couple of us had gone out bar-hopping in Tucson, and I'd put on makeup and swept my hair back in a ponytail. My hair is one of my best features, actually, so thick you can't see a trace of scalp even when it's dripping wet from the shower—and it's got body to spare, despite the low humidity. Stevie's a blonde, part in the middle, no bangs, as if she's trying out for a part in a surf movie, but her hair's a lot thinner than mine and it just hangs limp most of the time, unless she puts it up in rollers, and who'll have time for that after closure? But, as I said, she was in and Linda was out, or that was my best guess anyway, and it had nothing to do with the fact that Linda was Asian, but only how she looked in a two-piece. And the degree, of course. It might have hurt to admit it, but Stevie had her on both counts, and if I was going to get in it would have to be over Linda's back and not Stevie's or Gretchen's or Diane's because I couldn't begin to match their qualifications. My own degree was in environmental studies, which pretty well matched Linda's B.S. in animal sciences, so that was a wash.

As for the other three women on the extended crew, they weren't really in the running, or not that Linda or I could see.

Eight, that was the number. Eight slots. Four men, four women. And if we've been criticized for lack of diversity, just think about it. In the history of the planet, only twelve astronauts have walked on the moon, and all of them were men. Counting the second mission, we would number sixteen, and fully half that number would be women. Including, I hoped, me.

By the time I'd finished up in the cafeteria, hugged Linda goodbye and whispered luck in her ear, I was running late and that just ramped up my anxiety one extra degree I didn't need at all. I hurried across the courtyard, dodging the odd tourist, slammed into my room and stripped down for a quick two-minute shower (of which I was a past master, training myself for the mission, when we'd be limited to just seventy-five gallons of water apiece each day—for all purposes). I'd washed my hair the night before and laid out the dress, a pair of Mary Janes and the coral necklace I was going to wear, so it didn't take me long. Lipstick, eye shadow, a dab of hi-lighter, and I was out the door.

The air held the same faint sweetness I'd noticed earlier, though now it carried a taint of diesel from the pair of bulldozers scooping out the foundation for a new dormitory that would house visiting dignitaries, scientists and any friends of the project willing to contribute at one of three levels—brass, silver, gold—to its success. I didn't run into anybody I knew on my way over to Mission Control, which was just as well given the way I was feeling. The tourists were gathered round in clusters, sprouting cameras, binoculars and daypacks, but none of them gave me a second glance—and really, why would they bother? I was nobody. But tomorrow—if things worked out the way I envisioned—they'd be lining up for my autograph.

I took the stairs up to the third floor of Mission Control and if I broke out in a light sweat, so be it: the exercise calmed me. A simple thing: foot, ankle, knee, hip joint, breathe-in, breathe-out. I was in reasonably good shape from working the test plots and the Intensive Agriculture Biome and taking extended walks in the desert when I got the chance, but I wasn't a runner and didn't train with weights like so many of the others.

No need, that was my thinking. The Mission One crew experienced rapid weight loss, the men averaging an 18% drop in body weight, the women 10%, and it was probably healthier to put on a few pounds before closure—Linda and I had gone over this time and again. The trick was, you had to distribute those extra pounds in the right places, because Mission Control was watching and Mission Control definitely did not want to present fat Terranauts to the public.

Josie Muller, the secretary, waved me in with a smile, which I tried to return as if everything was normal, as if what was going to transpire in the next few minutes in the control room with its dull white plasterboard walls, oatmeal carpeting and panoptic views of E2 itself was the most ordinary thing in the world. "Just take a seat," she said, "—it'll be a minute." We both looked to the polished oak door that gave onto the inner sanctum.

I hadn't expected this—a wait. I'd assumed my eight o'clock must have been the first interview of the day and I'd timed it to the minute, thinking to walk right in and let the tension flow out of me like water down a drain. "Is there somebody in there?"

She nodded.

"A seven-thirty? I didn't know they'd scheduled that early?"

"Well, there *are* sixteen of you and they want to give everybody a full half hour at least—you know, for . . . well, final things. To wrap things up."

"Who is it, just out of curiosity?"

Early on, in the first or maybe second week after I'd been selected to join the project, Josie and I had shared a pitcher of mango margaritas at El Caballero in downtown Tillman and after that I'd always thought she was on my side. Or at least sympathetic. More sympathetic to me, I mean, than to some of the others. She was in her late forties, her hair already gone gray and her face composed around a pair of tortoiseshell frames that pinched her temples and marginalized her eyes—and she leaned now across the desk to mouth the name: "Stevie."

Stevie. Well, that was all right. Stevie was in and I'd already accepted that. At least it wasn't Tricia Berner, one the three women both Linda and I had agreed didn't stand a chance, even though, when I lay awake nights staring at the ceiling till the darkness pooled and dissolved into something darker still, I could see that she did. She was attractive in her own way, if you discounted her style, which was right off the street, short skirts, too much makeup, jewelry that might as well have been encrusted on her, and she was the best actress, hands-down, among the crew. And that meant more than you might think—from the start, right from the building phase to Mission One Closure and on through the course of our training, the project was as much about theater as it was science, and even more so now, with Mission Two, and the pledge we'd all taken. But more on that later. Suffice it to say that that closed door, no matter who was behind it, made my stomach clench till I could taste the pancakes all over again.

It was ten past eight and I'd already been in and out of the easy chair in the corner half a dozen times and studied the framed photos of the Mission One crew that lined the walls till I could have reproduced them from memory, when the door swung open and there was Stevie, in heels no less, giving me a blank stare as if she didn't recognize me, as if we hadn't hauled lines together and shoveled cow dung in hundred-ten-degree heat and crouched elbow-to-elbow over one table or another through too many meals to count. I saw that she'd hi-lighted her hair and layered on enough makeup to be clearly visible from the cheap seats, but I couldn't tell yet whether she was playing comedy or tragedy. They had to have taken *her*, hadn't they? For a fraction of a second I let myself soar, seeing Linda in her place and both of us in, a gang of two, bulwark against the autocracy of Mission Control on the one hand and the tyranny of the majority on the other, but then Stevie's eyes came into focus—hard blue, cold blue, blue so dark it was almost black—and I saw the triumph there. Her lips curled in a smile that showed off her flawless dentition and firm pink gums and then she was giving me the thumbs-up sign and it all came clear. We might have embraced—we should have, sisters in solidarity, the mission above all else—but I stiffened and the moment passed and she was by me, cranking her smile to the limit and gushing over Josie and Josie gushing right back.

The door stood open before me. I didn't even have to knock.

There were four people inside, seated casually, two on the couch and two in a pair of Posturepedic office chairs, three of whom I'd expected and one whose presence came as a total surprise. And, to be honest, something of a shock. *They're not leaving anything to chance here*, that was my first thought. And then I was thinking, *Good sign or bad?*

But let me explain. The two seated on the couch were a given: Jeremiah Reed and Judy Forester, the visionary who'd dreamed up the project and saw it through its creation and his chief aide and confidante. Privately we called Jeremiah G.C., short for God the Creator, and Judy, in keeping with the religious theme, Judas, because she was a betrayer, or at least that was her potential. We all felt that. It was just the way she was wound, a hair's breadth from turning on you, the kind of person who would have gone straight to the top in the Stasi, but by 1994 the Stasi was no more, so here she was, among us. Lately, Linda and I had been calling her Jude the Obscure, given some of her counterintuitive pronouncements from on high. She wasn't much older than I, but she was Jeremiah's right hand—the right hand of God—and that gave her a power over us that was out of all proportion to who she was. Or would have been, if it weren't for the fact that she was sleeping with the deity himself. Did I toady up to her though I hated myself for it? You can bet I did. And I wasn't the only one.

The third person in this trinity was newly anointed, brought in from outside to oversee day-to-day operations by way of cost-cutting and efficiency. His name was Dennis Roper and he affected a ducktail haircut and slash sideburns, à la 1982. We called him Little Jesus. About a month after they installed him at Mission Control, he hit on Linda, which to my mind was not only unprofessional but sleazy too, given the power he wielded. Linda slept with him a couple of times, though it was wrong and we both knew it whether there was a quid pro quo involved or not—*especially* if there was a quid pro quo—and when he was done with her he came onto me, but I wasn't having it. I wouldn't sink that low even if he was halfway good-looking, which he wasn't. I never liked short men—and beyond that, short or tall, I liked them to have personalities.

Anyway, there I was, hovering in the middle of the room, the door standing open behind me because I'd been too agitated to think to shut it, and the four of them (I'll get to the fourth in a minute) gazing up patiently at me, as if they had all day to do whatever they were going to do, though by my accounting they were already running ten minutes late. "Hi," I said, nodding at each of them in turn, then motioned to the straight-backed chair set there facing them and murmured, "you want me to sit here?"

"Hi, Dawn," Judy said, giving me a big smile that could have meant anything, and the others smiled in succession, everything as routine and amenable as could be, no pressure here, all for one and one for all.

No one had answered my question so I took it on my own initiative to ease into the chair—was this part of the test?—gazing straight into their eyes as if to say *I'm not at all intimidated because I'm one hundred percent certain I'm as vital to this crew as anybody out there walking the planet today.*

"Don't worry, we won't keep you long," Dennis said, getting up to tiptoe across the room and ease the door shut before sitting back down. He drew in a deep breath and let it out again, then bent forward in the office chair so that his elbows rested on his knees and he could screw his eyes into mine. "I know it's a big day for all the candidates and we're all looking forward to finalizing things and moving toward closure, so all we want really is to ask you a few things, little details, minor things, that's all, just to set the record straight—you on board with that?"

The fourth person in the room, and he didn't say a word or unfreeze his face or even shift in his seat to relieve the tension in his buttocks and hip flexors, was Darren Iverson, the millionaire—billionaire—who'd financed the project from its inception to the tune of something like a hundred-fifty million dollars and picked up the operating costs too, which were in the neighborhood of ten million a year, a million of that for power alone. He was a few years younger than Jeremiah, which would have put him in his mid-fifties, and he didn't really look like a billionaire—or what I suppose anybody would have expected a billionaire to look like. He wore matching shirt and pants combinations he might have picked up at Sears, in desert brown, with waffle-tread workboots, also in brown. His eyes were brown too and so was his hair, or what was left of it. We called him Mr. Iverson to his face. Otherwise he was G.F., short for God the Financier.

I looked to G.F., then to G.C. and Judy and finally came back to Dennis. "I feel like I'm on *Star Trek* or something," I said, but nobody laughed. *Star Trek* was one of our touchstones, as was *Silent Running*, for obvious reasons. "You know, 'Where No Man Has Gone Before?'" Still no reaction. I was feeling giddy, maybe a bit light-headed from the tension and all the energy my gastrointestinal system was putting into digesting breakfast, and whether it was ill-advised or not, I couldn't help adding, "Or no woman."

Dennis pushed himself back up to a sitting position. "Great, but we just want to ask you a few things that really haven't come up, to this point, that is"—and here he made it a question—"about your personal life?"

If this caught me by surprise, I didn't let it show. I'd assumed they'd be asking me about food values, estimated crop yields, milk production and minimum protein requirements, that sort of thing, the technical aspects of the job I'd be expected to fill, but this came out of nowhere. I just nodded.

"Are you currently seeing anyone?"

"No," I said, too quickly, and that was because I was lying. Despite myself, I'd been drawn into a relationship—or no, I'd fallen, full-on, no parachute—with Johnny Boudreau, who'd been second boss of the construction crew when E2 was in the building stages, and who played guitar and sang in a bar band on weekends.

Dennis—Little Jesus!—flipped a note card in his hand and made a show of squinting at the name written on the back of it. "What about John Boudreau?"

I wanted to say, *Are you spying on me now?*, but I kept my composure. I couldn't summon Johnny just then, couldn't picture him or take a snapshot in the lens of my mind, and I realized that if he really did mean anything lasting to me we'd have this month to make our peace with wherever that was going to go, and then there'd be closure, 730 days of it. I shrugged.

Into the incriminatory silence Judy said, "You are using birth control, right?"

I nodded.

"And—forgive me, but you do understand how vital this is, don't you?—have you had multiple partners in recent months, anything that might endanger . . . or, what do I mean?" She looked to Dennis.

"E.," he said, using my crew sobriquet, E. being short for Eos, rosy-limbed goddess of dawn, which I took to be a compliment even if it came by way of left field, "what we mean is we can't risk any sort of infection arising after closure—"

"You mean STDs, right?" I wasn't angry, or not yet—they were just doing what was best for the mission and what was best for the mission was best for me. "You don't have to worry," I said, and I gave Dennis a meaningful look. "It's been only Johnny, Johnny and nobody else."

Judy: "And he's, uh—?"

"Clean? Yes, as far as I know."

Dennis: "He does play in a band, doesn't he?"

"Listen," and here I shot a look past the two of them to where G.C. sat there on the couch like a sphinx and then to the brown hole of G.F., "I don't really see the point of all this. The medical officer, which I assume is going to be Richard, right?" Nothing. Not a glimmer from any of them. "The medical officer's going to do a thorough exam, and even if I had gonorrhea, syphilis and chlamydia—or if any of the men had it—it'd just be treated, right?"

There was a silence. Distantly, as if it were being piped in over a faulty sound system, there came the muffled clank of the bulldozers going about their business across campus. G.C.—lean, pale as a cloud with his fluffed-up hair and full white beard—uncrossed his legs and spoke for the first time. His voice was a fine tenor instrument, capable of every shading and nuance—when he was younger, long before the project, he'd performed on Broadway in things like *Hair* and *Man of La Mancha*. "But the issue is birth control," he said. "You do understand, don't you, that we can't risk having any of our female crew getting, well, knocked up. To put it bluntly."

It wasn't a question and I didn't answer it. "I'll take a pregnancy test, if it'll make you rest easier. Believe me, it won't be a problem."

"Yes," he said, tenting his fingers to make a cradle for his chin so he could stare directly into me, "but what about post-closure?"

And now—I couldn't help myself—I gave each of them a smile in turn and said, as sweetly as I could, "You'll have to ask the men about that."

***

If I mentioned the term "marathon" earlier, it was just a metaphor really, since as I said, I'm not a runner—why waste energy on something so unproductive?—but when I came out of that room I knew for the first time in my life what a finisher must feel like. Or not simply a finisher, but a winner. *The* winner. I was in. They liked me, liked my commitment and hard work and the pluses on my balance sheet that far outweighed the minuses (which in their congratulatory fervor no one bothered to enumerate). Everybody was grinning, all the way round, even Dennis. G.C., who was always pushing comparisons with NASA, sprang up out of his chair in a confusion of limbs to pump my hand and assure me I had the right stuff and that he'd known it all along. Judy embraced me. And G.F., who'd sat there like a catatonic the whole time, actually rose out of his seat and came forward to congratulate me with a minimalist handshake involving two fingers only.

I don't remember much beyond that though I'm sure my face must have been flushed and the vein on my forehead pulsing like heat lightning. I felt so grateful—and relieved—I could have kissed them all, but I didn't. Or at least I don't think I did. Dennis later told me I'd practically bowed my way across the floor before pausing at the door to give them all a broad valedictory wave as if I were ducking into the wings after an ovation, but I don't remember that either. It was heady, at any rate, even if I can't say for sure what was true and what wasn't. And it didn't really matter. Not anymore.

Unfortunately—and here you had to appreciate the subtlety of their scheduling—the first person I saw on coming through the door was Linda. She was seated in the chair I'd vacated, head down, studying her notes on closed systems, group dynamics, technics, Vernadsky and Brion and Mumford, boning up, though there was no point in it now. I saw that she'd put on a dress—a bronze rayon shift that only managed to look dowdy on her—and pinned up her hair, which was usually such a mess. What did I feel? Honestly? Sad, of course, but in that moment it was no more than a fluctuation in the flight I was on, the first stage of the rocket falling away while the payload hurtles higher and ever higher.

She didn't notice me. Didn't lift her head. I could see her lips moving over the phrases we'd chanted together like incantations—*Thought isn't a form of energy. So how on Earth can it change material processes?*—as if the people inside that room would care. They'd asked about my sex life. Asked things like, "How do you feel about Ramsay? Gretchen? Stevie? You think you can work with them inside?" And what did I say? *Of course,* I said. *Of course. They're the best people in the world. I look forward to the challenge. We'll make it work, make it click,* everything. *It's going to be awesome!*

I could feel Josie's eyes on me, but I didn't turn to her, not yet. I glided across the room as if I were riding a conveyor belt and then I was right there in front of Linda and I said her name, once, very softly, and she looked up. That was all it took. I didn't have to say a word. I watched the new calculus flicker like a current across her face and saw her put it all behind her and with an effort raise up her arms for a hug. "Dawn," she murmured, "Dawn, oh, Dawn, I'm so glad, I am—"

It was an awkward embrace. I was standing and she was sitting, the notebook spread open in her lap, her feet planted on the carpet, and I could feel the strain in the muscles of my lower back. Her grip was fierce, almost as if we were wrestling and she was trying to pull me down. I couldn't say anything because there was nothing to say that wouldn't sound like I was congratulating myself—and I couldn't do that, not at her expense.

"Dawn," she said, "Dawn," and drew it out till it was a bleat even as Josie moved forward to get into the act and Judy appeared at the door of the control room. I let go then and Linda sank back into the chair.

"Congrats," Josie mouthed for me alone, an expert at conveying meaning without sound, and then Judy was saying, "Linda? Linda, come on in. We're all ready for you."

* * *

I waited there the full half hour, settling myself into the chair and chattering away at Josie as one thought after another came cascading into my head, already wondering about the closure ceremony and measurements for our uniforms and whether we'd have our choice of living quarters or if they'd been pre-assigned (if Josie knew, she wasn't letting on). At nine, on the stroke, Ramsay appeared, in T-shirt and jeans, a baseball cap reversed on his head and the fingers of his right hand rooting at the beginnings of a shadowy growth of beard. I hadn't seen him the last couple of days, our schedules at odds, and the beard surprised me. If I'd assumed he was in, Dennis' question had pretty well confirmed it—pointedly, he hadn't asked how I felt about any of the men or women Linda and I had relegated to the second tier but only the ones we'd handicapped as the frontrunners—and if that was the case he'd have to shave before we were presented to the press or Mission Control would have something to say about it. Beyond that, the way he was dressed—his whole attitude, from the minute he slouched in the door, flashed a grin at Josie and me and perched himself on the corner of the desk as if it belonged to him—bespoke a level of confidence that verged on arrogance. Or inside knowledge. Maybe that was it. He'd been chummy with G.C. and Judy from the beginning, all in the name of public relations, of course, and I realized how naïve I'd have to have been not to understand that there was a pecking order here.

"Hi, girls," he said, "what's happening? Everybody feeling just unconquerable this morning? But wait, wait, wait—E., let me be the first, or maybe"—here he snatched a look at Josie—"the second to congratulate you. Well done! All for one and one for all, right?"

I just stared at him in astonishment. "But how did you know?"

"How did I know? Just look at your face. Quick, Josie, you got your compact? Here, come on, take a look at yourself." Going along with him, Josie fished her compact out of her purse and handed it to him so he could snap it open and bound across the room to hold the little rectangular mirror up in front of my face. "See? See there?" He swung his head round comically to where Josie sat at her desk. "Look at the way the Zygomaticus muscles are stretching that smile, and wait a minute, the Risorius too, which, in laymen's terms is called the look-how-proud-I-am muscle."

I couldn't help myself: I felt dazzled. And all his cutting-up, which I might have found sophomoric and more than a little annoying in another place or time, seemed witty and genuine, touching even. "What about you?" I asked. "You hear anything yet?"

"I'm the nine o'clock," he said, giving nothing away. He snapped the compact shut and gestured toward the door with it. "Who's in there now?"

"Linda."

"Oh," he said. "Oh, Linda, yeah. Of course. *Linda.*" He was watching me closely—he knew as well as I did that if I was in, Linda was out, or that was how it looked, unless Mission Control relented and decided to send all sixteen of us inside.

I didn't have a chance to say anything more, either in her defense or my own, because the door swung open then and Linda was coming through it and you didn't have to be clairvoyant to see the way things were. She was trying to control her face—there was no love lost between her and Ramsay and he was probably the last person she wanted to break down in front of, especially if he was in and she was out. Behind her, at the door, an expressionless Judy was beckoning to Ramsay, who flipped the compact back to Josie and exclaimed, to no one in particular, "What, am I up already?," and walked right by Linda without even glancing at her.

I might have hesitated for just an instant before I rose from the chair to go to her, ready to wrap her in my arms and murmur whatever needed to be said by way of consolation, though there could be no consolation and we both knew it. I'd be lying if I said I hadn't anticipated this moment, rehearsing it in my head over and over, but in every scenario I'd come up with I saw her giving in to the inevitable the way I would have if I were in her position and then the two of us regrouping and fighting through the storm together. She surprised me, though. She made straight for the door without raising her eyes, her shoulders slumped and her feet digging at the carpet as if the room had somehow tilted on her and she was climbing the side of a mountain. By the time I caught up with her she was already out in the hallway, heading for the stairs. "Linda!" I called sharply, more stunned than anything else. "Linda!"

She didn't turn to acknowledge me, just started down the stairs, her pinned-up hair shining like cellophane under the overhead lights. She was short—five-two to my five-eight—and looking down on her from that angle she seemed so reduced she might have been a child clacking down the stairs after a bad day at school. And it had been a bad day, the worst, and I needed to talk it out with her—for my own sake as well as hers.

"Linda!"

Still she didn't turn and I think she would have made it all the way down to the first floor and out the door and into the heat if it weren't for the fact that she was wearing heels (and that was another thing: we'd discussed how inappropriate it would be to wear heels, tacky even, because this wasn't a beauty contest, and here she was in a pair of pumps in the same shade as her dress). I hurried down the steps and actually took hold of her arm in mid-stride so she had no choice but to stop and turn her face to me. "I'm sorry," I said. "It's horrible. It's shit. I mean, how *could* they?"

"*You're* sorry? What have you got to be sorry about? You're in." She shot me a furious look and snatched her arm away.

"I know, I know. It's wrong. Way wrong. They're idiots, G.C., Judy, all of them—we knew it all along. I mean, how many times did we say how out of touch they were, how they wouldn't recognize true merit, if, if—"

"They picked *you*, though, didn't they?"

I ducked my head as if to acknowledge the blow. Two people we both knew, support staff, made their way past us, heading up to the second floor. They knew what the score was as soon as they caught a glimpse of Linda's face and they went on by without a word. I waited till they reached the next landing, struggling with myself. What I said next was false and we both knew it the minute it was out of my mouth: "They should have taken you instead."

"Don't make me laugh. You know what this is all about, and so what if I have the qualifications—better than yours, if you want to know the truth. I'm Asian, that's the fact. And I'm fat."

"You're not fat," I said automatically.

"Fat and short and not half as pretty as you. Or Stevie. Or even Gretchen."

I didn't know what to say.

"Blondes, that's what they want. Or what?" She gestured angrily in my face. "Redheads. Or is it strawberry blonde? Isn't that what you're always calling it?"

I couldn't believe what I was hearing. Did she really think hair color had anything to do with it? When I'd put all that time into food production while she was flapping around in her flippers and wetsuit trying to go head-to-head with Stevie? "Come on, Linda," I said, "this is me you're talking to. I know you're hurting right now, but we'll get through this just like we got through everything else they tossed at us—"

"Screw you," she said, and then she was clattering down the stairs, unsteady on the heels, which I realized she must have bought just for the interview since I'd never seen them before. It made me sad. I didn't want this. I wanted to go someplace, anyplace, shout out the news, phone my mother, phone Johnny, but Linda was dragging me down. I called her name again and she swung round abruptly. "What?" she demanded.

I was still poised there on the third step from the bottom. "Don't you want to go someplace and talk things over? I mean, for coffee. Or maybe a drink?"

"A drink? At five past nine in the morning? Are you out of your mind?"

"Why not? They gave us the day off, right? Why not do something crazy, like go shoot pool and get plastered?"

"No," she said. "No way."

"Coffee then?"

She made a face, but she was standing there motionless now, the heels thrusting her up and away from the gleaming surface of the floor and the shift bunched across her midsection, half a size too small. (The whole outfit was wrong, too blocky on her, which was typical of Linda, whose style sense was always a bit off, and why she hadn't shown it to me beforehand I couldn't imagine. Or maybe I could.) I came down the steps and crossed the lobby to her and she let me loop my arm through hers and lead her toward the door. "Tell you what," I said, "let's go into town to that place with the Napoleons. Your fave? Okay?"

She didn't answer but I felt some of the rigidity go out of her and we kept on walking.

This was better, much better, and I suppose I never should have said what came next, but I was trying to be positive, you can appreciate that. "Listen," I said, as we stepped through the door and into the glare of the sun, "I know how you feel, I do, but like you said, there's always Mission Three."

***

We drove the forty miles to Tucson with the radio cranked and the windows down, our hair beating round our heads in the old way of freedom and the open road, the way it had been before I'd met Johnny and we'd go off on day trips whenever we could just to get away from E2 and all the focus and pressure surrounding it. The car was a hand-me-down from my mother, a Camry in need of tires and paint, with a hundred thousand miles on it, but good still, solid, and it came to me then that I didn't know what I was going to do with it. Put it up on blocks? Isn't that what people did with cars? But where? There was no way I'd have time to drive across country and leave it at my parents' house. Mission Control would give us a stipend to store our personal things, furniture, clothes and whatever, but they hadn't said anything about cars—would they let us leave them on campus? The more I thought about it the more I realized they wouldn't—the cars would just deteriorate and become an eyesore and nobody wanted the press or the tourists to see that. And it wasn't as if I could just park the car someplace and expect it to be there when I got back. But then maybe I was worrying over nothing. Who knew, by the time the mission was over, cars might be obsolete—or mine would be, anyway.

I turned to Linda, who understandably hadn't had much to say since we'd got in the car, which, I suppose, was part of my strategy though I hadn't been aware of it till now—let the wind and the music stand as an excuse while we both privately took the opportunity to sort out our feelings—and had an inspiration. "Linda, I was just thinking," I said, and I had to shout to be heard over the noise of the wind and the radio, "do you want a car? I mean for like when it's too hot to bicycle? Or when you need groceries?"

She was staring straight ahead, her hair down now and floating round her face as if we'd been plunged underwater. "What, you mean this one?"

I nodded, though she wouldn't have seen it since she still wouldn't look at me. The radio was playing a tune by a singer who would kill himself a month after closure, not that the two were related in any way, just that it helps put the time in perspective for me. *Here we are now, entertain us.* That was the lyric. And it droned through the speakers as I stole a glance at Linda, then flicked my eyes to the rearview—trucks, eternal trucks—and back to the road ahead of us.

"You want me to car-sit, is that what you're saying?"

"Yeah," I said. "I guess. If you think you can get some use out of it, I mean. Otherwise, it'll just sit there and rust. Or not rust—dry up, right?"

"And when Mission Three comes around and it's my turn—if it's ever going to be my turn—then what? You're going to want it back?"

I shrugged. The singer droned, soon to be dead, though he didn't know it yet—or maybe he did. There was hair in my mouth. A truck swung out to pass and I winced at the intrusion. I was feeling generous—feeling ecstatic, actually, and what I was doing here and would do for the next four hours on the road and in the pastry shop and the handbag store we both liked was feeling more and more like a duty—and I said, "You can keep it. I'll sign it over and everything. For nothing, gratis, free, it's yours. And when you go in, I'll watch it for you—change the oil, keep it washed and waxed, everything. Deal?"

She shook her head in denial. She didn't want a car. And she didn't want to be here pretending any more than I did. What she wanted, she wasn't going to get. Not now—and I think I knew it even then—and not two years from now either.

***

When I got back it was past two, the message light was blinking on the phone and I needed to call Johnny and my mother, in that order. I'd already tried Johnny twice, once from the phone in the hallway of the pastry shop and once from a gas station on the way back while Linda was getting us Diet Cokes, and both times, as I'd expected, I got his machine.

He was at work, obviously, and he'd get the message when he got it. The thing was, how would he react? He'd be happy for me, or make a show of being happy, but then he'd drop the pose and let his sarcasm take over and that could be harsh. Lately he'd been calling me his girlfriend in a bottle and introducing me around as the woman going into stir. And my mother. She'd go gaga because now she could tell people her daughter wasn't just breaking her back doing menial labor in a greenhouse in the Arizona desert for less than minimum wage, but getting somewhere, getting famous, making use of her degree and participating in a project *Time* magazine had proclaimed to be as significant for the future of humanity as the Apollo missions to the moon. Of course, that was back then, before Mission One soured, and yet it wouldn't make an iota of difference to my mother: *Time* had proclaimed and that was enough for her. And if you want to know the truth, it was enough for me too.

Anyway, there I was, standing in the middle of the room, sweating rivulets, my hair a tangle, the endorphin high of the morning still lifting me right up off the ground and the sugar rush (we'd shared a Napoleon and a creampuff) running like rocket fuel through my veins, staring at the pulsing yellow button on the phone console as if I didn't know what it was for. Add to that the fact that I was feeling lightheaded from caffeine overload because I'd wound up having two cafes au lait at the pastry shop while Linda and I tried to talk things through. Not to mention the Diet Coke. I was rattled, flying high, but in the best possible way. The message would have been from my mother, I was sure of it, because she was as keyed up about the interview as I was—*Just be yourself*, that was her advice—and I was about to press *Play* when the phone rang.

All that caffeine, all that sugar—the sound startled me and it wasn't till the third ring that I picked up.

It was Johnny. "Hey, you hear anything yet?"

"Yes," I said, "I'm in." I'd anticipated this for a long while, weighing the pros and cons, thinking of what I'd say, but now that the moment had come, now that I'd said it, I was surprised at how neutral my tone was. This was dancing-around-the-room news, shouting-it-out-the-windows, but I just dropped it there like a stone.

There was a pause. I could hear sounds in the background, an engine straining against the gear, the clank of metal on metal. When he finally spoke, if anything his voice was even less inflected than mine. "That's great," he said. "I'm happy for you, I really am."

"But not so much for yourself, right?"

"What am I supposed to do while you're in there, get an inflatable sex doll?"

"Dream about me."

"If only. Girlfriend in a bottle. Bottled girlfriend. Girlfriend under glass."

"Sealed-in sweetness," I said.

"What about the four guys—you know who's in?"

"Ramsay for sure. And Richard Lack. The other two I haven't heard yet—the interviews are still going on. Linda's out. But you probably guessed that. She's taking it hard."

Another pause. "So you expect me to wait for you? And what about you—you're going to be locked up in there with four guys and you tell me nothing's going to happen?"

"I never said that. You knew from the beginning—"

He cut me off: "I don't want to bicker. This is a day for celebration, right? When we going to get together—five okay?"

"Five's perfect."

"Dinner at the Italian place, maybe. Or if you want a steak—you won't be getting many of those, will you? Then drinks and dancing, and after we'll go back to my place and talk this over like sensible adults—with our clothes off."

"Sounds like a plan," I said.

"Five," he said, and hung up.

The minute I set the phone down it rang again, the very instant, as if it had been timed to go off like a bomb fabricated of dynamite and a ticking clock. The voice that came at me, high-pitched and demanding, was Judy's: "Jesus, Dawn, where have you been? I've been ringing the phone off the hook for the past three hours now. Don't you realize how short the time is? We need you over here right now for your fitting—*now*, do you hear me?"

I don't know if I'd call myself overly apologetic, but when I'm in the wrong I'll admit it, and here I was in the wrong already (though if they wanted me on call, they should have said so, or that was how I felt anyway). "Sorry," I said.

"What were you thinking? From now on we're going to need you available twenty-four/seven. We're counting down to closure, don't you realize that?"

"Sorry," I repeated. And then, before she could go on I said, "Who's in? Who made it? Who am I going to be living with?"

"You'll find out when you get here—"

"Stevie I know—and Ramsay, right? Richard, I presume, because—"

"One other thing, and we'll fill you in when you get here, there'll be a dinner tonight, five o'clock, at Alfano's, just Mission Control and the final eight, and I've asked two or three journalists—and a photographer—to join us, nothing official, that'll come tomorrow at the press conference—"

From where I was standing, if I tugged at the phone cord and canted my head to the right, I could see out the window to where E2 caught the sun in its glass panels and showered light over the campus, the white interlocking struts of the spaceframe like the superstructure of a vast beehive—honeycomb, that was the term that came into my head just then in all its sweetness, a sweetness so intense it cloyed.

I blocked out Judy for a just a moment there, adrift on the future and what it meant and what was happening to me in the here and now. "Yes," I said, "yes, okay," though I didn't know what I was agreeing to.

"So we'll brief you on all this, of course—this is just the beginning, believe me. But for now, for tonight, just remember you're representing the mission from here on out and that means you're going to want to look your best..."

"What about the dress I was wearing this morning, would that be okay?"

"What dress?"

"For the interview? You know, it's like a light green, almost a mint?"

"I'm drawing a blank here."

"You know, the tank dress?"

I watched a sparrow clip its wings tight and plummet from the balcony to the lawn below. And what was that? A cloud in the cloudless sky, dragging a moving shadow across the courtyard. Dark, then light, then dark again. "Oh, yeah, yeah, of course," Judy said. "A tank dress, right?"

I didn't say anything

"I don't know." She let out a sigh. "Haven't you got something with maybe a little more style?"

You've just read an excerpt from The Terranauts.

ABOUT THE AUTHOR

T. C. Boyle has published fifteen novels and ten volumes of short stories, including the PEN/Faulkner Award-winning *World's End*; *The Tortilla Curtain*, which was awarded France's prestigious Prix Médicis étranger; and most recently, the *New York Times* bestseller *The Harder They Come*. He lives in Santa Barbara, California.

IMPRINT: Ecco
PRINT ISBN: 9780062349408
PRINT PRICE: $26.99
EBOOK ISBN: 9780062349460
EBOOK PRICE: $21.99
PUBLICATION DATE: 10/25/16
PUBLICITY CONTACT: Sonya Cheuse Sonya.cheuse@harpercollins.com
RIGHTS CONTACT: Michele Corallo michele.corallo@harpercollins.com
EDITOR: Daniel Halpern
AGENT: Georges Borchardt
AGENCY: Georges Borchardt, Inc.

No Witness But The Moon

Suzanne Chazin

"A tremendous talent."
—Lee Child

SUMMARY

In this powerful novel from award-winning author Suzanne Chazin, a tense stand-off between a Hispanic police detective and an undocumented immigrant leads to the shooting death of one, the shattered life of the other, and the shocking connection between them. Detective Vega's need for answers propels him back to his old Bronx neighborhood, a raw, menacing place where he is viewed as a disgraced cop, not a homegrown hero. It also puts him at odds with his girlfriend, Adele Figueroa, head of a local immigrant center, who must weigh her own doubts about his behavior. When a shocking piece of evidence surfaces, it becomes clear that someone doesn't want Vega to put all the pieces together—and is willing to do whatever it takes to bury the truth. Only by risking everything will Vega be able to find justice, redemption, and the most elusive goal of all: the ability to forgive himself.

EXCERPT

Chapter One

He hoped this day would never come. He hoped he'd never have to cross the divide.

On one side were cops who never had to second-guess their instincts, never had to shield their consciences—that soft tissue of the soul—from the razor-sharp judgments of colleagues, friends, even strangers.

On the other were those who had to look in the mirror at three A.M. with a belly full of booze and a heart full of lead. The ones who had to whisper the worst question a cop can ask himself and then listen for that tumor of self-doubt in the echo: *Did I do the right thing?*

Jimmy Vega never wanted to be a cop in the first place. He wanted to be a musician. He wanted to move people with rhythm, not muscle. Then his girlfriend—later wife, later ex-wife—got pregnant. You could say he became a cop the same way he became a father: by backing into it and then trying his hardest to make it work out.

And it had. For eighteen years, it had.

Until tonight.

It was a Friday evening in early December, too early for real snow, even here some fifty miles north of New York City where the deer sometimes outnumber the people. There had been a dusting earlier today—the first of the season. Most of it had melted away but a sugary glaze still clung to the trees and stone walls, lending a festive atmosphere to the rolling hills and horse farms of Wickford, NY.

Vega, a detective assigned to the county police's homicide task force, had been in Wickford most of the day helping the local cops investigate a fatal robbery. The homeowner, a retired school principal, had suffered a heart attack during the break-in. Vega suspected the crime was part of a string of increasingly violent home invasions in the area. Four weeks earlier, just over the border in Connecticut, a rookie cop had been disarmed and pistol-whipped by four Hispanic men involved in a burglary there. Two weeks ago, a teenage babysitter in nearby Quaker Hills had been raped and savagely beaten by what appeared to be the same gang.

"Every day I'm getting a dozen suspicious vehicle calls," Mark Hammond, a Wickford detective, told Vega. "I swear, if we don't catch these mutts soon, we're gonna have some dead Wall Street CEO on our hands."

"Perish the thought," said Vega dryly.

Hammond made a face. Vega suspected the Wickford detective played golf with a few of them. He certainly dressed like he did.

At six P.M Vega and Hammond had progressed as far as they could in the case. Vega was ready to call it quits for the evening. He phoned his girlfriend, Adele Figueroa, from the parking lot of the Wickford Police station, a brick and clapboard structure that looked like George Washington still slept inside. The entire village, with its cobblestoned sidewalks and whitewashed New England storefronts, could have sprung whole from a Currier and Ives lithograph. It was a cold clear night, the moon so bright it bleached the surrounding sky. A gust of wind bit right through Vega's dark blue insulated jacket. The air felt sharp enough to crack a tree branch. Tomorrow would have been his mother's sixty-fourth birthday. Vega had been trying to distract himself and not focus on it so much this year. It was supposed to get easier with time. That's what everyone told him.

"I just need to drop my car back at the station," Vega told Adele. "Then I'll be right over." He heard what he thought was a bark through the phone.

"*Nena?*" His term of endearment for her. *Babe* in Spanish. "Did I just hear a dog?"

"Don't ask." She blew her nose. "It's just for a little while."

"But you're allergic to dogs."

"Yeah, but Sophia isn't." Adele's daughter had been begging for a dog ever since Vega first met the girl eight months ago when he and Adele started dating. But even so, Adele's plate was full. Besides being the founder and executive director of La Casa, the largest immigrant outreach center in the county, Adele was on the board of the local food pantry and had also recently joined the advisory board of a Hispanic think tank in Washington, D.C. She barely had time to deal with the drama of being a divorced mother raising a nine-year-old, let alone take on a pet.

"One of my clients at La Casa had to move into a friend's apartment temporarily," Adele explained. "The landlord doesn't allow dogs. Sophia cried when she found out he might have to go to a shelter. It's just for a couple of weeks."

"Huh. Famous last words."

"I figure the walks will do me good. Lately my hourglass figure has too many hours and too little glass."

Vega laughed then wished he could take it back. He never understood why a woman with a Harvard law degree couldn't accord her body the same confidence she accorded her mind. "I think you look beautiful, *nena*. Even if you are picking up steaming piles of—"

"Mock me, *mi amado,* and I'll make you do it. See you in—what? An hour?"

"Sure thing." Vega hung up and drove his unmarked Pontiac Grand Am out of the parking lot. He'd pulled the short straw getting this silver hunk of junk this morning. It had four wheels and working brakes but the interior lights worked only intermittently and the heater was lukewarm at best. He preferred the cars he used to get when he worked undercover in narcotics: Humvees and Land Rovers and Escalades. Drug dealers drove in style.

He kept his police radio on and listened for any reports of car emergencies or accidents in the area. Wickford was a lousy place to break down, especially in winter after dark. There were almost no streetlights and the estates were set so far back from the road, it would be difficult for anyone to summon help. Vega was anxious to be off duty. But even so, he'd never leave someone stranded if he had the power to help.

The radio was quiet so he took a shortcut he knew through the back roads of Wickford that would put him on the highway. He made a left then a right down several narrow, winding streets, some of them unpaved, all of them no wider than a cow path. He passed huge, dark velvet expanses of lawns slashed by moonlight and shadowed by hundred-year-old trees. A few miles to the west where Adele lived, Lake Holly's downtown blazed with delis, pizzerias, and row frames strung with Christmas lights and inflatable Santas on thumbprint lawns. But here, the darkness was broken only by the occasional high beams of a car.

A dispatcher's voice broke the silence. "Ten-thirty-two in Wickford. Report of shots fired."

Vega sat up straight. A ten-thirty-two was local police code for a home invasion. From the sound of it, an *armed* home invasion. Vega listened for the address.

"Private residence at Six Oak Hill. Homeowner reports push-in robbery and assault. One confirmed suspect though there may be others. Suspect is male. Hispanic. Medium build and complexion. Late forties or early fifties. Wearing a black puffy jacket, dark jeans, and a tan baseball cap. Suspect may be armed."

This is it. These are the guys we've been looking for. All of Vega's senses turned razor-sharp, as if he'd just gulped a double espresso. He'd stood next to the body of that retired school principal, dead of a heart attack these bastards caused. He'd seen pictures of that poor teenage girl in Quaker Hills, her flesh a map of swellings and bruises that only hinted at the even greater violation beneath. He'd heard the water-cooler rumors that that poor rookie in Connecticut was so traumatized after his encounter; he'd quit the force. If Vega could be the guy to stop it all, right now, that would be an absolute high—the kind of high every cop lives for.

He typed Six Oak Hill into his GPS. He was two streets away. He could be on the scene long before any of the Wickford patrols or an ambulance responded. He grabbed the speaker on his department radio.

"County twenty-nine," he said, identifying his unmarked vehicle to dispatchers. "I'm on Perkins Road in Wickford. I'll take this in. Alert local PD that a plainclothes Hispanic detective will be on scene in a silver Pontiac Grand Am." Vega didn't want to get shot by some townie cop who mistakenly took him for the perp.

He turned off Perkins Road and raced over to Oak Hill—a steep ridge of newly constructed estates on four-acre expanses of lawn. Deep pockets of woods blocked the road from any of its neighbors and its high elevation kept the trees on adjoining roads from spoiling the view. There were only a few houses on the cul-de-sac. Six Oak Hill was a sprawling red-tile-roofed hacienda at the end of a long circular driveway. There were no vehicles parked on the street but that didn't mean one wasn't parked nearby. From what Vega had learned about the gang's operations, they sent a forward party of one or two guys. Only after they'd secured the property did they bring a getaway car.

He pulled the Grand Am to the curb and switched on his police grill lights. They bathed the perfectly trimmed boxwood hedge and pale stucco arches of the house in alternating flashes of red and blue. There was a fountain at the center of the driveway but it looked as if it had been turned off for the winter. The night air was still and silent save for the voice of a female dispatcher over his police radio giving the estimated time of arrival for backup. It would be at least four minutes.

Vega sprang from his car and began walking briskly down the driveway. He tensed as a door along the side of the house swung open. A short, Hispanic-looking man in a puffy black jacket and jeans stumbled onto the driveway. Floodlights bounced off the brim of his tan baseball cap. The man's right hand clutched his left shoulder as he tried to regain his footing. On his heels was a taller, movie-star-handsome man, also Hispanic-looking, waving a gun.

Vega pulled his Glock 19 service pistol from his holster and sprinted down the driveway.

"Police!" he shouted, pointing his weapon at the good-looking man. "Drop the gun! Hands up!"

The man immediately obeyed. "I'm Ricardo Luis," he called out in a Spanish accent. "Don't shoot! This is my home." His name sounded vaguely familiar but Vega was too pumped up to remember where he'd heard it.

The man in the baseball cap pitched forward and ran into the rear yard, still clutching his left shoulder. Then he disappeared.

"Stay where you are," Vega ordered Luis. "Keep your hands where I can see them. More police are coming." Vega scooped Luis's weapon off the driveway and tucked it into his waistband next to his handcuffs. Then he took off after the other figure in the baseball cap.

Bright floodlights blinded Vega as he plastered his body up against the side of the house and scanned the backyard for movement. Colored strands of Christmas lights flashed from a white columned pergola, illuminating a patio and pool covered over for the winter and a fenced tennis court to the far right. Nothing moved. Vega tried to catch his breath. He waited. And then he saw it—the shadow of a figure inching along the edge of the tennis courts. As soon as Vega took a step forward, the suspect broke from the bushes and began running straight for the woods in back.

"Police! Stop!" Vega shouted again. The man kept running. Even with a full moon out tonight, Vega knew the canopy of dense branches and pines would seal off the light. He had no idea how far the woods extended. In Wickford, it could easily go a half mile in any direction. Still, he couldn't hang back. He couldn't take the chance that once again, this gang would get away.

He ran to the pergola and took cover behind one of the columns. He felt like a pinball in an arcade game, zigzagging between bumpers, trying to stay out the line of fire as he made his way across the lawn. His heart beat hard against his rib cage. Sweat poured down his body. The homeowner's gun was digging into the small of Vega's back. The cold had begun to numb his fingers around the handle of his gun. Vega wished he were back in uniform. At least he'd have a radio on his collar—not this bulky handheld unit that only served to weigh him down. At least he'd be wearing his Kevlar vest. He still owned one but he hadn't expected to need it today.

Vega was at the edge of the woods now. He'd lost the suspect entirely. The darkness was like a wool blanket. Overhead, bright moonlight dusted the tops of the trees. But on the ground, there were only shapes and silhouettes. Thorny branches snagged Vega's pants and jacket. Logs and stumps half-hidden by leaves tripped up his feet. The cold made his nose run and his fingers tingle. He heard the whoosh of his own hard breathing in his ears. He couldn't turn on his flashlight. He had to mute the volume on his radio. Both would give away his location. So he was forced to stagger blindly across the uneven terrain, guided only by sound and shadow.

The land sloped steeply downward. Vega felt drawn by gravity and momentum. Ahead, he heard the snap of dry branches and the crunch of dead leaves. That made it easier to track the suspect's location but also for the suspect to track his. If there was a gang waiting to ambush Vega at the bottom of this hill, he was as good as dead.

Then Vega's right eye caught something in his peripheral vision. He swung his whole body in the direction of the movement and listened. He heard a crackle of dead branches. A scuff of pebbles. Vega's heart fisted up in his chest. He aimed his gun. The milliseconds felt like hours. Something darted out of the bushes. Something sleek and fast. Moonlight caught the white of its tail. A deer. It leapt over a log and scampered away. Was that all it was? Vega couldn't be sure. His own sandpaper breathing trumped every other sound.

And then—luck. Fifty feet farther down the hill, the suspect stumbled, his forward momentum carrying him right into a clearing that was lit up by a neighbor's floodlight. The man got to his feet, but before he could start running again, Vega caught up just short of the pool of light and took cover behind a tree.

"Police! Stop! Put your hands over your head!"

The suspect froze. He had his back to Vega but he was hunched over slightly, breathing hard, his jacket rising and falling with each intake of breath. Vega trained his gun on the man's torso and waited for him to straighten and put his hands in the air.

He didn't.

The suspect's left hand remained somewhere in front of him out of Vega's line of sight. His right one stayed planted on his left shoulder. *Was he shot? Reaching for a weapon?* From this angle, Vega couldn't be sure. In the time it would take to *be* sure, it could all be over. Several years ago while working undercover, Vega had witnessed one drug dealer shoot and kill another. One minute, they were standing around arguing the disputed weight of the merchandise. The next, one of the dealers was lying on the ground, bleeding out. It had happened that fast. Vega never saw it coming.

"Let me see your hands!" Vega shouted again.

No response. No compliance. *Was he stalling?* Vega scanned the woods. This was just how that rookie in Connecticut got disarmed. He thought he'd gotten the drop on one of the gang only to find himself surrounded by three more.

Vega switched to Spanish. *"Soy el policía! Déjeme ver sus manos!"* I'm the police! Let me see your hands!

Nothing.

"Are you deaf, *pendejo? Está usted sordo?"*

The man straightened but kept his back to Vega and his hands hidden. *"Hay una razón"*—the man choked out between gasps of air—*"por la que…hice esto."* There's a reason I did this.

So they were going to conduct this interchange in Spanish. Fine. At least now Vega knew. But why wasn't the suspect cooperating? What could he possibly hope to gain by refusing to obey a police officer with a gun pointed at him? "I don't care about your reason, *pendejo,*" Vega replied in Spanish. "Put your hands where I can see them."

"You are making a mistake," said the man in Spanish.

Was that a threat? "Show me your hands! Now!"

Vega felt a burning in his gut—that fight or flight instinct that every officer has to conquer in order to survive. You can't back down when you're a cop. You can't negotiate a command or turn it into a request—or, God forbid, a plea. You're no good to anybody if you do. Not to other cops.

Not to civilians. Not even to yourself. You have to own the situation or one way or another, it will own you.

"I'm not gonna tell you again," shouted Vega.

"But you don't understand. You can't do this—"

The man lifted his right hand off his left shoulder. Vega thought he was going to raise it in the air. Instead, he shoved it into the right front pocket of his jeans and spun around to face Vega.

One. Two. Two seconds. That's all the time a police officer has to make a decision.

One. Two. A lot can happen in two seconds.

An object can fall sixty-four feet.

A bullet can travel a mile.

And an indecisive cop can become a dead one.

Vega wasn't aware of squeezing the trigger. But he heard the shots. Like burst balloons.

Bam.

Bam.

Bam.

Bam.

The man crumpled to the ground. The confrontation was over.

The pain had just begun.

Chapter Two

Jimmy Vega's hands were shaking so much, it took him several tries before he could press the button on his radio.

"This is County twenty-nine," he said, trying to squeeze the breathlessness and panic from his voice. "I'm in the woods behind Oak Hill Road. Suspect on the ten-thirty-two is down on a four-four-four." Local code for an officer-involved-shooting.

It was like waking from a dream. Just fifty or sixty feet farther down the hill Vega could see the flashing lights of police cars bathing the woods in a strange, otherworldly glow. *Did they just show up? Or have they been there all along?* He'd been so focused on the suspect, he'd blotted out all other sensations.

Two uniformed patrol officers with heavy-duty flashlights began climbing cautiously toward him. Vega took a step forward into the pool of light. The suspect was lying on his back, not moving. From this angle on the hillside, all Vega could see were the soles of his sneakers and his tan baseball cap, now lying on the ground near him, soaked with blood. Vega wanted to rush over and begin CPR. That's what he was trained to do after a shooting. But he couldn't—not until these officers cleared him to move. He wasn't in uniform. For all the police knew, he was another perp. He dropped his gun to the ground, slowly removed his gold detective's shield from his belt, and cupped it in his left hand. Then he raised both hands in the air.

"Police officer! Don't shoot!" he shouted, waving his shield.

The two Wickford cops stepped into the floodlight. A man and a woman. The woman had a soft chin and frizzy bleached hair that reminded Vega of a dandelion. The man was shaped like a torpedo—with a shaved head beneath his cap and a wide torso made wider by his Kevlar vest. Both officers holstered their weapons as soon as they recognized him from the station house earlier. They were closer to the suspect than Vega was. Vega noticed the woman's mouth form a perfect *O* at the sight of the man. Torpedo raised an eyebrow and stepped back.

"No ambulance needed here, Detective. You got him good."

"Did you find anyone else?" asked Vega. He was still panting hard. His side had a stitch in it like he'd just run a marathon. "I think I heard someone else in the woods."

"There are police everywhere down there," said Torpedo. "If there's anyone else, we'll find them."

Vega retrieved his gun from the ground and ran over to the man he'd just shot. He was a homicide cop. He was used to pulling up on bloody, sometimes gory crime scenes. But he was unprepared for the damage he himself had inflicted. He'd aimed, as he'd been taught in his police training, for the center mass of the body—the torso. But as the man collapsed and fell backward, one of the bullets must have caught him in the chin and gone through his skull, cracking it open as easily as an egg. Blood and brain matter glistened, dark and gelatinous, across the fallen leaves. The suspect was unrecognizable from the neck up.

I've killed a man. Dear God, I fucking blew his head off! In Vega's eighteen years as a police officer, including five in undercover narcotics dealing with hardened gangbangers and felons, he'd never had to shoot anyone. He'd pointed his gun plenty of times and had guns pointed at him. He'd seen people killed. He'd wrestled suspects into handcuffs while they were trying to take a swing at him. But he'd never fired his weapon in the line of duty. The vast majority of police officers never do You practice for it. Every couple of months you go out to the shooting range and train. But it's like a fire drill. You do it to stay sharp. You don't expect to ever really need it.

"Are you okay, Detective?" asked the woman cop with the dandelion hair.

"Yeah." Vega was shaking badly but he tried to cover it by pretending he was just cold. He began frantically walking the perimeter of the body. "Where's the gun? He had a gun."

Torpedo felt the dead man's jacket then stepped to the side and conferred with his partner.

"Anything?" Dandelion murmured. Torpedo shook his head. "He seems pretty sure he had one."

Vega paced impatiently. "No," he muttered to himself. "I just blow people's brains out for the fun of it." He hadn't even realized they'd heard him until he noticed the two officers looking his way. Both dropped their gazes and shined their flashlights on the ground to give them some extra wattage over and above the floodlights. They nudged the leaves with their boots. Nothing.

"He had one," Vega insisted. "I know he did!"

"We'll find it," Dandelion assured him.

More cops were heading up the hill now. Wickford's Detective Sergeant Mark Hammond was with them, carefully maneuvering his perfectly pressed khakis past the twigs and brambles that had snagged Vega's own pants.

Vega ignored them all. He crouched down next to the dead man. The suspect's bloody right hand was turned palm-side down. There was something underneath. It was too small to be a gun. *A knife, perhaps? A box cutter?* Vega knew he wasn't supposed to touch anything. But he had to know. He uncurled the fingers slightly. Staring up at him was a creased, blood-smeared photograph of two Hispanic men and a teenage boy.

There was nothing else in the dead man's hand.

Vega's stomach lurched. He felt light-headed and dizzy. He pushed himself unsteadily to his feet, ran over to the nearest tree, and vomited. He heaved again and again until there was nothing left inside of him. *The man I killed was involved in a home invasion robbery,* Vega reminded himself. *He ran after I identified myself as a police officer. He refused to surrender. He turned on me.*

He had no weapon.

That thought beat out every other in Vega's brain.

The other officers on the scene gave Vega space. No one said anything to him. They probably thought that's what he needed right now, and a part of him did. But another part of him would have given anything for someone to tell him he'd done the right thing. Instead, everyone went about their business like actors on a stage waiting for someone to feed them their lines. Nobody knew what to say. Two EMTs started up the hill but were quickly turned back. Vega watched their faces absorb the news in the ghoulish alternating flashes of red and blue light.

Hammond eventually walked over and patted Vega gently on the back.

"Come sit in my car, Jimmy. Okay? Maybe call your family? No sense you being out here."

Vega nodded, not trusting himself to speak as Hammond led him down the hill and into the front passenger seat of Hammond's unmarked Toyota.

"I thought for a moment you were gonna put me in back," said Vega.

It was meant to be a weak joke but Hammond's response gave Vega pause. "Take as long as you need to get your thoughts together, okay, Jimmy?" The detective's smile had too many teeth in it.

Hammond's unmarked Toyota smelled of peppermints and Lysol, but it calmed Vega down to be encased in this tomb away from the murmurs of other cops. He felt certain everyone was judging him. How could they not? He would.

Hammond got in the driver's side and radioed a request for the medical examiner and the county crime scene unit. The uniforms began cordoning off the area with yellow police tape. Vega felt like he was watching it all unfold underwater. Voices and sounds came at him disconnected from their sources. The dispatcher's voice over the radio provided a constant update of all the additional vehicles and agencies that were now being directed to this tiny lane in Wickford. All because of Vega. Because of what he'd done.

When Hammond left the car to go back up the hill, Vega took out his cell phone and dialed Adele. He could barely get the words out before he started to choke up.

"I just shot and killed a man."

"*What?* Oh my God! *Mi amado*, what happened? Are you okay?"

Vega's head was pounding. His eyes burned like someone had rubbed them with sand. He took a deep breath and heard it catch in his lungs. He hadn't felt the urge to cry this strongly since that day nearly two years ago when a Bronx detective called to tell him his mother had been found beaten to death in her apartment. At least then, no one would have blamed him if he'd broken down. The crime was brutal. It was still unsolved. But now? This was different. The police officers on the scene would take it as a sign of weakness. Worse, they'd take it as a sign of guilt.

Whatever you do, stay strong, he told himself. If he stopped believing that he'd had no choice about what he'd done, why would anyone else believe it either?

He tried to steady his voice and state the facts as dispassionately as possible. "Dispatch reported a home invasion and shots fired at a residence here in Wickford. I was nearby so I took in the call. The suspect refused to surrender and turned on me."

"Oh, Jimmy, how awful. Are you hurt?"

"No." He couldn't bring himself to tell her that the man he'd killed probably wasn't armed. He needed time to wrap his head around that one. He still didn't want to believe it was true.

A silence hung between them. It was just a moment's worth but Vega felt the sting. Was she judging him? Or was he judging himself so much that he read every hesitation as a criticism?

"It's going to be all right," she cooed softly. "Where are you? Peter was going to drop Sophia off after he took her to the movies." Peter was Adele's ex. "Maybe I can get her babysitter Marcela to come over."

"There's no point," said Vega. "They won't let you within a hundred feet of me."

"Have you given a statement yet? Spoken to counsel?" Adele had been a criminal defense attorney before she started La Casa. It was still in her blood.

"No." Vega squinted through the windshield. Already things were heating up. On the other side of the yellow crime-scene tape were civilian onlookers, news cameras, and more police cars. A lot more police cars. "It's going to be a long night," said Vega. "Can you call Joy and let her know?" Vega's eighteen-year-old daughter was a freshman at the local community college. She lived with Vega's ex-wife.

"Of course. I'll do that now." Adele hung on the line for a moment without speaking. "A delicate question," she said finally. "The uh—suspect. Was he white? Black?"

"Hispanic. He spoke to me in Spanish."

"Good."

"Why good?" asked Vega.

"Well, you're Puerto Rican," said Adele. "So you'll probably get a pass on the race issue."

Vega couldn't contain himself. "There is no race issue, Adele! I wasn't thinking about the color of his skin or the color of mine. My only thought was not getting shot!"

"Calm down, *mi amado*," she said softly. "I understand. I'm just trying to think ahead."

Ahead? Vega couldn't think through the next hour. "I don't need you to be my lawyer, *nena*. I'll have lawyers up the yin yang soon enough."

"Sorry." She exhaled. "You're right. I'll get in touch with Joy and check in with you later, okay? I love you."

"I love you, too." Vega hung up just as the driver's side door opened and Hammond slid in.

"Hey, Jimmy"—Hammond patted his shoulder and gave him a big, fake smile that was all pink gums and white teeth—"how you holding up?"

Vega wasn't interested in small talk. "Did you find a gun?"

"Not yet."

"A knife? Any sort of weapon?"

Hammond ran a finger along the pleats in his slacks without looking at Vega or answering his question—which was answer enough, Vega supposed.

"So that photograph?" asked Vega. "That was that all you found in his hands?"

"At the moment."

"How about accomplices?"

"The homeowner says he only saw one man."

"When I was in the woods, it felt like somebody else was there."

"My guys were at the bottom of the hill. Not sixty feet away. They didn't see anyone."

Vega winced. How could he not have seen them? "They were that close?"

Hammond nodded. "They had their lights and sirens on and everything."

"I guess I just—blocked it out or something."

Hammond put a hand on Vega's arm and squeezed it for emphasis. "Don't talk, Jimmy—okay? You can only go through this story once. You go through it more than once and change something, some attorney's gonna eat you alive—or put me on a witness stand and eat us both alive."

Vega nodded. "Any indications that he was part of that gang?"

The temperature inside the car seemed to plummet twenty degrees. Vega could feel it instantly.

"Listen, Jim—I don't even know if I'm supposed to be saying this yet. But I just got a call from the chief of police? Over in Greenfield, Connecticut?"

Vega narrowed his gaze at Hammond. Cops aren't teenage girls. They don't frame statements as questions unless they'd rather not deliver the answers.

"Spit it out, Mark."

"The Greenfield PD just arrested the whole gang. Like maybe an hour ago. Four Hispanic men coming out of a big estate over there."

"The gang responsible for these home invasions? Are you sure?"

"One of the guy's prints matches a print we picked up on that robbery. The DNA on another matches semen from the rape in Quaker Hills. That Connecticut rookie they pistol-whipped positively ID'd two of them from mug shots. "

"So you're saying—"

"The man you killed probably wasn't connected to those other crimes."

You've just read an excerpt from No Witness But the Moon.

ABOUT THE AUTHOR

Suzanne Chazin's work has appeared in *American Health, Family Circle, Ladies Home Journal, People* and *The New York Times.* She has twice been the recipient of the Washington Irving Book award for fiction. Her short fiction appeared in the anthology, *Bronx Noir,* which won the 2008 Book of the Year Award for special fiction from the New Atlantic

Independent Booksellers Association. *Land of Careful Shadows* was shortlisted for the 2016 RUSA Reading List. She lives in Chappaqua, NY. Visit her at suzannechazin.com.

IMPRINT: Kensington
PRINT ISBN: 9781496705174
PRINT PRICE: $25.00
EBOOK ISBN: 9781496705181
EBOOK PRICE: $21.25
PUBLICATION DATE: 10/25/16
PUBLICITY CONTACT: Morgan Elwell Melwell@kensingtonbooks.com
RIGHTS CONTACT: Jackie Dinas Jdinas@kensingtonbooks.com
EDITOR: Michaela Hamilton
AGENT: Stephany Evans
AGENCY: FinePrint Literary Management

PROMOTIONAL INFORMATION:
Major outreach to national print and online media; Extensive blogger campaign, Goodreads giveaways and early NetGalley placement; National print and online advertising; Trade magazine advertising; Podcast advertising; Multilayered social-media campaign and online advertising; Shareable images, dedicated hashtags, and exclusive content; Giveaway opportunities leading up to the book's release.

BOOKSELLER BLURBS:
"Chazin's latest again deftly weaves some difficult and topical subjects into a police procedural."—Kirkus Reviews on *A Blossom of Bright Light*

"Well-paced...Fascinating, multidimensional lead characters."—Publishers Weekly on *A Blossom of Bright Light*

"Suzanne Chazin's *A Blossom of Bright Light* is terrific, a compulsively readable police procedural that builds to the pace of a thriller with an explosive ending. Entertaining and much more with characters who resonate as people and a story that explores complex issues played out on a human scale."—Hallie Ephron, *New York Times* bestselling author of *Night Night, Sleep Tight*

"The most difficult jobs in our society require a fine balance of empathy and emotional distance. In Suzanne Chazin's new novel, a detective and his activist girlfriend struggle to maintain order in a beleaguered community threatened by an inconceivable horror. It is their efforts to hang on to their humanity—and each other—that make *A Blossom of Bright Light* unforgettable. This timely novel sets a taut mystery against a compelling exploration of innocence, obligation, and the redeeming power of love."— Sophie Littlefield, Anthony Award-winning author of *The Guilty One*

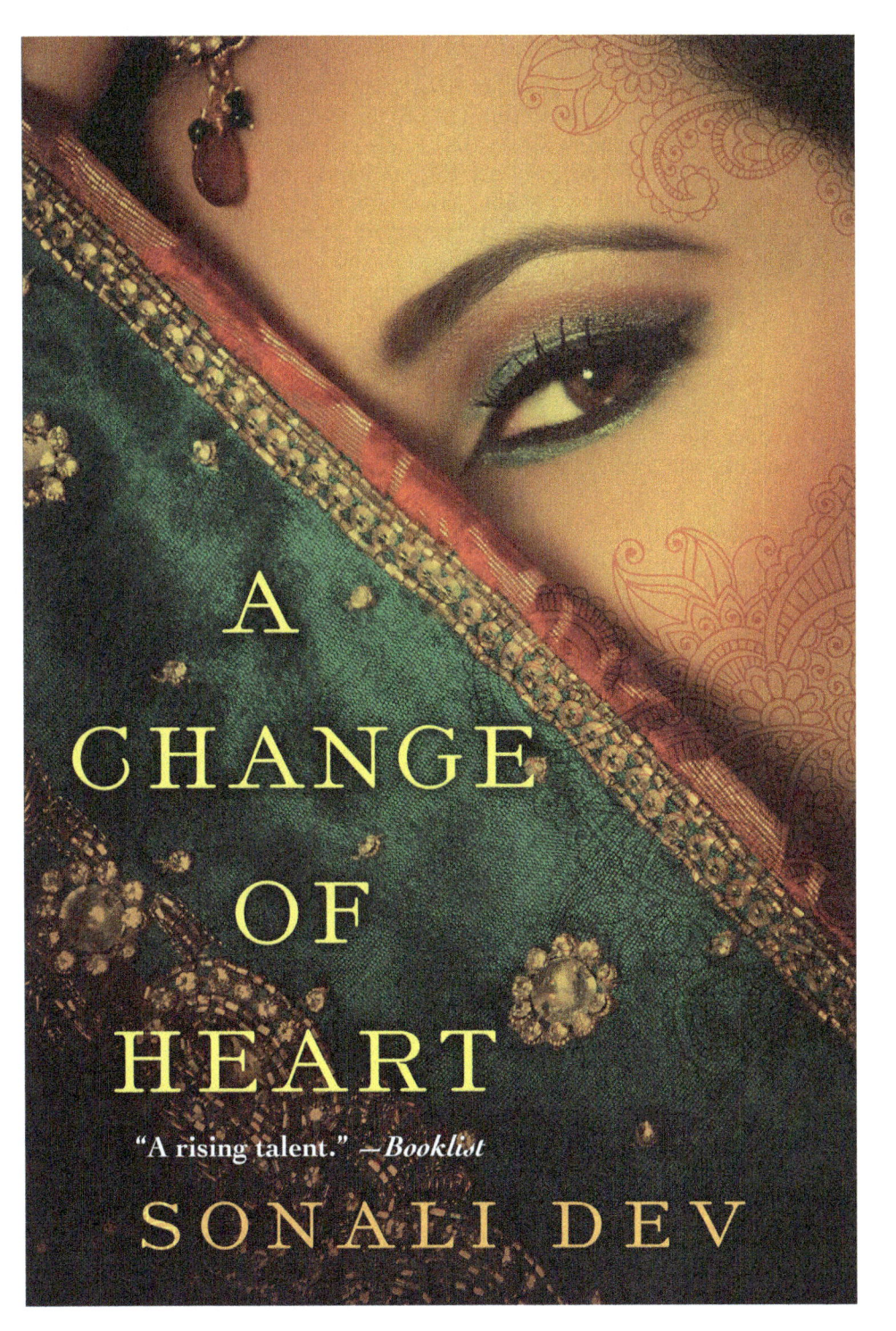

A CHANGE OF HEART

"A rising talent." —*Booklist*

SONALI DEV

SUMMARY

Sonali Dev's highly acclaimed previous two novels, *A Bollywood Affair* (2014) and *The Bollywood Bride* (2015) have been featured on over 20 "Best Of" lists, including NPR's Best Books, Kirkus Reviews' Best of the Year, and *The Washington Post*. Her third and most technically skilled novel yet, *A Change of Heart* delves beyond the surface of modern Indian-American life, an extraordinary story of secrets, danger, and the risks we take in the name of love. . .Dr. Nikhil 'Nic' Joshi had it all until, while working for Doctors Without Borders in a Mumbai slum, his wife, Jen, discovered a black market organ transplant ring. Before she could expose the truth, Jen was killed. Two years after the tragedy, Nic is a cruise ship doctor who spends his days treating seasickness and sunburn and his nights in a boozy haze. On one of those blurry evenings on deck, Nic meets a woman who makes a startling claim: she received Jen's heart in a transplant and has a message for him...

EXCERPT

Chapter One

Nikhil's here and I could just die of happiness. Shit, I shouldn't have said that. Especially not now. Please, Universe, scratch that.—Dr. Jen Joshi

Nikhil's head felt like someone had squeezed it through a liquidizer. Whiskey burn stung his brain as if he had snorted the stuff instead of pouring it down his gullet. He leaned into the polished brass railing, letting the wind pummel his face. The ship, all twenty-four floors of behemoth decadence, was like the damn Burj Al Arab speeding across the Caribbean. And yet the only way to know they were moving was to watch the waves. His fingers released the glass sitting on the railing and it flew into the night, disappearing long before it hit the inky water.

He imagined hopping on the railing, imagined being that glass. Boom! And it would be over. Finally, there'd be peace.

The sky was starting to ignite at the edges, as though the glass of Jack he'd just tossed into the night had splattered amber flecks across the horizon. It would go up in flames soon. All of it orange and gold when the sun broke through the rim of the ocean. It was time for him to leave. The last thing he needed was the mockery of another breaking dawn.

"Sir, why don't you stay and watch today?" A man leaned on his mop, staring at Nikhil from under his windblown hair, that tentative, guilty look firmly in place. The look people couldn't seem to keep off their faces when they talked to Nikhil—the one that announced, rather loudly, that they were terrified of intruding. Because The Pathetic Dr. Joshi with the giant hole in his heart might break down right before their eyes.

"Very beautiful it is, no?" The man pointed his chin at the burgeoning sunrise that had just pumped Nikhil's lungs full of pain and waited for a response. But while the blazing pain in Nikhil's heart was functioning at full capacity, the booze incapacitated his tongue. He wanted to react, wanted to have a conversation with the man who was obviously starved for it. He searched for words to say, but he came up empty.

Now there was a word: *empty*.

Still empty after two years.

The deck hand's smiling mouth drooped into a frown. He turned away and started working the spotless floor with his mop. Shit, had he just thought of the man as a deckhand? Jen would have clonked him upside the head for it. Jen would've—

"What's your name?" Conversation was better than the high definition telecast of memories that kicked off in his brain.

"Gavin." The man looked surprised. "From Goa. In India."

Great. Goa. Jen's favorite place in the whole world.

The steady boat pitched beneath Nikhil's feet. His stomach lurched. The world summersaulted around him. He leaned over the brass railing and tried not to throw up his guts.

He failed. When the heaving stopped the world was still spinning too fast. He lifted his T-shirt and wiped the foul-smelling puke off his mouth. Gavin from Goa was walking across the deck with a bottle of water in his hand.

Nikhil should have thanked him, should've told him he was fine. Instead he turned toward the stairs. In the light of day he could talk to people, pretend to be alive, but now when the world was as dark as his insides, he couldn't. The stairs dived into the lower deck. He grabbed the railing and stumbled down, landing on his ass on the last step.

The smell of chlorine from the three-tiered pool cut past the smell of regurgitated Jack on his shirt, setting off the churning in his stomach again. He pulled himself up and dragged himself to the elevator, rubbing his face on his shoulder like the snotty, cranky brat he used to be. But no tears came to dilute the unrelenting burn of wanting.

How could it be that he was still here? The sunset, the sunrise, it was all still here when she was gone.

He wanted her back. God. Please. Give her back to me.

"Look what you've done to yourself, Spikey."

His head snapped up. He didn't remember stepping out of the elevator, but he spun around now, his breath loud in the absolute silence. The brightly lit corridor swirled around him. The bloodred carpet, the gold-striped walls, every inch of garish splendor echoed that word.

"Spikey."

There wasn't a soul in sight.

He followed the echoing word across the hallway and around the corner, his racing heart dragging the rest of his body along. He turned the corner, expecting to see nothing. Expecting to chase the sound the way he'd been chasing his dead wife's memories for two years.

A shadow clad in black stood all the way across the corridor. A wisp of dark against the overpowering gold of the walls. Bright red strands cascaded around her face and into her jaw in a razor-sharp edge. Hair he knew better than he knew his own name.

He reached out and leaned into the wall, but the ship continued to seesaw beneath him. She held steady for a moment and then she was gone, melting around the corner.

He sprang after her, running until he was standing in the spot she'd been in. Another long corridor stretched out in front of him. It showed no signs of life, only an endless line of doors connected by endless golden molding, and the endless buzz of the lights overhead.

The walls closed in around him, forcing him to stumble forward. His breath ricocheting against the heavily textured wallpaper.

And then there she was again, a flash of red hair peeking around the corner. He ran at it, at her. But his drunken legs tripped over themselves and he splattered flat on his face, arms and legs splayed like a dead arthropod someone had swatted into the floor.

When he lifted his head she was gone.

His face fell back on the rough, deep pile of the carpet with its polythene smell, and everything went black. Everything except the panacean sound of that name.

Spikey.

Only one person called him that.

Jen, his wife. And she'd been dead for two years.

***

Nikhil woke up to the sound of drums beating inside his cerebral cortex. And to claws plucking at his spinal cord as if it were a string on the guitar that still hung on the wall of his childhood room in his parents' home.

Pain vibrated down each vertebra, his usual wake-up call. He knew enough not to sit up immediately, because steady as the boat was, his inner boat would pitch and rock like a rabid Jell-O cup until he made it to the toilet and emptied his innards through his mouth and nose. So much for the comfort of morning rituals.

He was in his own bed. Although he didn't remember getting here. He lifted the sheet off his bare chest and rubbed his wife's misspelled name tattooed across his left pec. His running shorts were still in place over his jutting pelvic bones. They had always been prominent after he'd lost his chubby-kid fat in college. But now they were sharp enough to cut through skin. He pressed his hand into the knife-edged rise of bone, the exact place Jen had liked to hold when—

He sat up too fast. Bile jelly-wobbled up his esophagus along with everything that had happened before he had passed out in that corridor. The over-deodorized smell of carpet. The flash of red hair. He tried to fight it, but his brain traced back his steps until it hit up against that word.

Spikey.

His wife had taken to calling him that after he'd told her how Spikey The Dinosaur had been his favorite TV show in elementary school. He had been a little obsessed with the young stegosaurus who wanted nothing more than for everyone to be happy, who always did the right thing, who had everything a little dinosaur could ask for but was always on the verge of losing it all. Nikhil's mother still had his Spikey toy collection stored in the basement.

When he'd shown it to Jen she had twirled her fingers in his hair, finding that sensitive spot at the top of his head. *Your hair stands up in spikes just like Spikey, Spikey.*

He scrubbed his hand over the hair he now kept cropped down to a skull trim, over the scar slashing down the back of his head where they had cracked open his skull. Sometimes that sort of thing took your memories. With him it had jackhammered the memories into his brain. And what did you do with memories of your wife having her neck snapped in an alley while they held you down and made you watch what they did to her?

The newly grown hair scraped like a hundred two-sided needles into his palm and his scalp. Jen would have hated his shaved head. Hated it. She had loved his hair. She had loved every stupid thing about him. For the life of him he hadn't known why.

"What is wrong with you?" he'd asked her once.

"Actually, my weakness for men with pathetic self-esteem is my only flaw," she'd told him. She'd been more than a little pissed at him for asking.

He threw the sheets back and pushed his legs off the bed.

Look what you've done to yourself, Spikey.

She had been so real. The hair framing her face, that blasted hair color he'd hated so much. It had been so damn real. Maybe it was time to stop chugging the Jack. The whole point of it was to shut the memories down, not to bring them to life.

He reached out and gripped the nightstand to steady the endless pitching in his stomach. Then yanked his hand back when his fingers landed on two bright white pills on a writing pad. His thumb found its way to his wedding band and went to work, rotating it around his finger at a maddening skip. Around and around.

He knew the slanting scrawl on the pad. The *T* flying off the page; the *g* looping around on itself.

He knew what the note said even before he read it.

Take two aspirin and call me in the morning.

Fuck.

His Jen was back.

Chapter Two

My husband's G-spot is on his head. There's this point right at his crown under where his hair gets all spiky, and rubbing it makes him totally hard.—Dr. Jen Joshi

One of these days she'd get used to calling herself Jess. *Just think of it as a role,* he had told her. Of course she thought of it as a role. How else could she possibly do this?

There had been a time when she would have given anything to be someone else, to have a new name, a new history. A fresh slate. Pure again. But there was nothing pure about what she was doing. It was yet another rebirth right into the gutter.

Speaking of gutters, she tried not to think about the smell of vomit in Dr. Nikhil Joshi's room when she had dragged him there last night and left him sprawled on his bed. Maybe pulling off his shirt had been stupid. What if he had woken up? But knowing he was Jen's husband, she just hadn't been able to leave him in soiled clothes. Which was definitely stupid because the sympathy squeezing in her chest was an indulgence she absolutely could not afford.

The good doctor*saab*'s vomit had smelled like the hell he seemed to be trapped in. Booze and bile. Excess and starvation.

His ribs had been so stark against his skin, shades lighter than the burned tan of his forearms and face. The desire to toss his T-shirt into the trash had been strong, but only because she couldn't burn it. Instead she had dumped it on the scattered pile of laundry in the corner of his room, done what she needed to do, and left. Hanging around his kind of pain gouged out all her scabs, and she needed her scabs.

It had been a week. A full week away from her baby. The garish splendor of her shoebox-sized room did nothing to keep it from feeling like a jail cell. All she wanted was to be back in her little flat in Mumbai, with her baby in her arms. Being so far away from him made her feel scattered, as though all of her was parts and pieces floating around without glue. Before this she'd never left him for so much as a day. Those two days when he'd disappeared, when they'd taken him from her were something she couldn't think about right now. If she thought about that she wouldn't be able to get through this.

She picked up her phone. She needed to hear his voice. Calls to Mumbai from the cruise ship were obscenely priced. Good. Because she wasn't the one paying for them. The thought of making the bastard who was paying for the calls pay for something, for anything, gave her a breath of satisfaction.

"Hello, darling." The husky sweetness of Sweetie Raja's voice released some of the tension in her body. Putting people at ease was her flatmate's special gift, not hers. She sank into the tiny bunk bed and slipped off her ballet flats, flexing her toes and stretching out her calves. If she wasn't able to dance soon, she was going to explode.

"Hi, Sweetie, is Joy up yet?"

"I'm fine, darling, thank you so much for asking."

"I'm sorry. Everything okay with you?"

He laughed. She could imagine his gorgeous ponytail swaying to his laughter, his kohl-lined eyes sparkling beneath lashes that drove women wild with envy and men wild with confusion.

"You're apologizing? Who are you and what did you do with my best friend?" he asked, still laughing.

"Ignore me. I'll be my unapologetic bitchy self when I get back. Promise."

The laughter in his voice turned to worry. "Listen to you. You sound exhausted. When was the last time you got some sleep?"

"I'm fine."

Sweetie knew she couldn't talk about it. He hadn't once asked for details. This was why he was her best friend. He was completely at ease around secrets.

"Joy's brushing his teeth. You know you need your strength for the audition next month," he said.

She mumbled something. She knew Sweetie had pulled every string he could to get her the audition with Bollywood's top dance troupe. A dream she could almost touch after working toward it for five years. And here she was a million miles away, where the last thing on her mind was which bloody troupe she danced with.

He called out to Joy. "Joy, Mamma's on the phone, son. Brushing done?"

Her baby's sweet mouth had to be dripping white foam. The bubblegum smell of his toothpaste lumped in her throat. She always made him count ten brushstrokes for each tooth and he did it as though her word was law. Seven-year-olds were supposed to be willful, but it had probably never even occurred to Joy that he could argue with her.

"Mamma?"

With every one of her senses she gathered up his voice. "Hi, Joyboy."

"Ten times on each tooth. I counted." Her sweet, sweet baby.

"You sure?" she said as sternly as she could manage. "Because, you don't—"

"I know, I know, I don't want worms to dig holes in my enalbum."

"Germs, *babu*, not worms."

She heard a soft smack. His palm striking his forehead and a self-conscious cluck. "Yeah, yeah, that."

"Are you taking good care of Sweetie-mamu?"

"I'm trying, but he won't stop drinking so many coffees. I told him you'd be angry if you found out. But..." There was a pause, and he lowered his voice to a whisper. "But he told me not to tell you."

She laughed, and the sweet pain in her heart made her whole again. "You keep trying. All we can do is try, remember?"

"Mamma?"

"Yeah, babu?"

"I made you something in school. But you don't have to come home soon to see it. Sheila-teacher said she'll keep it carefully for you, okay?"

It took her a moment to respond without letting her voice crack. "Mamma will be home as soon as she can. And you know what?"

"Yes, yes, I know. I know your heart is with me. And yes, yes, I'm taking care of it for you."

"Good, because hearts are important." Her hand went to her chest. The still unfamiliar raised scar pushed into her hand. It was only fair that it still hurt. "I love you, my Joy-baby-boy. Mamma's kissing you and holding you. Can you feel it?"

There was silence on the phone, and she knew he had squeezed his eyes shut, imagining her arms around him. "Did you feel mine?"

"Of course I did. But I didn't hear the kiss."

The smacking of his lips was so loud and clear she soaked up the sound and held on to it.

"I love you most in the world, Mamma."

"Hey!" Sweetie's voice was back on the phone. "What about me?"

"Is he rolling his eyes at you?" she asked, biting her lip.

"Of course he is. And he does it even better than you."

"Thanks, Sweetie." Her teeth dug into her lip. Tears were a luxury she couldn't afford either.

"Thank me by coming home safe."

She made an incoherent sound and let him go. Her safety wasn't the issue. How she wished it was, but it wasn't.

***

She watched Jen's Nikhil tuck his white uniform shirt into his white pants and walk out of the clinic. He always seemed to move as if an invisible crane were pulling him forward, always against his will.

Why a doctor had to dress like a cruise ship purser she had no idea, but despite the fact that the uniform was ironed and clean, he managed to make it look almost as soiled as his vomit- streaked T-shirt from last night.

For all the effort she had put into preparing herself to come face-to-face with him, seeing him fall flat on his face like a roadside drunkard while trying to chase her down a corridor was the last thing she had expected. Actually, the horrid sadness it set off inside her was the last thing she had expected. Usually, she liked nothing more than to see a man fall flat on his face and get hurt. It was like poetry to her, watching them in pain instead of inflicting it.

She took a deep breath, adjusted the hood of her sweatshirt so it covered her head, and followed him into the elevator, sliding into the back corner behind him. Not that he noticed her. Not that he noticed anything. He seemed to have no idea that there was a world around him and that it was spinning away with or without him.

Even if he did happen to wake up from his stupor, there was no chance in hell that he would recognize her from yesterday. Not with her hair stuffed into a hairband and hidden away under the thick fleece-lined fabric.

She still couldn't believe what hair extensions could do. All her life she had hated her wispy hair. Now that the heavier healthier strands had been tacked on to her head, all she felt was the awful weight of them. But if his dead wife's hair was what it took to get his attention, then that's what it took.

He had been at the clinic since nine in the morning. It was almost seven p.m. now. He hadn't stepped out of the clinic for ten hours, not even to eat lunch. He had the look of someone who had spent a year in a famine-ridden nation. Skin over bone.. No quilting of muscle or fat. But unlike those pictures of starving people from famines, there was no hunger in his eyes. There was, in fact, absolutely nothing in his eyes.

The elevator started to move, and the strange tension in her belly heightened. Closed spaces made her jittery, especially when she was trapped in one with a man. The elevator bounced to a halt. Nikhil didn't move.

This was his floor. He was messing up her plan. She cleared her throat. He straightened and dragged himself out.

With a finger on the door-open button, she waited for him to be far enough away that he couldn't reach her before the door closed. Then she yanked back her hood, tugged Jen's hair out of the band, and shook it out so it covered most of her face.

"Spikey..." She whispered the word as the door started to slide. It was almost as though she could see the syllables float across the lobby toward him. The instant they struck like a harpoon between his shoulder blades he spun around. His suddenly alert gaze slammed into her cascading hair and clung to it. Now there was hunger. Crazed, desperate hunger.

He leapt forward. But of course he didn't reach her outstretched hand before the door closed. She had timed her words perfectly.

She stepped out of the elevator on the eighth floor, then slipped quietly into a corridor and then her room. Before long the sound of running feet passed outside the door she was leaning against. The desperate edge to the sound had to be her imagination, the thudding in her heart just adrenaline. With over three thousand rooms on *The Oasis*, there was no way he would find her.

Actively bringing her heartbeat under control, she pulled out her bag from the closet, gripping the rough black canvas with its red stitching so hard her fingers cramped. She hadn't bothered to unpack. If she had her way she was getting off the ship with Dr. Joshi in a few days, so why bother? Under her neatly folded clothes—black sweats, black jeans, black tanks—there was a zipper that opened the false bottom of the bag. She unzipped it and pulled out a glossy photograph of Joy and pressed it to her heart.

The memory of her baby boy's smell wrapped around her, the sweetness of milk and Bournvita and baby soap all mixed in with his breath and his sweat and his drool. His Joy smell. From that first time they'd laid him on her breast in the hospital he'd grown and changed every day, but that smell of him, that had stayed exactly the same. It was her stamp on him and his on her.

Pressed against the photo her scar prickled and tightened. The blasted thing had a life of its own and it refused to let her forget it was there. As if she needed a reminder. As if she could ever be the person she had been before she got it.

The sound of footsteps echoed outside her door again. She imagined Nikhil's starved body racing up and down all the corridors on the ship and refused to acknowledge the squeezing in her chest it set off. She could open the door, let him in and tell him everything. But he'd never believe her. She needed him ready. Ripe, and desperate enough to suspend all that he held as true.

Amazingly enough, he had jumped down the rabbit hole rather more easily than she had expected.

You're right, Jen, she thought, *your Spikey does have reverse trust issues.*

Thank heavens for small mercies. She wasn't about to stare a gift horse in the mouth, given that gift horses weren't a problem she'd ever had to deal with.

She gave the photograph one last look, filled her mind with her baby's sweet smile, pulled out the only other thing she had stashed away in the false bottom of the bag, and settled in to read.

You've just read an excerpt from A Change of Heart.

ABOUT THE AUTHOR

Sonali Dev's first literary work was a play about mistaken identities performed at her neighborhood Diwali extravaganza in Mumbai. She was eight years old. Despite this early success, Sonali spent the next few decades getting degrees in architecture and written communication, migrating across the globe, and starting a family while writing for magazines and websites. With the advent of her first gray hair her love for telling stories returned full force, and she now combines it with her insights into Indian culture to conjure up stories that make a mad tangle with her life as supermom, domestic goddess, and world traveler. Sonali is an active member of RWA and WFWA. She lives in Chicago with her family. Visit her online at www.sonalidev.com.

IMPRINT: Kensington
PRINT ISBN: 9781496705747
PRINT PRICE: $25.00
EBOOK ISBN: 9781496705754
EBOOK PRICE: $13.50
PUBLICATION DATE: 9/27/16
PUBLICITY CONTACT: Vida Engstrand vengstrand@kensingtonbooks.com
RIGHTS CONTACT: Jackie Dinas jdinas@kensingtonbooks.com
EDITOR: Martin Biro
AGENT: Claudia Cross
AGENCY: Folio Literary Management

PROMOTIONAL INFORMATION:
Print and online advertising; Select author events; Extensive publicity campaign; Email marketing and promotion; Early reviewer promotions through Goodreads and Netgalley; Social media advertising and promotions.

BOOKSELLER BLURBS:
"Dev's exquisitely written second novel seamlessly integrates the explosive tension of Ria and Vikram's love story with the universal complications of family, identity, and feeling like an outsider, even in your own skin. The modern Indian-American setting offers a glimpse of a rich culture and enhances the book's overt and subtle messages of love, compassion, hope, and common ground. A bright, beautiful gem."—Kirkus Reviews, STARRED REVIEW, Best Books of 2015 for *The Bollywood Bride*

"A vibrant, emotional story… There is much about this book to love. Dev deftly weaves themes of family and friendship into a beautiful romance, setting the story against a backdrop of a massive Indian American wedding, all while tackling issues of mental illness, family expectations and celebrity…readers will rejoice at the results."—*The Washington Post* on *The Bollywood Bride*

"Filled with complexity of characters, rich sense of family love and enticing peeks into a culture… Dev's ability to weave these elements throughout the story is admirable, and she has created a lush, satisfying second-chance-at-love tapestry."—BookPage on *The Bollywood Bride*

"Appealing protagonists, a diverse supporting cast and a colorful multicultural backdrop lend this charming story unexpected emotional depth."—ALA The Reading List, Best Romance of 2014 for *A Bollywood Affair*

THE ONE MAN

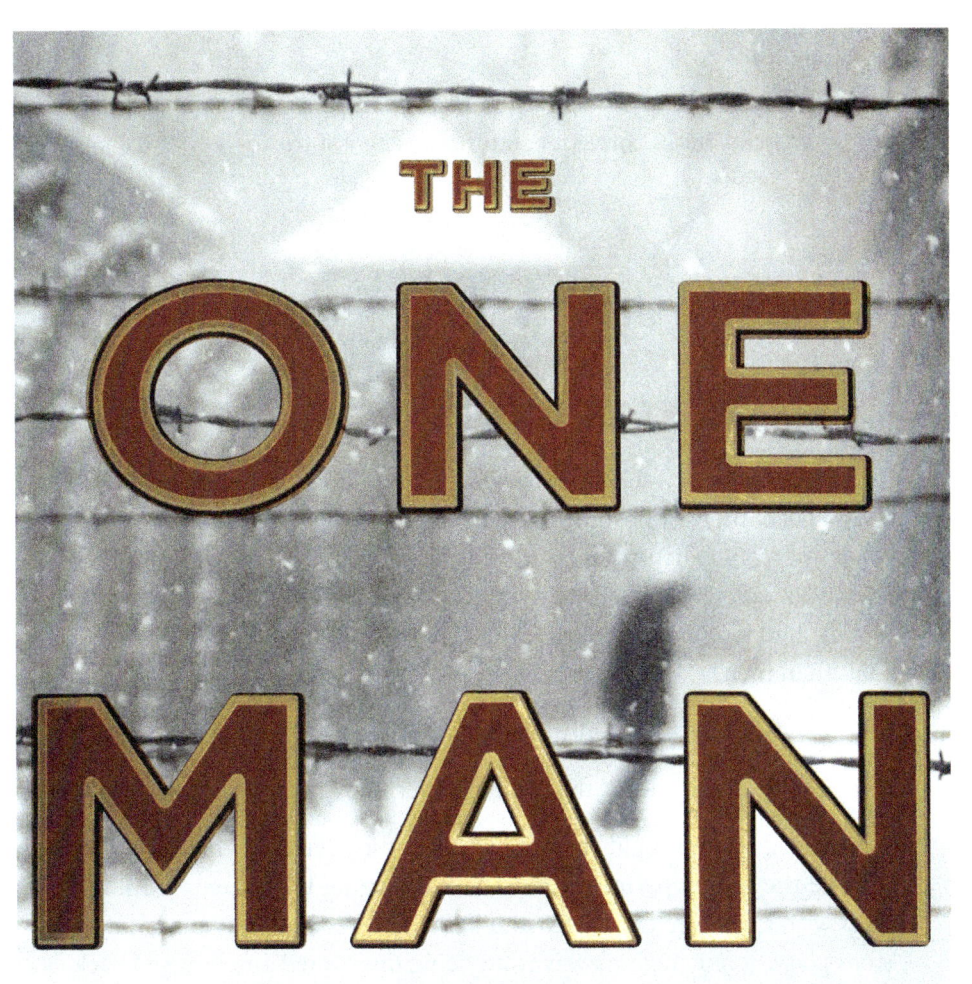

A NOVEL

ANDREW GROSS

NEW YORK TIMES BESTSELLING AUTHOR

SUMMARY

In this riveting historical thriller from *New York Times* bestselling author Andrew Gross, a U.S. intelligence officer is sent into Auschwitz to help one man escape.

EXCERPT

Chapter One

April 1944

The barking of the dogs was closing in on them, not far behind now.

The two men clawed through the dense Polish forest at night, clinging to the banks of the Vistula, only miles from Slovakia. Their withered bodies cried out from exhaustion, on the edge of giving out. The clothing they wore was tattered and filthy; their ill-fitting clogs, useless in the thick woods, had long been discarded; and they stank, more like hunted animals than men.

But now the chase was finally over.

"*Sie sind hier!*" they heard the shouts in German behind them. This way!

For three days and nights they had buried themselves in the woodpiles outside the camp's perimeter wire. Camouflaging their scents from the dogs with a mixture of tobacco and kerosene. Hearing the guards' bootsteps go past, only inches away from being discovered and dragged back to the kind of death no man could easily contemplate, even in here.

Then, the third night, they clawed their way out under the cover of darkness. They traveled only at night, stealing whatever scraps of food they could find on the farms they came upon. Turnips. Raw potatoes. Squash. Which they gnawed at like starving animals. Whatever it was, it was better than the rancid swill they'd been kept barely alive on these past two years. They threw up, their bodies unaccustomed to anything solid. Yesterday, Alfred had turned his ankle and now tried to carry on with a disabling limp.

But someone had spotted them. Only a couple of hundred yards behind, they heard the dogs, the shouts in German, growing louder.

"*Hier entlang!*" This way! "Over here!"

"Alfred, come on, quick!" the younger one exhorted his friend. "We have to keep going."

"I can't. I can't." Suddenly the limping man tripped and tumbled down the river embankment, his feet bloody and raw. He just sat there on the edge of exhaustion. "I'm done." They heard the shouts again, this time even closer. "What's the use? It's over." The resignation in his voice confirmed what they both knew in their hearts: that it was lost. That they were beaten. They had come all this way but now had only minutes before their pursuers would be upon them.

"Alfred, we have to keep moving," his friend urged him on. He ran down the slope and tried to lift his fellow escapee, who even in his weakened condition felt like a dead weight.

"Rudolf, I can't. It's no use." The injured man just sat there, spent. "You go on. *Here—*" He handed his friend the pouch he'd been carrying. The proof they needed to get out. Columns of names. Dates. Maps. Incontrovertible proof of the unspeakable crimes the world needed to see. "Go! I'll tell them I left you hours ago. You'll have some time."

"No." Rudolf lifted him up. "Did you not vow not to die back there in that hell, just to let yourself die here . . . ?"

Rudolf saw it in his friend's eyes. What he'd seen in hundreds of other sets of eyes back at the camp, when they'd given up for good. A thousand.

Sometimes death is just simpler than continuing to fight.

Alfred lay there, breathing heavily, almost smiling. "Now go."

From the woods, only yards away, they heard a click. The sound of a rifle being cocked.

They froze.

It's over, they both realized at once. *They'd been found.* Their hearts leapt up with fear.

Out of the darkness, two men came forward. Both dressed in civilian garb, with rifles, their faces gritty and smeared with soot. It was clear they weren't soldiers. Maybe just local farmers. Maybe the very ones who had turned them in.

"*Resistance?*" Rudolf asked, a last ember of hope flickering in his eyes.

For a second, the two said nothing. One merely cocked his gun. Then the larger one, bearded, in a rumpled hunting cap, nodded.

"Then help us, please!" Rudolf pleaded in Polish. " We're from the camp."

"*The camp?*" The man looked at their striped uniforms without understanding.

"Look!" Rudolf held out his arms. He showed them the numbers burned into them. "Auschwitz."

The barking of the dogs was almost on them now. Only meters away. The man in the cap glanced toward the sound and nodded. "Take your friend. Follow me."

Chapter Two

Early May

Washington, DC

This was the first time he'd been asked to sit in with such esteemed company, and Captain Peter Strauss hoped, after what he had to propose, it wouldn't be the last.

It was a drizzly Monday eve, and the mood around the table inside the Oval Office of the White House was as somber as the leaden skies outside. News of the two escapees, Rudolf Vrba and Alfred Wetzler, had reached President Roosevelt's inner circle within days of them making it across the Polish border to Slovakia.

As one of Bill Donovan's youngest, but chief, OSS operations officers and a Jew, Strauss knew that suspicions of Nazi extermination camps—not just forced labor camps—went as far back as 1942, when reports filtered out from European Jewish groups of some 100,000 Jews forced from the ghettos in Warsaw and Lodz and likely killed. But the firsthand accounts from the two Auschwitz escapees, strengthened by actual documents they brought with them from the camp's administrative offices listing names, numbers, and the factory-like process of mass liquidation, gave credence to everyone's worst fears.

Around the oval table, Roosevelt, his secretary of war, Henry Stimson, Treasury Secretary Robert Morgenthau, William Donovan, his chief spymaster and head of the Office of Strategic Services, and Donovan's aide, Captain Peter Strauss, in this company for the very first time, pored over the grim report and pondered just what it meant. Even more troubling was the escapees' claims that the death camp was rapidly expanding and that the pace of the exterminations, by mass gassing, had increased. Thousands upon thousands were being systemically wiped out each week.

"And this is only one of many such places of death," Morgenthau, a Jew himself whose prominent New York banking family had seen that the escapees' firsthand accounts got into the president's hands, uttered grimly. "Reports suggest there are dozens more. Entire families are being sent to the gas chambers as soon as they arrive. Towns."

"And our options are what, gentlemen?" A disheartened FDR looked around the table. A third, bloody year at war and worry of the upcoming invasion, the decision of whether to run for a fourth term, and the advance of his crippling disease had all taken their toll on him but did not diminish the fight in his voice. "We can't just sit back and allow these unconscionable acts to continue."

"The Jewish Congress and the World Refugee Board are imploring us to bomb the camp," the treasury secretary advised him. "We cannot simply sit on our hands any longer."

"Which will accomplish what, exactly?" Henry Stimson, who had served in the administrations of two presidents prior to FDR and who had come out of public retirement to run the country's war effort, asked. "Except to kill a lot of innocent prisoners ourselves. Our bombers can barely make it all the way there and back with a full payload. We'd suffer considerable losses. And we all know we need every one of those aircraft for what's coming up."

It was May 1944, and word had leaked even to Strauss's level of the final preparations under way for the forthcoming invasion of Europe.

"Then at least we can disrupt their plans and bomb the railway tracks," Morgenthau pleaded, desperate to convince the president to take action. "The prisoners are brought there on sealed trains. That would at least slow down the pace of the exterminations."

"Bombers flying all over Europe at night . . . Making precision strikes on rail tracks? And as you say, there are many such camps?" Stimson registered his skepticism. "I believe the best thing we can do for these poor people, Mr. President, is to get to them and liberate them as swiftly as possibly. Not by sponsoring any ill-conceived raids. At least, that's my view."

The president drew in a breath and took off his wire glasses, the deep channels around his eyes reflecting the pallid cast of a conflicted man. Many of his closest friends were Jews and had urged action. His administration had brought more Jews into the government than any before it. And, as a humane and compassionate being, always seeking to give hope and rise to the common man, he was more repelled by the report of the atrocities he'd just read through than by any that had crossed his desk in the war, even more than the tragic losses of American lives on the beaches in the Pacific or the loss of troops at sea on their way to England.

Yet as a realist, Roosevelt knew his secretary of war was right. Too much lay ahead, and all of it far too important. Plus, the anti-Jewish lobby was still a strong one in the country, and reports of soldiers lost trying to save exclusively Jewish lives would not go well as he sought to gain a fourth term. "Bob, I know how hard this is for you." He put his hand on the treasury secretary's shoulder. "It's hard for all of us, to be sure. Which brings us to the reason we are all here tonight, gentlemen. Our special project. What's it called, 'Catfish'?' " He turned toward the head of the OSS, Colonel Donovan. "Tell me, Bill, do we have any real hope that this project is still alive?"

"Catfish" was the name known only to a very few for the secret operation Strauss was in charge of to smuggle a particular individual out of Europe. A Polish Jew, whom FDR's people claimed was vital to the war effort.

As far back as 1942, it had been discovered that bearers of certain Latin American identity papers were awarded special treatment in Warsaw. For several months, hundreds of Polish and Dutch Jews were issued counterfeit papers from Paraguay and El Salvador to gain exit from Europe. Many had made their way to northern France, where they were interned at a detention center in the village of Vittel, while their cases were gone over by skeptical German officials. As doubtful as the Nazis were about the origin of these papers, they could not afford to upset these neutral Latin American countries, whose authoritarian rulers were, in fact, sympathetic to their cause. How these particular refugees were able to acquire these papers, purchased secretly through anti-Nazi emissaries in the Paraguayan and Salvadoran embassies in Bern, and their dubious provenance, was always clouded. What also remained unclear was how contacts friendly to the United States had been able to get them into the hands of the very subject and his family (aka "Catfish") they were attempting to smuggle out. For a while, the prospects looked hopeful. Twice, transport out of Europe had been arranged, via Holland and France. Yet each time the Germans blocked their exit. Then, just three months ago, an informer from Warsaw had blown the papers' suspect origins wide open, and now the fates of all the Vittel Jews, including the one they so desperately wanted, were completely up in the air.

"I'm afraid, we've hit a snag, Mr. President," Donovan said. "We don't know for certain if he's even there."

"Or if he is, if he's even still alive . . ." Secretary of War Stimson added. "Our intelligence on the matter has all gone dark."

The emissaries who had passed along these documents had been arrested and were now in Nazi jails.

"So I'm told we still need this man. At all costs." The president turned to his secretary of war. "Is this still true?"

"Like no other." Stimson nodded. "We were close in Rotterdam. There was even transport booked. *Now* . . ." He shook his head somberly, then took his pen and pointed to a tiny spot on the map of Europe that was on a stand next to the conference table.

A place called Oswiecim. In Poland.

"*Oswiecim?*" Roosevelt put back on his glasses.

"Oswiecim is the Polish name for Auschwitz, Mr. President," the secretary of war said. "Which, in light of the report we've all just read, is why we're here."

"I see." The president nodded. "So now he's one of five million faceless Jews, forced out of their homes against their will, without papers or identity?"

"And to what fate, we do not know . . ." Secretary of the Treasury Morgenthau shook his head gravely.

"It's all our fates that are in the balance, gentlemen." Roosevelt pushed his wheelchair back from the table. "So you're here to tell me we've done everything we can to find this man and get him out. And now it's lost. *We've* lost."

He went around the table. For a moment, no one replied.

"Perhaps not completely lost, Mr. President." The OSS chief leaned forward. "My colleague Captain Strauss has looked at the situation closely. And he believes there might be one last way . . ."

"A last way?" The tired president's gaze fell on the young aide.

"Yes, Mr. President."

The captain appeared around thirty, slightly balding already, the son of a cantor, and a graduate of Columbia Law School. A smart cookie, Roosevelt had been told. "All right, son, you've got my attention," the president said.

Strauss cleared his throat and glanced one more time at his boss. He opened his folder.

"Go on." Donovan nodded to him. "Tell him your plan."

Chapter Three

January, Four Months Earlier

The Vittel Detention Center, Occupied France

"Papa, Papa, wake up! They're here!"

The shrill of whistles knifed through the frigid morning air. Dr. Alfred

Mendl awoke in his narrow bunk, his arm wrapped around his wife, Marte, protecting her from the January cold. Their daughter, Lucy, stood over them, both nervous and excited. She'd been at the blanket-covered window of the cramped room that was fit at most for four, but which they now shared with fourteen others. This was no place for a girl to pass her twenty-second birthday, as she had just the night before. Huddled on lice-infested mattresses, sleeping amidst their haphazard suitcases and meager belongings, every one slowly stirred out of their blankets and greatcoats with the anticipation that something clearly was up.

"Papa, look now!"

On the landing outside, the French *milice* were going room to room, banging on doors with their batons. "Get up! Out of bed, you lazy Jews. All those holding foreign passports, take your things and come down. You're leaving!"

Alfred's heart leapt. After eight hard months, was this finally the time?

He jumped out of bed, still dressed in his rumpled tweed pants and woolen undershirt, all that kept them warm. They had all slept in their warmest clothes most every night for months now, washing them whenever they could. He nearly tripped over the family stretched out on the floor next to them. They rotated the sleeping arrangements a month at a time.

"Everyone holding foreign passports packed and out!" a black-clad policeman threw open the door and instructed them.

"Marte, get up! Throw everything together. Maybe today is the day!" he said to his wife with a feeling of hopefulness. Hope that had been dashed many times over the past year.

Everyone in the room was murmuring, slowly coming to life. Light barely crept through the blanket-covered sills. Vittel was a detention camp in the northeast corner of France, actually four, six-story hotels that formed a ring around a large courtyard, not exactly "four stars," so the joke went, as it was all surrounded by three rows of barbed wire manned by German patrols. Thousands were held there—political prisoners, citizens of neutral or enemy countries whom the Germans were hoping to exchange—

although the Jews, mostly of Polish and Dutch descent, whose fate was being decided by Berlin, were kept together on the same ward. The French policeman who entered their room stepped between the rustling bodies, prodding people along with his stick. " Didn't you hear me? All of you, up, packed. Quick, quick! Why are you dallying? You're shipping out."

Those who were slow to move, he nudged sharply with his stick and kicked open their suitcases that were strewn on the floor.

"We are we going?" people questioned in various languages and accents: Polish, Yiddish, and awkward French, everyone scurrying to get their things together.

"You'll see. Just get yourself moving. That's my only job. And take your papers. You'll find out downstairs."

"Take our papers!" Alfred looked at Marte and Lucy with a lift in his heart. *Could this finally be their time?* He and his family had waited so long there. Eight harsh months, after making their way with the forged identity papers gotten into his hands by the emissary from the Paraguayan embassy in Warsaw. First to the Swiss border through Slovakia and Austria, where they were turned away; then by train through occupied France to Holland, all the while under the protection of the Paraguayan embassy in Warsaw as a foreign national on a teaching assignment at the university in Lvov. Once, they literally got as far as the pier in Rotterdam where they were to board a Swedish cargo ship, the *Prinz Eugen*, to Stockholm, transport papers in hand, only to be turned back again as their papers needed to be authenticated. Literally in limbo, they were sent here to Vittel, while Jewish organizations in Switzerland and the United States' and British governments argued their cases and pressured the Paraguayan and Salvadoran governments to honor their documents. Since then, they had been kept here in a kind of diplomatic hell. Always promised that the matter was being looked into. One more day, just another day, while the German foreign office and Latin American embassies worked it out. Alfred and his family had even taught themselves Spanish, to make their case all the more convincing. Of course they knew their documents were not worth the paper they were printed on. Alfred was Polish, had been born in Warsaw, and had taught electromagnetic physics at the university in Lvov after years in Prague and Gottingen with some of the best minds in the atomic field. At least until he was stripped of his position a year ago and his diplomas were trashed and burned. Marte was from Prague, now overrun by the Nazis, but had been a Polish citizen for years. They all knew that the only thing that had kept them from being shipped off somewhere and never heard from again was these papers, suspect as they were, that had been arranged by he knew not who with the promise that they would get the family out and to America, where he would be greeted warmly by Szilard and Fermi, his old colleagues. Still, whatever they had suffered these past months was far better than what they would have faced back home. Months ago he'd heard the university in Lvov had been cleared out just like those in Warsaw and Krakow. The last of his colleagues shot, kicked in the streets, or shipped off somewhere with their families, never heard from again.

Bring your papers, the *milice* said now. Was this a good sign or a bad one? Alfred didn't know. But everyone around him was springing to life, pulsing with both nerves and anticipation. Maybe it had all been cleared up at last. Maybe they were finally leaving.

A day hadn't passed where he hadn't dreamed of presenting his work to people who pursued good and not these Nazis.

"Darling, come on, quick!" He helped his wife fill up her suitcase. Marte was frail these days. She'd caught a cold in November, and it seemed to have never left her chest. She looked like she'd aged ten years since they'd begun their journey.

They'd had to leave everything behind. Their fine china. Their collection of antique pharmacy jars. All the awards that had been given to him. Anything of value other than a few photo graphs and, of course, his work. They stuffed whatever they had taken into their small bags. When the time came to leave, it had to be in a day.

"Lucy, quick!" Alfred assembled his papers and threw them into his leather briefcase along with the few books he'd been able to bring along. He could lose his clothing, his academic diplomas, the photographs of his parents on the Vistula in Warsaw, the personal effects dearest to him. Even his best shoes. But his work—his work must remain. His formulas and studies. Everything depended on getting them out. One day that would become clear. He hastily bundled it all together in his case and fastened the lock. "Marte, Lucy, we must go."

A few in the crowded room remained behind and wished those who were leaving well, like prisoners saying goodbye to a fellow inmate who'd been pardoned. "See you in a better life," they said, as if they knew their fates would not be as rosy. A strange familiarity had built up among people whose lives had been thrown together for months in such close quarters.

"God be with you! Goodbye!"

Alfred, Marte, and Lucy made their way outside, melding into the river of people heading along the outside corridors and down to the courtyard. Parents held onto their children; sons and daughters helped the elderly as they slowly went down the stairs, so as not to be trampled in the rush. On the ground, they were herded into the large yard, shivering from the January chill, murmuring, wondering to their neighbors what was going to happen next. Above them, a crowd of those left behind pressed against the banisters, looking on.

"Papa, what's going to happen to us?" Lucy asked, eyeing the German guards with their submachine guns.

Alfred looked around. "I don't know."

There were Germans—there always were—but not so many as one would think if something bad was going to happen to them. They all huddled together in the cold. Merchants, teachers, accountants, rabbis. In long woolen coats and homburgs and fedoras.

Whistles sounded. A officious-looking captain in the local French militia, a German officer following behind, stepped in front of the throng and ordered everyone to line up with their papers. The German was in a gray wool officer's coat with the markings of the secret intelligence division, the Abwehr, which worried Alfred.

He and his family grabbed their suitcases and joined the queue.

The French officer went down the line, family by family, inspecting their papers closely and checking their faces. Some he instructed to remain where they were; others he waved to the side of the yard. Armed guards stood everywhere. And dogs, barking loudly and pulling on their leashes, scaring the young children, and some of the parents too.

"It will be a joy to be rid of this place," Marte said. "Wherever we end up."

"It will," Alfred said, though he was sensing something in the mood of the soldiers that didn't seem right. They had their caps low and their hands on their weapons. There was no levity. No fraternizing.

Those who didn't speak French were directed to the side without knowing what was going on. One family, Hungarian, Alfred suspected, shouted loudly in their native tongue as a French militia man tried to move them and then kicked open a suitcase, filled with religious articles, which the old man and his wife scampered vainly to pick up. Another man, clearly a rabbi with a long white beard, kept showing his papers to the *milice* captain in frustration. The French officer finally flung them back at him, the old man and his wife bending to pick them off the ground as eagerly as if they were thousand-zloty notes.

No, Alfred thought, it didn't seem right at all.

The captain and his German overseer made their way down the line. The soldiers and the guards gradually began to use more force to restrain everyone.

"Don't worry, these have been checked many times," Alfred assured Marte and Lucy. "They will definitely pass."

But a worrisome feeling rose up in him as each interaction seemed to be met only by frustration and anger, and then people were brusquely shuffled into the growing throng ringed by heavily armed guards.

Outside the walls they heard a train hiss to a stop.

"See, they are taking us somewhere." Alfred tried to sound optimistic to his family.

At last the French officer made his way up to them. "*Papers*," he requested impassively. Alfred handed him the travel documents showing that he and his family were under the protection of the Paraguayan government and had merely been residents in Poland these past seven years.

"We have been waiting a long time to get home," Alfred said in French to the officer, whose shifting black eyes never really looked at him, just back and forth, from the documents to their faces, as had been done many times these past eight months without incident. The SS officer stood behind him, hands clasped behind his back, with a stone-like look that made Alfred feel uneasy.

"Have you enjoyed your stay here in France, senorita?" the *milice* captain asked Lucy in passable Spanish.

"*Sí*, sir," she replied, nervously enough so that Alfred could hear it in her voice. Who wouldn't be? "But I am ready to finally get home."

"I'm sure you are," the captain said. Then he stepped in front of Alfred. "It says you are a professor?"

"Yes. Electromagnetic physics."

"And where did you acquire these papers, monsieur?"

"What? Where did we acquire them . . . ?" Alfred stammered back, his insides knotting with fear. "These were issued by the Paraguayan embassy in Warsaw. I assure you they are valid. Look, there, you can see . . ." He went to show the officer the official seal and signatures.

"I'm afraid these papers are forgeries," the *milice* captain declared.

"I beg your pardon?"

"They are worthless. They are as bad as your Spanish, I'm afraid, mademoiselle. *All of you* . . . " He raised his voice so that the entire crowd could hear. "You are no longer under the protection of the Paraguayan and El Salvadoran governments. It is determined that these visas and passports are not valid. You are prisoners of the French government now, who have no recourse, given your situation, but to turn you over to the German authorities."

There was an audible gasp from the crowd. Some wailed, "*My God, no!*" Others simply looked to the person next to them and muttered, "What did he say . . . ? That these are not valid?"

To Alfred's horror, the French officer began to tear his documents into shreds. All that had kept them alive these past ten months, their only route to freedom, letting them scatter from his hands like ashes onto Alfred's shoes.

"You three, over there," the officer pushed them brusquely, "with the rest." Then he moved down the line without another word. "Next."

"What have you done?" Alfred bent to scoop the shredded documents off the ground. He pulled at the arm of the officer. "Those papers are perfectly valid. They have been inspected many times. Look, look . . ." He pointed to the torn signature page. "We are Paraguayan citizens, looking to return home. We demand transit!"

"You *demand* transit?" The SS officer following the *milice* captain finally spoke. "Be assured, transit is arranged."

Two guards edged their way in and pushed them with their guns from the line. "Take your bags. Over there!" They pointed toward the throng of other Latin American passport holders who were now being penned in by guards, a deepening hopelessness beginning to envelop them.

People began to shout out cries of outrage and objection, holding up their documents, eight months of waiting, hoping, being kept in pens, their dreams of freedom suddenly dashed. The French officer announced in several languages that those holding these travel papers had five minutes to gather their belongings and board transportation that had been arranged outside the camp grounds.

"Where are you taking us?" a terrified woman yelled. For months, rumors of dark places where no one was ever heard from again had spread through the detention camp like an outbreak of typhus.

"To the beach," one of French militia laughed. "To the South of France. Where else? Isn't that where you are looking to go?"

"We have an express train for you. Do not worry," another chortled with the same sarcasm. "You Latin American aristocrats will be traveling first class."

Pandemonium spread like wildfire. Some just refused to accept their fate. The old rabbi in the white beard and his wife sat down on their luggage, refusing to budge. Others screamed back in anger at the black-clad guards, who, now that the true purpose of what they were doing had come out and the crowd had grown unruly, began to close in, herding them like sheep toward the front gate, brandishing their weapons.

"Stay together," Alfred instructed Marte and Lucy, tightly clutching their bags. They were separated for a moment by people charging to the front, cursing and showing their discredited papers in fits of rage. The crowd began to surge. The guards closed in, using their rifle shafts like cattle prods. The white-bearded rabbi and his wife still refused to move; a German guard had now taken over and was screaming at them like they were deaf. "*Aussen.*" Out. "Get up! Now." Fights began to break out. Some faces were bloodied, struck by rifle shafts. A few old-timers fell to the ground, and the crowd moved over them despite desperate pleas and shrieks from those who stopped to help.

But family by family, there was no choice but to go. Worried, everyone grabbed their things. The *milice* herded them with their sticks and rifles in the direction of the front gate. Some prayed, others whimpered, but all, except the rabbi and his wife, went. Guards infiltrated the crowd, kicking along luggage. "Is this yours? Take it, or it stays!" Moving them like cattle through Vittel's makeshift wire gate, dogs barking, pulling on their leashes, amid outraged shouts everywhere, wails, cries, every one giving themselves over to their worst fears.

"Papa, what's happening?" Lucy said, afraid.

"Come on, stay close," Alfred said, clutching his and Marte's valise along with his briefcase. "Maybe it will just be another detention center like this. We've lived through worse." He tried to appear as positive as he could, though he knew in his heart it would not be. Now they had no papers. And Marte's health was growing worse. They moved through the front gate, the first time in eight months they were beyond the wire.

A cargo train waited for them on the tracks. At first, people assumed it was not for them. More for cattle or horses. Then everyone was startled by the sudden rattle of the doors being flung open. The French guards remained behind. The soldiers along the tracks were now German, which sent terror into every one's heart.

"Here are your fancy carriages, Jews," one of them cackled. "Please, let me help you." He cracked a man in the head with his rifle stock. "Everyone up and in."

There was resistance at first, people objecting, fighting back. This was transport fit for swine, not people. Then there were two short bursts of machine gun fire from behind them and everyone turned. The white-bearded rabbi and his poor wife were now lying on the ground in a pool of blood next to their luggage.

"Oh my God, they're going to massacre us," a woman screamed. Everyone headed for the trains. One by one they hurried in, pushing the old and young, dragging their belongings with them. If it couldn't be carried, or if someone stopped to load another article first, their bags were torn from them and tossed aside, clothing and pictures and toiletries spilling over the platform.

"No, those are my possessions!" a woman yelled.

"Get in. Get in. You won't need them." A guard pushed her inside.

"There are no seats in here," someone said. Alfred helped Marte and Lucy up and someone pushed him up from behind. When they all thought the car was filled, they pushed more in. In minutes, you could barely breathe.

"There's no room! There's no more room! Please . . ." a woman wailed. "We'll suffocate in here."

They filled it even more.

"Please, I don't want to go," a man shouted over the wailing.

"C'mon, do you want to end up like them?" another urged him onward, glancing back to the rabbi and his wife in the courtyard.

"My daughter, my daughter. *Sophie . . . !*" a woman cried. A young girl, forced by the crowd into another car, cried out from afar, "Mama!"

The guards kept loading and packing people in with whatever they could carry, until the train car grew tighter and more crowded than Alfred could ever have imagined.

Then the door was slammed shut.

There was only darkness at first. The only light from outside angled through narrow slits in the side door. There were a few whimpers in the pitch black, but then everyone just became silent. The kind of silence when no one has any idea what will happen next. There was barely room to move, to even adjust your arms, to breathe. The car smelled, the odor of eighty people jammed together in a space that would hold half that, many of whom hadn't bathed in weeks.

They stayed that way, listening to the shouts and cries from outside, until they heard a whistle and with a jerk the train began to move. Now people were whimpering, sobbing, praying. They stayed upright by leaning against each other in the dark. In a corner there two jugs, one filled with water—but hardly enough, given the number of them in the car. The other empty. Alfred realized what it was for.

"Where are they taking us, Alfred?" Marte asked under her breath as the rail cars picked up speed.

"I don't know." He sought out her and Lucy's hands and clasped them tightly in his. "But at least we are together."

You've just read an excerpt from The One Man.

ABOUT THE AUTHOR

Andrew Gross is the author of *New York Times* and international bestsellers *The Blue Zone*, *Don't Look Twice*, and *The Dark Tide*, which was nominated for the Best Thriller of the Year award by the International Thriller Writers, *Reckless*, *Eyes Wide Open*, and most recently, *One Mile Under*. He is also coauthor of five number one bestsellers with James Patterson, including *Judge & Jury* and *Lifeguard*. He lives in Westchester County, New York, with his wife, Lynn.

IMPRINT: Minotaur Books
PRINT ISBN: 9781250079503
PRINT PRICE: $26.99
EBOOK ISBN: 9781466892187
EBOOK PRICE: $12.99
PUBLICATION DATE: 8/23/16
PUBLICITY CONTACT: Hector DeJean hector.dejean@stmartins.com
RIGHTS CONTACT: Kerry Nordling kerry.nordling@stmartins.com
EDITOR: Kelley Ragland

AGENT: Simon Lipskar
AGENCY: Writer's House

BOOKSELLER BLURBS:
"The horrors of Holocaust are never less than gut-wrenching. When focused on one man, the imperative of his rescue bringing with it knowledge essential to defeating the Axis Powers, the suspense of that story becomes gut-wrenching, too. High stakes indeed. And Andrew Gross brings a full arsenal of the novelist's skills to *The One Man*, yet none is so essential as the personal outrage powering the narrative, driving him deep into each character portrayed to create an immersive experience for the reader. When you turn the last page, be sure to read on to the Epilogue."—Barbara Peters, The Poisoned Pen

"*The One Man* is totally engrossing—I read it in two sittings!—and full of twists and turns. I was particularly moved that so much of this fantastic story was based on truth and clearly so personal to write. Do not miss this book."—Candice Cohen, Palm Beach Books, Florida

"So powerful, authentic. An ode to courage, daring, family and secrets. I can't wait for August 2016 to put *The One Man* in everyone's hands."—Diane Garrett, Diane's Books, Greenwich, CT

"If you can read this book without your heart in your mouth or finish without a tear in year eye, I'd be very surprised. This is a wonderful and memorable book, definitely one of the reads of the year."—Robin Agnew, Aunt Agatha's

"*The One Man* is a superb tale of espionage and heroism in WWII with the highest stakes. Gross knows how to ratchet up the suspense—and then some, to an emotional finale. I'm still shaking."—Otto Penzler, Mysterious Bookshop, New York, NY

"Andrew Gross has found his calling in his new book, *The One Man*. . . I have been a fan of Andrew Gross and his books since he began his career and I believe *The One Man* is outstanding. It surpasses even some of the top writers of our time. *The One Man* captures the lingering horrors of World War II and its long-lasting residual effects on not only the victims of Nazi soldiers, but their families as well. It focuses mostly on people, rather than the crimes committed by the Nazis. But is also shows how the Nazis exterminated some of the greatest minds the world will ever see.

Andrew Gross did extensive research for this project, interviewing numerous survivors, studying documents, books, journals. Among the interviews he conducted was that of his 95-year-old father-in-law who escaped Warsaw just months before the war. He was the only one in his family to survive. The book is written with compassion and sheds light on little known aspects of the war. Don't miss this as it shows Andrew Gross's wonderful talent."—Cheryl Kravitz, Classic Books, FLA

EVERY MAN A MENACE

A NOVEL

PATRICK HOFFMAN

SUMMARY

Patrick Hoffman burst onto the crime fiction scene with *The White Van*, a captivating thriller set in the back streets of San Francisco, which was named a *Wall Street Journal* best mystery of the year and was shortlisted for the CWA Ian Fleming Steel Dagger Award. Hoffman returns with *Every Man a Menace*, the inside story of an increasingly ruthless ecstasy-smuggling ring.

San Francisco is about to receive the biggest delivery of MDMA to hit the West Coast in years. Raymond Gaspar, just out of prison, is sent to the city by his boss—still locked up on the inside—to check in on the increasingly erratic dealer expected to take care of distribution. In Miami, meanwhile, the man responsible for shipping the drugs from Southeast Asia to the Bay Area has just met the girl of his dreams—a woman who can't seem to keep her story straight. And thousands of miles away, in Bangkok, someone farther up the supply chain, a former conscript of the Israeli army, is about to make a phone call that will put all their lives at risk.

Stretching from the Golden Triangle of Southeast Asia to the Golden Gate of San Francisco, *Every Man a Menace* offers an unflinching account of the making, moving, and selling of the drug known as Molly—pure happiness sold by the brick, brought to market by bloodshed and betrayal.

EXCERPT

Part One

Getting out of prison is like having a rotten tooth pulled from your mouth: it feels good to have it gone, but it's hard not to keep touching at that hole. Raymond Gaspar served four years this time. He served them at a place in Tracy called the Deuel Vocational Institution, DVI. The only vocation he learned was making sure the drugs kept moving. By the time he was done, he'd become something like a football coach. He told the players where to stand, what to do. He wasn't the head coach. That would be his boss, a man named Arthur.

Raymond fell in with Arthur because one of his uncles used to associate with him. As soon as Raymond got bounced from San Quentin up to DVI, his uncle told him to find a man named Arthur. *Don't worry,* he said. *There'll only be one Arthur on the yard.* That ended up being true. Arthur smiled big when he heard who Raymond was.

It turned out Arthur was a good man to know at DVI. He was big business, and not just there either; he kept a low profile, but his fingers stretched well beyond the yard. He associated as white, but he dealt with blacks and Latins, too; as far as Raymond knew, Arthur was the only man in the California Department of Corrections who could make a call to the Black Guerrila Family or the Aryan Brotherhood and get action from either group. That's how he was.

Raymond had been locked up for trying to sell a stolen boat to a man in San Francisco. He had walked right into a police investigation that didn't have anything to do with him. It was simple bad luck. They wrapped him up outside the garage on Sixth Street. When the cops searched his car they found an ounce of crystal meth. It was a bad day. They had him on tape talking about the boat, which led them to the boat itself, back in a garage in Richmond, and they had the drugs. Two months later, his public defender, a good lawyer, lost a motion to suppress at the preliminary hearing, and Raymond was forced to take a deal: four years.

Arthur must've thought that stolen boat made Raymond something of a businessman. He kept him off the front lines, didn't use him as muscle, and right off the bat made him a supervisor. It was a fine thing to be doing: make the rounds, see where things were with the supply, let Arthur know that everything was good. He didn't have to touch the dope, and he didn't have to play rough either.

Raymond swore he saw a shine in Arthur's eyes when he reminded him that his release date was approaching. It was uncharacteristic. "I got a little situation you could help me with," the older man said. They were sitting near the handball courts in the south yard. A few of Arthur's men sat near them. Arthur was a big man, with a big head and big shoulders; he sat hunched over with his elbows on his knees. In his country accent— he'd been raised on a horse farm in western Colorado—he explained that he had a little side thing going in San Francisco.

"I got this lady that buys a little pack of Molly every month and sells it to this other dude. Thirty, forty, fifty pounds a month. Real weight. I set it up—everything's good. She cuts me a little percentage off the deal each time." He made a gesture like he was flicking water off his hands. Raymond wanted to ask what kind of percentage, but he didn't. Arthur told him anyway.

"Thing is, that ten percent is not enough." He looked at Raymond like he was confirming his level of interest. Raymond nodded.

"What I'd like to do is replace at least one of these two parties with you. I mean, unless you're planning on going straight or some bullshit? Accepting the Lord into your heart?" Raymond shook his head.

"It's a complicated situation, though," Arthur went on. "We can't just go and push a motherfucker out on this one." He made his face look like the very idea was distasteful. "Nah, you can't just push 'em out. I want you to go there and—acquaint yourself with the situation. It's hard for me to see everything from here." He pointed at the walls, turned, and looked at Raymond.

"Go and look?" Raymond asked. He felt a sense of uneasiness come over him.

"That's it," Arthur said. "Just go and look around, get to know these two skunks, see wassup. Do some of that fancy bullshitting you do; make sure this next deal goes through. I'll cut you half of my ten, put you at thirty thousand or something around there, let you land on your feet. After that, if we gotta do the same shit the next month, we'll drop it to a quarter of the ten, two-point-five, put you at fifteen or something. It's not bad." He smiled; Raymond did, too. Fifteen thousand a month was good.

Arthur continued: "Even if we don't make a move, it won't hurt to have you on the ground. You did your thing in here, man. And I still owe that fucking uncle of yours, so …"

He held his fist out. Raymond bumped it.

***

It felt good to step off that Greyhound bus and put his feet down on Mission Street. It was late in the afternoon, cold and damp around the bus station, but the air smelled clean to Raymond. He walked all the way to the Prita Hotel, on Nineteenth and Mission. He always stayed there when he was in the city. The Prita was the kind of place where you needed to get buzzed in at the front door, then buzzed in again at a second door at the top of some filthy stairs. You talked to the clerk through a dirty Plexiglas window. The hallways smelled like cigarettes and crack smoke.

They charged by the day, week, or the month. The rooms consisted of a bed, a small TV, and a locked door. Raymond paid for a week.

When he'd gotten his room, Raymond laid down and thought about the situation he was about to get into. Arthur had outlined the arrangement. Gloria Ocampo, a Filipina woman was bringing the ecstasy in. Every month she got a shipment from some Israelis and sold it to a guy named Shadrack Pullman. Arthur had set the whole deal up, hence the 10 percent cut. "But you gotta watch this chick," he'd said. "She's paranoid, nasty, and smart." He tapped on the side of his head with his pointer finger. "A capital-G Gangster, you understand? Don't let her looks fool you."

Raymond had asked about Shadrack next.

"Served his time right here," Arthur said, pointing out at the yard. "He's all right—you know—a little on the eccentric side. He's got a little Pomo in him, you know? Indian, Native American. He's the type of character gonna let you know what he thinks, one way or the other. He don't keep it close to the chest, but he's all right." Arthur waved his hand like Shadrack was nothing to worry about.

"Truth of the matter is, if we do end up having to move someone, it's gotta be Shadrack first, 'cause trying to get rid of Gloria would be like kicking a damn hornets' nest." He shook his head like he wasn't ready for the idea. "You never know, though. Her time might come, too."

Raymond asked what he was supposed to say he was doing there.

"I talk to Gloria somewhat regularly," Arthur said. "I check in, thank her for her timely payments. Last time she made mention of Shadrack turning eccentric—that's her word. She called him eccentric. I said, 'All right, I'll send someone, have a little talk with the boy, straighten him out.' She said, 'No, don't worry.' She got a Pinoy accent. I said, 'No, it's fine.' Bottom line, you know, it's grounds for entry. But you just gotta say your lines, man. Say you're there watching over my interests, making sure the deal keeps clicking. She'll probably ask you. You can tell her you getting two-point-five on my ten."

Raymond asked if his showing up was going to cause any kind of undue worry.

"Maybe so, maybe not," Arthur said. "But what the fuck they gonna do about it? You're working for me. Those two aren't about to make a move on me."

Lying there on the bed, Raymond pictured the whole thing. He could handle it. He could make a threat, or follow through on one. But, the way he saw it, the ideal thing would be to let these two carry on. Collect his two-point-five and stay mellow. He didn't want to kick a hornets' nest if he didn't have to.

***

A few hours later, Raymond walked up Mission Street and bought himself a prepaid cell phone. The sidewalk was crowded, but he felt tense and lonely. The city had changed. It seemed richer. When he got back to the Prita, he sent a text message to Gloria Ocampo.

She texted back right away. Said she'd come by at eight. For a brief moment, Raymond wondered what he was getting himself into.

He had vague plans of using the money he'd make from this job to start something straight. Buy some tools, start working carpentry or something like that. But he wasn't about to go fully clean. He didn't really want to leave the grimy life behind. He liked making money from drugs, from illegal shit. It made him feel high. He'd been doing it most of his life, and he wasn't about to quit now. He didn't really care for carpentry all that much.

Gloria Ocampo showed up exactly at eight. She was slightly plump, nothing like Raymond had expected. He had pictured a club girl: skinny, with tight jeans. Gloria was probably in her fifties. She had dark circles under her eyes that made her look tired. But she was still pretty; she dressed nice, and she smelled good, too.

When she came in she looked the room over like she was making sure nobody else was there. Then she walked to the one window and looked out into the light well.

"You just got out?" she asked, turning back around. She had a strong accent, just like Arthur had said.

"Just today," Raymond said, feeling a wave of embarrassment at the poorness of the room. He wiped at his face.

Gloria dug into her inside jacket pocket and pulled out a folded sheet of paper. When she handed it to Raymond he saw that there were three hundred-dollar bills inside—crisp and clean, the faces up.

"That's all I have now, but I give you more later," she said.

Raymond shrugged and put the money in his back pocket. He realized he was thirsty, and licked his lips. He wanted to ask Gloria if she was Arthur's girlfriend, but he worried that she'd think he was hitting on her. He looked at her body instead, imagined having sex with her, then looked away again, aware of the silence. He could feel his heart pumping in his chest; it occurred to him that he might already be in over his head.

"How's Arty?" Gloria asked. Raymond had never heard anyone call him that before.

"He's fine."

"What he say you doing here?"

The curiosity on her face, the intensity of it, struck Raymond for a second. "He wants me to look in on one of your partners," he said. "Make sure everything stays clicking."

She nodded. Then she walked back to the door, which was still cracked open, and closed it. "Don't say anything stupid," she said, pointing at her ear and then at the ceiling. "But what'd he say about this partner?"

"He said the boy was acting reckless," Raymond said.

"Shadrack's not a boy," Gloria said, shaking her head. "And he's not acting reckless. He's acting crazy. He's acting like one of these homeless men that shouts at walls. You know this kind of crazy? A lot of people are not happy with him, Mr. Gaspar." She looked at Raymond for a moment, made sure he was listening. Then she continued.

"These people, they want to know if you're the right man to take care of this. You know what I mean? They don't want you to start something and then decide that you can't finish it."

This wasn't what Raymond had been expecting. He'd thought Gloria would meet him with resistance, say that Shadrack was fine, that she didn't need his help. Raymond hadn't heard of any other people. He didn't know what to think of this news, but he felt his interest tick up. He watched her for a second and reminded himself not to get too eager. *Sit, breathe, wait.*

"I'm worried about it," Gloria went on. "I'm worried he's going to ruin the entire arrangement. You fix that. You come at the right time." She raised her eyebrows and looked into Raymond's eyes searchingly.

He felt his neck get warm. "Well, that's why I'm here," he said. He prided himself on his ability to read people, and right at that moment his bullshit detectors were sounding.

"Tell me now," Gloria said. "Why'd Arthur send you?" She turned her head, worked at removing something from her teeth with her tongue, and turned back to him. "As opposed to that other guy?"

Raymond didn't know who she was talking about. "I guess he thinks I'm a people person," he said. "I guess he thinks I got a gift for fixing problems. Truth of the matter is I couldn't tell you. You should ask him."

Her face did something resembling a smile when she heard this. "Tomorrow's Sunday," she said. "On Monday I take you to get a new ID." She raised her finger like Raymond had protested. "I take you to get an ID. Arthur told me to. On Tuesday you go to Shadrack's house and we'll see what kind of people person you are." Her face transformed itself into a friendly thing. She said good-bye, and left.

As soon as she was gone, Raymond sent a text message to Arthur. An inmate named Duck held a phone for him in prison.

New number. Met your girlfriend. She on one.

***

On Monday, after checking in with his parole officer, Raymond went back to his room and texted Gloria. She picked him up in a tan minivan driven by a silent young Asian man with a thin mustache. The driver barely looked at Raymond when he got in. There were crumbs on the floor of the van, like someone had been tearing up loaves of bread. Raymond sat in back, feeling stressed by all the activity around him.

They drove to an industrial neighborhood lined with barbwire in South San Francisco. A few semitrucks sat parked and quiet on the shady side of the road. When the van stopped, Gloria handed him an envelope and said it contained seven hundred dollars. She told him to give it to a man named Javier.

"Don't worry," she said. She pointed at the building. "Go on."

There was a garage door open. The place looked like an auto-body shop. Inside Raymond noticed a bank of security monitors within an office on the right. He saw himself in black and white on one of the screens. Farther in, two men stood hunched, working on the door of a car. One of them sensed Raymond standing there, and turned.

Raymond said he was looking for Javier. The man said something in Spanish to the other man, who walked over to a doorway toward the back. *What the hell am I doing this for?* Raymond thought.

The man who'd spoken stood there smiling and nodding like they'd shared some kind of joke. Then he shifted his eyes toward the lot. Raymond told himself to calm down. He took a deep breath, let his shoulders relax.

After a short time another man came from the back with his eyebrows raised. He wore blue coveralls, like the other men. He had the look and walk of a convict. Raymond pulled out the envelope and handed it to him.

"Who sent you?" the man asked, in a casual way. He opened the envelope and counted the money with his head tilted.

"Gloria," Raymond said, pointing without conviction over his shoulder.

Javier walked Raymond into the back room and had him stand against a blue backdrop. A camera was already set up on a tripod. Javier looked through the viewfinder, adjusted the tripod, adjusted the camera, and snapped three pictures of Raymond. The flash from the camera popped with each shot.

"Real cards with holograms," he said. "We'll call you when it's ready."

As Raymond walked back out to the car he realized he hadn't given Javier his number, but he kept going.

"What the fuck was that for?" he asked when he got back into the van. He felt genuinely angry.

"Got to have a backup plan," said Gloria. She was using the passenger-side visor mirror to apply wine-colored lipstick. She didn't stop what she was doing to look at him.

They rode without talking all the way back to the Mission. Raymond had an uneasy feeling in his gut; it felt like a test of wills. He didn't like having his picture taken. He didn't like being told what to do, either. He remembered Arthur saying how crafty Gloria was and he wondered if he'd just been played.

Before he got out, she handed him another envelope, this one holding a thousand dollars. His silence suddenly felt immature, but he realized that's exactly how she wanted it. "It's from Arthur," she said.

"Well, thanks," Raymond said. For a moment, he felt, inexplicably, like crying—but it passed.

"Fifty-six Colby," Gloria said when he got out. "Five-six Colby, C-O-L-B-Y. Got it?"

"Fifty-six Colby," he said.

"That's Shadrack Pullman's address. Go see him tomorrow evening."

***

Colby Street was off Silver Avenue. Raymond took a taxi there, which, after four years in prison, felt luxurious. He arrived about an hour before the sun set. The house was plain, a box on a block filled with similar-looking ones. He stared at it for a moment and then made his approach. There was a garage on the bottom, with a gated front entrance beside it and stairs leading up to the living area. Plastic blinds covered the windows on the second floor. The walls were dirty; even on a rundown block, they stood out.

Raymond felt nerves swimming in his stomach as the doorbell buzzed upstairs. After a few moments, he heard the metallic sounds of locks being unbolted, chains being undone, and finally the door—around a corner and out of sight, at the top of the stairs—being pulled open.

"Who is it?" called an angry voice.

"It's Raymond Gaspar," he said. "Arthur's friend."

Silence. Raymond studied the stairway, noticing dust and hair on the ground, dark smudges on the walls. He felt his heart speed up a little.

"What's the password?"

Gloria hadn't mentioned any password. "Arthur," he said, trying his best to sound confident.

During all the talk about Shadrack Pullman, Raymond had never been told how he looked. The man coming down the stairs now must have been about six feet four, 180 pounds. He wore loose jeans and no shirt, and he had long hair, though the hair up top was receding a little. He was white Raymond thought, but there was something Asian-looking about his face. No, not Asian, Raymond remembered. Native.

He was angry. Raymond couldn't tell if he'd heard what he'd said, so he repeated it once the man had reached the bottom of the stairs.

Shadrack came right up to the metal gate and looked down at his visitor. Raymond took a step back.

"Arthur's not the password," Shadrack said.

His eyes seemed speedy; he was looking at Raymond wrong, focusing behind him. He held his face tight, scanning the block to see if Raymond had come alone before settling his eyes back behind Raymond.

"They call you Ray, Raymond, or Raymundo?" he asked.

"Well, Ray, or Raymond."

"Shit, then come on," he said, opening the gate. "Get on up."

Raymond walked in past Shadrack and up the stairs, then turned and waited. Shadrack waved him forward. In his mind, Raymond pictured throwing an elbow at his host's throat if the man tried anything. The doorway led to a living room. The lights were off, but a huge television played a nature show with the volume muted. As Raymond's eyes adjusted, he saw that the room was cluttered with stacks of books, with boxes and newspapers. A female mannequin leaned against the wall in one corner, bald and white. She had been drawn on with a marker; it looked like a child had scribbled out her breasts and face. The house smelled dirty.

"Shh—turn," said Shadrack.

Raymond turned. The man held a pistol in his hand.

You've just read an excerpt from Every Man a Menace.

ABOUT THE AUTHOR

Patrick Hoffman is a writer and private investigator based in Brooklyn. His first novel, *The White Van*, was a finalist for the CWA Ian Fleming Steel Dagger Award and was named a *Wall Street Journal* best book of the year. He was born in San Francisco and lived there for half his life, working as an investigator, both privately and at the San Francisco Public Defenders Office.

IMPRINT: Atlantic Monthly Press
PRINT ISBN: 9780802125446
PRINT PRICE: $25.00
EBOOK ISBN: 9780802190130
EBOOK PRICE: $25.00
PUBLICATION DATE: 10/4/16
PUBLICITY CONTACT: Deb Seager dseager@groveatlantic.com
RIGHTS CONTACT: Amy Hundley ahundley@groveatlantic.com
EDITOR: Morgan Entrekin
AGENT: Charlotte Sheedy
AGENCY: Charlotte Sheedy Literary Agency

PROMOTIONAL INFORMATION:
Prepublication reading copies, eGalleys on NetGalley and Edelweiss, major review coverage, targeted outreach to crime fiction media, promotion at regional trade shows and BookExpo America, library marketing including ALA, prepublication buzz campaign with giveaways on Shelf Awareness, PW, and Goodreads, mystery and thriller advertising and media campaign.

THE ORPHAN'S TALE

PAM JENOFF

SUMMARY

Seventeen-year-old Noa has been cast out in disgrace after becoming pregnant by a Nazi soldier during the occupation of her native Holland. Heartbroken over the loss of the baby she was forced to give up for adoption, she lives above a small German rail station, which she cleans in order to earn her keep. When Noa discovers a boxcar containing dozens of Jewish infants, unknown children ripped from their parents and headed for a concentration camp, she is reminded of the baby that was taken from her. In a moment that will change the course of her life, she steals one of the babies and flees into the snowy night, where she is rescued by a German circus. The circus owner offers to teach Noa the flying trapeze act so she can blend in undetected, spurning the resentment of the lead aerialist, Astrid. At first rivals, Noa and Astrid soon forge a powerful bond. But as the façade that protects them proves increasingly tenuous, Noa and Astrid must decide whether their unlikely friendship is enough to save one another—or if the secrets that burn between them will destroy everything.

EXCERPT

Prologue

Paris

They will be looking for me by now.

I pause on the granite steps of the museum, reaching for the railing to steady myself. Pain, sharper than ever, creaks through my left hip, not perfectly healed from last year's break. Across the Avenue Winston Churchill, behind the glass dome of the Grand Palais, the March sky is rosy at dusk.

I peer around the edge of the arched entranceway of the Petit Palais. From the massive stone columns hangs a red banner two stories high: *Deux Cents ans de Magie du Cirque (Two Hundred Years of Circus Magic.)* It is festooned with elephants, a tiger and a clown, their colors so much brighter in my memories.

I should have told someone I was going. But they would have only tried to stop me. My escape, months in the planning since I'd read about the upcoming exhibit in the *Times*, had been well-orchestrated: I had bribed an aide at the nursing home to take the photo I needed to mail to the passport office, paid for the plane ticket in cash. I'd almost been caught when the taxi cab I'd called pulled up in front of the home in the pre-dawn darkness and honked loudly. But the guard at the desk remained asleep.

Summoning my strength now, I begin to climb again, taking each painful step one by one. Inside the lobby, the opening gala is already in full swing, clusters of men in tuxedos and women in evening gowns mingling beneath the elaborately painted dome ceiling. Conversations in French bubble around me like a long forgotten perfume I am desperate to inhale. Familiar words trickle back, first in a stream then a river, though I've scarcely heard them in half a century.

I do not stop at the reception desk to check in; they are not expecting me. Instead, dodging the butlered hors d'oeuvres and champagne, I make my way along the mosaic floors, past walls of murals to the circus exhibit, its entrance marked by a smaller version of the banner outside. There are photos blown up and hung from the ceiling by wire too fine to see, images of a sword swallower and dancing horses and still more clowns. From the labels below each picture, the names come back to me like a song: Lorch, D'Augne, Neuhoff—great European circus dynasties felled by war and time. At the last of these names, my eyes begin to burn.

Beyond the photos hangs a tall, worn placard of a woman suspended from silk ropes by her arms, one leg extended behind her in a mid-air arabesque. Her youthful face and body are scarcely recognizable to me. In my mind, the song of the carousel begins to play tinny and faint like a music box. I feel the searing heat of the lights, so hot it could almost peel off my skin. A flying trapeze hangs above the exhibit, fixed as if in mid-flight. Even now, my almost ninety year-old legs ache with yearning to climb up there.

But there is no time for memories. Getting here took longer than I thought, like everything else these days, and there isn't a minute to spare. Pushing down the lump in my throat, I press forward, past the costumes and headdresses, artifacts of a lost civilization. Finally, I reach the rail car. Some of the side panels have been removed to reveal the close, tiny berths inside. I am struck by the compact size, less than half my shared room at the nursing home. It had seemed so much larger in my mind.

Had we really lived in there for months on end? I reach out my hand to touch the rotting wood. Though I had known the rail car was the same the minute I had seen it in the paper, some piece of my heart had been too afraid to believe it until now.

Voices grow louder behind me. I glance quickly over my shoulder. The reception is breaking up and the attendees drawing closer to the exhibit. In a few more minutes, it will be too late.

I look back once more, then crouch to slip beneath the roped stanchion. Hide, a voice seems to say, the long-buried instinct rising up in me once more. Instead, I run my hand under the bottom of the rail car. The compartment is there, exactly as I remembered. The door still sticks, but if I press on it just so… It snaps open and I imagine the rush of excitement of a young girl looking for a scribbled invitation to a secret rendezvous.

But as I reach inside, my fingers close around cold, dark space. The compartment is empty and the dream I had that it might hold the answers evaporates like cool mist.

Chapter One

Noa

Germany, 1944

The sound comes low like the buzzing of the bees that once chased Papa across the farm and caused him to spend a week swathed in bandages.

I set down the brush I'd been using to scrub the floor, once-elegant marble now cracked beneath boot heels and set with fine lines of mud and ash that will never lift. Listening for the direction of the sound, I cross the station beneath the sign announcing in bold black: *Riedstadt Hauptbahnhof*. A big name for nothing more than a waiting room with two toilets, a ticket window and a wurst stand that operates when there is meat to be had and the weather is not awful. I bend to pick up a coin at the base of one of the benches, pocket it. It amazes me the things that people forget or leave behind.

Outside, my breath rises in puffs in the February night air. The sky is a collage of ivory and gray, more snow threatening. The station sits low in a valley, surrounded by lush hills of pine trees on three sides, their pointed green tips poking out above snow-covered branches. The air has a slightly burnt smell. Before the war, Riedstadt had been just another tiny stop that most travelers passed through without noticing. But the Germans make use of everything it seems, and the location is good for parking trains and switching out engines during the night.

I've been here almost four months. It hadn't been so bad in the autumn and I was happy to find shelter after I'd been sent packing with two days' worth of food, three if I stretched it. The girls' home where I lived after my parents found out I was expecting and kicked me out had been located far from anywhere in the name of discretion and they could have dropped me off in Mainz, or at least the nearest town. They simply opened the door, though, dismissing me on foot. I'd headed to the train station before realizing that I had nowhere to go. More than once during my months away, I had thought of returning home, begging forgiveness. It was not that I was too proud. I would have gotten down on my knees if I thought it would do any good. But I knew from the fury in my father's eyes the day he forced me out that his heart was closed. I could not stand rejection twice.

In a moment of luck, though, the station had needed a cleaner. I peer around the back of the building now toward the tiny closet where I sleep on mattress on the floor. The maternity dress is the same one I wore the day I left the home, except that the full front now hangs limply. It will not always be this way, of course. I will find a real job—one that pays in more than not-quite-moldy bread—and a proper home.

I see myself in the train station window. I have the kind of looks that just fit in, dishwater hair that whitens with the summer sun, pale blue eyes. Once my plainness bothered me; here it is a benefit. The two other station workers, the ticket girl and the man at the kiosk, come and then go home each night, hardly speaking to me. The travelers pass through the station with the daily edition of *Der Sturmer* tucked under their arms, grinding cigarettes into the floor, not caring who I am or where I came from. Though lonely, I need it that way. I cannot answer questions about the past.

No, they do not notice me. I see them though, the soldiers on leave and the mothers and wives who come each day to scan the platform hopefully for a son or husband before leaving alone. You can always tell the ones who are trying to flee. They try to look normal, as if just going on vacation. But their clothes are too tight from the layers padded underneath and bags so full they threaten to burst at any second. They do not make eye contact, but hustle their children along with pale, strained faces.

The buzzing noise grows louder and more high-pitched. It is coming from the train I'd heard screech in earlier, now parked on the far track. I start toward it, past the nearly empty coal bins, most of their stores long taken for troops fighting in the east. Perhaps someone has left on an engine or other machinery. I do not want to be blamed, and risk losing my job. Despite the grimness of my situation, I know it could be worse—and that I am lucky to be here.

Lucky. I'd heard it first from an elderly German woman who shared some herring with me on the bus to Den Hague after leaving my parents. "You are the Aryan ideal," she told me between fishy lip smacks, as we wound through detours and cratered roads.

I thought she was joking; I had plain blond hair and a little stump of a nose. My body was sturdy—athletic, until it had begun to soften out and grow curvy. Other than when the German had whispered soft words into my ear at night, I had always considered myself unremarkable. But now I'd been told I was just right. I found myself confiding in the woman about my pregnancy and how I had been cast out. She told me to go Wiesbaden, and scribbled with a note saying I was carrying a child of the Reich. I took it and went. It did not occur to me whether it was dangerous to go to Germany or that I should refuse. Somebody wanted children like mine. My parents would have sooner died than accepted help from the Germans. But the woman said they would give me shelter; how bad could they be? I had nowhere else to go. I was lucky, they said again when I reached the girls' home. Though Dutch, I was considered of Aryan race and my child (otherwise shamed as an *uneheliches kind*, conceived out of wedlock) might just be accepted into the Lebensborn program and raised by a good German family. I'd spent nearly six months there, reading and helping with the housework until my stomach became too bulky. The facility, if not grand, was modern and clean, designed to deliver babies in good health to the Reich. I'd gotten to know a sturdy girl called Eva who was a few months further along than me, but one night she awoke in blood and they took her to hospital and I did not see her again. After that, I kept to myself. None of us would be there for long.

My time came on a cold October morning when I stood up from the breakfast table at the girls' home and my water broke. The next eighteen hours were a blur of awful pain, punctuated by words of command, without encouragement or a soothing touch. At last, the baby had emerged with a wail and my entire body shuddered with emptiness, a machine shutting down. A strange look crossed the nurse's face.

"What is it?" I demanded. I was not supposed to see the child. But I struggled against pain to sit upright. "What's wrong?"

"Everything is fine," the doctor assured. "The child is healthy." His voice was perturbed, though, face stormy through thick glasses above the draped cream sheet. I leaned forward and a set of piercing coal eyes met mine.

Those eyes that were not Aryan.

I understood then the doctor's distress. The child looked nothing like the perfect race. Some hidden gene, on my side or the German's, had given him dark eyes and olive skin. He would not be accepted into the Lebensborn program.

My baby cried out, shrill and high-pitched, as though he had heard his fate and was protesting. I had reached for him through the pain. "I want to hold him."

The doctor and the nurse, who had been recording details about the child on some sort of form, exchanged uneasy looks. "We don't, that is, the Lebensborn program does not allow that."

I struggled to sit up. "Then I'll take him and leave." It had been a bluff; I had nowhere to go. I had signed papers giving up my rights when I arrived in exchange for letting me stay, there were hospital guards… I could barely even walk. "Please let me have him for a second."

"Nein." The nurse shook her head emphatically, slipping from the room as I continued to plead.

Once she was out of sight, something in my voice forced the doctor to relent. "Just for a moment," he said, reluctantly handing me the child. I stared at the red face, inhaled the delicious scent of his head that was pointed from so many hours of struggling to be born and I focused on his eyes. Those beautiful eyes. How could something so perfect not be their ideal?

He was mine, though. A wave of love crested and broke over me. I had not wanted this child, but in that moment, all the regret washed away, replaced by longing. Panic and relief swept me under. They would not want him now. I'd have to take him home because there was no other choice. I would keep him, find a way…

Then the nurse returned and ripped him from my arms.

"No, wait," I protested. As I struggled to reach for my baby, something sharp pierced my arm. My head swam. Hands pressed me back on the bed. I faded, still seeing those dark eyes.

I awoke alone in that cold, sterile delivery room, without my child, or a husband or mother or even a nurse, an empty vessel that no one wanted anymore. They said afterward that he went to a good home. I had no way of knowing if they were telling the truth.

I swallow against the dryness of my throat, forcing the memory away. Then I step from the station into the biting cold air, relieved that the Schutzpolizei des Reiches, the leering state police that patrol the station, are nowhere to be seen. Most likely they are fighting the cold in their truck with a flask. I scan the train, trying to pinpoint the buzzing sound. It comes from the last box car, adjacent to the caboose—not from the engine. No, the noise comes from something inside the train. Something alive.

I stop. I have made it a point to never go near the trains, to look away when they pass by—because they are carrying Jews.

I was still living at home in our village the first time I had seen the sorry round up of men, women and children in the market square. I had run to my father, crying. He was a patriot and stood up for everything else—why not this? "It's awful," he conceded though his graying beard, stained yellow from pipe smoke. He had wiped my tear-stained cheeks and given me some vague explanation about how there were ways to handle things. But those ways had not stopped my classmate Steffi Klein from being marched to the train station with her younger brother and parents in the same dress she'd worn to my birthday a month earlier.

The sound continues to grow, almost a keening now, like a wounded animal in the brush. I scan the empty platform and peer around the edge of the station. Can the police hear the noise too? I stand uncertainly at the platform's edge, peering down the barren railway tracks that separate me from the boxcar. I should just walk away. Keep your eyes down, that has been the lesson of the years of war. No good ever came from noticing the business of others. If I am caught nosing into parts of the station where I do not belong, I will be let go from my job, left without a place to live, or perhaps even arrested. But I have never been any good at not looking. Too curious, my mother said when I was little. I have always needed to know. I step forward, unable to ignore the sound which, as I draw closer now, sounds like cries.

Or the tiny foot which is visible through the open door of the rail car.

I pull back the door. "Oh!" My voice echoes dangerously through the darkness, inviting detection. There are babies, tiny bodies too many to count, lying on the hay-covered floor of the rail car, packed close and atop one another. Most do not move and I can't tell whether they are dead or sleeping. From amidst the stillness, piteous cries mix with gasps and moans like the bleating of lambs.

I grasp the side of the rail car, struggling to breathe over the wall of urine and feces and vomit that assaults me. Since coming here, I have dulled myself to the images, like a bad dream or a film that couldn't possibly be real. This is different, though. So many infants, all alone, ripped from the arms of their mothers. My lower stomach begins to burn.

I stand helplessly in front of the box car, frozen in shock. Where had these babies come from? They must have just arrived, for surely they could not last long in the icy temperatures.

I have seen the trains going east for months, people where the cattle and sacks of grain should have been. Despite the awfulness of the transport, I had told myself they were going somewhere like a camp or a village, just being kept in one place. The notion was fuzzy in my mind, but I imagined somewhere maybe with cabins or tents like the seaside campsite south of our village in Holland for those who couldn't afford a real holiday or preferred something more rustic. Resettlement. In these dead and dying babies, though, I see the wholeness of the lie.

I glance over my shoulder. The trains of people are always guarded. But here there is no one—because there is simply no chance of the infants getting away.

Closest to me lays a baby with gray skin, its lips blue. I try to brush the thin layer of frost from its eyelashes but the child is already stiff and gone. I yank my hand back, scanning the others. Most of the infants are naked or just wrapped in a blanket or cloth, stripped of anything that would have protected them from the harsh cold. But in the center of the car, two perfect pale pink booties stick stiffly up in the air, attached to a baby who is otherwise naked. Someone had cared enough to knit those, stitch by stitch. A sob escapes through my lips.

A head peeks out among the others. Straw and feces cover its heart-shaped face. The child does not look pained or distressed, but wears a puzzled expression, as if to say, "Now what am I doing here?" There is something familiar about it: coal dark eyes, piercing through me, just as they had the day I had given birth. My heart swells.

The baby's face crumples suddenly and it squalls. My hands shoot out, and I strain to reach it over the others. My grasp falls short of the infant, who wails louder. I try to climb into the car, but the children are packed so tightly, I can't manage for fear of stepping on one. Desperately, I strain my arms once more, just reaching. I pick up the crying child, needing to silence it before the guard hears. Its skin is icy as I pluck it from the car, naked save for a soiled cloth diaper.

The baby in my arms now, only the second I'd ever held, seems to calm in the crook of my elbow. Could this possibly be my child, brought back to me by fate or chance? The child's eyes close and its head bows forward, whether it is sleeping or dying, I cannot say. Clutching it, I start away from the train. Then I turn back: if any of those other children are still alive, I am their only chance. I should take more.

But the baby I am holding cries again, the shrill sound cutting through the silence. I cover his mouth and run back into the station.

I walk toward the closet where I sleep. Stopping at the door, I look around desperately. I have nothing. Instead I walk into the women's toilet, the usually dank smell scarcely noticeable after the box car. At the sink, I wipe the filth from the infant's face with one of the rags I use for cleaning. The baby is warmer now, but two of its toes are blue and I wonder if it might lose them. I search the child for some marking as to where it came from; but there is nowhere that anyone could have identified it.

I open the filthy diaper. The child is a boy like my own had been. Closer now I can see that his tiny penis looks different than the German's, or that of the boy at school who had shown me his when I was seven. Circumcised. Steffi had told me the word once, explaining what they had done to her little brother. The child is Jewish. Not mine.

I step back as the reality I had known all along sinks in: I cannot keep a Jewish baby, or a baby at all, by myself and cleaning the station twelve hours a day. What had I been thinking?

The baby begins to roll sideways from the ledge by the sink where I had left him. I leap forward, catching him before he falls to the hard tile floor. I am alone with an infant for the first time and I hold him at arm's length now, like a dangerous animal. But he moves closer, nuzzling against my neck. I clumsily make a diaper out of the other rag, then carry the child from the toilet and out of the station, heading back toward the rail car. I have to put him back on the train, as if none of this ever happened.

At the edge of the platform, I freeze. One of the guards is now walking along the tracks, blocking my way. I search desperately in all directions. Close to the side of the station sits a milk delivery truck, the rear stacked high with large cans. Impulsively I start toward it. I slide the baby into one of the empty jugs, trying not to think about how icy the metal must be against his bare skin. He does not make a sound but just stares at me helplessly

I duck behind a bench as the truck door slams. In a second, it will leave, taking the infant with it.

And no one will know what I have done.

You've just read an excerpt from The Orphan's Tale.

ABOUT THE AUTHOR

Pam Jenoff holds a bachelor's degree in international affairs from George Washington University and a master's degree in history from Cambridge, and she received her Juris Doctor from the University of Pennsylvania. Jenoff's novels are based on her experiences working at the Pentagon and also as a diplomat for the State Department handling Holocaust issues in Poland. She lives with her husband and three children near Philadelphia where, in addition to writing, she teaches law school.

IMPRINT: Mira Books
PRINT ISBN: 9780778319818
PRINT PRICE: $15.99
EBOOK ISBN: 9781460396421
EBOOK PRICE: $7.99
PUBLICATION DATE: 1/31/17
PUBLICITY CONTACT: Emer Flounders emer.flounders@harpercollins.com
RIGHTS CONTACT: Reka Rubin reka.rubin@harlequin.com
EDITOR: Erika Imranyi
AGENT: Susan Ginsburg
AGENCY: Writers House

PROMOTIONAL INFORMATION:
Extensive consumer advertising campaign, including national print media; Targeted trade support, including library and independent bookseller outreach; Book club promotion, including a reader's guide inside the book; In-book advertising in selected Harlequin MIRA® imprint titles; National galley distribution and press kit mailings; Blogger outreach; Extensive online promotion, including social media and Bookclubbish.com; Featured title at www.Harlequin.com.

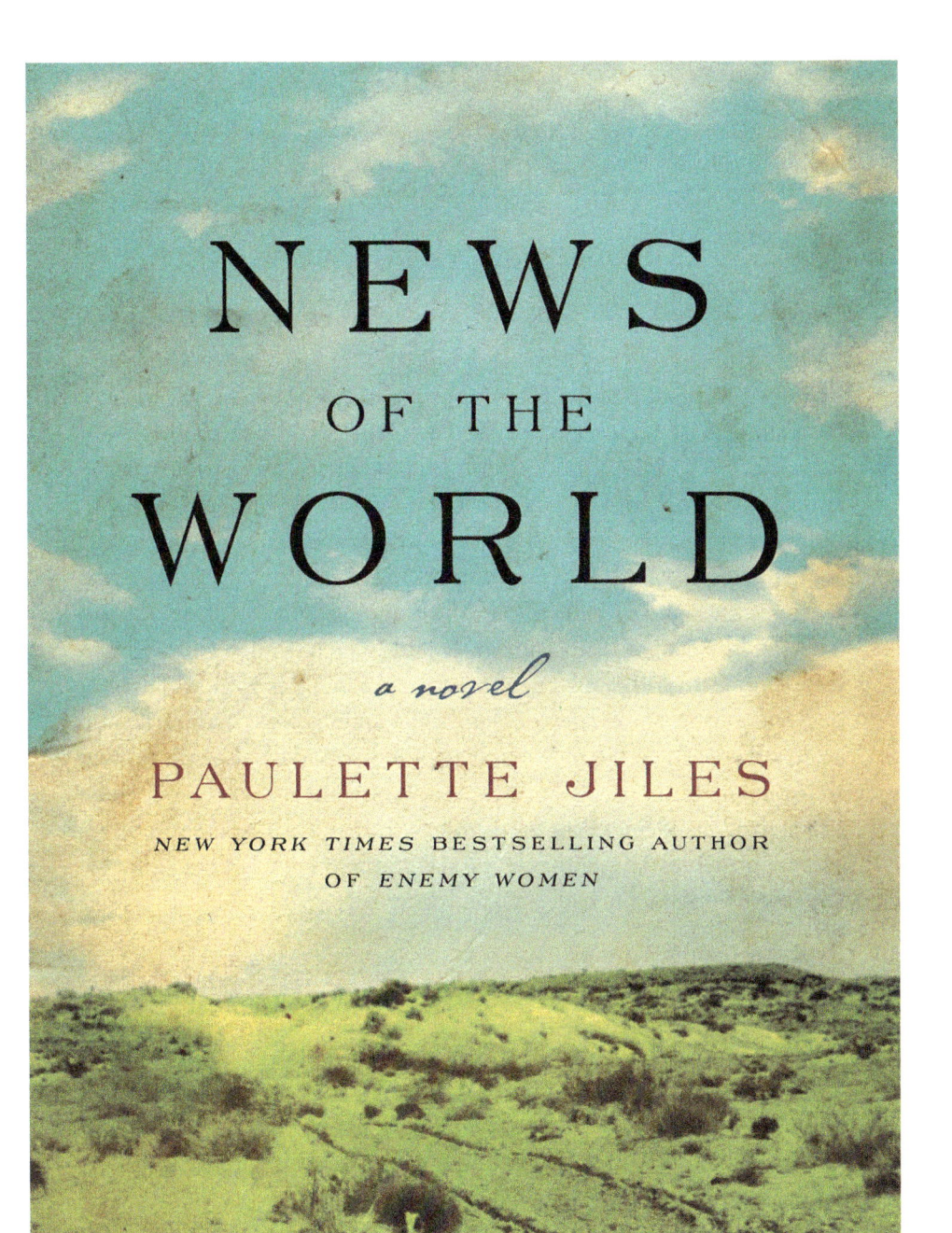

NEWS
OF THE
WORLD

a novel

PAULETTE JILES

NEW YORK TIMES BESTSELLING AUTHOR
OF *ENEMY WOMEN*

SUMMARY

In the aftermath of the Civil War, an aging itinerant news reader agrees to transport a young captive of the Kiowa back to her people in this exquisitely rendered, morally complex, multilayered novel of historical fiction from the author of *Enemy Women* that explores the boundaries of family, responsibility, honor, and trust.

EXCERPT

Chapter One

Wichita Falls, Texas, Winter 1870

Captain Kidd laid out the *Boston Morning Journal* on the lectern and began to read from the article on the Fifteenth Amendment. He had been born in 1798 and the third war of his lifetime had ended five years ago and he hoped never to see another but now the news of the world aged him more than time itself. Still he stayed his rounds, even during the cold spring rains. He had been at one time a printer but the war had taken his press and everything else, the economy of the Confederacy had fallen apart even before the surrender and so he now made his living in this drifting from one town to another in North Texas with his newspapers and journals in a waterproof portfolio and his coat collar turned up against the weather. He rode a very good horse and was concerned that someone might try to take the horse from him but so far so good. So he had arrived in Wichita Falls on February 26th and tacked up his posters and put on his reading clothes in the stable. There was a hard rain outside and it was noisy but he had a good strong voice.

He shook out the *Journal*'s pages.

The Fifteenth Amendment, he read, which has just been signed between the several states February 3rd, 1870, allows the vote to all men qualified to vote without regard to race or color or previous condition of servitude. He looked up from the text. His reading glasses caught the light. He bent slightly forward over the lectern. That means colored gentlemen, he said. Let us have no vaporings or girlish shrieks. He turned his head to search the crowd of faces turned up to him. I can hear you muttering, he said. Stop it. I hate muttering.

He glared at them and then said, Next. The Captain shook out another newspaper. The latest from the *New York Herald Tribune* states that the polar exploration ship *Hansa* is reported by a whaler as being crushed in sunk in the pack ice in its attempt to reach the North Pole; sunk at seventy degrees north latitude off Greenland. There is nothing in this article about survivors. He flipped the page impatiently.

The Captain had a clean-shaven face with runic angles, his hair was perfectly white and he was still six feet tall. His hair shone in the single hot ray from the bull's-eye lantern. He carried a short-barreled Slocum revolver in his waistband at the back. It was a five-shot, thirty-two caliber and he had never liked it all that much but then he had rarely used it.

Over all the bare heads he saw Britt Johnson and his men, Paint Crawford and Dennis Vesey, at the back wall. They were free black men. Britt was a freighter and the other two were his driving crew. They held their hats in their hands, each with one booted foot cocked up against the wall behind them. The hall was full. It was a broad open space used for wool storage and community meetings and for people like himself. The crowd was almost all men, almost all white. The lantern lights were harsh, the air was dark. Captain Kidd traveled from town to town in north Texas with his newspapers and read aloud the news of the day to assemblies like this in halls or churches for a dime a head. He traveled alone and had no one to collect the dimes for him but not many people cheated and if they did somebody caught them at it and grabbed them by the lapels and wrenched them up in a knot and said *You really ought to pay your Goddamned dime, you know, like everybody else.*

And then the coin would ring in the paint can.

***

He glanced up to see Britt Johnson lift a forefinger to him. Captain Kidd gave one brief nod, and completed his reading with an article from the *Philadelphia Inquirer* concerning the British physicist James Maxwell and his theories of electromagnetic disturbances in the ether whose wavelengths were longer than infrared radiation. This was to bore people and calm them down and put them into a state of impatience to leave; leave quietly. He had become impatient of trouble and other people's emotions. His life had lately seemed to him thin and sour, a bit spoiled, and it was something that had only come upon him lately. A slow dullness had seeped into him like coal gas and he did not know what to do about it except seek out quiet and solitude. He was always impatient to get the readings over with now.

The Captain folded the papers, put them in his portfolio. He bent to his left and blew out the bull's eye lantern. As he walked through the crowd people reached out to him and shook his hand. A pale-haired man sat watching him. With him were two Indians or half-Indians that the Captain knew for Caddoes and not people of a commendable reputation. The man with the blond hair turned in his chair to stare at Britt. Then others came to thank the Captain for his readings, asked after his grown children. Kidd nodded, said *tolerable, tolerable*, and made his way back to Britt and his men to see what it was Britt wanted.

***

Captain Kidd thought it was going to be about the Fifteenth Amendment but it was not. Yes sir, Captain Kidd, would you come with me? Britt straightened and lifted his hat to his head and so did Dennis and Paint. Britt said, I got a problem in my wagon.

She seemed to be about ten years old, dressed in the horse Indians' manner in a deerskin shift with four rows of elk teeth sewn across the front. A thick blanket was pulled over her shoulders. Her hair was the color of maple sugar and in it she wore two down puffs bound onto a lock of her hair by their minute spines and also bound with a thin thread was a wing-feather from a golden eagle slanting between them. She sat perfectly composed, wearing the feather and a necklace of glass beads as if they were costly adornments. Her eyes were blue and her skin that odd bright color that occurs when fair skin has been burnt and weathered by the sun. She had no more expression than an egg.

I see, said Captain Kidd. I see.

He had his black coat collar turned up against the rain and the cold and a thick wool muffler around his neck. His breath moved out of his nose in clouds. He bit his lower lip on the left side and thought about what he was looking at in the light of the kerosene hurricane lantern Britt held up. In some strange way it made his skin crawl.

I am astonished, he said. The child seems artificial as well as malign.

Britt had backed one of his wagons under the roof of the fairway at the livery stable. It didn't fit all the way in. The front half of the wagon and the driver's seat was wild with the drumming noise of the rain and a bright lift of rain-spray surrounded it. The back end was under shelter and they all stood there and regarded the girl the way people do when they come upon something strange they have caught in a trap, something alien whose taxonomy is utterly unknown and probably dangerous. The girl sat on a bale of Army shirts. In the light of the lantern her eyes reflected a thin and glassy blue. She watched them, she watched every movement, every lift of a hand. Her eyes moved but her head was still.

Yes sir, said Britt. She's jumped out of the wagon twice between Fort Sill and here. As far as Agent Hammond can figure out she is Johanna Leonberger, captured at age six four years ago, from near Castroville. Down near San Antonio.

I know where it is, said Captain Kidd.

Yes sir. The Agent had all the particulars. If that's her, she's about ten.

Britt Johnson was a tall, strong man but he watched the girl with a dubious and mistrusting expression. He was cautious of her.

My name is Cicada. My father's name is Turning Water. My mother's name is Three Spotted. I want to go home.

But they could not hear her because she had not spoken aloud but the Kiowa words in all their tonal music lived in her head like bees.

Captain Kidd said, Do they know who her parents are?

Yes sir, they do. Or, as much as he can figure out from the date she was taken. The Agent, here, I'm talking about. Her parents and her little sister were killed in the raid. He had a paper from her relatives, Wilhelm and Anna Leonberger, an aunt and uncle. And he gave me a fifty-dollar gold piece to deliver her back to Castroville. The family sent it up to him by a Major from San Antonio, transferred north. He was to give it to somebody to transport her home. I said I would get her out of Indian Territory and across the Red. It wasn't easy. We like to drowned. That was yesterday.

The Captain said, It's come up two foot since yesterday.

I know it. Britt stood with one foot on the drawbar. The hurricane lantern burnt with its irresolute light on the tailgate and shone into the interior of the freight wagon as if revealing some alien figure in a tomb.

Captain Kidd took off his hat and shook water from it. Britt Johnson had rescued at least four captives from the red men. From the Comanche, from the Kiowa, and once from the Cheyenne up north in Kansas. Britt's own wife and two children had been taken captive three years ago, in 1867, and he had gone out and got them back. Nobody knew quite how he had done it. He seemed to have some celestial protection about him. He usually went alone. Britt was a rescuing angel, a dark man of the Red Rolling Plains, cunning and strong and fast like a nightjar in the midnight air. But Britt was not going to return this girl to her parents, not even for fifty dollars in gold.

Why won't you go? said Captain Kidd. You have come this far already. Fifty dollars in gold is a considerable amount.

I figured I could find somebody to hand her off to here, Britt said. It's a three-week journey down there. Then three weeks back. I have no haulage to carry down there.

Behind him Paint and Dennis nodded. They crossed their arms in their heavy waxed-canvas slickers. Long bright crawls of water slid across the livery stable floor and took up the light of the lantern like a luminous stain and the roof shook with the percussion of drops as big as nickels.

Dennis Crawford, thin as a spider, said, We wouldn't make a dime the whole six weeks. Unless we could get something to haul back up here, said Paint.

Shut up, Paint, said Dennis. You know people down there?

Well all right, said Paint. I can hear you.

Britt said, There it is. I can't leave my freighting that long. I have orders to deliver. And the other thing is, if I'm caught carrying that girl it would be bad trouble. He looked the Captain straight in the eye and said, She's a white girl. You take her.

Captain Kidd felt in his breast pocket for his tobacco. He didn't find it. Britt rolled a cigarette for him and handed it to him and then snapped a match in his big hand. Captain Kidd had not lost any sons in the war and that was because he had all daughters. Two of them. He knew girls. He didn't know Indians but he knew girls, and what was on that girl's face was contempt.

He said, Find a family going that way, Britt. Somebody to drown her in sweetness and light and improving lectures on deportment.

Good idea, said Britt. I thought of it already.

And so? Captain Kidd blew out smoke. The girl's eyes did not follow it. Nothing could move her gaze from the men's faces, the men's hands. She had a drizzle of freckles across her cheekbones and her fingers were blunt as noses with short nails lined in black.

Can't locate any. Hard to find somebody to trust with this.

Captain Kidd nodded. But you've delivered girls before now, he said. The Blainey girl, you got her back.

Not that far a trip. Besides I don't know those people down there. You do.

Yes, I see.

Captain Kidd had spent years in San Antonio. He knew the way, knew the people. In North and West Texas there were many free black men, they were freighters and scouts and now after the war, the 10th US Cavalry, all black. However, the general population had not settled the matter of free black people in their minds yet. All was in flux. Flux; a soldering aid that promotes the fusion of two surfaces, an unstable substance that catches fire.

The Captain said, You could ask the Army to deliver her. They take charge of captives. Not any more, said Britt.

What would you have done if you hadn't come across me?

I don't know.

I just got here from Bowie. I could have gone south to Jacksboro.

I saw your posters when we pulled in, Britt said. It was meant.

One last thing, said Captain Kidd. Maybe she should go back to the Indians. What tribe took her? Kiowa.

Britt was smoking as well. His foot on the drawbar was jiggling. He snorted blue fumes from his nostrils and glanced at the girl. She stared back at him. They were like two mortal enemies who could not take their eyes from one another. The endless rain hissed in a ground-spray out in the street and every roof in Wichita Falls was a haze of shattered water.

And so?

Britt said, The Kiowa don't want her. They finally woke up to the fact that having a white captive gets you run down by the cav. The Agent said to bring all the captives in or he was cutting off their rations and sending the 12th and the 9th out after them. They brought her in and sold her for fifteen Hudson's Bay four-stripe blankets and a set of silver dinnerware. German coin silver. They'll beat it up into bracelets. It was Aperian Crow's band brought her in. Her mother cut her arms to pieces and you could hear her crying for a mile.

Her Indian mother. Yes, said Britt. Were you there? Britt nodded.

I wonder if she remembers anything. From when she was six.

No, said Britt. Nothing.

The girl still did not move. It takes a lot of strength to sit that still for that long. She sat upright on the bale of Army shirts which were wrapped in burlap, marked in stencil for Fort Belknap. Around her were wooden boxes of enamel wash basins and nails and smoked deer tongues packed in fat, a sewing machine in a crate, fifty-pound sacks of sugar. Her round face was flat in the light of the lamp and without shadows, or softness. She seemed carved. Doesn't speak any English?

Not a word, said Britt.

So how do you know she doesn't remember anything?

My boy speaks Kiowa. He was captive with them a year.

Yes, that's right. Captain Kidd shifted his shoulders under the heavy dreadnaught overcoat. It was black, like his frock coat and vest and his trousers and his hat and his blunt boots. His shirt had last been boiled and bleached and ironed in Bowie; a fine white cotton with the figure of a lyre in white silk. It was holding out so far. It was one of the little things that had been depressing him. The way it frayed gently on every edge.

He said, Your boy spoke with her.

Yes, said Britt. For as much as she'd talk to him.

Is he with you?

Yes. Better on the road with me than at home. He's good on the road. They are different when they come back. My boy nearly didn't want to come back to me.

Is that so? The Captain was surprised.

Yes sir. He was on the way to becoming a warrior. Learned the language. It's a hard language.

He was with them how long?

Less than a year.

Britt! How can that be?

I don't know. Britt smoked and turned to lean on the wagon tailgate and looked back into the dark spaces of the stable with the noise of horses and mules eating, eating, their teeth like grindstones moving one on another and the occasional snort as hay dust got up their noses, the shifting of their great cannonball feet. The good smell of oiled leather harness and grain. Britt said, I just don't know. But he came back different.

In what way?

Roofs bother him. Inside places bother him. He can't settle down and learn his letters. He's afraid a lot and then he turns around arrogant. Britt threw down his smoke and stepped on it. So, gist of it is, the Kiowa won't take her back.

Captain Kidd knew, besides the other reasons, that Britt trusted him to return her to her people because he was an old man.

Well, he said.

I knew you would, said Britt.

Yes, said the Captain. So.

Britt's skin was saddle-colored but now paler than it usually was because the rainy winter had kept the sun from his face for months. He reached into the pocket of his worn ducking coat and brought out the coin. It was a shining sulky color, a Spanish coin of eight escudos in twenty-two carat, and all the edge still milled, not shaved. A good deal of money; everyone in Texas was counting their nickels and dimes and glad to have them since the finances of the state had collapsed and both news and hard money were difficult to come by. Especially here in North Texas, near the banks of the Red River, on the edge of Indian Territory.

Britt said, That's what the family sent up to the Agent. Her parents names were Jan and Greta. They were killed when they captured her. Take it, he said. And be careful of her.

As they watched the girl slid down between the freight boxes and bales as if fainting and pulled the thick blanket over her head. She was weary of being stared at.

Britt said, She'll stay there the night. She's got nowhere to go. She can't get hold of any weapons that I can think of. He took up the lamp and stepped back. Be really careful.

You've just read an excerpt from News of the World.

ABOUT THE AUTHOR

Paulette Jiles is a poet and the author of *Cousins*, a memoir, and the bestselling novels *Enemy Women*, *Stormy Weather*, and *The Color of Lightning*. She lives on a ranch near San Antonio, Texas.

IMPRINT: William Morrow
PRINT ISBN: 9780062409201
PRINT PRICE: $22.99
EBOOK ISBN: 9780062409225
EBOOK PRICE: $17.99
PUBLICATION DATE: 10/4/16
PUBLICITY CONTACT: Camille Collins camille.collins@harpercollins.com

RIGHTS CONTACT: William Morrow: 2nd serial, permissions, book club, reprint, audio, ebook
Agent: 1st serial, translation, film/TV, multimedia
EDITOR: Jennifer Brehl
AGENT: Liz Darnso
AGENCY: Darhansoff and Verrill

TERRITORIES SOLD:
World English (Morrow in US and Canada; Harper 360 in UK)

PROMOTIONAL INFORMATION:
National online advertising, including Shelf Awareness and Goodreads; National print media campaign; National radio interviews; Online publicity; Author appearances in Texas; National advertising campaign, including *The New Yorker*, *New York Times Book Review*, and *NPR*; 15-stop blog tour, including reviews, features and giveaways; Outreach to historical fiction bloggers; Pre-publication online buzz campaign, including early consumer reads and author video; Major reading group outreach, including online reading group guide and features on Bookclubgirl.com and in the Book Club Girl newsletter; Social networking campaign; Authorperk email marketing campaign; ebook backlist price promotions with excerpt from *News of the World*; Official author website: http://www.paulettejiles.com; Deep distribution of reader's edition.

BOOKSELLER BLURBS:
"After reading *News of the World*, I need to go back and see Captain Kidd's backstory from *Enemy Women*. How did I miss that one? Paulette Jiles is talented on every level—true voices, character development, historical accuracy, humor and poignancy. She proves that a fantastic book can be accomplished in under 225 pages. What a gem! The story itself is beautiful. But the bonus for me was the geography and demographic of the Captain and Johanna's journey thru post-Civil War Texas—an era and area with which I was unfamiliar, along with the relationships between the free blacks, war veterans, various native tribes and civilians. Just another example of Jiles' mastery of historical fiction."—Karen McCue, McLean & Eakin Booksellers, Petosky, MI

"As I finished the final pages of *News of the World* I realized just how much I enjoyed this story of an unlikely relationship developing under difficult circumstances. Jiles is a gifted wordsmith whose descriptive prose creates vivid physical and emotional landscapes that you slip into without effort. It is filled with interesting and lesser known historical facts of the time period and culture but it is the portrayal of the evolving relationship between two unique characters that is particularly moving and beautiful. At times I found the story so engaging I couldn't turn the pages fast enough, at other times I lingered. In the end I found *News of the World* to be a subtle yet powerful story about compassion and transformation. Jiles could have drawn out the story, could have packed in more details but she didn't need to. It's a wholly satisfying story as is."—Sharon Gambin, Literati Bookstore, Ann Arbor, MI

"This was a winner. This was a lot of story packed in a relatively short book, and very well done. Jiles created two outstanding characters with Captain Kidd and Johanna and I immediately engaged with them and their story. They are both brave, humble and honorable individuals for whom I felt deep respect. Kidd's sharp, indignant humor made me laugh—'Young man, stop speaking in explanation points.' I look forward to selling this book."—Tina Smith, Joseph-Beth Booksellers, Lexington, KY

"Jiles' characters are completely captivating and will draw you in leaving you asking for more! I cannot wait to handsell this book."—Vicki Burger, Windy City Books, Casper, WY

"*News of the World* is a beautifully written story about a travelling news reader and his quest to return a 10 year old girl to her family after being captured and living with native Americans. Jiles brings to life the challenges facing 70-year old Captain Kidd in the virtually lawless frontier in central Texas in the 1870s and his struggles to develop a relationship with a young girl torn from everything and everyone she has ever truly known. Wonderfully lyrical language and stunning descriptions of landscape propel this captivating and original tale into the best of the year!"—Phyllis Spinale, Wellesley Books, Wellesley, OH

"Jiles captures the flavor of the post-Civil War American West perfectly in this tale built around two very strong characters. Captain Kidd brings news to isolated Texans by giving paid readings drawn from East Coast and European news articles. The elderly widower accepts the task of returning a ten-year-old girl to her faraway relatives. She had earlier been captured by the Kiowa and adapted to their Indian ways. Now her crafty intelligence and surprising skill helps to save them both from attack. I do love westerns and recommend this page turner highly!"—Karen Bakshoian, Letterpress Books, Portland, ME

THE COUPLE NEXT DOOR

a novel

SHARI LAPENA

SUMMARY

How well do you know the couple next door? Or your husband? Or even—yourself? People are capable of almost anything. . . A domestic suspense debut about a young couple and their apparently friendly neighbors—a twisty, rollercoaster ride of lies, betrayal, and the secrets between husbands and wives. . . Anne and Marco Conti seem to have it all—a loving relationship, a wonderful home, and their beautiful baby, Cora. But one night when they are at a dinner party next door, a terrible crime is committed. Suspicion immediately focuses on the parents. But the truth is a much more complicated story. Inside the curtained house, an unsettling account of what actually happened unfolds. Detective Rasbach knows that the panicked couple is hiding something. Both Anne and Marco soon discover that the other is keeping secrets, secrets they've kept for years. What follows is the nerve-racking unraveling of a family—a chilling tale of deception, duplicity, and unfaithfulness that will keep you breathless until the final shocking twist.

EXCERPT

Chapter One

Anne can feel the acid churning in her stomach and creeping up her throat; her head is swimming. She's had too much to drink. Cynthia has been topping her up all night. Anne had meant to keep herself to a limit, but she'd let things slide—she didn't know how else she was supposed to get through the evening. Now she has no idea how much wine she's drunk over the course of this interminable dinner party. She'll have to pump and dump her breast milk in the morning.

Anne is wilting in the heat of the summer's night and watches her hostess with narrowed eyes. Cynthia is flirting openly with Anne's husband, Marco. Why does she put up with it? Why does Cynthia's husband, Graham, allow it? Anne is angry but powerless; she doesn't know how to put a stop to it without looking pathetic and ridiculous. They are all a little tanked. So she ignores it, quietly seething, and sips at the chilled wine. Anne hasn't been brought up to create a scene, isn't one to draw attention to herself.

Cynthia, on the other hand.

All three of them—Anne, Marco, and Cynthia's mild-mannered husband, Graham—are watching her, as if fascinated. Marco in particular can't seem to take his eyes off Cynthia. She leans in a little too close to Marco as she bends over and fills his glass, her clingy top cut so low that Marco's practically rubbing his nose in her cleavage.

Anne reminds herself that Cynthia flirts with everyone. Cynthia has such outrageous good looks that she can't seem to help herself.

But the longer Anne watches, the more she wonders if there could actually be something going on between Marco and Cynthia. Anne has never had such suspicions before. Perhaps the alcohol is making her paranoid.

No, she decides—they wouldn't be carrying on like this if they had anything to hide. Cynthia is flirting more than Marco is; he is the flattered recipient of her attentions. Marco is almost too good-looking himself—with his tousled dark hair, hazel eyes, and sensual mouth, he's always attracted attention. They make a striking couple, Cynthia and Marco. Anne tells herself to stop it. Tells herself that of course Marco is faithful to her. She knows he is completely committed to his family. She and the baby are everything to him. He will stand by her, no matter what—she takes another gulp of wine—no matter how bad things get.

But watching Cynthia drape over her husband, Anne is becoming more and more anxious and upset. She is still more than twenty pounds overweight from her pregnancy, six months after having the baby. She thought she'd be back to her pre-pregnancy figure by now, but apparently it takes at least a year. She must stop looking at the tabloids in the grocery store checkout and comparing herself to all those celebrity moms with their personal trainers who look terrific after a couple of months.

But even at her best, Anne could never compete with the likes of Cynthia, her taller, shapelier, neighbour—with her long legs, nipped-in waist, and big breasts, her porcelain skin and tumbling jet-black hair. And Cynthia always dressed to kill, in high heels and sexy clothes—even for a dinner party at home with one other couple.

Anne can't focus on the conversation around her. She tunes it out and stares at the carved marble fireplace, exactly like the one in her own living-dining room, on the other side of the common wall Anne and Marco share with Cynthia and Graham; they live in an attached brick row houses, typical of upstate New York, solidly built in the late nineteenth century. All the houses in the row are similar—Italianate, restored, expensive—except that Anne and Marco's house is at the end of the row, and each one reflects slight differences in decoration and taste; each one is a small masterpiece.

Anne reaches clumsily for her cell phone on the dining table and checks the time. It is almost one o'clock in the morning. She'd checked on the baby at midnight. Marco had gone to check on her at twelve thirty. Then he'd gone out for a cigarette on the back patio with Cynthia, while she and Graham sat rather awkwardly at the littered dining table, making stilted conversation. She should have gone out to the back yard with them; there might have been a breeze. But she hadn't, because Graham didn't like to be around cigarette smoke, and it would have been rude, or at least awkward, to leave Graham there all alone at his own dinner party. So for reasons of propriety, she had stayed. Graham, a WASP like herself, is impeccably polite. Why he had married a tart like Cynthia is a mystery. Cynthia and Marco had come back in from the patio a few minutes ago, and Anne desperately wants to leave, even if everyone else is still having fun.

She glances at the baby monitor sitting at the end of the table, its small red light glowing like the tip of a cigarette. Suddenly she has doubts, feels the wrongness of it all. Who goes to a dinner party next door and leaves their baby alone in the house? What kind of mother does such a thing? She feels the familiar agony set in—*she is not a good mother.*

So what if the sitter cancelled? They should have brought Cora with them, put her in her portable playpen. But Cynthia had said no children. It was to be an adult evening, for Graham's birthday. Which is another reason Anne has come to dislike Cynthia, who was once a good friend—Cynthia is not baby-friendly. Who says a six-month-old baby isn't welcome at a dinner party? How had Anne ever let Marco persuade her that it was okay? It was irresponsible. She wonders what the other mothers in her mom's group would think, if she ever told them. *We left our six-month-old baby home alone, and went to a party next door.* She imagines all their jaws dropping in shock, the uncomfortable silence. But she will never tell them. She'd be shunned.

She and Marco had argued about it, before the party. When the sitter called and cancelled, Anne had offered to stay home with the baby—she hadn't wanted to go to the dinner anyway. But Marco was having none of it.

"You can't just stay home," he insisted, when they argued about it in the kitchen.

"I'm fine staying home," she said, her voice lowered. She didn't want Cynthia to hear them arguing about going to her party.

"It will be good for you to get out," Marco countered, lowering his own voice. And then he'd added, "You know what the doctor said."

All night long, she's been trying to decide whether that last comment was mean-spirited, or self-interested, or whether he was simply trying to help. Finally, she had given in. Marco persuaded her that with the monitor on next door, they could hear the baby any time she stirred or woke. They would check on her every half hour. Nothing bad would happen.

It is one o'clock. Should she go check on Cora now, or just try to get Marco to leave? She wants to go home to bed. She wants this night to end.

She pulls her husband's arm. "Marco," she urges, "we should go. It's one o'clock."

"Oh, don't go yet," Cynthia says. "It's not that late!" She obviously doesn't want the party to be over. She doesn't want Marco to leave. She wouldn't mind at all if Anne left though, Anne is pretty sure.

"Maybe not for you," Anne says, and she manages to sound a little stiff, even though she is drunk, "but I have to be up early, to feed the baby."

"Poor you," Cynthia says, and for some reason, this infuriates Anne. Cynthia has no children, nor has she ever wanted any. She and Graham are childless by choice.

Getting Marco to leave the party is difficult. He seems determined to stay. He's having too much fun, but Anne is getting anxious.

"Just one more," Marco says to Cynthia, holding up his glass, avoiding his wife's eyes.

He is in a strangely boisterous mood tonight—it seems almost forced. Anne wonders why. He's been quiet lately, at home. Distracted, even moody. But tonight, with Cynthia, he's the life of the party. For some time now, Anne has sensed that something is wrong, if only he would tell her what it is. He isn't telling her much of anything these days. He's shutting her out. Or maybe he's withdrawing from her because of her depression, her "baby blues." He's disappointed in her. Who isn't? Tonight he clearly prefers the beautiful, bubbly, sparkly Cynthia.

Anne looks at the time and loses all patience. "I'm going to go. I was supposed to check on the baby at one." She looks at Marco. "You stay as late as you like," she adds, her voice tight. Marco looks sharply at her, his eyes glittering. Suddenly Anne thinks he doesn't look that drunk at all, but she feels dizzy. Are they going to argue about this? In front of the neighbours? Really? Anne begins to look around for her purse, gathers up the baby monitor, realizes then that it is plugged into the wall, and bends over to unplug it, aware of everyone at the table silently staring at her fat ass. Well, let them. She feels like they are ganging up on her, seeing her as a spoilsport. She feels tears start to burn and fights them back. She does not want to burst into tears in front of everyone. Cynthia and Graham don't know about her post-partum depression. They wouldn't understand. Anne and Marco haven't told anyone, with the exception of Anne's mother. Anne has recently confided in her. She knows her mother won't tell anyone, not even her father. Anne doesn't want anyone else to know, and she suspects Marco doesn't either, although he hasn't said as much. But pretending all the time is exhausting.

While her back is turned, she hears Marco's change of heart.

"You're right. It's late, we should go," he says. She hears him set his wine glass down on the table behind her with a *clunk*.

Anne turns around, brushing the hair out of her eyes with the back of her hand. She desperately needs a haircut. She gives a fake smile and says, "Next time, it's our turn to host." And adds, silently—*you can come to our house, where our child lives with us, and I hope she cries all night and spoils your evening. I'll be sure to invite you when she's teething.*

They leave quickly after that. They have no baby gear to gather up, just themselves, Anne's purse and the baby monitor, which she shoves into it. Cynthia looks annoyed at their swift departure, Graham is neutral—and make their way out the impressively heavy front door and down the steps. Anne grabs hold of the elaborately carved hand rail to help her keep her balance. It is just a few short steps along the sidewalk until they are at their own front steps, with a similar hand rail and an equally impressive front door. Anne is walking slightly ahead of Marco, not speaking. She may not speak to him for the rest of the night. She marches up the steps and stops dead.

"What?" Marco says, coming up behind her, his voice tense.

Anne is staring. The front door is ajar; it is open about three inches.

"I know I locked it!" Anne says, her voice shrill.

Marco says, his voice tight, "Maybe you forgot. You've had a lot to drink."

But Anne isn't listening. She's inside and running up the staircase and down the hall to the baby's room, with Marco right behind her.

When she gets to the baby's room and sees the empty crib, she screams.

Chapter Two

Anne feels her scream inside her own head and reverberating off the walls—her scream is everywhere. Then she falls silent and stands in front of the empty crib, rigid, her hand to her mouth. Marco fumbles with the light switch behind her. They both stare at the empty crib where their baby should be. It is impossible that she not be there. There is no way Cora could have gotten out of the crib by herself. She is barely six months old.

"Call the police," Anne whispers, then throws up, the vomit cascading over her fingers and onto the hardwood floor as she bends over. The baby's room, painted a soft butter yellow, with stencils of baby lambs frolicking on the walls, immediately fills with the smell of vomit and panic.

Marco doesn't move. Anne looks up at him. He is paralysed, in shock, staring at the empty crib, as if he can't believe it. Anne sees the panic and guilt in his eyes and starts to wail—a horrible, keening sound, like an animal in pain.

Marco still doesn't budge. Anne bolts across the hall to their bedroom, grabs the phone off the bedside table and dials 911, her hands shaking, getting vomit all over the phone. Marco finally snaps out of it. She can hear him walking rapidly around the second floor of the house while she stares across the hall at the empty crib. He checks the bathroom, at the top of the stairs, then he passes quickly by her on his way to the other room down the hall, the one they have turned into an office. But even as he does, Anne wonders, in a detached way, why he is looking there. It's as if part of her mind has split off and is thinking logically. It's not like their baby could get out of her crib and crawl around the rooms and hide. She is not in the bathroom, or the office.

Someone has taken her.

When the Emergency operator answers, Anne cries, "Someone has taken our baby!" She is barely able to calm herself enough to answer the operator's questions. "I understand, Ma'am. Try to stay calm. The police are on their way." The operator assures her.

Anne hangs up the phone. Her whole body is trembling. She feels like she is going to be sick again. It occurs to her how it will look. They'd left the baby alone in the house. Was that illegal? It must be. Even through the horror she feels about their baby, some part of her brain is thinking about self-preservation. How will they explain it?

Marco appears at the bedroom door, pale and sick-looking.

"This is your fault!" Anne screams, wild-eyed, and pushes past him. She rushes into the bathroom at the top of the stairs and throws up again, this time into the pedestal sink, then washes the vomit from her shaking hands and rinses her mouth. She catches a glimpse of herself in the mirror. Marco is standing right behind her. Their eyes meet in the mirror.

"I'm sorry," he whispers. "I'm so sorry. It's my fault."

And he is sorry, she can tell. Even so, Anne brings her hand up and smashes at the reflection of his face in the mirror. The mirror shatters, and she breaks down, sobbing. He tries to take her in his arms, but she pushes him away and runs downstairs. Her hand is bleeding, leaving a trail of blood along the handrail.

***

An air of unreality permeates everything that happens next. Anne and Marco's comfortable home immediately becomes a crime scene.

Anne is sitting on the sofa in the living room. Someone has placed a blanket around her shoulders, but she's still trembling. She is in shock. Police cars are parked on the street outside the house, their red lights flashing. The lights pulse through the front window and circle the pale living room walls. Anne sits, immobile, on the sofa and stares ahead as if hypnotised by the lights.

Marco, his voice breaking, has given the police a quick description of the baby—six months old, blonde, blue eyes, about sixteen pounds, wearing a disposable diaper and a plain, pale pink onesie. A light summer baby blanket, solid white, is also missing from the crib.

The house is crawling with uniformed police officers. They fan out and methodically begin to search the house. Some of them wear latex gloves and carry evidence kits. Anne and Marco's fast, frantic look through of the house in the short minutes before the police arrived had turned up nothing. The forensic team is moving slowly; clearly they are not looking for Cora, they are looking for evidence. The baby is already gone.

Marco sits down on the sofa next to Anne and puts his arm around her, holds her close. She wants to pull away, but she doesn't. She lets his arm stay there. How would it look if she pulled away? She can smell the alcohol on him.

Anne now blames herself. It's her fault. She wants to blame Marco, but she agreed to leave the baby alone. She should have stayed home. No—she should have brought Cora with them next door, to hell with Cynthia. She doubts Cynthia would have actually thrown them all out, and had no party for Graham at all. This realization comes too late.

They will be judged, by the police, and by everybody else. Serves them right, leaving their baby all alone. She would think that, too, if it had happened to someone else. She knows how judgmental mothers are, how good it feels to sit in judgement of someone else. She thinks of her own mothers' group, meeting with their babies once a week in each other's homes for coffee and gossip, what they will say about her.

Someone else has arrived—a composed man in a well-cut dark suit. The uniformed officers treat him with deference. Anne looks up, meets his piercing blue eyes, and wonders who he is.

He approaches and sits down in one of the arm chairs across from Anne and Marco. and introduces himself. Then he leans forward. "Tell me what happened."

Anne immediately forgets the detective's name, or rather, it hasn't registered at all. She only catches "detective." She looks at him, encouraged by the frank intelligence behind his eyes. He will help them. He will help them get Cora back. She tries to think. But she can't think. She is frantic and numb at the same time. She simply looks into the detective's sharp eyes and lets Marco do the talking.

"We were next door," Marco begins, clearly agitated. "At the neighbours." Then he stops.

"Yes?" the detective says.

Marco hesitates.

"Where was the baby?" the detective asks.

Marco doesn't answer. He doesn't want to say.

Anne, pulling herself together, answers for him, the tears spilling down her face. "We left her here, in her crib, with the monitor on." She watches the detective for his reaction—*what awful parents*—but he betrays nothing. "We had the monitor on over there, and we checked on her constantly. Every half hour." She glances at Marco. "We never thought…" but she can't finish. Her hand goes to her mouth, her fingers press against her lips.

"When was the last time you checked on her?" the detective asks, taking a small notebook from the inside pocket of his suit jacket.

"I checked on her at midnight," Anne says. "I remember the time. We were checking on her every half hour, and it was my turn. She was fine. She was sleeping."

"I checked on her again at twelve thirty," Marco says.

"You're absolutely certain of the time?" the detective asks. Marco nods; he is staring at his feet, as if he finds it hard to meet the detective's eyes. "And that was the last time anyone checked on her, before you came home?"

"Yes," Marco says, looking up at the detective, running a nervous hand through his dark hair. "I went to check on her at twelve thirty. It was my turn. We were keeping to a schedule."

Anne nods.

"How much have you had to drink tonight?" the detective asks Marco.

Marco flushes. "They were having a small dinner party, next door. I had a few," he admits.

The detective turns to Anne. "Have you had anything to drink tonight, Mrs. Conti?"

Her face burns. Nursing mothers aren't supposed to drink. She wants to lie. "I had some wine, with dinner. I don't know how much, exactly," she says. "It was a dinner party." She wonders how drunk she looks, what this detective must think of her. She feels like he can see right through her. She remembers the vomit upstairs in the baby's room. Can he smell alcohol on her the way she can smell it on Marco? She remembers the shattered mirror in the upstairs bathroom, her bloodied hand. She's ashamed of how they must look to him, drunken parents who abandoned their six-month-old daughter. She wonders if they will be charged with anything.

"How is that even relevant?" Marco says to the detective.

"It might affect the reliability of your observations," the detective says evenly. He is not judgemental. He is merely after the facts, it seems. "What time did you leave the party?" he asks.

"It was almost one thirty," Anne answers. "I kept checking the time on my cell. I wanted to go. I—I should have checked on her at one, it was my turn, but I thought we'd be leaving any minute, and I was trying to get Marco to hurry up." She feels agonizingly guilty. If she had checked on her daughter at one o'clock would this have been prevented? But then, there were so many ways this could have been prevented.

"You placed the call to 911 at 1:27," the detective says.

"The front door was open," Anne says, remembering.

"The front door was open?" the detective repeats.

"It was open three or four inches. I'm sure I locked it behind me when I checked on her at midnight," Anne says.

"How sure?"

Anne thinks about it. Was she sure? She had been positive, when she saw the open front door, that she had locked it. But now, with what had happened, how can she be sure of anything? She turns to her husband. "Are you sure you didn't leave the door open?"

"I'm sure," he says curtly. "I never used the front door. I was going through the back to check on her, remember?"

"You used the back door," the detective repeats.

"I may not have locked it every time," Marco admits, and covers his face with his hands.

* * *

Detective Rasbach observes the couple closely. A baby is missing. Taken from her crib—if the parents, Marco and Anne Conti, are to be believed—between approximately 12:30 a.m. and 1:27 a.m., by a person or persons unknown, while the parents were at a party next door. The front door had been found partly open. The back door may have been left unlocked by the father—it had in fact been found closed, but unlocked, when the police arrived. There is no denying the distress of the mother. And of the father, who looks badly shaken. But the whole situation doesn't feel right. Rasbach wonders what is really going on.

Detective Jennings waves him over silently. "Excuse me," Detective Rasbach says, and leaves the stricken parents for a moment.

"What is it?" Rasbach asks quietly.

Jennings holds up a small vial of pills. "Found these in the bathroom cabinet," he says.

Rasbach takes the small clear plastic container from Jennings and studies the label. *Anne Conti, Sertraline, 20 mg.* Sertraline, Rasbach knows, is a powerful anti-depressant.

"The bathroom mirror upstairs is smashed," Jennings tells him.

Rasbach nods. He hasn't been upstairs yet. "Anything else?"

Jennings shakes his head. "Nothing so far. House looks clean. Nothing else taken, apparently. We'll know more from forensics in a few hours."

"Okay," Rasbach says, handing the vial of pills back to Jennings.

He returns to the couple on the sofa and resumes his questioning. He looks at the husband. "Marco—is it okay if I call you Marco?—what did you do after you checked on the baby at twelve thirty?"

"I went back to the party next door," Marco says. "I had a cigarette in the neighbour's back yard."

"Were you alone when you had your cigarette?"

"No. Cynthia came out with me." Marco flushes; Rasbach notices. "She's the neighbour who had us over for dinner."

Rasbach turns his attention to the wife. She's an attractive woman, with fine features and glossy brown hair, but right now she looks hollowed out. "You don't smoke, Mrs. Conti?"

"No, I don't. But Cynthia does," Anne says. "I was sitting at the dining room table with Graham, her husband. He hates cigarette smoke, and it was his birthday, and I thought it would be rude to leave him alone inside." And then, inexplicably, she volunteers, "Cynthia had been flirting with Marco all evening, and I felt bad for Graham."

"I see," Rasbach says. He studies the husband, who looks utterly miserable. He also looks nervous and guilty. Rasbach turns to him. "So you were outside in the back yard next door shortly after twelve thirty. Any idea how long you were out there?"

Marco shakes his head helplessly. "Maybe fifteen minutes, give or take?"

"Did you see anything, or hear anything?"

"What do you mean?" The husband seems to be in some kind of shock. He is slurring his words slightly. Rasbach wonders just how much alcohol he's had.

Rasbach spells it out for him. "Someone apparently took your baby sometime between twelve thirty and one twenty-seven. You were outside in the back yard next door for a few minutes shortly after twelve thirty." He watches the husband, waits for him to put it together. "To my mind, it's unlikely that anyone would carry a baby out your front door in the middle of the night."

"But the front door was open," Anne says.

"I didn't see anything," Marco says.

"There's a lane running behind the houses on this side of the street," Detective Rasbach says. Marco nods. "Did you notice anyone using the lane at that time? Did you hear anything, a car?"

"I—I don't think so," Marco says. "I'm sorry, I didn't see or hear anything." He covers his face with his hands again. "I wasn't paying attention."

Detective Rasbach had already checked out the area quickly before coming inside and interviewing the parents. He thinks it unlikely—but not impossible—that a stranger would carry a sleeping child out the front door of a house on a street like this one, and risk being seen. The houses are attached row houses set close to the sidewalk. The street is well lit, and there is a fair bit of vehicular and foot traffic, even late at night. So it is odd—perhaps he is being deliberately misled?—that the front door was open. The forensics team is dusting it for fingerprints now, but somehow, Rasbach doesn't think they'll find anything.

The back holds more potential. Most of the houses, including the Contis', have a single detached garage opening onto the lane—behind the house. The back yards are long and narrow, fenced in between, and most, including the Contis', have trees and shrubs and gardens. It is relatively dark back there; there are no street lights as there are in the front. It's a dark night, with no moon. Whoever has taken the child, if he had come out the Contis' back door, would only have had to walk across the back yard to the lane. The chances of being seen carrying an abducted child out the back to a waiting vehicle are much less than the chances of being seen carrying an abducted child out the front door.

The house, yard and garage are being thoroughly searched by Rasbach's team. So far, they have found no sign of the missing baby. The Contis' garage is empty, and the garage door has been left wide open to the lane. It's possible that even if someone had been sitting out back on the patio next door they might not have noticed anything. But not likely. Which narrows the window of the abduction to between approximately 12:45 a.m. and 1:27 a.m.

"Are you aware that your motion detector isn't working?" Rasbach asks.

"What?" the husband says, startled.

"You have a motion detector on your back door, a light that should go on when someone approaches it. Are you aware that it isn't working?"

"No," the wife whispers.

The husband shakes his head vigorously. "No, I—it was working when I checked on her—what's wrong with it?"

"The bulb has been loosened." Detective Rasbach watches the parents carefully. He pauses. "It leads me to believe that the child was taken out the back, to the garage, and away, probably in a vehicle, via the lane." He waits, but neither the husband nor the wife says anything. The wife is shaking, he notices.

"Where is your car?" Rasbach asks, leaning forward.

"Our car?" Anne echoes.

Chapter Three

Rasbach waits for their answer.

She answers first. "It's on the street."

"You park on the street when you've got a garage in back? Rasbach asks.

"Everybody does that," Anne answers. "It's easier than going through the lane, especially in the winter. Most people get a parking permit and just park on the street."

"I see," Rasbach says.

"Why?" the wife asks. "What does it matter?"

Rasbach explains. "It probably made it easier for the kidnapper. If the garage was empty, and the garage door was left open, it would be relatively easy for someone to back a car in, and put the baby in the car while the car was in the garage, out of sight. It would obviously be more difficult—certainly riskier—if the garage already had a car in it. The kidnapper would run the risk of being seen in the lane with the baby."

Rasbach notices that the husband has turned another shade paler, if that is even possible. His pallor is quite striking.

"We're hoping we will get some imprints from the garage," Rasbach adds.

"You make it sound like this was planned," the mother says.

"Do you think it wasn't?" Rasbach asks her.

"I—I don't know. I guess I thought Cora was taken because we left her alone in the house, that it was a crime of opportunity. Like if someone had snatched her from the park when I wasn't looking."

Rasbach nods, as if trying to see it from her point of view. "I see what you mean," he says. "For example, a mother leaves her child playing in the park while she fetches an ice cream from the ice cream truck. The child is snatched while her back is turned. It happens." He pauses. "But surely you realize the difference here."

She looks back at him blankly. He has to remember that she is probably in shock. But he sees this sort of thing all the time, it is his job. He is analytical, not at all sentimental. He must be, if he is to be effective. He will find this child, dead or alive, and he will find whoever took her.

He tells her, his voice matter of fact, "The difference is, whoever took your baby, probably knew she was alone in the house."

The parents look at one another blankly.

"But nobody knew," the mother whispers.

"Of course," Rasbach adds, "it is possible that she might have been taken even if you were sound asleep in your own bedroom. We don't know for sure."

The parents look desperately at each other; they would like to believe that it isn't their fault, after all, for leaving their baby alone. That this might have happened anyway.

Rasbach asks, "Do you always leave the garage door open like that?"

The husband answers. "Sometimes."

"Wouldn't you close the garage door at night? To prevent theft?"

"We don't keep anything valuable in the garage," the husband says. "If the car's in there, we generally lock the door, but we don't keep much in there otherwise. All my tools are in the basement. This is a nice neighbourhood, but people break into garages here all the time, so what's the point of locking it?"

"Some people leave the garage doors up on purpose to prevent the graffiti artists from tagging them," the wife puts in.

Rasbach nods. Then he asks, "What kind of car do you have?"

"It's an Audi," Marco says. "Why?"

"I'd like to have a look. May I have the keys?" Rasbach asks.

Marco and Anne look at one another in confusion. Then Marco gets up and goes to a side table near the front door and grabs a set of keys from a bowl. He hands them over to the detective silently and sits back down.

"Thank you," Rasbach says. Then he leans forward and says deliberately, "We will find out who did this." They stare back at him, meeting his eyes, the mother's entire face swollen from crying, the father's eyes puffy and bloodshot with distress and drink, his face pasty.

Rasbach nods to Jennings, and together they leave the house to check the car. The couple sit on the sofa silently and watch them go.

**

Anne doesn't know what to make of the detective. All this about their car—he seems to be insinuating something. She knows that when a wife goes missing, the husband is usually the prime suspect, and probably vice versa. But when a child goes missing, were the parents usually the prime suspects? Surely not. Who could harm their own child? Besides, they both have solid alibis. They can be accounted for, by Cynthia and Graham. There is obviously no way they could have taken and hidden their own daughter. And why would they?

She is aware that the neighbourhood is being searched, that there are police officers going up and down the streets, knocking on doors, interviewing people roused from their beds. Marco has provided the police with a recent photo of Cora, taken just a few days ago. The photo shows a happy blonde baby girl smiling up at the camera, with big blue eyes.

Anne is angry at Marco—she wants to scream at him, pummel him with her fists—but their house is full of police officers—she doesn't dare. And when she looks at his pale, bleak face, she sees that he is already blaming himself. She knows she can't get through this on her own. She turns to him and collapses into his chest, sobbing. His arms come up around her and he hugs her tightly back. She can feel him shaking, can feel the painful thumping of his heart. She tells herself that together they will get through this. The police will find Cora. They will get their daughter back.

And if they don't, she will never forgive him.

***

Detective Rasbach, in his lightweight summer suit, steps out the front door of the Contis' house and down the front steps into the hot summer night, closely followed by Detective Jennings. They have worked together before. They have each seen some things that they would like to be able to forget.

Together they walk toward the opposite side of the street, lined bumper to bumper with parked cars. Rasbach presses a button and the headlights of the Audi flash briefly. Already the neighbours are out on their front steps, in their pajamas and summer bathrobes. Now they watch as Rasbach and Jennings walk toward the Contis' car.

Rasbach hopes that someone on this street might know something, might have seen something, and will come forward.

Jennings says, his voice low, "What's your take?"

Rasbach answers quietly, "I'm not optimistic."

Rasbach pulls on a pair of latex gloves that Jennings hands him, and opens the door on the driver's side. He looks briefly inside and then silently walks to the back of the car. Jennings follows.

Rasbach pops open the trunk. The two detectives look inside. It's empty. And very clean. The car is just over a year old. It still looks new.

"Love that new car smell," Jennings says.

Clearly, the child isn't there. That didn't mean she hadn't been there, however briefly. Perhaps forensic investigation will reveal fibres from a pink onesie, DNA from the baby—a hair, a trace of drool, or maybe blood. Without a body, they will have a tough case to make. But no one puts their baby in the trunk with good intentions. If they find any trace of the missing child in the trunk, he would see that the parents rotted in hell. Because if there's anything Rasbach has learned in his years on the job, it is that people are capable of almost anything.

Rasbach is aware that the baby could have gone missing at any time before the dinner party. He has yet to question the parents about the previous day in detail, has yet to determine who, other than the parents, last saw the child alive. But he will find out. Perhaps there is a mother's helper who comes in, or a cleaning lady or a neighbour—someone who had seen the baby, alive and well, earlier that day. He will establish when the baby was last known to be alive, and work forward from there. This leaving the monitor on, checking every half hour while they dined next door, the disabled motion detector, the open front door, could all simply be an elaborate fiction, a carefully constructed fabrication of the parents, to provide them with an alibi, to throw the authorities off the scent. They might have killed the baby at any time earlier that day—either deliberately, or by accident—and put her in the trunk and disposed of the body before going to the party next door. Or, if they were still thinking clearly, they might not have put her in the trunk at all, but in the car seat. A dead baby might not look that different from a sleeping baby. Depending on how they killed her.

Rasbach knows that he's a cynic. He hadn't started out that way.

He says to Jennings, "Bring in the cadaver dogs."

You've just read an excerpt from The Couple Next Door.

ABOUT THE AUTHOR
Shari Lapena worked as a lawyer and as an English teacher before turning to writing fiction. She has written two award-winning literary novels, and *The Couple Next Door* is her suspense debut. Connect with Shari Lapena online sharilapena.com, and on Twitter @sharilapena.

IMPRINT: Pamela Dorman Books
PRINT ISBN: 9780735221086
PRINT PRICE: $26.00
EBOOK ISBN: 9780735221116
EBOOK PRICE: $12.99
PUBLICATION DATE: 8/23/16
PUBLICITY CONTACT: Meredith Burks mburks@penguinrandomhouse.com
RIGHTS CONTACT: Lorna Henry lohenry@penguinrandomhouse.com
EDITOR: Pamela Dorman
AGENT: Helen Heller
AGENCY: Helen Heller Agency Inc
TERRITORIES SOLD:
Euromedia (Czech-Republic)
Gyldendal DK (Denmark)
Prometheus (The Netherlands)
Otava (Finland)
Presses de la Cite (France)
Luebbe (Germany)
Miskal (Israel)
Alexandra (Hungary)
Bjatur (Iceland)
Mondadori (Italian)
Random House (Spain)
Gyldendal Norsk (Norway)
Zysk (Poland)
Record (Brazil)
AST (Russia)
Fortuna (Slovakia)
Modernista (Sweden)
Dogan Kitap (Turkey)
China Times (China)
Trei (Romania)
Presenca (Portugal)
Soulbookstore (Korea)

PROMOTIONAL INFORMATION:
Print and online reviews and features; Mystery media attention; National radio campaign; Online advertising, social media and online promotion; Academic marketing and library promotions.

MERCURY

MARGOT LIVESEY

A NOVEL

SUMMARY

Donald believes he knows all there is to know about seeing. An optometrist in suburban Boston, he is sure that he and his wife Viv, who runs the local stables, are both devoted to their two children, and to each other. Then Mercury—a gorgeous young thoroughbred with a murky past—arrives at Windy Hill and everything changes. Hilary, a newcomer to town, has inherited Mercury from her brother after his mysterious death. When she first brings Mercury to board at Windy Hill everyone is struck by his beauty and prowess, particularly Viv. As she rides him, Viv begins to dream of competing again, embracing the ambitions that she harbored before she settled for a career in finance. Her daydreams soon morph into consuming desire, and her infatuation with the thoroughbred escalates to obsession. Donald may have 20:20 vision, but he is slow to notice how profoundly Viv has changed and how these changes threaten their quiet, secure world. By the time he does it is too late to stop the catastrophic collision of Viv's ambitions and his own myopia. *Mercury* is a riveting tour de force that showcases this "searingly intelligent writer at the height of her powers." (Jennifer Egan).

EXCERPT

Part One
Donald

Chapter One

My mother called me after a favorite uncle, who was in turn called after a Scottish king. Donald III was sixty when he first ascended the throne in 1093. He went on to reign twice, briefly and disastrously. As a child I hated my name—other children sang "Donald, where's y'er troosers?" in the playground—but as an adult I have come to appreciate being named after a valiant late bloomer: a man who seized the day. Of course most Americans, when I introduce myself, are thinking not about Scottish history but about a cartoon duck. They are surprised when I tell them that a Scot invented penicillin and that James VI, for whom the Bible was so gloriously translated, was a keen amateur dentist. I used to believe that in my modest fashion, I was contributing to the spread of Scottish values: thrift, industry, integrity. I have my own business, a full-service optometrist's, in a town outside Boston. More than most people, I have tested the hypothesis that the eye is the window to the soul.

Give us a child until the age of seven and he is ours for life, the Jesuits famously claimed, so perhaps it was my first ten years in Scotland that inoculated me against American optimism. I am pleased by an average day, and I know I am neither great nor awesome. What's more, I don't believe other people are either, although I am too polite to say so. Before I started my business, I practiced as a surgeon, which taught me precision and humility.

It was my mother who brought us to the States. In 1981 she was offered a two-year position in the Boston office of her advertising company. My father, a manager for British Rail in the days when there still was a British Rail, was happy to have an adventure. On the plane over, while my little sister, Frances, made her dolls cups of tea, the three of us studied a map of America and made a list of places we wanted to see. We rented a house on Avon Hill in Cambridge. I attended a nearby school where I gradually made friends but my real friend was Robert, whose parents ran a flower shop in Edinburgh, round the corner from the house I still regarded as home. Every week I wrote to him on a blue aerogram, and every week I received a reply to my previous aerogram. Despite the stingy American holidays, my parents worked hard at our list, and from each place we visited—Washington, DC; Yosemite; the Berkshires; New York; Montreal—I sent Robert a postcard.

During our second Christmas I sent him a card from Key West, and it was there, beside the hotel swimming pool, that my parents announced that we were not going back to Scotland. In June, when the tenants left, our house would be sold. I had already written my Christmas thank-you letter to Robert—we'd exchanged model airplanes—and week after week, as I put off breaking the news, my aerograms grew briefer. I was suddenly aware that he would never see the Frog Pond on Boston Common, where my mother had taught us to skate, or the famous glass flowers that I had tried so hard to describe; that my new friends—Dean, David, Jim, Gerry—would never be more than names to him.

At Easter Robert wrote that he and his family had spent a week in a caravan near Montrose. They had played cricket with the family in the next caravan, and he and his brother had slept in their own wee tent. "It was fab," he wrote, "though Ian thrashes around in his sleep like a maniac." I didn't answer. I planned to, almost daily, but I could not bring myself to write even "Dear Robert." After three more letters, which I didn't open, he stopped writing, and when we went back to pack up our house, he was visiting cousins on the Isle of Wight. In the years that followed, my parents returned for a fortnight every August, but I chose to go to summer camp; a brief visit was worse than none. One of the first things I did after I returned to Edinburgh at the age of eighteen to study medicine was to go to the flower shop. Over the door hung a sign: Bunty's Bakery. They moved, the woman said vaguely. The new owners of his house were equally unhelpful. During eight years in that small city I never glimpsed him, even from afar. I still have all his aerograms in a shoebox that, although I have no plans to reread them, it would grieve me sharply to lose.

Fran was six when we moved. Within a year, her memories of Scotland had faded; she was a robust American. She has always been on easier terms with life than I have. My mother claims I didn't smile until I was nearly eight months old, and then was miserly with my new skill. "You'd look at your father and me playing peek-a-boo," she said, "as if we'd lost our minds." Even now I sometimes have to remind myself to tighten my cheek muscles, raise the corners of my mouth. I would fit in well in one of those countries—Iceland, say, or Latvia—where people seldom smile. Which is not to say I don't have a sense of humor. I enjoy puns, and have a weakness for silly jokes and slapstick. One of the things that drew me to Viv—you will not see much evidence of it in this narrative—was that she made me laugh. She is the only person I know well who calls me Don. We have been married for nine years and have two children, aged ten and eight. At the wedding reception Viv, already six months pregnant with Trina, carried Marcus instead of a bouquet. Our parents were, at that time, all four, still alive.

The year before Marcus was born, I qualified as an ophthalmologist in Massachusetts. But four years later, when Trina was fourteen months old, I gave up practicing surgery, and we moved out of Boston to be closer to my parents. One unexpected consequence of the move was that Viv, who had loved horses as a teenager, began to ride more often. Her old friend Claudia lived nearby and ran a stable that belonged to her great-aunt. One day, as she knelt to tie Trina's shoes, Viv announced that Claudia had suggested they run Windy Hill together. I knew at once, from the way she focused on the laces, that she had already agreed. One of the things I first admired about Viv was her impulsiveness. She was born saying, "Yes." And I was born saying "Let me figure that out."

The three of us, Viv, Claudia, and I, met with Claudia's accountant, who made it clear that even in a good season, Viv would earn a small fraction of her current salary working in mutual funds. While the accountant went over the numbers, Viv and Claudia exchanged the kind of look that might have passed between members of Shackleton's expedition as he described the challenges ahead. What did they care about horrendous odds? They were bound for glory.

But after the accountant had packed up her spreadsheets, and Claudia had gone home to the house she shared with her great aunt, Viv turned to me. "You have to say, Don, if you don't want me to do this. It was never part of our deal for you to earn all the money."

She had spent most of our second date describing Nutmeg, the horse she rode as a girl in Ann Arbor. What I recall even now, more than a decade later, are not so much the details—his chestnut coat and four white socks, how he whinnied at the sight of her—but the wistfulness with which she recounted them. When I asked if she still rode, she said, "Just enough to know how bad I've gotten." We had both had previous relationships, but this was the only one Viv cared to describe. You could say I'd been duly warned.

So, even as she offered to refuse Claudia, I knew that to accept her offer would change a certain balance between us. Instead I reminded her of her favorite quotation from Margaret Fuller: "Men for the sake of getting a living forget to live." Her earning less, I said, was fine with me. I was happy to support our household. And for several years that was true. I enjoyed my work, enjoyed my egalitarian marriage. I learned to speed around the huge American supermarket; my cooking improved; I bought a vacuum cleaner and found a person to use it. In Brazil, Alice had designed commercial spaces; in Massachusetts she cleaned houses with surprising cheer. My life, despite frequent emergencies, fit me like a well-made suit.

Most of the emergencies then had to do with my parents. My father had

Parkinson's, and my mother and I wanted to keep him at home for as long as possible. I arranged for Alice to clean and cook for them, and several days a week I brought Marcus and Trina over after school. I had been a dreamy child, but I became an adult without a minute to spare. As a boy in Edinburgh I had loved visiting the orrery at the Chamber Street Museum. At the turn of a switch each of the eight planets—Pluto had not yet been discovered—would begin spinning on its own axis, at the same time orbiting the sun. That was what my life, and the life of my family, was like in the years when everything worked. Unlike the planets, Viv and I touched often.

When Viv and I visited Edinburgh the spring she was pregnant with Marcus, I took her to see the orrery. It had been moved to the ground floor of the museum, and the mechanism that spun the planets had been disconnected. Standing beside the glass sphere with its painted constellations, I had done my best to describe the various orbits.

None of us shared Viv's passion for horses. I was neutral, Marcus hostile, and Trina, who loved most animals, had fallen off a pony when she was four and remained wary. I tried to make up for my lack of enthusiasm by being a good listener. But there is listening, and listening. When my patients talk during an exam, I respond appropriately even when 90 percent of my attention is focused on the cornea, the iris, the lens. And that, I fear, is how I listened when Viv first told me about a horse named Mercury.

We were in the kitchen. I was doing the dishes after a not-bad lamb curry—Marcus and Trina are adventurous eaters—and Viv was leaning against the counter, eating a peach in greedy mouthfuls. It was early September, and the peaches would soon be gone. Nearby in his cage, Nabokov, my father's African grey parrot, was also eating a peach; I had cut his into wedges and removed the poisonous pit. As I rinsed plates, as Viv talked, I was thinking about the woman who had come into my office that morning, so upset she could barely speak; the undertaker had forgotten her father's glasses.

"Mercury," I repeated, the schoolboy's trick for feigning attention. "Commonly known as quicksilver. Also the smallest planet."

"Quicksilver," Viv said. "That would suit him."

His owner, she went on, was the mother of their worst student. When

Hilary phoned, Viv had been sure it was to say that her daughter was quitting—but no, she had inherited a horse and wanted to board him at Windy Hill. Mercury had arrived that day. Five years old, a dapple-gray Thoroughbred, the most beautiful animal Viv had ever seen.

"I'm hungry," cried Nabokov, eyeing her peach. "I'm starving."

I took advantage of his interruption to tell Viv about the dead man's glasses. "His daughter was beside herself. We gave her a display pair. I only hope they fit him."

"I can't imagine Dad without his glasses," Viv said. "Mom either."

Even after all my years in the States, the word *mom,* so similar to the British *mum,* still strikes me as a simpleminded palindrome. Our children are resigned to my calling Viv by name, another palindrome, or saying "your mother" like some stern Victorian parent. I tell them they're growing up in a bilingual household. We used to make lists of words that are different in funny ways: *vest* and *waistcoat, pants* and *trousers, sidewalk* and *pavement, sick* and *ill.* I explained that "I quite like him" in Scottish means you don't, and in American means you do.

But I don't blame our two languages for the chasm that opened between Viv and me, so much as Mercury and my poor listening skills—and also, only now as I write this, my father's death. The road to his final exit was paved with so many losses, so many diminutions, that his end should have been a relief. But the psyche is capable of endless surprises; perhaps that's why it was named after a nymph. Looking back over the months following his departure, I can see that I lost track of certain things. So that September evening I failed to notice Viv's excitement. She was eating a peach, she was talking about a horse, she looked just like herself, her hair, fair when we first met now closer to brown, hanging down her back like a girl's. I did not understand that grief has many guises. It can make a man oblivious to his wife's needs, or susceptible to a hazel-eyed woman, or a thief of keys and codes, or an outright liar. It can obscure the direction of his moral compass. Or utterly change that direction.

I was saying that Viv's father had nice glasses when we heard a sound unusual on our small street: the wail of a siren, growing rapidly louder.

"Something's wrong," said Viv. She dropped her peach stone, I dried my hands, we hurried out into the street. Two fire engines, lights flashing, were parked outside the yellow house five doors down. Dirty smoke billowed from the doors and windows, but there were no flames.

Other people, strangers and neighbors we knew, were making their way towards the fire, drawn by whatever draws us to disaster. Someone tugged my sleeve, and I saw that Marcus and Trina had followed us. "Will the house burn down?" said Trina.

"No," I said. "The firemen will save it." I bent down and picked her up, more for my sake than for her safety.

A policeman stepped from between two cars and told the small crowd to stand back. "Does anyone know how many people live here?" he asked.

"There's three apartments," a man called out. "The guy at the top works nights at the post office."

Someone else added that the woman on the ground floor worked at a health club.

The house was less than a hundred yards from ours, but I had never seen anyone enter or leave. Even after blizzards, when everyone else appeared with shovels and snow blowers, no one emerged from the yellow house; their stretch of pavement was cleared, or sometimes ignored, by a service. We watched while two firemen forced the front door. Another climbed a ladder, checking windows. Trina started coughing—the smoke had an acrid odor—and I remember thinking we should not be exposing our children to this scene. What if someone jumped from a window, or was carried out unconscious? But neither Viv nor I could tear ourselves away. There were still no flames.

Finally a fireman stepped out of the building, waving his arms above his head: all clear. People began to return home. Viv was talking to a neighbor; Marcus was chatting to our babysitter. Suddenly Trina exclaimed, "Look, Dad."

Following her gesture, I made out the dark shape of a cat in the downstairs window. "It's trapped," she said, her voice rising. "It can't get out."

I tried to tell her that the cat was fine, it lived indoors, but Trina wriggled out of my arms. We made our way over to the policeman. "Excuse me, Officer," I said. "There's a cat at the window."

"You have to rescue it," said Trina.

Now that we were closer, the cat did have a desperate look, its body pressed against the glass. The policeman took in the situation, looking from me, to Trina, to the house.

"Hey, Tim," he called, "can you get that cat out? Don't want to stress its nine lives."

A fireman, presumably Tim, loped towards the building and disappeared inside. A minute later he appeared behind the cat, and a minute after that he was back in the street, holding the cat, gray and squirming, in his gloved hands. "Now what?" he said as he approached.

"We'll take—," Trina started to say.

On the word *take*, there was a noise like a huge inhalation of breath. Suddenly our faces were lit not by the lights of the engines but by flames leaping from the windows on the first floor, the second, the third.

***

In the weeks that followed, the fire became a local scandal. How was it possible, with fire engines standing by, that the house had been gutted? The woman who came to retrieve the cat two days later said she had lost everything.

"I'm sorry," I said. We were standing in the hall of my unburned home.

"Fuck it." She pushed her hands deeper into the pockets of her turquoise tracksuit. "Maybe it's time to head west. At least I still have my wheels."

"And Fred," said Trina. After two days of hiding under our sofa, resisting Trina's entreaties, the cat was weaving around his owner's legs.

"That's right," said the woman. "I still have my damned cat." She picked him up and buried her face in his neck. "West," I discovered, as we walked to her car, meant her hometown of Pittsfield.

***

I used to wonder if there was anything that I loved as much as Viv loved her horses—I mean, besides the handful of people for whom I would step in front of a speeding train. At university I smoked grass and took enough coke (once) and Ecstasy (twice) to know that, for me, drugs are not the doors of perception. I play tennis, I garden until it gets too hot, I read, mostly Scottish history, but for the last four years both hobbies and friends have taken second place to my father. I suppose my equivalent to horses is eyes, those pearls, those vile jellies. From the moment we studied them at university, I was fascinated by the intricate mechanism, by the emotions we attribute to the eyes of others, the visions we claim for our own. When I first saw a painting by Josef Albers, I stared and stared at the yellow square within the green square. How had he persuaded the colors to shift and tremble at their margins?

In childhood I was blessed with excellent vision. Then, within a few months of my eighteenth birthday, I quite suddenly found myself squinting at street signs and blackboards. Now I wear a pair of elegant progressives that I reach for first thing in the morning and part from last thing at night; I scarcely recognize myself without them. Viv, so far, has 20/20 vision in both eyes. One of these days, I used to tell her, you'll grow up.

I was in my second year of training as an ophthalmologist at Edinburgh University when my father was diagnosed with Parkinson's. As soon as my mother phoned to break the news, the several incidents I had noticed, and ignored, at Christmas came together in an irrefutable declaration: the way my father dragged his foot through the snow on our Christmas walk, the way he delegated pouring the wine and carving the turkey, the odd jerks of head or hand.

Parkinson's is an idiopathic condition, which means it has no known cause, although smoking, infuriatingly, lowers the risk. There is, as yet, no cure. Often it progresses slowly for years, but my father, once diagnosed, grew rapidly worse, as if the illness had only been waiting to be acknowledged. On the phone my mother's voice was frightened, and when I visited at Easter I was shocked by the changes only a few months had brought. That summer I moved back to the States.

As a manager at the MBTA in Boston, my father was ambitious for his life, not his job. He did not seem to mind that he had never been promoted beyond area manager. He liked to travel, to tend his garden, to kayak and fish; in winter he took tai chi lessons and, intermittently, studied Japanese. He went walking in the Adirondacks and wrote haiku in the manner of Basho. Illness brought out the best in him. He followed a strict diet, did his exercises, and campaigned for better health care. He asked often how he could make my mother's life easier. More recently, he submitted with good grace to the presence of caregivers.

One evening, the second autumn after I moved back, he summoned my mother and me to his study. When we were settled with our drinks, he announced that he was planning to file for a no-fault divorce.

"I'd still want to see you, Peggy," he said earnestly, "but you'd be free to find another husband, one who can make you supper and put in the storm windows. I might linger for years, especially if you keep taking such good care of me."

My mother was wearing a blue cardigan that matched her eyes and well-cut jeans; she was at that time fifty-two, lively, sociable, passionate about her job. Gently she set down her glass. "Edward, did I upset you? I know sometimes I'm cranky, but I never mean to make you feel you're a nuisance. You're not. I'm glad we get to spend so much time together."

My father laughed, and Nabokov, nearby in his cage, gave a gruff imitation. "I'm a huge nuisance," he said. "Elephantine. Actually I find it reassuring when you're cranky. Makes me feel less of a charity case. No, I've been thinking about this for a while. You're in the prime of life. You deserve a companion who can do the things you enjoy."

As my mother walked towards him, I left the room and drove home to my fit and lovely partner, who, unbeknownst to me, was pregnant with Marcus. Would she have made that offer to me? Or I to her? The answer, I thought then, was yes, and yes.

I met Viv the spring after I returned to Boston, when she sat down beside me on the subway and opened her copy of the *New Yorker* to the article I was reading in mine. Later she confessed she had already read it but hoped the coincidence might draw my attention—which, along with her elegant profile and crooked left pinkie (an accident with Nutmeg), it did. As the train emerged onto the bridge over the Charles River, we both paused in our reading to look at the gray water, and I asked what she thought of the article. Until that very morning I had been carrying a torch for Ruth, my girlfriend of four years, who was still in Edinburgh, studying to be an anesthesiologist. We had talked often but vaguely about her coming to Boston. Walking home after I got off the train, with Viv's phone number written in the margin of my magazine, I had finally understood that Ruth would never move to the States.

I lived then on the pleasingly named Linnaean Street, where, more than two decades earlier, Fran and I had gone to school. We both recalled our teacher telling us about the famous taxonomist, a brilliant man who believed that the swallows in Sweden wintered at the bottom of frozen ponds. The forsythia was just coming into bloom, and as I neared my apartment, I picked up a bright red cardinal's feather. I slipped it into the letter I wrote to Ruth that weekend. Only after the envelope disappeared into the mailbox did I realize that I now faced a modern dilemma: namely, how to avoid e-mail until my letter arrived. I could not bear the childishness of being caught in an excuse—computer problems, a hospital emergency—or the mendacity of writing as if nothing had changed. So, as with Robert, I hid. I deleted Ruth's e-mails unread, her phone messages unheard, until they dwindled and then ceased.

Viv, as I've mentioned, at that time worked in mutual funds. I liked that her job was so different from mine, and I liked that she knew so much about current events. My patients were not, for the most part, affected by changes in weather and regime, but in her world a storm in the Indian Ocean, or a new president in Chile, could change everything. She followed international politics in a way that only a few of my American friends did, and she was reassuringly left-wing, believing not only in the obvious causes—gay marriage, women's rights, abolition of the death penalty, gun control, recycling, universal health care—but in the more obscure ones like proportional representation, job sharing, and death with dignity. She had grown up in Ann Arbor, where her mother still lived, and had seldom met a Republican. One of the things she envied about my profession was that I met all kinds of people. "And you make them better," she said. "We try," I said, "but sometimes it's too late, or we make mistakes." Viv nodded, and said fund managers made mistakes too. She tried never to forget that money always represented something precious: a house, a goat, a violin. Later that night she took me to a club, where we flung ourselves around on the dance floor. Need I say I was equally charmed by her highmindedness and her exuberance.

After qualifying as an ophthalmologist in Massachusetts, I practiced for two years. I found surgery deeply satisfying, but when Trina was born, and my father's condition worsened, I needed a job with shorter, more predictable hours. My sister worked as a publicist for a music company in Nashville, and was as helpful as a person living a thousand miles away can be, phoning frequently and visiting when she could, but the brunt of my father's care fell to my mother and to me. Viv and I moved to our town outside Boston. I started my business, and Viv joined Claudia at the stables.

Since our father's death, Fran and I have been much less in touch, so it was a pleasant surprise when, the Sunday after the fire, she phoned. Viv talked to her for twenty minutes before handing me the phone.

"How's it going?" Fran said. "Viv seems really excited about this new horse. It's nice to hear her being enthusiastic again."

As I said, there is listening and listening. At the time Fran's "again" did not register. Viv's job in our marriage was to be the enthusiast. Over the years she has taken lessons in boxing, salsa, and more recently, Pilates. She had learned to make a gâteau Saint-Honoré. She campaigned for Clinton, Gore, and Obama. She protested the start of the Iraq war and the threatened closure of our Montessori school. Her ability to enter wholeheartedly into a cause or an activity is one of the many things I admire about her. Or, I should say, used to admire.

Chapter Two

The day after Fran's phone call, Merrie greeted me at the office with the news that our UPS delivery was late, and my first patient was already waiting. Her glasses were pushed up on her forehead, and she spoke in the extra-calm voice she uses on busy days. I can claim no special intelligence in hiring Merrie; she was the receptionist for the business that previously occupied these premises, a dermatologist's, and when I took over the lease, she phoned to ask if I needed help. "I know zilch about optometry," she said, "but I can talk to anyone, and I'm a whiz on computers." Both of which turned out to be true. She is also tall, a serious runner, a devout Catholic, and the single mother of three daughters, two of whom share her coffee-colored complexion while the third, the youngest, is much darker. She has never mentioned a father, singular or plural. On the rare occasions when she steps out from behind her desk to give me advice, I pay attention.

Besides Merrie and myself there is Leah, who is trained in optometry, and Jo, who is in her twenties and still taking classes. Merrie had urged me to hire Jo. "We need some young blood around here," she said, and she was right. Jo is good with our older patients, talking them into more flattering frames, urging them to give progressives a chance. The four of us get on famously and rarely meet outside the office.

My first patient was seated in a corner of the waiting room, wearing the uniform of the local Catholic school, reading a magazine. The older girls roll up their skirts and loosen their ties, but this girl's skirt was knee length, her tie neatly knotted. She did not look up as I said, "Good morning. I'm Dr. Stevenson." It was her mother, in her own short skirt, who gave me a girlish smile and said that Diane was having trouble seeing the blackboard.

"No, I'm not," said Diane quietly.

While she continued to gaze at the magazine, her mother said they'd moved to our town in June. Diane had always been a good student, but her new teachers were complaining that she never volunteered in class, and sometimes confused assignments.

In my office Diane read the first two charts and then guessed wildly, mistaking P for X, N for O. At last, not turning on the light, I sat down beside the chair.

"What is it?" she said. "What's the matter?"

"Stand up," I said. "Close your eyes and walk towards the door."

Arms outstretched, she took a couple of hesitant steps then stopped. I urged her on, and she shuffled forward until her hand touched the door.

"What's the matter?" she said again. "Am I going blind?"

"No"—I reached for the light—"but you are shortsighted, and no amount of willpower will change that. If you don't wear glasses, you'll miss most of what's going on around you. You may have an accident, or cause one. Let me show you how things will look."

Diane returned to the chair. "Can't I have contact lenses?"

"When you're older," I said. "Within a week you'll barely notice your glasses."

We bargained our way to a prescription. Back in the waiting room, her mother thanked me. Her voice went up at the end of her sentences in a way I couldn't place until later, when Viv told me that she had grown up in Canada. While we waited for Merrie to finish a phone call, I asked Diane if she knew my friend Steve Abrahams, the biology teacher at her school.

She nodded. They were doing a cool project on soil. Her mother chimed in that Diane preferred micro-organisms to people.

So my first meeting with Hilary ended, neither of us knowing the part we already played in each other's lives.

***

In the months following my father's death, I missed him in every way imaginable. I also found myself, as I had not since Marcus was born, with odd stretches of time, sometimes as long as half an hour, when I had no immediate task, and in those empty intervals I also missed surgery. The week after I saw Diane, I met with a patient to discuss his cataract operation. As I held out my model eye, twelve times life-size, and explained how the new lens would be folded to fit through a small incision in the sclera and then unfolded behind the pupil, I wished that I were the one sliding the lens into place.

I put the feeling away to examine later and drove to Windy Hill. In the decades since she inherited the farm, Claudia's great-aunt had sold off most of the land, but the stables were still surrounded by fields and woods. The nearest neighbor, half a mile away, was a fancy farm stand and nursery. As I drove up the hill to the barn, several of the horses grazing in the paddocks on either side raised their heads. I recognized Dow Jones, the bay Viv used to ride in competitions. I parked in my usual spot beside the row of horse trailers. In the large field half a dozen riders were circling under Claudia's instruction.

"Shoulders back, Louie," I heard her call.

I was searching for the slouching rider when a flash of white caught my peripheral vision. During my years with Viv, I have, inadvertently, learned a good deal about *Equus caballus*. Horses have been domesticated for over six thousand years. They appear in early cave paintings at Lascaux and Pech Merle. The wealthy King Croesus had a soothsayer who described the horse as a warrior and a foreigner, and another king, I forget his name, was buried surrounded by a dozen stuffed horses. Until the twentieth century, horses fought on many battlefields and were part of most people's daily lives. They have the largest eyes of any land mammal and are blessed with both binocular and monocular vision. Historically horses are divided by a kind of class system. Hardworking horses—cart horses and plow horses—are described as cold-blooded. Racehorses, Thoroughbreds, and Arabians are hot-blooded. Those in between—the warm-blooded horses—are bred to combine the best of the other two.

Mercury, true to his name, was unmistakably hot-blooded. The lines of his body, the arch of his neck, the rise and fall of his stride, were, I agreed with Viv reluctantly, beautiful. I was so absorbed in watching him that I paid no heed to his rider until, nearing the fence, she waved. Then I recognized Diane's mother. Turning back to the circling ponies, I saw that the girl on the brown pony, not quite trotting, was my patient, minus her carefully chosen glasses.

Besides the indoor arena, the stables consist of a large barn that houses most of the stalls, a tack room, a feed room, and the office, and a smaller building that houses additional stalls and storerooms. Inside the barn I made my way to the office, a modest room furnished with various castoffs. My mother donated the red curtains and the table and chairs. I contributed two filing cabinets that Merrie wanted to replace and a coffeemaker. That afternoon Marcus and Trina were working at opposite ends of the table: Marcus on homework, Trina on an elaborate drawing.

"Hi, Daddy," they said.

"How was your patient?" added Marcus. He has Viv's fair coloring, but his high forehead, straight eyebrows, and slightly blocky nose are, according to my mother, a direct throwback to my namesake: Uncle Donald. He is an ardent swimmer and almost always smells faintly of chlorine.

"My patient was all right," I said. "He liked knowing about his surgery. Some people do, some people don't."

"Which are you?" Trina reached for another crayon. Small for her age, pale-skinned and dark-haired, she is the barometer of our household, monitoring approaching storms, pleading for calm weather. She can work on a single picture for an hour.

"I like to know about things in advance," I said, "but I tend to worry. What about you?"

"I don't like surprises," she declared. "And I don't want anyone to cut me open."

"Surprises, yes," said Marcus. "Definitely no cutting."

Like many children, mine are deeply interested in bodily functions: how long they can hold their breath, or stand on one foot, whether they can walk in a straight line with their eyes closed, where sweat comes from. When Marcus broke his leg on the playground last May, they were both fascinated by the X-ray showing the thin dark line across the tibia. And when my father, in a last vain effort to control his illness, had an operation that involved cauterizing areas of the brain, Trina drew a picture of him, his head haloed in sparks.

"Where's Viv?" I asked.

"With the horses," said Marcus, unhelpfully.

She was not in the feed room or the tack room. She was not in the first row of stalls. At last I heard her voice coming from a stall in the second row. She was talking to Charlie, one of the stable girls, who was grooming the school's oldest pony, the stalwart Samson. I rode him once, and it was like riding a carousel; whatever I did, he followed the horse in front. Now I patted his whiskery nose and joked that they were getting him ready for the rodeo.

"Poor Samson," said Viv. "You don't give him enough credit."

"We're putting him on a diet," Charlie added. "He's going to be our most improved pony." A slender girl with a loud laugh, she had been working at Windy Hill for nearly three years and was Viv's favorite among the stable girls.

I explained that I wanted a quick word with Diane Blake before I took the children home. Viv said her lesson ended at five. How did I know her?

"She's one of my patients. Her mother was riding that gray horse you told me about."

"Mercury. Isn't he amazing?"

"He's fantastic," said Charlie, her voice as dazzled as Viv's.

Back in the office I asked Trina and Marcus if we could wait for ten minutes. While they returned to their projects, I studied the calendar on the wall. Each day displayed a list of lessons, deliveries, vet's and farrier's visits, which stable girls were on duty. Merrie kept a similar calendar in my office. Of course there were surprises—Marcus's leg, a horse struck by colic—but for the most part, I thought, as I sat in that cozy room with my industrious children, we knew what we were doing next week, next month, next year.

The lesson ended. From nearby came the stamp of hooves as the riders dismounted. When I stepped out of the office, half a dozen girls were milling around the lockers that had been installed last year, after a student's purse went missing. Claudia had argued against them. "I worry they make the stables seem less safe," she said. "Like a dog wearing a muzzle." But Viv had prevailed, and within a week everyone took the lockers for granted.

Diane was not among the girls. Maybe she's outside, Claudia suggested, and there she was, leaning on the fence that bordered the field, pretending to watch her mother, although, without her glasses, I knew that horse and rider were a blur. I greeted her and asked why she wasn't wearing them.

"I thought I only had to wear them at school."

"Don't you want to see what's going on the rest of the time? Wouldn't you like to see your mum riding?"

She responded to my question with one of her own: her teacher had posed the old ethical dilemma about who to save when a museum catches fire, your grandmother or a Rembrandt. "Most people said Grandma," said Diane, "but I said the painting because it will give thousands of people pleasure. Which is the total opposite of Grandma."

As she spoke, Mercury broke into a trot; Hilary lurched perilously and grabbed the saddle. Maybe it was just as well that Diane couldn't see what her mother was doing. "Do you like Rembrandt?" I asked.

She shrugged. "Mom and I saw a painting by him in New York, of a guy on a gray horse. He looks as if he's going on an important errand. I liked that painting, and I bet I could get to like others."

Later, when Viv showed me a copy of the painting, I agreed with her description. Dusk is falling, and the young man, the Polish rider, gazes intently at the viewer as if he is on his way to save someone he loves. But that afternoon, before I could question her further, Trina appeared; she had finished her drawing and wanted to go home. As I drove down the hill, it came to me that the test I had set Diane in my office was one my father had set me. When we lived in Edinburgh, our next-door neighbor had been blind. My mother instructed me to say, "Hello, Valerie, it's Donald," when I met her in the street. But sometimes I simply walked past her or, on bolder days, ran. One afternoon my mother caught me in this cruel game. After supper my parents sat me down. My mother said Valerie had come to the hospital when I was born, and until her eyesight failed, she often babysat for me. My father said he had once asked her what was the worst thing about being blind.

"And do you know her answer?" he said. "Never knowing who's there."

Then he had blindfolded me, led me out into the street, and told me to walk to the corner.

Chapter Three

I met Viv, as I have said, the spring after I returned to Boston. With most of my previous girlfriends, we had been friends before we became lovers. With Viv, I at last understood the expression "falling in love." We slept together on our second date, and I felt as if I were tumbling off a high wall, a wall I had built, brick by brick, out of self-control and hard work. But suddenly I didn't care about control; all I wanted was to be entwined with this woman. I was enthralled by her intelligence, her ambition, her gift, like that of Donald III, for seizing the day, her American confidence that all would be well, and if it wasn't, it could be fixed. When, eight months later, she told me she was pregnant, I picked her up and carried her around the room. At last, I thought, I would feel at home in America. And Viv and I, I was certain, would be good parents. We agreed on the importance of rules and routines—plenty of books, not too much sugar or television—and on public education. When her friend Lucy sent her son to private school, Viv had begged her to reconsider. So our quarrel about private school for Marcus was notable as both our first major disagreement about the children and my first experience of Viv abandoning a deeply held belief.

A couple of weeks after Mercury's arrival, we were having supper at a Mexican restaurant when Viv announced that Greenfield School had an open house in early November. "It's on a Thursday," she said, "so we can all go." Her tone suggested some long-agreed plan.

I set down my beer. Why on earth, I asked, would we want to visit Greenfield? If we needed an outing with the children, we could go to Louisa May Alcott's house, or Drumlin Farm.

Viv set down her own beer and clasped her hands, pleating her crooked finger in with the others. "Don," she said, "I've been talking about this for months. The middle school is a disaster."

As she listed the problems—broken computers, too few textbooks, large classes, wacked-out teachers—I realized it was true: since soon after Marcus broke his leg, she had been complaining about the school. But I had heard her complaints as a to-do list: the things we would, as committed parents, work to change.

"These are the crucial years," she went on, "when the pathways in the brain are formed."

She spoke as if she was quoting someone, and I was sure I knew who. The morning after we moved into our house, Anne had knocked on the door with a tray of cinnamon rolls. She, her husband, and two daughters lived across the street; she worked part-time as an architect. Last year the older daughter had bitten another girl. Anne had enrolled her at Greenfield and begun fervently promoting the school.

"If you're worried about Marcus's pathways," I said, "why not help him study rain forests and follow his chess tournament?"

Twice in the last week Viv had arrived home too late to help with homework. Now, as the server brought our enchiladas, she ignored my criticism. No amount of help at home, she said, smiling firmly, could compensate for a bad school. When I repeated the arguments she had made to Lucy, her smile vanished. She accused me of being stingy. We Scots, as I have already remarked, have a long and honorable tradition of thrift, but the word "stingy" made me grasp my knife like a scalpel.

"Viv, you're talking about spending what would be a year's salary for many people on a child's education."

"Please, Don." She reached across the table. "I know it's a lot of money, but let's take a look at Greenfield. Marcus is my son. I want the best for him."

Marcus was my son too; I would have given him my kidneys, my lungs. Let me think about it, I said.

Recognizing a major victory, Viv changed the subject. Mercury was already gaining weight, she said. He preferred a snaffle bit, not too thin. I ate, I nodded. I was still bristling at her charge of meanness. Had she forgotten that my going to the office, day in, day out, was what kept us afloat, and allowed her to ride her beautiful horse?

***

I wish I did not have to bring Jack into this story, but without him there would be no story. Until three years ago, when retinitis pigmentosa rendered him legally blind, he was my patient. The last time I checked, the vision in his good eye was 10/200; what is visible to a normal person at two hundred feet, he can only see at ten. He can make out the burners on his stove, and sort white socks from dark ones. His bad eye detects only the brightest lights. I have had to break grim tidings to many people, but telling Jack, a man my age, a man in love with books—he teaches classics at the university—that nothing could be done about his failing vision was particularly hard.

I was tiptoeing around the subject when he interrupted.

"Forgive me, Doc," he said, "but the short version is, I'm going blind. Farewell the daylight world, farewell the winged chariot, aka Apollo."

He was my last patient of the day, and we had walked together to the nearest bar, where we drank Scotch and he told me how Odysseus finally, by guile and strength, gets rid of the suitors. As he spoke, he kept his vivid blue eyes fixed on my face. Even knowing what I did, it was hard to believe how little he could see. A few weeks later I invited him to dinner, and a few weeks after that, at his insistence, I took him to meet my father, who was still living at home. They had enjoyed a lively conversation about the Adirondacks, where each had hiked in better days. Jack was one of the few people I had kept in touch with during the awful last year of my father's life. His apartment was on the edge of the campus, and it was easy to drop in on the way to and from the children's various lessons. The week after Viv and I argued about private school, I stopped by while Marcus was swimming.

"Screw tops," Jack said, opening the bottle I'd brought. "God's gift to the blind."

He poured two glasses of merlot and led the way to the sofa. I asked about his book. That summer he had begun to write about blindness, his own and the wider history of the condition.

"I'm working on a topic near to my heart," he said cheerfully. "Namely what I find most annoying about sighted people. Number one is people asking if I want to touch their faces. To which the answer is, Christ, no. Stay away from me with your Helen Keller fantasies. The couple of times I tried it, I could only make out major features: noses, eyebrows. Cheers."

"Cheers." I clinked my glass to his. "Maybe it only works if you've been blind from birth."

"Maybe it only works if you're a kinky person who likes to feel faces. Another thing that drives me crazy"—he was warming to his subject—"is when I ask someone where I am, and instead of telling me, they say, 'Where do you want to be?' As if they could transport me by magic carpet. Let me show you something."

Jack's apartment consists of three large rooms. The bedroom and the living room open off the hall, and the kitchen, which is large enough to eat in, opens off the living room. He got up and, carrying his almost full wineglass, stepped around the coffee table, crossed the room, skirted his desk, and disappeared into the kitchen. He came back again without spilling a drop.

"Okay," he said. "Close your eyes. You do it."

I closed my eyes, picked up the glass, took two steps, and stopped. That evening in Edinburgh when my father blindfolded me, I had come to a standstill after three or four steps. I tried to turn around, banged into a parked car, called for help. Now, still with my eyes closed, I said, "I can't."

"Give me your glass."

With a glass in each hand, Jack took only a couple of steps before he too stopped. "One glass, yes. Two glasses, no. I need one hand free to 'see.' "

We had talked on several occasions about facial vision, that sense that allows the blind to detect obstacles. Now I suggested he keep a record of how soon he sensed an obstacle, whether size or surroundings made a difference.

"The library at the Perkins school must have the latest research," I said. "Speaking of schools, I wanted to ask you about Greenfield. Viv has a bee in her bonnet about Marcus going there."

Jack frowned. "That doesn't sound like Viv. Did something rattle her?"

I brushed his question aside. "Not that I know of," I said. "Can you tell me anything about the school?"

He began to list its virtues: a great classics department, a firstrate library, a music teacher who was a terrific jazz trumpeter, school trips to Tanglewood and Storm King. "But," he said, "I can't imagine spending thirty grand a year to send a kid there."

Neither, I said, could I.

***

My life, first as an ophthalmologist, now as an optometrist is one of close quarters, peering into eyes, studying charts and lenses. Most days at lunchtime I go for a brisk walk, as much for the luxury of gazing at birds and buildings as for the exercise. The day after my drink with Jack, I was striding down our main street when I caught sight of a couple seated in the window of a Thai restaurant. Something about their attitudes—the woman with one hand outstretched; the man watching her—drew my attention.

In Edinburgh Robert and I used to play a game that involved staring at a person and seeing how long it took for them to notice. The answer was usually less than a minute. I stopped staring, walked to the traffic light, crossed the street, and headed back on the far side. From a distance my mother's expression was hard to decipher, but her posture conveyed the same information: she liked this man.

Only a few weeks before Viv had remarked, not for the first time, how great it would be if Peggy met someone; I had agreed. But as I retraced my steps to the office, a small part of me was drifting loose. Dead leaves fluttered across the street, and suddenly I was back with my girlfriend Ruth on an autumn day in Scotland. We had walked along the Firth of Forth to the Hawes Inn in South Queensferry. As we sat by the fire, drinking beer, I had told her about Robert Louis Stevenson. He had come here to drink when he was a mediocre law student. Later, he had set a crucial scene in his novel *Kidnapped*, at the Inn.

In a far corner of the office parking lot, someone had abandoned two beer bottles. As I carried them over to recycling, it came to me that I had deleted Ruth's messages not only because I dreaded her anger but also because I was afraid that suddenly, at the eleventh hour, she would offer to come to Boston. Even before I met Viv, my patience with our long-distance relationship was utterly gone, drained, like the bottles, to the last drop.

***

That evening I did not mention seeing my mother to Viv. Instead we talked about whether Marcus was ready for the advanced diving class, and which of us should undertake the delicate task of asking our neighbors not to park so close to our driveway. And the following evening, when my mother came over, I again said nothing. At supper she described her art history course. They were studying William Morris and his attempts to create a utopian community.

"Hands up who'd like to live in a commune," my mother said.

Trina said she liked summer camp, but only for two weeks, and Viv said her dormitory at Yale had made her want to spend a decade in solitary confinement. I volunteered that I'd enjoyed the summer I picked grapes in France, sharing a house with half a dozen other pickers.

"What about you, Peggy?" said Marcus. "Would you like to share your house with lots of people?" He and my mother took each other seriously.

"I wouldn't like to share my present house," she said, "but I like the idea of friends living nearby. Maybe a big house divided into condos so that you could have privacy and company."

You mean assisted living, Viv suggested, and my mother's eyes flashed. "Absolutely not. Those are segregated communities, our version of putting the elderly on an ice floe. I mean people of all ages, living together and learning from each other. That's one of the utopian beliefs: everyone has something to teach."

"You could give Ping-Pong lessons," said Marcus.

"And you could teach people to swim."

After she left and the children were in bed, Viv said, "Peggy's on the move. Did you notice her earrings? And she's gotten highlights. She'll be off on the Orient Express soon."

Here was my chance; but still I said nothing. I could not bear the prospect of Viv's delighted exclamations. Instead I asked if she had fed Nabokov.

Jack told me once that the word *secret* has the same root as *separate*. I think of that now as I parse out this history of how our family ceased to be Viv's sun. We both kept secrets, and our secrets kept us separate.

You've just read an excerpt from Mercury.

ABOUT THE AUTHOR

Margot Livesey is the *New York Times* bestselling author of the novels *The Flight Of Gemma Hardy, The House On Fortune Street, Banishing Verona, Eva Moves The Furniture, The Missing World, Criminals*, and *Homework*. Her work has appeared in *The New Yorker, Vogue*, and *The Atlantic*, and she is the recipient of grants from both the National Endowment for the Arts and the Guggenheim Foundation. *The House On Fortune Street* won the 2009 L.L. Winship/PEN New England Award. Livesey was born in Scotland and grew up on the edge of the Highlands. She lives in the Boston area and is a professor of fiction at the Iowa Writers' Workshop.

IMPRINT: Harper
PRINT ISBN: 9780062437501
PRINT PRICE: $26.99
EBOOK ISBN: 9780062437532
EBOOK PRICE: $21.99
PUBLICATION DATE: 9/27/16
PUBLICITY CONTACT: Jane Beirn jane.beirn@harpercollins.com
EDITOR: Jennifer Barth
AGENT: Amanda Urban
AGENCY: ICM

PROMOTIONAL INFORMATION:
National print and radio campaign; 8-city author tour to Boston/New England, Chicago, Milwaukee, New York, Philadelphia, San Francisco, Seattle, and Washington, DC; Early buzz-building campaign with ARE giveaways on Goodreads and The Reading Room; Targeted ads and video trailer on Facebook, and ebook promotions with Livesey's backlist titles; Coordinated month-long blog tour; targeted outreach to book clubs as well as to library and academic markets.

I WILL SEND RAIN

A NOVEL

RAE MEADOWS

AUTHOR OF *MERCY TRAIN*

SUMMARY

A luminous, tenderly rendered novel of a woman fighting for her family's survival in the early years of the Dust Bowl; from the acclaimed and award-winning Rae Meadows.

In this novel, set in the Dust Bowl, each member of the Bell family is pulled in different directions—toward a strong temptation, toward a first love, toward a strange calling, and toward an inner voice—as they brave the early years of a grueling drought that tests their will, their strength as a family, and will profoundly change them all.

EXCERPT

Chapter One

Annie Bell awoke in the blue darkness before dawn, her nightdress in a damp tangle at her knees. She'd dreamed about the baby, ten years gone, but all that stayed with her were stray details: the tang of sour milk, a bleating cry she couldn't soothe. Samuel slept beside her, his hand clenched, his face scrunched into the pillow. She inched away from him and sat up. There had been no rain for seventy-two days and counting. The mercury would climb past a hundred today and no doubt again tomorrow.

She rose quickly, quietly, and padded downstairs through the kitchen and out the back door. They would all be up soon, but in these last moments before the sun, cool air still hid in the shadows, and the hushed morning wind whispered against her arms. She stepped gingerly to avoid the grasshopper husks that littered the yard. As she rounded the barn and the darkness faded to gray, she noticed a mound of half-darned socks lumped on a hay bale.

Oh, Birdie. How often she'd thought this recently. About her daughter's lack of urgency, her inability to see what needed to get done. To her they were only socks with holes; but Annie knew, like any farmer's wife, that they were one of a thousand things that kept the place going.

Annie brushed the hair from her forehead; after nineteen years on the farm, it was now mapped with lines, making her look, she thought, older than thirty-seven. It was getting harder to stretch their means. Provide, provide, provide, she repeated in her head as she kneaded bread or wrung out the sheets or ground old wheat into porridge, while her daughter frittered away the afternoons. Thinking about a boy, she had little doubt.

Really it was Birdie's daydreaming that rankled Annie most of all. This wasn't fair, she knew. Part of being young was giving in to the feeling that your life was full of possibility. Annie knew she had done the same when she'd first met Samuel all those years ago, remembered what it was like to want things for herself. But now, here were the land, the farm, the house, her children, her husband.

She dropped the socks where she'd found them. Let Birdie be for now, she thought, try and give her a little space. She slid her toe in an arc across the hard-packed dirt.

A jackrabbit knifed in front of her and then was gone. The sun appeared, and, as it rose, would slowly take with it any respite from the heat. Birdie would soon drag her feet to the barn to milk, Fred would charge out to see the hens, Samuel would look around for a way he hadn't yet thought of to beckon life from the fields.

It was time to make the biscuits.

**

Birdie stepped outside the kitchen door into the arid wind. She rounded the house and made a visor with her hand. Nothing. Always nothing. Land as flat as a razor in every direction, a burned-out watery mirage. To the north was Kansas, and to the south, Texas; to the west were New Mexico and Colorado, and to the east, the rest of Oklahoma. The windmill was the tallest point on the farm, flanked by the barn. Her father had built the small shed off in front a few years ago, now mostly full of burlap sacks of grasshopper bait. The wind buzzed against her ears, blowing her hair in her face. Relentless.

She grabbed her hair into a ponytail with her fist, unwilling yet to tie it back with string or rubber band. Where had she left her green ribbon? She pulled down the bucket from the windmill and pumped the water up, brown at first before it ran clean. Now taller than the house, the grove of locust trees her father had planted in that first year on the farm offered better shade than the scraggly mesquites. She carried the bucket over and emptied it around the base of the trees. Last week her father had poured water on the roof of their house, which had made it sizzle and steam, but hadn't done much to cool anything down inside. At least she'd never had to live in the old sod dugout, which was little more than a roof on a mound of dirt beyond the barn. At least they now had running water and electricity in the house.

"Birdie," her father said from the open door of the shed.

Samuel Bell's ropy arms were reddish brown from the sun, and his hair had grown thin, as if the drought were eroding him, too. He used to laugh readily at Fred's clowning, even sing sometimes in the evening, stomping his foot to keep time, some lively tune he'd picked up in the barracks in his sharecropper days. But now any leftover energy went into worry, into thumbing through the tissuethin pages of his Bible, its cover cracked like the veins of a longdead leaf. You needed at least sixteen inches of rain to grow anything and they had had four. With only weeks until harvest, the plants should have been at grain filling, at milk stage, or even soft dough, but the kernels were still as small and hard as tacks.

Last week a man from Amarillo had come with charts and graphs, talking about rain.

"Haven't you waited long enough?" he'd asked a packed school gymnasium.

Here was a chance to do something, the farmers nodded. A way out of the drought. None of them had the money to spare but there was no choice, really.

"How do you go about that?" Samuel asked.

"Explosives. A heck of a lot of them," the man answered. "Give her a little shake up there," he said pointing at the sky. "We done it north of Las Cruces. And down there at Toad Creek, East Texas. Those boys in Washington could do it for y'all but they don't want to spend the money."

The farmers grumbled. Of course, of course. It would be up to them to help themselves.

"Let's bomb it to hell!" someone had shouted.

The man had smiled and clapped, had kept on clapping until the farmers had joined in, even pounding their feet on the wooden floor.

The farm's small remaining patch of grass crunched under Samuel's feet, chewed to its roots by the cows and desiccated by the sun. The man from Amarillo would arrive midweek. Samuel was skeptical, of course, but they had all paid their share, come what may.

"Make yourself useful," Samuel said to Birdie. "Get some of that thistle off the fence." It was all that seemed to grow now and it tormented him to watch it cartwheel across the dry yard.

Birdie hated hauling tumbleweeds, which scratched her arms and face. Cy Mack had run his thumb along her chin and told her she was the softest thing in Oklahoma. He said he loved her freckled nose and the dimple in her cheek. He said she smelled like clover.

"That pile's too tall already," she said to her father.

"Start a new one."

She sighed and wiped the sweat off her lip with her arm.

"It's so hot," she said.

Samuel laughed a little. "You don't say."

Out on the western fence, at the edge of the largest field, she plied a tumbleweed thatch from the barbed wire and tossed it to the side. And then the wind paused. Birdie felt the quiet like a shiver, and in that still breath she could hear the meadowlarks chirping and beating their wings. In the distance, a black haze that looked like mountains. The heaviest clouds she'd ever seen were rolling toward them. Delight rose up in her as if she'd been handed a big, pink-bowed package. She ran back to her father.

"Look, Pop."

Her father looked up from the fence post he was rewiring. He took his hat off, ran his hand over his hair, and put his hat back on. Relief bloomed in his face.

"Well, hallelujah," he said. "Go get your mother. The rains have come."

**

Fred balanced a twig across two rocks as a bridge for the ants. He made a line of biscuit crumbs up the side to entice them to climb.

"Come on, little fellows," he thought. "Eat up."

Fred was knock-kneed and pallid, younger than his eight years. He had never spoken. His parents had given up trying to get him to, and he'd settled into his own way of communicating, a proficiency of expressions and gestures that his family knew well. Now he wrote on a small chalkboard, which he carried to school, and he kept notebooks stashed around the house, pencils attached with yarn and tape.

The anthill was the size of a bread box. He was tempted to jump on it and watch the little black workers scurry, but he resisted. One of the ants skittered out, elbowed antennae quivering. Fred crouched down and pressed the marcher down softly into the dirt with his finger. He'd learned in school about how an ant colony operates as a unified whole, the ants working together for the good of the group. He wondered how many would need to die before the colony would notice.

It was getting hard to see, the dark specks of the ants indistinguishable from the ground. He blinked and rubbed his eyes with his fists. He stood, confused by the sudden darkness, and then he saw the clouds.

Rain would mean wheat would mean money would mean a bicycle.

***

"Mama!" Birdie cried, the door snapping shut behind her. Inside the farmhouse it was hot and close, the windows covered against the sun.

"Now what is it, Barbara Ann?" Annie said. A lost button? A dress she'd seen in town? A splinter in her thumb that would keep her from milking? Her daughter found drama everywhere, her emotions so quick to bubble up to the surface. "I'm in the kitchen," Annie said. "No need to yell."

The ivy wallpaper Annie had put up five years before was curling away from the wall in the corners. The green leaves, the indulgence, felt mocking now, bumpy under her hand. She felt as if she had faded along with the ivy print, all the work and the wait had slowly leached her of color, too.

"Mama, come out. Come quick." Birdie was breathless.

Annie untied her apron in the doorway. She'd traded three dozen eggs for a last quart of mulberries from the Jensens, which she'd just finished baking into a pie. It was a rare extravagance. Her garden was still strong, at least. She watered it each night, bucket by bucket from the well.

"What's all your clatter about?" she asked.

She wondered if Birdie would finally tell her about Cy Mack. Annie already knew the girl was moony for him, that much was obvious. She had sensed for a while that Birdie had her eye on something beyond Mulehead. She would press for details about Kansas City, where Annie herself had only been once. Did the women have red-painted fingernails? Were the buildings taller than the grain elevator? When the radio had worked—the oiled-walnut box now on the floor shoved next to the sofa—Birdie would lose herself to the stories of *Ann of the Airlanes* or *The Romance of Helen Trent*, always eager for news of places far away. So the idea of Cy Mack courting her daughter needled at Annie, concerned her more than she wanted to admit. He was a farmer's son, already farming full time. No matter what he might be telling Birdie now, Annie knew that Cy would never leave.

"Rain, Mama. It's rain," Birdie said.

Annie felt her face soften and rise. At last.

They ran outside together, mouths agape when they saw the wall of thick black clouds headed their way. Annie put her hand on Samuel's shoulder, a gesture of relief and solidarity both. Birdie noticed. It was more than she had seen pass between her parents in months.

"Where's your brother?" Samuel asked.

"Maybe over in that gulch near Woodrow's place," Birdie said. "I don't know."

"What if there's lightning?" Annie asked.

"He'll come when the rain starts," he said. "It seems it'll be hard to miss."

"We should celebrate," she said. "No need to wait for supper."

Birdie loved the musty, sweet fruit and larded crust of mulberry pie. Before she turned toward the house, though, she saw what her father now saw. The clouds were not gathering overhead as they should have been, they were instead moving at them like a wall, the sun lost in a hazy scrim, the winds picking up, dry and popping with electricity, biting and raw against her skin.

"What in God's name?" Her father squinted against the darkening sky, which turned brownish and then dark gray, even green in places where the sun was trying to burn through. It was midday but it looked like dusk, the sweep of an otherworldly hand.

Birdie started to cough.

"Fred," her mother said.

"I'll go," Samuel said. "Get inside."

He nodded his head to the old dugout, two rooms they'd gouged from the earth, where he and Annie had first lived when they'd arrived as newlyweds. Almost fully underground, it was the closest thing they had to a cellar.

He ran east toward Woodrow's place, hoping the boy had sense enough to head for home. If he even saw the clouds. Samuel knew his son could spend all day counting cow chips or following coyote tracks, oblivious, his face as open as a sunflower.

"Fred!" he yelled, though it was pointless given the wind. Dirt began to blow. The world had gone dark and haywire. Dear God, Samuel thought, what is this ugliness?

***

Fred ran in from the fence, scared. How close was he to home? Was that the barn up ahead? His spindly legs took him blindly forward, his flailing arms searching for anything solid around him. His name, faint and carried by the wind. Louder this time.

He barreled into Samuel, jolting them both with a zinger of a shock, a hundred times what he could get from rubbing his feet on the rug and then touching the doorknob. The dust generated electricity all around them. He held onto his father's hand as they ran, the wind whipping their clothes and burning their eyes, to the dugout door.

They closed themselves in and Fred scampered to his mother's feet. She smoothed her hand over his wiry hair. He is safe, she thought, be thankful for that. But she could not hold on to her relief. Surprise—she swallowed dryly—things can always get worse.

They sat atop sacks of surplus wheat from three years ago. Outside the wind groaned, grating against the roof. Birdie knew she should be ashamed for feeling excited, but her heart thumped, loud in her ears, like the time they'd waited out a twister in the Macks' cellar after a Sunday supper, she next to Cy, then sixteen to her thirteen. He'd leaned over and said, "You're safe down here," and her ears had burned.

"Samuel? What is this?" Annie asked. She pulled her dress over her knees and rocked her feet against the floor.

"I don't know, Ann. I don't hear any hail, though," Samuel said. "I suppose that's a good sign."

Annie stood and straightened the canned beets, parsnips, and beans, the dugout now their makeshift storehouse. When had he stopped calling her Annie? They had become more formal with each other, more careful. She could feel herself retreating. Today, though, standing next to him when she'd seen the clouds and, thinking they held rain, felt the tightness in her jaw ease, she had imagined again a carpet of wildflowers, trumpet vines, and pale green buffalo grass all around them, and she'd felt an old tenderness swelling. You and me and this family, she had wanted to say. She had offered her silent hand instead.

"Seems to have passed," Samuel said. "I don't hear much."

"How could there be no rain with clouds like that?" Fred thought. He was disappointed. There would be no bicycle.

***

Samuel dislodged the old door with his shoulder and climbed out into the light. The sun was out again, that much they could see. A moment later Birdie and her mother followed through the door, Fred trailing behind.

"Dust," Samuel said, as if they couldn't see for themselves.

The world was buried under it: the garden, the window ledges, the wheat. Birdie wiped her hand across her face, trailing a mix of sweat and grit. The wind blew the fine sand over her shoes. She could feel it in her eyes and in her throat. Her father looked dolefully out at his buried fields, but he seemed unable to move, unwilling yet to acknowledge what had befallen his land. Annie trudged straight to the garden.

"You ever hear of a dust storm before?" Birdie asked.

"I never did," Samuel said.

"Think it'll make the papers?"

"I think it will."

Birdie wanted to talk to Cy about it, to see how he looked at her. His eyes were the color of an April sky before you started to wish for clouds.

Fred coughed and hacked up blackened phlegm and spat it into the dirt.

"Learn some manners," Birdie said.

"Pill," Fred thought, squinting his eyes at her. Bossy pill. Wash your hands, Fred. Fill the trough, Fred, Leave me alone, Fred. The rest of the time she only cared about Cy. He'd seen her slip out of the house last night.

"Birdie, go check on the cows. Take a rag for their noses. Fred, see to the coop."

Fred tripped as he ran off and he narrowly missed the corner of the shed. He liked his sister, too. He could make her laugh. When they were smaller they would run into the fields and spin around to get lost and she would sing "Baa, Baa, Black Sheep" until he found her sitting, feet out in front of her, in the tall-as-him wheat.

Samuel watched Birdie walk away, her hair bleached like straw from the sun, and then started toward the fields to see how much had been destroyed.

**

The pea shoots were lost, as if trampled by a horse. The pole beans hung limp, flopped over, pulled from the trellis and weighed down with dirt. Annie gently lifted a stalk and brushed the dust off its bruised leaves.

She refused to read the destruction of the garden as a larger sign. God doesn't use weather as a weapon, she thought. Even her father would agree on that. But she wasn't so sure about Samuel. With less to do on the farm, he had more time to pray, more time to listen for the still, small voice. "God is displeased," he had said when she'd found him staring off from the porch a few days before. There was a time when she would have tried to shake him out of it, but his new searching look, his eyes wild and cast up, kept her from saying anything.

As she set to work tending to her wounded plants, Annie saw how the years out here had ravaged her hands—her skin creased and dry, her nails thick and short. They were capable hands, though, and she did not begrudge them. On the night she'd first met Samuel, she knew she would choose the soil, the sun, the work, over a steady life as the wife of a minister like her mother.

***

"One, two, three, four, five, six, seven, eight, nine," Fred said in his head, counting the leghorns, their white feathers now dirty brown, as they bobbed around. "Where are you, ten?" He counted again, but still came up one short. The birds screeched and pecked at his skinny legs, agitated from the storm, as he scattered the kafir corn.

He wanted it to be like it was before. When Miss Miller taught his class and he gave her a box of chocolate for Christmas before she left to get married. In the fall he would have sour Miss Peterson and they didn't have the money to give her anything and she would never leave because no one would ever want to marry her.

Where was that hen?

In back of the coop he found her on her side, dust clogging her eyes, panting through an open beak, her wattle limp against the floor. His lip quivered and he balled his fists to stop the tears. "Get up, get up, get up," he thought. He wiped the hen's eyes with the hem of his shirt. He loved these birds. He rubbed lard on their combs in the winter so they wouldn't get frostbite. He kept meticulous counts of their eggs—some 230 apiece last year—on a yellow ledger pad under his bed. Leghorns were a nervous breed, and he knew how to hold them in the crook of his arm to calm them.

He looked at the ravaged bird and knew there was only one thing for him to do. He put his foot on its body, grasped its small quivering head in his hands, and yanked as hard as he could. The neck gave way with a pop. Fred kneeled down and cradled the creature to his chest like a gift.

***

Birdie swept the kitchen floor. Dust had made its way through every crack and window seam, settled on every surface. The counters, the clock, the sink, the table, the telephone. But it felt good to clean up the mess, she was strangely invigorated by the excitement of the day. As she wiped a wet rag across the windowsill, she wondered what it would be like if she and Cy lived someplace like Oregon, where she heard everything was green and blackberries grew in wild thickets.

Later, when the storms kept coming, she would think back on this day and try to recall the expectation she had felt when the kitchen was clean and she'd sat down with a fork and the mulberry pie.

She scraped the dust off the crust, and dug in.

You've just read an excerpt from I Will Send Rain.

ABOUT THE AUTHOR

Rae Meadows is the author of *Calling Out*, which received the 2006 Utah Book Award for fiction, *No One Tells Everything*, a Poets & Writers Notable Novel, and most recently the widely praised novel, *Mercy Train*. She lives with her husband and two daughters in Brooklyn, New York.

IMPRINT: Henry Holt
PRINT ISBN: 9781627794268
PRINT PRICE: $26.00
EBOOK ISBN: 9781627794275
EBOOK PRICE: $12.99
PUBLICATION DATE: 8/9/16
PUBLICITY CONTACT: Tracy Locke tracy.locke@hholt.com
RIGHTS CONTACT: Devon Mazzone Devon.Mazzone@fsgbooks.com
EDITOR: Sarah Bowlin
AGENT: Elisabeth Weed
AGENCY: Book Group
PROMOTIONAL INFORMATION:
Feature title on the Henry Holt Fall list; Expect national review and feature attention; National media attention; 10 city author tour; Online promotion includes Goodreads and Librarything giveaway campaign; National and targeted advertising, blogger campaign.

AUTHOR BLURBS:
"*I Will Send Rain* is meticulously researched, deeply felt, and beautifully written, and I loved immersing myself in its harsh and elegant world."—Curtis Sittenfeld

"As lush and powerful as the novel's Dust Bowl setting is dry and cracked—Meadows paints the Bell family's desperation with compassion and warmth, and her precise language turns grit into gold."—Emma Straub

Commonwealth

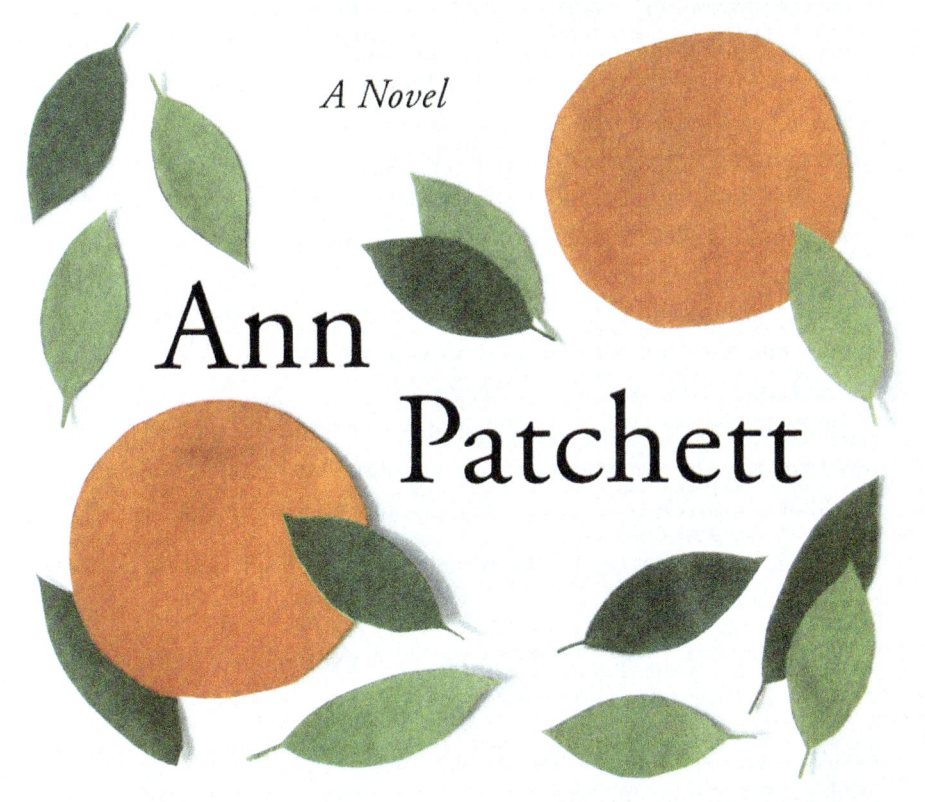

A Novel

Ann Patchett

SUMMARY

The acclaimed, *New York Times* bestselling author—winner of the PEN/Faulkner Award and the Orange Prize—tells the enthralling story of how an unexpected romantic encounter irrevocably changes two families' lives.

EXCERPT

Chapter One

The christening party took a turn when Albert Cousins arrived with gin. Fix was smiling when he opened the door and he kept smiling as he struggled to make the connection: it was Albert Cousins from the district attorney's office standing on the cement slab of his front porch. He'd opened the door twenty times in the last half hour—to neighbors and friends and people from church and Beverly's sister and all his brothers and their parents and practically an entire precinct worth of cops—but Cousins was the only surprise. Fix had asked his wife two weeks ago why she thought they had to invite every single person they knew in the world to a christening party and she'd asked him if he wanted to look over the guest list and tell her who to cut. He hadn't looked at the list, but if she were standing at the door now he would have pointed straight ahead and said, *Him*. Not that he disliked Albert Cousins, he didn't know him other than to put his name together with his face, but not knowing him was the reason not to invite him. Fix had the thought that maybe Cousins had come to his house to talk to him about a case: nothing like that had ever happened before but what else was the explanation? Guests were milling around in the front yard, and whether they were coming late or leaving early or just taking refuge outside because the house was packed beyond what any fire marshal would allow, Fix couldn't say. What he was sure of was that Cousins was there uninvited, alone with a bottle in a bag.

"Fix," Albert Cousins said. The tall deputy DA in a suit and tie put out his hand.

"Al," Fix said. (Did people call him Al?) "Glad you made it." He gave his hand two hard pumps and let it go.

"I'm cutting it close," Cousins said, looking at the crowd inside as if there might not be room for him. The party was clearly past its midpoint—

most of the small, triangular sandwiches were gone, half the cookies. The tablecloth beneath the punch bowl was pink and damp.

Fix stepped aside to let him in. "You're here now," he said.

"Wouldn't have missed it." Though of course he had missed it. He hadn't been at the christening.

Dick Spencer was the only one from the DA's office Fix had invited. Dick had been a cop himself, had gone to law school at night, pulled himself up without ever making any of the other guys feel like he was better for it. It didn't matter if Dick was driving a black-and-white or standing in front of the judge, there was no doubt where he came from. Cousins on the other hand was a lawyer like all the others—DAs, PDs, the hired guns—friendly enough when they needed something but unlikely to invite an officer along for a drink, and if they did it was only because they thought the cop was holding out on them. DAs were the guys who smoked your cigarettes because they were trying to quit. The cops, who filled up the living room and dining room and spilled out into the backyard beneath the clothesline and the two orange trees, they weren't trying to quit. They drank iced tea mixed with lemonade and smoked like stevedores.

Albert Cousins handed over the bag and Fix looked inside. It was a bottle of gin, a big one. Other people brought prayer cards or mother-of-pearl rosary beads or a pocket-sized Bible covered in white kid with gilt-edged pages. Five of the guys, or their five wives, had kicked in together and bought a blue enameled cross on a chain, a tiny pearl at the center, very pretty, something for the future.

"This makes a boy and a girl?"

"Two girls."

Cousins shrugged. "What can you do?"

"Not a thing," Fix said and closed the door. Beverly had told him to leave it open so they could get some air, which went to show how much she knew about man's inhumanity to man. It didn't matter how many people were in the house. You didn't leave the goddamn door open.

Beverly leaned out of the kitchen. There were easily thirty people standing between them—the entire Meloy clan, all the DeMatteos, a handful of altar boys plowing through what was left of the cookies—but there was no missing Beverly. That yellow dress.

"Fix?" she said, raising her voice over the din.

It was Cousins who turned his head first, and Cousins gave her a nod.

By reflex Fix stood straighter, but he let the moment pass. "Make yourself at home," he said to the deputy district attorney and pointed out a cluster of detectives by the sliding glass door, their jackets still on. "You know plenty of people here." Maybe that was true and maybe it wasn't. Cousins sure as hell didn't know the host. Fix turned to cut his way through the crowd and the crowd parted for him, touching his shoulder and shaking his hand, saying congratulations. He tried not to step on any of the kids, his four-year-old daughter Caroline among them, who were playing some sort of game on the dining room floor, crouching and crawling like tigers between the feet of adults.

The kitchen was packed with wives, all of them laughing and talking too loud, none of them being helpful except for Lois from next door who was pulling bowls out of the refrigerator. Beverly's best friend, Wallis, was using the side of the bright chrome toaster to reapply her lipstick. Wallis was too thin and too tan and when she straightened up she was wearing too much lipstick. Beverly's mother was sitting at the breakfast table with the baby in her lap. They had changed her from her lacy christening gown into a starched white dress with yellow flowers embroidered around the neck, as if she were a bride who'd slipped into her going-away dress at the end of the reception. The women in the kitchen took turns making a fuss over the baby, acting like it was their job to keep her entertained until the Magi arrived. But the baby wasn't entertained. Her blue eyes were glazed over. She was staring into the middle distance, tired of everything. All this rush to make sandwiches and take in presents for a girl who was not yet a year old.

"Look how pretty she is," his mother-in-law said to no one, running the back of one finger across the baby's rounded cheek.

"Ice," Beverly said to her husband. "We're out of ice."

"That was your sister's assignment," Fix said.

"Then she failed. Can you ask one of the guys to go get some? It's too hot to have a party without ice." She had tied an apron behind her neck but not around her waist. She was trying not to wrinkle her dress. Strands of yellow hair had come loose from her French twist and were falling into her eyes.

"If she didn't bring the ice, then she might at least come in here and make some sandwiches." Fix was looking right at Wallis when he said this but Wallis capped her lipstick and ignored him. He had meant it to be helpful because clearly Beverly had her hands full. To look at her anyone would think that Beverly was the sort of person who would have her parties catered, someone who would sit on the couch while other people passed the trays.

"Bonnie's so happy to see all those cops in one room. She can't be expected to think about sandwiches," Beverly said, and then she stopped the assembling of cream cheese and cucumbers for a minute and looked down at his hand. "What's in the bag?"

Fix held up the gin, and his wife, surprised, delivered the first smile she'd given him all day, maybe all week.

"Whoever you send to the store," Wallis said, displaying a sudden interest in the conversation, "tell them to get tonic."

Fix said he would buy the ice himself. There was a market up the street and he wasn't opposed to slipping out for a minute. The relative quiet of the neighborhood, the order of the bungalows with their tight green lawns, the slender shadows the palm trees cast, and the smell of the orange blossoms all combined with the cigarette he was smoking to have a settling effect on him. His brother Tom came along and they walked together in companionable silence. Tom and Betty had three kids now, all girls, and lived in Escondido, where he worked for the fire department. Fix was starting to see that this was the way life worked once you got older and the kids came, there wasn't as much time as you thought there was going to be. The brothers hadn't seen each other since they'd all met up at their parents' house and gone to Mass on Christmas Eve, and before that it was probably when they'd driven down to Escondido for Erin's christening. A red Sunbeam convertible went by and Tom said,

"That one." Fix nodded, sorry he hadn't seen it first. Now he had to wait for something he wanted to come along. At the market they bought four bags of ice and four bottles of tonic. The kid at the register asked them if they needed any limes and Fix shook his head. It was Los Angeles in June. You couldn't give a lime away.

Fix hadn't checked his watch when they'd left for the market but he was a good judge of time. Most cops were. They'd been gone twenty minutes, twenty-five tops. It wasn't long enough for everything to change, but when they came back the front door was standing open and there was no one left in the yard. Tom didn't notice the difference, but then a fireman wouldn't. If the place didn't smell like smoke then there wasn't a problem. There were still plenty of people in the house but it was quieter now. Fix had turned on the radio before the party started and for the first time he could hear a few notes of music. The kids weren't crawling in the dining room anymore and no one seemed to notice they were gone. All attention focused on the open kitchen door, which was where the two Keating brothers were heading with the ice. Fix's partner, Lomer, was waiting for them and Lomer tipped his head in the direction of the crowd. "You got here just in time," he said.

As tight as it had been in the kitchen before they'd left, there were three times as many people crammed in there now, most of them men. Beverly's mother was nowhere in sight and neither was the baby. Beverly was standing at the sink, a butcher's knife in her hand. She was slicing oranges from an enormous pile that was sliding across the counter while the two lawyers from the L.A. County District Attorney's Office, Dick Spencer and Albert Cousins—suit jackets off, ties off, and shirtsleeves rolled up high above the elbow—were twisting the halves of oranges on two metal juicers. Their foreheads were flushed and damp with sweat, their opened collars just beginning to darken, they worked as if the safety of their city relied on the making of orange juice.

Beverly's sister Bonnie, ready now to be helpful, plucked Dick Spencer's glasses from his face and wiped them with a dish towel, even though Dick had a capable wife somewhere in the crush. That was when Dick, his eyes relieved of the scrim of sweat, saw Fix and Tom and called out for the ice.

"Ice!" Bonnie cried, because it was true, it was hot as hell and ice sounded better than anything. She dropped her towel to lift the two bags from Tom, placing them in the sink atop the neat orange cups of empty rinds. Then she took the bags from Fix. Ice was her responsibility.

Beverly stopped slicing. "Perfect timing," she said and dug a paper cup into the open plastic bag, knocking out three modest cubes as if she knew to pace herself. She poured a short drink—half gin, half orange juice, from the full pitcher. She made another and another and another as the cups were passed through the kitchen and out the door and into the waiting hands of the guests.

"I got the tonic," Fix said, looking at the one bag still in his hands. He wasn't objecting to anything other than the feeling that he and his brother had somehow been left behind in the time it had taken them to walk to the market and back.

"Orange juice is better," Albert Cousins said, stopping just long enough to down the drink Bonnie had made for him. Bonnie, so recently enamored of cops, had shifted her allegiance to the two DAs.

"For vodka," Fix said. Screwdrivers. Everyone knew that.

But Cousins tilted his head towards the disbeliever, and there was Beverly, handing her husband a drink. For all the world it looked like she and Cousins had a code worked out between them. Fix held the cup in his hand and stared at the uninvited guest. He had his three brothers in the house, an untold number of able-bodied men from the Los Angeles Police Department, and a priest who organized a Saturday boxing program for troubled boys, all of whom would back him up in the removal of a single deputy district attorney.

"Cheers," Beverly said in a low voice, not as a toast but a directive, and Fix, still thinking there was a complaint to be made, turned up his paper cup.

***

Father Joe Mike sat on the ground with his back against the back of the Keating house, staking out a sliver of shade. He rested his cup of juice and gin on the knee of his standard-issue black pants. Priest pants. The drink was either his fourth or his third, he didn't remember and he didn't care because the drinks were very small. He was making an effort to write a sermon in his head for the following Sunday. He wanted to tell the congregation, the few who were not presently in the Keatings' backyard, how the miracle of loaves and fishes had been enacted here today, but he couldn't find a way to wring enough booze out of the narrative. He didn't believe that *he* had witnessed a miracle, no one thought that, but he had seen a perfect explanation of how the miracle might have been engineered in the time of Christ. It was a large bottle of gin Albert Cousins had brought to the party, yes, but it was in no way large enough to fill all the cups, and in certain cases to fill them many times over, for the more than one hundred guests, some of whom were dancing not four feet in front of him. And while the recently stripped Valencia trees in the backyard had been heavy with fruit, they never would have been able to come up with enough juice to sate the entire party. Conventional wisdom says that orange juice doesn't go with gin, and anyway, who was expecting a drink at a christening party? Had the Keatings just put the gin in their liquor cabinet no one would have thought less of them. But Fix Keating had given the bottle to his wife, and his wife, worn down by the stress of throwing a good party, was going to have a drink, and if she was going to have a drink then by God everyone at the party was welcome to join her. In many ways this was Beverly Keating's miracle. Albert Cousins, the man who brought the gin, was also the one who suggested the mixer. Albert Cousins had been sitting beside him not two minutes before, telling Father Joe Mike that he was from Virginia and even after three years in Los Angeles he was still shocked by the abundance of citrus fruit hanging from trees. Bert—he told the priest to call him Bert—had grown up with frozen concentrate mixed into pitchers of water which, although he hadn't known it at the time, had nothing to do with orange juice. Now his children drank fresh-squeezed juice as thoughtlessly as he had drunk milk as a boy. They squeezed it from the fruit they had picked off the trees in their own backyard. He could see a new set of muscles hardening in the right forearm of his wife, Teresa, from the constant twisting of oranges on the juicer while their children held up their cups and waited for more. Orange juice was all they wanted, Bert told him. They had it every morning with their cereal, and Teresa froze it into Tupperware popsicle molds and gave the popsicles to the children for their afternoon snacks, and in the evening he and Teresa drank it over ice with vodka or bourbon or gin. This was what no one seemed to understand—it didn't matter what you put into it, what mattered was the juice itself. "People from California forget that, because they've been spoiled," Bert said.

"It's true," Father Joe Mike admitted, because he'd grown up in Oceanside and couldn't quite believe the extent to which this guy was going on about orange juice.

The priest, whose mind was wandering like the Jews in the desert, tried to focus again on his sermon: Beverly Keating went to the liquor cabinet, which she had not restocked for the christening party, and what she found there was a third of a bottle of gin, a nearly full bottle of vodka, and a bottle of tequila that Fix's brother John had brought back from Mexico last September which they had never opened because neither one of them knew exactly what to do with tequila. She carried the bottles to the kitchen, at which point the neighbors who lived on either side of their house and the neighbors across the street and three of the people who lived near Incarnation offered to go home and see what they had in their own cabinets, and when those neighbors returned it wasn't just with bottles but oranges. Bill and Susie came back with a pillowcase full of fruit they'd run home to pick, saying they could go back and get three pillowcases more: what they gave to the party hadn't made a dent. Other guests followed suit, running home, raiding their fruit trees and the high boozy shelves of their pantries. They poured their bounty into the Keatings' kitchen until the kitchen table looked like a bar back and the kitchen counter looked like a fruit truck.

Wasn't that the true miracle? Not that Christ had rolled out a buffet table from His holy sleeve and invited everyone to join Him for fishes and loaves, but that the people who had brought their lunches in goatskin sacks, maybe a little more than they needed for their family but certainly not enough to feed the masses, were moved to fearless generosity by the example of their teacher and His disciples. So had the people at this christening party been moved by the generosity of Beverly Keating, or they were moved by the sight of her in that yellow dress, her pale hair twisted up and pinned to show the smooth back of her neck, the neck that disappeared into the back of the yellow dress. Father Joe Mike took a sip of his drink. And when it was done the people collected eleven baskets of scraps. He looked around at all the cups on the tables and chairs, on the ground, many of which had a sip or two left in the bottom. Were they to gather up all the leftovers, how much would they have? Father Joe Mike felt small for not having offered to go back to the rectory to see what was there. He had been thinking about how it would look for a priest to show his congregants just how much gin he had squirreled away, instead of taking the opportunity to participate in the fellowship of a community.

There was a gentle tapping against the toe of his shoe. Father Joe Mike looked up from his knee, where he had been meditating on the contents of his cup, and saw Bonnie Keating. No, that wasn't right. Her sister was married to Fix Keating, which made her Bonnie-Something-Else. Bonnie-of-Beverly's-Maiden-Name.

"Hey, Father," she said, a cup just like his held loosely between finger and thumb.

"Bonnie," he said, trying to make his voice sound like he wasn't sitting on the ground drinking gin. Though he wasn't sure that this was still gin. It may have been tequila. "I was wondering if you'd dance with me."

Bonnie X was wearing a dress with blue daisies on it that was short enough to make a priest wonder where he was supposed to rest his gaze, though when she'd gotten dressed this morning she probably hadn't taken into account that there would be men sitting on the ground while she remained standing. He wanted to say something avuncular about not dancing because he was out of practice, but he wasn't old enough to be her uncle, or her father for that matter, which is what she'd called him. Instead he answered her simply. "Not a great idea."

And speaking of not great ideas, Bonnie X then dropped down to sit on her heels, thinking, no doubt, that she and the priest would then be closer to eye level and could have a more private conversation, and not thinking about where this would bring the hem of her dress. Her underwear was also blue. It matched the daisies.

"See, the thing is, everybody's married," she said, her voice not modulated to reflect her content. "And while I don't mind dancing with a guy who's married because I don't think dancing means anything, all of them brought their wives."

"And their wives think it means something." He was careful now to lock his eyes on her eyes.

"They do," she said sadly, and pushed a chunk of straight auburn hair behind one ear.

It was at that moment that Father Joe Mike had a sort of revelation: Bonnie X should leave Los Angeles, or at the very least she should move to the Valley, to a place where no one knew her older sister, because when not juxtaposed to that sister, Bonnie was a perfectly attractive girl. Put the two of them together and Bonnie was a Shetland pony standing next to a racehorse, but he realized now that without knowing Beverly the word "pony" never would have come to mind. Over Bonnie's shoulder he could see that Beverly Keating was dancing in the driveway with a police officer who was not her husband, and that the police officer was looking like a very lucky man.

"Come on," Bonnie said, her voice somewhere between pleading and whining. "I think we're the only two people here who aren't married."

"If what you're looking for is availability, I don't fit the bill."

"I just want to *dance*," she said, and put her free hand on his knee, the one that wasn't already occupied by a cup.

Because Father Joe Mike had just been chastising himself about placing the propriety of appearances over true kindness, he felt himself waver. Would he have given two seconds' thought to appearances if it had been his hostess asking for a dance? If Beverly Keating were crouching in front of him now instead of her sister, her wide-set blue eyes this close to his own, her dress slipping up so that the color of her underwear was made known to him—he stopped, giving his head an imperceptible shake. Not a good thought. He tried to take himself back to the loaves and the fishes, and when that proved impossible he held up his index finger. "One," he said.

Bonnie X smiled at him with such radiant gratitude that Father Joe Mike wondered if he had ever made another living soul happy before this moment. They put down their cups and endeavored to pull one another up, though it was tricky. Before they were fully standing they were in each other's arms. From that point it wasn't very far to Bonnie clasping her hands behind Joe Mike's neck and hanging there like the stole he wore to hear confessions. He rested an awkward hand on either side of her waist, the narrow place where her ribs curved down to meet his thumbs. If anyone at the party was looking at them he was not aware of it. In fact, he was overcome by the sensation of invisibility, hidden from the world by the mysterious cloud of lavender that rose up from the hair of Beverly Keating's sister.

In truth, Bonnie had already managed one dance before enlisting Father Joe Mike, though in the end it wound up being not even half a dance. She had pulled the hardworking Dick Spencer away from the oranges for a minute, telling him he should take a break, that union rules applied to men who juiced oranges. Dick Spencer wore thick horn-rimmed glasses that made him look smart, lots smarter than Fix's partner Lomer, who refused to give her the time of day despite the fact that she had twice leaned up against him, laughing. (Dick Spencer *was* smart. He was also so myopic that the couple of times his glasses had gotten knocked off while wrestling with a suspect he had been as good as blind. The thought of fighting a man who may well have a gun or a knife he couldn't see was enough to make him sign up for night school, then law school, then ace the bar exam.) Bonnie took Spencer's sticky hand and led him out to the back patio. Right away they were making a wide circle, bumping into other people. With her arms around his back she could feel how thin he was under his shirt, thin in a nice way, a thin that could wrap around a girl twice. The other deputy DA, Cousins, was better-looking, sort of gorgeous really, but he was stuck on himself, she could tell. Dick Spencer was a sweetheart in her arms.

That was about as far as her thoughts had progressed when she'd felt a strong hand gripping her upper arm. She'd been trying very hard to concentrate on Dick Spencer's eyes behind his glasses and the effort was making her dizzy, or something was making her dizzy. She was holding on to him tight. She hadn't seen the woman approaching. If she'd seen her, Bonnie might have had time to dodge, or at least come up with something clever to say. The woman was talking loud and fast, and Bonnie was careful to lean away from her. Just like that Dick Spencer and his wife were leaving the party.

"Going?" Fix said as they sailed past him in the living room.

"Keep an eye on your family," Mary Spencer said.

Fix was on the couch, his older girl Caroline stretched out across his lap, sound asleep. He mistakenly thought Mary was complimenting him on watching his daughter. Maybe he had been half asleep himself. He patted Caroline lightly on the small of her back and she didn't move.

"Give Cousins a hand," Dick said over his shoulder, and then they were gone without his jacket or tie, without a goodbye to Beverly.

Albert Cousins hadn't been invited to the party. He'd passed Dick Spencer in the hallway of the courthouse on Friday talking to a cop, some cop Cousins didn't know but who maybe looked familiar the way cops do. "See you Sunday," the cop had said, and when he walked away, Cousins asked Spencer, "What's Sunday?" Dick Spencer explained that Fix Keating had a new kid, and that there was going to be a christening party.

"First kid?" Cousins had asked, watching Keating retreat down the hall in his blues.

"Second."

"They do all that for second kids?"

"Catholics," Spencer said and shrugged. "They can't get enough of it."

While Cousins hadn't been looking for a party to crash, it wasn't an entirely innocent question either. He hated Sundays, and since Sundays were thought to be a family day, invitations were hard to come by. Weekdays he was out the door just as his children were waking up. He would give their heads a scratch, leave a few instructions for his wife, and be gone. By the time he got home at night they were asleep, or going to sleep. Pressed against their pillows, he found his children endearing, necessary, and that was how he thought of them from Monday morning all the way to Saturday at dawn. But on Saturday mornings they refused to keep sleeping. Cal and Holly would throw themselves onto his chest before the light of day had fully penetrated the vinyl roll-down shades, already fighting over something that had happened in the three minutes they'd been awake. The baby would start pulling herself over the bars of her crib as soon as she'd heard her siblings up—it was her new trick—and what she lacked in speed she made up for in tenacity. She would throw herself onto the floor if Teresa didn't run to catch her in time, but Teresa was up already and vomiting. She closed the door to the bathroom in the hall and ran the tap, trying to be quiet about it, but the steady sound of retching filled the bedroom. Cousins threw off his two older children, their weightless selves landing in a tangle on the bedspread folded at the foot of the bed. They lunged at him again, shrieking with laughter, but he couldn't play with them and he didn't want to play with them and didn't want to get up and get the baby, but he had to.

And so the day went from there, Teresa saying she needed to be able to go to the grocery store by herself, or that the people who lived on the corner were having a cookout and they hadn't gone to the last cookout. Every minute a child was howling, first one at a time, then in duet, with the third one waiting, then the third one joining in, then two settling down so as to repeat the cycle. The baby fell straight into the sliding glass door in the den and cut open her forehead before breakfast. Teresa was on the floor, butterflying tiny Band-Aids, asking Bert if he thought she needed stitches. The sight of blood always made Bert uncomfortable and so he looked away, saying no, no stitches. Holly was crying because the baby was crying. Holly said that her head hurt. Cal was nowhere in evidence—though screaming, be it that of his sisters or his parents, usually brought him running back. Cal liked trouble. Teresa looked up at her husband, her fingers daubed in the baby's blood, and asked him where Cal had gone.

All week long Cousins waded through the pimps and the wife-beaters, the petty thieves. He offered up his best self to biased judges and sleeping juries. He told himself that when the weekend came he would turn away from all the crime in Los Angeles, turn towards his pajama-clad children and newly pregnant wife, but he only made it to noon on Saturdays before telling Teresa that there was work at the office he had to finish before the first hearing on Monday. The funny thing was he really did go to work. The couple of times he'd tried slipping off to Manhattan Beach to eat a hot dog and flirt with the girls in their bikini tops and tiny cutoff shorts, he'd gotten a sunburn which Teresa was quick to comment on. So he would go to the office and sit among the men he sat among all week long. They would nod seriously to one another and accomplish more in three or four hours on a Saturday afternoon than they did on any other day.

But by Sunday he couldn't do it again, not the children or the wife or the job, and so he pulled up the memory of a christening party he hadn't been invited to. Teresa looked at him, her face bright for a minute. Thirty-one years old and still she had freckles over the bridge of her nose and spreading over her cheeks. She often said that she wished they took their kids to church, even if he didn't believe in church or God or any of it. She thought it would be a good thing for them to do as a family, and this party might be the place to start. They could all go together.

"No," he said. "It's a work thing."

She blinked. "A christening party?"

"The guy's a cop." He hoped she wouldn't ask the cop's name because at that particular moment he couldn't remember it. "Sort of a deal maker, you know? The entire office is going. I just need to pay respects."

She'd asked him if the baby was a boy or a girl, and if he had a present. The question was followed by a crash in the kitchen and a great clattering of metal mixing bowls. He hadn't thought about a present. He went to the liquor cabinet and picked up a full bottle of gin. It was a big bottle, more than he would have wanted to give, but once he saw the seal was still intact the matter was decided.

That was how he came to be in Fix Keating's kitchen making orange juice, Dick Spencer having abandoned his post for the consolation prize of the blonde's unimpressive sister. He would wait it out, showing himself to be reliable in hopes of scoring the blonde herself. He would juice every orange in Los Angeles County if that's what it took. In this city where beauty had been invented she was possibly the most beautiful woman he had ever spoken to, certainly the most beautiful woman he had ever stood next to in a kitchen. Her beauty was the point, yes, but it was also more than that: there had been a little jolt between their fingers whenever she passed him another orange. He felt it every time, an electric spark as real as the orange itself. He knew that making a move on a married woman was a bad idea, especially when you were in the woman's house and her husband was also in the house and her husband was a cop and the party was a celebration of the birth of the cop's second child. Cousins knew all of this but as the drinks stacked up he told himself there were larger forces at work. The priest who he'd been talking to earlier out on the back patio wasn't as drunk as he was and the priest had definitely said there was something out of the ordinary going on. Saying something was out of the ordinary was as good as saying all bets were off. Cousins reached for his cup with his left hand and stopped to roll his right wrist in a circle the way he'd seen Teresa do before. He was cramping up.

Fix Keating was standing in the doorway, watching him like he knew exactly what he had in mind. "Dick said I was on duty," Fix said. The cop wasn't such a big guy but it was clear that his spring was wound tight, that he spent every day looking for a fight to throw himself into. All the Irish cops were like that.

"You're the host," Cousins said. "You don't need to be stuck back here making juice."

"You're the guest," Fix said, picking up a knife. "You should be out there enjoying yourself."

But Cousins had never been a man for a crowd. If this had been a party Teresa had dragged him to he wouldn't have lasted twenty minutes. "I know what I'm good at," he said, and took the top off the juicer, stopping to rinse the buildup of pulp from the deep metal grooves of the top half before pouring the contents of the juice dish into a green plastic pitcher. For a while they worked next to one another not saying anything. Cousins was half lost in a daydream about the other man's wife. She was leaning over him, her hand on his face, his hand going straight up her thigh, when Fix said, "So I think I've got this figured out."

Cousins stopped. "What?"

Fix was slicing oranges and Cousins saw how he pulled the knife towards himself instead of pushing it away. "It was auto theft."

"What was auto theft?"

"That's where I know you from. I've been trying to put it together ever since you showed up. I want to say it was two years ago. I can't remember the guy's name but all he stole were red El Caminos."

The details of a particular auto theft were something Cousins wouldn't remember unless it had happened in the last month, and if he was very busy his memory might go out only as far as a week. Auto theft was the butter and the bread. If people didn't steal cars in Los Angeles then cops and deputy district attorneys would be playing honeymoon bridge at their desks all day, waiting for news of a murder. Auto thefts ran together—those cars flipped exactly as they were found, those run through a chop shop—one theft as unmemorable as the next but for a guy who stole only red El Caminos.

"D'Agostino," Cousins said, and then he repeated the name because he had no idea where that particular gift of memory had come from. That's just the kind of day this was, no explanation.

Fix shook his head in appreciation. "I could have sat here all day and not come up with that. I remember him though. He thought it showed some kind of class to limit himself to just that one car."

For a moment Cousins felt nearly clairvoyant, as if the case file were open in front of him. "The public defender claimed an improper search. The cars were all in some kind of warehouse." He stopped turning the orange back and forth and closed his eyes in an attempt to concentrate. It was gone. "I can't remember."

"Anaheim."

"I never would have gotten that."

"Well, there you go," Fix said. "That was yours."

But now everything was gone and Cousins couldn't even remember the outcome. Forget the defendant and the crime and sure as hell forget the cops, but he knew verdicts as clearly as any boxer knew who had knocked him down and who he had laid out cold. "He went up," Cousins said, deciding to take the bet on himself, believing that any crook stupid enough to steal nothing but red El Caminos had gone up.

Fix nodded, trying not to smile and smiling anyway. Of course he went up. In a certain stretch of the imagination they had done this thing together.

"So you were the detective," Cousins said. He could see him now, that same brown suit all detectives wore to court, like there was only one and they shared it.

"Arresting," he said. "I'm up for detective now."

"You've got a death card?" Cousins said it to impress him without having any sense of why he would want to impress him. He might be a grade-one deputy DA but he knew how cops kept score. Fix, however, took the question at face value. He dried his hands and pulled his wallet out of his back pocket, fingering past a few bills.

"Fourteen to go." He handed his list to Cousins, who dried his hands before taking it.

There were many more than fourteen names on the folded piece of paper, probably closer to thirty, with "Francis Xavier Keating" printed at the bottom, but half the names had a single line drawn through them, meaning Fix Keating was moving up. "Jesus," Cousins said. "This many of them are dead?"

"Not dead." Fix took back the list to check the names beneath the straight black lines. He held it up to the kitchen light. "Well, a couple of them. The rest were either promoted already or they moved away, dropped out. It doesn't make any difference—they're off."

Two older women in their best church dresses and no hats leaned against one another in the frame of the open kitchen door. When Fix looked over they gave him a wave in unison.

"Bar still open?" the smaller one said. She meant to sound serious but the line was so clever she hiccupped and then her friend began to laugh as well.

"My mother," Fix said to Cousins, pointing to the one who had spoken, then he pointed to the other, a faded blonde with a cheerful, open face. "My mother-in-law. This is Al Cousins."

Cousins dried his hand a second time and extended it to one and then the other. "Bert," he said. "What're you ladies drinking?"

"Whatever you've got left," the mother-in-law said. You could see just a trace of the daughter there, the way she held her shoulders back, the length of her neck. It was a crime what time did to women.

Cousins picked up a bottle of bourbon, the bottle closest to his hand, and mixed two drinks. "It's a good party," he said. "Everybody out there still having a good time?"

"I thought they were waiting too long," Fix's mother said, accepting her drink.

"You're morbid," the mother-in-law said to her with affection.

"I'm not morbid," the mother corrected. "I'm careful. You have to be careful."

"Waiting for what?" Cousins asked, handing over the second drink.

"The baptism," Fix said. "She was worried the baby was going to die before we got her baptized."

"Your baby was sick?" he asked Fix. Cousins had been raised Episcopalian, but he had let go of that. To the best of his knowledge, dead Episcopal babies were passed into heaven regardless.

"She's fine," Fix said. "Perfect."

Fix's mother shrugged. "You don't know that. You don't know what's going on inside a baby. I had you and your brothers baptized in under a month. I was on top of it. This child," she said, turning her attention to Cousins, "is nearly a year old. She couldn't even fit into the family christening gown."

"Well, there's the problem," Fix said.

His mother shrugged. She drank down her entire drink and then waggled the empty paper cup as if there had been some mistake. They'd run out of ice, and the ice had been the only thing to slow the drinkers down. Cousins took the cup from her and filled it again.

"Someone's got the baby," Fix said to his mother, not a question, just a confirmation of fact.

"The what?" she asked.

"The baby."

She thought for a minute, her eyes half closed, and nodded her head, but it was the other one who spoke, the mother-in-law. "Someone," she said without authority.

"Why is it," Fix's mother said, not interested in the question of the baby, "that men will stand in a kitchen all day mixing drinks and juicing oranges for those drinks but won't so much as set a foot over the threshold to make food?" She stared pointedly at her son.

"No idea," Fix said.

His mother then looked back at Cousins but he only shook his head. Dissatisfied, the two women turned as one and tipped back out into the party, cups in hand.

"She has a point," Cousins said. He never would have stood back here making sandwiches, though he felt he could use a sandwich, that he wanted one, and so he poured himself another drink.

Fix returned to the business of the knife and the orange. He was a careful man, and took his time. Even drunk he wasn't going to cut off his finger. "You have kids?" he asked.

Cousins nodded. "Three and a third."

Fix whistled. "You stay busy."

Cousins wondered if he meant *You stay busy running after kids*, or, *You stay busy fucking your wife*. Either way. He put another empty orange rind in the sink that overflowed with empty orange rinds. He rolled his wrist.

"Take a break," Fix said.

"I did."

"Then take another one. We've got juice in reserve, and if those two are any indication of where things are going most of the people here won't be able to find the kitchen much longer."

"Where's Dick?"

"He's gone, ran out of here with his wife."

I bet he did, Cousins thought, a vision of his own wife flashing before him, the shrieking bedlam of his household. "What time is it, anyway?"

Fix looked at his watch, a Girard-Perregaux, a much nicer watch than a cop might be wearing. It was three forty-five, easily two hours later than either man would have guessed in his wildest estimation of time.

"Jesus, I should get going," Cousins said. He was fairly certain he'd told Teresa he would be home no later than noon.

Fix nodded. "Every person in this house who isn't my wife or my daughters should get going. Just do me a favor first—go find the baby. Find out who has her. If I go out there now everybody's going to want to start talking and it'll be midnight before I find her. Take a quick walk around, would you do that? Make sure some drunk didn't leave her in a chair."

"How will I know it's your baby?" Cousins asked. Now that he thought about it, he hadn't seen a baby at the party, and surely with all these Micks there were bound to be plenty of them.

"She's the new one," Fix said, his voice gone suddenly sharp, like Cousins was an idiot, like this was the reason some guys had to be lawyers rather than cops. "She's the one in the fancy dress. It's her party."

***

The crowd shifted around Cousins, opening to him, closing around him, pushing him through. In the dining room every platter was stripped, not a cracker or a carrot stick remained. The conversation and music and drunken laughter melted into a single indecipherable block of sound from which the occasional clear word or sentence escaped—*Turns out he's had her in the trunk the entire time he's talking*. Somewhere down a distant hallway he couldn't see, a woman was laughing so hard she gasped for breath, calling, *Stop! Stop!* He saw children, plenty of children, several of whom were pulling cups straight from the unwitting fingers of adults and downing the contents. He didn't see any babies. The room was overwarm and the detectives had their jackets off now, showing the service revolvers clipped to their belts or holstered under their arms. Cousins wondered how he had failed to notice earlier that half the party was armed. He went through the open glass doors to the patio and looked up into the late-afternoon sunlight that flooded the suburb of Downey, where there was not a cloud and never had been a cloud and never would be a cloud. He saw his friend the priest standing still as stone, holding the little sister in his arms, as if they'd been dancing for so long they had fallen asleep standing up. Men sat in patio chairs talking to other men, many of them with women in their laps. The women, all the ones he saw, had taken off their shoes at some point and ruined their stockings. None of them was holding a baby, and there was no baby in the driveway. Cousins stepped inside the garage and flipped on the light. A ladder hung on two hooks and clean cans of paint were lined up on a shelf according to size. There was a shovel, a rake, coils of extension cord, a bench of tools, a place for everything and everything in its place. In the center of the clean cement floor was a clean navy-blue Peugeot. Fix Keating had fewer children and a nicer watch and a foreign car and a much-better-looking wife. The guy hadn't even made detective. If anyone had bothered to ask him at that moment, Cousins would have said it seemed suspicious.

About the time he started really looking at the car, which seemed somehow sexy just by virtue of its being French, he remembered the baby was missing. He thought of his own baby, Jeanette, who had just learned to walk. Her forehead was bruised from where she had careened into the glass yesterday, the Band-Aids were still in place, and he panicked to think he was supposed to be watching her. Little Jeanette, he had no idea where he'd left her! Teresa should have known he wasn't any good at keeping up with the baby. She shouldn't have trusted him with this. But when he came out of the garage to try and find her, his heart punching at his ribs as if it wanted to go ahead of him, he saw all the people at Fix Keating's party. The proper order of the day was returned to him and he stood for another moment holding on to the door, feeling both ridiculous and relieved. He hadn't lost anything.

When he looked back up at the sky he saw the light was changing. He would tell Fix he needed to go home, he had his own kids to worry about. He went inside to find a bathroom and found two closets first. In the bathroom, he stopped to splash some water on his face before coming out again. On the other side of the hallway there was yet another door. It wasn't a big house but it seemed to be made entirely of doors. He opened the door in front of him and found the light inside was dim. The shades were down. It was a room for little girls—a pink rug, a pink wallpaper border featuring fat rabbits. There was a room not unlike this in his own house that Holly shared with Jeanette. In the corner he saw three small girls sleeping on a twin bed, their legs crossed over one another's legs, their fingers twisted in one another's hair. Somehow the only thing he failed to notice was Beverly Keating standing at the changing table with the baby. Beverly looked at him, a smile of recognition coming over her face.

"I know you," she said.

She had startled him, or her beauty startled him again. "I'm sorry," he said. He put his hand on the door.

"You're not going to wake them up." She tilted her head towards the girls. "I think they're drunk. I carried them in here one at a time and they never woke up."

He went over and looked at the girls, the biggest one no more than five. He couldn't help but like the look of children when they were sleeping. "Is one of them yours?" he asked. They all three looked vaguely similar. None of them looked like Beverly Keating.

"Pink dress," she said, her attention on the diaper in her hand. "The other two are her cousins." She smiled at him. "Aren't you supposed to be fixing drinks?"

"Spencer left," he said, though that didn't answer the question. He couldn't remember the last time he'd been nervous, not in the face of criminals or juries, certainly not in the face of women holding diapers. He started again. "Your husband asked me to find the baby."

Finished with her work, Beverly rearranged the baby's dress and lifted her up from the table. "Well, here she is," she said. She touched her nose to the baby's nose and the baby smiled and yawned. "Somebody's been awake a long time." Beverly turned towards the crib.

"Let me take her out to Fix for a minute," he said. "Before you put her down."

Beverly Keating tilted her head slightly to one side and gave him a funny look. "Why does Fix need her?"

It was everything, the pale pink of her mouth in the darkened pink room, the door that was closed now though he didn't remember closing it, the smell of her perfume which had somehow managed to float gently above the familiar stench of the diaper pail. Had Fix asked him to bring the baby back or just to find her? It didn't make any difference. He told her he didn't know, and then he stepped towards her, her yellow dress its own source of light. He held out his arms and she stepped into them, holding out the baby.

"Put your hand under her head," she said. "Do you have children?" But by then she was very close and she lifted up her face. He put one arm under the baby, which meant he was putting his arm beneath her breasts. It wasn't a year ago she'd had this baby and while he didn't know what she'd looked like before it was hard to imagine she had ever looked any better than this. Teresa never pulled herself together. She said it wasn't possible, one coming right after the next. Wouldn't he like to introduce the two of them, just to show his wife what could be done if you cared to try. Scratch that. He had no interest in Teresa meeting Beverly Keating. He put his other arm around her back, pressed his fingers into the straight line of her zipper. It was the magic of gin and orange juice. The baby balanced between the two of them and he kissed her. That was the way this day was turning out. He closed his eyes and kissed her until the spark he had felt in his fingers when he touched her hand in the kitchen ran the entire shivering length of his spine. She put her other hand against the small of his back while the tip of her tongue crossed between his parted teeth. There was an almost imperceptible shift between them. He felt it, but she stepped back. He was holding the baby. The baby cried for a second, a single red-faced wail, and then issued a small hiccup and pressed into Cousins's chest.

"We're going to smother her," she said, and laughed. She looked down at the baby's pretty face. "Sorry about that."

The small weight of the Keating girl was familiar in his arms. Beverly took a soft cloth from the changing table and wiped over his mouth. "Lipstick," she said, then she leaned over and kissed him again.

"You are—" he started, but too many things came into his head to say just one.

"Drunk," she said, and smiled. "I'm drunk is all. Go take the baby to Fix. Tell him I'll be there in just a minute to get her." She pointed her finger at him. "And don't tell him anything else, mister." She laughed again.

He realized then what he had known from the first minute he saw her, from when she leaned out the kitchen door and called for her husband. This was the start of his life.

"Go," she said.

She let him keep the baby. She went to the other side of the room and started to arrange the sleeping girls into more comfortable positions. He stood at the closed bedroom door for one more minute to watch her.

"What?" she said. She wasn't being flirtatious.

"Some party," he said.

"Tell me about it."

In one sense only had Fix been right to send him out to find the baby: nobody knew him at this party and it had been easy for him to move through the crowd. It was something Cousins hadn't realized until now when everyone turned their head in his direction. A woman as trim and tan as a stick stepped right in front of him.

"There she is!" she cried, and leaned in to kiss the yellow curls that feathered the baby's head, leaving a wine stain of lipstick. "Oh," she said, disappointed in herself. She used her thumb to try to wipe it up and the baby tightened up her features as if she might cry. "I shouldn't have done that." She looked up at Cousins and smiled at him. "You won't tell Fix it was me, will you?"

It was an easy promise to make. He'd never seen the tan woman before.

"There's our girl," a man said, smiling at the baby as he patted Cousins on the back. Who did they think he was? No one asked him. Dick Spencer was the only person who knew him at all and he was long gone. As he cut a slow path to the kitchen he was stopped and encircled over and over again. *Oh, the baby*, they said in soft voices. *Hey there, pretty girl.* The compliments and kind words surrounded him. She was a very good-looking baby, he could see it now that they were in the light. This one looked more like the mother, the fair skin, the wide-set eyes, everybody said so. *Just like Beverly.* He jostled her up in the crook of his arm. Her eyes would open and then close again, blue beacons checking to see if she was still in his arms. She was as comfortable with him as any of his own children were. He knew how to hold a baby.

"She sure likes you," a man wearing a gun in a shoulder harness said.

In the kitchen a group of women sat smoking. They tapped their ashes in their cups, signaling they were done. There was nothing left to do but wait for their husbands to tell them it was time to go home. "Hey there, baby," one of them said, and they all looked up at Cousins.

"Where's Fix?" he asked.

One of them shrugged. "I don't know," she said. "Do you have to go now? I'll take her." She held out her hands.

But Cousins wasn't about to turn her over to strangers. "I'll find him," he said, and backed away.

Cousins felt like he had been walking in a circle around Fix Keating's house for the last hour, first looking for the baby and then looking for Fix. He found him on the back patio talking to the priest. The priest's girl was nowhere in sight. There were fewer people outside now, fewer people everywhere. The angle of the light coming through the orange trees had lowered considerably. He saw a single orange high above his head, an orange that had somehow been overlooked in the frenzy to make juice, and he raised up on his toes, the baby balanced in one arm, and picked it.

"Jesus," Fix said, looking up. "Where have you been?"

"Looking for you," Cousins said.

"I've been right here."

Cousins nearly made a crack about Fix not bothering to try and find him but then he thought better of it. "You're not where I left you."

Fix stood up and took the baby from him without gratitude or ceremony. She issued a small sound of discontent at the transfer, then settled against her father's chest and went to sleep. Cousins's arm was weightless now and he didn't like it. He didn't like it one bit. Fix looked at the stain on the top of her head. "Did somebody drop her?"

"It's lipstick."

"Well," said the priest, pushing out of his chair. "That's it for me. We've got a spaghetti supper back at the church in half an hour. Everyone's welcome."

They said their goodnights, and as Father Joe Mike walked away he grew a tail of parishioners who followed him down the driveway, Saint Patrick marching through Downey. They waved their hands at Fix and called goodnight. It wasn't night, but neither was it fully day. The party had gone on entirely too long.

Cousins waited another minute, hoping that Beverly would come back for the baby like she'd said, but she didn't come, and it was hours past time for him to go. "I don't know her name," he said.

"Frances."

"Really?" He looked again at the pretty girl. "You named her for yourself?"

Fix nodded. "Francis got me into a lot of fights when I was a kid. There was no one in the neighborhood who forgot to tell me I had a girl's name, so I figured, why not name a girl Frances?"

"What if she'd been a boy?" Cousins asked.

"I would have named him Francis," Fix said, yet again making Cousins feel he had asked a stupid question.

"When the first one was a girl we named her after Kennedy's daughter. I thought, that's fine, I'll wait, but now—" Fix stopped, looking down at his daughter. There had been a miscarriage between the two girls, fairly late. They were lucky to get this second one, that's what the doctor had said, though there was no point in telling that to the deputy district attorney. "It works out this way."

"It's a good name," Cousins said, but what he thought was, *Lucky you didn't wait.*

"What about you?" Fix said. "You've got a little Albert at home?"

"My son's name is Calvin. We call him Cal. And the girls, no. No Albertas."

"But you've got one coming up."

"In December," he said. Cousins remembered how it was before Cal was born, how he and Teresa would lie in bed at night saying names to one another in the dark. One name would remind her of a kid who got picked on in grade school, a kid who wore stained shirts and bit his thumbs. Some other name would remind him of a boy he never liked, a bully, but when they got to Cal both of them were happy. It was something like that when they were thinking up names for Holly, too. Maybe they'd spent less time on it, maybe they didn't talk about it in bed, her head up on his shoulder, his hand on her stomach, but they'd picked it out together. She wasn't named for anybody, just for herself, because her parents thought it was a beautiful name. And Jeanette? He didn't even remember talking about a name for Jeanette. He'd been late getting to the hospital just that one time and if memory served he'd gone into the room and Teresa said, *This is Jeanette.* She would have been Daphne if anyone had asked him about it. They should talk about what they were going to name this new one. It would give them something to talk about.

"Name this one Albert," Fix said.

"If it's a boy."

"It'll be a boy. You're due."

Cousins looked at Frances asleep in her father's arms. It wouldn't be the worst thing if they had another girl, but if it was a boy then maybe they would call him Albert. "You think?"

"Absolutely," Fix said.

***

He never did talk about it with Teresa but he was there in the waiting room when the baby was born and he filled out the birth certificate—Albert John Cousins—after himself. Teresa had never much liked her husband's name but when would there have been an opportunity to bring that up? As soon as they were home from the hospital she started calling the baby Albie, Al-*bee*. Cousins told her not to but he wasn't ever around. What was he going to do, stop her? The other kids liked it. They called the baby Albie, too.

You've just read an excerpt from Commonwealth.

ABOUT THE AUTHOR

Ann Patchett is the author of *The Patron Saint of Liars*, *Taft*, *The Magician's Assistant*, *Bel Canto*, *Run*, and *State of Wonder*. She was the editor of *Best American Short Stories, 2006*, and has written three books of nonfiction, *Truth & Beauty*, *What now?*, and the essay collection *This is the Story of a Happy Marriage*. She has won numerous prizes, including the PEN/Faulkner Award and the Orange Prize for Fiction, and her work has been translated into more than thirty languages. Patchett is the co-owner of Parnassus Books in Nashville, Tennessee, where she lives with her husband, Karl VanDevender, and their dog, Sparky.

IMPRINT: Harper
PRINT ISBN: 9780062491794
PRINT PRICE: $27.99
EBOOK ISBN: 9780062491817
EBOOK PRICE: $16.99
PUBLICATION DATE: 9/13/16
PUBLICITY CONTACT: Jane Beirn jane.beirn@harpercollins.com
EDITOR: Jonathan Burnham
AGENT: Daniel Kirschen
AGENCY: ICM Partners

BY GASLIGHT

A NOVEL

STEVEN PRICE

SUMMARY

London, 1885. A severed head is dredged from the Thames, while a woman's body is discovered ten miles away. The famed American detective William Pinkerton is summoned by Scotland Yard to investigate. The dead woman fits the description of a grifter Pinkerton had been pursuing for a long time—someone he believed would lead him to Edward Shade, a man he has been hunting since his father's death. Steven Price's *By Gaslight* is an atmospheric portrait of a man on the brink. It's the story of the most unlikely of bonds: between Pinkerton, the greatest detective of his age, and Shade, the one criminal he cannot outwit. Moving from the diamond mines of South Africa to the fog-enshrouded streets of Victorian London, the novel is a journey into a cityscape of grief, trust, and its breaking, where what we share can bind us even against our better selves.

EXCERPT

Chapter One

He was the oldest son.

He wore his black moustaches long in the manner of an outlaw and his right thumb hooked at his hip where a Colt Navy should have hung. He was not yet forty but already his left knee went stiff in a damp cold from an exploding Confederate shell at Antietam. He had been sixteen then and the shrapnel had stood out from his knee like a knuckle of extra bone while the dirt heaved and sprayed around him. Since that day he had twice been thought killed and twice come upon his would-be killers like an avenging spectre. He had shot twenty-three men and one boy outlaws all and only the boy's death did not trouble him. He entered banks with his head low, his eyebrows drawn close, his huge menacing hands empty as if fixed for strangling. When he lurched aboard crowded streetcars men instinctively pulled away and women followed him with their eyelashes, bonnets tipped low. He had not been at home more than a month at a stretch for five years now though he loved his wife and daughters, loved them with the fear a powerful man feels who is given to breaking things. He had long yellow teeth, a wide face, sunken eyes, pupils as dark as the twist of a man's intestines.

So.

He loathed London. Its cobbled streets were filthy even to a man whose business was filth, who would take a saddle over a bed and huddle all night in a brothel's privy with his Colt drawn until the right arse stumbled in. Here he had seen nothing green in a month that was not holly or a cut bough carted in from a countryside he could not imagine. On Christmas he had watched the poor swarm a man in daylight, all clutched rags and greed; on New Year's he had seen a lady kick a watercress girl from the step of a carriage, then curse the child's blood spotting her laces. A rot ate its way through London, a wretchedness older and more brutal than any he had known in Chicago.

He was not the law. No matter. In America there was not a thief who did not fear him. By his own measure he feared no man living and only one man dead and that man his father.

**

It was a bitter January and that father six months buried when he descended at last into Bermondsey in search of an old operative of his father's, an old friend. Wading through the night's fog, another man's blood barnacling his knuckles, his own business in London nearly done.

He was dressed like a gentleman though he had lost his gloves and he clutched his walking stick in one fist like a cudgel. A stain spotted his cuffs that might have been soot or mud but was not either. He had been waiting for what passed for morning in this miserable winter and paused now in a narrow alley at the back of Snow Fields, opera hat collapsed in one hand, frost creaking in the timbers of the shopfronts, not sure it had come. Fog spilled over the cobblestones, foul and yellow and thick with coal fumes and a bitter stink that crusted the nostrils, scalded the back of the throat. That fog was everywhere, always, drifting through the streets and pulling apart low to the ground, a living thing. Some nights it gave off a low hiss, like steam escaping a valve.

Six weeks ago he had come to this city to interrogate a woman who last night after a long pursuit across Blackfriars Bridge had leaped the railing and vanished into the river. He thought of the darkness, the black water foaming outward, the slapping of the Yard sergeants' boots on the granite setts. He could still feel the wet scrape of the bridge bollards against his wrists.

She had been living lawful in this city as if to pass for respectable and in this way absolve herself of a complicated life but as with anything it had not helped. She had been calling herself LeRoche but her real name was Reckitt and ten years earlier she had been an associate of the notorious cracksman and thief Edward Shade. That man Shade was the one he really hunted and until last night the Reckitt woman had been his one certain lead. She'd had small sharp teeth, long white fingers, a voice low and vicious and lovely.

The night faded, the streets began to fill. In the upper windows of the building across the street a pale sky glinted, reflected the watery silhouettes below, the passing shadows of the early horses hauling their waggons, the huddled cloth caps and woollens of the outsides perched on their sacks. The ironshod wheels chittering and squeaking in the cold. He coughed and lit a cigar and smoked in silence, his small deep-set eyes predatory as any cutthroat's.

After a time he ground the cigar under one heel and punched out his hat and put it on. He withdrew a revolver from his pocket and clicked it open and dialed through its chambers for something to do and when he could wait no longer he hitched up one shoulder and started across.

***

If asked he would say he had never met a dead nail didn't want to go straight. He would say no man on the blob met his own shadow and did not flinch. He would run a hand along his unshaved jaw and glower down at whatever reporter swayed in front of him and mutter some unprintable blasphemy in flash dialect and then he would lean over and casually rip that page from the reporter's ring-coil notebook. He would say lack of education is the beginning of the criminal underclass and both rights and laws are failing the country. A man is worth more than a horse any day though you would never guess it to see it. The cleverest jake he'd ever met was a sharper and the kindest jill a whore and the world takes all types. Only the soft-headed think a thing looks like what it is.

In truth he was about as square as a broken jaw but then he'd never met a cop any different so what was the problem and whose business was it anyway.

***

He did not go directly in but slipped instead down a side alley. Creatures stirred in the papered windows as he passed. The alley was a river of muck and he walked carefully. In openings in the wooden walls he glimpsed the small crouched shapes of children, all bones and knees, half dressed, their breath pluming out before them in the cold. They met his eyes boldly. The fog was thinner here, the stink more savage and bitter. He ducked under a gate to a narrow passage, descended a crooked wooden staircase, and entered a nondescript door on the left.

In the sudden stillness he could hear the slosh of the river, thickening in the runoffs under the boards. The walls creaked, like the hold of a ship.

That rooming house smelled of old meat, of water-rotted wood. The lined wallpaper was thick with a sooty grime any cinderman might scrape with a blade for half a shilling. He was careful not to touch the railing as he made his way upstairs. On the third floor he stepped out from the unlit stairwell and counted off five doors and at the sixth he stopped. Out of the cold now his bruised knuckles had begun to ache. He did not knock but jigged the handle softly and found it was not locked. He looked back the way he had come and he waited a moment and then he opened the door.

Mr. Porter? he called.

His voice sounded husky to his ears, scoured, the voice of a much older man.

Benjamin Porter? Hello?

As his eyes adjusted he could see a small desk in the gloom, a dresser, what passed for a scullery in a nook beyond the window. A sway-backed cot in one corner, the cheap mattress stuffed with wool flock bursting at one corner, the naked ticking cover neither waxed nor cleaned in some time. All this his eye took in as a force of habit. Then the bed groaned under the weight of something, someone, huddled in a blanket against the wall.

Ben?

Who's that now?

It was a woman's voice. She turned towards him, a grizzled Negro woman, her grey hair shorn very short and her face grooved and thickened. He did not know her. But then she blinked and tilted her face as if to see past his shoulder and he saw the long scar in the shape of a sickle running the length of her face.

Sally, he said softly.

A suspicion flickered in her eyes, burned there a moment. Billy?

He stepped cautiously forward.

You come on over here. Let me get a look at you. Little lantern-box Billy. Goodness.

No one's called me that in a long time.

Well, shoot. Look at how you grown. Ain't no one dare to.

He took off his hat, collapsed it uneasily before him. The air was dense with sweat and smoke and the fishy stench of unemptied chamber pots, making the walls that much closer, the ceiling that much lower. He felt big, awkward, all elbows.

I'm sorry to come round so early, he said. He was smiling a sad smile. She had grown so old.

Rats and molasses, she snorted. It ain't so early as all that.

I was just in the city, thought I'd stop by. See how you're keeping.

There were stacks of papers on the floor around the small desk, the rough chair with its fourth leg shorter than the others. He could see the date stamp from his Chicago office on several of the papers even from where he stood, he could see his father's letterhead and the old familiar signature. The curtains though drawn were thin from long use and the room slowly belled with a grey light. The fireplace was dead, the ashes old, an ancient roasting jack suspended on a cord there. On the mantel a glazed pottery elephant, the paint flecking off its shanks. High in one corner a bubble in the plaster shifted and boiled up and he realized it was a cluster of beetles. He looked away. There was no lamp, only a single candle stub melted into the floor by the bed. He could see her more clearly now. Her hands were very dirty.

Where's Ben? he asked.

Oh he would of wanted to seen you. He always did like you.

Did I miss him?

I guess you did.

He lifted his face. Then her meaning came clear.

Aw, now, she said. It all right.

When?

August. His heart give out on him. Just give right out.

I didn't know.

Sure.

My father always spoke well of him.

She waved a gruff hand, her knuckles thick and scarred.

Why didn't you write us? We would've helped with the expenses. You know it.

Well. You got your own sorrows.

I didn't know if you got my letter, he said quietly. I mean if Ben got it. I sent it to your old address—

I got it.

Ben Porter. I always thought he was indestructible.

I reckon he thought so hisself.

He was surprised at the anger he felt. It seemed to him a generation was passing all as a whole from this earth. That night in Chicago, almost thirty years gone. The rain as it battered down over the waggon, the canvas clattering under its onslaught, the thick waxing cut of the wheels in the deep mud lanes of that city. He had been a boy and sat beside his father up front clutching the lantern box in the rain, struggling to keep it dry and alight as his father cursed under his breath and slapped the reins and peered out into the blackness. They were a group of eleven fugitive slaves led by the furious John Brown and they had hidden for days in his father's house. Each would be loaded like cargo into a boxcar and sent north to Canada. They had journeyed for eight weeks on stolen horses over the winter plains and had lost one man in the going. He had known Benjamin and Sally and two others also but the rest were only bundles of suffering, big men gone thin in the arms from the long trek, women with sallow faces and bloodshot eyes. Their waggon had lurched to a halt in a thick pool of muck just two miles shy of the rail yards and he remembered Ben Porter's strong frame as he leaned into the back corner, squatted, hefted the waggon clear of its pit, the rain running in ropes over his arms, his powerful legs, and the strange low sound of the women singing in the streaming dark.

Sally was watching him with a peculiar expression on her face. You goin to want some tea, she said.

He looked at her modest surroundings. He nodded. Thank you. Tea would be just fine. He made as if to help her but she shooed him down.

I ain't so old as all that. I can still walk on these old hoofs.

She got heavily to her feet, gripping the edge of one bedpost and leaning into it with her twisted forearm, and then she shuffled over to the fireplace. She broke a splint from a near-toothless comb of parlour matches and drew it through a fold of sandpaper. He heard a rasp, smelled a grim whiff of phosphorous, and then she was lighting a twist of paper, bending over the iron grate, the low rack of packing wood stacked there. The bricks he saw were charred as if she had failed to put out whatever fire had burned there last.

How you take it? she asked.

Black.

Well I see you got you lumps already. She gestured to his swollen knuckles.

He smiled.

She was wrestling the cast iron kettle over the grating. You moved, he said delicately. He did not want to embarrass her. I didn't have your new address.

She turned back to look at him. One eye scrunched shut, her spine humped and malformed under her nightgown. You a detective ain't you?

Maybe not a very good one. What can I do to help?

Aw, it boil in just a minute. Ain't nothin to be done.

I didn't mean with the tea.

I know what you meant.

He nodded.

It ain't much to look at but it keep me out of the soup. An I got my old arms and legs still workin. I ain't like to complain.

He had leaned his walking stick against the brickwork under the mantel and he watched Sally run her rough hands over the silver griffin's claw that crested its tip. Over and over, as if to buff it smooth. When the water had boiled she turned back and poured it out and let it steep and shuffled over to the scullery and upended one fine white china teacup.

You say you been here workin? she called out to him.

That's right.

I allowed maybe you been lookin for that murderer we been readin bout. The one from Leicester.

He shrugged a heavy shoulder. He doubted she was doing any reading at all, given her eyes. I've been tailing a grifter, she had a string of bad luck in Philadelphia. Ben knew her.

Sure.

I caught up with her last night but she jumped into the river. I'd guess she'll wash up in a day or two. I told Shore I was here if he needs me. At least as long as the Agency can spare me.

Who's that now. Inspector Shore?

Chief Inspector Shore.

She snorted. Chief Inspector? That Shore ain't no kind of nothin.

Well. He's a friend.

He's a scoundrel.

He frowned uneasily. I'm surprised Ben talked about him, he said slowly.

Wasn't a secret between us, not in sixty-two years. Specially not to do with no John Shore. Sally carried to him an unsteady cup of tea, leaned in close, gave him a long sad smile as if to make some darker point. You got youself a fine heart, Billy. It just don't always know the cut of a man's cloth.

She sat back on her bed. She had not poured herself a cup and he saw this with some discomfort. She looked abruptly up at him and said, How long you say you been here? Ain't you best be gettin on home?

Well.

You got you wife to think about.

Margaret. Yes. And the girls.

Ain't right, bein apart like that.

No.

Ain't natural.

Well.

You goin to drink that or leave it for the rats?

He took a sip. The delicate bone cup in his big hand.

She nodded to herself. Yes sir. A fine heart.

Not so fine, he said. I'm too good a hater for much. He set his hat on his head, got slowly to his feet. Like my father was, he added.

She regarded him from the wet creases of her eyes. My Mister Porter always tellin me, you got to shoe a horse, best not ask its permission.

I beg your pardon?

You goin to leave without sayin what you come for?

He was standing between the chair and the door. No, he said. Well. I hate to trouble you.

She folded her hands at her stomach, leaned back thin in her grey bedclothes. Trouble, she said, turning the word over in her mouth. You know, I goin to be eighty-three years old this year. Ain't no one left from my life who isn't dead already. Ever morning I wake up surprised to be seein it at all. But one thing I am sure of is next time you over this side of the ocean I like to be dead and buried as anythin. Aw, now, dyin is just a thing what happen to folk, it ain't so bad. But you got somethin to ask of me, you best to ask it.

He regarded her a long moment.

Go on. Out with it.

He shook his head. I don't know how much Ben talked to you about his work. About what he did for my father.

I read you letter. If you come wantin them old papers they all still there at his desk. You welcome to them.

Yes. Well. I'll need to take those.

But that ain't it.

He cleared his throat. After my father passed I found a file in his private safe. Hundreds of documents, receipts, reports. There was a note attached to the cover with Ben's name on it, and several numbers, and a date. He withdrew from his inside pocket a folded envelope, opened the complicated flap, slid out a sheet of drafting paper. He handed it across to her. She held the paper but did not read it.

Ben's name goin to be in a lot of them old files.

He nodded. The name on this file was Shade. Edward Shade.

She frowned.

It was in my father's home safe. I thought maybe Ben could help me with it.

A brougham clattered past in the street below.

Sally? he said.

Edward Shade. Shoot.

You've heard of him?

Ain't never *stopped* hearin bout him. She cast her face towards the weak light coming through the window. You father had Ben huntin that Shade over here for years. Never found nothin on him, not in ten years. She looked disgusted. Everyone you ask got they own version of Edward Shade, Billy. I won't pretend what I heard is the true.

I'd like to hear it.

It's a strange story, now.

Tell me.

She crushed her eyes shut, as if they pained her. Nodded. This were some years after the war, she said. Sixty-seven, sixty-eight. Shade or someone callin hisself Shade done a series of thefts in New York an Baltimore. Private houses, big houses. A senator's residence is the one I heard about. Stole paintings, sculptures, suchlike. All them items he mailed to you father's home address in Chicago, along with a letter claimin responsibility an namin the rightful owner. Who was Edward Shade? No one knew. No one ever seen him. It was just a name in a letter far as anyone known. First packages come through, you father he return them on the quiet to they owners an get a heapful of gratitude in turn. But when it keep on happenin, some folk they start to ask questions. All of it lookin mighty suspicious, month after month. Like he was orchestratin the affair to make the Agency look more efficient. Some daily in New York published a piece all about it, kept it goin for weeks. That newspaper was mighty rough on the Agency. It embarrassed you father something awful, it did.

I remember something about that.

Sure. But what else was he goin to do? They was stolen items, ain't no choice for a man like you father but to return them rightfully back.

Yes.

An then the case broke an the whole affair got cleaned up. Turned out

Shade weren't no one after all. It were a ring of bad folk had some grudge against you father. They was lookin for some leverage an if that weren't possible they was hopin to embarrass the Agency out of its credibility. Edward Shade, that were just a name they made up.

But he had Ben hunting Shade for years after.

Right up until the end. You father had his notions.

None of that was in the file.

Sally nodded. Worst way to keep a secret is to write it down.

Ben ever mention a Mary Reckitt?

Sally touched two fingers to her lips, studied him. Reckitt?

Mary Reckitt. In the file on Shade there was a photograph of her. Her measurements were on the back in Ben's handwriting. There was a transcript attached, an interview between Ben and Reckitt from seventy-nine. In it he asks her about some nail she worked with, someone she couldn't remember. Ben claimed there were stories about them in the flash houses in Chicago but she didn't know what he was talking about or claimed she didn't. He left it alone eventually. Diamond heists, bank heists, forgeries circulating through France and the Netherlands, that sort of thing. According to my father's notes, he was certain this nail was Shade. In September I sent out a cable here and to Paris and to our offices in the west with a description of Mary Reckitt. Shore got back to me in November, said she was here, in London. Where my father had Ben on the payroll.

Billy.

Before he died, the last time I saw him, he looked me in the eye and he called me Edward.

Billy.

It was almost the last thing he said to me.

She looked saddened. My Mister Porter got mighty confused hisself, at the end, she said. You know I loved you father. You know my Mister Porter an me we owe him our whole lives. But that Edward Shade, now?

You take them papers, go on. You read them an you see. It ain't like you father made it out to be. He were obsessed with it. Shade were like a sickness with him.

He studied her in the gloom. I found her, Sally. The woman I was following last night, the woman who took her life. It was Mary Reckitt.

Shoot.

I talked to her before she jumped, I asked her about Shade. She knew him.

She told you that?

He was silent a long moment and then he said, quietly, Not in so many words.

Sally opened her hands. Aw, Billy, she said. If you huntin the breath in a man, what is it you huntin?

He said nothing.

My Mister Porter used to say, Ever day you wake up you got to ask youself what is it you huntin for.

Okay.

What is it you huntin for?

He walked to the window and stared out through the frost and soot on the pane at the crooked rooftops of the warehouses at the river feeling her eyes on him. The sound of her breathing in the darkness there. What are you saying? That Shade didn't exist?

She shook her head. There ain't no catchin a ghost, Billy.

***

When does a life begin its decline.

He thought of the Porters as they had once been and still were in his mind's eye. The glistening rib cage of the one in the orange lantern light and the rain, wool-spun shirt plastered to his skin, his shoulders hoisting that cart up out of the muck. The low plaintive song of the other as she kneeled coatless in the waters. He thought of the weeks he had tailed Mary Reckitt from her terrace house in Hampstead to the galleries in Piccadilly, trailed her languidly down to the passenger steamers on the Thames, watched in gaslight the curtained windows of her house. Hoping for a glimpse of Edward Shade. She was a small woman with liquid eyes and black hair and he thought suddenly of how she had regarded him from the steps of that theatre in St. Martin's Lane, one gloved wrist bent back. The fear in her eyes. Her small hands. She had leaped a railing into a freezing river and they would find her body in the morning or the day after.

So.

He would be thirty-nine years old this year and he was already famous and already lonely. In Chicago his wife was dying from a tumour the size of a quarter knuckled behind her right eye though neither he nor she knew it yet. It would be another ten years before it killed her. He had held the rope as his father's casket went in and turned the first shovel of earth over the grave. That scrape of dirt would echo in him always. Whether he lived to eighty or no the greater part of his life lay behind him.

When does a life begin its decline? He stared up at the red sky now and thought of the Atlantic crossing and then of his home. The fog thinning around him, the passersby in their ghostly shapes. Then he went down to Tooley Street to catch the rail line back to his hotel.

His name. Yes that.

His name was William Pinkerton.

You've just read an excerpt from By Gaslight.

ABOUT THE AUTHOR

Steven Price's first collection of poems, *Anatomy of Keys* (2006), won Canada's 2007 Gerald Lampert Award for Best First Collection, was short-listed for the BC Poetry Prize, and was named a Globe and Mail Book of the Year. His first novel, *Into That Darkness* (2011), was short-listed for the 2012 BC Fiction Prize. His second collection of poems, *Omens in the Year of the Ox* (2012), won the 2013 ReLit Award. He lives in Victoria, British Columbia, with his family.

IMPRINT: Farrar, Straus and Giroux
PRINT ISBN: 9780374160531
PRINT PRICE: $27.00
EBOOK ISBN: 9780374714116
EBOOK PRICE: $12.99
PUBLICATION DATE: 10/04/16
PUBLICITY CONTACT: Lottchen Shivers Lottchen.Shivers@fsgbooks.com
RIGHTS CONTACT: Pauline Post pauline.post@fsgbooks.com
EDITOR: Jonathan Galassi
AGENT: Ellen Levine
AGENCY: Trident Media Group

PROMOTIONAL INFORMATION:
Author appearances; National publicity; National advertising; Web marketing campaign; Library marketing campaign; Reading group guide; Advance Reader's Edition.

"A fiercely compassionate story about the bonds and the bounds of motherhood and, ultimately, of love." —Cristina Henríquez, author of *The Book of Unknown Americans*

LUCKY BOY

a novel

shanthi Sekaran

SUMMARY

A heart-wrenching novel that gives voice to two mothers: a young undocumented Mexican woman and an Indian-American wife whose love for one lucky boy will bind their fates together.

Solimar Castro-Valdez is eighteen and drunk on optimism when she embarks on a perilous journey across the U.S./Mexican border. Weeks later she arrives on her cousin's doorstep in Berkeley, CA, dazed by first love found then lost, and pregnant. But amid the uncertainty of new motherhood and her American identity, Soli learns that when you have just one precious possession, you guard it with your life.

Kavya Reddy has always followed her heart. A mostly contented chef, the unexpected desire to have a child descends like a cyclone in Kavya's mid-thirties. When she can't get pregnant, this desire sets Kavya on a collision course with Soli, when she is detained and her infant son comes under Kavya's care. As Kavya learns to be a mother—the singing, story-telling, inventor-of-the-universe kind of mother she fantasized about being—she builds her love on a fault line, her heart wrapped around someone else's child. *Lucky Boy* is an emotional journey that will leave you certain of the redemptive beauty of this world.

EXCERPT

Prologue

Clara, patron saint of television and eye disease, stood three feet tall in the church at the end of the road. The road was known generally as la calle, for it was the only one in the village. Scattered along it were one church, one store, and a one-room schoolhouse, recently closed. The road sprouted caminos and footpaths as it went, and ended in a small square, where the town hall stood, and a cantina with the town's only television, which sat atop a folding table. When the men weren't hunched around it watching fútbol, it spun lazy afternoon offerings of love and betrayal, murder and long-lost sons.

Clara, beauty of Assisi, nobleman's daughter, ran away one night to a friar at the roadside, was brought to Saint Francis and shorn. Her hair fell like cornsilk to the ground and she traded her dress for a rough brown habit. She walked barefoot and lived in silence and begged for her daily bread. But she didn't mind. She'd fallen in love with something larger than her world.

Clara was ill one day, Papi said, and couldn't go to mass. She lay faded in her bed, and what flickered on her wall but a vision of the daily service, from processional to homily to eucharist? And so they made her patron of eye disease, because what could have visited her but a dance of glaucomic flashes? And then television came along and needed a patron, and the pope said Clara. And how about the time, Papi once said, when she faced down an invading army, alone at the convent window with nothing but the sacrament in hand? Now Clara spent her days tucked into a dim chapel. Day in, day out, alone in the shadows, and if anyone did visit, it was only because they wanted something.

But that night was La Noche del Maíz. The village priest brought her down from her perch and wiped tenderly her web of whisper-fine cracks. He wrapped her in finery, silk robes and nylon flowers, and loaded her on her platform. Four strong men raised her high and she wobbled down the road but didn't fall—not once had she fallen—and so it began: a line of altar boys, a trumpet's cry, the swing of a cloud-belching censer.

Fine for a saint, thought Solimar, to wait all year for a single tromp through the village. Fine for a saint to spend all of eternity with her mouth shut, her feet still. Solimar Castro Valdez was no saint. She was breaking out. She'd come out that evening to meet a man, not a friar. His name was Manuel. He owned a car and a passport—the right kind—and he'd be taking her away from this place. And he was there. Right there in Santa Clara Popocalco.

For months, the idea of leaving had lain dormant. But it was stirring now, snuffling to life. Every cell in her body strained against its casing. It was time to leave. It was time.

Manuel would meet her at the entrance to the town hall. Slowly, slowly, the procession moved on. She walked hand in hand in hand with her mother and father. She squeezed their papery old fingers and pulled harder with each step. When they turned a corner, she spotted the clock tower by the church. Seven minutes late already. She flung off her parents' hands. "See you there!" she cried, and ran.

At the town hall doors: no Manuel. No one who looked like he owned an American passport. A man like that would have to be handsome—not that handsome mattered, not when all she wanted was the land beyond the border, except that she was eighteen and helpless against the nether-murmur of romance.

At the town hall doors, breathless still, she waited. Papi found her and brought her a plate of tamales, which she was too jumbled inside to eat. Mama would be milling through the village plaza and finding old friends from nearby towns, stretching spools of gossip that had begun a month, a year, a decade before.

As the sky dimmed, drums and horns throbbed through the square. Drink had been drunk and around her the village swarmed with new faces: Where had they come from? A pair of teenagers leaned and kissed against a tree, a flutter of children linked arms in a circle, running themselves off their feet, a perilous carousel of arms and legs and fevered teeth. Still, no Manuel. She felt she should smoke a cigarette, though she'd never tried one before. She believed a cigarette would make her feel like less of a fool.

Never had she seen so many people here, in her little village. Most days, it seemed the world had forgotten Santa Clara Popocalco. It was the sort of place that existed only because no larger town had cared to claim it. It lay dry and hollow, anchored to this earth by the Sierra Norte to the east, Oaxaca city to the west. Every morning a cold front rolled in from a distant shore. It collided with the hillside and smothered the valley in fog that smelled faintly, sweetly of corn. Every afternoon, the sun burned through the fog and houses regained their low and addled forms.

Popocalco offered no work, only the growing and eating of a few stalks of corn. When the money left, the people followed, except for the very poor and very old, who still grew crops to feed themselves and sell in local markets, who gurgled through the village square every morning and in the evenings, visiting the church, nodding to the faces, always the same faces, and napping and cooking and eating and washing, sweeping their front steps each day, not exactly waiting to die, Soli believed, but not quite living, either.

For too long, she'd pushed away the thought of leaving. Papi! She was his only one. And Mama. Mama would crawl into bed and never crawl out.

But decay had spread like the valley fog, until it found its way to Soli. She'd breathed so much of it in that she couldn't breathe it out again. She was filling up with silence and heavy bones. She was eighteen. And then, the letter from Silvia. Inside, somewhere between her chest and chin, a seed split open to the sun and she began to wonder: Could she? And how? And eventually: When? And why not? And how soon? Her life lay elsewhere. If she stayed in Popocalco, she'd be staying for them, the gentle old souls, her mother and father and the sullen corn, watching all those lives wind down to their modest end.

The fireworks family entered the square, pushing the castillo de luces, a tower of scaffolding rigged with rockets and sparklers.

In the big picture, Popocalco was nowhere. In the big picture, it was a thin and spiny stretch of the past.

She waited for an hour at the church door, until all her readiness had been sighed away. Papi wandered off. She stood deflated and alone, certain she'd missed Manuel by seven minutes. A brass band began to play, the somber nasal tune Soli had heard every year, for as long as she could remember, at la Noche del Maíz. She closed her eyes. Applause. She didn't need to open them to know that a teenage boy was climbing the castillo, lifting a fiery pole to the highest joints of the tower. In a moment, the first sparks would pinwheel through the night. And they would begin, one small explosion followed by the next, a rapturous storm.

Punctuality. Seven minutes. Time was religion in America, Papi had warned. If she'd missed her chance by seven minutes, it was her own wretched fault.

But then, a layer beneath the noise, a rustle. "Solimar." She opened her eyes. At first, all she saw were the bushy jut of his chin and the gleam of hair slicked back. He could have been the Devil in the firelight, for all she could see. He stepped forward. Papi, all at once, beside her. He shook Papi's hand.

Now this, now here, was a man with a passport. Manuel would visit the next day to go over their plan. He'd get Soli to California, he said, no matter what it took. She was leaving! The promise of it stoked a flame that blazed through her. Already, Popocalco, this house of smoke, was shrinking away. Already, this existence was nothing but a distant prick of light. Electrified by the promise of forward motion, Soli stretched up to kiss the sky, growing and growing, until she too was a flaming tower, a castle of light, sparking from the eyes, spitting streaks of joy.

Chapter One

Preeti Patel was getting married. Kavya was wearing black.

The decision wasn't a symbolic one. She'd bought a black Mysore silk sari on University Avenue on a whim one day. Also on a whim, she'd had the sari blouse stitched in the provocative new cut, held together by nothing more than a thin ribbon tied across her back. She wanted to surprise her husband, so she tied the blouse herself, guided by the bony hills of her scapulae. Eight yards of silk, woven with silver thread. At the end hung a swathe embroidered with banyan trees and antlered deer. She straightened the pleats that cascaded from her hips to her ankles, climbed tidily over her chest and down her back. She clipped on a pair of heavy silver earrings that spilled down to her shoulders and matched her silver choker. Her feet she slipped into silver stiletto heels.

Rishi looked up when she emerged from the bedroom. He was striking in a blue silk kurta. "You're wearing black," he said.

"It's classy," she answered.

He crossed his arms, then walked over and kissed the junction of her neck and shoulder.

The sun beat down as they drove. Coastal waters gave way to outlet malls and farmland. It was warm, even for July. Kavya was getting over warm, but when she turned the AC dial, nothing happened. "What's going on?"

"Push it in."

"I did."

Rishi shrugged. "Open a window then. It's better for you." It's what they did in Berkeley, where the air was crisp enough most days. But Kavya knew well this strain of windshield glare. An open window would bring nothing more than a blast of sick heat. She spun the knob, jiggled it, pounded at it. She was sweating now, itching, moisture beading above her lip. She grunted at Rishi, who seemed to have no intention of helping.

"Sorry?" He sent her a sidelong glance, a wan smile. He glowed in the heat, the way a woman should, his face a collection of plains and fine ridges. He placed a hand on her knee as he drove, which he seemed to think would disarm her. In the old days, Rishi would have pulled over and inspected the air-conditioning himself. He would have pulled out the manufacturer's manual or even reset their route to take them through more temperate territory. Those were the days when they'd first met, undergrads at UC Berkeley, when Rishi would make his daily appearance in the student cafe where Kavya was barista. He'd spend too long at the counter, ignoring the line behind him, asking her about the coffee beans (about which she knew nothing) or the pastries (delivered weekly by a supplier). He'd do anything, those days, to get their brief transactions to last longer than they should have; he'd show up on campus where he knew she'd be, find reasons to bump into her, leave behind his desi posse to linger on Sproul Plaza, where she recruited for activist groups and ran teach-ins and sit-ins. She was his object of fascination, though she'd been plain without makeup, and he a sculpted ideal. Back then, she wondered why he would be interested in her, aside from the fact that she was tall and reasonably fit. She concluded that a person as immaculately beautiful as Rishi might stop looking for beauty in others. He'd search instead for the non-physical: intelligence, humor, all around chutzpah. Kavya reasoned that she must have possessed some combination of these—or was it simply the fact that she seemed, for a while, to want nothing to do with him? In a world that admired handsome men, obeyed them, promoted them, Kavya became the unattainable, the object of Rishi's devotion.

But this: This wasn't devotion. The hand on her knee was a gentle plea to please be quiet, to let him drive and think in peace of whatever it was he was thinking. She jerked her knee, and the hand slid off.

What Rishi was thinking about was the wedding, specifically, the wedding invitation, and more specifically, the groom's name, Vikram Sen, etched in crimson. Vikram Sen was CFO of Weebies, the Silicon Valley megapolis where Rishi worked. The Internet super-site had cornered the market on baby and children's gear, social networking for parents, and a steady feed of articles designed to affirm a reader's existing parenting style while simultaneously triggering worries—the smallest and most niggling—that trying one notch harder might make the difference between decency and brilliance for their wee ones.

Sen was rumored to have a stuffed Bengal tiger in his office and a liquor cabinet that took up an entire wall. At Weebies, they called him the Don. Rishi read in a *Forbes* profile that he'd graduated from Harvard business school, moved into a two-bedroom apartment in San Francisco with five other software engineers, and helped build the walls of the empire over which he now presided. Yes, there had to have been closed doors and failures along the way, but no one spoke of those now. All anyone talked about now were share prices and visits from Brangelina and the boom-boom-boom of unmitigated industry success. Vikram Sen was indisputably an Internet wonder boy, a divinity of the Silicon Valley pantheon, walking proof of the pulsing, breathing American dream. And Rishi was going to his wedding. His gut twisted at the thought of possibly, very probably, meeting Vikram Sen, face-to-face, palm to palm.

Rishi himself worked in a remote corner of the Weebies campus. He had a desk in the PR office, where he managed ventilation, an engineering oddity in a building full of well-groomed image slingers. Only once had he stood outside Vikram Sen's office, sent to test-run an air-quality monitor. He'd lingered, hoping to meet the man himself, but the Don hadn't emerged.

Kavya let out the sort of deep, tremulous sigh that begged for commentary. "Hey," Rishi said. "You'll be fine. We'll have fun. I promise." Though he knew where the sigh came from, he knew asking about it would invite an outpouring that would throw the afternoon so far off course that they'd end up ditching the wedding and turning the car back to Berkeley. If Kavya wasn't going to start, he most definitely wouldn't.

When they arrived, he waved his way past the valets and parked more than a block away, along the neighborhood sidewalk. He turned to Kavya. "Ready?" She frowned and touched her hair. The wind from the open windows had plucked ringlets from her updo, and they sprang off her head like confetti. He opened his door and paused. "Hey, beautiful." He tucked a ringlet behind her ear, "We'll have fun. I promise." He kissed her cheek, then her hand.

"Okay." She took a deep breath and opened the door with a thrust of her toe.

A mandap was set up at the far end of the Patels' backyard, three acres on the outskirts of Sacramento, land that used to be gold territory but now lay fallow. It belonged to Hitesh and Suma Patel, her parents' oldest friends. Hitesh Patel moved among his guests, his belly shaking with every back he slapped. Above the land floated gold, pounds and pounds of it, on earlobes and chests and wrists of ladies wrapped in silk, their brows arched and perfectly threaded, scanning the land like aging lionesses.

In the beginning, Kavya's parents had befriended the Patels because they had little choice. The scarcity of Indians in the 1970s had propelled this North-South friendship. Preeti grew up three blocks from Kavya in a modest, tree-lined neighborhood. Three blocks in India might have kept them from ever meeting, but among the Caucasian tundra of suburban Sacramento, it had felt essential that the girls be friends. Soon enough, their parents realized that they got along as well, that they shared more than nationality, and that the neutralizing effects of American soil would allow their friendship to flourish.

Kavya hitched up the folds of her sari to walk over the wet grass. After the girls grew up and left home, the Patels moved here, to a gated community on the outskirts of town, at the foot of the Sierra Nevadas. Houses here had bathrooms the size of Berkeley bungalows and lawns that stretched without purpose, unfettered by other plant life, disrupted only by swimming pools and the occasional gazebo. Calling it a community was a stretch. Houses—mansions, really—were spread so thinly across the grassy hills that neighbors went mostly undetected.

She wouldn't have gone, except that not to go would have made a stronger statement than she was willing to make. Preeti Patel was getting married and sealing forever her victory over Kavya. Over the years, the girls had grown from playmates to rivals and begrudging friends. To be fair, it was Kavya who begrudged; Preeti was endlessly gracious, completely unimpeachable in her maintenance of friendship. Preeti was infallibly interested and interesting, and if she felt superior to Kavya, she never spoke of it, never mentioned her own achievements; that was left to the mothers.

And also to be fair, there wasn't much rivalry to speak of. Rivalry suggested equality, and Preeti beat Kavya at every step, in a flurry of accomplishment, beautifully and without comment: The day Kavya smoked her first spliff, Preeti won the state spelling bee. The night Kavya first let a boy's hand crawl up her blouse, Preeti won the national spelling bee. The day Kavya gave away the drum set she had failed to master, Preeti became first-chair violinist of the Central Valley Youth Symphony. The week Kavya got into Berkeley, Preeti got into Berkeley. A week later, Preeti received fat envelopes from Stanford, Brown, Yale, UPenn, and Princeton. Harvard had said no, most likely a typographical error that the Patels didn't bother to pursue. When Kavya spent her weekday afternoons trying to free Tibet and bring back affirmative action, Preeti ensconsed herself in the Stanford library, resting only to call her mother. When Kavya spent her weekends cocooned in Rishi's unwashed sheets, Preeti returned home to eat her mother's food. When Kavya graduated from Berkeley and became a barista, Preeti won a Fulbright and spent a year studying diabetic blindness in rural Gujarat. The year Kavya started culinary school, Preeti moved back to California with a degree in epidemiology from Johns Hopkins. The week Kavya got audited for misfiling her taxes, Preeti bought her first house, a three-story Victorian in San Francisco's Noe Valley. They were the Goofus and Gallant of the Central Valley Indians, and most people knew it.

For seven years, as the girls slipped from their twenties to their thirties, Kavya had this over Preeti: She was married. Matrimonial completion had always been her trump card. Today, it would be swept from her grasp.

If there had been a belly to stroke, a smooth hill of skin rising bare and brown from the front folds of her sari, she would have had something that Preeti didn't have, and even when Preeti did have sweet-faced and well-behaved children, it wouldn't have mattered, because Kavya would have had her own. Even if she'd been mid-cycle, still trying that month, she might at least have declined to drink and felt the murmur of a harbored secret when asked, one hundred times or more, when she and Rishi were having children. But she'd lost again that month. She had tried and failed. She would try and fail and try again.

Kavya's mother was the first to see them. She broke from a group of ladies to stalk across the lawn. Still yards away, she cried out, "Where is your mangala sutra?" Kavya only wore her wedding necklace, a thick gold rope with a cluster of pendants, when she knew her mother would be checking. She'd forgotten.

"Why you're wearing black?" her mother asked.

"Hi, Amma."

("Hi, Mom," Rishi eeked from behind.)

"Why you didn't wear the green sari?"

"I like this one."

"Come, maybe Suma Aunty has something you can change. I'll ask."

"No, thank you. I'm wearing this." Kavya kissed her mother's cold cheek and caught there the scent of white wine.

"Are you drinking? Is that alcoholic punch?"

"Why you couldn't dress like Preeti? See how lovely she looks!"

"She's the bride."

Preeti Patel stood at the head of a receiving line, revealing herself, unconventionally, before the ceremony began. She wore a red sari, her hands laced with henna, her neck, face, and hair meshed in gold.

"Preeti has her head on the right way," Uma said, her gaze flickering like a moth wing over her own daughter. "Did you eat? Go eat. They have pakoras and some samosas. The samosas are too oily. All this fried food. And go get something to drink." In the distance was what looked like a fully stocked bar. Rishi spotted an appetizer table and was gone.

Uma Mahendra clicked her tongue. "See who all is wearing black?" She swung her nose to the group at the far corner of the lawn: Maya Gulati, divorced. Sapna Kumari, lesbian. Aparna Dutta, some sort of filmmaker. Neha Murthy, single. Rakhi Viswant, single. Geetha Nallasivan, Sheela Chatterjee, Veena Jain, all belligerently single. They glided to the bar in black saris and stilettos, a coven of the shameless. They seemed to be having an excellent time. Kavya patted her mother's shoulder, stuck her purse under her arm, and stalked off to join them.

"Drink juice," her mother called. "No boozing!"

Kavya hadn't done any boozing for approximately nine months, the length of a pregnancy, but in her case, a steady parade of losses. That evening, her ovulation yet to start, faced with hours of this place, these people, boozing was precisely what Kavya planned to do. A great deal of booze would be required to outlast the mingling, the questions, the ceremony, the post-ceremony mingling, the reception, the speeches, the tearful send-off of bride and groom. Her mission was to reach the bar without interruption, but the odds of making it across the grass without being grabbed for embraces and interrogations were slim. The grass sucked at her heels and halted her step. She was a slow-moving target, easily detected.

"Kav-YAH!"

A fierce clamp on her forearm spun her around to face a woman with buttery arms and an enormous and complex, somewhat frightening bindi. "Hi, Aunty," Kaya said and fell into the warm cushion of an embrace. The woman pulled Kavya into the waiting gully of aunties, where arms circled her waist, fingered her hair, pinched the skin of her abdomen.

"Is this Kavya?" came the cry. "Looking just the same, darling! Still working at the pizza parlor, Kavya? Hello, beta, looking sooo lovely, why so skinny, Kavya, where is the belly fat, hah?"

Like gulls thrown a crust of bread, they frenzied around her, their voices rising to shrieks.

"Remember ladies, we got married and fat and that was the way it was, isn't it, and now these girls are staying so slim, it is good, it is good I think, no, to stay healthy, my knees! My knees are paining me day and night and I think if only I had stayed slim like this, it is good, Kavya, good to stay healthy, but what is this flat belly, hah, when will we see some you-know-what in there Kavya, if no fat then how about a baby, no? How handsome that Rishi is, nothing stopping you, isn't it? Your poor mother is probably wanting a little one, isn't it, something to keep her young, nobody's getting younger, Kavya, we need some grandchildren, isn't it, that's what I told my Raju, Raju go do hanky-panky and bring me the baby, Raju! Go eat, Kavya, you're looking so tired, these girls work too hard now, isn't it, remember ladies we got married and sat down and that was it, we had to watch the servants, to make sure they didn't steal, isn't it, but then we could relax, these young girls stress themselves too much, and then they cannot conceive, isn't it, no, no, Kavya beta, not saying anything, you will have no trouble noooo trouble having a baby, you will have a hundred babies!"

Kavya broke from the group and ran, her heels sinking into the lawn, threatening to topple her. As she neared the group in black, they turned to receive her. Maya Gulati plucked a fresh glass of prosecco from the bar. Turning back to Kavya, she lobbed her a small smile, nodded, and raised her glass.

Chapter Two

Arno, the boy next door, was the first Soli had ever kissed. She was fourteen at the time, and he was an altar boy, noble and broad-shouldered in his white robes. They would meet in the dark and humid side chapel, beneath the saint's gaze. Soli had thought for twenty-six days that she loved Arno, that they would marry and live together in the village, but then Arno left. Set your heart free, Solimar, Doña Alberta would say. My boy's doing so well up there, he's never coming back. Never! Arno went north to work, and Soli, heart-weary, had moved on to the altar boy who replaced him, falling again with gusto, only to lose this second love to the temptations of the north. She wound her heart around the next altar boy, and the two, three, four that followed, resigning herself to the knowledge that she would have to unwind it again, lest it break. When Arno did come back, no longer a boy married now to a woman from Veracruz, he came back with creases around his eyes and dollars tumbling from his pockets and built his mother a home. Soli didn't want Arno anymore. She wanted a life that moved.

"She's the proudest woman in town, that Alberta," Mama said. "She's friendly enough, yes, to your face. But I can tell there's something devilish in there, some devilish kind of pride." Arno was building a solid American brick house, a dollar house, and from her crumbling adobe cube, Soli watched it every day, rising from the ground, one proud wall and then another. Four brick walls and a tidy flat roof, and then, when they thought it was finished, metal spindles sprang from the roof, the anchors of a second floor. Arno's mother would have the tallest house in the village. Arno, who had left school at fifteen, who worked like a donkey up north, who had borne humiliation and solitude, had made it all worthwhile.

"It's time for me to leave," Soli had said that spring, for maybe the hundredth time. It had been weeks since Silvia's letter. This time, her mother turned to her. Her father put down his mug.

"And what would you do?"

The conversation, at last, had begun. Soli felt her future, like a winter-shriveled bloom, begin to soften to the sun.

She watched the dollar house grow, and so did Mama and Papi. They didn't gawk like Soli did—Mama couldn't look at it when they walked by. She would lift her eyes to the sky. Soli knew her mother wanted a dollar house. She knew she needed to give her one. She wanted to buy her parents a new roof, so they wouldn't have to patch the tin that warped and leaked every spring. She wanted to buy them their own telephone line, so they could call her and she them, like the laughing families in the commercials. Papi had raised her to be as focused as a man; Mama had raised her not to depend on one. If she was as independent as they'd raised her to be, then she had no choice but to leave. She could have gone to the city, but who knew what waited there? If she was going to leave, she would leave like a man.

There were certain risks, of course, to leaving as a woman.

"*Violacion!*" Mama hissed the word, a spark of spittle flying from her lips. It was a word never to be said aloud, lest it caught and flared. "If they rape the ugly ones, think what they'll do to you."

Soli hadn't known what to say to this. She didn't know where to begin.

"Manuel seems to be a good man," Mama comforted herself.

"How do you know?" Soli asked, and regretted it immediately.

"Señora Ruiz. Juanita's mother? You know the old one with the mole? You know she was born with that thing? The doctors said it would grow into her eye socket and blind her, but her parents said no, no—"

"Mama."

"Okay, so. Señora Ruiz has another daughter. This is her daughter's nephew, this Manuel."

"And?"

"And so we know him, don't we?"

Soli knew there was only one answer.

"I will be fine."

"Yes. You will."

No one's nephew, she wanted to say, could be anything but a saint. Surely the mere fact of having an aunt would fill a man with virtue. But she kept her mouth shut. It seemed like a good time to start.

***

Manuel came to the house the day after the festival. When he pulled up in front of their home, the neighbors seeped out of their doorways and gathered on the drive. They stood with their arms crossed, examining the man—still handsome in the daylight—who'd come for their Soli. A few gazed solemnly at the Cadillac.

He wore a tie and shiny black shoes. He had a neat black mustache and a small patch of hair on his chin. He spoke respectfully to her parents and showed them what he'd be driving. It was a lion of a car, long and black, with a red-and-gold crest on its hood. Papi ran his hand over its roof and nodded. Manuel's eyes rested on the fingerprints left behind.

She remembers this: the prospect of riding in such a car with such a man made her feel like she could lift off the ground, soaring.

"Look here," Manuel said. He had a radio in there and a cell phone. He had cases of bottled water in the trunk. And he whipped from his pocket a navy blue passport with a crisp picture of him on one page, stamped with symbols that winked in the light. Soli would ride with him to the border, and then she would hide. Manuel, with his blue-and-gold passport, would be welcomed home to America. He showed them how the backseat lifted up to reveal a small compartment, big enough for a girl like Soli to fold herself into. She'd stay hidden until they crossed safely, cleared the guards and vigilantes, and then she'd emerge, an American butterfly.

The compartment looked as small as Popocalco felt.

Papi took one look at it and shook his head. "No," he said. "No, no, no. Thank you, señor, for your time, but no way will my daughter be climbing into a trap like that."

"Papi! I can do it. I'll be okay." And with Papi, Manuel, and all of Popocalco watching, Soli climbed in to prove it. "See," she called, her lips smashed against her knees. "No problem!"

Manuel said, "Señor, you have my word. She will be safe in there. She will spend thirty minutes. Forty. And see? Breathing vents. Cut into the fabric." He grinned at Papi. "Pretty smart, right?"

Soli climbed out. "Please, Papi."

"She's lucky she's small, señor. A man could never do this," Manuel said. Papi walked away. He would help her go, she knew, but he would never say yes.

***

Papi was a corn farmer. His father and his grandfather were corn farmers. It was what the family did, until the corn became too expensive to farm, and then impossible to sell. The strain of corn from Soli's valley was eleven thousand years old, an age beyond her understanding. But now the stalks bent to the ground, or lay heaped like dead grasshoppers.

The day before Soli left Popocalco, her father took her on a walk through town. They walked to the church and lit a candle at Clara's altar. The saint gazed down. She knew things of Soli that no one else did. Soli believed in saints, mostly because she'd been told to, but as she grew from a child to a woman, she'd started to question the parameters of the arrangement. Could this supposed patron be two places at once? Was she confined to the village? Would she follow Soli down the highway and across the border, or hang hovering above the cantina television, keeping the picture from fizzling to static in the crucial seconds before Granados broke from the defensive line to strike?

They walked past the cantina and ignored the buzzing television and the voices that called out to them. They walked past the village's only billboard, hand-painted: Señora *Garza makes the freshest tortillas! 57 La Calle!* Señora *Garza's for the best and the freshest!* Her father held her hand. "Listen, m'ija," he said. "The place you're going? Not everyone makes it there. It isn't easy. People die from the heat, they die from hunger. They get shot. You take care of yourself. Make sure you get fed. Call the cantina from every phone you can find or borrow. They'll come get me. Stick with Manuel. He is a good man, a trustworthy man, and we're giving him all the money we could find. You hear that? We're paying him. You don't need to pay him. You don't pay him in any way."

***

Manuel came for her on a Wednesday morning before dawn. It was strange, thinking back, that the day was nothing but a Wednesday, that it had no more momentous name than that. There were people who woke that day and did nothing to change their lives. And then there was Soli. Manuel waited with the engine running. She had a coat and one rucksack. Inside the house, Papi said goodbye. He pressed a folded American bill—five dollars—into his daughter's palm. Then he hugged her. Papi held her for a very long time, until her ear ached from the press of his sternum. Instead of wrapping her arms around him, Soli lifted the bill and studied it. She'd never held American money before and couldn't pull her gaze from the ashen green.

Mama wouldn't say goodbye. She locked herself in the bedroom. "Mama," Soli called. She banged on the door. "Mama, come and say goodbye to me. Mama?" She said it twice, and then she shouted it. She commanded that her mother come out. She scraped at the door, as she used to when she was small and her parents would shut themselves in there some afternoons.

"Mama," she said. "Don't be angry."

From inside, she heard her mother sob. "M'ija, get out of here."

"Mama! This is your last chance."

But she didn't come out. Later, Soli would realize that if her mother had come out, if she had wrapped herself around her girl the way Papi had, she would never have let her go.

**

Soli spent two days in a car with Manuel, and the one good thing she could say about him was that he didn't lay a finger on her. He didn't talk much, either. When she asked him questions, he answered them and fell silent again. Mostly he hummed to the radio, American music she recognized from youth nights at the church, which she'd stopped going to because eventually she and not-all-there Torta were the only youths left. They drove first from Popocalco to a place near Oaxaca City. Soli had been to the city before, but never beyond it. After a night in Morelia with her mother's aunt, they were meant to head up through Mazatlán, then Obregon, as Manuel had shown Papi, tracing his map with his highlighter pen. Soli was no genius, but she could read a map. And so, when Manuel veered right and sped off on a junction marked for Monterrey, she sat up fast. All this time, they'd been heading west. Without warning, Manuel had turned east.

"What do you think you're doing?" she asked.

"What do you mean?"

"You're going the wrong way. You're going east."

"You mind your business."

"This is my business. Where are we going?"

"I've got business to take care of this way, okay?"

"With who?"

He waited before answering. "With a contact." His eyes slid from Soli to the road.

"That's not what you told my family," she said. "You need to get me to California. You gave your word!"

He said nothing.

"Get me out of here! Let me out!" She pulled at the door handle. She beat on the window.

"Who's the driver?" His roar filled the car. *"Who is the driver?"*

Soli cowered in her seat, certain he would strike her. The doors were the high-tech kind that locked while the car was moving. A good thing, too, because if she'd opened the door and jumped from that car, her story would have ended there.

Later, it would make sense that this handsome man who was supposed to be her companion, her easy ticket in, had veered east when Papi had given everything for a promised west. She'd had a lot of time in the car to think—sixteen hours, precisely—enough time to come to a few conclusions.

First. A man like Manuel doesn't do things to be kind. Soli had heard how other people crossed, in the backs of trucks, stacked like tortillas, one atop the other. Sitting in the cool cushion of that car, she realized that her parents could not have begged, borrowed, or stolen enough money to pay for a chauffeured, air-conditioned ride through the border. It was a conclusion that could come to light only when she'd broken from her parents, when the speed and sky and solitude of her journey opened new vistas of logical thought. When they took the eastern route to Monterrey, she knew for sure that polite Manuel, handsome Manuel, Manuel with the gleaming, purring lion of a car, had told her father a big, sweaty lie.

Second. Never trust a man who plucks his chin. Manuel plucked his chin every time he thought she was asleep. Sometimes he'd do it at high speeds, one hand on the steering wheel, the other plying his devil-beard with a pair of gold tweezers.

Third. With the ship sinking, she'd have to rescue what she could. When Manuel walked off for a piss in the bushes that day, she opened the trunk and crammed as many bottles as she could into her backpack. Later that afternoon, he stopped the car and said he had to make a call. When he was out of sight, she opened his glove compartment and found three things: a tape cassette from someone named Prince, a tube of hand cream, and a blade, nine inches long and sharp enough to make her fingers tingle through its sheath. She took all three.

***

Soon they came to an encampment with red trucks and large tents, dusty men and a few women sitting in groups, waiting in lines. Like her, they were heading for the border, but the camp was a place to stop, sleep, and, if they were lucky, eat.

"This is where you stay tonight," Manuel said.

"And then what?"

Manuel sighed through his nose, turned to Soli, and said, "Okay. I'll show you." He pulled over at the outer edge of the camp, hopped from the driver's seat to the back.

"The compartment?" he asked. "Remember that?"

He yanked at the backseat and the cushion lifted. The compartment into which Soli had folded herself, all those days ago, was packed now with cloudy green plastic, wrapped around blocks of white. Even through the green, she could see how pure the white was.

"You want me to do something with that?"

"Good girl. Fast learner." Soli listened with equal parts denial and fascination as Manuel explained his plans for her, speaking with a buoyancy she'd never seen in him. In Manuel's mind, Soli would get to the United States, all right, but she wouldn't be going through the border, not in his Cadillac, and certainly not in the secret compartment. He held his sides, laughing high and wheezy, when she reminded him that she'd planned to hide in there. "I can't believe you fit in that thing," he said and giggled. "I couldn't believe it when you got in! I was like *Oh, shit, she's getting in!*" He broke into full-gale laughter, and then paused. "Soli." He took her hand in his. "We've spent many days together, and I feel like maybe we're friends." He searched for her gaze. "Are we friends? Yes?"

She nodded slowly.

"Then I feel like I can trust you. I feel like you can do this, like you're smart enough. Take a walk with me." As they walked toward the camp, Manuel explained to Soli that he would drive her to Piedras Negras, on the Texas border.

"Texas? You said California. Is California close to Texas?"

He looked into her eyes then, and she caught a shimmer of irritation. "Yes, Soli, Texas is very close to California."

She waited for more.

"I'll take you to a market run by my friends, very nice people. Good people, Soli. And from there, you'll pass into America. With a few small packages."

"The ones from the car?"

He closed his eyes, smiled, and nodded. "That's it! Easy, don't you think?"

"But what about the border? And what about the car? Can't I just come with you?"

"The border, Soli, is up here." With his foot he drew a line in the dirt. "And the passage you'll be taking? He pointed at the ground. "The passage you'll be taking is way down there. Under the ground." He took a step closer to her, his lips at her ear. The base of her spine caught a warm shiver. He murmured low. He murmured like a lover. "You'll be crawling under the feet of the pinche idiota border guards, Soli, and they won't have a clue. I urge you to give them the finger as you pass. They'll never know. From Mexico to the States, just like that." He began to laugh, quietly, through his teeth. "Good, right? Right, Soli?"

"I'll be crawling? Through a tunnel?"

"You're small. You fit in that compartment? You'll have no problem with a tunnel." He gripped her elbow, leaned in until she hardly had space to breathe. "It's *good*, right, Soli?"

Soli searched for words, for voice, for a gust of air. "Yes," she whispered. "It's good."

"Good! Now go get yourself some food, chula. Beans are hot!" He gave a small hop and spun around. "The beans are hot and good, Soli," he called, as she walked away. She turned to watch him lean back, open his arms, and roar to the sky: "THE BEANS ARE HOT AND GOOD!"

You've just read an excerpt from Lucky Boy.

ABOUT THE AUTHOR

Shanthi Sekaran teaches creative writing at California College of the Arts, and is a member of the Portuguese Artists Colony and the San Francisco Writers' Grotto. Her work has appeared in *Best New American Voices* and *Canteen*, and online at *Zyzzyva* and *Mutha Magazine*. A California native, she lives in Berkeley with her husband and two children.

IMPRINT: Putnam
PRINT ISBN: 9781101982242
PRINT PRICE: $27.00
EBOOK ISBN: 9781101982259
EBOOK PRICE: $13.99
PUBLICATION DATE: 1/10/17
PUBLICITY CONTACT: Alexis Welby awelby@penguinrandomhouse.com
RIGHTS CONTACT: Tom Dussel tdussel@penguinrandomhouse.com
EDITOR: Tara Singh Carlson
AGENT: Lindsay Edgecombe
AGENCY: Levine Greenberg Rostan

PROMOTIONAL INFORMATION:
Author events; National print reviews and features; Online reviews and features; Online advertising; Book club promotions; Reading group guide; Social media promotions; Giveaways at BEA.

TODAY WILL BE DIFFERENT

MARIA SEMPLE

SUMMARY

A genius novel from the author of *Where'd You Go, Bernadette*, about a day in the life of Eleanor Flood, forced to abandon her small ambitions when she awakes to a strange, new future unfolding. *Today Will Be Different* is a hilarious, heart-filled story of reinvention, sisterhood, and how sometimes it takes facing up to our former selves before we can really begin living.

EXCERPT

Today will be different. Today I will be present. Today, anyone I'm speaking to, I will look them in the eye and listen deeply. Today I'll play a board game with Timby. I'll initiate sex with Joe. Today I will take pride in my appearance. I'll shower, get dressed in proper clothes and only change into yoga clothes for yoga, which today I will actually attend. Today I won't swear. I won't talk about money. Today there will be an ease about me. My face will be relaxed, its resting place a smile. Today I will radiate calm. Kindness and self-control will abound. Today I will buy local. Today I will be my best self, the person I'm capable of being. Today will be different.

The Trick

Because the other way wasn't working. The waking up just to get the day over with until it was time for bed. The grinding it out was a disgrace, an affront to the honor and long shot of being alive at all. The ghost-walking, the short-tempered distraction, the hurried fog. (All of this I'm just assuming, because I have no idea how I come across, my consciousness is that underground, like a toad in winter.) The leaving the world a worse place just by being in it. The blindness to the destruction in my wake. The Mr. Magoo.

If I'm forced to be honest, here's an account of how I left the world last week: worse, worse, better, worse, *mezzo mezzo*, worse, *mezzo mezzo*. Not an inventory to make one swell with pride. I don't necessarily need to make the world a better place, mind you. Today, I will live by the Hippocratic Oath: first do no harm.

How hard can it be? Dropping off Timby, having my poetry lesson (my favorite part of life!), taking a yoga class, eating lunch with Sydney

Madsen who I can't stand but at least I can check her off the list (more on that later), picking up Timby, and giving back to Joe, the underwriter of all this mad abundance.

You're trying to figure out, Why all the drama surrounding one normal day of white people problems? Because there's me and there's the beast in me. It would be kind of brilliant if the beast in me played out on a giant canvas, shocking and awing, causing fabulous destruction, talked about forever. If I could swing that, I just might: self-immolate gloriously for the performance art spectacle. The sad truth? The beast in me plays out on a painfully small scale: micro-transactions usually involving Timby, my friends, or Joe. I'm irritable and consumed by anxiety when I'm with them; maudlin and shit-talking when I'm not. Ha! Aren't you glad you're at a safe distance, doors locked, windows rolled up? Okay, come on. I'm nice. I'm exaggerating for effect. It's not really like that.

And so the day began, the minute I whipped off my sheets. The click-click-click of Yo-Yo's nails across the hardwood, stopping outside the bedroom. Why, when Joe whips off his sheets, doesn't Yo-Yo trot-trot-trot and wait in abject hope? How can Yo-Yo, on the other side of a closed door, tell it's me and not Joe? It was once depressingly explained by a dog trainer: it's my smell Yo-Yo's caught whiff of. That his idea of Nirvana is a dead seal washed up on the beach leaves me begging the question: is it time for bed yet? Nope, I'm not doing that. Not today.

I didn't mean to be coy about Sydney Madsen.

When Joe and I arrived in Seattle from New York ten years ago, we were ready to start a family. I was fried, having given five solid years to *Looper Wash*. Everywhere you looked it was *Looper Wash* T-shirts, bumper stickers, mouse pads. "I'm a Vivian." "I'm a Dot." You remember. If not, check your nearest dollar store, the two-for-one bin, it's been a while.

Joe, a hand surgeon, had become a legend of sorts for reconstructing the hand of that quarterback whose thumb bent back in a playoff game and nobody thought he'd ever play again but the next year he went on to win the Super Bowl. (I can't remember his name, but even if I did, I couldn't say, due to doctor/patient/nosy-wife confidentiality.) Joe could move anywhere. Why Seattle? Joe, a nice Catholic boy from outside Buffalo, couldn't see raising kids in Manhattan, my first choice. We struck a deal. We'd move anywhere he wanted for ten years; then back to New York for ten; his city for ten, my city for ten; back and forth, unto death. (A deal he's conveniently forgotten his end of, I might add, seeing as we're coming up on year ten and not a peep on packing up.)

As everybody knows, being raised Catholic with half a brain means becoming an atheist. At one of our skeptic conventions (yes, our early years were actually spent doing things like driving to Philadelphia to watch Penn Gillette debate a rabbi! Oh, to be childless again... or not) Joe heard that Seattle was the least religious city in America. Seattle it was.

A Doctors Without Borders board member threw Joe and me a welcome-to-Seattle party. I swanned into her Lake Washington mansion filled with modern art and future friends, mine for the picking. My whole life, I've been liked. Okay, I'll say it: I've been adored. I don't understand why, on account of my disgraceful personality, but somehow it works. Joe says it's because I'm the most male woman he's ever met, but sexy and with no emotional membrane. (A compliment!) I went from room to room, being introduced to a series of women, interchangeable in their decency and warmth. It was the thing where you meet somebody who tells you they like camping and you say, "Oh! I was just talking to someone who's going on a ten day rafting trip down the Snake River, you should totally meet them" and the person says, "That was me."

What can I say? I'm terrible with faces. And names. And dates. And times.

The whole party was a blur with one woman eager to show me funky shops, another hidden hikes, another Mario Batali's father's Italian restaurant in Pioneer Square, another the best dentist in town who has a glitter painting on his ceiling of a parachuting tiger, another willing to share her housekeeper. One of them, Sydney Madsen, invited me to lunch the next day at the Tamarind Tree in the International District.

(Joe has a thing he calls the "magazine test." It's the reaction you have when you open the mailbox and pull out a magazine. Instantly, you know if you're happy to see this magazine or bummed. Which is why I don't subscribe to the *New Yorker* and do subscribe to *Us Weekly*.) Sydney Madsen has turned out to be the human equivalent of *Tinnitus Today*.

That first lunch: she was so careful with her words, so sincere in her gaze, noticed a small spot on her fork and was overly solicitous of the waiter when asking for a new one, brought her own tea bag and asked for hot water, said she wasn't very hungry so how about we split my green papaya salad, told me she'd never seen *Looper Wash* but would put a hold on the DVDs at the library.

Am I painting a clear enough picture of the tight-assed dreariness, the selfish cluelessness, the cheap creepiness? A water-stained fork never killed anybody! Buy the DVD's, how about? Eat the food at the restaurant, that's how they stay in business! Worst of all, Sydney Madsen was steady, earnest, without a speck of humor, and talked... very... slowly... as... if... her... platitudes... were... little... gold... coins.

I was in shock. Living too long in New York does that to a girl, gives her the false sense that the world is full of interesting people. Or at least people who are crazy in an interesting way.

At one point I writhed so violently in my chair that Sydney actually asked, "do you need to use the powder room?" ("Powder room?" "Powder room?!" Kill her!) The worst part? All those women with whom I'd gladly agreed to go hiking and shopping? They weren't a bunch of women. They were all Sydney Madsen! Damn that blur! It took everything I had to kink her fire hose of new invitations: a weekend at her cabin on Vashon Island, introducing me to the wife of someone for this, the playwright of something for that.

I ran home screaming to Joe.

Joe: You should have been suspicious of someone so eager to make friends, because it means she probably doesn't have any.

Me: This is why I love you, Joe. You just boil it all down. (Joe the boiler. Don't we just love him?)

Forgive me for long-hauling you on Sydney Madsen. My point is: for ten years I haven't been able to shake her. She's the friend I don't like, the friend I don't know what she does for a living because I was too stultified to ask the first time and now it would be rude (because I'm not rude), the friend I can't be mean enough to so she gets the message (because I'm not mean), the friend to whom I keep saying, no, no, no, yet she still chases me. She's like ALS, you can't cure her, you can just manage the symptoms.

Today the lunch bell tolls.

Please know I'm aware that the horror of lunch with a boring person *is* a white person's problem. When I say I have problems, I'm not talking about Sydney Madsen.

***

Yo-Yo trotting down the street, the prince of Belltown. Oh, Yo-Yo, you foolish creature with your pep and your blind devotion and your busted ear flapping with every prance. How poignant it is, the pride you take in being walked by me, your immortal beloved. If you only knew.

What a disheartening spectacle it's been, a new month, a new condo higher than the last, each packed with blue-badged Amazon squids, every morning squirting by the thousands from their studio apartments onto my street, heads in devices, never looking up. (They work for Amazon, so you know they're soulless. The only question, how soulless?) It makes me pine for the days when Third Avenue was just me, For Lease signs and the one tweaker yelling, *That's* how you spell America.

Outside our building, Kevin stood by his wheely trash can and refilled the poop-bag dispenser. "Good morning, you two."

"Good morning, Kevin!" I stopped and took a focused breath in. "How's your day so far?" Just that minor interaction and my chest grew weak, my heart became thin as a bird's.

"Oh, can't complain," he said. "You?"

"Can complain, but won't."

Kevin chuckled.

Today, already a net gain.

***

I opened the front door of our apartment. Down the hallway: Joe face down at the dining room table, his forehead flat on the newspaper, arms splayed with bent elbows as if under arrest. It was a jarring image, one of pure defeat, the last thing I'd ever associate with Joe—

THUNK.

The door shut. I unclipped Yo-Yo from his harness. By the time I straightened, my stricken husband had hopped up and disappeared into his office.

My attitude? Works for me!

Yo-Yo raced to his food, greyhound-style, back legs reaching past his front. Realizing it was the same dry food that had been there before his walk, he became overwhelmed with confusion and betrayal. He took one step and stared at a spot on the floor.

Timby's light clicked on. God bless him, up before the alarm. I went into his bathroom and found him in his PJs, on the step stool.

"Morning, darling. Look at you, up and awake."

Timby stopped what he was doing. "Can we have bacon?"

Timby, in the mirror, waited for me to leave. I lowered my eyes. The little Quick Draw McGraw beat my glance. He pushed something into the sink before I could see it. The unmistakable clang of lightweight plastic. The Sephora 200!

It was nobody's fault but my own, Santa putting a makeup kit in Timby's stocking. It's how I'd buy myself extra time at Nordstrom: telling Timby to roam cosmetics. The girls there loved his gentle nature, his sugar sack body, his squeaky voice. Soon enough, they were making him up. I don't know if he liked the makeup as much as being doted on by a gaggle of blondes. On a lark, I picked up a kit the size of a paperback which unfolded and fanned out to reveal six different makeup trays (!) holding 200 (!) colors of shadows, glosses, blushes, and whatever-they-were's. Whoever had found a way to cram so much into so little should seriously be working for NASA.

"You do realize you're not wearing makeup to school," I told him.

"I know, Mom." The sigh and shoulder heave right out of the Disney Channel. Again, my bad for letting it take root. After school, a jigsaw puzzle!

When I emerged from Timby's room, Yo-Yo was standing there, overcome with relief that I still existed. Knowing I'd be heading to the kitchen to make breakfast, he raced me to his food bowl. This time he deigned to eat some, one eye on me.

Joe was back and making himself tea.

"How's things?" I asked.

"Don't you look nice," he said.

True to my grand scheme for the day, I'd showered and put on a dress and oxfords. If you beheld my closet, you'd see a woman of specific style. Dresses from France and Belgium, price tags ripped off before I got home because Joe would have an aneurysm, and every iteration of flat black shoe... again, no need to discuss price. Buy them? Yes. Put them on? On most days, too much energy.

"Olivia's coming tonight," I said with a wink, already tasting the wine flight and rigatoni at Tavolata.

"How about she take Timby out so we can have a little alone time?" Joe grabbed me by the waist and pulled me in as if we weren't practically fifty.

Here's who I envy: lesbians. Why? Lesbian Bed Death. Apparently, after a lesbian couple's initial flush of hot sex, they stop having it altogether. It makes perfect sense. Left to their own devices, women would stop having sex after they have children. There's no evolutionary need for it. Our brains know it, our body knows it. Who feels sexy during the slog of motherhood, the middle-aged fat roll and flattening butt? Who wants anyone to see them naked, let alone fondle their breasts droopy like tube socks or touch their stomachs spongy like breadfruit? Who wants to pretend they're all sexed up when the honey pot is dry?

Me, that's who, if I don't want to get switched out for a younger specimen.

"Alone time it is," I said to Joe.

"Mom, this broke." Timby came in with his ukulele and plonked it on the counter. Suspiciously near the trash. "The sound's all messed up."

"What do you propose we do?" I asked, daring him to say, Buy a new one.

Joe grabbed the ukulele and gave it a strum. "It's a little out of tune, that's all." He began to adjust the strings.

"Hey," I said. "Since when can you tune a ukulele?"

"I'm a man of many mysteries," Joe said. He gave the instrument a final strum and handed it back.

***

The bacon and French toast were being wolfed, the smoothies being drunk. Timby was deep into an Archie *Double Digest*. My smile was on lockdown.

Two years ago when I was getting all martyr-y about having to make breakfast every morning, Joe said, "I pay for this circus. Can you please climb down off your cross and make breakfast without the constant sighing?"

I know what you're thinking. What a jerk! What a sexist thug! But Joe had a point. Lots of women would gladly do worse for a closet of Antwerp. From that moment on, it was service with a smile. It's called knowing when you've got a weak hand.

Joe showed Timby the newspaper. "The Pinball Expo is coming back to town. Wanna go?"

"Do you think the KISS machine is still broken?"

"Almost certainly," Joe said.

I handed over the poem I'd printed out and heavily annotated.

"Okay, who's going to help me?" I asked.

Timby didn't look up.

Joe took it. "Ooh, Robert Lowell."

I began from memory: "Nautical Island's hermit heiress still lives through winter in her Spartan cottage; her sheep still graze above the sea. Her son's a bishop. Her farmer's first selectman"

"Almost," Joe said. "Her farmer *is* first selectman."

"Shoot. Her farmer *is* first selectman."

"Mom!"

"Shh!" I continued reciting. "Thirsting for the hierarchic privacy of Queen Victorian's century, she buys up all the eyesores facing her shore, and lets them fall. The season's ill—we've lost our summer millionaire, who seemed to leap from an L.L. Bean catalogue—"

"Mommy, look at Yo-Yo. See how his chin is sitting on his paws?"

Yo-Yo was positioned on his pink lozenge so he could watch for dropped food, his little white paws delicately crossed.

"Aww," I said.

"Can I have your phone?" Timby asked.

"Just enjoy your pet," I said. "This doesn't have to turn into electronics."

"And it's very cool what Mom is doing," Joe said to Timby. "She's always learning."

"Learning and forgetting," I said. "But thank you."

He shot me an air-kiss.

I continued. "His nine-knot yawl was auctioned off to lobstermen—"

"Don't we love Yo-Yo?" Timby asked.

"We do." The simple truth. Yo-Yo is the world's cutest dog, part Boston Terrier, part Pug, part something else... brindle-and-white with a black patch on one eye, bat ears, smooshed face and curlicue tail. Before the Amazon invasion, when it was just me and hookers on the street, one remarked, "It's like if Barbie had a pit bull."

"Daddy," Timby said. "Don't you love Yo-Yo?"

Joe looked at Yo-Yo and considered the question. More evidence of Joe's superiority: he thinks before he speaks.

"He's a little weird," Joe said with a shrug and returned to the poem. "Keep going. You're doing great."

Timby dropped his fork. I dropped my jaw.

"Weird?!" Timby cried.

Joe looked up. Now he was the bemused one. "Yeah, what?"

"Oh, Daddy! How can you say that?"

"He just sits there all day looking depressed," Joe said. "When we come home, he doesn't greet us at the door. When we are here, he just sleeps, waits for food to drop or stares at the front door like he has a migraine."

For Timby and me, there were simply no words.

"I know what he's getting out of us," Joe said. "I just don't know what we're getting out of him."

Timby jumped out of his chair and laid across Yo-Yo, his version of a hug. "Oh, Yo-Yo! *I* love you."

Joe flicked the poem. "Let's get this. 'The season's ill'...."

"The season's ill," I said. "We've lost our summer millionaire, who seemed to leap from an L.L. Bean catalogue—" To Timby, "You. Get ready."

"Are we driving through or are you walking me in?"

"Driving. I have Alonzo at 8:30."

Breakfast over, Yo-Yo got up from his pillow. Joe and I watched as he walked to the front door and stared at it.

"I didn't realize I was being controversial," Joe said. "The season's ill."

***

It's easy to tell who went to Catholic school by how they react when they first see Galer Street. I didn't, so to me it's an old, stately brick building with a huge flat yard and improbably dynamite view of Puget Sound. Joe did, so he goes white with flashbacks of nuns whacking his hands with rulers, priests threatening him with God's wrath, and spectacle-snatching bullies roaming the halls unchecked.

By the time we pulled into drop-off, I'd recited the poem twice perfectly and was doing it a third time for charm. "One dark night, my Tudor Ford climbed the hill's skull...."

Ominous silence from the back seat. "Hey," I said. "Are you even following along?"

"I am, Mom. You're doing perfect."

"Perfectly. Adverbs end in l-y." Timby wasn't in the rear view mirror. I figure-eighted it to see him hunched over something. "What are you doing?"

"Nothing." Followed once again, by that high-pitched rattle of plastic.

"Hey! No makeup."

"Then why did Santa put it in my stocking?"

I turned around but Timby's door had opened and shut. By the time I swung back, he was scudding up the front steps. In the reflection of the front door, I caught Timby's eyelids smeared with rouge. I rolled down my window. "You little sneak, get back here!"

The car behind me honked. Ah, well, he was school's problem now.

Me peeling out of Galer Street with seven child-free hours on the horizon? Cue the banjo getaway music.

You've just read an excerpt from Today Will Be Different.

ABOUT THE AUTHOR

Maria Semple's first novel, *This One Is Mine*, was set in Los Angeles, where she also wrote for television shows including *Arrested Development*, *Mad About You,* and *Ellen*. She escaped from Los Angeles and lives with her family in Seattle, where her second novel, national bestseller *Where'd You Go, Bernadette*, took place.

IMPRINT: Little, Brown and Company
PRINT ISBN: 9780316403436
PRINT PRICE: $27.00
EBOOK ISBN: 9780316403443
EBOOK PRICE: $13.99
PUBLICATION DATE: 10/4/16
EDITOR: Judy Clain
AGENT: Anna Stein
AGENCY: Aitken Alexander Associates

PROMOTIONAL INFORMATION:
National media campaign, including television, print, radio, and online interviews; Digital marketing and publicity campaign, including features and reviews, blog outreach, and shareable graphics; Prepublication buzz campaign; Presell tour; Select author appearances.

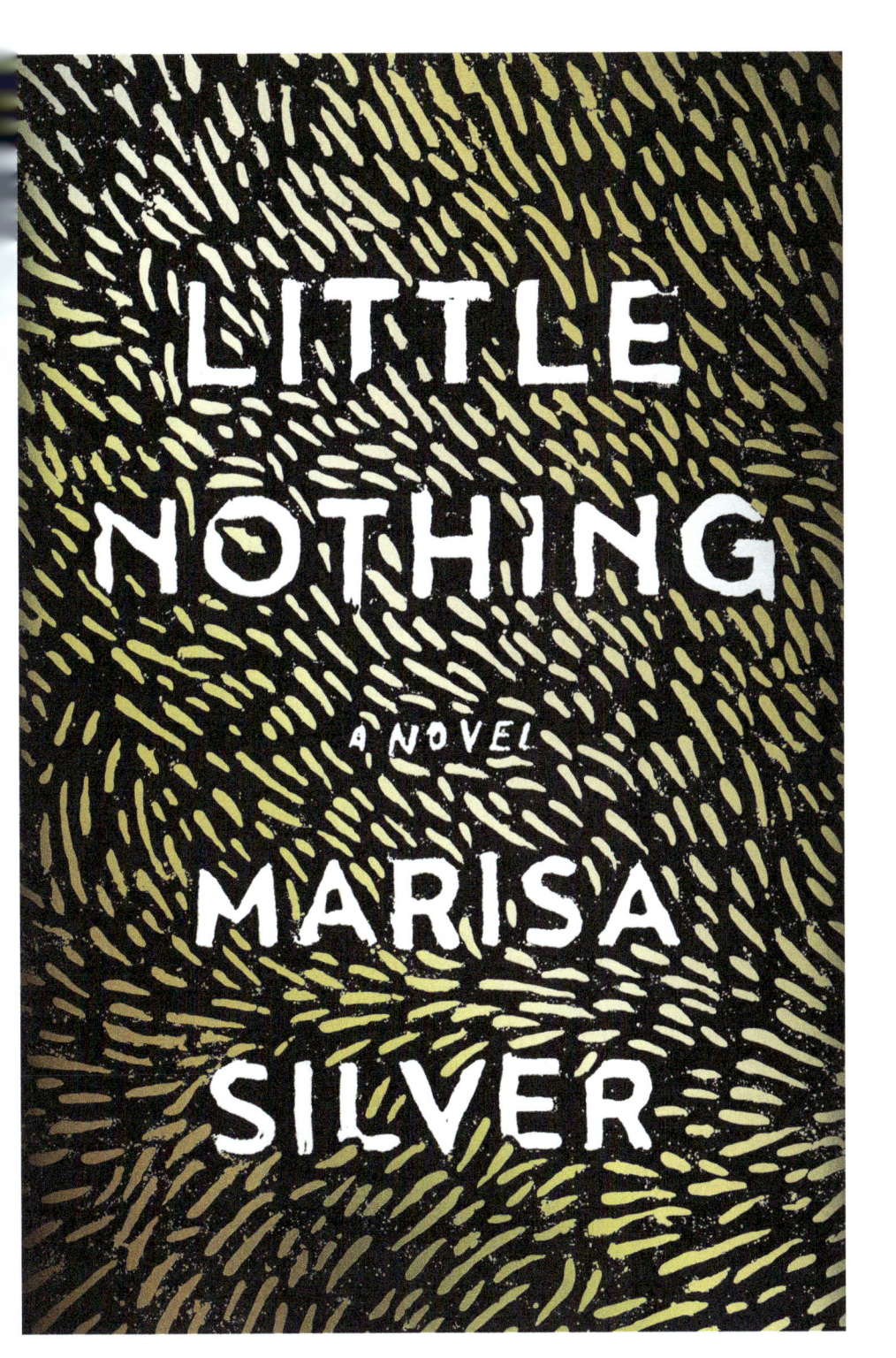

LITTLE NOTHING

A NOVEL

MARISA SILVER

SUMMARY

A stunning, provocative new novel from *New York Times* bestselling author Marisa Silver, *Little Nothing* is the story of Pavla, a child scorned for her physical deformity, whose passion and salvation lie in her otherworldly ability to transform herself and the world around her.

EXCERPT

Once in wintertime, when everything was covered in a deep bed of snow, a poor boy had to go out on his sled to fetch wood. After he had finished gathering and loading the wood, feeling frozen to the bone, before heading home he wanted to build a fire and warm himself a bit. So he scraped away the snow and cleared a patch of earth, when lo and behold, he found a little golden key lying there. Well, he figured where there's a key there must also be a lock to fit it in, so he dug into the ground and found a little iron box. If only the key fits! he thought to himself. There must surely be precious things in the box. He looked and looked but could not find a keyhole; finally he found one, but it was so small he could hardly see it. He tried to insert the key and fortunately it fit. Then he turned it one time around, and now we will have to wait until he manages to open the lock and lift the lid to discover what sort of wondrous things are in the box. —From *The Golden Key*, Brothers Grimm

"Představte si květinu!" the midwife yells, her voice reaching the baby as warped and concave sounds. "Pictuuure a flowaahhherrr."

Next, another voice, closer this time, the sound so near that if the baby could stretch its arm it might touch it. "You bitch!" the voice howls. "You monster! Get out of me now!" Agáta Janáček is enraged that this should be happening to her even though she has wished for it and prayed for it, consulted the gypsy witch Zlata, and buried amulets of animal bones wrapped in the hair of a virgin for it. But old as she is—and tough threads of gray streak her hair and sprout from the colorless mole on her chin and thinly veil her pubis where there was once a dark, luxurious thatch— the old stories of childhood hold sway. Her mother warned her about this moment. It was a cautionary bedtime story chanted night after night: little Agáta, the prettiest girl in the village, lives in a magical paradise filled with delicious honey-scented medovnik and talking bunny rabbits. Then one day, a terrible monster comes and whispers in her ear words sweeter than any jam, sweeter even than her favorite candies that hang from the Christmas tree each year and which she is forbidden to pull off until Christmas Day, even though this means surrendering the low-hanging chocolate treasures to the mice and rats who skitter across the floorboards at night and gorge themselves, their nocturnal pleasures mapped by a trail of black pellets. But little Agáta cannot resist the tantalizing whispers of the monster and she allows him to touch her face and stroke her body and climb on top of her and shove his hard sausage between her soft thighs. *Unh . . . unh*, her mother would grunt, her voice a striking imitation of the guttural efforts Agáta heard most nights coming from behind the thin lace curtain that separated her parents' bed from the one she shared with her five brothers and sisters. And then, what next? Pretty Agáta grows fat as a pig, fat as a cow. Her little *tzitzis*, once tender and delicate as meringue, become achy and so swollen they have to be held up by a harness of cloth that winds round her back and halters at the nape of her neck. Months go by and the beautiful, smooth skin of her belly becomes striped like a zebra's as her flesh stretches and pulls. And then finally, after backache and fat fingers and a burning in her gut so fierce she will think a match has been struck inside her, Agáta's body will split in two.

First the body and then the heart. Good night. Sleep tight. The bedbugs will surely bite.

But her mother is long dead and is not here to sigh and shake her head with false sympathy for her daughter's pain.

"A *flowwerrrr openingggg*," the midwife calmly insists.

"You bitch, you whore, you fucking fuck!" Agáta rages, her voice becoming clearer to the baby as it begins to swim through the dark tunnel, its head pushing against something hard, then something soft, then something hard again, as if it were a paper boat in a swift current, banging up against rocks then drifting into a calm eddy only to be drawn back helplessly into the propelling current once more. "You ugly whore who no man will fuck even with his eyes closed!"

The midwife laughs. She has heard far worse. "A rose opening," she persists, "the petals pushing out . . . out . . . *Ano. Ano.*"

The baby twists down and up a U valve, which is something it will get to know very well when Václav Janáček, the father (who, by the way, is nowhere to be heard, who is hiding in the chicken coop that smells like hell, having been neglected by his wife these past twenty-seven hours of her hair-raising labor) will set his child to crawling around the crude plumbing of the first sinks and toilets in the village.

And the midwife shouts: "It's blooooming, blooming, I can see the bud . . ."

"A whore with so much hair growing on your face a man thinks he is making love to a mirror—"

"It reaches for the sunlight, up and up and up and—"

Agáta lets loose with a wretched sound that is so loud in the baby's narrow ear canal that the dawning light is occluded by the sheer thickness of the roar.

"Yes! Yes! A rose! A beautiful pink . . . a beautiful. . . . a—"

And now, Václav hears nothing coming from the house, not the curses of his wife, nor the scream of an infant, nor the triumphant exclamations of the midwife who can add one more to her tally of live births, only the infernal squawking of the hens. In his panic he picks up a cackling rooster and stuffs its head under his armpit, an action he will regret when he has to buy a replacement for the suffocated bird.

The silence is so dense that it is just as hard on the baby's eardrums as any sound. It is the silence that will become a refrain, when a stranger falls speechless in the child's presence, or when a villager pushes her children behind her skirts as she passes in the narrow market lanes to protect them from what might be catching. The child will learn to hear the complicated messages that fill these silences just the way, years later, imprisoned, it will stare into the night sky until all the hues that exist in the darkness have been accounted for and named, a painstaking ritual that proves that out of nothing comes everything.

Just as now, out of that hush comes a sound at first so soft that it could be a whisper traveling from the farthest star, from the outer reaches of the universe where all time goes, where all history, all wars, all arguments between husbands and wives, all the unanswered wishes of mothers for their children to be perfect and to live long and happy lives gather and mingle, making small talk about the deluded humans who thought that the past was something that could be put away and forgotten, who believed that the future was a story they could make their own. The small sound begins to stretch and expand until it finally ruptures:

"Ayeeeee!" Agáta howls in fright. "What is this thing?"

This thing, of course, is a baby. Forty centimeters of baby to be precise although no one bothers to measure. No one thinks to enact the rituals of inspection that normally attend a birth—the delicate washing, the finger and toe counting, the near-scholarly examination of genitalia for signs of future procreative success. No one offers that the child looks like the father (eyes shaped like the downward smile of nail parings) or that it has a mouth shaped like a perfect raspberry-colored bow that Agáta will finally but not now, not yet, claim as her legacy even though she is so old that her lips are no longer supported by a full set of teeth and have nearly collapsed inside her mouth. No one mentions that the baby has hair the color of dead grandmother Ljuba, whose flaxen locks were her pride, for to make these comparisons is to lay claim, to stamp the child as family so that when the cord is cut and the baby is finally free of Agáta's body, everyone will know to whom it belongs. For Václav and Agáta to assert ownership would be to admit that they are cursed, that this child they have prayed for, waited for, that comes to them after neighbors have joked about Václav still being able to stand at attention and about Agáta's womb being filled with cobwebs has turned out to be this *thing*, this foreshortened object, this disproportionate dollhouse version of an infant. It is as though, coming so late to the feast, the plumber and his wife have been given only leftovers, the hardened heels of bread and the tough ends of beef that others have passed over.

"A girl," Václav says, still smelling of feathers and dead rooster. He hasn't yet touched the child, only ordered the midwife to unwrap the swaddling to reveal the naked declaration of its worth. He speaks with a little hitch of satisfaction as if the sex somehow proves that the fault is not his. Agáta, who has not yet looked at her daughter since that first, alarming view, lies on the bloodstained bed with her back turned away from the onion basket that serves as a cradle, staring at the varicose cracks in the wall, praying either to sleep herself to death or to wake from what must surely be a nightmare. All the while she murmurs: *Is it real? It isn't real. Is it?* Even when the baby mews from hunger, Agáta does not reach for her. What use are her false comforts?—her milk has not yet begun to flow. The midwife shows Václav how to settle the baby with sugar water, collects her money, then leaves the house in a hurry, not eager to prolong her association with this blighted birth and damage her reputation.

A day later, Agáta's milk has still not come in, but she is not surprised that it is unwilling to spend itself on such a lost cause. Exhausted by the birth, she sleeps and wakes and then, remembering what she has brought into the world, sleeps again, leaving her husband to administer the sugar water. Perhaps she hopes that if she pays the baby no mind the child will simply disappear, return to the land of wishes it came from and that she will wake up with only a memory of a vague but unnameable disappointment that will be forgotten in the daily skirmish of cleaning and cooking and arguing vegetable prices with market cheats. But her crotch will not let her forget. A thing so small ripping her from fore to aft so that she has to bite down on the handle of a wooden spoon when she pees. Returning to her bed, she glances at the baby girl who is so tiny, so nearly not there. Her head is too large for her torso, her arms and legs too short. She looks like a rag doll sewn together from cast-off parts. Each time Agáta wakes, it seems possible that the baby's existence is just a magician's trick, and that if Agáta were to look in the basket, she would find only newly pulled scallions.

"My little mouse," Judita, the village wet nurse sings as she rocks the baby against her bosoms that are long and heavy as giant zucchinis. Her brown nipples are so thick that the infant girl gags each time Judita pushes her small face into her curd-smelling skin. "Every one of my little mice grows big and strong and so will you," she commands, shaking the baby in order to get her to suck.

Judita's house, a dirt-floored room with walls blackened from a haphazardly swept chimney, smells sweetly of infant puke. Here, along with three other newborns, the plumber's daughter is rotated from the left breast to the right, then into the hands of Judita's eldest daughter, Vanda, whose job it is to strip and wipe. The sixteen-year-old's expression seesaws between the crinkle of disgust she feels for these shitting machines that are her daily burden and the hard fury of hatred she bears toward her mother whose body and its uses signal her own utilitarian future. Vanda's task complete, she hands the baby off to her younger sister, Sophia, who diapers the child in sun-starched, wind-smelling cloth that has just been taken down from the line. It is Tomás, Judita's idiot son, who is in charge of washing the dirty diapers in a barrel whose water is not changed often enough, a job he has been given because he performs his mucky task without complaint. After the baby is cleaned and freshly attired in diapers that are much too large for her tiny body, she is placed in a hay-filled crate where she dozes and wakes and waits for her turn on the line once again. It is as efficient a system as any being implemented in the new factories in the faraway city where, the villagers have heard, men in white smocks hold stopwatches and notebooks and workers are occasionally sucked up into the machines so that who knows what accounts for the brilliant red of a bolt of cloth? Still, after weeks, when it becomes evident that even Judita's rich milk, responsible for so many of the village's pudgy, no-necked boys and girls, will not work miracles on this tiny, misshapen body, she grows frustrated. By the second month, her little mouse becomes her little rat; by the third, her little cockroach, a freakish, thumb-sized enemy determined to bring down shame on the wet nurse and ruin her business.

"Enough!" she declares one day. She carries the baby from her house down the main street, stomping past the corn chandler and the harness maker and the town gossips with her recalcitrant package held out in front of her as if she were returning bad meat to the butcher and making sure that everyone in the village can smell the proof. She crosses the rickety bridge that spans the river that splits the town in two then marches to the plumber's cottage. There she finds Agáta on her knees in the garden yanking a clutch of knobby, dirt covered beets from the ground. Agáta's eyes grow fearful at the unexpected sight of her child who she had hoped not to see for at least another month or perhaps never again. She stands and backs up a few steps, her pickings shielding her useless breasts. But Judita is adamant, and the final payment for services is rendered: root vegetables for the baby.

"But what am I supposed to do with her?" Agáta says, cradling her baby awkwardly so that the child's head flops over her forearm like a heavy bulb.

"First," Judita says, "you could try giving her a name."

Bronislava means weapon of glory, Rosta, seizer of glory, Ceslav, honor and glory, and Miroslav, great glory. But these names that Agáta chose for each seed Václav planted inside her over the decades of their attempts were the ones she buried along with the residue of every miscarriage. The couple's imagination is dulled by thwarted hope and, unable to project any glorious future for the stubby child they have managed to bring to life, this dwarf child who mocks their years of effort, they can only conjure the prosaic. They call the baby Pavla, which means exactly what she is, which is little. She is narrow of body and short of limbs. Her eyes are round and watchful, her gaze both passive and disarmingly intrusive. Although it is impossible, her parents cannot help but feel she can see inside their minds and that she knows their private, and sometimes horrible, thoughts. She is an uncomplaining baby, as if she knows any kindness turned her way is provisional and that she ought not to draw more attention to herself than is necessary. She remains as quiet as any object in the cottage, as still as the portrait of dead Teta Ivana who picked a rose, pricked her finger, and died of infection, as still as the cuckoo clock that is never wound because Agáta and Václav have no need for timepieces. They feel the passage of the day in their bones, know instinctively when it is the hour to rise, to eat, to work, to sleep, when to commence the weekly argument when Agate tells Václav that he is courting a terrible fate by refusing to go to Mass and Václav tells Agáta that he will not believe that God intends for Father Matyáš, who as a boy did questionable things with the back end of a sheep (As did you! Agáta always reminds him. But I grew up to be a plumber! Václav replies) to be the conveyer of His word.

Left mostly to her own devices, which, at four months, are considerably few, Pavla lies in the wooden crib Václav barters from one of his neighbors in exchange for a cracked commode. The slats create the frame through which Pavla watches Agáta excavate the dark eyes of potatoes with a bent-knuckled knife, yank stringy, gray tendons from chicken legs, wring out newly washed laundry, throttling wet sheets and Václav's undershirts in her muscular hands, and make the soap that she sells at the market.

Agáta heats the rendered cooking fat then mixes it with lye that she makes using ashes from the hearth. The blue glass bottle in which she stores the poison catches the sunlight and Pavla's attention so that the very first object she attempts to grasp is this ephemeral cobalt sparkle. Then Agáta stirs and stirs and stirs, stripping off her sweater, then her apron, then her shirt, then her skirt until she is down to her underclothes. Her skin drips with sweat, her arms and breasts and stomach shake with her exertions. Of course Pavla knows nothing of rendered fat or lye or the laborious process of making soap, or that her mother drops chamomile flowers or rose petals into her molds because with this small, inexpensive effort her soaps can fetch a few more coins at the market. But what she does understand is that her mother is a digger, yanker, wringer, twister, and an aggressive and sometimes angry stirrer and so is somewhat relieved to be left alone. Pavla also observes her mother in the rare moments when the potatoes are boiling and the laundry is hung and there is no fault in the world of her home that she must immediately attack and remedy. Then Agáta will stand next to the open window without moving, barely breathing, as if the wind that charges her hours and days has unexpectedly died down and she has been left stranded in the incomprehensible sea of her life, suddenly aware that she has no purpose except to avoid the purpose that is staring at her though the bars of the crib. To counter her creeping terror, Agáta tells stories. She speaks not to her audience of one but to herself, the sound and memory of the old fairy tales as soothing as the bit of worn, soft chamois cloth she carried in her pocket when she was a girl and that she rubbed between her thumb and forefinger when her mother first told her these same stories, the bit of cloth she kept hidden for so many years in a small wooden box, intending to pass down the comfort to her own child. But now, this sentiment seems foolish. Maybe it is even the cause of her heartbreak, because everyone knows it is bad luck to second-guess fate.

In the Land of Pranksters there reigned a king . . . There once lived a poor, penniless man, truly a pauper . . . A good many years back it must be since the goblin used to dwell on Crow Mountain . . . and the story she told again and again, the one that little Pavla, even though she could not yet understand it, would remember all her life:

Once there was an old grandfather who went to work in his field. When he got there, he saw that an enormous turnip was growing there. He pulled and pulled, but he could not yank the turnip out of the ground, so he called his old wife. The man held onto the turnip and his wife held onto him and they pulled and pulled, but still, they could not pull the turnip from the ground. So they called their little granddaughter. The grandpa held onto the turnip and the grandma held onto the grandpa and the granddaughter held onto the grandma and they pulled, but still no luck. And so they called their dog. And the dog held onto the granddaughter and the granddaughter held onto the grandmother and the grandmother held onto the grandfather, who pulled the turnip, but still nothing. And so they called their kitty, who got in the back of the line and pulled the dog, but the turnip wouldn't budge. Suddenly, they heard a little voice coming from a hole in the ground. It was the voice of a mouse. The grandfather said, "Oh, little mouse, you do not have the strength to help us," but the grandmother said, "Let her help us if she wants to." So the grandfather held onto the turnip and the grandmother held onto the grandfather and the granddaughter held onto the grandmother and the dog held onto the granddaughter and the kitty held onto the dog and the mouse held onto the kitty and they pulled and pulled and pulled and . . . the turnip came out of the ground! And the grandmother said to the grandfather, "Sometimes the littlest one can be the biggest help."

Each time Agáta reaches the end of the story, she dismisses the stupidity of the moral. "What a ridiculous bunch," she might mutter, or, "Anyway, everyone knows that a giant turnip would be as sour as an old shoe."

As the hours pass and the light in the room softens and the corners recede into shadows, and, as she listens to the low drone of her mother's recitation, Pavla sees both less and more, for Agáta in shadow is somehow the purer distillation of her character: dark, wary, certain that this world she lives in is not as real as the one she visits in her tales where mountain kings and speaking rams are more comprehensible to her than the day's weather or the queer human being she has made.

"Oh ho, my wife!"

It is evening and twilight gives up its fight and the night sky closes over the village. Agáta shakes herself out of her reverie and becomes all energy and spin, engaging herself importantly with whatever is at arm's length—a sock that needs darning, a soup that requires stirring, even, because she can no longer ignore the sweet stink of baby shit, her daughter. The door of the cottage opens and a dark shape fills it: Pavla's father is home. The tools of his trade hang off Václav's thick leather belt and he jangles when he moves. This inadvertent music provokes his daughter who waggles her little arms. When Václav notices this reaction, he shakes his hips again, and to his pleasure, his daughter's eyes grow wide and her mouth forms its first, wobbly smile. This is the opening conversation of Pavla's life and she does not want it to end so she manifests a noise that sounds like the bleating of a goat.

"Don't upset her," Agáta warns, not wanting to have her maternal skills put to the test.

"She's not upset. She's laughing!" Václav says, taking off his tool belt and jangling it over the crib. Pavla makes her sound again and watches as her father's astonishment turns to pleasure, his smile unmasking a mouthful of brown and rotted teeth that emerge from his swollen gums at odd angles like the worn picket fence that surrounds Agáta's garden and fails to keep out the scavenger deer. Pavla will do anything to keep seeing these teeth and so she laughs and waves her arms and feels, for the first time in her life but not the last, the exquisite pain of love. In a few years, she will put Václav's screwdrivers and wrenches and bolts of all different sizes to use, dressing the long tools in bits of cloth to make faceless dolls and stringing washers on twine to fashion necklaces for her mother. For now, she follows the symphony of her father as he crosses the room and sits on a hard chair and waits for his wife to pull off his high boots whose soles are impacted with sludge. It is Agáta's great shame that the handsome farrier she married so long ago, the boy who rode the horses he shod back and forth along the main street supposedly to try out his work but really to show off his powerful thighs to the village maidens, saw advantage in turning his skill with iron and his eye for chance to, of all things, indoor plumbing. "Horses will soon be a thing of the past," he explained to Agáta, the girl who was most impressed by those powerful flanks, as he lay on top of her in their marriage bed, pushing her knees closer to her face to improve his angle of entry. "But everyone shits once a day. Sometimes twice, if they're lucky."

The work was slow at first. The villagers were used to chamber pots and being able to study their bodies' expulsions for signs of good or ill health, and the notion of what was once inside them disappearing before their eyes made them suspicious. Even Agáta refused the improvement, not fully believing that it was possible for a body to eliminate its waste anywhere but in a boiling-in-summer, freezing-in-winter, always pungent outhouse. Time and again, people would fold their arms and narrow their gazes and ask Václav, "But where does it go, really?" His answer did not satisfy them because even though they talked a good game about heaven and hell to keep their children in line and satisfy that idiot, Father Matyáš, these were realistic people who had a pretty good idea of where they would end up for the rest of time, and who did not fancy the notion of sharing eternity with piles of their neighbor's crap. But eventually the idea caught on. Now, years later, Agáta is the wife of a man who makes a decent living unclogging the drains and pipes of villagers who have finally stopped squatting in the fields or pouring their slops out of windows to fertilize their flowers but who have yet to learn the idiosyncrasies of modern waste disposal. They are forever putting all manner of objects down their toilets as if to bury their secrets. Love letters from mistresses or the bill for a frivolous hat purchase, fistfuls of hair cut off to approximate some newfangled style advertised in a gazette brought from the city by a peddler, the gazette itself—all these things and more create odiferous backups that warp floorboards and stain rugs. His clients regard plumbing as a sin-exonerating miracle, a daily confession, which is reasonable given the narrow confines of the indoor WCs that are built into the corners of rooms or fashioned from standing wardrobes, and owing to the contemplative and sometimes prayerful minutes spent therein. The villagers have no interest in Václav's explanations about the curved and narrow pipes that render their efforts at secrecy useless. More than useless, as it turns out, for all it takes for a marriage to crumble is for a husband to be present when the plumber exhumes a clot of bloody towels flushed away because a mother of six has decided a seventh will be the death of her. In fact, Václav turns out to be the opposite of what people assume. He is not a man devoted to the eradication of unmentionable things but one whose very presence brings them to light. When he enters a house, the owners will not look him in the eye, as if he were judge and jury and taxman all at once. He has taken to demanding his fee up front because no man pays another to witnesses his humiliation. But Agáta cannot complain. Her husband provides a living for her and now, she supposes, for the unfortunate issue of her aged womb.

During the first half year of Pavla's life, except at mealtimes when she is fed warm goat's milk and vegetables macerated to a soupy pulp, or during diaper changes, she has little contact with her mother who doesn't know what to make of her fractional child. Every seven days, she lifts her baby from the crib, removes whatever oversized garments have been left on the doorstep by pitying neighbors, and washes Pavla in a basin. When her daughter is naked, Agáta will sometimes let her eyes wander over her child, but just as she feels her tears begin to collect, she sets to scrubbing, using not a perfumed soap but one that is as harsh on the skin as gravel. Let silly women spend money on fancy toiletries they think will keep their husbands close. A body needs to be scoured like the inside of a pot. Holding up one arm, then the other in order to get into the creases of bunched-up baby fat, she reduces her daughter to parts and eradicates the implications of the deformed whole. If Václav is home, he might do his hip-shaking, tool-jangling dance to entertain Pavla and distract her from her mother's ministrations, but more often than not, he stands next to the basin and tilts his head to the side, studying his baby as if she were another plumbing problem in need of a fix.

But like a rat or icy wind, love creeps in. When winter comes, and there are no vegetables to pull, and the life of the village turns hushed and isolated, Agáta comes to Pavla's crib more often and lifts her up, even when she has been cleaned and fed and still smells of—yes, lately, she cannot resist—roses.

"Who are you?" Agáta says, holding Pavla so that they are face-to-face. She is finally curious about this strange being who she has brought into the world and whose musical sounds, those triplet thirds that move up and down the scale, and whose beginning words, despite their rubbery incoherence, quicken her heart. If the child could speak she would say, "I am Pavla," for that is all she knows about herself at this point having not been subject to the fantasies of a besotted mother spinning her baby's fairytale future of whirlwind romance, loyal children, and wealth. During the next months, as the cast-iron lid of sky settles heavily on the land, and as villagers are less eager to go outside to throw chicken bones where they belong, when the logic of "If I ate this piece of paper/bit of twine/pig's knuckle, it would come out the other end anyway" holds sway against the ice that seeps through the soles of boots and the bitter air that slices cracks into the lips and hands on a journey to the compost heap, Václav's plumbing business picks up. As soon as he leaves the house each morning, Agáta opens the standing wardrobe, pulls up a chair, and with her daughter on her lap, gazes into the mirror that hangs inside the door. The reflective glass has browned and crackled around the edges so that only in its center does it allow for a true, if fuzzy, reflection. The two study each other. What Pavla sees: a woman whose occasional smile sneaks out only to be snatched back, as if Agáta recognizes her error.

And what does Agáta see?

She tells a story:

"A mother had her baby stolen from his cradle by a wolf, and in his place lay a changeling, a little monster with a great thick head and staring eyes who did nothing but eat and drink. In distress she went to a neighbor and asked her advice. The neighbor told her to take the changeling into the kitchen, lay him on the hearth, and make a fire. Then she should take two eggshells and boil some water in them. That would make the changeling laugh, and as soon as he laughed, it would be all up with him. The woman did everything just as the neighbor said. And when she put the eggshells on the fire to boil, the blockhead sang out: *"I'm as old as the Westerwald but I've never seen anyone try to boil water in an eggshell!"* And he roared with laughter. As soon as he did that, a pack of wolves appeared carrying the rightful child. They set him on the hearth and took the changeling away, and the woman never saw them again."

When she finishes, Agáta looks at her daughter in the mirror. Certainly she must be a replacement for the child Agáta expected. But then again, Pavla was taken away to Judita's milking house, and now has returned to take her rightful place in her crib. Agáta tries to ignore a passing shadow of self-doubt. Holding her daughter against her breast, she feels Pavla's tiny heart pulsing against her wing-like backbones. Her daughter relaxes in her arms and grows heavy with sleep, and Agáta feels the pride all mothers feel when they have successfully ushered their children into the land of gentle dreaming. She holds her girl close and, she can't help it, she sings the song her mother sang to her so very long ago: *Good night, my dear, good night. May God himself watch over you. Good night, sleep well. May you dream sweet dreams!*

Should she be allowed to invoke God? Wasn't it against God that she took the gypsy's remedies? Wasn't it He who paid her back for her pagan infidelity? Would God now, after all this, place within her the feelings that are stirring her heart? She pictures Father Matyáš and cannot help but see him through Václav's eyes: a man too ignorant for the words he delivers, too sullied to touch the wafer that he places on extended, hopeful tongues, too wracked by drunken tremors to hold the cup steady with his long, boney fingers. The same fingers that he uses to pat the heads of his alter boys and smooth the collars of their frocks even when they don't need smoothing. "No!" she says out loud without intending to, startling the baby. A God that makes that sheep fucker his emissary cannot deny her this feeling that fills her withered breasts and makes her nipples tingle. *Dream a little dream, oh dream it.* She sings in full voice, not caring that she cannot hold a tune or that the neighbors out tending their black pigs might hear. How many years has she had to listen to them laugh at their children, scream at them, chide them, praise them, wish them well and safe as they troop off to school, off to the fields, off to life? *When you wake up, trust the dream, that I love you. That I'm going to give you my heart!*

By the time Pavla is five years old, Agáta has enfolded her little daughter into her daily routine. The girl's tasks: sweep the floor, clean the chicken coop, carry the fresh eggs to the house in the cradle of her skirt, walking slowly so that the warm and delicate ovals do not jostle against one another and crack. Pavla is handy with a knife and she makes quick work of shelling peas or pitting cherries. Her arms and legs remain short relative to her torso, and when she walks or runs, she moves side to side to propel herself forward, her arms pumping double time. Watching her daughter race after an errant chicken or leap up to try and catch a petal-white butterfly, Agáta feels her chest expand to make room for the brew of awe and heartache that she has come to identify as happiness. Václav has fashioned a step stool so that Pavla can reach the basin in order to scrub dishes, scour her teeth, and wash her face, and he has made her a special riser that sits on the seat of a chair so that, at mealtimes, the rising sun of her round, fair head surfaces above the lip of the table. When Agáta takes Pavla to the shops, the children stare and often laugh, while their mothers *tsk tsk* at Agáta's misfortune and their relative good luck. "Leave me home," Pavla begs each time her mother announces the dreaded weekly trip, but Agáta slaps her. "If I have to do it, then you have to do it, too," she says, not clarifying whether she means enduring the humiliation or selling soap.

Because the majority of houses in the village date from the previous century and have not been constructed with plumbing in mind, the work of retrofitting them for underground pipes is a job suited for the small. By the time Pavla is seven years old, Václav, recognizing both his daughter's quick wit and her unique suitability, begins to take her on his rounds. It is the girl's job to crawl into caverns beneath houses that hold eons worth of cold. Once she has studied these spaces and judged where the dirt is soft enough for digging and where rock forms too much of an impediment, she emerges, dusts herself off, then draws maps of the underground geographies. Because of the incessant comparisons she has been subjected to and is the subject of—*but she's half as tall as my Jurek and they share the same year and name day! But look: her hand is just a quarter the size of my darling Katarina's!*—Pavla has an innate grasp of scale, and from her crude yet accurate diagrams, Václav can determine where the pipes should be laid. Once he has done the laborious work of digging trenches, he hitches up his pants, drops to his knees, and wriggles underground. Pavla stands by the mouth of the hole, and when her father calls for the parts he needs, she hands them to him, sometimes using a pulley system that she and Václav devise with a rope and her Easter basket. She quickly learns the vocabulary of his trade—gaskets and bastard neck bolts, couplings and stems—and she is able to predict what her father will need before he asks for it. Václav and Pavla often work for hours without speaking, the only sound passing between them the clank of metal, Václav's muffled grunts, his occasional, frustrated profanities, and her corresponding giggles. Often, a client will comment about what a good man Václav is to keep his poor daughter close and make her feel useful. Although Pavla can see her father's expression harden, he never responds. That his stoicism is read as heroic forbearance helps his business: villagers are eager for a saint to install and sanctify their toilets. When a job is complete and a client examines his new plumbing, flushing and then watching in astonishment as the water disappears from the toilet bowl, Václav will give Pavla a conspiratorial wink, and she knows they share the secret of her true value.

The crib remains Pavla's sleeping bower long after other children in the village have moved into proper beds where the sweating or freezing bodies of their four or six or eight brothers and sisters keep them from rolling onto the hard floor. With no siblings and only one bed in the house, Pavla would sleep between her beloved parents, but she resists the transition. She is reassured by her crib, whose geometry is so conducive to her size. Confined, she feels that she occupies a comprehensible space relative to her mattress, the house, the village, the world. She teaches herself to add, subtract, and even multiply using the slats, and by the time she turns eight and finally convinces her fearful and protective mother and her father, who frets the loss of a good assistant, to let her attend school, she is well ahead of the other children. She is sought after as a seatmate on test days and she obliges by angling her tablet to the advantage of her dull-witted neighbor. That lucky student's result is never questioned because the teacher, Mr. Kublov, no student of science or of much else, believes that Pavla's smallness of stature is mirrored by a corresponding puniness of brain, and that she is the one who cheated her way to a perfect score. She is forced to stand in the corner with her back to the classroom, and Mr. Kublov does not bother to admonish the boys who make a game of pitching nuggets of wadded paper at her back. The girls call her Little Nothing as though there are descending versions of nothingness. These girls want to assure Pavla that she counts for much less than the next-to-nothings their mothers tell them they are by virtue of their laziness when it comes to household chores, or the big nothings their fathers insinuate they are by only speaking directly to their brothers. During outdoor break time, the boys devise a game of chase where Pavla is the chicken and they are the farmers. The winner is the one who wrestles her to the ground and administer the coup de grâce. Then she must flap her arms and dance like a decapitated bird. The girls, led by their ring-leader Gita Blažek, are no less eager—they place her in the middle of their circle while they hold hands and raise their arms in an arch and chant: *The golden gate was opened, unlocked by a golden key. Whoever is late to enter, will lose their head. Whether it's him or her . . . Whack him with a broom!* They close their arms around her head like a vice, then administer the punishment. Mr. Kublov watches from his post at the top of the schoolhouse stairs where he smokes his cigarettes and steals nips from the flask hidden in his coat pocket, relieved that the children have found a united purpose so that he doesn't have to break up a fight and risk getting punched or scratched in the process.

These humiliations continue until heavy rains swell the river that separates Pavla and her neighbors' homes from the other side of the village where the school stands. The bridge is demolished. A fallen poplar now stretches from one bank to the other, but the drop is precipitous and the spindly trunk does not fill the children with confidence. One boy tries to cross, but immediately falls off and lands in the muddy bank below. No one wants to make another attempt, but no one wants to return home and be beaten for playing hooky and forced to spend the day mucking out stalls. Pavla runs back to her house as quickly as her short legs will carry her. Her mother is busy stirring lard and lye. The steam from the boiling pot clouds the cottage's window, and she doesn't notice when her daughter slips into Václav's toolshed and gathers a mallet, a rope, and a set of pulleys. Once back at the river, she hammers one of the pulleys to a standing tree and feeds the rope through it. She puts the remaining tools into her school satchel and tightens the strap across her back. Holding the ends of the rope in one hand, she hoists herself onto the fallen tree. A wind created by the high and swift current makes balancing difficult, but her center of gravity is low enough to stabilize her and her small feet find purchase on the narrow trunk. She envisions the makeshift bridge as just another subterranean corridor below the houses where she and her father work, a tight, enclosed space that enfolds her, and her imagination sees her safely to the other side. There, she hammers the second pulley into a firm root, feeds the rope through until it is taut, and ties a knot. Holding tightly to one of the two ropes, the others nervously make their way across the trunk while Pavla slowly pulls the other through the pulley to guide them forward.

The games of chase-the-chicken stop, and if Pavla is remanded to the corner by Mr. Kublov, the other students leave her alone. They begin to seek her out not only to help with their schoolwork but for the more important work of sneaking into the cloakroom in order to put a dead mouse in Kublov's coat pocket or smear glue inside his hat. Once the students begin their geography study, aided by a wildly inaccurate roll-up map suspended from the top of the chalkboard that shows their tiny country, which is routinely tossed back and forth between sovereign empires as a consolation prize for greater losses, to be the continent's largest territory, Pavla's precise and wholly proportional mapmaking skills are discovered. The children enlist her to draw a detailed schematic of the male genitalia on a large sheet of paper. Selflessly, Petr Matejcek offers himself as a model. During the following day's recess, he and Pavla hide behind the outhouse that is still in use because the mayor does not consider the school, or the children, or education in general worthy of the expense of Václav's services. Without ceremony, Petr drops his trousers. She has never seen a penis before. It looks like a pale and very narrow and really quite useless section of piping.

"It moves if you kiss it," Petr says.

"By itself?"

"Try it."

Pavla leans forward and puts her lips to the skin that is as soft as the belly of a newborn pig and smells just as musky and tantalizingly complex. When she leans back, she watches in wonder as Petr's penis reddens and swells. For the first time, she witnesses something she has never thought possible—that a small, runty thing can magically transform.

"I stick it in things," Petr says, touching himself tenderly.

It makes perfect sense to Pavla who thinks of washers and fittings.

"You better draw it before it shrinks," he says.

The following day, when Kublov yanks the string and unfurls the map, there is Petr, or at least the truly marvelous part of him, drawn with a hand so deft that were this a lesson in anatomy, the children would know exactly the location of the dorsal vein and they would be able to count the folds of the scrotal sac. The ensuing geography lesson is a huge success. Petr is particularly proud, and even though the children agreed to protect his anonymity, he cannot help but boast of his contribution. He is suspended from school for a month. Pavla and the others lean over their desks, pants and stockings lowered and dresses hiked, their naked bottoms pink and proud, Pavla's no less for being lower to the ground, and wait for the stinging crack of Kublov's walking stick.

They still call her Little Nothing, but the name is now a sign of inclusion, no more incendiary than Toes, which is what they call Tabor Svoboda on account of his ability to write with his feet. These nicknames mark them as a group separate from parents and teachers and Father Matyáš, whose aim it is to separate children from their delights. Pavla revels in her name because she knows that if nothing is little, then it must be something indeed.

You've just read an excerpt from Little Nothing.

ABOUT THE AUTHOR

Marisa Silver is the author of the novel *Mary Coin*, a *New York Times* bestseller. She is also the author of *The God of War* (a *Los Angeles Times* Book Prize finalist), *No Direction Home*, and two story collections, *Alone With You* and *Babe in Paradise* (a *New York Times* Notable Book and *Los Angeles Times* Best Book of the Year). Her first short story appeared in *The New Yorker* when she was featured in the magazine's first "Debut Fiction" issue. Winner of the O. Henry Prize, Silver's fiction has been included in *The Best American Short Stories*, *The O. Henry Prize Stories*, and other anthologies. She lives in Los Angeles.

IMPRINT: Blue Rider Press
PRINT ISBN: 9780399167928
PRINT PRICE: $27.00
EBOOK ISBN: 9780698146808
EBOOK PRICE: $13.99
PUBLICATION DATE: 9/13/16
PUBLICITY CONTACT: Aileen Boyle aboyle@penguinrandomhouse.com
EDITOR: Sarah Hochman
AGENT: Henry Dunow
AGENCY: Dunow, Carlson & Lerner Agency

PROMOTIONAL INFORMATION:
Targeted outreach to book clubs; Early reads programs; Major online promotion campaign; Reading group guide.

A GENTLEMAN IN MOSCOW

AMOR TOWLES

SUMMARY

From the *New York Times* bestselling author of *Rules of Civility*—a transporting novel about a man who is ordered to spend the rest of his life inside a luxury hotel. With his breakout debut novel, *Rules of Civility*, Amor Towles established himself as a master of absorbing, sophisticated fiction, bringing late 1930s Manhattan to life with splendid atmosphere and a flawless command of style. Readers and critics were enchanted; as NPR commented, "Towles writes with grace and verve about the mores and manners of a society on the cusp of radical change." *A Gentleman in Moscow* immerses us in another elegantly drawn era with the story of Count Alexander Rostov. When, in 1922, he is deemed an unrepentant aristocrat by a Bolshevik tribunal, the count is sentenced to house arrest in the Metropol, a grand hotel across the street from the Kremlin. Rostov, an indomitable man of erudition and wit, has never worked a day in his life, and must now live in an attic room while some of the most tumultuous decades in Russian history are unfolding outside the hotel's doors. Unexpectedly, his reduced circumstances provide him a doorway into a much larger world of emotional discovery. Brimming with humor, a glittering cast of characters, and one beautifully rendered scene after another, this singular novel casts a spell as it relates the count's endeavor to gain a deeper understanding of what it means to be a man of purpose.

EXCERPT

1922

The Ambassador

At half past six on the twenty-first of June 1922, when Count Alexander Ilyich Rostov was escorted through the gates of the Kremlin onto Red Square, it was glorious and cool. Drawing his shoulders back without breaking stride, the Count inhaled the air like one fresh from a swim. The sky was the very blue that the cupolas of St. Basil's had been painted for. Their pinks, greens, and golds shimmered as if it were the sole purpose of a religion to cheer its Divinity. Even the Bolshevik girls conversing before the windows of the State Department Store seemed dressed to celebrate the last days of spring.

"Hello, my good man," the Count called to Fyodor, at the edge of the square. "I see the blackberries have come in early this year!"

Giving the startled fruit seller no time to reply, the Count walked briskly on, his waxed moustaches spread like the wings of a gull. Passing through Resurrection Gate, he turned his back on the lilacs of the Alexander Gardens and proceeded toward Theatre Square, where the Hotel Metropol stood in all its glory. When he reached its threshold, the Count gave a wink to Pavel, the afternoon doorman, and turned with a hand outstretched to the two soldiers trailing behind him.

"Thank you, gentlemen, for delivering me safely. I shall no longer be in need of your assistance."

Though strapping lads, both of the soldiers had to look up from under their caps to return the Count's gaze—for like ten generations of Rostov men, the Count stood an easy six foot three.

"On you go," said the more thuggish of the two, his hand on the butt of his rifle. "We're to see you to your rooms."

In the lobby, the Count gave a wide wave with which to simultaneously greet the unflappable Arkady (who was manning the front desk) and sweet Valentina (who was dusting a statuette). Though the Count had greeted them in this manner a hundred times before, both responded with a wide-eyed stare. It was the sort of reception one might have expected when arriving for a dinner party having forgotten to don one's pants.

Passing the young girl with the penchant for yellow who was reading a magazine in her favorite lobby chair, the Count came to an abrupt stop before the potted palms in order to address his escort.

"The lift or the stairs, gentlemen?"

The soldiers looked from one another to the Count and back again, apparently unable to make up their minds. *How is a soldier expected to prevail on the field of battle*, the Count wondered, *if he cannot be decisive about ascending to an upper floor?*

"The stairs," he determined on their behalf, then vaulted the steps two at a time, as had been his habit since the academy.

On the third floor, the Count walked down the red-carpeted hallway toward his suite—an interconnected bedroom, bath, dining room, and grand salon with eight-foot windows overlooking the lindens of Theatre Square. And there the rudeness of the day awaited. For before the flung-open doors of his rooms stood a captain of the guards with Pasha and Petya, the hotel's bellhops. The two young men met the Count's gaze with looks of embarrassment, having clearly been conscripted into some duty they found distasteful. The Count addressed the officer.

"What is the meaning of this, captain?"

The captain, who seemed mildly surprised by the question, had the good training to maintain the evenness of his affect.

"I am here to show you to your quarters."

"These *are* my quarters."

Betraying the slightest suggestion of a smile, the captain said, "No longer, I'm afraid."

Leaving Pasha and Petya behind, the captain led the Count and his escort to a utility stair hidden behind an inconspicuous door in the core of the hotel. The ill-lit ascent turned a sharp corner every five steps in the manner of a belfry. Up they wound three flights to where a door opened on a narrow corridor servicing a bathroom and six bedrooms reminiscent of monastic cells. This attic was originally built to house the butlers and ladies' maids of the Metropol's guests; but when the practice of traveling with servants fell out of fashion, the unused rooms had been claimed by the caprices of casual urgency—thenceforth warehousing scraps of lumber, broken furniture, and other assorted debris.

Earlier that day, the room closest to the stairwell had been cleared of all but a cast-iron bed, a three-legged bureau, and a decade of dust. In the corner near the door was a small closet, rather like a telephone box, that had been dropped in the room as an afterthought. Reflecting the pitch of the roof, the ceiling sloped at a gradual incline as it moved away from the door, such that at the room's outer wall the only place where the Count could stand to his full height was where a dormer accommodated a window the size of a chessboard.

As the two guards looked on smugly from the hall, the good captain explained that he had summoned the bellhops to help the Count move what few belongings his new quarters would accommodate.

"And the rest?"

"Becomes the property of the People."

So this is their game, thought the Count.

"Very well."

Back down the belfry he skipped as the guards hurried behind him, their rifles clacking against the wall. On the third floor, he marched along the hallway and into his suite where the two bellhops looked up with woeful expressions.

"It's all right, fellows," the Count assured and then began pointing: "This. That. Those. *All* the books."

Among the furnishings destined for his new quarters, the Count chose two high-back chairs, his grandmother's oriental coffee table, and a favorite set of her porcelain plates. He chose the two table lamps fashioned from ebony elephants and the portrait of his sister, Helena, which Serov had painted during a brief stay at Idlehour in 1908. He did not forget the leather case that had been fashioned especially for him by Asprey in London and which his good friend Mishka had so appropriately christened the Ambassador.

Someone had shown the courtesy of having one of the Count's traveling trunks brought to his bedroom. So, as the bellhops carried the aforementioned upward, the Count filled the trunk with clothes and personal effects. Noting that the guards were eyeing the two bottles of brandy on the console, the Count tossed them in as well. And once the trunk had been carried upstairs, he finally pointed to the desk.

The two bellhops, their bright blue uniforms already smudged from their efforts, took hold of it by the corners.

"But it weighs a ton," said one to the other.

"A king fortifies himself with a castle," observed the Count, "a gentleman with a desk."

As the bellhops lugged it into the hall, the Rostovs' grandfather clock, which was fated to be left behind, tolled a doleful eight. The captain had long since returned to his post and the guards, having swapped their belligerence for boredom, now leaned against the walls and let the ashes from their cigarettes fall on the parquet floor while into the grand salon poured the undiminished light of the Moscow summer solstice.

With a wistful eye, the Count approached the windows at the suite's northwest corner. How many hours had he spent before them? How many mornings dressed in his robe with his coffee in hand had he observed the new arrivals from St. Petersburg disembarking from their cabs, worn and weary from the overnight train? On how many winter eves had he watched the snow slowly descending as some lone silhouette passed under a street lamp? At that very instant, at the square's northern extreme a young Red Army officer rushed up the steps of the Bolshoi, having missed the first half hour of the evening's performance.

The Count smiled to remember his own youthful preference for arriving *entr'acte*. Having insisted at the English Club that he could only stay for one more drink, he stayed for three. Then leaping into the waiting carriage, he'd flash across the city, vault the fabled steps, and like this young fellow slip through the golden doors. As the ballerinas danced gracefully across the stage, the Count would be whispering his *excusez-moi*'s, making his way to his usual seat in the twentieth row with its privileged view of the ladies in the loges.

Arriving late, thought the Count with a sigh. What a delicacy of youth.

Then he turned on his heels and began to walk his rooms. First, he admired the salon's grand dimensions and its two chandeliers. He admired the painted panels of the little dining room and the elaborate brass mechanics that allowed one to secure the double doors of the bedroom. In short, he reviewed the interior much as would a potential buyer who was seeing the rooms for the very first time. Once in the bedroom, the Count paused before the marble-topped table on which lay an assortment of curios. From among them, he picked up a pair of scissors that had been prized by his sister. Fashioned in the shape of an egret with the long silver blades representing the bird's beak and the small golden screw at the pivot representing its eye, the scissors were so delicate he could barely fit his thumb and finger through the rings.

Looking from one end of the apartment to the other, the Count took a quick inventory of all that would be left behind. What personal possessions, furnishings, and *objets d'art* he had brought to this suite four years before were already the product of a great winnowing. For when word had reached the Count of the Tsar's execution, he had set out from Paris at once. Over twenty days, he had made his way across six nations and skirted eight battalions fighting under five different flags, finally arriving at Idlehour on the seventh of August 1918, with nothing but a rucksack on his back. Though he found the countryside on the verge of upheaval and the household in a state of distress, his grandmother, the Countess, was characteristically composed.

"Sasha," she said without rising from her chair, "how good of you to come. You must be famished. Join me for tea."

When he explained the necessity of her leaving the country and described the arrangements he had made for her passage, the Countess understood that there was no alternative. She understood that although every servant in her employ was ready to accompany her, she must travel with two. She also understood why her grandson and only heir, whom she had raised from the age of ten, would not be coming with her.

When the Count was just seven, he was defeated so soundly by a neighboring boy in a game of draughts that, apparently, a tear was shed, a curse was uttered, and the game pieces were scattered across the floor. This lack of sportsmanship led to a stiff reprimand from the Count's father and a trip to bed without supper. But as the young Count was gripping his blanket in misery, he was visited by his grandmother. Taking a seat at the foot of the bed, the Countess expressed a measure of sympathy: "There is nothing pleasant to be said about losing," she began, "and the Obolensky boy is a pill. But Sasha, my dear, why on earth would you give him the satisfaction?" It was in this spirit that he and his grandmother parted without tears on the docks in Peterhof. Then the Count returned to the family estate in order to administer its shuttering.

In quick succession came the sweeping of chimneys, the clearing of pantries, and the shrouding of furniture. It was just as if the family were returning to St. Petersburg for the season, except that the dogs were released from their kennels, the horses from their stables, and the servants from their duties. Then, having filled a single wagon with some of the finest of the Rostovs' furniture, the Count bolted the doors and set out for Moscow.

'Tis a funny thing, reflected the Count as he stood ready to abandon his suite. From the earliest age, we must learn to say good-bye to friends and family. We see our parents and siblings off at the station; we visit cousins, attend schools, join the regiment; we marry, or travel abroad. It is part of the human experience that we are constantly gripping a good fellow by the shoulders and wishing him well, taking comfort from the notion that we will hear word of him soon enough.

But experience is less likely to teach us how to bid our dearest possessions *adieu*. And if it were to? We wouldn't welcome the education. For eventually, we come to hold our dearest possessions more closely than we hold our friends. We carry them from place to place, often at considerable expense and inconvenience; we dust and polish their surfaces and reprimand children for playing too roughly in their vicinity—all the while, allowing memories to invest them with greater and greater importance. This armoire, we are prone to recall, is the very one in which we hid as a boy; and it was these silver candelabra that lined our table on Christmas Eve; and it was with this handkerchief that she once dried her tears, et cetera, et cetera. Until we imagine that these carefully preserved possessions might give us genuine solace in the face of a lost companion.

But, of course, a thing is just a thing.

And so, slipping his sister's scissors into his pocket, the Count looked once more at what heirlooms remained and then expunged them from his heartache forever.

You've just read an excerpt from A Gentleman in Moscow.

ABOUT THE AUTHOR

Amor Towles was born and raised in the Boston area. He graduated from Yale University and received an MA in English from Stanford University. An investment professional for more than twenty years, he now devotes himself full time to writing. His first novel, *Rules of Civility*, published in 2011, was a *New York Times* bestseller in both hardcover and paperback. Towles lives in Manhattan with his wife and two children. Connect with Amor Towles online at AmorTowles.com, and on Facebook and Twitter @AmorTowles.

IMPRINT: Viking Books
PRINT ISBN: 9780670026197
PRINT PRICE: $27.00
EBOOK ISBN: 9780399564048
EBOOK PRICE: $13.99
PUBLICATION DATE: 9/6/16
PUBLICITY CONTACT: Meredith Burks mburks@penguinrandomhouse.com
RIGHTS CONTACT: Tracy Fisher tf@wmeentertainment.com
EDITOR: Paul Slovak
AGENT: Dorian Karchmar
AGENCY: William Morris Endeavor

TERRITORIES SOLD:
UK and British Commonwealth (Hutchinson)
Holland (A.W. Bruna/ Arbeiderspers)
Germany (Ullstein)
Poland (Znak)

PROMOTIONAL INFORMATION:
12-city author tour; Print and online reviews and features; Fiction media attention; NPR interviews; Radio satellite tour; Major advertising campaign; Book club promotion; Social media and online promotion; Academic marketing and library promotions.

PART TWO: DEBUT FICTION

THE MOTHERS

BRIT BENNETT

SUMMARY

A dazzling debut novel from an exciting new voice, *The Mothers* is a surprising story about young love, a big secret in a small community—and the things that ultimately haunt us most. Set within a contemporary black community in Southern California, Brit Bennett's mesmerizing first novel is an emotionally perceptive story about community, love, and ambition. It begins with a secret. "All good secrets have a taste before you tell them, and if we'd taken a moment to swish this one around our mouths, we might have noticed the sourness of an unripe secret, plucked too soon, stolen and passed around before its season." It is the last season of high school life for Nadia Turner, a rebellious, grief-stricken, seventeen-year-old beauty. Mourning her own mother's recent suicide, she takes up with the local pastor's son. Luke Sheppard is twenty-one, a former football star whose injury has reduced him to waiting tables at a diner. They are young; it's not serious. But the pregnancy that results from this teen romance—and the subsequent cover-up—will have an impact that goes far beyond their youth. As Nadia hides her secret from everyone, including Aubrey, her God-fearing best friend, the years move quickly. Soon, Nadia, Luke, and Aubrey are full-fledged adults and still living in debt to the choices they made that one seaside summer, caught in a love triangle they must carefully maneuver, and dogged by the constant, nagging question: What if they had chosen differently? The possibilities of the road not taken are a relentless haunt. In entrancing, lyrical prose, *The Mothers* asks whether a "what if" can be more powerful than an experience itself. If, as time passes, we must always live in servitude to the decisions of our younger selves, to the communities that have parented us, and to the decisions we make that shape our lives forever.

EXCERPT

Chapter One

We didn't believe when we first heard because you know how church folk can gossip.

Like the time we all thought First John, our head usher, was messing around on his wife because Betty, the pastor's secretary, caught him cozying up at brunch with another woman. A young, fashionable woman at that, one who switched her hips when she walked even though she had no business switching anything in front of a man married forty years. You could forgive a man for stepping out on his wife once, but to romance that young woman over buttered croissants at a sidewalk café? Now that was a whole other thing. But before we could correct First John, he showed up at Upper Room Chapel that Sunday with his wife and the young, hip-switching woman—a great-niece visiting from Fort Worth—and that was that.

When we first heard, we thought it might be that type of secret, although, we have to admit, it had felt different. Tasted different, too. All good secrets have a taste before you tell them, and if we'd taken a moment to swish this one around our mouths, we might have noticed the sourness of an unripe secret, plucked too soon, stolen and passed around before its season. But we didn't. We shared this sour secret, a secret that began the summer Nadia Turner got knocked up by the pastor's son and went to the abortion clinic downtown to take care of it.

She was seventeen then. She lived with her father, a Marine, and without her mother, who had killed herself six months earlier. Since then, the girl had earned a wild reputation—she was young and scared and trying to hide her scared in her prettiness. And she was pretty, beautiful even, with amber skin, silky long hair, and eyes swirled brown and gray and gold. Like most girls, she'd already learned that pretty exposes you and pretty hides you and like most girls, she hadn't yet learned how to navigate the difference. So we heard all about her sojourns across the border to dance clubs in Tijuana, the water bottle she carried around Oceanside High filled with vodka, the Saturdays she spent on base playing pool with Marines, nights that ended with her heels pressed against some man's foggy window. Just tales, maybe, except for one we now know is true: she spent her senior year of high school rolling around in bed with Luke Sheppard and come springtime, his baby was growing inside her.

Luke Sheppard waited tables at Fat Charlie's Seafood Shack, a restaurant off the pier known for its fresh food, live music, and family-friendly atmosphere. At least that's what the ad in the *San Diego Union-Tribune* said, if you were fool enough to believe it. If you'd been around Oceanside long enough, you'd know that the promised fresh food was day-old fish and chips stewing under heat lamps, and the live music, when delivered, usually consisted of ragtag teenagers in ripped jeans with safety pins poking through their lips. Nadia Turner also knew things about Fat Charlie's that didn't fit on a newspaper ad, like the fact that a platter of Charlie's Cheesy Nachos was the perfect drunk snack or that the head cook sold the best weed north of the border. She knew that inside, yellow life preservers hung above the bar and kelp, dark and crispy, dripped from the ceiling, so after long shifts, the three black waiters called it a slave ship. She knew secret things about Fat Charlie's because Luke had told her.

"What about the fish sticks?" she would ask.

"Soggy as shit."

"The seafood pasta?"

"Don't fuck with that."

"What could be so bad about pasta?"

"You know how they make that shit? Take some fish that's been sitting around and stuff it in ravioli."

"Fine, the bread then."

"If you don't finish your bread, we just give it to another table. You about to touch the same bread as some dude that's been digging in his nuts all day."

The winter her mother killed herself, Luke saved Nadia from ordering the crab bites. (Imitation crab deep-fried in lard.) She'd begun disappearing after school, riding buses and hopping off wherever they took her. Sometimes she rode east to Camp Pendleton, where she watched a movie or bowled at Stars and Strikes or played pool with Marines. The young ones were the loneliest, so she always found a pack of privates, awkward with their shorn heads and big boots, and by the end of the night, she usually ended up kissing one of them until kissing made her feel like crying. Other days she rode north, past Upper Room Chapel, where the coast became frontier. South, and she hit more beach, better beaches, beaches with sand as white as the people who lay on it, beaches with boardwalks and roller coasters, beaches behind gates. She couldn't ride west. West was the ocean.

She rode buses away from her old life, where after school, she'd lingered with her friends in the parking lot before driver's ed or climbed the bleachers to watch the football team practice or caravanned to In-N-Out. She'd goofed around at Jojo's Juicery with her coworkers and danced at bonfires and climbed the jetty when dared because she always pretended to be unafraid. She was startled by how rarely she had been alone back then. Her days felt like being handed from person to person like a baton, her calculus teacher passing her to her Spanish teacher to her chemistry teacher to her friends and back home to her parents. Then one day, her mother's hand was gone and she'd fallen, clattering to the floor.

She couldn't stand to be around anyone now—her teachers, who excused her late work with patient smiles; her friends, who stopped joking when she sat down at lunch, as if their happiness were offensive to her. In AP Government, when Mr. Thomas assigned partner work, her friends quickly paired off with each other, and she was left to work with the other quiet, friendless girl in the class: Aubrey Evans, who skirted off to Christian Club meetings at lunch, not to pad her college resume (she hadn't raised her hand when Mr. Thomas asked who had turned in applications) but because she thought God cared if she spent her free period inside a classroom planning canned food drives. Aubrey Evans, who wore a plain gold purity ring that she twisted around her finger when she talked, who always attended service at Upper Room by herself, probably the poor holy child of devout atheists who was working hard to lead them into the light. After their first time working together, Aubrey had leaned closer to her, dropping her voice.

"I just wanted to say I'm sorry," she said. "We've all been praying for you."

She seemed sincere, but what did that matter? Nadia hadn't been to church since her mother's funeral. Instead, she rode buses. One afternoon, she climbed off downtown in front of the Hanky Panky. She was certain someone would stop her—she even looked like a kid with her backpack—but the bouncer perched on a stool near the door barely glanced up from his phone when she ducked inside. At three on a Tuesday, the strip club was dead, empty silver tables dulled under the stage lights. Black shades pulled in front of the windows blocked the plastic sunlight; in the man-made darkness, fat white men with baseball caps pulled low slouched in chairs facing the stage. Under the spotlight, a flabby white girl danced, her breasts swinging like pendulums.

In the darkness of the club, you could be alone with your grief. Her father had flung himself into Upper Room. He went to both services on Sunday mornings, to Wednesday night Bible study, to Thursday night choir practice although he did not sing, although practices were closed but nobody had the heart to turn him away. Her father propped his sadness on a pew, but she put her sad in places no one could see. The bartender shrugged at her fake ID and mixed her a drink and she sat in dark corners, sipping rum-and-Cokes and watching women with beat bodies spin onstage. Never the skinny, young girls—the club saved them for weekends or nights—just older women thinking about grocery lists and child care, their bodies stretched and pitted from age. Her mother would've been horrified at the thought—her in a strip club, in the light of day—but Nadia stayed, sipping the watery drinks slowly. Her third time in the club, an old black man pulled up a chair beside her. He wore a red plaid shirt under suspenders, gray tufts peeking out from under his Pacific Coast Bait & Tackle cap.

"What you drinkin'?" he asked.

"What're *you* drinking?" she said.

He laughed. "Naw. This a grown man drink. Not for a little thing like you. I'll get you somethin' sweet. You like that, honey? You look like you got a sweet tooth."

He smiled and slid a hand onto her thigh. His fingernails curled dark and long against her jeans. Before she could move, a black woman in her forties wearing a glittery magenta bra and thong appeared at the table. Light brown streaked across her stomach like tiger stripes.

"You leave her be, Lester," the woman said. Then to Nadia. "Come on, I'll freshen you up."

"Aw, Cici, I was just talkin' to her," the old man said.

"Please," Cici said. "That child ain't even as old as your watch."

She led Nadia back to the bar and tossed what was left of her drink down the drain. Then she slipped into a white coat and beckoned for Nadia to follow her outside. Against the slate gray sky, the flat outline of the Hanky Panky seemed even more depressing. Further along the building, two white girls were smoking and they each threw up a hand when Cici and Nadia stepped outside. Cici returned the lazy greeting and lit a cigarette.

"You got a nice face," Cici said. "Those your real eyes? You mixed?"

"No," she said. "I mean, they're my eyes but I'm not mixed."

"Look mixed to me." Cici blew a sideways stream of smoke. "You a runaway? Oh, don't look at me like that. I won't report you. I see you girls come through here all the time, looking to make a little money. Ain't legal but Bernie don't mind. Bernie'll give you a little stage time, see what you can do. Don't expect no warm welcome though. Hard enough fighting those blonde bitches for tips—wait till the girls see your light-bright ass."

"I don't want to dance," Nadia said.

"Well, I don't know what you're looking for but you ain't gonna find it here." Cici leaned in closer. "You know you got see-through eyes? Feels like I can see right through them. Nothin' but sad on the other side." She dug into her pocket and pulled out a handful of crumpled ones. "This ain't no place for you. Go on down to Fat Charlie's and get you something to eat. Go on."

Nadia hesitated, but Cici dropped the bills into Nadia's palm and curled her fingers into a fist. Maybe she could do this, pretend she was a runaway, or maybe in a way, she was. Her father never asked where she'd been. She returned home at night and found him in his recliner, watching television in a darkened living room. He always looked surprised when she unlocked the front door, like he hadn't even noticed that she'd been gone.

In Fat Charlie's, Nadia had been sitting in the booth toward the back, flipping through a menu, when Luke Sheppard stepped out of the kitchen, white apron slung across his hips, black Fat Charlie's T-shirt stretched across his muscular chest. He looked as handsome as she'd remembered from Sunday School, except he was a man now, bronzed and broad-shouldered, his hard jaw covered in stubble. And he was limping now, slightly favoring his left leg, but the gimpiness of his walk, its uneven pace and tenderness, only made her want him more. Her mother had died a month ago and she was drawn to anyone who wore their pain outwardly, the way she couldn't. She hadn't even cried at the funeral. At the repast, a parade of guests had told her how well she'd done and her father placed an arm around her shoulder. He'd hunched over the pew during the service, his shoulders quietly shaking, manly crying but crying still, and for the first time, she'd wondered if she might be stronger than him.

An inside hurt was supposed to stay inside. How strange it must be to hurt in an outside way you couldn't hide. She played with the menu flap as Luke limped his way over to her booth. She, and everyone at Upper Room, had watched his promising junior season end last fall. A routine kick return, a bad tackle, and his leg broke, the bone cutting clear through the skin. The commentators had said he'd be lucky if he walked normal again, let alone played another down, so no one had been surprised when San Diego State pulled his scholarship. But she hadn't seen Luke since he'd gotten out of the hospital. In her mind, he was still in a cot, surrounded by doting nurses, his bandaged leg propped toward the ceiling.

"What're you doing here?" she asked.

"I work here," he said, then laughed, but his laugh sounded hard, like a chair suddenly scraped against the floor. "How you been?"

He didn't look at her, shuffling through his notepad, so she knew he'd heard about her mother.

"I'm hungry," she said.

"That's how you been? Hungry?"

"Can I get the crab bites?"

"You better not." He guided her finger down the laminated menu to the nachos. "There. Try that."

His hand curved soft over hers like he was teaching her to read, moving her finger under unfamiliar words. He always made her feel impossibly young, like two days later, when she returned to his section and tried to order a margarita. He laughed, tilting her fake ID toward him.

"Come on," he said. "Aren't you, like, twelve?"

She narrowed her eyes. "Oh fuck you," she said, "I'm seventeen."

But she'd said it a little too proudly and Luke laughed again. Even eighteen—which she wouldn't turn until late August—would seem young to him. She was still in high school. He was twenty-one and had already gone to college, a real university, not the community college where everyone loafed around a few months after graduation before finding jobs. She had applied to five universities and while she waited to hear back, she asked Luke questions about college life, like were dorm showers as gross as she imagined or did people actually stick socks on door handles when they wanted privacy? He told her about undie runs and foam parties, how to maximize your meal plan, how to get extra time on tests by pretending you had a learning problem. He knew things and he knew girls, college girls, girls who wore high heels to class, not sneakers, and carried satchels instead of backpacks, and spent their summers interning at Qualcomm or California Bank & Trust, not making juice at the pier. She imagined herself in college, one of those sophisticated girls, Luke driving to see her, or if she went out of state, flying to visit her over spring break. He would laugh if he knew how she imagined him in her life. He teased her often, like when she began doing her homework in Fat Charlie's.

"Shit," he said, flipping through her calculus book. "You a nerd."

She wasn't, really, but learning came easily to her. (Her mother used to tease her about that—must be nice, she'd say, when Nadia brought home an aced test she only studied for the night before.) She thought her advanced classes might scare Luke off, but he liked that she was smart. See this girl right here, he'd tell a passing waiter, first black lady president, just watch. Every black girl who was even slightly gifted was told this. But she liked listening to Luke brag and she liked it even more when he teased her for studying. He didn't treat her like everyone at school, who either sidestepped her or spoke to her like she was some fragile thing one harsh word away from breaking.

One February night, Luke drove her home and she invited him inside. Her father was gone for the weekend at the Men's Advance, so the house was dark and silent when they arrived. She wanted to offer Luke a drink—that's what women did in the movies, handed a man a boxy glass, filled with something dark and masculine—but moonlight glinted off glass cabinets emptied of liquor and Luke pressed her against the wall and kissed her. She hadn't told him it was her first time but he knew. In her bed, he asked three times if she wanted to stop. Each time she told him no. Sex would hurt and she wanted it to. She wanted Luke to be her outside hurt.

By spring, she knew what time Luke got off work, when to meet him in the deserted corner of the parking lot, where two people could be alone. She knew which nights he had off, nights she listened for his car crawling up her street and tiptoed past her father's shut bedroom. She knew the days he went to work late, days she slipped him inside the house before her father came home from work. How Luke wore his Fat Charlie's T-shirt a size too small because it helped him earn more tips. How when he dropped to the edge of her bed without saying much, he was dreading a long shift so she didn't say much either, tugging his too-tight shirt over his head and running her hands over the expanse of his shoulders. She knew that being on his feet all day hurt his leg more than he ever admitted and sometimes, while he slept, she stared at the thin scar climbing toward his knee. Bones, like anything else, strong until they weren't.

She also knew that Fat Charlie's was dead between lunch and happy hour, so after her pregnancy test returned positive, she rode the bus over to tell Luke.

"Fuck" was the first thing he said.

Then, "Are you sure?"

Then, "But are you *sure* sure?"

Then, "Fuck."

In the empty Fat Charlie's, Nadia drowned her fries in a pool of ketchup until they were limp and soggy. Of course she was sure. She wouldn't have worried him if she weren't already sure. For days, she'd willed herself to bleed, begging for a drop, a trickle even, but instead, she stared at the perfect whiteness of her panties. So that morning, she rode the bus to the free pregnancy center outside of town, a squat gray building in the middle of a strip mall. In the lobby, a row of fake plants nearly blocked the receptionist, who pointed Nadia to the waiting area. She joined a handful of black girls who barely glanced up at her as she sat between a chubby girl popping purple gum and a girl in overall shorts who played Tetris on her phone. A fat white counselor named Dolores led Nadia to the back, where they squeezed inside a cubicle so cramped, their knees touched.

"Now, do you have a reason to think you might be pregnant?" Dolores asked.

She wore a lumpy gray sweater covered in cotton sheep and spoke like a kindergarten teacher, smiling, her sentences ending in a gentle lilt. She must've thought Nadia was an idiot—another black girl too dumb to insist on a condom. But they had used condoms, at least most times, and Nadia felt stupid for how comfortable she had felt with their mostly safe sex. She was supposed to be the smart one. She was supposed to understand that it only took one mistake and her future could be ripped away from her. She had known pregnant girls. She had seen them waddling around school in tight tank tops and sweatshirts that hugged their bellies. She never saw the boys who had gotten them that way—their names were enshrouded in mystery, as wispy as rumor itself—but she could never unsee the girls, big and blooming in front of her. Of all people, she should have known better. She was her mother's mistake.

Across the booth, Luke hunched over the table, flexing his fingers like he used to when he was on the sidelines at a game. Her freshman year, she'd spent more time watching Luke than watching the team on the field. What would those hands feel like touching her?

"I thought you were hungry," he said.

She tossed another fry onto the pile. She hadn't eaten anything all day—her mouth felt salty, the way it did before she puked. She slipped out of her flip-flops, resting her bare feet against his thigh.

"I feel like shit," she said.

"Want something different?"

"I don't know."

He pushed away from the table. "Let me get you something else—"

"I can't keep it," she said.

Luke stopped, halfway out his seat.

"What?" he said.

"I can't keep a baby," she said. "I can't be someone's fucking mother, I'm going to college and my dad is gonna—"

She couldn't bring herself to say out loud what she wanted—the word *abortion* felt ugly and mechanic—but Luke understood, didn't he? He'd been the first person she told when she'd received her acceptance e-mail from the University of Michigan—he'd swept her into a hug before she even finished her sentence, nearly crushing her in his arms. He had to understand that she couldn't pass this up, her one chance to leave home, to leave her silent father whose smile hadn't even reached his eyes when she showed him the e-mail, but who she knew would be happier with her gone, without her there to remind him of what he'd lost. She couldn't let this baby nail her life in place when she'd just been given a chance to escape.

If Luke understood, he didn't say so. He didn't say anything at first, sinking back into the booth, his body suddenly slow and heavy. In that moment, he looked even older to her, his stubbled face tired and haggard. He reached for her bare feet and cradled them in his lap.

"Okay," he said, then softer, "okay. Tell me what to do."

He didn't try to change her mind. She appreciated that, although part of her had hoped he might do something old-fashioned and romantic, like offer to marry her. She never would've agreed but it would've been nice if he'd tried. Instead, he asked how much money she needed. She felt stupid—she hadn't even thought of something as practical as paying for the surgery—but he promised he'd come up with the cash. When he handed her the envelope the next day, she asked him not to wait with her at the clinic. He rubbed the back of her neck.

"Are you sure?" he said.

"Yes," she said. "Just pick me up after."

She'd feel worse if she had an audience. Vulnerable. Luke had seen her naked—he had slipped inside her own body—but somehow, his seeing her afraid was an intimacy she could not bear.

The morning of her appointment, Nadia rode the bus to the abortion clinic downtown. She had driven past it dozens of times—an unremarkable tan building, slunk in the shadows of a Bank of America—but she had never imagined what it might look like inside. She stared out the window as the bus wound its way toward the beach, envisioning sterile white walls, sharp tools on trays, fat receptionists in baggy sweaters herding crying girls into waiting rooms. Instead, the lobby was open and bright, the walls painted a creamy color that had some fancy name like *taupe* or *ochre*, and on the oak tables, beside stacks of magazines, there were blue vases filled with seashells. In a chair farthest from the door, Nadia pretended to read a *National Geographic*. Next to her, a redhead mumbled as she struggled with a crossword puzzle; her boyfriend slumped beside her, staring at the dark insides of his sunglasses. He was the only man in the room so maybe the redhead felt superior—more loved—since her boyfriend had joined her, even though he didn't seem like a good boyfriend, even though he wasn't even talking to her or holding her hand, like Luke would have done. Across the room, a black girl in a clingy yellow dress sniffled into her jean jacket sleeve. Her mother, a heavy woman with a purple rose tattooed on her arm, sat beside her, arms folded across her chest. She looked angry or maybe just worried. The girl looked fourteen, broad-shouldered like a swimmer, and the louder she sniffled, the harder everyone tried not to look at her.

Nadia thought about texting Luke. I'm here. I'm okay. But he'd just started his shift and he was probably worried enough as it is. She flipped through the magazine slowly, her eyes gliding off the pages to the blonde receptionist smiling into her headset, the traffic outside, the blue vase of seashells beside her. Her mother had hated the actual beach—messy sand and cigarette butts everywhere—but she loved shells so whenever they went, she always spent the afternoon padding along the shore, bending to peel shells out of the damp sand.

"They calm me," she'd said once. She'd clutched Nadia on her lap and turned a shell carefully, flashing its shiny insides. In her hand, the shell had glimmered lavender and green.

"Turner?"

In the doorway, a black nurse with graying dreadlocks read her name off a metal clipboard. As Nadia gathered her purse, she felt the nurse give her a once-over, eyes drifting past her red blouse, skinny jeans, black pumps.

"Should've worn something more comfortable," the nurse said.

"I am comfortable," Nadia said. She felt thirteen again, standing in the vice-principal's office as he lectured her on the dress code.

"Sweatpants," the nurse said. "Someone should've told you that when you called."

"They did."

The nurse shook her head, starting back down the hall. She seemed weary, unlike the chipper white nurses squeaking down the hallways in pink scrubs and rubber shoes. Like she'd seen so much that nothing surprised her anymore, not even a girl with a sassy mouth wearing a silly outfit, a girl so alone, she couldn't find one person to sit with her in the waiting room. No, there was nothing special about a girl like this—not her good grades, not her prettiness. She was just another black girl who'd found herself in trouble and was finding her way out of it.

In the sonogram room, a technician asked Nadia if she wanted to see the screen. Optional, he said, but it gave some women closure. She told him no. She'd heard once about a sixteen-year-old girl from her high school who'd given birth and left her baby on the beach. The girl was arrested when she doubled back to tell a cop she'd seen a baby and he discovered that she was the mother. How could he tell, Nadia had always wondered. Maybe, in the floodlights of his patrol car, he'd spotted blood streaking the insides of her thighs or smelled fresh milk spotting her nipples. Or maybe it was something else entirely. The ginger way she'd handed the baby over, the carefulness in her eyes when he brushed sand off its downy hair. Maybe he saw, even as he backed away, the maternal love that stretched like a golden thread from her to the abandoned baby. Something had given the girl away, but Nadia wouldn't make the same mistake. Double back. She wouldn't hesitate and allow herself to love the baby or even know him.

"Just do it already," she said.

"What about multiples?" the technician asked, rolling toward her on his stool. "You know, twins, triplets . . ."

"Why would I want to know that?"

He shrugged. "Some women do."

She already knew too much about the baby, like the fact that it was a boy. It was too early to actually tell, but she felt his foreignness in her body, something that was her and wasn't her. A male presence. A boy child who would have Luke's thick curls and squinty-eyed smile. No, she couldn't think about that either. She couldn't allow herself to love the baby because of Luke. So when the technician swirled the sensor in the blue goo on her stomach, she turned her head away.

After a few moments, the technician stopped, pausing the sensor over her belly button.

"Huh," he said.

"What?" she said. "What happened?"

Maybe she wasn't actually pregnant. That could happen, couldn't it? Maybe the test had been wrong or maybe the baby had sensed he wasn't wanted. Maybe he had given up on his own. She couldn't help it—she turned toward the monitor. The screen filled with a wedge of grainy white light, and in the center, a black oval punctuated by a single white splotch.

"Your womb's a perfect sphere," the technician said.

"So? What does that mean?"

"I don't know," he said. "That you're a superhero, maybe."

He chuckled, swirling the sensor around the gel. She didn't know what she expected to see in the sonogram, the sloping of a forehead, maybe, the outline of a belly. Not this, white and bean-shaped and small enough to cover with her thumb. How could this tiny light be a life? How could something this small bring hers to an end?

When she returned to the waiting room, the girl in the yellow dress was sobbing. No one looked at her, not even the heavy woman, who was now sitting one seat over. Nadia had been wrong—this woman couldn't be the girl's mother. A mother would move toward a crying child, not away. Her mother would've held her and absorbed her tears into her own body. She would've rocked her and not let go until the nurse called her name again. But this woman reached over and pinched the crying girl's thigh.

"Cut all that out," she said. "You wanted to be grown? Well, now you grown."

The procedure only takes ten minutes, the dreadlocked nurse told her. Less than an episode of television.

In the chilly operating room, Nadia stared at the monitor that hung in front of her flashing pictures from beaches around the world. Overhead, speakers played a meditation CD—classical guitar over crashing waves—and she knew she was supposed to pretend she was lying on a tropical island, pressed against grains of white sand. But when the nurse fit the anesthesia mask on her face and told her to count to a hundred, she could only think about the girl abandoning her baby in the sand. Maybe the beach was a more natural place to leave a baby you couldn't care for. Nestle him in the sand and hope someone found him—an old couple on a midnight stroll, a patrol cop sweeping his flashlight over beer cases. But if they didn't, if no one stumbled upon him, he'd return to his first home, an ocean like the one inside of her. Water would break onto the shore, sweep him up in its arms, and rock him back to sleep.

When it was over, Luke never came for her.

An hour after she'd called him, she was the only girl still waiting in the recovery room, curled in an overstuffed pink recliner, clutching a heat pad against her cramping stomach. For an hour, she'd stared into the dimness of the room, unable to make out the faces of the others but imagining they looked as blank as hers. Maybe the girl in the yellow dress had cried into the arms of her recliner. Or maybe the redhead had just continued her crossword puzzle. Maybe she'd been through this before or maybe she already had children and couldn't take another. Was it easier if you already had a child, like politely declining seconds because you were already full?

Now the others were gone and she had pulled out her phone to call Luke a third time when the dreadlocked nurse dragged over a metal chair. She was carrying a paper plate of crackers and an apple juice box.

"Cramps'll be bad for a while," she said. "Just put some heat on 'em, they'll go away. You got a heat pad at home?"

"No."

"Just heat you up a towel. Works just as fine."

Nadia had hoped she might get a different nurse. She'd watched the others swish through the room to dote on their girls, offering smiles, squeezing hands. But the dreadlocked nurse just shook the plate at her.

"I'm not hungry," Nadia said.

"You need to eat. Can't let you go until you do."

Nadia sighed, taking a cracker. Where was Luke? She was tired of this nurse, with her wrinkled skin and steady eyes. She wanted to be in her own bed, wrapped in her comforter, her head on Luke's chest. He would make her soup and play movies on his laptop until she fell asleep. He would kiss her and tell her that she had been brave. The nurse uncrossed, then recrossed her legs.

"Heard from your friend yet?" she asked.

"Not yet, but he's coming," Nadia said.

"You got someone else to call?"

"I don't need someone else, he's coming."

"He's not coming, baby," the nurse said. "Do you have someone else to call?"

She glanced up, startled by the nurse's confidence that Luke would not show, but even more jolted by her use of the word *baby*. A cotton soft *baby* that seemed to surprise the nurse herself, like it had tripped off her tongue. Just like how after the surgery, in her delirium, Nadia had looked into the nurse's blurred face and said "Mommy?" with such sweetness, the nurse had almost answered yes.

You've just read an excerpt from The Mothers.

ABOUT THE AUTHOR

Born and raised in Southern California, Brit Bennett graduated from Stanford University and later earned her MFA in fiction at the University of Michigan, where she won a Hopwood Award in Graduate Short Fiction as well as the 2014 Hurston/Wright Award for College Writers. Her work is featured in *The New Yorker*, *The New York Times Magazine*, *The Paris Review*, and *Jezebel*. Connect with Brit Bennett online at Brit-Bennett.tumblr.com, and on Twitter @britrbennett.

IMPRINT: Riverhead Books

PRINT ISBN: 9780399184512

PRINT PRICE: $27.00

EBOOK ISBN: 9780399184536

EBOOK PRICE: $13.99

PUBLICATION DATE: 10/11/16

PUBLICITY CONTACT: Liz Hohenadel lehohenadel@penguinrandomhouse.com

RIGHTS CONTACT: Danya Kukafka dkukafka@penguinrandomhouse.com

EDITOR: Sarah McGrath

AGENT: Julia Kardon

AGENCY: Mary Evans, Inc.

PROMOTIONAL INFORMATION:
Author tour; National electronic media; National print campaign including reviews and features, and NPR interviews; Online advertising; Social media content; Academic marketing and library promotions.

THE WANGS VS. THE WORLD

A NOVEL

JADE CHANG

SUMMARY

A hilarious debut novel about a wealthy but fractured Chinese immigrant family that had it all, only to lose every last cent—and the road trip they take across America that binds them back together.

EXCERPT

Bel-Air, CA

Charles Wang was mad at America. Actually, Charles Wang was mad at history.

If the death-bent Japanese had never invaded China, if a million—a billion—misguided students and serfs had never idolized a balding academic who parroted Russian madmen and couldn't pay for his promises, then Charles wouldn't be standing here, staring out the window of his beloved Bel-Air home, holding an aspirin in his hand, waiting for those calculating assholes from the bank—the bank that had once gotten down on its Italianate-marble knees and kissed his ass—to come over and repossess his life.

Without history, he wouldn't be here at all.

He'd be there, living out his unseen birthright on his family's ancestral acres, a pampered prince in silk robes, writing naughty, brilliant poems, teasing servant girls, collecting tithes from his peasants, and making them thankful by leaving their tattered households with just enough grain to squeeze out more hungry babies.

Instead, the world that should have been his fell apart, and the great belly of Asia tumbled and roiled with a noxious foreign indigestion that spewed him out, bouncing him, hard, on the tropical joke of Taiwan and then, when he popped right back up, belching him all the way across the vast Pacific Ocean and smearing him onto this, this faceless green country full of grasping newcomers, right alongside his unclaimed countrymen: the poor, illiterate, ball-scratching half men from Canton and Fujian, whose highest dreams were a cook's apron and a back-alley, back-door fuck.

Oh, he shouldn't have been vulgar.

Charles Wang shouldn't even know about the things that happen on dirt-packed floors and under stained sheets. Centuries of illustrious ancestors, scholars and statesmen and gentlemen farmers all, had bred him for fragrant teas unfurling in fresh springwater, for calligraphy brushes of white wolf hair dipped in black deer-glue ink, for lighthearted games of chance played among true friends.

Not this. No, not this. Not for him bastardized Peking duck eaten next to a tableful of wannabe rappers and their short, chubby, colored-contact-wearing Filipino girlfriends at Mr. Chow. Not for him shoulder-to-shoulder art openings where he sweated through the collar of his paper-thin cashmere sweater and stared at some sawed-in-half animal floating in formaldehyde whose guts didn't even have the courtesy to leak; not for him white women who wore silver chopsticks in their hair and smiled at him for approval. Nothing, nothing in his long lineage had prepared him for the Western worship of the Dalai Lama and pop stars wearing jade prayer beads and everyone drinking goddamn boba chai.

He shouldn't be here at all. Never should have set a single unbound foot on the New World. There was no arguing it. History had started fucking Charles Wang, and America had finished the job.

America was the worst part of it because America, that fickle bitch, used to love Charles Wang.

She had given him this house, a beautiful Georgian estate once owned by a minor MGM starlet married to a studio lawyer who made his real money running guns for Mickey Cohen. At least that's what Charles told his guests whenever he toured them around the place, pointing out the hidden crawl space in the wine cellar and the bullet hole in the living room's diamond-pane window. "Italians don't have nothing on gangster Jews!" he'd say, stroking the mezuzah that he'd left up on the doorway. "No hell in the Old Testament!"

Then he'd lead his guests outside, down the symmetrical rows of topiaries, and along the neat swirls of Madame Louis Lévêque roses until he could arrange the group in front of a bowing lawn jockey whose grinning black face had been tactfully painted over in a shiny pink. He'd gesture towards it, one eyebrow arched, as he told them that the man who designed this, this house destined to become the Wang family estate, had been Paul Williams, the first black architect in the city. The guy had built Frank Sinatra's house, he'd built that ridiculous restaurant at LAX that looked like it came straight out of The Jetsons—stars and spaceships, and a castle for Charles Wang.

Martha Stewart had kvelled over this house. She'd called it a treasure and lain a pale, capable hand on the sleeve of Charles Wang's navy summer-silk blazer with the burnished brass buttons, a blazer made by his tailor who kept a suite at the Peninsula Hong Kong and whose name was also Wang, though, thank god, no relation. Martha Stewart had clutched his jacket sleeve and looked at him with such sincerity in her eyes as she'd gushed, "It's so important, Charles, so essential, that we keep the spirit of these houses whole."

It was America, really, that had given him his three children, infinitely lovable even though they'd never learned to speak an unaccented word of Mandarin and lived under their own roofs, denying him even the bare dignity of being the head of a full house. His first wife had played some part in it, but he was the one who had journeyed to America and claimed her, he was the one who had fallen to his knees at the revelation of each pregnancy, the one who had crouched by the hospital bed urging on the birth of each perfect child who walked out into the world like a warrior.

Yes, America had loved him once. She'd given him the balls to turn his father's grim little factory, a three-smokestack affair on the outskirts of Taipei that supplied urea to fertilizer manufacturers, into a cosmetics empire. Urea. His father dealt in piss! Not even real honest piss—artificial piss. Faux pee. A nitrogen-carrying ammonia substitute that could be made out of inert materials and given a public relations scrubbing and named carbamide, but that was really nothing more than the thing that made piss less terribly pissy.

The knowledge that his father, his tall, proud father with his slight scholar's squint and firmly buttoned quilted vests, had gone from quietly presiding over acres of fertile Chinese farmland to operating a piss plant on the island of Taiwan—well, it was an indignity so large that no one could ever mention it.

Charles's father had wanted him to stay at National Taiwan University and become a statesman in the New Taiwan, a young man in a Western suit who would carry out Sun Yat Sen's legacy, but Charles dropped out because he thought he could earn his family's old life back. An army of well-wishers—none of whom he'd ever see again—had packed him onto a plane with two good-luck scrolls, a crushed orchid lei, and a list of American fertilizer manufacturers who might be in need of cheap urea.

Charles had spent half the flight locked in the onboard toilet heaving up a farewell banquet of bird's-nest soup and fatty pork stewed in a writhing mass of sea cucumber. When he couldn't stomach looking at his own colorless face for another second, he picked up a miniature bar of waxpaper-wrapped soap and read the label, practicing his English. It was a pretty little package, lily scented and printed with purple flowers. "Moisturizing," promised the front, "Skin so soft, it has to be Glow." And in back, there was a crowded list of ingredients that surprised Charles. This was before anything in Taiwan had to be labeled, before there was any sort of unbribable municipal health department that monitored claims that a package of dried dates contained anything more than, say, "The freshest dates dried in the healthy golden sun."

Charles stood there, heaving, weaving forward and back on his polished custom-made shoes, staring cross-eyed at the bar of soap, trying to make out the tiny type. Sweet almond oil, sodium stearate, simmondsia chinensis, hydrolyzed wheat proteins, and then he saw it: UREA. Hydroxyethyl urea, right between shea butter and sodium cocoyl isethionate.

Urea!

Urea on a pretty little American package!

Charles stood up straight, splashed cold water on his face, and strode back to his seat, the miniature soap tucked in his palm. He pulled his gray checked suit jacket down from the overhead bin, took out the list of fertilizer manufacturers, and tucked it into the seat pocket right behind the crinkly airsick bag. When Charles walked off the plane, the scrolls and the pungent lei also stayed behind. He stuck the soap in his shirt pocket, slung his jacket over his shoulder, and swallowed the last trace of bile. Charles Wang was going to come out of America smelling sweet. He was sure of it. "Shit into Shinola," he said to himself aloud, repeating one of his favorite American movie phrases.

And he'd done it.

Turned shit into two hundred million dollars' worth of Shinola. Made himself into a cosmetics king with eight factories in Los Angeles, factories that he'd gone from supplying with urea to owning outright—each one turning out a glossy rainbow-scented sea of creams and powders and lipsticks and mascaras.

In the beginning, he'd operated all eight of them separately, sending the clients of one into the disguised folds of another anytime they complained about his steadily rising prices. They'd get hooked in again—"Special offer! Just for you my prices go so low!"—and find their invoices once again mysteriously padded, just a little bit, just enough to be uncomfortable. Later, as it became clear that women were willing to pay twenty, twenty-five, thirty dollars for a tube of lipstick, that sort of subterfuge became unnecessary, and there was no end to the number of hotel chains who wanted to brand their shampoos and makeup artists ready to launch their own lines.

One of them, a tiny Japanese girl who stared out at the world through anime eyes, came to him with empty pockets and a list of celebrity clients. He'd fronted her the first set of orders for KoKo, a collection of violently hued shadows that came in round white compacts with her face, framed by its perfect bob cut, embossed on the front, the fuchsia and monarch yellow and electric blue powders glaring out through two translucent holes cut through her printed irises. The line was an immediate smash hit, going from runways and editorial layouts straight to department store makeup counters and into the damp suede reaches of a million teenage purses. And Charles, somehow, got credit for being a visionary, a risk taker, an integral part of a new generation of business talents who made their millions on mass customization, on glamorizing the role of the middleman, on merchandizing someone else's talent.

Yes, America had loved him. America was honest enough with him to include chemical piss in a list of pretty ingredients; America saw that the beautiful was made up of the grotesque.

Makeup was American, and Charles understood makeup. It was artifice, and it was honesty. It was science and it was psychology and it was fashion; but more than that, it was about feeling wealthy. Not money—wealth. The endless possibility of it and the cozy sureness of it. The brilliant Aegean blues and slick wet reds and luscious blacks, the weighty packaging, with its satisfying smooth hinges and sound closures.

Artifice, thought Charles, was the real honesty. Confessing your desire to change, being willing to strive, those were things that made sense. The real fakers were the ones who denied those true impulses. The cat-loving academic who let her hair frizz and made no attempt to cover her acne scars was the most insidious kind of liar, putting on a false face of unconcern when in her heart of hearts she must, must want to be beautiful. Everyone must want to be beautiful. The fat girl who didn't even bother to pluck her caterpillar eyebrows? If life were a fairy tale, her upturned nose would grow as long as her unchecked middle was wide. And for a time, a long and lucrative time, the good people of America had agreed.

By the turn of the millennium, he was rich already. Rich enough, probably, to buy back all the land in China that had been lost, the land that his father had died without ever touching again. Never mind that the Communists would never have allowed it to be privately owned. The simple fact that he could afford it was enough. He wouldn't even have done anything with those fallow acres, just slipped the deed in his pocket, received the bows of his peasants, and directed his driver towards Suzhou, where the women were supposed to be so beautiful it didn't matter that they were also bold and disobedient.

But really, Charles Wang was having too much fun in America to dwell on the China that might have been his.

Just four years ago he'd had the hull of his sexy little cigarette speedboat painted with twenty-seven gallons of Suicide Blonde, his best-selling nail polish color—a perfect blue-toned red that set off the mahogany trim and bright white leather seats. As soon as the paint dried, the boat ripped from Marina del Rey to Costa Careyes with a delectable payload of models for an ad campaign shoot, four morning-to-midnight days that Charles remembered mostly as a parade of young flesh in a range of browns and pinks interrupted only by irrelevant slashes of bright neoprene.

Now the boat was gone. Some small-hearted official with a clipboard and a grudge had probably plastered notices on the entrance to his slip or routed some ugly tugboat into the dock and dragged his poor Dragon Lady away—how Charles had laughed when the registrar at the marina asked if he knew that term was racist—leaving her to shiver in a frigid warehouse.

He never should have fallen for America.

As soon as the happy-clappy guitar-playing Christian missionary who taught him English wrote down Charles's last name and spelled it W-AN-G, he should have known.

He should have stayed leagues away from any country that could perpetrate such an injustice, that could spread this glottal miscegenation of a language, with its sloppy vowels and insidious Rs, across the globe.

In Chinese, in any Chinese speaker's mouth, Wang was a family name to be proud of. It meant king, with a written character that was simple and strong. And it was pronounced with a languid drawn-out diphthong of an o sound that suggested an easy life of summer palaces and fishing for sweet river shrimp off gilded barges. But one move to America and Charles Wang's proud surname became a nasally joke of a word; one move and he went from king to cock.

No boat. No car. No house. No factories. No models. No lipstick. No KoKo. No country. No kingdom. No past. No prospects. No respect. No land. No land. No land.

Now, now that he had lost the estate in America, all Charles could think of was the land in China.

The life that should have been his.

China, where the Wangs truly belonged. Not America. Never Taiwan.

If they were in China, his ungrateful children would not be spread out across a continent. If they were in China, his disappointed wife would respond to his every word with nothing but adoration. Angry again, Charles turned away from the window and back to his bare desk. Almost bare. In the center, dwarfed by the expanse of mahogany, was a heavy chop fashioned from a square block of prized mutton-fat jade.

Most chops underlined their authority with excess, an entire flowery honorific crowded on the carved base, but this one, once his grandfather's, had a single character slashed into its bottom.

王

Just the family name. Wang.

Over a century ago, when the seal was first made, its underside had started out a creamy white. Now it was stained red from cinnabar paste. His grandfather had used the chop in lieu of a signature on any documents he'd needed to approve, including the land deeds that were once testament to the steady expansion of Wang family holdings. Charles was thankful that his grandfather had died before all the land was lost, before China lost herself entirely to propaganda and lies. The men of the Wang family did not always live long lives, but they lived big.

The land that had anchored the Wangs and exalted them, the land that had given them a place and a purpose, that was gone. But Charles still had the seal and the deeds, everything that proved that the land was rightfully his.

And in a few fevered hours of searching the Internet, he'd uncovered stories, vague stories, of local councils far from central Party circles returning control to former owners, of descendants who, after years in reeducation camps, managed to move back into abandoned family houses that had been left to rot, entire wings taken over by wild pigs because peasants persuaded to deny their history could never appreciate the poetry and grandeur of those homes. He stored each hopeful tale away in a secret chamber of his heart, hoarding them, as he formed a plan. He would make sure that his three children were safe, that his fearsome and beloved second wife was taken care of, that his family was all under one roof, and then, finally, Charles Wang was going to reclaim the land in China.

He popped an aspirin in his mouth, pushing back that new old feeling of a tunnel, a dark and almost inevitable tunnel, closing in on him, and crunched down on the pill as he picked up the phone.

You've just read an excerpt from The Wangs Vs. The World.

ABOUT THE AUTHOR

Jade Chang has covered arts and culture as a journalist and editor. She is the recipient of a Sundance Fellowship for Arts Journalism, the AIGA/Winterhouse Award for Design Criticism, and the James D. Houston Memorial scholarship from the Squaw Valley Community of Writers. She lives in Los Angeles.

IMPRINT: Houghton Mifflin Harcourt
PRINT ISBN: 9780544734098
PRINT PRICE: $26.00
EBOOK ISBN: 9780544734203
EBOOK PRICE: $26.00
PUBLICATION DATE: 10/4/16
PUBLICITY CONTACT: Taryn Roeder taryn.roeder@hmhco.com
RIGHTS CONTACT: Debbie Engel debbie.engel@hmhco.com
EDITOR: Helen Atsma
AGENT: Marc Gerald
AGENCY: United Talent Agency

TERRITORIES SOLD:
US, HMH
Canada, Harper Canada
UK, Fig Tree / Penguin
Brazil, Intrinseca
Netherlands, Signatuur
France, Belfond
Italy, Ponte alle Grazie
Spain, Kailas

PROMOTIONAL INFORMATION:
Pre-pub media event in New York; Pre-pub bookseller event in Los Angeles; Author tour New York, San Francisco, Seattle, and Los Angeles; Early giveaways on Goodreads and Library Thing; NetGalley newsletters and promotion; Major print and online advertising including the *New York Times Book Review*, *Entertainment Weekly*, and Goodreads; Online reader's guide and placement with Reading Group Choices and Reading Group Guides; Online promotion, including book and make-up giveaways, Spotify playlists, Pinterest boards, hashtag campaigns on Instagram and Twitter, Facebook advertising, and promotion with fashion and lifestyle bloggers/Instagrammers.

HISTORY OF WOLVES

EMILY FRIDLUND

SUMMARY

Set in the austere woods of northern Minnesota, *History of Wolves* is a coming-of-age-plus-crime story that explores, in the words of Emily Fridlund's young narrator Linda, "the difference between what you want to believe and what you do." Pivoting around a morally complex question—how complicit is the observer of a 'crime', a girl who neither fully understands her world, nor the consequences of her inaction?—*History of Wolves* is a beautifully paced, gorgeously written novel about guilt, innocence, negligence, well-meaning belief, and the loss of a child.

EXCERPT

Chapter One

It's not that I never think about Paul. He comes to me occasionally before I'm fully awake, though I almost never remember what he said, or what I did or didn't do to him. In my mind, the kid just plops down on my lap. Boom. That's how I know it's him: there's no interest in me, no hesitation. We're sitting in the Forest Center on a late afternoon like any other, and his body moves automatically towards mine—not out of love or respect, but simply because he hasn't yet learned the etiquette of minding where his body stops and another begins. He's four, he's got an owl puzzle to do, don't talk to him. I don't. Outside the window, an avalanche of cottonwood fluff floats by, silent and weightless as air. The sun sets, the puzzle cleaves into an owl and comes apart again, I prod Paul to standing. Time to go. It's time. But in the second before we rise, before he whines out his protest and asks to stay a little longer, he leans back against my chest, yawning. And my throat cinches closed. Because it's strange, you know? It's marvelous, and sad too, how good it can feel to have your body taken for granted.

Before Paul, I'd known just one person who'd gone from living to dead. He was Mr. Adler, my eighth-grade history teacher. He wore brown corduroy suits and white sneakers, and though his subject was America he preferred the Russian Czars. He once showed us a photograph of Rasputin, and that's how I think of him now—cyclone-bearded, bullet in the head—though in fact Mr. Adler was always clean-shaven as a deacon. I was in English class when his second-period student burst in, saying he'd fallen. We all crowded across the hall, and there lay Mr. Adler face down on the floor, looking like Lily Holburn's dad after a weekend drunk. "Does he have epilepsy?" someone asked. "Does he have pills?" We were all repulsed. The Boy Scouts argued over proper CPR techniques, while the Gifted and Talented kids reviewed his symptoms in hysterical whispers. I had to force myself to go to him. I crouched down and took Mr. Adler's dry-meat hand. It was early November. He was darkening the carpet with drool, sucking in air between longer and longer intervals, and there was a distant bonfire scent, I remember. Someone was burning garbage in plastic bags, some janitor getting rid of leaves and pumpkin rinds before the first big snow.

When the paramedics finally loaded Mr. Adler's body onto a stretcher, the Boy Scouts trailed behind like puppies, hoping for an assignment. They wanted a door to open, something heavy to lift. Girls stood crying in the hallway, and a few teachers held palms to their chests, embarrassed and hesitant about what to do next.

"That a Doors' song?" one of the paramedics asked. He'd stayed behind to pass out packets of Saltines to lightheaded students. I shrugged. I must have been humming out loud. He gave me orange Gatorade in a Dixie cup, saying—as if I was the one he'd come to save, as if his duty was to root out sickness in whatever living thing he could find—"Drink slow now. Do it in sips."

The Walleye Capital of the World, we were called back then. There was a sign to this effect out on Route 10 and a mural of three mohawked fish painted on the side of the diner. Those guys were always waving a finny hello, all grins and eyebrows, all teeth and gums, but no one came from out of town to fish—or do much at all—by the time the big lakes froze up in November. Downtown went: diner, hardware, bait and tackle, bank. The most impressive place in Loose River back then was the old paper mill, I think, and that was because it was half-burned down, charred black planks soaring up over the banks of the river. Almost everything official, the hospital and DMV and Burger King and police station, were twenty-plus miles down the road in Whitehead.

I remember the day the Whitehead paramedics picked Mr. Adler up, they tooted the ambulance horn as they left the school parking lot. We all stood at the windows and watched, even the hockey players in their yellowed caps, even the cheerleaders with their static-charged bangs. Snow was coming down by then, hard. As the ambulance slid around the corner, its headlights zigzagged crazily over the mural on the diner, and those big happy fish just looked on. "Shouldn't there be sirens?" someone asked, and I thought—measuring the last swallow of Gatorade in my little waxed cup—how stupid can people be?

Mr. Adler's replacement was Mr. Grierson, and he arrived just before Christmas with a deep, otherworldly tan. He wore one gold hoop earring and a brilliant white shirt with pearly buttons. We learned later that he'd come from California, from a private girls' school on the sea. No one knew what brought him all the way to northern Minnesota, midwinter, but after the first week of class, he took down Mr. Adler's maps of the Russian Empire, replacing them with enlarged copies of the U.S. Constitution. He announced he'd double-majored in theater in college, which explained why he stood in front of the class one day with his arms outstretched, reciting the whole Declaration of Independence by heart. Not just the soaring parts about life, liberty, and the pursuit of happiness, but the needling, wretched list of tyrannies against the colonies. I could see how badly he wanted to be liked. "What does it mean?" Mr. Grierson asked, when he got to the part about mutually pledging our sacred honor.

The hockey players slept innocently on folded hands. Even the Gifted and Talented kids were unmoved, clicking their mechanical pencils so that the lead protruded obscenely, like hospital needles. They jousted each other across the aisles. "*En garde!*" they hissed, contemptuously.

Mr. Grierson sat down on Mr. Adler's desk. He was a little breathless from his recitation, and I realized?in an odd flash, like a too-bright light passing over him?that he was middle-aged. I could see greasy sweat on his face, his pulse pounding under his gray stubble. "People. *Guys*. What does it mean that the rights of Man are *self-evident*? Come on. You know this."

I saw his gaze rest on Lily Holburn, who had sleek black hair and was wearing, despite the cold, a sheer crimson sweater. He seemed to think her beauty could rescue him, that she would be, because she was prettier than the rest of us, kind. It was Lily's predicament to appear pliant and eager, even when she had no clue what to say, even though she had no idea how to answer him. She had big brown eyes, dyslexia, no pencil, a boyfriend. Her face was turning red as Mr. Grierson watched her.

She blinked. He nodded at her, promising implicitly that, whatever she said, he'd agree. She gave him a deer-like lick of her lips.

I don't know why I raised my hand. It wasn't that I felt sorry for her exactly. Or him.

It was just that I felt his need unbearable for a moment?embarrassing, out of all proportion to the occasion. "It means some things don't have to be proven," I offered. "Some things are simply true. There's no changing them."

"That's right!" he said, grateful—I knew—not to me in particular, but to some hoop of luck he felt he'd stumbled into. I could do that. Give people what they wanted without them knowing it came from me. Without saying a word, Lily could make people feel encouraged, blessed. She had dimples on her cheeks, nipples that flashed like signs from God through her sweater. I was flat-chested, plain as a banister. I made people feel judged.

Winter collapsed on us that year. It just knelt down, exhausted, and stayed. In the middle of December so much snow fell that the gym roof buckled under and caved in, so school was cancelled for a week. With school out, the hockey players went ice fishing. The Boy Scouts played hockey on the ponds. Then came Christmas with its strings of colored lights up and down Main Street, and the competing nativity scenes at the Lutheran and Catholic churches—one with painted sandbags standing in as sheep, and one with baby Jesus sculpted out of a lump of ice. New Year's brought another serious storm. By the time school started again in January, Mr. Grierson was wearing nondescript sweaters like our other teachers, and he'd replaced his hoop earring with a stud. Someone had taught him to use the Scantron machine, I guess, because after a week's worth of lectures on Louis and Clark, he gave us our first test. While we hunched at our desks filling in bubbles, he walked up and down the aisles, clicking a ballpoint pen.

The next day, Mr. Grierson asked me to stay after class. He sat behind his desk and touched his lips, which were chapped and scaling off under his fingers. "You didn't do very well on your exam," he told me.

He was waiting for an explanation, I thought, so I lifted my shoulders defensively. But before I could say a word, he said, "Look, I'm sorry." He twisted the stud—delicate, difficult screw—into his ear. "I'm still working out the kinks in my lesson plan. What were you studying before I arrived?"

"Russia."

"Ah." A look of scorn passed over his face, followed immediately by pleasure. "The Cold War lingers in the back country."

I defended Mr. Adler. "It wasn't the Soviet Union we were talking about. It was *Czars*."

"Oh, Mattie." My name was Madeline. No one ever called me that. It was like being tapped on the shoulder from behind, spooked by a gust of wind that brought down leaves from another season. Usually I was called Linda, or Commie, or Freak. I pulled my hands into balls in my sleeves. Mr. Grierson went on. "No one cared about the Czars before Stalin and the bomb. They were little puppets on a far-away stage, utterly insignificant. Then all the Mr. Adlers went to college in 1961 and there was general nostalgia for the old Russian toys, the inbred princesses from another century. Their ineffectuality made them interesting. You understand?" He smiled then, closing his eyes a little. I saw his front teeth were white, and his canines were yellow. "But you're thirteen."

"Fourteen."

"I just wanted to say I'm sorry if this has started off badly. We'll get on better footing soon."

The next week he asked me to drop by his classroom after school. This time, he'd taken the stud out of his ear and set it on his desk. Very tenderly, with his forefinger and thumb, he was probing the flesh around his earlobe.

"Mattie," he said, straightening up.

He had me sit in a blue plastic chair beside his desk. He set a stack of glossy brochures in my lap, made a teepee of his fingers. "Do me a favor? But don't blame me for having to ask. That's my job." He squirmed.

That's when he asked me to be the school's representative in History Odyssey.

"This will be great," he said, unconvincingly. "What you do is you do a speech about Vietnam War registers, border crossings to Canada, etcetera. Maybe the desecration of the Ojibwa peoples? Or those back-to-the land folks that came up here in the seventies? Something local, something ethically ambiguous. Something with Constitutional implications."

"I want to do wolves," I told him.

"What, a history of wolves?" He was puzzled. Then he shook his head and grinned. "Right. You're a fourteen-year-old girl." The skin bunched up around his eyes. "You all have a thing for horses and wolves. I love that. I love that. That's so weird. What is that *about*?"

Because my parents didn't own a car, this is how I got home when I missed the bus. I walked four miles down the plowed edge of Route 10 and then turned left at Long Lake Road. The left-hand side followed the lake back around towards Bearfin, and the right-hand side turned steeply into an unplowed hill. At that fork, I stopped, stuffed my jeans into my socks and readjusted the cuffs on my woolen mittens. In winter, the trees against the orange sky looked like veins. The sky between the branches looked like sunburn. It was twenty minutes through snow and sumac before the dogs heard me and started braying against their chains.

By the time I got home, it was dark. When I opened the door, I saw my mom hunched over the metal sink, arms elbow-deep in inky water. Her white hair curtained down her back, which gave her a stagy, theatrical look, like someone in a silent movie. But her voice was all Midwestern vowels, all twangy Kansas. "Is there a prayer for clogged drains?" she asked, without turning around.

I set my wool mittens on the wood stove, where they would stiffen and no longer fit my hands just right in the morning.

My mom nudged a stool with her hip and sat down. But she kept her greasy hands in the air like they were something precious—something wiggling and still alive—that she'd snatched up from a pond. Something she might feed us on, a pretty little pair of carp. "We need Drano. Crap." She looked up into the air, then very slowly wiped her palms on her sweater. "Please help. God of infinite pity for the pathetic farce that is human living."

She was only half kidding. I knew that. I knew from stories how my parents had ridden in a stolen van to Loose River in the early eighties, how my father had stockpiled rifles and pot, and how, when their commune fell apart, my mother had traded whatever hippie fanaticism she had left for Christianity. For as long as I could remember she went to church three times a week—Wednesday, Saturday, and Sunday—because she held out hope that penance worked, that some of the past could be reversed, slowly and over years.

My mother believed in God, but grudgingly, like a grounded daughter.

"Do you think you could take one of the dogs with you and go back?"

"Back into town?" I was still shivering. The thought made me furious for a second, wiped clean of everything. I couldn't feel my fingers.

"Or not." She swung her long hair back and swiped her nose with her wrist. "No, not. It's probably below zero out there. I'm sorry. I'll go get another bucket." But she didn't move from her stool. She was waiting for something. "I'm *sorry* I asked. You can't be mad at me for asking." She clasped her greasy hands together. "I'm sorry, I'm sorry, I'm sorry."

For each *sorry*, her voice rose a half-step.

I waited a second before I spoke. "It's okay," I said.

You've just finished reading an excerpt from History of Wolves.

ABOUT THE AUTHOR

Emily Fridlund has a PhD in creative writing from the University of Southern California and is currently a postdoctoral associate at Cornell University. She has fiction published or forthcoming in the *ZYZZYVA, Boston Review, FiveChapters, New Orleans Review, Sou'wester, New Delta Review, The Chariton Review, The Portland Review*, and *Painted Bride Quarterly*, among other journals. Fridlund's collection of stories,

Catapult, was a finalist for the Noemi Book Award for Fiction, and the Tarrt First Fiction Award. It won the Mary McCarthy Prize—the prize includes a cash award and publication by *Sarabande* in 2017. The opening chapter of *History Of Wolves* was published in Southwest Review and won the 2013 McGinnis-Ritchie Award for Fiction.

IMPRINT: Atlantic Monthly Press
PRINT ISBN: 9780802125873
PRINT PRICE: $25.00
EBOOK ISBN: 9780802189776
EBOOK PRICE: $25.00
PUBLICATION DATE: 1/3/17
PUBLICITY CONTACT: Deb Seager dseager@groveatlantic.com
RIGHTS CONTACT: Amy Hundley ahundley@groveatlantic.com
EDITOR: Elisabeth Schmitz
AGENT: Nicole Aragi
AGENCY: Aragi, Inc.

PROMOTIONAL INFORMATION:
Prepublication reading copies available; E-galleys available on NetGalley and Edelweiss; 12-city tour (Boston, New York City, Ithaca, NY, Washington, D.C., Ann Arbor, Chicago, Milwaukee, Madison, Minneapolis/St. Paul, Los Angeles, San Francisco, Seattle); Major review coverage; National media campaign including print and radio interviews; Promotion at regional trade shows and BookExpo America; Library marketing including ALA; Prepublication buzz campaign with giveaways on Shelf Awareness, PW, and Goodreads; IndieBound bookseller outreach campaign.

THE NEXT

A NOVEL

STEPHANIE GANGI

SUMMARY

Is there a right way to die? If so, Joanna DeAngelis has it all wrong. She's consumed by betrayal, spending her numbered days cyberstalking Ned McGowan, much younger ex, and watching him thrive in the spotlight with someone new, while she wastes away. She's every woman scorned, fantasizing about revenge. . .except she's out of time.

Joanna falls from her life, from the love of daughters and devoted dog, into an otherworldly landscape, a bleak infinity she can't escape until she rises up and returns and sets it right—makes Ned pay—so she can truly move on.

From the other side into right this minute, Jo embarks on a sexy, spiritual odyssey. As she travels beyond memory, beyond desire, she is transformed into a fierce female force of life, determined to know how to die, happily ever after.

EXCERPT

Chapter One

This is not my beautiful life.

Far away, in the kitchen, water runs. What's that for? Tea? God help me, no more tea.

The water runs and runs, far more than a kettle requires. I can't hear anything under the damned running water, but I know the conversation is intense. Anna's antennae are already up. Anytime she comes in here, she scans the room for my phone and drops her voice, assessing and conferring with her sister or the hospice nurse like she's the mother, not me.

I can feel the twitch at the corner of her right eye. I can feel Laney's mouth draw in and pucker with the effort not to cry. They are mine. Both girls, trying to do the right thing. It drags me like a rip current. I can't get pulled along. I have my own problems. And I don't want them in here. I'm busy.

Yes, okay, I fell. I was on a mission, I needed my phone. I got out of the bed and made my way over to the dresser, to where it was charging. I leaned on Tom, he braced for me, he paced himself for me, he's a good dog, but I stumbled. Not his fault. Yes, I cracked a rib, my compromised bones gave way, yes, yes, high alert.

Now Anna wants caregivers around the clock. Now Anna wants to confiscate the phone. Now Anna wants me in a special bed, secured, so I can rest and revive and survive, for how long? Another week, another month? She wants to fix me, fix everything. She is trying to will a miracle.

Laney's stunned. I need to leverage that. She's still in her kid mindset, waiting for direction, not wanting to disrespect me, wanting to believe I have enough mother left in me to rally, to assert control over this, too, the process of my dying. I have only so much energy left, and now, with the rib, every breath hurts. They want to strap me down and take the phone. I need that phone. Like I said, I'm busy.

Let me think. Not easy. My bedroom hums with monitors. Soft, steady beeps track my ... I was going to say "progress," but that's not right. What's the opposite of progress? Regress? If only I *could* go back.

I remember when this bed, surrounded now by equipment, was a raft that rocked and rolled as we navigated the briny seas of each other. In the mornings, after he left, waves rose in me again, knocked me off balance, made me blush as I untangled sheets, retrieved pillows, tried to restore order.

This bed is not that bed. Here, I am anchored by a line embedded in the back of my hand, and an analgesic, morphine, keeps me bobbing and drifting, a little ways away from the pain. I've noticed everyone seems eager to press that button on my behalf.

Not me. I prefer the pain. Anna cannot possibly understand that. The pain keeps me sharp. When I am sharp I go inside, and I make myself feel it again, how it was with him, how I was, when everything was slippery with the chemistry of new love greasing the rusty mechanisms of my heart, and, I'll say it, my soul.

I shouldn't do that. Idealize the past. It's not healthy, hahaha.

But memory is seductive, especially here at the end, and I follow and it lures me down the same old hole, I follow it back, back, until it turns on me and I'm where I started, without him, in the land of the left-behind, two hours out from the next morphine push. Swapping one pain for another, cancer for heartbreak, down in the hole, alone.

He's moved on. Meaning Ned.

Meaning, love of my life, mate to my soul, late-night listener curved around my body, with late-night fingers stepping across my lines and furrows, the terrain of me, and into me as the light rose pink like me over the Hudson River, through our window, and lit me up, and opened up my folded desire. I showed myself.

He put his hands on me and he stopped time. He put his hands on me and he stopped cells. I came alive. This, after chemo and the menopause that comes with it. I got my period again. That happened. My skin glowed. My hair, my wayward hair, flowed back shining. I trusted my body again, and forgot to run my visualization exercise, the daily action movie, bad cells in black Speedos and swim caps poised to jackknife into my bloodstream, while good cells, valiant surfer boys in board shorts and hippie hair, built dams.

I told Dr. Keswani, "He's younger," as if that fact might be another symptom, which, in retrospect, it was. She laughed and said, "The best medicine." Which, in retrospect, it was.

Well, the medicine was addictive, and then it was poisonous.

But that first night, when we were up against each other, I had to halt his hand. My shirt was off. He was working at my bra. "Wait, wait a second. I need to tell you something." He looked stricken. Sexually-transmittable disease? Pre-op transgender? Or any number of other show-stoppers I was too old-school, or just too old, to count.

I reached behind and undid the hooks and let the bra drop to the floor. I said, "I've been sick. I have scars. Here. And here." I closed my eyes and took his fingertips on a walk along the ropy ridges underneath each new breast, and finger-stepped him along the scar higher on my chest, the one the bathing suit did not hide.

Five years ago. I was a topless, middle-aged woman splayed on a grad-student sofa. Did we even pause to sweep away strewn papers, his mess of a novel? A window was open somewhere, the room was chilled and I was tense with the cold and the reveal, I was like a sensor, every nerve distended, my hand guiding his hand, feeling for the slightest recoil from him.

A recoil that did not come. I opened my eyes, expecting to see his face clouded with disappointment by my body. He pushed up. He looked into me. He said, "You okay?"

"Yes, yes, I'm fine. I think. I hope." I gave a little smile, a little shrug, to protect myself against the gods of irony, who were surely listening, waiting for me to get cocky, to drop my guard and let myself feel a future. "I mean, I am. I'm fine." I had to add another, "I hope."

"Does this mean we can't…?" He was concerned only that the slide inside, so close, was in jeopardy. It was so normal a thing to say that it took me by surprise. He was not repelled. He was worried he wasn't going to get laid. Ned had a reassuringly male, one-track mind that made cancer irrelevant for a little while.

I wanted him. I was wearing the pricey lingerie to prove it.

Even though technically they were nerveless, with cosmetic nipples, created from belly fat and tattoo ink, my new breasts remembered what my real breasts once responded to. Like phantom limbs, they were gone but there.

"Does this mean we can't…?"

Relief flowed, loosening my thighs. I pulled him in. After, he touched his lips to the ridges where his fingers walked, kissing away my self-consciousness. That's when I came up with the nickname. *Doc.* I felt healed.

I was 46 and he was 31. I was by far the oldest woman he'd ever been with. "Is it weird for you? Do I feel old?"

He said, "Of a certain vintage, maybe, but not old."

I hid my face. "That's just code for old!" He pulled my hands away.

He said, "Textured," in his smoke voice, and stroked the skin at the corners of my eyes.

He said, "Wise," and let his fingers flutter over a scar.

"Complex," he said, and put his hands between my legs. He moved over me again and pushed in again and whispered, "No more talking."

I am not healed. He did not stop time, he did not stop cells. Did I mention? He's moved on. Ned's living the high life now with someone younger, richer. Healthy. She's iconic. She's a celebrity skin doctor. She's one of the best-known women in the world. She's everywhere and he's right next to her. Smiling. Can you believe that? He's smiling. Swipe, tap, scroll. See? There they are again, those lucky ducks, at last night's events. There you are again, Doc, you moved-on, up-trading, lucky-duck bastard. It's like I never existed.

Jealousy, whoa. I hadn't ever experienced it, never really related to the scorned-woman thing. Not like this. I guess I was always the dumper, rather than the dumpee. But now. Wow. I see them and my brain whirs like an old juke box gearing up to search and reach and set the disk on the turntable and drop the needle into the open vein of an Adele song, any Adele song. I feel ennobled by jealousy, diva-like. I have been wronged. I have been betrayed on a level that is Adele-esque.

Still I want him back, even if it's only on the small screen in the palm of my hand.

Swipe, tap, scroll. I'm fascinated. I'm disgusted. The display, the showing off, the bragging. When did that become okay? Didn't that used to be discouraged? Look at our expensive objects, look at our famous friends. This is what we are eating, wearing. Here's where we are, here's where we're going. Everyone is healthy, everything is special. Everyone and everything poses in a sunny, filtered future where the unphotogenic sick are not allowed. Well, I'm sick. I'm unphotogenic. I'm invisible.

Refresh, refresh, refresh. Talk about ironic. I'm pushing my own buttons. I need my phone so I can check Twitter, instagram, newsfeeds, posts. So I can see. Good morning, Doc. Good morning, Doc's new woman.

Trudi Mink, dermatologist to the stars.

Trudi. I don't like that name.

He's moved on. I have to accept it and move on too. If only.

If only he would acknowledge what we had. What we meant to each other.

If only he would apologize for walking out on me in the hour before my darkest hour.

If only he would stop ignoring me.

If only cyberstalking weren't so easy.

The truth is, I want nothing more than to move on. Except it's too late. Where am I going, in this condition?

Where is my fucking phone?

I'm sobbing now, that's what happens when the morphine is at the end of its shift. Sobbing brings coughing. I try and stifle myself with a small pillow so my daughters don't hear, so they won't come in, and then the pain in my ribs sears me, and I can't hold the coughing back, and then the pain in my ribs sets me on fire. Tom, who has been resting hard against me, like ballast, raises his big dog head and looks at me with anxious eyes. He steps off the bed. He paces. He pants.

The silence outside my door is full. Someone listening. Someone entering. Here comes the tea. Elena murmurs and fusses, but now there is something formal in her voice, something harder than before, something not-Laney, something more Anna, adapted from the kitchen conference. Things have been decided.

Caregivers, around the clock. New bed, no phone. No phone, no reason. I can't face it. I push the button myself this time. The morphine blur spreads thick like gel across my brain, such as it is, and it doesn't take long, I fall away just as Laney enters, I mumble nonsense as she approaches, I'm going under and I won't have to face her. I pretend if I can't see her, she can't see me.

Chapter Two

Joanna DeAngelis was dying wrong. It was one thing the sisters could agree upon.

She had fractured a rib, and now, surprise, an interloper, pneumonia, outpaced the cancer in her chest. Her breathing was inhibited; when she slept, half sitting up so she didn't choke, her breath sounded like it scraped her lungs. Keswani, the oncologist, recommended they install a high hospital bed with railings and restraints, which she would not be able to leave without help.

Laney rinsed the porcelain cup and saucer, her grandmother's, for the third time that grey February day. She set the kettle under the faucet and let the water run cold, for tea, again. "You're not living here. I'm here all day. She's … she's okay."

"She is not okay, Lane. She's not. You have to deal with it."

"I am not saying she's fine. I said she was 'okay.' Not fine. I'm not stupid. And stop telling me to 'deal with it.' You deal with it."

"We need someone here full time. And she needs the special bed. Or she's going to have to go back to Sloan. We can't have her wandering all over the place!"

"Anna, no one is wandering all over the place. She went from the bed to the … bathroom, probably. She had Tom to lean on. She's done it before with no problem."

"Well, it's a problem now, isn't it? I'm getting that bed installed this week." Anna tapped at her phone and waved it at Laney. "Jules agrees with me."

Laney said, "Well, Tom agrees with me, but neither of us are doctors, so I guess our votes don't count."

By nature, nurture, and now, profession as a pediatric resident, Anna was devoted to her mother's care. She'd put her own life on hold, or more accurately, double-timed it, fitting in long days of tending to the kids at Kravis, stealing time with Jules, and supervising an environment of efficiency at her mother's apartment. Captain of the team, guardian at their mother's door, Anna wanted only to protect Joanna—who seemed kind of deranged, frankly—from more pain, of any kind.

"I don't like the idea of Tom in there all the time, either. He's too big to be on the bed! What if he knocks into the machines? Or pulls out the line? And she's … recruited him or something, to help her get around. She's supposed to be using the bedpan, not the bathroom. He's her accomplice!"

"First you go for the bed, now you want to take away the dog. Tom's watching over her. He's not an accomplice. And Mama's not a criminal."

"Something's off, I'm telling you. She's not right. Maybe something going on in the brain? What is up with the phone thing? I never saw her so into her phone before. What's she doing on the internet all the time?"

"Tinder?"

"Is that supposed to be funny?" Anna watched Laney, who assembled components for tea on a tray. "Lane, the water. Shut the water! You've got a flame open, and the water's running, and …"

"It might be hard for you to believe, but I do know how to make a cup of tea." Laney set the kettle on the stove. "Fine, see about the caregivers' schedule. Order the bed. But leave Tom alone." By giving Anna a win and throwing down about Tom, Laney thought she might distract sister her from their mother's obsession with her phone.

Tom was not Joanna's only accomplice.

Anna scrolled her contacts, made the call and set the date for the bed's delivery. "I have to go, Jules is waiting. It's Valentine's Day." She went to Laney and touched her forehead to her sister's. "We're okay, we're doing okay. Right?"

"It's Valentine's Day?" Laney's eyes welled. "I'm such a loser. Yes, of course. We're okay." They hugged tight.

Anna said, "You do make a fine cup of tea, I'll give you that. And …"

Laney waited for the parting shot.

"You're almost good at manipulating me. Do not let her have that phone."

Before Christmas, when Joanna came home from Sloan Kettering for the last time, Laney moved back home too, to help. She was secretly relieved to flee the clutter and grime of expensive floor-through rooms she shared with three others in Brooklyn. Aside from the circumstances, being home was respite from watching for signs of what to do with her life, in her first year as an official grown-up after the four-year undergraduate fairy tale in Boston.

Laney was tired of her Boston-Brooklyn friends and their opinions, their naiveté and cynicism, their distressed clothes and hair and outlooks, and most of all, their healthy mothers. She was tired of alcohol and technology, which had turned once-friends into posers with poor eye contact who seemed unable to form a sentence without reaching for a device. She worked as an intern helping the former hippie-boomer publishers "deploy" social media at Personal Growth & Human Development Books, PGHD, the company where her mother had been an editor, but that gig was on hold for the duration. She'd had to leave every normal thing, pals and work and mindless fun, everything with which her friends were preoccupied, outside the dying-mother bubble she inhabited.

Tray in hand, she tapped her toe at the bedroom door, and whispered, "Mama?"

Her mother drifted, drugged, in her blue bed at the Master, the Art Deco apartment building standing sentinel over 103rd Street and Riverside Drive. The bedrooms windows were high enough and wide enough so that the Hudson River was a presence. The river, flat glass or chop, played on every surface in the bedroom. The watery reflection shimmered like a lure across the bed, catching the sun's rise and set and the moods of the moon.

Always cold, her mother had huddled and gone small under blue quilts. All Laney could see was the beanie that Anna bought a couple of years back at a skateboard shop downtown on Lafayette, white with a black skull, when the skull was still ironic. Joanna was attached to the hat. Laney hated seeing it on her mother's head, daring death.

Joanna had stopped eating. Bringing tea was all Laney could think to do. She set the tray down on the night table as quietly as she could. Joanna moaned from a dream.

Laney had brought up a few never-unpacked boxes from basement storage to go through, a project, something to distract her mother and herself from the exhausting mix of drama and tedium of care-giving. She started with cartons that looked the oldest, liquor boxes advertising brands she never heard of, marked "Loretta," her grandmother's things.

She took up a spot on the floor at Joanna's bedside, slit through yellowed tape, opened cardboard flaps, unwrapped glass, ceramic, porcelain vessels and dishes, plaques and ashtrays, figurines, once precious, now useless, stopping now and then to smooth and read from crumpled newspaper.

Laney, at least, was diverted by the treasures, and thought it would lift her mother's spirit to see Loretta's porcelain cup and saucer show up in rotation. Joanna had given Laney one dip of her head to acknowledge, days ago.

Laney wanted more. More Mama. She was finding it tough to stay connected—to stay kind—to this person, sunken in pillows, agitated or absent, in sleep or drugs or a private darkness all her own.

Anna felt it was their duty to make the final-days experience what Joanna said she wanted when she lobbied to leave Sloan Kettering: a tranquil passage at home with loved ones nearby. No fear, no worries, everything understood, everything absolved, and with luck, eyes would close, and she would sigh with acceptance, and simply stop.

Laney thought, *Like in the movies, like Beaches.* She was conflicted. It was Mama, after all, not an erratic stranger messing up the choreography of some big dying-with-dignity plan, not a kid abusing cellphone privileges. Laney was trying to hold on to her, respect her, by delaying more strangers and equipment encroaching, more indignities accumulating.

It was hard to argue with Doctor Know-it-All, as Laney was coming to think of her sister. But Anna did not know it all.

Laney knew and Anna did not, that the phone expedition was not random. Joanna was technically still there, still with them, still alive, but she was secretly—secretly!—preoccupied to the point of online obsession with Ned, so much more compelling to her than food or her daughters or her own life ebbing away. Laney could see it was a fierce force keeping Joanna going. But the force was overtaking her, hijacking her, which is why Anna, who thought Ned McGowan long gone, assumed there was something wrong with her brain.

Laney was surprised her sister had not yet figured it out. She could tell Ned was back on the scene last summer by Joanna's voice on the telephone, girlish. She knew he was gone again a couple of months later, when her mother's voice was heavy and flat. Laney did not share this insight with Anna, who loathed Ned from the start, who'd never considered Ned anything but a hijacker. Now, once again, he had stolen their mother.

The room was dim but not dark. Laney could feel her mother's eyes slide, watching through the split of swollen eyelids. Tom lay against her, and his eyes followed Laney, too, as she closed up the boxes as quietly as she could and set them in a corner for another day, another attempt at reclaiming something of her mother.

"Hey, Mama, hi." Laney sat at her mother's side. "You awake? You hot?" She reached to remove the beanie. Joanna moved away from Laney's touch.

"Okay, I'll leave it. What do you need? Tea? I brought some, fresh." She poured. "Can you try and sit up a little?" She reached to adjust the pillow. Joanna shut her eyes and turned her head.

"How about some water, then?" She went to the bathroom and filled a mint-green plastic hospital pitcher from the tap. She thought, *I need to get rid of this hideous hospital pitcher*. Rejected, guilty and angry all at the same time, she checked herself, *Then again, why bother? She can barely look at me.*

She knew it was ridiculous, but she was pissed at her mother. Where was the cancer-movie version, selfless and dying in a way that made everything okay for her kids? The three of them had watched Beaches enough times to know there was protocol, there was supposed to be a good ending, with cozy sweaters and cups of tea and looking out to sea, the three of them, their best, loving selves.

This was not that.

Laney pulled aqua sheets with white ruffled edges, her mother's favorites, up under Joanna's chin. She straightened and tucked. "It's Valentine's Day, Mama. Anna reminded me." She leaned down, touched her cheek to her mother's forehead. She couldn't judge Joanna for not dying according to Hollywood movie standards. Laney was twenty-two, it was the hallmark of her generation to not judge. And death, it was so heavy, so personal. Was it even possible to die wrong? On the other hand, it wasn't only happening to Joanna. Their mother's death was happening to Anna and Laney too. Chasing down an ex-boyfriend? Ignoring your kids?

Her mother was definitely not dying right.

"How about some drops?" Laney separated the sliver-thin skin of her eyelids, easing them open. Joanna's eyes were blue and black, much darker than Laney's. The whites were yellow and the rims were flaked with dried tears.

Laney said, "This will feel really good," and carefully let a drop fall into her mother's eye. Joanna squeezed her eyes shut against this comfort, and again pulled from her daughter's touch. Weary tears ran. She coughed for a full minute, and Laney's heart raced for twice as long.

She dabbed at Joanna's eyes with a tissue. She murmured, "Oh, don't cry, Mama, don't cry. You're making it worse. I'm here." She used the same soggy tissue to dab at her own eyes.

Tom wriggled closer to Joanna on the bed, and dropped his heavy head on to her thigh. "No," Joanna rasped. "No." She shook her head.

Laney grabbed the dog's collar and dragged him away. "Come on, Tom, you gotta get off. You're too heavy. Come on, off now."

Joanna shook her head again.

"What is it, Mama? What are you trying to say?"

Joanna twisted under the mask.

"Are you in pain?"

No, no. She shook her head. *No.*

"What do you need?" Laney adjusted the mask. "I can't take it off right now. You don't sound good. Try to relax a little bit, and then I can give you a break from the mask. Should I press the button?"

Again, Joanna shook her head, this time, forcefully. She said, "Phone," and Laney stalled and pretended not to understand, an attempt to heed Anna's admonition, but she and her mother had made a wordless pact. It had become routine, when Anna wasn't around. Wasn't it better than leaving Joanna to struggle to find the phone again?

"You need to try and slow down your breathing. Concentrate on the oxygen."

Joanna said, "Elena," and grasped Laney's hand.

Tom watched as Laney-the-accomplice delivered the charged phone to Joanna and said, "Just for a few minutes." She brought Joanna her sunglasses, because the bright light and colors on the small screen hurt her mother's eyes. She pulled Tom along by his ruff and stepped out to give her mother privacy and to give herself a break. As she shut the door of the bedroom, she looked back to see a shadow of her mother, an apparition of her mother, surrounded by machinery, sprouting tubes, the white beanie with the black skull pulled down low on her brow, behind sunglasses, bent over the phone, Joanna DeAngelis, Mama, a stranger acting strange.

Chapter Three

I fall into a morphine dream. We are in the Met, our old haunt. We circle a sculpture, the Kouros, the big, nude boy. I press my fingers along the cool, stone phallus, the round bulk of shoulders, the torpedo thighs. Marble calf and ass muscles undulate under my touch. I am turned on. I need Ned inside me, but he is gone, striding the way he does, down impossibly long hallways. Is he leading me or running away from me? I push through a door into an empty auditorium. Ned is on stage. A television camera circles, a woman blots his shine away, another tames his hair. I want him and I am on him and he tries to fight me off. I get stronger and stronger and I tear at his clothes. I pull at bristle of white that strafes the black, his famous hair, and it rips away from his scalp. I hold a handful. The camera circles. The auditorium is full. Hundreds of students, nineteen, twenty years old, film too, with their phones. I force Ned inside. My skin is tagged and mottled and rippled. It sways as I move. My breasts have broken off, leaving flat, rough stone where they had been. My hair, everywhere, is grey. An artillery of cell phones aims. I don't care. I move up and straddle his mouth. I bear down. He struggles. The students film.

I wake up hot, aroused, with a pulse, just like the old days, between my legs. I don't want to move. I want to stay alive inside the dream. Traffic motors along on Riverside Drive. It must be rush hour. I hear the hum of the dishwasher in the kitchen. NPR plays on the radio in the living room, an unstoppable current of events. It all keeps going, even as the dream dissolves, even as I disintegrate.

"Tch tch tch." I attempt clicking sounds with my tongue for Tom. Laney put my phone back on the dresser to charge, but forgot to bring the bedpan close. I need Tom for my trip to the bathroom, and then I can grab the phone again, that's the important thing. I need to check in on Dr. Trudi and her boyfriend—my boyfriend. Tom noses in and puts his long muzzle along the bed, ready to be of service.

"Let's go, man." He positions himself, and stares intently at me as if to say, *Really? This didn't go so well last time we tried it.*

I take the oxygen mask off, and detach the IV line embedded in a vein on the back of my hand. My poor veins. I'm covered in bruises in bloom, purple and green and grey and yellow. Lifting the quilt is an event. I am frustrated to the point of tears as I untangle my legs, so pale and thin they look like someone else's, from the bedding. Finally, I have feet on the floor, but I am sweaty and freezing and nauseated from the effort.

I sit a minute. Tom waits. I put a hand on his back, his long, strong back, ninety pounds of poodle covered in chocolate brown curls, and I feel him shift to take my weight. He knows what to do. This, a couple of times a day, our little secret. This, the way his body shifts and braces for me, releases fresh tears. Tom. My friend.

I rasp out, "Thank you, buddy," and off we go, fifteen feet that might as well be fifteen miles. I am only half upright, bent around the burn in my bones. I grip Tom and shuffle forward, shuffle again, two steps more. I have to gasp back a cough, I don't want Elena to come running.

Laney is the weak link. She's lying to Anna. Not only is she slipping me my smartphone, she knows what I'm doing with it. She's suspected about Ned since last summer. She will cave under pressure if—when—her sister exerts it. Allegiances are fluid right now.

Shuffle, cough, rest. Shuffle, cough, rest. Tom pants, too, with anxiety. It's not easy for a dog to measure his steps, it's awkward, he has to step and stop, step and stop. He presses—not too hard—against my leg for constant contact, to feel what I need from him. I lean against the wall to rest, and he noses my hand to ask if I'm okay. Not really, buddy.

I struggle to position myself properly on the cold bowl. I am queasy, I can feel a sheen of perspiration on the back of my neck. An awful essence rises up from inside me into my throat, a mouthful of foamy fluid, and I worry that I should be crouching instead of sitting.

Tom waits politely with his head turned away.

I pull myself up, I hang on to Tom for the trip back to bed. I rush a little, queasiness abated, I've got the hang of walking again for the moment, I've got the phone, and I'm busy. The phone's days are numbered, or mine are. Either way, I need to see. Swipe. Tap. Scroll.

Swipe. Here we go. Tap to parties, clubs, galleries, charity events. Scroll and score, new images. Last Night's Parties. A red carpet. He's half a step behind her, with his arm extended and a hand on the small of her back.

I follow a twitter trail of betrayal to Page Six, The Cut, The Gloss, Style, the Style Section, the New York Social Register, Patrick-somebody's photographs. It's incredible how close you can feel with strangers by following them online. I check instagram to see how Trudi is doing, I study her emojis, I note her LOLs and exclamation points, I know what they are up to for the weekend. I'm familiar with her OMG besties, selfies, fancy plates, lush flower arrangements, wine labels, boutique shopping bags, her trending nail color.

Like the old song says, they gavotte. They cavort, they preen. I pinch my fingers and expand the screen to examine Ned's two-faced face. To see if I can find the taut upper lip, the tension that wires his smile when he is only pretending to be happy. Pinch, expand the screen. Ah, she's got a fresh mani-pedi. I know her fingers and her toes. Ah, there's the ring.

My boyfriend. I sound crazy, I know. Look, I'm sick, I'm on drugs, I don't know whether it's night or day, I am not feeling anything good, except good ol' pain over every inch of my ruined body, and from the corkscrew to my heart. I am hurting my daughters. Of course Anna wants to enforce lock-down. Of course Elena is terrified. But I'm not crazy.

I'm righteous.

I'm struggling to let go and move on, and I don't mean from the relationship. I mean from life, my life, mine, the version that began again last July when he knocked, again. He'd had a dream He had to come.. Of course I let him in.

Just last summer. Here we go. Down the hole. I can't prop the pillows. My chest tightens.

Just last summer, only I knew I was sick and only I knew I was not getting better. Keswani showed me the film and I nodded, polite down to my radiant backlit bones, and I nodded at the luminous ghostly shapes gathered in my lungs, I nodded, understanding nothing, seeing nothing, hearing nothing, I just nodded, and Keswani gave me options—"It's your choice"—none of which suggested a life worth living, the options being not-bad days and bad days and very bad days in a fight to the finish, more chemo, more hospital, more strangers and drugs and machinery with increasing authority over my body and my mind, more iterations of not-dead-yet, stops along the way, stops along the way. Caregiving. Submission.

That was me. Single, dying, dragging it out. No partner "in sickness," no partner "for worse." I thought about Anna and Laney, building their lives, interrupted, detoured, dutiful. For who knew how long. It felt immoral. I had dark thoughts of swift exits executed to save us all.

Then there was Ned, in my inbox. He'd had a dream, he had to come. You can't make this stuff up. Can you imagine? I could not resist!

Just last summer. He still loved me, not her.

So yes, Doc, come in, come in, of course, yes, it's the beginning of the end of me, yes, come back, yes, come home and love me till my heart stops. Love of my life, my beautiful life, unto my beautiful death.

For eight weeks, hot as hell, he took care of me. Trudi Mink, his soon-to-be-ex—I believed him when he said, *It's over, I promise*—was globetrotting fashion week to fashion week tending famous skin, doing business, he was free as a bird, he was nearly moved back in, walking Tom, whistling in the kitchen, washing my hair. He took notes at doctor's appointments.

I dodged the girls. They didn't even know I'd recurred. Anna had started her residency, and she'd met Jules, she was in love, she was in that bubble. Elena, newly graduated, was bumming around Brooklyn, piecing together dollars for rent and a social life. I, Mama, was out of sight, I was out of mind, they were doing their lives, they were doing their twenties, so all-consuming, right? Normal! Exactly what it's supposed to be.

I put aside the ways he'd hurt me before. Burned me. Doc was back, and he loved me and I loved him, that fucker. Love. I told myself that was all that mattered. I let myself trust Ned to help me be strong. Who would flake out on a woman with Stage Four breast cancer?

We slow strolled the shady promenade on Riverside with Tom, who looked over his shoulder, tongue lolling, grinning at his reunited puppy-parents. We watched television. Ned worked on his novel, draft five or six or seven, year four or five, he'd lost count, and I read his pages, my trusty green Flair in hand. Our old routine. We retreated to bed, this bed, where we swayed and floated with languid desire. Ned on his knees. Cries of pleasure rising from my center. I remember looking to the window and mouthing, *Thank you, thank you,* to the sky, to the river, for giving me all this, at this late stage. Cries of pleasure!

I showed myself. He promised. *I won't let you be alone. I'm here. I've got you.* He promised.

Imagine my surprise.

In humid August, I was tossing and turning on the sofa. I could not get comfortable. I'd lost weight, and my bones hurt. It was hard to find a way to be. It was hot but I was cold. I don't like air conditioning in the first place, but air conditioning when you're sick is a nightmare. The noise. The faint chemical smell, what is that? Freon? The steady chill. I could not get warm. Tom was stretched out on the floor next to me. Ned was set up in Laney's old room, tapping away, working on something, excited by it, I could tell by the way he hit the keyboard. The tapping stopped, he came to me, he didn't ask, he didn't have to, he arranged a quilt on top of me, and he went to the air conditioner and adjusted the setting. He said, *Errands, I'll be home soon, you sleep.* He said, *Take care of her for me,* to Tom. He stepped out and he never came back. They call that an Irish exit.

Under the monitor's soft bleats, I remember his voice. *Errands.* I'm still waiting, Doc. I bleat too, a noise like laughing and I choke on it.

I'm not crazy. I'm righteous. Bitches are made, not born.

I have fallen past rational thinking. I have fallen past the edge of myself. I have fallen into purple despair, into red, red fury, into bloody black hatred deep and dark as, well, death. Me hating him has turned into me hating me. I'm rancid, body and brain. I'm unrecognizable to myself. Unrecognizable to my daughters.

A bitter mantra beats inside me: *You taught him how to treat you. You taught him how to treat you.*

What I taste, the foamy fluid in my throat, that's bile.

Whatever. I only care about the phone. Swipe, tap, scroll. There's Trudi. Did I mention the baby bump? No? Oh.

There. Ned has his arm around Trudi Mink. She is in couture, something Grecian, red, one-shouldered, fitted tight under her tiny breasts, from whence it flows and drapes over a tidy baby bump. A baby bump made by Ned. He fucked her and he knocked her up, probably right around the time he sent me the I-had-a-dream email last July.

It's all over the internet, has been for a few months, so I'm not surprised, but the shock of the new photos—she's really popped—has me … I am at a loss. For words, comprehension, sanity.

Okay, maybe I am crazy. Maybe I am. I've earned it.

I'm sweating again. I'm freezing. My fingers tremble. I need to sit up, I'm choking, I need to stop crying, I'm choking, I need to stop crying and choking so I can see the screen. Pinch, expand. A new burn rises from my heart, up into my throat, up into my nostrils. My eyes boil. I blink to clear my vision. I imprint this image, the pregnant woman in the red dress, behind my eyes and it joins all the other invaders inside me, taking me down. I can't believe it.

He has an arm around her shoulders and a hand on her belly. I'm blind with pain and I'm sick, I'm dying, but I'm jealous, I'm blinking, I'm peering, I'm bent over the small screen, I'm trying to see: Is that his tight smile? Is he faking?

The phone flies from my grip, so I can't tell.

You've just read an excerpt from The Next.

ABOUT THE AUTHOR

Stephanie Gangi is a NYC novelist, poet, and by day, a corporate communications strategist. She is working on her second novel, and a chapbook of poems, *More Than Four*.

IMPRINT: St. Martin's Press
PRINT ISBN: 9781250110565
PRINT PRICE: $26.99
EBOOK ISBN: 9781250110589
EBOOK PRICE: $12.99
PUBLICATION DATE: 10/18/16
PUBLICITY CONTACT: Dori Weintraub dori.weintraub@stmartins.com
RIGHTS CONTACT: Chris Scheina chris.scheina@stmartins.com
Kerry Nordling kerry.nordling@stmartins.com
EDITOR: Jennifer Enderlin
AGENT: Meg Ruley and Andrea Cirillo
AGENCY: Jane Rotrosen Agency

TERRITORIES SOLD:
World

PROMOTIONAL INFORMATION:
National print publicity; Online publicity; National print advertising; Online advertising; Book club/ site outreach; eMail marketing; Pre-publication trade advertising; eBlasts to regional trade organizations; Early reader reviews; Blog outreach; Discussion guide online; IndieBound Whitebox mailing; Library marketing campaign.

AUTHOR BLURBS:
"A profound and provocative page-turner about love and loss, revenge and redemption, this debut novel will stick with you for a long time. Stephanie Gangi is an instant, new favorite."—Emily Giffin

"I was instantly hooked by Gangi's vivid writing, her psychological acumen and her sharp observation of love and life. She is a fascinating writer who understands love, sex, men and women. I truly could not stop reading. *The Next* is a riveting debut by a fiercely talented writer."—Erica Jong

"*The Next* isn't just a ghost story—it's a love story, a family story, an illness story, and a revenge story as well. Stephanie Gangi's novel is fast-paced, wickedly observant, and haunting in the best sense of the word."—Tom Perrotta

THE NIX

Nathan Hill A novel

SUMMARY

A Nix can take many forms. In Norwegian mythology, it is a spirit who appears as a white horse that steals children away. In Nathan Hill's remarkable first novel, a Nix is anything you love that one day disappears, taking with it a piece of your heart. It's 2011, and Samuel Andresen-Andersen—college professor, stalled writer—has a Nix of his own: his mother. Decades ago, when he was a small boy, she abruptly walked out on the family. Now she's reappeared, having committed an absurd crime that electrifies the nightly news and beguiles the internet. She needs Samuel's help. To save her he'll have to uncover the secrets of her life, and in so doing perhaps reclaim his own. Moving from the suburban Midwest to New York City to the 1968 riots that rocked Chicago and beyond, *The Nix* explores—with both biting, side-splitting humor and fierce tenderness—the resilience of love and home, even in times of radical change.

EXCERPT

Prologue

Late Summer 1988

If Samuel had known his mother was leaving, he might have paid more attention. He might have listened more carefully to her, observed her more closely, written certain crucial things down. Maybe he could have acted differently, spoken differently, been a different person.

Maybe he could have been a child worth sticking around for.

But Samuel did not know his mother was leaving. He did not know she had been leaving for many months now—in secret, and in pieces. She had been removing items from the house one by one. A single dress from her closet. Then a lone photo from the album. A fork from the silverware drawer. A quilt from under the bed. Every week, she took something new. A sweater. A pair of shoes. A Christmas ornament. A book. Slowly, her presence in the house grew thinner.

She'd been at it almost a year when Samuel and his father began to sense something, a sort of instability, a puzzling and disturbing and sometimes even sinister feeling of depletion. It struck them at odd moments. They looked at the bookshelf and thought: *Don't we own more books than that?* They walked by the china cabinet and felt sure something was missing.

But what? They could not give it a name—this impression that life's details were being reorganized. They didn't understand that the reason they were no longer eating Crock-Pot meals was that the Crock-Pot was no longer in the house. If the bookshelf seemed bare, it was because she had pruned it of its poetry. If the china cabinet seemed a little vacant, it was because two plates, two bowls, and a teapot had been lifted from the collection.

They were being burglarized at a very slow pace.

"Didn't there used to be more photos on that wall?" Samuel's father said, standing at the foot of the stairs, squinting. "Didn't we have that picture from the Grand Canyon up there?"

"No," Samuel's mother said. "We put that picture away."

"We did? I don't remember that."

"It was *your* decision."

"It was?" he said, befuddled. He thought he was losing his mind. Years later, in a high-school biology class, Samuel heard a story about a certain kind of African turtle that swam across the ocean to lay its eggs in South America. Scientists could find no reason for the enormous trip. Why did the turtles do it? The leading theory was that they began doing it eons ago, when South America and Africa were still locked together. Back then, only a river might have separated the continents, and the turtles laid their eggs on the river's far bank. But then the continents began drifting apart, and the river widened by about an inch per year, which would have been invisible to the turtles. So they kept going to the same spot, the far bank of the river, each generation swimming a tiny bit farther than the last one, and after a hundred thousand years of this, the river had become an ocean, and yet the turtles never noticed.

This, Samuel decided, was the manner of his mother's departure. This was how she moved away—imperceptibly, slowly, bit by bit. She whittled down her life until the only thing left to remove was herself.

On the day she disappeared, she left the house with a single suitcase.

Part One

The Packer Attacker

Late Summer 2011

Chapter One

The headline appears one afternoon on several news websites almost simultaneously: Governor Packer attacked!

Television picks it up moments later, bumping into programming for a Breaking News Alert as the anchor looks gravely into the camera and says, "We're hearing from our correspondents in Chicago that Governor Sheldon Packer has been attacked." And that's all anyone knows for a while, that he was attacked. And for a few dizzying minutes everyone has the same two questions: Is he dead? And: Is there video?

The first word comes from reporters on the scene, who call in with cell phones and are put on the air live. They say Packer was at the Conrad Hilton Hotel hosting a dinner and speech. Afterward, he was making his way with his entourage through Grant Park, glad-handing, baby-kissing, doing all your typical populist campaign maneuvers, when suddenly from out of the crowd a person or a group of people began to attack.

"What do you mean *attack*?" the anchor asks. He sits in a studio with shiny black floors and a lighting scheme of red, white, and blue. His face is smooth as cake fondant. Behind him, people at desks seem to be working. He says: "Could you describe the attack?"

"All I actually know right now," the reporter says, "is that things were thrown."

"What things?"

"That is unclear at this time."

"Was the governor struck by any of the things? Is he injured?"

"I believe he was struck, yes."

"Did you see the attackers? Were there many of them? Throwing the things?"

"There was a lot of confusion. And some yelling."

"The things that were thrown, were they big things or small things?"

"I guess I would say small enough to be thrown."

"Were they larger than baseballs, the thrown things?"

"No, smaller."

"So golf-ball-size things?"

"Maybe that's accurate."

"Were they sharp? Were they heavy?"

"It all happened very fast."

"Was it premeditated? Or a conspiracy?"

"There are many questions of that sort being asked."

A logo is made: *Terror in Chicago*. It whooshes to a spot next to the anchor's ear and flaps like a flag in the wind. The news displays a map of Grant Park on a massive touch screen television in what has become a commonplace of modern newscasting: someone on television communicating via another television, standing in front of the television and controlling the screen by pinching it with his hands and zooming in and out in super-high definition. It all looks really cool.

While they wait for new information to surface, they debate whether this incident will help or hurt the governor's presidential chances. Help, they decide, as his name recognition is pretty low outside of a rabid conservative evangelical following who just loves what he did during his tenure as governor of Wyoming, where he banned abortion outright and required the Ten Commandments to be publicly spoken by children *and teachers* every morning before the Pledge of Allegiance and made English the official and only legal language of Wyoming and banned anyone not fluent in English from owning property. Also he permitted firearms in every state wildlife refuge. And he issued an executive order requiring state law to supersede federal law in all matters, a move that amounted to, according to constitutional scholars, a fiat secession of Wyoming from the United States. He wore cowboy boots.

He held press conferences at his cattle ranch. He carried an actual live real gun, a revolver that dangled in a leather holster at his hip.

At the end of his one term as governor, he declared he was not running for reelection in order to focus on national priorities, and the media naturally took this to mean he was running for president. He perfected a sort of preacher-slash-cowboy pathos and an antielitist populism and found a receptive audience especially among blue-collar white conservatives put out by the current recession. He compared immigrants taking American jobs to coyotes killing livestock, and when he did this he pronounced *coyotes* pointedly with two syllables: *ky-oats*. He put an *R* sound in Washington so it became *Warshington*. He said *bushed* instead of *tired*. He said *yallow* for *yellow* and *crick* for *creek*.

Supporters said that's just how normal, nonelite people from Wyoming talk.

His detractors loved pointing out that since the courts had struck down almost all of his Wyoming initiatives, his legislative record was effectively nil. None of that seemed to matter to the people who continued to pay for his $500-a-plate fund-raisers (which, by the way, he called "grub-downs") and his $10,000 lecture fees and his $30 hardcover book *The Heart of a True American,* loading up his "war chest," as the reporters liked to call it, for a "future presidential run, maybe."

And now the governor has been attacked! Though nobody seems to know how he's been attacked, what he's been attacked with, who he's been attacked by, or if the attack has injured him. News anchors speculate at the potential damage of taking a ball bearing or marble at high velocity right in the eye. They talk about this for a good ten minutes, with charts showing how a small mass traveling at close to sixty miles per hour could penetrate the eye's liquid membrane. When this topic wears itself out, they break for commercials. They promote their upcoming documentary on the ten-year anniversary of 9/11: *Day of Terror, Decade of War.* They wait.

Then something happens to save the news from the state of idleness into which it has drifted: The anchor reappears and announces that a bystander caught the whole spectacular thing on video and has now posted it online.

And so here is the video that's going to be shown several thousand times on television over the next week, that will collect millions of hits and become the third-most-watched internet clip this month behind the new music video from teen pop singing sensation Molly Miller for her single "You Have Got to Represent," and a family video of a toddler laughing until he falls over. Here is what happens:

The video begins in whiteness and wind, the sound of wind blowing over an exposed microphone, then fingers fumbling over and pressing into the mic to create seashell-like swooshing sounds as the camera adjusts its aperture to the bright day and the whiteness resolves to a blue sky, indistinct unfocused greenishness that is presumably grass, and then a voice, a man's voice loud and too close to the mic: "Is it on? I don't know if it's on."

The picture comes into focus just as the man points the camera at his own feet. He says in an annoyed and exasperated way, "Is this even on? How can you tell?" And then a woman's voice, calmer, melodious, peaceful, says, "You look at the back. What does it say on the back?" And her husband or boyfriend or whoever he is, who cannot manage to keep the picture steady, says "Would you just help me?" in this aggressive and accusatory way that's meant to communicate that whatever problem he's having with the camera is her responsibility. The video through all this is a jumpy, dizzying close-up of the man's shoes. Puffy white high-tops. Extraordinarily white and new-looking. He seems to be standing on top of a picnic table. "What does it say on the back?" the woman asks.

"Where? What back?"

"On the screen."

"I know *that*," he says. "Where on the screen?"

"In the bottom right corner," she says with perfect equanimity.

"What does it say?"

"It says *R*."

"That means it's recording. It's on."

"That's stupid," he says. "Why doesn't it say *On*?"

The picture bobs between his shoes and what seems to be a crowd of people in the middle distance.

"There he is! Lookit! That's him! There he is!" the man shouts. He points the camera forward and, when he finally manages to keep it from trembling, Sheldon Packer comes into view, about thirty yards away and surrounded by campaign staffers and security. There is a light crowd. People in the foreground becoming suddenly aware that something's happening, that someone famous is nearby. The cameraman is now yelling: "Governor! Governor! Governor! Governor! Governor! Governor! Governor!" The picture begins shaking again, presumably from this guy waving or jumping or both.

"How do you make this thing zoom?" he says.

"You press Zoom," says the woman. Then the picture begins to zoom, which causes even more focus and exposure-related problems. In fact, the only reason any of this footage is at all usable on television is because the man eventually hands the camera to his partner, saying, "Here, would you just take this?" He rushes over to shake the governor's hand.

Later all of this blather will be edited out, so the clip that will be repeated hundreds of times on television will begin here, paused, as the news puts a small red circle around a woman sitting on a park bench on the right side of the screen. "This appears to be the perpetrator," the anchor says. She's white-haired, probably sixty, sitting there reading a book, in no way unusual, like an extra in a movie, filling out the frame. She's wearing a light blue shirt over a tank top, black leggings that look elastic and yoga-inspired. Her short hair is tousled and falls in little spikes over her forehead. She seems to have an athletic compactness to her—thin but also muscular. She notices what's happening around her. She sees the governor approaching and closes her book and stands and watches. She's on the edge of the frame seemingly trying to decide what to do. Her hands are on her hips. She's biting the inside of her mouth. It looks like she's weighing her options. The question this pose seems to ask is: *Should I?*

Then she starts walking, quickly, toward the governor. She has discarded her book on the bench and she's walking, taking these large strides like suburbanites doing laps around the mall. Except her arms stay steady at her sides, her fists in balls. She gets close enough to the governor that she's within throwing range and, at that moment, fortuitously, the crowd parts, so from the vantage point of our videographer there's a clear line of sight from this woman to the governor. The woman stands on a gravel path and looks down and bends at her knees and scoops up a handful of rocks. Thus armed, she yells—and this is very clear, as the wind dies down exactly at this moment and the crowd seems to hush, almost as if everyone knows this event is going to happen and so they all do what they can to successfully capture it—she yells, "You pig!" And then she throws the rocks.

At first there's just confusion as people turn to see where the yelling is coming from, or they wince and flinch away as they are struck by the stones. And then the woman scoops another handful of rocks and throws, and scoops and throws and scoops and throws, like a child in an all-out snowball war. The small crowd ducks for cover and mothers protect their children's faces and the governor doubles over, his hand covering his right eye. And the woman keeps throwing rocks until the governor's security guards reach her and tackle her. Or not really *tackle* but rather embrace her and slump to the ground, like exhausted wrestlers.

And that's it. The whole video lasts less than a minute. After the broadcast, certain facts become available in short order. The woman's name is released: Faye Andresen-Anderson, which everyone on the news mistakenly pronounces as "Anderson-Anderson," making parallels to other infamous double names, notably Sirhan Sirhan. It is quickly discovered that she is a teaching assistant at a local elementary school, which gives ammunition to certain pundits who say it shows how the radical liberal agenda has taken over public education. The headline is updated to teacher attacks gov. packer! for about an hour until someone manages to find an image that allegedly shows the woman attending a protest in 1968. In the photo, she is wearing big round glasses and appears to be leaning on someone just out of frame. Behind her is a great mass of people, all of them sitting, many of them holding homemade banners or signs, one of them holding an American flag.

The headline changes to sixties radical attacks gov. packer!

And as if the story isn't delicious enough already, two things happen near the end of the workday to vault it into the stratosphere, water-coolerwise. First, it's reported that Governor Packer is having emergency surgery on his eyeball. And second, a mug shot is unearthed that shows the woman was arrested in 1968—though never officially charged or convicted—for *prostitution*.

This is just too much. How can one headline possibly gather all these amazing details? radical hippie prostitute teacher blinds gov. packer in vicious attack!

The news plays over and over the part of the video where the governor is struck. They enlarge it so it's all pixelated and grainy in a valiant effort to show everyone the exact moment that a sharp piece of gravel splashes into his right cornea. Pundits argue about the meaning of the attack and whether it represents a threat to democracy. Some call the woman a terrorist, others say it shows how far our political discourse has fallen, others say the governor pretty much asked for it by being such a reckless crusader for guns. Comparisons are made with the Weather Underground and the Black Panthers. The NRA releases a statement saying the attack never would have happened had Governor Packer been carrying his revolver. The people working at their desks behind the TV anchor, meanwhile, do not appear at this moment to be working any harder or less hard than they were earlier in the day.

It takes about forty-five minutes for a clever copywriter to come up with the phrase "Packer Attacker," which is promptly adopted by all the networks and incorporated into the special logos they make for the coverage.

The woman herself is being kept in a downtown jail awaiting arraignment and is unavailable for comment. Without her explanation, the narrative of the day forms when opinion and assumption combine with a few facts to create an ur-story that hardens in people's minds: The woman is a former hippie and current liberal radical who hates the governor so much that she waited in a premeditated way to viciously attack him.

Except there's a glaring logical hole in this theory, which is that the governor's jaunt through the park was an impromptu move that not even his security detail knew about. Thus the woman couldn't have known he was coming and so couldn't have been waiting in ambush. However, this inconsistency is lost in the more sensational news items and is never fully investigated.

Chapter Two

Professor Samuel Anderson sits in the darkness of his small university office, his face lit grayly by the glow of a computer screen. Blinds are drawn over the windows. A towel blocks the crack under the door. He has placed the trash bin out in the hall so the night janitor won't interrupt. He wears headphones so nobody will hear what he's doing.

He logs on. He reaches the game's intro screen with its familiar image of orcs and elves torqued in battle. He hears the brass-heavy music, triumphant and bold and warlike. He types a password even more involved and intricate than the password to his bank account. And as he enters the *World of Elfscape* landscape, he enters not as Samuel Anderson the assistant professor of English but rather as Dodger the Elven Thief, and the feeling he has is very much like the feeling of coming home. Coming home at the end of a long day to someone who's glad you're back, is the feeling that keeps him logging on and playing upward of forty hours a week in preparation for a raid like this, when he gathers with his anonymous online friends and together they go kill something big and deadly.

Tonight it's a dragon.

They log on from basements, offices, dimly lit dens, cubicles and workstations, from public libraries, dorm rooms, spare bedrooms, from laptops on kitchen tables, from computers that whir hotly and click and crackle like somewhere inside their plastic towers a food item is frying. They put on their headsets and log on and materialize in the game world and they are together again, just as they have been every Wednesday and Friday and Saturday night for the past few years. Almost all of them live in Chicago or very close to Chicago. The game server on which they're playing—one of thousands worldwide—is located in a former meatpacking warehouse on Chicago's South Side, and for lagand latency-related issues, *Elfscape* always places you in the server nearest your location. So they are all practically neighbors, though they have never met in real life. "Yo, Dodger!" someone says as Samuel logs in.

Yo, he writes back. He never talks here. They think he doesn't talk because he doesn't have a microphone. The truth is he does have a microphone, but he's worried that if he talks during these raids some wandering colleague out in the hall might hear him saying things about dragons. So the guild knows really nothing about him except that he never misses a raid and has the tendency to spell out words rather than use the accepted internet abbreviations. He will actually write "be right back" instead of the more common "brb." He will write "away from keyboard" rather than "afk." People are not sure why he insists on this reverse anachronism. They think the name Dodger has something to do with baseball, but in fact it is a Dickens reference. That nobody gets the reference makes Samuel feel smart and superior, which is something he needs to feel to offset the shame of spending so much time playing a game also played by twelve-year-olds.

Samuel feels conflicted about these *Elfscape* friends: happy for the camaraderie while also resenting that he's become one of them. One of those guys who spends his Friday nights playing video games. He tries to remind himself that millions of other people do this. On every continent. Twenty-four hours a day. At any given moment, the number of people playing *World of Elfscape* is a population about the size of Paris, he thinks, sometimes, when he feels that rip inside him because this is where his life has ended up.

One reason he never tells anybody in the real world that he plays *Elfquest* is that they might ask what the point of the game is. And what could he say? *To slay dragons and kill orcs.*

Or you can play the game as an orc, in which case the point is to slay dragons and kill elves.

But that's it, that's the tableau, the fundamental premise, this basic yin and yang.

He began as a level-one elf and worked his way up to a level-ninety elf and this took roughly ten months. Along the way, he had adventures. He traveled continents. He met people. He found treasure. He completed quests. Then, at level ninety, he found a guild and teamed up with his new guild mates to kill dragons and demons and most especially orcs. He's killed so many orcs. And when he stabs an orc in one of the vital places, in the neck or head or heart, the game flashes CRITICAL HIT! and there's a little noise that goes off, a little orcish cry of terror. He's come to love that noise. He drools over that noise. His character class is thief, which means his special abilities include pickpocketing and bombmaking and invisibility, and one of his favorite things is to sneak into orcheavy territory and plant dynamite on the road for orcs to ride over and get killed by. Then he loots the bodies of his enemies and collects their weapons and money and clothes and leaves them naked and defeated and dead.

Why this has become so compelling he isn't really sure.

Tonight it's twenty elves armed and armored against this one dragon because it is a very large dragon. With razor-sharp teeth. Plus it breathes fire. Plus it's covered in scales the thickness of sheet metal, which is something they can see if their graphics card is good enough. The dragon appears to be asleep. It is curled catlike on the floor of its magma-rich lair, which is set inside a hollowed-out volcano, naturally. The ceiling of the lair is high enough to allow for sustained dragon flight because during the battle's second phase the dragon will launch into the air and circle them from above and shoot fiery bombs onto their heads. This will be the fourth time they've tried to kill this dragon; they have never made it past phase two. They want to kill it because the dragon guards a heap of treasure and weapons and armor at the far end of the lair, the looting of which will be sweet vis-à-vis their war against the orcs. Veins of brightred magma glow just under the ground's rocky surface. They will break open during the third and final phase of the fight, a phase they have not yet seen because they just cannot get the hang of the fireball-dodging thing.

"Did you all watch the videos I sent?" asks their raid leader, an elf warrior named Pwnage. Several players' avatars nod their heads. He had e-mailed them tutorials showing how to defeat this dragon. What Pwnage wanted them to pay attention to was how to manage phase two, the secret to which seems to be to keep moving and avoid getting bunched up.

LETS GO!!! writes Axman, whose avatar is currently dry-humping a rock wall. Several elves dance in place while Pwnage explains the fight to them, again.

Samuel plays *Elfscape* from his office computer because of the faster internet connection, which can increase his damage output in a raid like this by up to two percent, usually, unless there's some bandwidth-traffic problems, like when students are registering for classes. He teaches literature at a small university northwest of Chicago, in a suburb where all the great freeways split apart and end at giant department stores and corporate office parks and three-lane roads clogged with vehicles driven by the parents who send their children to Samuel's school.

Children like Laura Pottsdam—blond, lightly freckled, dressed sloppily in logoed tank tops and sweatshorts with various words written across the butt, majoring in business marketing and communication, and who, this very day, showed up to Samuel's Introduction to Literature course, handed in a plagiarized paper, and promptly asked if she could leave.

"If we're having a quiz," she said, "I won't leave. But if we're not having a quiz, I really need to leave."

"Is there an emergency?" he said.

"No. It's just that I don't want to miss any points. Are we doing anything today worth points?"

"We're discussing the reading. It's information you'll probably want to know."

"But is it worth points?"

"No, I suppose not."

"Then, okay, I really have to leave."

They were reading *Hamlet*, and Samuel knew from experience that today would be a struggle. The students would be spent, worn down by all that language. The paper he had assigned was about identifying logical fallacies in Hamlet's thinking, which even Samuel had to admit was sort of a bullshit exercise. They would ask why they had to do this, read this old play. They would ask, *When are we ever going to need to know about this in real life?*

He was not looking forward to this class.

What Samuel thinks about in these moments is how he used to be a pretty big deal. When he was twenty-four years old a magazine published one of his stories. And not just any magazine, but *the* magazine. They did a special on young writers. "Five Under Twenty-Five," they called it. "The next generation of great American authors." And he was one of them. It was the first thing he ever published. It was the only thing he ever published, as it turned out. There was his picture, and his bio, and his great literature. He had about fifty calls the next day from big-shot book people. They wanted more work. He didn't have more work. They didn't care. He signed a contract and was paid a lot of money for a book he hadn't even written yet. This was ten years ago, back before America's current financial bleakness, before the crises in housing and banking left the world economy pretty much shattered. It sometimes occurs to Samuel that his career has followed roughly the same trajectory as global finance: The good times of summer 2001 seem now, in hindsight, like a pleasant and whimsical daydream.

LETS GOOOOOOOO!!! Axman writes again. He has stopped humping the cave wall and is now leaping in place. Samuel thinks: ninth grade, tragically pimpled, hyperactivity disorder, will probably someday end up in my Intro to Lit class.

"What did you think about *Hamlet*?" Samuel had asked his class today, after Laura's departure.

Groans. Scowls. Guy in the back held his hands aloft to show his two big meat-hook thumbs pointing down. "It was stupid," he said.

"It didn't make any sense," said another.

"It was too long," said another.

"*Way* too long."

Samuel asked his students questions he hoped would spark any kind of conversation: Do you think the ghost is real or do you think Hamlet is hallucinating? Why do you think Gertrude remarried so quickly? Do you think Claudius is a villain or is Hamlet just bitter? And so on. Nothing. No reaction. They stared blankly into their laps, or at their computers. They always stare at their computers. Samuel has no power over the computers, cannot turn them off. Every classroom is equipped with computers at every single seat, something the school brags about in all the marketing materials sent to parents: *Wired campus! Preparing students for the twenty-first century!* But it seems to Samuel that all the school is preparing them for is to sit quietly and fake that they're working. To feign the appearance of concentration when in fact they're checking sports scores or e-mail or watching videos or spacing out. And come to think of it, maybe this is the most important lesson the school could teach them about the American workplace: How to sit calmly at your desk and surf the internet and not go insane.

"How many of you read the whole play?" Samuel said, and of the twenty-five people in the room, only four raised their hands. And they raised their hands slowly, shyly, embarrassed at having completed the assigned task. The rest seemed to reproach him—their looks of contempt, their bodies slumped to announce their huge boredom. It was like they blamed *him* for their apathy. If only he hadn't assigned something so stupid, they wouldn't have had to not do it.

"Pulling," says Pwnage, who now sprints toward the dragon, giant ax in hand. The rest of the raid group follows, crying wildly in a proximate imitation of movies they've seen about medieval wars.

Pwnage, it should be noted, is an *Elfscape* genius. He is a video-game savant. Of the twenty elves here tonight, six are being controlled by him. He has a whole village of characters that he can choose from, mixing and matching them depending on the fight, a whole self-sustaining microeconomy between them, playing many of them simultaneously using an incredibly advanced technique called "multiboxing" that involves several networked computers linked to a central command brain that he controls using programmed maneuvers on his keyboard and fifteen-button gaming mouse. Pwnage knows everything there is to know about the game. It's like he's internalized the secrets of *Elfscape* like a tree that eventually becomes one with the fence it grows next to. He annihilates orcs, often delivering the killing blow to his signature phrase: *I just pwned ur face n00b!!!*

During phase one of the fight they mostly have to watch out for the dragon's tail, which whips around and slams onto the rock floor. So everyone hacks away at the dragon and avoids its tail for the few minutes it takes to get the dragon down to sixty percent health, which is when the dragon takes to the air.

"Phase two," says Pwnage in a calm voice made robot-sounding from being transmitted over the internet. "Fire incoming. Don't stand in the bad."

Fireballs begin pummeling the raid group, and while many players find it a challenge to avoid the fire while continuing their dragon-fighting responsibilities, Pwnage's characters manage this effortlessly, all six of them, moving a couple of taps to their left or right so that the fire misses them by a few pixels.

Samuel is trying to dodge the fire, but mostly what he's thinking about right now is the pop quiz he gave in class today. After Laura left, and after it became clear the class had not done the assigned reading, he got into a punishing mood. He told his students to write a 250-word explication of the first act of *Hamlet*. They groaned. He hadn't planned on giving a pop quiz, but something about Laura's attitude left him feeling passive-aggressive. This was an Introduction to Literature course, but she cared less about literature than she did about *points*. It wasn't the topic of the course that mattered to her; what mattered was the currency. It reminded him of some Wall Street trader who might buy coffee futures one day and mortgage-backed securities the next. The thing that's traded is less important than how it's measured. Laura thought like this, thought only about the bottom line, her grade, the only thing that mattered.

Samuel used to mark up their papers—with a red pen even. He used to teach them the difference between "lay" and "lie," or when to use "that" and when to use "which," or how "affect" is different from "effect," how "then" is different from "than." All that stuff. But then one day he was filling up his car at the gas station just outside campus—it's called the EZ-Kum-In-'n-Go—and he looked at that sign and thought, *What is the point?*

Really, honestly, why would they ever need to know *Hamlet*?

He gave a quiz and ended class thirty minutes early. He was tired. He was standing in front of that disinterested crowd and he began to feel like Hamlet in the first soliloquy: insubstantial. He wanted to disappear.

He wanted his flesh to melt into a dew. This was happening a lot lately: He was feeling smaller than his body, as if his spirit had shrunk, always giving up his armrests on airplanes, always the one to move out of the way on sidewalks.

That this feeling coincided with his most recent search for internet photos of Bethany—well, that was too obvious to ignore. His thoughts always turn to her when he's doing something he feels guilty about, which, these days, is just about all the time, his whole life being sort of barnacled by these layers of impenetrable guilt. Bethany—his greatest love, his greatest screwup—who's still living in New York City, as far as he knows. A violinist playing all the great venues, recording solo albums, doing world tours. Googling her is like opening this great spigot inside him. He doesn't know why he punishes himself like that, once every few months, looking at pictures late into the night of Bethany being beautiful in evening gowns holding her violin and big bunches of roses and surrounded by adoring fans in Paris, Melbourne, Moscow, London.

What would she think about this? She would be disappointed, of course. She would think Samuel hasn't grown up at all—still a boy playing video games in the dark. Still the kid he was when they first met. Samuel thinks about Bethany the way other people maybe think about God. As in: *How is God judging me?* Samuel has the same impulse, though he's replaced God with this other great absence: Bethany. And sometimes, if he thinks about this too much, he can fall down a kind of hole and it's like he's experiencing his life at a one-step remove, as if he's not leading his life but rather assessing and appraising a life that weirdly, unfortunately, happens to be his.

The cursing from his guild mates brings him back to the game. Elves are dying rapidly. The dragon roars from above as the raid unloads all its best long-range violence—arrows and musket balls and throwing knives and electrical lightning-looking things that emerge from the bare hands of the wizards.

"Fire coming at you, Dodger," says Pwnage, and Samuel realizes he's about to be crushed. He dives out of the way. The fireball lands near him. His health bar empties almost to zero.

Thanks, Samuel writes.

And cheers now as the dragon lands and phase three begins. There remain only a few attackers of the original twenty: There's Samuel and Axman and the raid's healer and four of Pwnage's six characters. They have never reached phase three before. This is the best they've done against this dragon.

Phase three is pretty much like phase one except now the dragon is moving all around and opening up magma veins under the floor and shaking loose huge deadly stalactites from the cave's ceiling. Most *Elfquest* boss fights end this way. They are not so much tests of skill as of pattern memorization and multitasking: Can you avoid the lava splashing up from the floor and dodge the rocks falling from above and watch the dragon's tail so that you're not in the way of it and follow the dragon around its lair to keep hitting it with your dagger using the very specific and complicated ten-move attack that achieves the maximum damage output per second necessary to bring the dragon's health bar to zero before its internal ten-minute timer goes off and it does something called "enrages" when it goes all crazy and kills everyone in the room?

In the throes of it, Samuel usually finds this exhilarating. But immediately after, even if they win the fight, he always feels this crashing disappointment because all the treasure they've won is fake treasure, just digital data, and all the weapons and armor they've looted will help them only so long, because as soon as people start beating this dragon the developers will introduce some new creature who's even more difficult to kill and who's guarding even better treasure—a cycle that endlessly repeats. There is no way to ever really win. There is no end in sight. And sometimes the pointlessness of the game seems to reveal itself all at once, such as right now, as he watches the healer try to keep Pwnage alive and the dragon's health bar is slowly creeping toward zero and Pwnage is yelling "Go go go go!" and they are right on the verge of an epic win, even now Samuel thinks the only things really happening here are a few lonely people tapping keyboards in the dark, sending electrical signals to a Chicagoland computer server, which sends them back little puffs of data. Everything else—the dragon and its lair and the coursing magma and the elves and their swords and their magic—is all window dressing, all a façade.

Why am I here? he wonders, even as he is crushed by the dragon's tail and Axman is impaled by a falling stalactite and the healer burns to ash in a lava crevice and so the only elf remaining is Pwnage and the only way they're going to win is if Pwnage can stay alive, and the guild cheers through their headsets and the dragon's health ticks down to four percent, three percent, two percent . . .

Samuel wonders, even now, so close to victory, *What is the point? What am I doing?*

What would Bethany think?

You've just read an excerpt from The Nix.

ABOUT THE AUTHOR

Nathan Hill's short stories have appeared in many literary journals, including *The Iowa Review, AGNI, The Gettysburg Review*, and *Fiction*, where he was awarded the annual Fiction Prize. A native Iowan, he now lives with his wife in Naples, Florida. This is his first novel.

IMPRINT: Alfred A. Knopf
PRINT ISBN: 9781101946619
PRINT PRICE: $27.95
EBOOK ISBN: 9781101946626
EBOOK PRICE: $12.99
PUBLICATION DATE: 8/30/16
PUBLICITY CONTACT: Gabrielle Brooks
gbrooks@penguinrandomhouse.com
RIGHTS CONTACT: Emily Forland eforland@bromasite.com
EDITOR: Timothy O'Connell
AGENT: Emily Forland
AGENCY: Brandt & Hochman

TERRITORIES SOLD:
UK Edition Picador
German Edition Piper Verlag
French Edition Gallimard
Spanish & Catalan Editions Salamandra
Dutch Edition De Bezige Bij
Danish Edition Lindhardt & Ringhof

Swedish Edition Brombergs
Norwegian Edition Gyldendal Norsk
Italian Edition Rizzoli
Finnish Edition Gummerus
Hebrew Edition Kinneret
Hungarian Edition Libri Kiado
Korean Edition Amberlit

PROMOTIONAL INFORMATION:
BEA Buzz Panel book; pre-pub events in Minneapolis/St.Paul, Chicago; ALA appearance in June; National media appearances, including NPR and print features; National online interviews, reviews, and literary blog coverage; Men's magazine coverage; Author tour, including Chicago, Miami, Minneapolis/St. Paul, Naples, New York for select pre-pub events; BEA Featured Title; Advance Reader's Edition (also available as an eGalley); Pre-pub advertising and promotion in *Shelf Awareness, Early Word, Library Journal*; early giveaways on Goodreads, Read It Forward, and First to Read; National print advertising, including *The New York Times Book Review*; Major online advertising campaign, including *New York Times, Chicago Tribune, The New Yorker*; Litbreaker Network; Major Facebook and Goodreads advertising and promotion campaign; Major social media campaign; Regional eblasts; Reading Group Guide; Library marketing promotion; Holiday Repromotion; Jacket blowups available.

THINGS WE HAVE IN COMMON

TASHA KAVANAGH

SUMMARY

Fifteen-year-old Yasmin Doner is a social misfit—obese, obsessive, and deemed a freak by her peers at school. Struggling to cope since the death of her father and feeling an outsider in her mother's new marriage, Yasmin yearns for a sense of belonging, finding comfort only in food and the fantasy of being close to Alice Taylor, a girl at school. Rejected by her classmates, Yasmin will do anything to become friends with pretty and popular Alice—even if Alice, like everyone else, thinks she's a freak. When Yasmin sees a sinister man watching Alice from the school fence, she believes he is planning to abduct her. Yasmin decides to find out more about this man so that, when he takes Alice, she will be the only one who can save her—and so, will finally win her friendship. But as Yasmin forges a relationship with this man, who is kinder to her than anyone else, her affections begin to shift. Perhaps, she was wrong about him. Perhaps, she doesn't need Alice after all. And then Alice vanishes.

EXCERPT

The first time I saw you, you were standing at the far end of the playing field near the bit of fence that's trampled down, where the kids that come to school along the wooded path cut across.

You were looking down at your little brown straggly dog that had its face stuck in the grass, but then you looked up in the direction of the tennis court, your mouth going slack as your eyes clocked her. Even if I hadn't followed your gaze, I'd have known you were watching Alice Taylor because she had that effect on me too. I used to catch myself gazing at the back of her head in class, at her silky fair hair swaying between her shoulder blades as she looked from her book to the teacher or said something to Katy Ellis next to her.

At that moment she was turning to walk backwards, saying something to the girls that were following her, the sketchbook she takes everywhere tucked under her arm. She looked so light and easy, it was like she created space around her: not space in the normal sense but something else I can't explain. Even in our green school uniform it was obvious she was special.

If you'd glanced just once across the field, you'd have seen me standing in the middle on my own, looking straight at you, and you'd have gone back through the trees to the path quick, tugging your dog after you. You'd have known you'd given yourself away, even if only to me.

But you didn't. You only had eyes for Alice.

I looked round to see who else had spotted you. There were loads of kids on the field, but they were all busy with each other, footballs or their phones.

I looked back at the windows of the school building. I thought I'd see a teacher behind one of them, fixed on you, like *I know* your *game, sunshine*. I saw Mr Matthews walk past the History window reading from a piece of paper and Miss Wilcox one floor down in the staffroom talking to Mrs Henderson.

Then the bell went.

I didn't see your reaction because Robert pushed Dan into me, shouting 'He wants you, Doner—don't deny him,' then staggered backwards, laughing as Dan swore at him and tried to get him in a headlock.

I caught a glimpse of your blue jacket disappearing between the branches, though. The saying *Saved by the bell* came into my head because Dad always used to say it, and as I walked back across the field, I whispered the words slowly—'Saved by the bell, saved by the bell'—even though I knew that you weren't saved by anything, that you'd be back.

My name's not really Doner. It's Yasmin. It's just Doner at school—which is hilarious by the way because it's short for *Doner Kebab* and as well as being overweight I'm half Turkish. It used to be plain 'Fatty' at junior school, then 'Blubber-Butt' when I came to Ashfield, or 'Lesbo' till Mel Raynor and Natalie Simms started publicly making out, making lesbianism *à la mode*, whatever that means.

Anyway, I didn't see you at school the following day, even though I watched for you. At break and lunch I sat against the Games Hut where all the PE stuff like nets and balls and bibs is kept. I could see the whole of the fence that runs alongside the wooded path from there. I ate the chocolate Hobnobs I buy every morning on the way to school, chewing slowly and trying to ignore the fact that my bum was going numb from the concrete, scanning the trees for a bit of your jacket and listening for the kind of bark your little dog might make.

I was *vigilant*, and I wouldn't have missed you because of being distracted by friends because I don't have any. People look at me and think the same as I thought when I saw you: freak. So I figured, as well as feeling compelled to stare at Alice Taylor, being freaks was something else we had in common.

English is the only classroom I go to that overlooks the playing field, so I looked out for you there too. I have to sit in the third row from the window, but I could just about see the fence at the bottom of the field if I sat up, except that it was difficult to look without being obvious about it—which I was, because Robert threw a screwed-up piece of paper that hit my ear, and because a few minutes later Miss Frances, my English teacher who's really a Borg, said '*Yasmin*' in that sarcastic tone teachers use just to waste everyone's time because they know you're not listening and won't be able to answer whatever it was they asked.

I looked at her, rolling my biro in my fingers.

What she was telling me with her ice-blue eyes and black triangular eyebrows was, *I hate you Yasmin Laksaris and wish with all my frozen heart that you'd leave this school I have to teach in, but while you're still here don't think I won't make you pay for it.* What she said was: 'Any ideas about why Robert Browning chooses to set his poem in a storm?'

I thought about what the weather had been like when you were watching Alice. Dull and grey and so still it was as if the world had been sucked into another dimension where everything moved in silent, super-slow motion.

'She doesn't know, Miss,' Robert said. 'She's a kebab' (said like *Shish a kebab*). Miss Frances didn't laugh, even though I'm sure she found it quite amusing. She didn't want Robert stealing her spotlight. She folded her arms till she had everyone's attention again, then said, 'Do you have any opinions about *any*thing, Yasmin?'

I stopped twirling my biro. It's chewed, the plastic split halfway to the tip and the blue bit that fits in the end isn't there (I'm a chewer as well as a freak). I thought about giving my opinion that her drawn-on eyebrows make her look like she's a member of an enemy alien race that's managed to infiltrate the education system. Then I thought about giving my opinion about you—about how you were watching our school and had your sights set on Alice Taylor and that, if I was asked, I'd say one day pretty soon you might even take her.

I don't think I realised till that second that I *did* think you were going to take her. I knew it then, though. I knew the way you'd looked at her was never just looking. It was *wanting*. I bet it was wanting in a way you'd never wanted anything before. Like you'd never seen anything so lovely, never even dreamt about having anything quite that good—being able to touch her hair, slide your hands beneath her crisp white shirt.

Anyway, luckily for you I didn't say anything. No one would've believed me in any case. I'd probably have been sent to Miss Ward, the Head, who'd have said something like *I've told you about telling lies before, haven't I, Yasmin?* Which she has, several times. Instead, I looked around. Everyone was staring at me and I realised they were all waiting for me to answer Miss Frances's question about having opinions. Dan sniggered.

'No?' I said. It came out like a question, like I didn't know whether I had any opinions or not.

The whole class fell about then, and even though I couldn't care less, I felt my face burn. I probably looked at Alice without thinking, *instinctively*, to see if she was laughing with the rest of them.

She wasn't. She was the *only* one that wasn't. She was just looking at me over her shoulder, her green eyes sort of observing me.

I thought maybe in some parallel universe or via telepathy she'd heard my opinion about what you were going to do and that she'd understood somehow that I was going to save her, so I smiled. A small, secret smile. And even though she frowned and wrinkled her nose up before she turned away, I knew she'd felt it too—the connection.

I've kept Alice's steady green eyes in my head ever since. I still think of them even now—usually when I'm alone in the house, doing something ordinary like wiping the worktop or changing the sheets on the bed. They appear as suddenly as they did that day in English, and float about the house with me, watching me wherever I go, whatever I do.

Anyway, that day after school, I didn't know Alice's eyes would watch me forever, so I concentrated all my efforts on not losing them—on keeping them there in my head. It was like a self-induced trance. I didn't speak to anyone and ate dinner gazing somewhere beyond the telly, ignoring

Gary pointing his knife at my plate and having a go at Mum for putting too much mash on it, saying, 'You're not doing her any favours you know,' and moving along the sofa without a word when Mum patted me to budge up, all the while only hearing things like they were far away and only seeing Alice's green eyes watching me, watching me, watching . . .

When the six o'clock news came on, I went up to my room. Mum had closed the curtains and it was nice and cosy. I shut the door, switched on my giant lava lamp and took Alice's Box out of my bedside cabinet. It's square like a cube and gold and probably had chocolates in it to start with. For years it had my hair things in, like clips and scrunchies, but I stopped wearing them when I went to senior school and threw them away.

The first thing I put in it—the thing that made it Alice's Box—was a piece of green foil that went round a snack she'd had at break. That was in Year 7 when we were all new. It was a nice green, sort of smoky. I'd watched her lay it on her French book and smooth it carefully outwards from the middle with her fingertips. I don't know if she meant to leave it behind, but when everyone'd gone and I'd slid it carefully between the pages of my textbook, I imagined she had. I imagined it was a secret message—her way of telling me she'd be my friend if she could, if Katy would let her.

I started keeping other things of Alice's I found after that. Not any old thing. I didn't want her used tissues or empty crisp packets out of the bin—just things that were nice, or personal to her. Apart from the green foil, which was special because it was the first thing, I loved the heart: Alice's heart. She drew it. If I try and describe it, it won't sound anywhere near as lovely as it was, so you'll have to imagine the black lines, finer than cat hairs, swirling in and out and around each other. She was amazing at art, better than anyone. It was the way she saw things, I think, like she wasn't just looking, but feeling them too.

The thing in Alice's Box that you'd probably think was the weirdest was one of her trainer socks. For a few days I wasn't sure myself if it should go in, but then because I liked holding it and smelling it, I decided it should. It didn't smell of feet, if that's what you think (even though she'd worn it)—just a soft cottony smell.

I got a nice feeling when I looked at her things, when I held them. They made me feel calm. I'd whisper to start with—just words, her name, things I'd like to say to her—turning and touching whatever I was holding till I got so calm I stopped needing to whisper, stopped needing to breathe, even. Till everything floated away and it was just me and her.

After I put Alice's Box away, I took the Cadbury's Dairy Milk Turkish Delight out of my bedside drawer. I broke off a row, broke that in half, then put both bits in my mouth and lay back on the duvet. I let the chocolate melt slowly across the roof of my mouth and held my eyelids almost closed so I was looking through my lashes. That way, the galaxy that Gary painted on my ceiling before Mum and me moved in two years ago looked more convincing. I think he forgot I was thirteen and not eight when he did it, but I suppose it was nice of him. He didn't have to.

I thought about how it'd be when you took Alice—where I'd be when it happened. I imagined myself walking into English after lunch break (which would make it a Friday). I notice that Alice isn't at her desk. Everything's normal apart from that; everyone's messing around. Katy's the first to act any different, looking up at the clock that's saying it's two minutes past and calling across to Sophie, *Where's Alice?* Miss Francis comes in then. Everyone settles down and then *she* asks, *Where's Alice?* I look out of the window but of course you're not there. Nobody's there. Katy says she was with Alice at lunch. *She went back to get her coat after the bell*, she says. *She left it by the tennis court.* Miss Frances starts the lesson, reading from a book. She's distracted, though, and ten minutes later she glances up at the clock and checks her watch. She tells us to carry on reading, that she'll be back in one minute, and leaves the room.

I thought about how you didn't know I even existed, which gave me a nice feeling, like that even though you thought you were the one in control of things, you weren't because I was. *I* was in charge. I could save Alice. I thought if I told anyone what you were going to do, they wouldn't believe me, but that if I found out more about you, I could tell the police when the time came . . . when you took her. I thought I might even catch you in the act, if you tried to take her while we were at school. I thought I wouldn't let her out of my sight.

Either way, whether I was there or not, I'd still be the one that saved her. I'd be a heroine—Alice's heroine—and afterwards me and Alice would be bonded forever in the way people are after something traumatic. And even though Alice's parents would try and give me thousands of pounds in reward money, which Mum and Gary would be pleading with me to take, I'd say all I wanted for my reward was your dog. And in the papers there'd be a picture of me holding him and it'd say I was a heroine in the true sense of the word.

I went downstairs to get a drink then, being quiet because I didn't want Mum, or especially Gary, to come out of the sitting room and catch me with a glass of his secret Coke stash. Fizzy drinks are strictly forbidden on my diet plan (along with Cadbury's Dairy Milk Turkish Delight and chocolate Hobnobs, in case you were wondering). Apparently I should drink water instead. Dr. Bhatt says it's nice when you get used to it. In his Indian accent he goes, '. . . and with a bit of lemon or lime squeezed in it's really something rather special', his eyebrows all high like he actually believes it! I love Dr. Bhatt. He's my dietician. He's sort of spiritual in the way he says things. He's kind as well, even though he's got to deal with me, which must be frustrating because I'm bigger now than when I first started going to him a year ago.

Anyway, I managed to get the Coke out from behind the Pledge Furniture Polish and Mr. Muscle Window & Glass Cleaner without making too much noise. Mum and Gary think I don't know he keeps it there under the sink, and even though, when he's having a go at me about my weight (like he's not pretty *rotund* himself), it'd give me great pleasure to be able to point out what a bloody hypocrite he is—I want to keep it that way. I poured myself a glass and drank it down quick, then had another one. It's not as nice when it's not cold but it was too risky to faff about getting ice out of the freezer. Then I rinsed the glass under the tap and filled the bottle up with water to the same level it was before, because Gary, I bet you anything, makes a mental mark on the bottle of *exactly* how much is left every time he's had some. That's the kind of person he is, which is why, normally, I buy my own drinks.

I heard Mum and Gary arguing, then—or rather Gary delivering one of his lectures, his voice raised. When I was going back down the hall, I heard him say, 'It's a bit more than just puppy fat, Jen! I hate to say it, but it seems to me like she growing *in*to it, not out.'

I stopped outside the sitting-room door. I suppose you just do that, don't you, when someone's talking about you, even if you really don't want to hear? Even if you couldn't care less what they're going to say.

'She's been much better recently,' Mum said. 'She's definitely lost a few pounds. Let's just wait until she's been to the hospital.'

'OK, fine. But I think you're avoiding the issue. You're burying your head in the sand.'

'And I think you expect too much.'

'It's not about what I *expect*, Jen. I want her to be happy.'

'She is happy.'

'Have a normal teenage life,' Gary went on. 'You know—friends. *Boy*friends. I mean, come on! Who's going to want to date her like . . . like she is?'

'Well, we're dealing with it, aren't we?' Mum said, her voice raised as well now. 'She's losing weight. Honestly, Gary, she's only fifteen. I don't really want her doing anything with boys.'

There was another silence. Then Gary, wanting to have the last word like always, said, 'OK then. Let's just pretend she's losing weight and everything's hunky-dory, shall we?'

'Everything *is* hunky-dory, Gary. Let's just wait and see.'

I did a silent cheer for Mum for beating Gary to the final word and started up the stairs, but she wasn't finished. She said—the words clipped like she was accusing him—'You weren't there.'

Yeah, I thought. You weren't there, Gary Thornton—Gary Thorn-in-my-bum. You weren't there. School felt different the next day, and it wasn't anyone else. Everyone was the same—basically either ignoring me or calling me names.

I was different, though. And I knew why. It was because I had a purpose now, because I had to save Alice. It put a new angle on everything. It's like the perspective thing we did in art last year: far away = small, close up = big. It's obvious, I know, till you've got to draw it (unless you're Alice, of course, who could even make rotting fruit look lush). What I'm trying to say with the perspective thing is that I've always felt like *I'm* far away, like *I'm* the dot in the distance, and that everyone else is close up—big—living. But suddenly that day I didn't feel like the dot anymore. I felt like I was the one that was close up—the one who knew the score, who could see the big picture—and I walked around the place like *Bring it on!*

You've just read an excerpt from Things We Have in Common.

ABOUT THE AUTHOR

Tasha Kavanagh lives in Hertfordshire with her family and three cats. She has an MA in Creative Writing from the University of East Anglia, has worked as an editor on feature films, including *The Talented Mr Ripley*, *Twelve Monkeys* and *Seven Years in Tibet*, and is a windsurfing champion, having raced all over the world. She has had 10 books for children published under her maiden name Tasha Pym, and her first adult novel *Things We Have in Common* was shortlisted for the Costa First Novel Award.

IMPRINT: MIRA Books
PRINT ISBN: 9780778326854
PRINT PRICE: $15.99
EBOOK ISBN: 9781460396391
EBOOK PRICE: $9.99
PUBLICATION DATE: 1/31/17
PUBLICITY CONTACT: Emer Flounders emer.flounders@harpercollins.com
RIGHTS CONTACT: Reka Rubin reka.rubin@harlequin.com
EDITOR: Liz Stein
AGENT: Susan Armstrong
AGENCY: Conville & Walsh

TERRITORIES SOLD:
UK, North America, Sweden

PROMOTIONAL INFORMATION:
Extensive consumer advertising campaign, including national print media; Targeted trade support, including library and independent bookseller outreach; Book club promotion, including a reader's guide inside the book; In-book advertising in selected Harlequin MIRA® imprint titles; National galley distribution and press kit mailings; Blogger outreach; Extensive online promotion, including social media and Bookclubbish.com; Featured title at www.Harlequin.com.

MISCHLING

a novel

"Reading [Affinity Konar]
makes us greater than we are."
—Lydia Millet

**AFFINITY
KONAR**

SUMMARY

"One of the most harrowing, powerful, and imaginative books of the year" (Anthony Doerr) about twin sisters fighting to survive the evils of World War II.

EXCERPT

Part One

Stasha

Chapter One

World After World

We were made, once. My twin Pearl and me. Or, to be precise, Pearl was formed and I split from her. She embossed herself on the womb, I copied her signature. For eight months we were afloat in amniotic snowfall, two rosy mittens resting on the lining of our mother. I couldn't imagine anything grander than the womb we shared, but after the scaffolds of our brains were ivoried and our spleens were complete, Pearl wanted to see the world beyond us. And so, with newborn pluck, she spat herself out of our mother.

Though premature, Pearl was a sophisticated prankster. I assured myself that it was just one of her tricks; she'd be back to laugh at me. But when Pearl failed to return, I lost my breath. Have you ever had to live with the best part of yourself adrift, stationed at some unknowable distance? If so, I am sure you are aware of the dangers of this condition. After my breath left me, my heart followed suit, and my brain ran with an unthinkable fever. In my fetal pinkness, I faced this truth: without her, I would become a split and unworthy thing, a human incapable of love.

That is why I followed my sister's lead and allowed the doctor's hands to tear me out and smack me and hold me to the light. Let us note that I never cried during the ruptures of this unwanted transition. Not even when our parents ignored my wishes to name me Pearl too.

I became Stasha instead. And with the chore of birth complete, we entered the world of family and piano and book, of days that baffled by in beauty. We were so alike—we were always dropping marbles from the window onto the paving stones and watching them descend the hill with our binoculars, just to see how far their little lives would take them.

That world, teeming with awe, ended too. Most worlds do.

But I must tell you: there was another world we knew. Some say it was the world that made us the most. I want to say that they are wrong, but for now, let me tell you that our entry into this world began in our twelfth year of life, when we were huddled side by side in the back of a cattle car.

During that journey of four days and four nights, we cheated our way into survival. For sustenance, we passed an onion back and forth and licked its yellow hide. For entertainment, we played the game Zayde made for us, a game called *The Classification of Living Things*. In this form of charades, you had to portray a living thing, and the players had to name the species, the genus, the family, and so on, all the way to the encompassing brilliance of a kingdom.

We passed through so many living things in the cattle car, we postured from bear to snail and back—it was important, Zayde emphasized in his thirst-cracked voice, that we organize the universe to the best of our too-human ability—and when the cattle car finally came to a stop I stopped my charade too. The way I remember it—I was in the middle of trying to convince Pearl that I was an amoeba. It's possible that I was portraying some other living thing, and that I am only remembering it as an amoeba now because I felt so small in that moment, so translucent and fragile. I cannot be sure.

Just as I was about to admit my defeat, the door to the cattle car rolled open.

And the incoming light was so startling that we dropped our onion on the floor, and it rolled down the ramp, a smelly and half-eaten moon that landed at the feet of a guard. I imagine that his face was full of disgust, but I couldn't see it—he held a kerchief over his nostrils while issuing a series of sneezes, and he stopped sneezing only to hover his boot over our onion and cast an eclipsing shadow over the tiny globe. We watched the onion weep as he crushed it, its tears a bitter pulp. He then resumed his approach, and we scrambled to hide in the shelter of Zayde's voluminous coat. Though we had outgrown Zayde as a hiding place long ago, fear made us smaller, and we contorted within the coat folds beside his dwindled body, leaving our grandfather a lumpy, many-legged figure. In this shelter, we blinked. Then we heard a sound—a stomp, a shuffle—the guard's boots were immediately before us.

"What kind of insect are you?" he asked Zayde, rapping each of the girlish legs that emerged beneath the coat with a walking stick. Our knees smarted. Then the guard struck Zayde's legs too. "Six legs? You are a spider?"

It was clear that the guard had no real understanding of living things at all. Already, he'd made an error. But Zayde didn't bother to point out that spiders aren't insects. Traditionally, Zayde enjoyed issuing playful, sing-song corrections, as he liked to see all the facts put to rights. In that place though—it was too dangerous to express any intimate knowledge of creatures that crawled or were considered lowly, lest you be accused of bearing too much in common with them. We should have known better than to make an insect of our grandfather.

"I asked you a question," the guard insisted, while issuing another rap to our legs with his stick. "What kind?"

In German, Zayde gave him facts: his name was Tadeusz Zamorski. He was sixty-five years old. He was a Polish Jew. He ended there, as if all were told.

And we wanted to continue for him, we wanted to give all the details: Zayde was a former professor of biology. He'd taught the subject at universities for decades, but was an expert in many things. If you wanted to know about the insides of a poem, he would be the one to ask. If you wanted to know how to walk on your hands or find a star, he'd show you. With him, we once saw a rainbow that ran only red, saw it straddle a mountain and a sea, and he toasted the memory of it often. *To unbearable beauty!* He'd cry, eyes abrim. He was so fond of toasts that he made them indiscriminately, for nearly any occasion. *To a morning swim! To the lindens at the gate!* And in recent years, there was this, his most common toast: *To the day my son returns, alive and unchanged!*

But as much as we would have liked to, we said nothing of these things to the guard—the details caught in our throats and our eyes were tearful because of the death of the nearby onion. The tears were the onion's fault, we told ourselves, nothing more, and we wiped the drops away so that we could see what was happening through the holes in Zayde's coat.

Encircled in the portholes of these flaws were five figures: three little boys, their mother, and a white-coated man who stood with a pen cocked over a little book. The boys intrigued us—we'd never seen triplets before. In Lodz, there had been another set of girl-twins, but a trio was the stuff of books. Though we were impressed by their number, we had to admit that we trumped them in terms of identicality. All three had the same dark curls and eyes, the same spindly bodies, but they wore different expressions—one squinted at the sun, while the other two frowned, and their faces fell into similarity only when the white-coated man distributed candy into each of their palms.

The triplets' mother was different than all the other mothers of the cattle car—her distress was neatly tucked away, and she stood as still as a stopped clock. One of her hands hovered over her sons' heads in some perpetual hesitation, as if she felt that she no longer had the right to touch them. The white-coated man did not share this attitude.

He was an intimidating figure, all shiny black shoes and dark hair of equal polish, his sleeves so expansive that when he lifted an arm the fabric below billowed and winged and claimed a disproportionate measure of sky. He was movie-star handsome and prone to dramatics; kindly expressions swelled across his face with obviousness, as if he was eager to let everyone near know the extremity of his good intentions.

Words passed between the mother and the white-coated man. They seemed like agreeable words, though the man did most of the talking. We wished we could hear the conversation, but it was enough, I suppose, to see what happened next: the mother passed her hands over the dark clouds of the triplets' hair, and then she turned her back, leaving the boys with the white-coated man.

He was a doctor, she said as she walked away, a falter in her step. They would be safe, she reassured them, and she did not look back.

Our mother, hearing this, gave a little squeak and a gasp, before reaching over to tug at the guard's arm. Her boldness was a shock. We were used to a trembling mother, one that always shook while making requests of the butcher and hid from the cleaning woman. Always, it was as if pudding ran through her veins, making her constantly aquiver and defeatable, especially since Papa's disappearance. In the cattle car, she'd steadied herself only by drawing poppies on the wooden walls. Pistil, petal, stamen—she drew with a strange focus, and when she stopped drawing, she went to pieces. But on the ramp she discovered a new solidity—she stood stronger than the starved and weary should ever stand. Was the music responsible for this alteration? Mama always loved music, and this place was teeming with bright notes, they found us in the cattle car and drew us out with a distrustful cheer. Over time, we'd learn the depths of this trick, we'd know to beware of the celebratory tune, as it only held suffering at its core, and that the orchestra had been entrusted with the deception of all that entered, they were compelled, these musicians, to use their talents to ensnare the unwitting, to convince us that where we arrived was a place not entirely without an appreciation for the humane and the beautiful. Music, it uplifted the arriving crowds, it flowed beside them as they walked through the gates. Was this why Mama was able to be bold? I would never know. But I admired her courage as she spoke.

"It is good here—to be a double?" she asked the guard.

He gave her a nod, and called to the doctor, who was squatting in the dust so that he could address the boys at eye-level. The group appeared to be having the warmest of chats.

"Zwillinge!" the guard called to him. "Twins!"

The doctor left the triplets to a female attendant, and strode over to us, his shiny boots disrupting the dust. He was courtly with our mother, taking her hand as he addressed her.

"You have special children?" His eyes were friendly, from what we could see.

Mama shifted from foot to foot, suddenly diminished. She tried to withdraw her hand from his grasp but he held it tight, and then he began to stroke it with his fingertips, as if it were some wounded, but easily soothed, thing.

"Only twins, not triplets," she apologized. "I hope they are enough."

The doctor's laugh was loud and showy and it echoed within the caverns of Zayde's coat. We were relieved when it subsided so that we could listen to Mama rattling off our gifts.

"They speak some German. Their father taught them. They'll turn thirteen in December. Healthy readers, the both of them. Pearl loves music—she is quick, practical, studies dance. Stasha, my Stasha," here Mama paused, as if unsure how to categorize me, before declaring, "She has an imagination."

The doctor received this information with interest, and requested that we join him on the ramp.

We hesitated. It was better within the suffocations of the coat. Outside, there was a grey, flame-licked wind that alerted us to our grief, and a scorched scent that underpinned it, there were guns casting shadows and dogs barking and drooling and growling as only dogs bred for cruelty can. But before we had a chance to withdraw further, the doctor pulled aside the curtains of the coat. In the sunlight, we blinked. One of us snarled. It might have been Pearl. It was probably me.

How could it be, the doctor marveled, that these perfect jaws could be wasted on such dour expressions? He drew us out, made us turn for him, and had us stand back to back so he could appreciate the exactitudes of us.

"Smile!" he instructed.

Why did we obey this particular order? For our mother's sake, I suppose. For her, we grinned, even as she clung to Zayde's arm, her face lit with panic, two drops of sweat tripping down her forehead. Ever since we'd entered the cattle car, I'd avoided looking at our mother. I looked at the poppies she drew instead, I focused on the fragile bloom of their faces. But something about her false expression made me acknowledge what Mama had become: a pretty but sleepless semi-widow, faded in her personhood. Once the primmest of women, she was undone; dust streaked her cheek, her lace collar limped. Dull gems of blood secured themselves to the corners of her lips where she'd gnawed on them in worry.

"They are mischlinge?" he asked. "That yellow hair!"

Mama pulled at her dark curls, as if ashamed of their beauty, and shook her head.

"My husband—he was fair," was all she could say. It was the only answer she had when asked about the coloring that made certain onlookers insist that our blood was mixed. As we'd grown, that word "mischling", we heard it more and more, and its use in our presence had inspired Zayde to give us *The Classification of Living Things*. Never mind this Nuremberg foolishness, he'd say. He'd tell us to forget this talk, of mixed-breeds, crossed genetics, of quarter-Jews and kindred, these absurd, hateful tests that tried to divide our people down to the last blood drop and marriage and place of worship. When you hear that word, he'd say, dwell on the variation of all living things. Sustain yourself, in awe of this.

I knew then, standing before the white-coated doctor, that this advice would be difficult to take in the days to come, that we were in a place that did not answer to Zayde's games,

"Genes, they are funny things, yes?" the doctor was saying.

Mama, she didn't even try to engage him in this line of conversation.

"If they go with you," and here she would not look at us, "when will we see them again?"

"On your Sabbath," the doctor promised. And then he turned to us and exclaimed over our details—he loved that we spoke German, he said, he loved that we were fair. He didn't love that our eyes were brown, but this, he remarked to the guard, could prove useful—he leaned in still closer to inspect us, extending a gloved hand to stroke my sister's hair.

"So you're Pearl?" His hand dipped through her curls too easily, as if it had done so for years.

She's not Pearl, I said. I stepped forward, to obscure my sister, but Mama pulled me away, and told the doctor that indeed, he had named the right girl.

"So they like to play tricks?" he laughed. "Tell me your secret—how do you know who is who?"

"Pearl doesn't fidget," was all Mama would say. I was grateful that she didn't elaborate on our identifiable differences. Pearl wore a blue pin in her hair. I wore red. Pearl spoke evenly. My speech was rushed, broken in spots, riddled with pause. Pearl's skin was as pale as a dumpling. I had summer flesh, as spotty as a horse. Pearl was all girl. I wanted to be all Pearl, but try as I might, I could only be myself.

The doctor stooped so that we could be face to face.

"Why would you lie?" he asked me. Again, there was his laugh, tinged with the familial.

If I was honest, I would have said that Pearl was—to my mind—the weaker of the two of us, and I thought I could protect her if I became her. Instead, I gave him a half-truth.

"I forget which one I am sometimes," I said lamely.

And this is where I don't remember. This is where I want to wander my mind back and under, past the smell, past the thump-bump of the boots and the suitcases, towards some semblance of a goodbye. Because we should have seen our loves go missing, we should have been able to watch them leave us, should have known the precise moment of our loss. If only we'd seen their faces turning from us, a flash of eye, a curve of cheek! A face turning—they would never give us that. Still, why couldn't we have had a view of their backs to carry with us, just their backs as they left, only that? Just a glimpse of shoulder, a flash of woolen coat? For the sight of Zayde's hand, hanging so heavy at his side—for Mama's braid, lifting in the wind!

But where our loved ones should have been, we had only the introduction to this white-coated man, Josef Mengele, the same Mengele that would become, in all his many years of hiding: Helmut Gregor, G. Helmuth, Fritz Ulmann, Fritz Hollman, Jose Mengele, Peter Hochbicler, Ernst Sebastian Alves, Jose Aspiazi, Lars Balltroem, Friedrich Edler von Breitenbach, Fritz Fischer, Karl Geuske, Ludwig Gregor, Stanislaus Prosky, Fausto Rindon, Fausto Rondon, Gregor Schklastro, Heinz Stobert, and Dr. Henrique Wollman.

The man who would bury his death-dealing within these many names— he told us to call him "Uncle Doctor". He made us call him by this name, once, then twice, just so we could all be acquainted, with no mistakes. By the time we finished repeating the name to his satisfaction, our family had vanished.

And when we saw the absence where Mama and Zayde once stood, an awareness collapsed me at the knees, because I saw that this world was inventing a different order of living things. I did not know then what kind of living thing I would become, but the guard didn't let me have a chance to think about it—he grasped my arm and dragged me, till Pearl assured him that she'd support me, and she put her arm around my waist as we were led away with the triplets, away from the ramp and into the dust, onto a little road that led past the sauna and towards the crematoria, and as we marched into this new distance with death rising up on either side of us, we saw bodies being still bodies on a cart, saw them heaped and blackened, and one of the bodies—it was reaching out its hand, it was grasping for something to hold, as if there were some invisible tether in the air that only the near-dead could see. The body's mouth moved. We saw the pinkness of a tongue as it flapped and struggled. Words had abandoned it.

I knew how important words were to a life. If I gave the body some of mine, I thought, it would be restored.

Was I stupid to think this? Or feeble-minded? Would the thought have occurred to me in a place free of flame-licked winds and white-winged doctors?

These are fair questions. I think of them often, but I have never tried to answer them. The answers don't belong to me.

All I know: I stared at the body, and the only words I could summon weren't my own. They were from a song I'd heard played by a smuggled record player in our ghetto basement. Whenever I'd heard the song, it had improved me. So I gave these words a try.

"Would you like to swing on a star?" I sang to the body.

Not a sound, not a stir. Was it the fault of my squeaky voice? I tried again.

"Carry moonbeams home in a jar?" I sang.

It was pathetic of me to try, I know, but I had always believed in the world's ability to right itself, just like that, with a single kindness. And when kindness is not around, you invent new orders and systems to believe in, and there, in that moment—whether it was stupidity or feeble-mindedness—I believed in a body's ability to animate itself, with the breath of a word. But it was obvious that these lyrics were not the right words at all. None of them could unlock the life of the body, or were powerful enough to repair it. I searched for another word, a good word, to give—there had to be a word, I was sure of it—but the guard wouldn't let me finish. He pulled me away and forced us to press on, anxious to have us showered and processed and numbered so that our time in Mengele's zoo could begin.

Auschwitz had been built to imprison Jews. Birkenau had been built to kill them with greater efficiency. Mere kilometers bridged their attached evils. What this zoo was designed for, I did not know—I could only swear that Pearl and I, we would never be caged.

***

The barracks of the Zoo were once stables for horses, but now, they were heaped with the likes of us: twins, triplets, quints. Hundreds upon hundreds of us, all slotted into beds that weren't beds but matchboxes, little slots to slip bodies into, we were piled from floor to ceiling, forced into these minute structures three or four bodies at a time, so that a girl hardly knew where her body ended, and another's began.

Everywhere we looked there was a duplicate, an identical. All girls. Sad girls, toddler girls, girls from faraway places, girls that could have been our neighborhood's girls. Some of these girls were quiet, they posed like birds on their straw mattresses and studied us. As we walked past them on their perches, I saw the chosen, the ones selected to suffer in certain ways while their other half remained untouched. In nearly every pair, one twin had a spine gone awry, a bad leg, a patched eye, a wound, a scar, a crutch.

When Stasha and I sat on our own bunk, the mobile ones descended on us. They scrambled over the rickety corrals with their straw mattresses, and appraised our similarities. Demands of our identities were made.

We were from Lodz, we told them. First, a house. Then, a basement in the ghetto. We had a grandpapa, a mother. Once, there had been a father. And Zayde had an old spaniel that could play dead when you pointed a finger at him, but he was easily brought back to life. Did we mention that our father was a doctor who helped others so much that he disappeared one night, he left us to tend to a sick child, and never returned? Yes, we missed him so much we could not even divide the weight of our grief between us. There were other things we dreaded too: germs, unhappy endings, Mama weeping. And there were things we loved: pianos, Judy Garland, Mama weeping less. But who were we really, in the end? There wasn't much to say beyond the fact that one of us was a good dancer, and the other one tried to be good, but wasn't really good at anything except at being curious. That one was me.

Satisfied by this information, the others offered their own, in a clamor of sentence-finishing.

"We get more food here," began Alize, a girl so pale that you could nearly see through her.

"But it's not kosher and it eats your insides," her equally transparent half pointed out.

"We keep our hair," nodded Sharon, pulling on her braid for show.

"Until the lice come," added her shorn sister.

"We get to keep our clothes too," contributed one of the Russians.

"But they put crosses on our backs," finished her double. She turned so I could see the cross that blared in red paint on her dress, but I needed no introduction. A red cross stood between my shoulderblades too.

Then the voices left off abruptly, and the uninvited silence hung over us all—it was as if a new cloud had installed itself within the rafters of the Zoo. The many doubles looked at each other searchingly—there had to be something, their faces said, something more than food and hair and clothes. Then a voice piped up from the bunk below us. We craned to see the speaker, but she and her twin were curled up together, flush with the brick wall. We never came to know her face, but her words stayed with us always.

"They keep our families safe for us," said this unseen stranger.

At this, all the girls nodded their approval, and Pearl and I were overwhelmed by a new rush of conversation, as everyone congratulated each other on belonging to families who would remain intact, unlike the others.

I didn't want to ask the obvious. So I pinched Pearl, to make her ask for us.

"Why are we more important than the others?" her voice shrank as it approached the end of the question.

A flurry of answers rose, all having something to do with purpose and greatness, of purity and beauty and being of use. We didn't hear a single one that made sense.

And before I could even try to understand this concept, the blokowa assigned to look after us entered. Behind her prodigious back, we called this person "Ox"; she had the appearance of a wardrobe with a toupee, and tendencies towards foot-stamping and nostril-flaring while caught in one of her passions, which our supposed disobedience frequently inspired. When Pearl and I were first introduced to her however, she was just a figure popping her head in at the door, half-shrouded in night and offended by our questions.

"Why are we called 'the zoo'?" I asked. "Who decided this?"

Ox shrugged. "It is not obvious to you?"

I said that it was not. The zoos we'd read about with Zayde were sites of preservation that presented the vastness of life. This place, it cared only for the sinister act of collection.

"It is a name that pleases Doctor Mengele," was all Ox would say. "You won't find many answers here. But sleep! That's something you can have. Now let me have mine!"

If only we could have slept. But the darkness was darker than any I'd known, and the smell clung within my nostrils. A moan drifted from the bunk below, and outside there was the barking of dogs and my stomach wouldn't stop growling back at them. I tried to amuse myself by playing one of our word games, but the shouts of the guards outside kept overpowering my alphabet. I tried to make Pearl play a game with me, but Pearl was busy tricking her fingertips over the silver web that embroidered our brick corner, the better to ignore my whispered questions.

"Would you rather be a watch made from the bones in God's hands," I asked her. "Or would you rather be a watch made from the heartstrings of Bing Crosby?"

"I don't believe in Bing Crosby."

"Me neither. Not anymore. But, would you rather be a watch—"

"Why do I have to be a watch at all?"

I wanted to argue that sometimes, as living things, human-type people who were presumably still alive, we had to treat ourselves as objects in order to get by, we had to hide ourselves away and seek repair only when repair was safe to seek. But I chose to press on with another query instead.

"Would you rather be the key to a place that will save you or the key to the place that will destroy your enemies?"

"I'd rather be a real girl," Pearl said dully. "Like I used to be."

I wanted to argue that playing games would help her feel like a real girl again, but even I wasn't sure of this fact. The numbers the Nazis had given us had made life unrecognizable, and in the dark, the numbers were all I could see, and what was worse was that there was no way to pretend them into anything less enduring or severe or blue. Mine were smudged and bleared—I'd kicked and spat, they had to hold me down—but they were numbers still. Pearl, she was numbered too, and I hated her numbers even more than mine, because they pointed out that we were separate people, and when you are separate people, you may be parted.

I told Pearl that I'd tattoo us back as soon as possible, to make us the same, but she only sighed the sigh traditional to moments of sisterly frustration.

"Enough with the stories. You can't tattoo."

I told her that I knew how to well enough. A sailor taught me, back in Gdansk. I inked an anchor on his bicep.

True, it was a lie. Or a half-lie, since I had seen such an anchor-inking take place. When we'd summered at the sea, I spent my time peering into the gray recess of a tattoo parlor, its walls bordered with outlines of swallows and ships, while Pearl found a boy to hold her hand near the barnacled prow of a boat. So it was that as my sister entered into the secrecies of flesh on flesh, the pang of a palm curled within one's own, I schooled myself in the intimacies of needles, the plunge of a point so fine that only a dream could light upon its tip.

"I'll make us the same again someday," I insisted. "I just need some needle and ink. There must be a way to get that, given that we are special here."

Pearl scowled and made a big show of turning her back on me—the bunk cried out with a creak—and her elbow flew up and jabbed me in the ribs. It was an accident—Pearl would never hurt me on purpose, if only because it would hurt her too. That was one of the biggest stings of this sisterhood—pain never belonged to just one of us. We had no choice but to share our sufferings, and I knew that in this place we'd have to find a way to divide the pain before it began to multiply.

As I realized this, a girl on the other side of the barracks found a light, some precious book of matches, and she decided that this scarcity would be put to use making shadow puppets for the audience in the barracks. And so it was that we drifted off to sleep with a series of shadow figures crossing the wall, walking two by two, each flanking the other, as if in a procession towards some unseen ark that might secure their safety.

So much world in the shadows there! The figures feathered and crept and crawled toward the ark. Not a single life was too small. The leech asserted itself, the centipede sauntered, the cricket sang by. Representatives of the swamp, the mountain, the desert—all ducked and squiggled and forayed in shadow. I classified them, two by two, and the neatness of my ability to do so gave me comfort. But as their journey lengthened, and the flames began to dim, the shadows were visited by distortions. Humps rose on their backs and their limbs scattered and their spines dissolved. They became changed and monstrous. They couldn't recognize themselves.

Still, for as long as the light lived, the shadows endured. That was something, wasn't it?

You've just read an excerpt from Mischling.

ABOUT THE AUTHOR

Affinity Konar received her MFA from Columbia and lives in Los Angeles.

IMPRINT: Lee Boudreaux Books/ Little, Brown and Company
PRINT ISBN: 9780316308106
PRINT PRICE: $27.00
EBOOK ISBN: 9780316308083
EBOOK PRICE: $13.99
PUBLICATION DATE: 9/6/16
EDITOR: Lee Boudreaux
AGENT: Jim Rutman
AGENCY: Sterling Lord Literistic

THE GENTLE-MAN

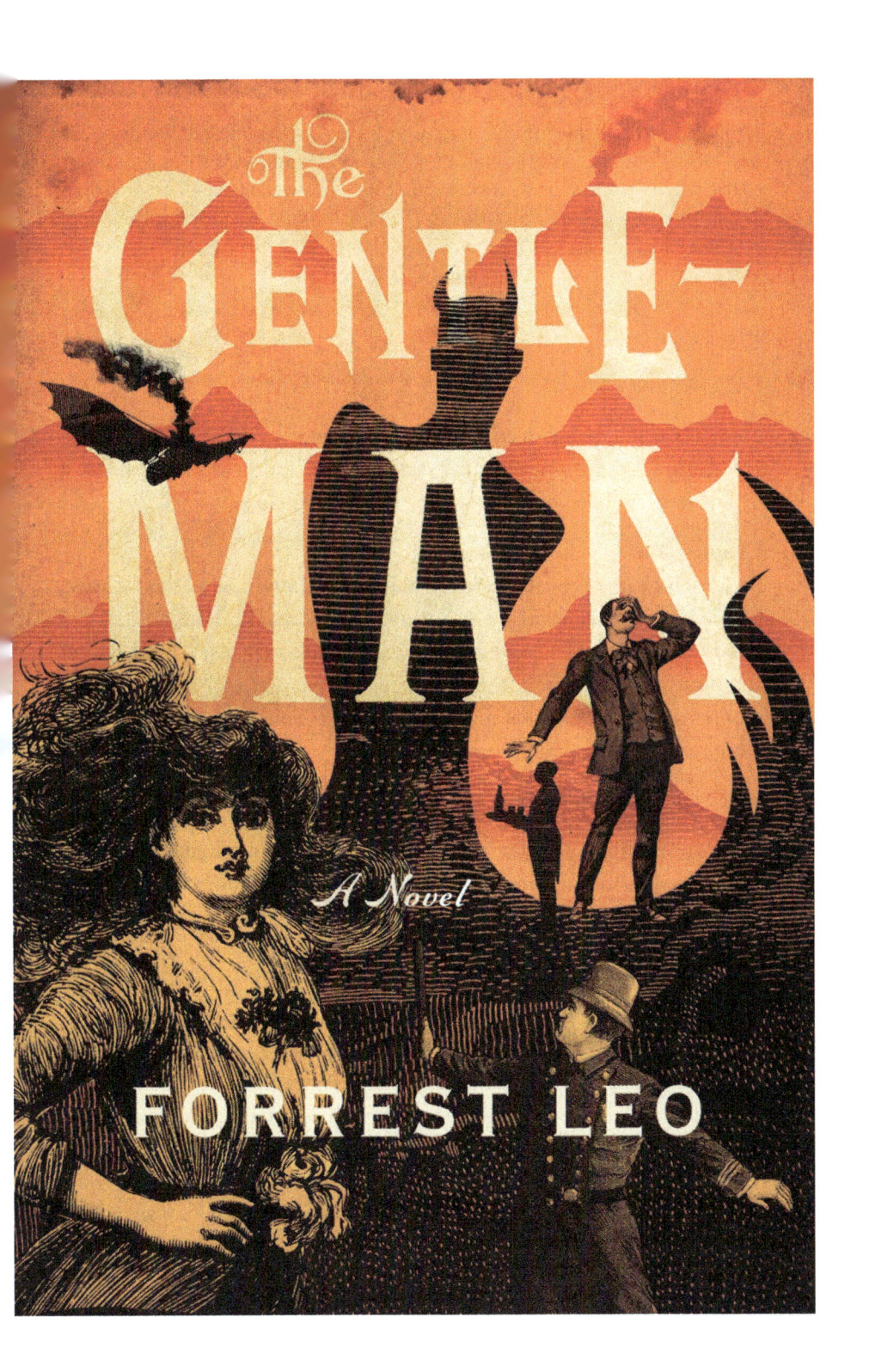

A Novel

FORREST LEO

SUMMARY

A funny, fantastically entertaining debut novel, in the spirit of Wodehouse and Monty Python, about a famous poet who inadvertently sells his wife to the devil—then recruits a band of adventurers to rescue her. The novel centers on a group of adventurers on a dangerous quest, spiked with literary allusions and fantastic mechanisms. And the gauzy England of yesteryear is infused with magic (and delightful footnotes).

EXCERPT

Editor's Note.

I have been charged with editing these pages and seeing them through to publication, but I do not like the task. I wish it on record that I think it better they had been burned.—*Hubert Lancaster, Esq*

Chapter One
In Which I Find Myself Destitute & Rectify Matters in a Drastic Way.
My name is Lionel Savage, I am twenty-two years old, I am a poet, and I do not love my wife. I loved her once, not without cause—but I do not any more. She is a vapid, timid, querulous creature, and I find after six months of married life that my position has become quite intolerable and I am resolved upon killing myself.

Here is how my plight came about.

Once upon a time about a year ago, I was very young and foolish, and Simmons informed me we hadn't any money left. (Simmons is our butler.)

'Simmons,' I had said, 'I would like to buy a boat so that I can sail the seven seas.'

I hadn't, I suppose, any real notion of actually sailing the seven seas—I am not an adventurous soul, and would relinquish my comfortable seat by the fire only with reluctance. But it seemed a romantic thing to own a boat in which one *could* sail the seven seas, should one suddenly discover he had a mind to. But Simmons (whose hair is grey like a thunderhead) said with some remonstrance, 'I'm afraid you cannot afford a boat, sir.'

'I can't afford it? Nonsense, Simmons, a boat cannot cost much.'

'Even if it cost next to nothing, sir, you still could not afford it.'

My heart sank. 'Do you mean to tell me, Simmons, that we haven't any money left?'

'I'm afraid not, sir.'

'Where on earth has it gone?'

'I don't mean to be critical, sir, but you tend toward profligacy.'

'Nonsense, Simmons. I don't buy anything except books. You cannot possibly tell me I've squandered my fortune upon books.'

'Squander is not the word I would have used, sir. But it was the books that did it, I believe.'

Well, there it was. We were paupers. Such is the fate of the upper classes in this modern world. I didn't know what to do, and I dreaded telling Lizzie—she was in boarding school at the time, but even from a distance she can be quite fearsome. (Lizzie is my sister. She is sixteen.) Despite the popularity of my poetry, I was not making enough money at it to maintain our household at Pocklington Place. Another source of income was necessary.

I set out to find one. Being a gentleman,* the trades were quite out of the question. Commerce is not a gentlemanly pursuit and sounds wretched besides. I considered physic or law, but lawyers turn my stomach and physicians are scoundrels all. I decided it must be marriage.

Finding a suitable family to marry oneself off to might sound a bore, but turned out to be rather a lark. I sought out only families of enormous means, without bothering myself too much about social position. As such, I had a few truly unpleasant experiences—but no dull ones.

The Babingtons were every bit as eccentric as one reads in the papers and proved entirely unsuitable. (Not that I object to eccentricity; but it is not

---

*It is for the attentive reader to decide for himself whether Mr Savage is deserving of that epithet.—HL.

a quality one searches for in a wife.) Sir Francis Babington and I are old friends, he having once savaged† a collection of my poetry.

'Frank,' I said one evening, having contrived to run into him while taking a turn about the Park,‡ 'I suppose it's about time I came over for dinner.' (I abhor taking turns about the Park. I only do so when I have ulterior motives.)

'Looking for a wife, Savage?' said he.

'Certainly not,' I replied coldly. I was thrown off. I had not thought myself so transparent. I groped for a new subject but was not quick enough.

'Never fear, lad, you'll find no judgment here.' He was laughing. Sir Francis is a ruddy and a rotund man, and his laugh is well matched to his person. 'Been looking to unload Agnes for a while now, as a matter of fact. Helen and I ain't particular as far as who to, and you'll do just fine. Why don't you come round Tuesday evening?'

This sort of impropriety I would ordinarily celebrate, but not when auditioning fathers-in-law. I declined.

The Pembrokes I enjoyed greatly, but the prospect of a half-dozen sisters-in-law was untenable. (One sister is quite enough.) I made it as far as a dinner, which was proceeding reasonably well, when the littlest one (Mary? Martha?) decided to be Mr Hyde. She jumped up on the table, thumped her chest with her tiny fists, and heaved a roasted pheasant at my head. That was that.

The Hammersmiths could have been the ticket, but their daughter was, I believe, replaced at infancy with a horse.

I could carry on and mention the Wellingtons, Blooms, and Chapmans—but my native discretion forbids it. Suffice it to say that the field was quickly emptied of players, and my options began to run low.

---

† I believe this is meant to be an unfortunate play upon my cousin's name. It is a literary offence typical of him.—HL.

‡ My cousin refers naturally to Hyde Park. This (in case the reader has the misfortune to be on the Continent or in the Colonies) is the London park which people of fashion and breeding frequent.—HL.

At the end of the day, in fact, the only real possibility was the Lancasters. They were rich, they were respectable and respected, and their daughter was beautiful. I will say that, whatever else I may lament—Vivien is very beautiful. Her hair is beaten gold, her eyes are a meteorological blue, her figure is—well, you have heard about her figure. It was her beauty I fell in love with first.

The dinner at which we met was unremarkable. It was not a private affair, but something of a party. I had contrived to procure myself an invitation on the grounds of my literary fame, and it seemed most of the guests had done the same. Whitley Pendergast was there, of course, as was Mr Collier, Mr Blakeney, Mr Morley, and Lord and Lady Whicher. (Whitley Pendergast is my rival and sworn enemy, and a terrible poet besides. The rest are literary personages of some reputation and indifferent talent. Benjamin Blakeney's *Barry the Bard* I hope you have not read, and Edward Collier's *Penthesilea's Progress* I fear you have. I have forgotten what mangled offspring crawled from the pens of the others.) A few ministers of state rounded out the meal, but it would be in poor taste to mention them by name.*

I was seated between Pendergast and Vivien.

—But I have forgotten to finish setting the scene! Easton Arms, which is the Lancasters' place in town, is a large town house in Belgravia furnished in the best and most modern taste. They are a very modern family, though very old in name. The art on the walls was unremarkable not in execution but in choice. If you were to close your eyes and name the six artists respectable and cultured persons of no particular taste ought to have on their walls, then you will have a very good idea of what hung in Easton Arms.† I haven't a clue as to their names, as I do not keep up with such things. But you take my meaning.

---

*I, too, was present. I dine often at Easton Arms. My father being brother to Lord Lancaster, I am Vivien's first cousin. As Mr Savage is my cousin's husband, he is thus by law my cousin also. It is for this reason I made bold to include an epigraph without obtaining his express permission. We harbour between us that particular and tenuous affection which marks the sobrinical bond.—HL.

†I beg you to note that this is equivalent to declaring popular art bad art—which would I am afraid quite condemn the poetry of Mr Savage. In addition, it should be mentioned that the collection at Easton Arms has a national reputation for excellence.—HL.

Everything seemed gilt-edged. The mirrors, the frames of the paintings, the books on the shelves (I pulled several down and found the pages to be uncut)—even the curtains were trimmed with gold lace. The situation seemed promising. I prepared to be charming.

I had a passing acquaintance with Lord Lancaster, who has a restless mind trapped by the constraints of domesticity and a portly person, but I had never met his wife. She turned out to be much as you imagine her to be from the papers, only rather shorter and even more terrible.

The gentlemen of the party were enjoying cigars before dinner. I have no fondness for cigars, but I appreciate the ritual of girding up one's loins in the fellowship of one's own gender before mingling at table. Besides, Lord Lancaster's smoking room is notably fine. The walls are decorated with intriguing memorabilia sent home by his son—a dozen tribal masks from a dozen countries, bits of colourful native costume, a gleaming blunderbuss—and the fireplace is large and the armchairs luxurious.

We sprawled in that peculiarly insolent way of the male gentry, smoking expensive cigars and speaking of nothing in particular.

Pendergast, a tragically short fellow with a peninsular nose, was attempting to be more pretentious than Collier, and was succeeding without too much effort. Every now and again he lobbed an insult my way, but I was not in the mood to test wits. I was too busy seducing Lancaster.

'Are you a political man, Mr Savage?'

'Not especially, my lord. I find that Politics and Art are rarely willing bedfellows; and when forced to it, Politics invariably takes Art's virtue without so much as a by-your-leave.'

He chuckled at that, but I did not. To never laugh at one's own wit is a thing I learned from Pendergast. (In a nearby armchair, Pendergast at that moment answered a question I did not hear with, 'Certainly not—I relegate such things to Mr Savage,' and laughed loudly.)

'Always wished I had time for art,' said Lancaster. 'Bought some paints, once, but Eleanor had 'em thrown out. Said it was an accident and blamed it on a maid, but you know how those things go. Probably for the best. Vivien, though—she inclines that way, you know.'

'Does she?' I murmured.

'Certainly,' said he. 'You and she ought to have a talk sometime. Think you'd get on famously.'

I was about to say something about how I should like that very much indeed, and to suggest future plans for such an acquaintance, when Lady Lancaster entered the room and curtly informed us that dinner was served and we were already late. I was nettled at the interruption. As it happened, though, I needn't have been—for when we took our places at the table I was upon Vivien's right.

Of all the literati at that salon, I was perhaps the most famous. It was because of this, I am certain, that I was seated next to Vivien. Lady Lancaster has a fondness for fame. She does not court it herself, but courts those touched by it. (It is this, rather than any actual interest in the arts, which causes her to hold dinners like the one I am describing.) I was also perhaps the handsomest at the table. I mention it not out of vanity—I am not a vain man—but to emphasise the importance the Lancasters attach to appearances, and also in case you have never seen a likeness of me. I am neither tall nor short, and very slender. I have very pale skin, very dark hair which is unruly, and very blue eyes—not a blue like Vivien's, but blue all the same. (The Lancaster blue is something akin to the sky at its bluest; the Savage blue is the sort of blue the sea turns when it is grey. If this does not make sense to you, you are not a poet.)*

I couldn't have known it at the time, but it was my good fortune that Vivien was approaching twenty-one and her mother felt it was past time she was married to someone in the public eye. Marriage is important to the Lancasters. It was and is a source of most acute pain to Lady Lancaster that her son is not yet domesticated. (He is at the moment in Siberia, I believe.)

I do a tolerable job of fitting into society.† I do not flaunt my native ec-

---

*It appears I am no poet.—HL.

†This, too, is open for debate. Mr Savage at all times displays such deep contempt for society that one wonders at the grudge he nurses. Whence comes it? Is it innate or learned? Can it be cured? Such questions are beyond the scope of your humble editor.—HL.

centricity, nor do I endeavour to seem any more mad than I am. The poetry published under my name displays vision, refinement, learning, wit, and taste—but not insanity. That I reserve for those offerings I distribute by secret means, under noms de plume.* My fame, as I have said, is not insignificant, and it was evident that Lady Lancaster, though dragonish in demeanour, was a dragon with a keen desire to impress. (It need not be pointed out that a mercenary dragon is far more dangerous than a work-a-day dragon.)

And so I was seated next to Vivien, and I do not believe it was an accident. Pendergast was on my right, which was a nuisance; but at the time I remember thinking it a small price to pay to sit beside one so fair.

The dining room at Easton Arms is very grand. The table is a mile or two long, and it was laid that evening with everything from venison to wild boar to caviar to quail eggs. There were sauces which defied description and puddings which boggled the mind. The serving trays were silver, but worked with the requisite gold filigree. I was not alone among the guests in my nervousness to take food from a platter worth more than I had ever owned. We were spared, however, the terror of actually holding one of those trays by the appearance of a flotilla of footmen who served us in frankly eerie silence, controlled apparently by minute signals of Lady Lancaster's head.

The dinner began, and though I stole many glances at my fair neighbour, I found myself for the only time in my memory unable to begin a conversation. I spent the first course searching for a subject and feeling a coward. I could not, try as I might, speak to Vivien. I once made it so far as to venture a remark upon the weather, but Pendergast swooped in and intercepted it.

'I've been considering a poem about the rain, you know,' he said, as though my comment had been meant for him.

'I trust the rain is magnanimous enough to forgive whatever offence you might give it,' I replied.

---

*These names include Horatio, Britannius Grammaticus, Iucundis Eremita, and Charles Greenley.—HL.

'You wrote a rain poem once, didn't you, Savage?' called Blakeney from across the table.*

'I can't recall,' said I. 'I might have, but it's foggy in my memory.'

'Foggy!' exclaimed Lady Whicher rapturously. 'Did you hear, Henry? He said his rain poem was foggy!'

'A sloppy pun, Savage,' declared Pendergast.

'I'd have made a better, but I can't hear myself think over the noise of your cravat.'

'This cravat,' he replied pompously, 'was given me by a French countess who expressed an affinity for my verse.'

'One hears at the club that the cravat wasn't the only thing she gave you.' A scandalised murmur went round the table and it seemed I had scored a hit—but Pendergast was a stauncher opponent than that.

'No,' he said without missing a beat, 'she gave me also an annuity of two hundred pounds and a promise to bring out a uniform edition of my published works. I asked her to pay you the same compliment, but she said your output was too slim to bear the cost.'

'Did she?' I said, taking the bait. He was building to something, and it amused me to let him see it through.

'She did, and very bad manners I thought it, too. So I said, "But madam, surely the sparsity of Mr Savage's verse makes it the more precious, rather like ambergris?" To which she replied, "Much like ambergris, Mr Pendergast, I can only stomach Mr Savage's poetry after it has been refined in the fire."'

The table applauded his thrust, but I remained unruffled. I have always enjoyed sparring with Pendergast, and that night it was also a means to delay converse with the divinity on my left. Besides, the key to success in a battle of wits is to maintain one's equanimity at all times. While the company lauded his hit, I calmly considered a riposte. I had almost got one when Vivien spoke up.

---

*See epigraph. It is for elucidation of this exchange as well as for other reasons that I elected to include it.—HL.

'It is a pity, Mr Pendergast,' said she, in a voice which was low and husky and altogether glorious and in retrospect rather like a siren's, 'that much like Mr Savage's poetry, ambergris needs no fiery refinement.'

'Does it not?' cried Lady Whicher.

'Not a bit. Its value comes from its unaltered chemical makeup.'

'Ambergris or Mr Savage's poetry?' demanded Blakeney. 'Precisely!' I interposed, and just like that I was again on top. I attempted to thank my fair saviour, but the words transmuted by some reverse alchemy into an attack on Pendergast and his countess.

I will not bore you with the continuation of our match, as it proceeded through the duration of the second and most of the third course. I won in the end, but the victory was hollow to me—the entire episode was nothing but a cover to hide the fact that I could not speak to the woman beside me.

It was Vivien who at last broke the silence between us, and so I may say without hesitation that the fault for my current predicament lies squarely upon her shoulders. Had she not said anything I would not have been able to, and would have returned home to Pocklington Place that evening with a feeling of cowardice and self-reproach which would have lasted for a day or a week and then given way to my accustomed cheer.*

Instead, I left that evening with a wife.

I do not mean literally, of course—our courtship, while brief, was not *that* brief. But later when Simmons asked how the dinner had gone, I believe my words to him were, 'I have found a wife, and I haven't the least intention of letting her go.'

Bitterest of ironies! If I could return to that night in March and relive it, I should have eaten my foie gras with relish, taunted Pendergast with pleasure, and never spared a second glance at that awful creature on my left. Could I even return as a spirit and whisper in my own corporeal ear, I should whisper with such urgency, 'Ignore her, sir! She will

---

*Like the unicorn, legends of my cousin's cheer persist only because they cannot be disproved.—HL.

be your death!' Well, but I cannot and I did not. Instead, when over the oysters she enquired, 'What are your thoughts on the matter, Mr Savage?' I turned and lost myself in those damned eyes and knew I was finished and did not mind a jot.

I will not here recount my wooing. It was, looking back, strangely joyous and brings me pain to recollect. There was throughout it a bizarre sense of burning happiness—a prickly feeling on the back of my neck, a pleasant tightness of the chest: something more than contentment, greater than the satisfaction of a match well made.

I thought it was the sensation of being in love. I have learned that it was not, it was the joy of the chase. I wonder now if I oughtn't have been a hunter. Perhaps I still could be one. I am certain that Simmons keeps an ancient musket somewhere, and I could steal a horse from my coachman and sally forth to murder foxes—or stow aboard an Arctic vessel and try my hand at clubbing seals, which cannot be difficult. But that is neither here nor there. I am a poet, I am a married man, and I am resolved upon my own immediate suicide—for I married for money instead of love, and when I did I discovered that I could no longer write.

You've just read an excerpt from The Gentleman.

ABOUT THE AUTHOR

Forrest Leo was born in 1990 on a homestead in remote Alaska, where he grew up without running water and took a dogsled to school. He holds a BFA in drama from New York University, and has worked as a carpenter, and a photographer, and in a cubicle.

IMPRINT: Penguin Press
PRINT ISBN: 9780399562631
PRINT PRICE: $26.00
EBOOK ISBN: 9780399562648
EBOOK PRICE: $12.99
PUBLICATION DATE: 8/16/16
EDITOR: Ed Park
AGENT: Mitchell Waters
AGENCY: Curtis Brown.

ALL OUR WRONG TODAYS

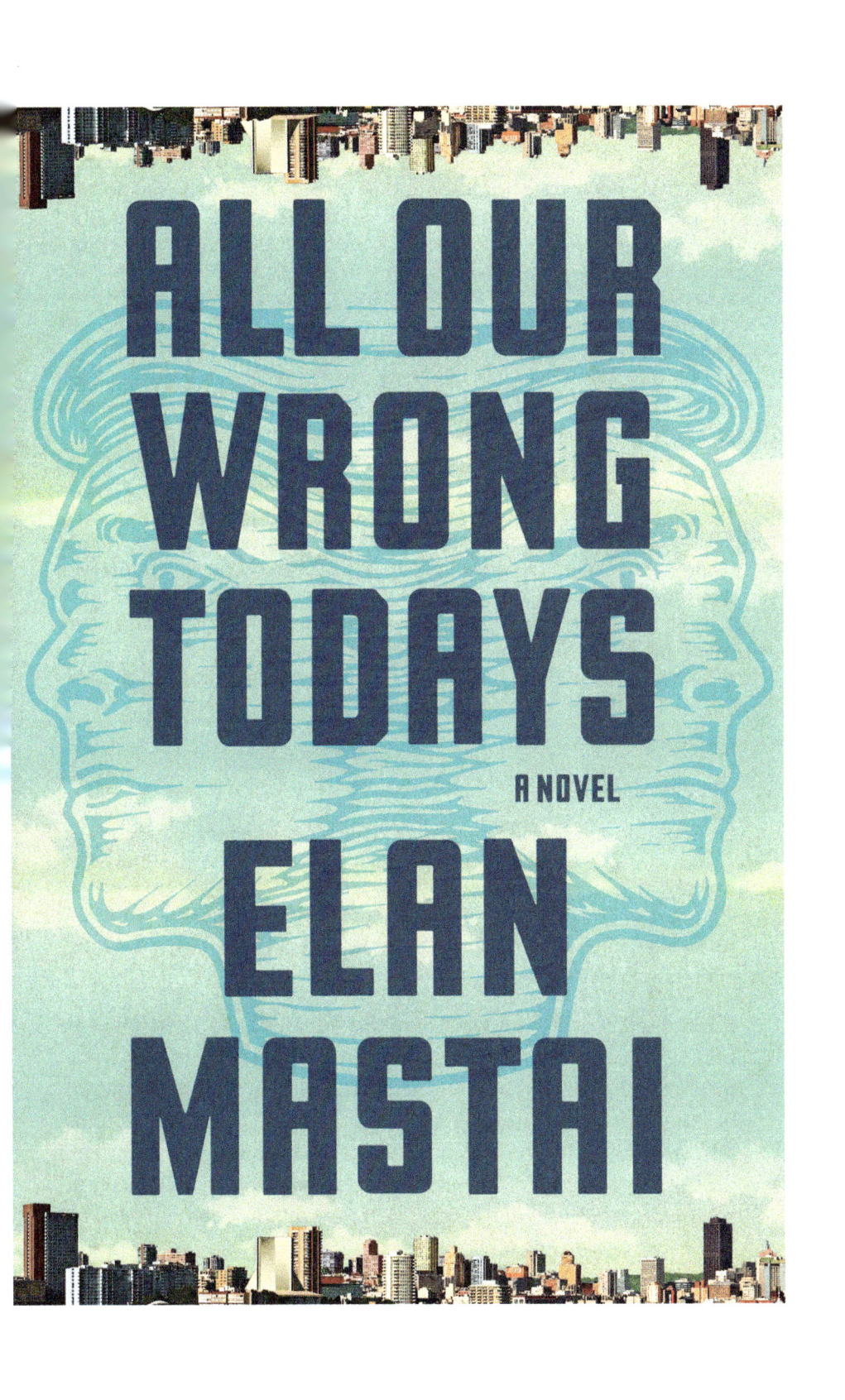

A NOVEL

ELAN MASTAI

SUMMARY

This stunningly assured debut novel is an emotionally compelling and intellectually persuasive novel about the complex and infinite possibilities of life. Tom Barren, the lackluster, ever-disappointing son of a haughty, emotionally-insulated super-genius scientist, lives in a version of our world in which an incredible discovery in 1965 profoundly changed the course of history, creating a futuristic utopia free of conflict, where punk rock never existed because it was never needed. Mourning his recently deceased mother and Penelope, the girl of his dreams who has just broken his heart, Tom steals his father's greatest invention and goes back in time to the moment of the world-changing discovery, his world erased in a fury of grief and stupidity as if it had never existed. Now stuck in our own 2015, he discovers a newly constituted version of his family and the woman he loved, and must decide whether to fix the flow of history, bring the billions of people living in edenic bliss back into existence and return to his natural dimension, or to try to make a life in our world where he has a girlfriend who just might believe his outrageous tale of alternate histories, a father who seems to genuinely love him, a mother who is very much not dead, and a soul mate of a sister who never existed in his original life. It is a story of friendship and family, of time machines and alternate realities, and of love in its multitude of forms.

EXCERPT

Chapter One

So, the thing is, I come from the world we were supposed to have.

That means nothing to you, obviously, because you live here, in the crappy world we *do* have. But it never should've turned out like this. And it's all my fault—well, me and to a lesser extent my father and, yeah, I guess a little bit Penelope.

It's hard to know how to start telling this story. But, okay, you know the future that people in the 1950s imagined we'd have? Flying cars, robot maids, food pills, teleportation, jetpacks, moving sidewalks, rayguns, hover-boards, space vacations, and moon bases. All that dazzling, transformative technology our grandparents were certain was right around the corner. The stuff of World's Fairs and pulp science-fiction magazines with titles like *Fantastic Future Tales* and *The Amazing World of Tomorrow*. Can you picture it?

Well, it happened.

It all happened, more or less exactly as envisioned. I'm not talking about the future. I'm talking about the *present*. Today, in the year 2016, humanity lives in a techno-utopian paradise of abundance, purpose, and wonder.

Except we don't. Of course we don't. We live in a world where, sure, there are iPhones and 3D-printers and, I don't know, drone-strikes or whatever. But it hardly looks like *The Jetsons*. Except it should. And it did. Until it didn't. But it would have, if I hadn't done what I did. Or, no, hold on, what I *will* have done.

I'm sorry, despite receiving the best education available to a citizen of the World of Tomorrow, the grammar of this situation is a bit complicated.

Maybe the first-person is the wrong way to tell this story. Maybe if I take refuge in the third-person I'll find some sort of distance or insight or at least peace of mind. It's worth a try.

Chapter Two

Tom Barren wakes up into his own dream.

Every night, neural scanners map his dreams while he sleeps so that both his conscious and unconscious thought-patterns can be effectively modeled. Every morning, the neural scanners transmit the current dream-state data into a program that generates a real-time virtual projection into which he seamlessly rouses. The dream's scattershot plot is made increasingly linear and lucid until a psychologically pleasing resolution is achieved at the moment of full consciousness…

I'm sorry—I can't write like this. It's fake. It's safe.

The third-person is comforting because it's in control, which feels really nice when relating events that were often so out of control. It's like a scientist describing a biological sample seen through a microscope. But I'm not the microscope. I'm the thing on the slide. And I'm not writing this to make myself comfortable. If I wanted comfort, I'd write fiction.

In fiction, you cohere all these evocative, telling details into a portrait of the world. But in everyday life, you hardly notice any of the little things. You can't. Your brain swoops past it all, especially when it's your own home, a place that feels barely separate from the inside of your mind or the outside your body.

When you wake up from a real dream into a virtual one, it's like you're on a raft darting this way and that according to the blurry, impenetrable currents of your unconscious, until you find yourself gliding onto a wide, calm, shallow lake, and the slippery, fraught weirdness dissolves into serene, reassuring clarity. The story wraps up the way it feels like it must and, no matter how unsettling the content, you wake up with the rejuvenating solidity of order restored. And that's when you realize you're lying in bed, ready to start the day, with none of that sticky subconscious gristle caught in the cramped folds of your mind.

It might be what I miss most about where I come from. Because in this world waking up sucks.

Here, it's like nobody has considered using even the most rudimentary technology to improve the process. Mattresses don't subtly vibrate to keep your muscles loose. Targeted steam valves don't clean your body in slumber. I mean, blankets are made from tufts of plant fiber spun into thread and occasionally stuffed with feathers. Feathers. Like from actual birds. Waking up should be the best moment of your day, your unconscious and conscious mind synchronized and harmonious.

Getting dressed involves an automated system that cuts and stitches a new outfit every morning, indexed to your personal style and body type. The fabric is made from laser-hardened strands of a light-sensitive liquid polymer that's recycled nightly for daily reuse. Breakfast involves a similar system that outputs whatever meal you feel like from a nutrient gel mixed with color, flavor, and texture protocols. And if that sounds gross to you, in practice it's indistinguishable from what you think of as real food, except that it's uniquely gauged to your tongue's sensory receptors so it tastes and feels ideal every time. You know that sinking feeling you get when you cut into an avocado, only to find that it's either hard and underripe or brown and bruised under its skin? Well, I didn't know that could even happen until I came here. Every avocado I ever ate was perfect.

It's weird to be nostalgic for experiences that both did and didn't exist. Like waking up every morning completely refreshed. Something I didn't even realize I *could* take for granted because it was simply the way things were. But that's the point, of course—the way things were… never was.

What I'm not nostalgic for is that every morning when I woke up, and got dressed, and ate breakfast in this glittering technological utopia, I was alone.

Chapter Three

On July 11th, 1965, Lionel Goettreider invented the future.

Obviously you've never heard of him. But where I come from, Lionel Goettreider is the most famous, beloved, and respected human on the planet. Every city has dozens of things named after him, streets, buildings, parks, whatever. Every kid knows how to spell his name using the catchy mnemonic tune that goes G-O-E-T-T-R-E-I-D-E-R.

You have no idea what I'm talking about. But if you were from where I'm from, it'd be as familiar to you as A-B-C.

Fifty-one years ago, Lionel Goettreider invented a revolutionary way to generate unlimited, robust, absolutely clean energy. His device came to be called the Goettreider Engine. July 11th, 1965 was the day he turned it on for the very first time. It made everything possible.

Imagine that the last five decades happened with no restrictions on energy. No need to dig deeper and deeper into the ground and make the skies dirtier and dirtier. Nuclear became unnecessarily tempestuous. Coal and oil pointlessly murky. Solar and wind and even hydro-power became quaint low-fidelity alternatives that nobody bothered with unless they were peculiarly determined to live off the main grid.

So, how did the Goettreider Engine work?

How does electricity work? How does a microwave oven work? How does your cell phone or television or remote control work? Do you actually understand on, like, a concrete technical level? If those technologies disappeared, could you reconceive, redesign, and rebuild them from scratch? And, if not, why not? You only use these things pretty much every single day.

But of course you don't know. Because unless your job's in a related field you don't need to know. They just *work*, effortlessly, as they were intended.

Where I come from, that's how it is with the Goettreider Engine. It was important enough to make Goettreider as recognizable a name as Einstein or Newton or Darwin. But how it functioned, like, technically? I really couldn't tell you.

Basically, you know how a dam produces energy? Turbines harness the natural propulsion of water flowing downward via gravity to generate electricity. To be clear, that's more or less *all* I understand about hydro-electric power. Gravity pulls water down, so if you stick a turbine in its path, the water spins it around and somehow makes energy.

The Goettreider Engine does that with the planet. You know that the Earth spins on its axis and also revolves around the Sun, while the Sun itself moves endlessly through the Solar System. Like water through a turbine, the Goettreider Engine harnesses the constant rotation of the planet to create boundless energy. It has something to do with magnetism and gravity and… honestly, I don't know—any more than I genuinely understand an alkaline battery or a combustion engine or an incandescent light bulb. They just work.

So does the Goettreider Engine. It just works.

Or it did. Before, you know, *me*.

Chapter Four

I am not a genius. If you've read this far, you're already aware of that fact.

But my father is a legitimate full-blown genius of the highest order. After finishing his third PhD, Victor Barren spent a few crucial years working in long-range teleportation before founding his own lab to pursue his specific niche field—time-travel.

Even where I come from, time-travel was considered more or less impossible. Not because of time, actually, but because of space.

Here's why every time-travel movie you've ever seen is total bullshit—because the Earth moves.

You know this. Plus I mentioned it last chapter. The Earth spins all the way around once a day, revolves around the Sun once a year, while the Sun is on its own cosmic route through the Solar System, which is itself hurtling through a galaxy that's wandering an epic path through the universe.

The ground under you is moving, really fast. The Earth rotates at about 1,000 miles per hour, 24 hours a day, while orbiting the Sun at a little over 130,000 miles per hour. That's 1,600,000 miles per day. Meanwhile our Solar System is in motion relative to the Milky Way galaxy at more than 1,300,000 miles per hour, covering just shy of 32,000,000 miles per day. And so on.

If you were to travel back in time to yesterday, the Earth would be in a different place in space. Even if you traveled back in time one second, the Earth below your feet would have moved nearly half a kilometer, 450 meters. In one second.

The reason every movie about time-travel is nonsense is that the Earth moves, constantly, always. You travel back one day, you don't end up in the same location, you end up in the gaping vacuum of outer space.

Marty McFly didn't appear thirty years earlier in his hometown of Hill Valley, California. His tricked out DeLorean materialized in the endless empty blackness of the cosmos with the Earth approximately 350,000,000,000 miles away. Assuming he didn't lose immediate consciousness from the lack of oxygen, the absence of air pressure would cause all the fluids in his body to bubble, partially evaporate, and freeze. He would be dead in less than a minute.

The Terminator would probably survive in space because he's an unstoppable robot killing machine, but traveling from 2029 to 1984 would've given Sarah Connor a 525,000,000,000 mile head start.

Time-travel doesn't just require traveling back in time, it also requires traveling back to a pinpoint-specific location in space. Otherwise, just like regular old everyday teleportation, you could end up stuck *inside* something.

Think about where you're sitting right now. Let's say on an olive green couch. A white ceramic bowl of fake green pears and real brown pinecones propped next to your feet on the teak coffee-table. A brushed steel floor-lamp glows over your shoulder. A coarse rug over reclaimed barnboard elm floors that cost too much but look pretty great…

If you were to teleport even a few inches in any direction, your body would be embedded in a solid object. One inch, you're wounded. Two inches, you're maimed. Three inches, you're dead.

Every second of the day, we're all three inches from being dead.

Which is why teleportation is only safe and effective if it's between dedicated sites on an exactingly calibrated system.

My father's early work in teleportation was so important because it helped him understand the mechanics of disincorporating and reincorporating a human body between discrete locations. It's what stymied all previous time-travel initiatives. Reversing the flow of time isn't even that complex. What's outrageously complex is instantaneous space-travel with absolute accuracy across potentially billions of miles.

My father's genius wasn't just about solving both the theoretical and logistic challenges of time-travel. It was about recognizing that in this, as in so many other aspects of everyday life, our savior was Lionel Goettreider.

Chapter Five

The first Goettreider Engine was turned on once and never turned off—it's been running without interruption since 2:03PM on Sunday, July 11th, 1965.

Goettreider's original Engine wasn't designed to harness and emit large-scale amounts of energy. It was an experimental prototype that performed beyond its inventor's most grandiose expectations. But the whole point of a Goettreider Engine is that it never has to be deactivated, just as the planet never stops moving. So, the original prototype was left running in the same spot where it was first switched on, in front of a small crowd of sixteen observers in a basement laboratory in section B7 of the San Francisco State Science and Technology Center.

Where I come from, every school kid knows the names and faces of the *Sixteen Witnesses*. Numerous books have been written about every single one of them, with their presence at this ultimate hinge in history shoved into the chronology of their individual lives as the defining event, whether or not it was factually true.

Countless works of art have depicted *The Activation Of The Goettreider*

Engine. It's *The Last Supper* of the modern world, those sixteen faces, each with its own codified reaction. Skeptical. Awed. Distracted. Amused. Jealous. Angry. Thoughtful. Frightened. Detached. Concerned. Excited. Nonchalant. Harried. There's three more. Damn it, I should know this…

When the prototype Engine was first turned on, Goettreider just wanted to verify his calculations and prove his theory wasn't completely misguided—all it had to do was actually *work*. And it did work, but it had a major defect. It emitted a unique radiation signature, what was later called *tau radiation,* a nod to how physics uses the Greek capital letter T to represent *proper time* in relativity equations.

As the Engine's miraculous energy-generating capacities expanded to power the whole world, the tau radiation signature was eliminated from the large-scale industrial models. But the prototype was left to run, theoretically forever, in Goettreider's lab in San Francisco—now among the most-visited museums on the planet—out of respect, nostalgia, and a legally rigid clause in Goettreider's last will and testament.

My father's idea was to use the original device's tau radiation signature as a breadcrumb trail through space and time, each crumb the size of an atom, a knotted thread to the past, looping through the cosmos with an anchor fixed at the most important moment in history—Sunday, July 11th, 1965, 2:03:48PM, the exact second Lionel Goettreider started the future. It meant that not only could my father send someone back in time to a very specific moment, the tau radiation trail would lead them to a very specific location—Lionel Goettreider's lab, right before the world changed forever.

With this realization, my father had almost every piece of the time-travel puzzle. There was only one last thing, minor compared to transporting a sentient human being into the past, but major in terms of not accidentally shredding the present—a way to ensure the time-traveler can't affect the past in any tangible way. There were several crucial safeguards in my father's design, but the only one I care about is the *defusion sphere*. Because that's how Penelope Weschler's life collided with mine.

Chapter Six

Nearly every object of art and entertainment is different in this world.

Early on, the variations aren't that significant. But as the late-1960s gave way to the vast technological and social leaps of the 1970s, almost everything changed, generating decades of pop culture that never existed—fifty years of writers and artists and musicians creating an entirely *other* body of work. Sometimes there are fascinating parallels, a loose story point in one version that's the climax in another, a line of dialogue in the wrong character's mouth, a striking visual composition framed in a new context, a familiar chord progression with radically altered lyrics.

July 11th, 1965 was the pivot of history even if nobody knew it yet.

Fortunately, Lionel Goettreider's favorite novel was published in 1963—*Cat's Cradle* by Kurt Vonnegut Junior.

Vonnegut's writing is different where I come from. Here, despite his wit and insight, you get the impression he felt a novelist could have no real effect on the world. He was compelled to write, but with little faith that writing might change anything.

Because *Cat's Cradle* influenced Lionel Goettreider so deeply, in my world Vonnegut was considered among the most significant philosophers of the late-twentieth century. This was probably great for Vonnegut personally but less so for his novels, which became increasingly homiletic.

I won't summarize *Cat's Cradle* for you. It's short and much better written than this book, so just go read it. It's weary, cheeky, and wise, which are my three favorite qualities in people and art.

Tangentially—Weary, Cheeky, and Wise are the three codified reactions I couldn't remember from the Sixteen Witnesses to The Activation.

Cat's Cradle is about a lot of things, but a major plot thread involves the invention of Ice-Nine, a substance that freezes everything it touches, which falls out of its creator's control and destroys all life on the planet.

Lionel Goettreider read *Cat's Cradle* and had a crucial realization, what he called *"The Accident"*—when you invent a new technology, you also invent the accident of that technology.

When you invent the car, you also invent the car accident. When you invent the plane, you also invent the plane crash. When you invent nuclear fission, you also invent the nuclear meltdown. When you invent Ice-Nine, you also invent unintentionally freezing the planet solid.

When Lionel Goettreider invented the Goettreider Engine, he knew he couldn't turn it on until he figured out its accident—and how to prevent it.

My favorite exhibit at the Goettreider Museum is the simulation of what *could've* happened if the Engine had somehow malfunctioned when Goettreider first turned it on. In the worst case scenario, the unprecedented amounts of energy pulled in by the Engine overwhelm its intake-core, triggering an explosion that melts San Francisco into a smoldering crater, poisons the Pacific Ocean with tau radiation, corrodes ten thousand square-miles of arable land into a stew of pain, and renders an impressive swath of North America uninhabitable for decades. Parents would occasionally complain to the Museum's curatorial staff that the simulation's nightmarish imagery was too graphic for children and, since the experiment obviously *didn't* fail, why draw attention away from Goettreider's majestic contributions to human civilization with grotesque speculation about imaginary global disasters? The simulation was eventually moved to an out-of-the-way corner of the Museum, where generations of teenagers on high school fieldtrips would huddle in the darkness and watch the world fall apart on a continuous loop.

I'm not a genius like Lionel Goettreider or Kurt Vonnegut or my father. But I have a theory too—*The Accident* doesn't just apply to technology, it also applies to people. Every person you meet introduces the accident of that person to you. What can go right and what can go wrong. There is no intimacy without consequence.

Which brings me back to Penelope Weschler and the accident of us. Of all of us.

You've just read an excerpt from All Our Wrong Todays.

ABOUT THE AUTHOR

Elan Mastai has had five films produced from his screenplays, most recently *What If* (released internationally as *The F Word*), which starred Daniel Radcliffe, Zoe Kazan, and Adam Driver. It premiered at the Toronto Film Festival, was released in more than 30 countries, and won Elan both the Canadian Academy Award and the Writers Guild of Canada Award for his script. In 2013, *Variety* named Elan one of its Ten Screenwriters To Watch. His previous features include *The Samaritan*, starring Oscar-nominees Samuel L Jackson and Tom Wilkinson, and he has developed movies for Warner Brothers, Paramount, Sony, Fox, and Dreamworks, and a TV series for the FX network. Upcoming film projects include *Get Over It*, based on an episode of the Peabody-winning radio show *This American Life* and produced by Ira Glass. Elan lives in Toronto with his family. *All Our Wrong Todays* has been pre-empted by Amy Pascal for Paramount Pictures.

IMPRINT: Dutton
PRINT ISBN: 9781101985137
PRINT PRICE: $27
EBOOK ISBN: 9781101985144
EBOOK PRICE: $13.99
PUBLICATION DATE: 2/7/17
PUBLICITY CONTACT: amwalker@penguinrandomhouse.com
RIGHTS CONTACT: skhan@penguinrandomhouse.com
EDITOR: Maya Ziv
AGENT: Simon Lipskar
AGENCY: Writers House

TERRITORIES SOLD:
Brazil: Intrinseca
Bulgaria: BARD
Canada: Doubleday/PRH
Canada: Doubleday/PRH
China: United Sky
Croatia: Znanje
Czech: Euromedia
France: Bragelonne
Germany: Goldmann/PRH
Greece: Enalios
Holland: Harper
Hungary: Agave
Israel: Keter
Italy: Sperling
Korea: Mirae
Macedonia: Toper

Poland: Sonia Draga
Portugal: Bertrand
Romanian: Grup Media Litera
Russia: Eksmo
Serbia: Vulkan
Slovak: Ikar
Slovenia: Ucla International
Spain: Alfaguara/PRH
Turkey: Pegasus
UK: Michael Joseph/PRH

PROMOTIONAL INFORMATION:
Major galley distribution; National publicity; National advertising; National print and radio publicity.

THE FIRE BY NIGHT

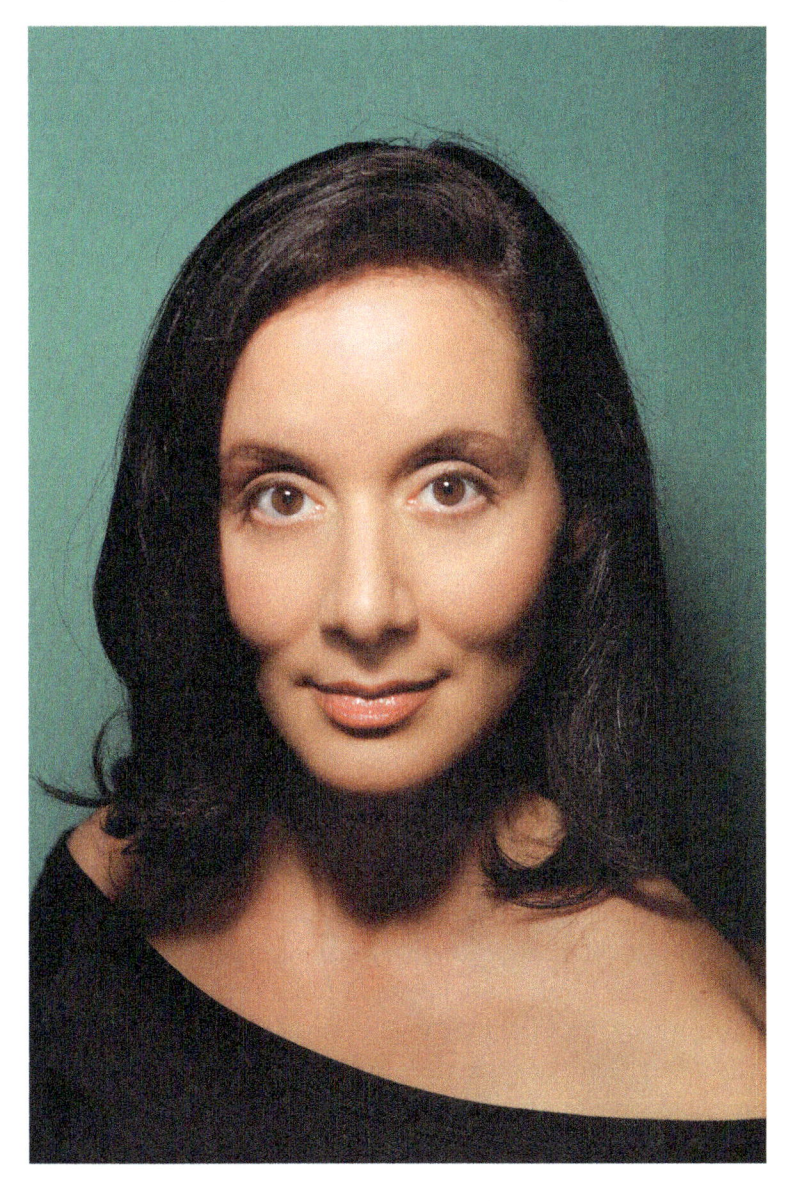

TERESA MESSINEO

SUMMARY

A powerful and gorgeously written debut about two military nurses working on the frontlines of WWII. Jo, raised in the Italian-Irish tenements of New York City, is in France, trapped behind enemy lines in a makeshift medical unit, where she refuses to leave her patients as the Germans advance and bombs fall around them. Jo's best friend from nursing school is Kay, a small-town girl from Pennsylvania, who the Army sends halfway around the world, first to Pearl Harbor, and then to the tunnels of Corregidor in the Philippines, where she is taken captive by the Japanese and must nurse civilians in a POW camp. Indelible and revelatory, *The Fire By Night* shines a light on the American women who were as brave as any band of brothers, but whose heroic roles in World War II have mostly been left unsung.

EXCERPT

Jo McMahon

Spring 1945

The Western Front

Chapter One

The main problem was her hands. They were raw and cracked and bleeding, and she couldn't get them to heal. A shell exploded outside the tent—somebody screamed and somebody laughed and someone else just said 'fuck.' Jo steadied the rickety supply rack in front of her, pressing her body against the shifting white boxes, pushing the brown glass bottles back into place with her thigh. The generator made a grinding noise as the lights flickered, went out, came back on. Her hands felt along the highest shelf, searching for a stray box of penicillin someone might have left behind in the initial rush to pack up, when the order to pull out had first come down. Her hands moved deftly, knowing exactly what they were searching for, by touch; and she found herself looking at them abstractedly, as if they were someone else's entirely, hands belonging to a brave and noble heroine in a novel or movie; a woman whose hands might be ugly, but whose face would be lit by an ethereal light; a person she could feel sorry for and admire at the same time; someone she could leave in the theatre, or shut up in a book, and never have to think of again. She would have to do something about her hands.

It was the surgeries that did it, really. Washing up in the freezing water basin, the caustic soap eating into open fissures; the thick brown gloves ripping off what was left of her knuckles when she tore them off, hurriedly, in between patients. But there was nothing for it; no way around it that she could see; she just couldn't figure this one out. Her aching fingers closed upon the elusive box and she wheeled around, just as a second explosion went off, this time on her bad side, where her eardrum had been punctured when the Newfoundland went down. She lost her footing, hitting the cold ground of the tent hard. She stuffed the medicine into the pocket of her six-fly pants—men's pants, with their buttons on the wrong side—then stopped for a moment to tie her shoe, thinking boots would have been nice for the nurses, but still no match for the mud as this, the coldest European winter on record, slowly thawed into an increasingly impassible mess. Two more shells went off, not as close as the last, but still, she noted absently, much too close—closer even than Anzio, and there the shells had been right on top of the them, it seemed, the shrapnel flying through the ineffectual canvas of the medical tents, killing surgeons were they stood, the orderlies removing their warm bodies and popping helmets onto the heads of the remaining doctors and nurses who carried on where they had left off.

Here, on this frigid night, the lines would have changed again, too quickly; they would be right up against the fighting, the enemy pushing through the center unexpectedly, perhaps, creating a new front; one they were near, or at, or even in front of. They were never supposed to be this close to the action, that's what they had been told during training—yet here they were, again. Jo remembered the time their truck had been commandeered, and another promised to pick them up. And how the nurses had waited patiently beside that little chicken coop in Southern Italy, resting their tired backs against its sun-drenched, white-washed warmth—until, hours later, after the hens had reluctantly gone in to roost, the girls had seen the first US scouts crawling cautiously towards them through the weeds. How the men had asked what they were doing there; how, if the scouts themselves were the very front of the front line, what the hell were the nurses doing here? Or again, that time they had been in Tunisia, waiting for a truck to move out the last of the wounded, watching the women and children run along the dirt road, or perch precariously on their camels forced into an unwilling trot; and the American MPs had brought up the rear on their motorcycles and yelled at the girls, demanding if they knew there was only ten miles between them and the German tanks and not a blessed thing in between. But they could not leave their men.

'How much we got left?' someone yelled outside in the rain, slamming the door of an idling truck. 'How long can it last?' Longer than I can last, Jo thought, wearily. Longer than any of us can last. The propaganda leaflets dropped by the Germans that the boys picked up showed exhausted American POWs, carefully carving tally marks into cell walls, keeping track of the date—1955. Another ten years. Jo smiled wryly at the Axis cartoonist's optimism. She'd be lucky to make it another ten months. She was just shy of her 26th birthday, and already her hair was streaked with iron gray and she had lost two teeth due to malnutrition. Queenie had told the captain she didn't mind when their molars fell out, but when her girls (Queenie always referred to the nurses in her charge as 'her girls'—they were her girls, heart and soul), started losing front teeth, too, well, then, even she had to say something about it. And they had gotten a few more C rations, after that.

Outside, someone was yelling 'retreat' in a voice too high and too shrill for a man's; he sounded more like a terrified schoolgirl than a soldier. 'Fall back, retreat,' he screamed again, as if anyone needed encouragement, as if everyone wasn't already running, already jostling, already scared. Easy enough for you, Jo thought listlessly, hearing the engines turning over and the men cursing at each other in their eagerness to pull out, their footsteps sounding loudly in the sucking mud. 'Just turn around and run, kid.' And as she said it aloud she suddenly felt incredibly seasoned and incredibly jaded and, above all else, incredibly tired. 'I've got a whole hospital to move first.'

***

It hadn't always been this way. She hadn't always been this way. There was a time when her hands had been lovely—when all of her had been lovely, all of her had been whole. She had been young then, and had curves—never enough curves, she had thought then, but good God, compared to the hard angles and bones she was now, she'd been a regular Rita Hayworth. Her skin had been smooth, her flesh firm and full—her tightly coiled chestnut hair with a lustre that betrayed her Irish father; a brown streak running through the blue of her left eye where her Italian mother always said she could see herself in her daughter. Giuseppina Fortunata 'Jo' McMahon. What a conglomerate she had felt, growing up in Brooklyn, where people identified so fiercely with their ethnicities. To be not fully one or the other but, somehow, both. To pray to both St. Patrick and St. Gennaro. To eat both lasagna, and corned beef and cabbage. But after nearly four years of field kitchens and alphabet rations, she couldn't think about real food. Not now. She couldn't bear it.

Jo walked into the last standing medical tent, the others having been arduously emptied and packed, dripping wet, onto the trucks that had already left. After hours of loading, now only half a dozen patients remained, their stretchers laid atop sawhorses, waiting to be transported farther back. How she and the other young nurses had memorized the transport chain when they first volunteered for the Army Corps! Front line. Aid man. Collection station. Clearing station. Field hospital. Evacuation hospital. General hospital. Safety. 'No female officers to serve closer to the front than field hospital, under any conditions.' Jo remembered that last clause had been underlined in their manuals, that the instructor had emphasized it, as if something like that were indecent, or could be guaranteed; as if war wasn't one step removed from chaos; as if she, serving in a field hospital, wasn't really at the front line right now. She emptied several tablets from the brown, cardboard box into her hand, reading without reading for the thousandth time, 'Penicillin G, 250,000 units, Chas. Pfizer & Co. Inc., N.Y., N.Y.,' remembering a time when she hadn't known the abbreviation for Charles, and had wondered why some mother back home would have ever named her baby Chas. She lifted the head of one of the conscious patients—conscious, if delirious; some poor Scot, in a kilt, no less, incongruous among all the GIs. 'Here, try to swallow, soldier,' as she lifted her canteen to his mouth. He tried to fight her, waving his hands ineffectually and cursing at phantoms standing somewhere behind her in a language all his own. But the typhus was too far-gone—not far enough yet for the dreaded seizures, but far enough advanced for the fever to have sapped him of his strength, of his will, of his right mind. She got the antibiotic down.

'Is there room on the truck for this one?' she asked the orderlies, who were dismantling the field x-ray machine in a corner of the tent. One of the hinges had stuck, and as they put their weight to it the table collapsed suddenly under their combined efforts, breaking off one of its legs. None of them answered her.

'Not on this truck, sweetpea. But we'll get him on the next one, for sure.'

And there was Queenie.

When Queenie walked into the tent from the cold and the rain and the muck outside, rubbing her frozen hands together, she managed to bring summer and honeysuckle and the smell of home cooking along with her. She was tiny—petite she always corrected—wearing the smallest men's regulation trousers she had taken in and taken in again and still had to wear cuffed. Her hair was, as usual, wrapped up in a clean white towel, under which one could imagine it still black and shiny as it once had been, instead of peppered with white. But Hollywood could have made a fortune casting Queenie as the girl-next-door-buy-war-bonds-today-tie-a-yellow-ribbon-round-her original sweetheart. Everyone loved Queenie—men and women alike—her quick laugh, her moxie, her indomitable spirit. Queenie herself defied description. On the one hand, she could drink—really drink—which was amazing, given her size. And curse as well as the men could. And gamble—she had laughed and laughed when she won a black silk negligee playing poker with some French officers in Algiers (she had given the beautiful, useless thing to Jo as a gift who, fresh to the war and still imbued with social mores herself, had been embarrassed and speechless and secretly delighted by it all). But if Queenie had a worldly side, this same nurse had stood with one doctor through 72 hours of surgery—72 hours—when all other medical personnel had been injured or killed. 200 litters lined up outside the tent, and they had gotten to them all, no coffee break. They had both received the Silver Star; but Queenie always said afterwards that she didn't deserve it. No false modesty, she honestly didn't believe she had done anything special. She was, in her own words, 'just doing my job.' And that, too, was Regina Carroll, whose first name had been, by now, all but usurped by her regal moniker. To the boys, she was their kid sister, the girl next door, the first girl they had ever kissed, all rolled into one. The person they were fighting the war for. Even now, with hell raining down on them again, Jo looked at Queenie and knew the war hadn't touched her, not underneath, not really; it hadn't gotten to her like it had gotten to everybody else, like it had gotten to Jo. Queenie didn't have to put up a shell to protect herself, to survive. She was still what they once had been; love and hope for dying boys. What all the girls had set out to become, ages ago, when they had first crossed the Atlantic in those rolling titans, heading for the European theatre of war, laughing and singing along the way as if it were going to be the best God-damned lawn party of all time.

One of the litters was half-in, half-out of an ambulance that had backed all the way up to the tent flap because of the rain. The orderlies paused to get their grip on the slippery wood of the handles just as the patient started flailing his arms, eyes wild, making a noise like a gagged hero in a gangster movie. In a second, Queenie was there, snatching up a wire-cutter that had been hooked to his stretcher, just as vomit shot through the man's nostrils, his mouth still tightly shut. The man was choking now, and crying, and panicking; Jo could see the whites of his eyes from across the tent. And Queenie kept smiling and talking to him nonstop.

'Poor baby, hold on there now, soldier, just a minute, sweetheart,' all the time, deftly cutting the wires the surgeons had so recently clamped into place to set his broken jaw. 'There you go now, you can breathe again, it's just the nasty anesthesia makes you so sick, I know, go ahead, baby, take a breath, they'll fix you up again at Evac, now don't worry about a thing, you're alright now, honey, it won't hurt for more than a second.' God, Jo thought, not hurt? What does it feel like to have your face shattered, then operated on, then 'barb wired' shut? But Queenie was true to her word, pulling out a 1/4 grain morphine syrette, ignoring its general warning, 'May be habit forming' and its less equivocal label, 'Poison.' After injecting it, she pinned the used needle to the man's bloodied collar; somewhere along the way, should he make it, someone would at least know what he had had.

And then she kissed him.

Just before they lifted him into the ambulance (the exhaust fumes were filling the tent, Jo felt sick), Queenie kissed him. The blood and the vomit and stench of fear and death, and she kissed him. And every person in that tent, who hadn't even known they were watching, stopped watching, envious of the dying man whose eyes were no longer scared; disgusted with themselves for what they had become, for how little they cared anymore; for how tired they were, for how much they hurt, how cold and hungry and filthy they felt, inside and out, with a kind of filth no water could wash away. Knowing they hadn't held a hand, let alone kissed someone, since they had stopped being humans themselves; how their world was now one of survival, an animal world of biting and ripping and tearing and, occasionally, licking each others' wounds. Sure, they might patch and bandage and send men further back along the chain to be patched and bandaged again; but they, the healers could no longer heal because they could not think and they could not feel and they could not remember when they had last thought or felt anything other than that they themselves were animals, hunted and trapped and cold.

And Queenie had kissed him.

***

When the command comes to fall back, it takes an infantryman less than ten seconds to simply turn around—and run. But not military nurses, whose only creed, whose one, unbreakable rule is never to leave their patients. Never. So begins the long task of finishing the surgeries already in progress; stabilizing those just coming into the post-op tent; of giving plasma, or whole blood when available; of lifting the 'heavy orthopoedics' with their colossal casts, arms and legs immobilized by a hundred pounds of plaster. The shock patients with their thready pulses; the boys with 'battle fatigue,' whimpering and taking cover under their cots, thinking themselves still in the field; the deaf; the maimed; the blind, heads carefully wrapped and bandaged, their tentative fingers reaching out in front of them, seared and melted together from clawing their way out of burning tanks. All these men had to be moved into an endless convoy of trucks and ambulances that could only hold so many, and only go so fast in the muddy ruts of what had once been a road. Jo remembered when they had been trying to move out, early on, before any of them knew anything; and she and a group of nurses had sewn together sheets to form an enormous cross to mark the field where the injured lay awaiting transport, smugly thinking the thin fabric would protect their men from strafing. And how the commanding officer himself had come up to them, livid, screaming at the naive girls for putting up not a red but a white cross, the symbol for airfield, and a legitimate military target under the Geneva Convention.

There were no more white sheets now.

The sound of the shells exploding outside mingled with thunder and it was all one cacophony of death. There had been a time when the girls would wince, or duck, or even jump into foxholes dug right into the dirt of the field hospital 'floor.' But there were no safe places left, not any more; and they walked around numb, oblivious to death hovering above them, packing up the more critical of their supplies—the scalpels, the clamps, the enormous steam sterilizer that would make everything usable when they set up again, somewhere. The ambulance was ready to leave, and the doctors already onboard were calling for Queenie.

'You can ride up front with me, sweetheart.'

'Yeah, on my lap.'

'No thank you, Doctors,' Queenie replied, her voice saccharine, 'I'll take my chances with the Germans first. I'll be fine in the back with my boys. Come on, Jo.'

Jo grabbed her green canvas musette bag—how could everything she owned fit into something the size of a handbag? But it did. Book. Rosary. Some thumbed-through letters from the Pacific. One faded photograph. Curity diapers. A nightshirt. Greying underwear. An extra tee shirt. Two C rations. The absurd negligee. A pen. Jo put on her helmet, the chinstrap long since burned off from years of using the helmet to heat water in for washing. Queenie was already in the back of the truck, instinctively reaching out a comforting hand without even realizing it, when a grating voice near Jo's ear said, 'Not so fast, Miss.'

It was Grandpa.

None of the girls remembered his real name anymore; if they had ever known it, it was just Grandpa now. The nickname originated when they found out he had served in the medical corps during the Great War; they joked, behind his back, of course, that he was old enough to have been a doctor in the Civil War, as well.

'You can stay with me, Miss McMahon. We'll get the next truck.'

Jo sighed. She hadn't noticed she was the only nurse left in the tent. Of course, she would not—she could not, ever—leave before the last of her patients did; but she would have rather sat through the long wait for the return truck with any of the other surgeons, even the fatherly ones in their forties who bored her kindly with talk of tobacco, and fly fishing back home. Anyone but Grandpa, who rambled on about the deep South, its nobility and 'gracious amenities.' Maybe, she thought, he really did remember it from antebellum times, after all.

'I'll stay,' Queenie began, but the truck had already shifted into gear; and, besides, two patients were holding onto her, looking at her with such intensity that it seemed she was the only thing rooting them to reality, tethering them to a spinning world.

'She'll be perfectly fine where she is, Miss Carroll,' Grandpa snapped irritably, her real name sounding like an insult as he grabbed a chart hanging crookedly off of one of the litters.

'I'll be perfectly fine,' Jo mouthed to Queenie, making a face. And Queenie laughed, her smile lighting up the interior of the cold ambulance already smelling of death; and Jo smiled, too, and made a little salute. And then the truck was pulling away, Queenie bending over one of the men, her hand gently caressing his forehead; then she was lost to them.

Jo took stock of what was left behind, in terms of supplies yet to be loaded; not much really. The x-ray and all but one of the operating tables had finally been collapsed and carried away; most of the medicines and supplies were already gone, except for one or two surgery kits neatly packed into their boxes, propped up against the center tent pole. One generator, still running; one oil-burning stove, now off and cooling before the journey; some lamps used for surgery; and the less important detritus that always littered the tent floor—disinfectant, bedpans, buckets, soap. Grandpa walked over to a chest marked linen and proceeded in his most officious voice.

'Miss McMahon, it is no secret to me that you and your fellow nurses refer to me as grandpa,' here he spat out the word, 'A term you use to convey my age and none of the honor one associates with that esteemed position.

Well, such being the case—and denying any fatigue on my part—I will oblige you by acting out the part insofar as setting down for a spell.'

And with that, he sat down stiffly. Jo noticed for the first time how pale and drawn the man looked, more so than he had in Italy, or Sicily or North Africa before that. He had always seemed aged to the nurses, their being just over twenty themselves. But this last push through France, closing in now on Germany itself, had been too much for him. Jo noted his lips were too white, his brows too closely knit together. He looked an old man who had just realized, suddenly, and with considerable annoyance, that he was, in fact, old.

'Yes, doctor,' Jo murmured demurely, moving off to check on the remaining patients—and to give the doctor some space. The tent flap suddenly opened, and a man with startlingly blue eyes pushed his way in.

'You still in here? You need to move out,' he said, breathlessly, dripping wet.

'We're almost ready, Captain,' Jo replied to the stranger, her eyes resting for a second on his shoulder; not one of their corps.

'Almost isn't good enough, bitch.'

Jo felt as if she had been slapped in the face. Nearly four years of war and how many thousands of brutal deaths later, this breach of courtesy still managed to shock Jo, more than the concussions outside that were shaking the tent. Jo and her fellow nurses were used to working side by side with surgeons and doctors who considered them almost as colleagues, allowing them to make independent decisions and perform difficult procedures no nurse would ever be permitted to do stateside (Jo thought of the first time she had had to do a spinal tap, hands shaking; and of the one she had done earlier that day, without thinking about it at all). Even the Germans (to give the devil his due) were respectful, if confused, by the women officers, having no such counterpart in their own armies (their krankenswesters held no rank; and, with their heavy, traditional dresses, were regarded by the men more as nuns than nurses). When taken as prisoner of war, enemy officers would awkwardly ask the captured American women for their word of honor not to attempt escape; then, in lieu of imprisonment, request they wait out the rest of the war serving in orphanages or makeshift civilian hospitals.

But this man had just called her a bitch.

Grandpa struggled to his feet as quickly as his ageing joints would allow, his mouth open in outrage.

'How—how dare you, sir,' he stammered, at last.

The captain stepped forward aggressively. 'What the hell are these men still doing here? You were supposed to be moved out hours ago. I've only got a God-damned patrol to hold this area, and you're gumming up the works with your ambulances blocking the roads and drawing fire.'

Jo recovered from her momentary shock, the thick shell she wove around herself adding yet another layer. She did not know this man, she would never see him again. Their paths were crossing for a second only, and that only by chance; soon she would be back with her medical corps, with the men—the hundreds of men—who needed her. This man, she made up her mind, needed no one. 'We're waiting for our truck to return, and then we'll be out of your way, sir.' She added the sir looking level in his eyes, eyes she noted as remarkably beautiful, almost turquoise in color, but cold and lifeless and blank, as if nothing, not even light, could penetrate them.

'Then you wait in the dark, sweetheart,' he said, ripping out the generator cord. Everything went dark; Jo heard him fumbling for a second and then the motor itself sputtered out, as if in protest. In a flash of lightning Jo could see the silhouette of the captain as he passed through the tent flap; then all was darkness. There was an explosion, but much farther away this time, to the south of them, maybe half a mile down the road, followed by two more, much quieter.

'Of all the, the -' Grandpa was still stuttering, incredulous. Then, in a lower voice, a voice Jo had never heard him use before, almost a whisper; 'You alright?'

'Don't be silly, of course,' Jo replied glibly, too glibly, feeling her way in the darkness for the nearest stretcher. 'Silly,' she repeated again. But it hadn't been silly at all.

'I'm sorry, soldier,' she addressed the blackness in front of her, still feeling for the stretcher in the dark. All the tent flaps had already been tightly shut to prevent light escaping; the ambulances would have been driving without headlights, as always; both precautions making the captain's behavior seem even more senseless and—no, I won't think of him anymore, he's gone. 'But we seem to have to make shift in the dark, here, for a little while.' She tried to force cheerfulness into her voice, like Queenie would have done; and failed. 'Would you mind telling me which one you are?'

A cockney voice came through the darkness, its edges seeming to curl up in a sympathetic smile. 'Jonesy, Miss. I'm not as bad off as some of these here other ones. Just the bad leg, if you remember, Miss.'

Jo smiled. The English patient. A Montgomery, the boys always called them. Now she remembered, broken leg; a heavy cast would be dangling on a wire in front of her somewhere. Whether or not it was just habit, his double repetition of 'Miss' had sounded almost reverential, as if he were trying to make up for what had just happened.

'Can you carry on for a little while here? I'm sorry, our lanterns and flashlights have already been packed up, so it's going to be catch as catch can for a bit.' Jo used the English expression for his sake; at least, she hoped it was English, she had read it once in a novel; certainly no one said that back home in Brooklyn.

'Not to worry, Miss,' came the grinning reply. 'I'm not going anywhere.'

Jo smiled automatically in the dark, moving now with more assurance from one cot to the next, better gauging the distance between them. The Scot was still cursing; at least he was conscious. There were two post-op patients next to him whose anesthesia hadn't worn off yet; she fumbled for their wrists, taking their vital signs as best she could, guessing without her watch—at least a stethoscope was still hanging around her neck. She bumped into Grandpa crossing the tent; 'Excuse me, Miss,' he said gently, all traces of his usual brusqueness gone from his voice. She played blind-man's bluff until she found the last two stretchers—one man was asleep, but breathing raspily and much too fast, his chest sounding like crackling tin foil when she listened to it. The last man was conscious, but groaning—his forehead hot and wet—he nearly screamed when she palpated his abdomen. So they had been right in their initial diagnosis; presenting appendicitis. Good God, right now. She reassured him as best she could—he didn't seem to be listening, although it was hard to tell in the inky blackness—his moans waxing and waning without a seeming connection to her words, bobbing, as he was, on a sea of pain. She made her way over to Grandpa, who was trying to take the pulse of one of the unconscious patients.

'This is a ludicrous situation, Miss McMahon,' he began, pausing to count as he found another wrist in the dark, lost count and gave up. 'These patients—with the exception of that Scotsman, whom I don't like the look, I mean, the sound of in the least—appear stable, if in various degrees of discomfort. Rather than knock our heads together walking around in the dark, may I suggest you stay by his bedside and I'll rotate between these two and that major over there—yes, he's a major, they were supposed to move him out first—with the overripe appendix.'

It was a plan, at least. Something to do until the truck came back, whenever that would be. Jo sidled over to her patient; he was easy to find. She wondered vaguely if they were really Scottish curse words, or the byproduct of his fever, or a combination of both. She sat down next to him on the packed ground. And then she thought of Gianni.

She had tried to stop thinking of him; there had been a time when she had tried to forget him altogether, to banish him from her thoughts each time he struggled to resurface, his body disfigured and floating, the dark blood spreading from his open wounds in all directions in the cold water of her consciousness. But she had lost the power to fight her brother anymore. Sometimes, when the pace of war made her unable to function except by memory or rote, then there would be a reprieve; he would still be there, but in the back of her mind, hiding in a dark corner of the tent, laying on the last stretcher in the ambulance. But, during the few hours of sleep allotted her; or now, with an enforced period of inactivity thrust upon her, Gianni in all his horror, in all his glory came flooding back. She loved him, and she hated him for haunting her, and wanted him to leave her alone, and felt she would die if he ever did.

'What were you thinking, Josie?'

She could see him now, looking down on her again, his dark olive skin, his even darker eyes, eyes that were so angry with her, eyes that would love her and pain her and punish her forever.

'What were you thinking?'

He had grabbed her arms rudely and held her in front of him, shaking her, shaking himself. He had to be brave now and he couldn't be brave, not with her doing this terrible thing, not with her leaving, too.

'I was drafted, that can't be helped. But mama and papa will be all alone when you leave; how could you sign up?' Again, that reproach, 'What were you thinking?'

She had stammered something about the war and about duty; about how they were calling for nurses, thousands of nurses, an army of nurses to fill the ranks; how the other girls were going, how it was the right thing to do. In her dreams (waking and sleeping) her words changed, got mumbled, turned around, twisted; it didn't matter, Gianni hadn't heard them then, he didn't hear them now.

Then he was crying. She had never seen him cry, not ever, not even when he broke his wrist in the park—where they weren't supposed to be playing in the rich kids' neighborhood—and he had turned white from the pain and wanted to scream but hadn't because of his scared baby sister looking up at him with her wide, blue eyes, one streaked with brown.

'It's not just mama and papa,' Gianni Rocco had begun, but couldn't finish. He had stopped shaking her now, and was holding her close, sobbing, wracking sobs, worse than his anger had been; this was goodbye. They were, to each other, all they had ever had. Their parents (a loveless marriage) had grown prematurely old from lives spent slaving away in navy yards and sweatshops; it had been the nuns at St. Cecelia's who raised the two immigrant waifs. But for affection, for compassion, for protection in a strange new world—Gianni and 'Josie' (his pet name for her; to everyone else she would be plain 'Jo') had only ever had each other; two people, one mind, always in agreement, always together; now, suddenly, about to be torn apart.

In her dreams he dies then. He dies in her arms, their parents coming into the small apartment looking older than ever, glancing up tiredly, mumbling they would like to come to the funeral but have to work in the morning, an extra shift, what can we do, if we don't, we'll lose our jobs. It is a nightmare, of course. But it is a dream, too, because he dies there; not later; not on that carrier; not with the hundreds of other boys screaming and choking and slipping on the decks wet with blood and water and gasoline, as the planes roar overhead and the explosions go off and they're hurled in the sea and he's dead before he hits the water; sinking, crushed by the incredible weight, his mouth filling with seawater, drowning out the last word he would never get to say, the last word he was saying to her now, the same word he always said to her.

'Josie.'

***

Jo started awake. Not that she had been asleep, but she hadn't been there, in that tent, sitting in the cold and the dark. The Scot was trying to get out of bed, he was asking for his shoes in English; then it was a jumble of words again, nonsense in any language, she got up and pushed him back onto the cot; pushed is too strong a verb, he was so weak, she held two fingers in place on his chest; he moaned, delirious, and fell back.

Gianni was dead, and her parents now, too, had died while she was overseas, what did it matter anymore, everywhere was death; and where it wasn't yet, it was coming. She noticed the bombing had stopped outside and switched to gunfire. The captain hadn't come back. He would have his work cut out for him, defending this useless patch of France—or was it Germany?—with only twenty to a platoon. The truck was taking forever, too. Had it been an hour yet? Two? Time was uncertain for her, her reveries sometimes lasted mere seconds, at other times, an entire night's sleep would be sacrificed to watching Gianni die again and again. The truck might not be back for hours now, even if the roads weren't taken out, even if they did find a way around the lowlands and the mud and the Germans. She tried looking at her wristwatch, angling it to pick up even the faintest glimmer of light, but it was useless; the darkness engulfed them completely, the tent was wrapped in its own envelope of blackness and rain and there wasn't even lightning anymore to split the sky.

After a long while, it grew quiet. For some time, the gunfire had come from farther and farther away until Jo thought it had stopped entirely, or continued on in some ravine or valley too deep or far away for the sound to carry. The Scot seemed to be praying, just by the cadence alone. There was a petition of some kind, a labored pause for breath, a response. None of it made sense to Jo; maybe God could unravel it in heaven. It seemed important to him, though, whatever it was; she tried to imagine what it could be. A litany? A rosary? Something embedded and a part of this man, surely, for it to rise to the surface like this when all other senses had left him. His voice rose and fell with the desperate intercessions; she felt for her musette bag, took out her rosary, held the weathered beads in her hands, pressing them hard between her fingers until they hurt, the pain clearing her mind for a second. But no prayer rose to her lips; at least, not the Our Fathers and Hail Marys she had anticipated, the prayers she had pleaded and begged with when the telegram had first come, when she had learned Gianni had been killed in action; when her own life had ended but, cruelly, her body had been forced to keep going through the motions of being alive. And lead us not into temptation, but deliver us from evil. From evil. She was surrounded by evil, it was everywhere. There was evil in Germany just ahead of them and there was evil in Japan, half a world away. There was evil in the bottom of the sea where dark things fed on the bodies of the lost, and there was evil in the mountains around them where the traitors and the deserters and the lovers fled.

But, now, there was evil, too, right among them; the captain tonight had seemed evil—but maybe she was still naive for all her experience, maybe this was the real world now, the world they were fighting to save. Maybe this would be as good as it ever got, even if the Axes were ultimately defeated; maybe the Allies had become little better than the thing they had set out to destroy. After all, what had just happened in Dresden? Even with their mail and radio so closely censored, they knew something obscene had happened there, something wicked and wrong, something that was not them, or not them as they still imagined themselves to be; that was the kind of thing the 'other side' did, not them, not the upholders of justice and freedom, not the liberators, not the good side.

But was she good, anymore? Was anyone good? This was hell, with no chance of heaven. She saw herself again as a little girl, her voluptuous hair severely restrained by tight braids, her second-hand school uniform fitting too tightly under her arms. She was reciting her catechism answers for Sister Jonathan, the nun's parted white hair peeking out from under her wimple. 'War is the punishment for sin, Sister', she had said from memory, along with a hundred other pat answers. Punishment for sin. What colossal sin had some fool committed for this to be its outcome? Or was this the fault of all of them, collectively? Was this everyone's sin, everyone's hatefulness; were these the small, petty, stupid crimes piled up, multiplied a million million times over; lust and envy and greed and betrayal, pressed down, running over; was this the whole world crying out, proclaiming through their lives their suicide creed of hate, vengeance, murder, power, death; and then their unholy prayer finally being answered with fire bombs raining down from the sky.

The wind picked up outside, buffeting the tent. Jo was deathly cold; if the truck didn't come soon, she would have to start the oil stove again, and the orderlies would curse when they had to load it onto the truck, still hot. The Scot was crying, not like a man, but like an exhausted toddler put into his crib to cry himself out, pitiable and whimpering and small. The major cried out, cutting off his yell mid-scream; he must have bitten his hand to stop himself. Grandpa was shushing his groggy patients who were asking where they were, what had happened, where was Bobby, Joey, Ted. The rain was pelting the side of the tent, running in under the canvas and into Jo's shoes. It seemed like forever until they heard noises outside; a faint rustling over the wind at first, then, certainly the sound of men surrounding the tent, coming closer; Jo tried and failed to make out if their muted words were in English or German. She wondered what would happen to them all if they were taken prisoner this far into the war. The Geneva Convention was still in place, on paper; she and Grandpa were noncombatants and protected. But food, the first and most powerful of man's weapons when withheld, was scarce; in a prison camp, at the end of winter, there would be hardly anything left. Jo did not relish the thought of dying that way, separated from her work, from her dying countrymen, from her dying cause.

The tent flap shot open, revealing a figure as he entered, his rifle level with the flashlight he now switched on. For a moment, everyone was blinded as the piercing light shone on them. Just as quickly, it was shut off, and the figure darted to the far end of the tent, opening the flap there. After what seemed like an eternity, they could feel the phantom relax, and hear him walk back to the center of the tent, turning on a flashlight and standing it, end up, on the cool iron of the stovetop. It was the American captain.

He looked at Jo and the doctor, the six men in turn, rubbing his stubbled chin in thought as if he were about to bid on them at auction. As her eyes adjusted to the light, Jo looked from litter to litter, noting instinctively where a line had to be removed, a cast adjusted. One of the post op patients looked straight at the light with his dilated pupils, dazed yet unable to turn away. Still, the captain was silent; he seemed uncertain how to begin.

'Here's the thing,' he started, then fell silent again.

'Captain Clark,' one of his men called hoarsely through the tent flap, walking up and hastily exchanging whispers with him. When the soldier left, the captain began again.

'Okay, well, there's nothing for it. Here goes. The fighting has moved off to the south of us for the time being. There's no telling how long that will last; and, at any moment, it could shift back this way. But for now, for the next couple of hours, anyway, possibly days, you should be okay.'

To Jo, the captain's manner seemed inconsistent with the (relatively) good news he was bringing them; he kept looking at the floor, then at the tent flap, never at the nurse or doctor directly. He turned almost angrily when one of the patients cried out in pain, lifted his hand as if to say something, shook his head hastily and turned away.

'When might we be moving out?' Grandpa ventured, uncertain if the captain might again disappear into the night.

'What?' came the puzzled reply of a man thinking along entirely different lines, jolted back into the here and now against his will. 'Oh, move out. No, no. You're not. I mean, you can't. The road's blocked. Gone, really.'

The man started pacing back and forth, looking at the patients as if, by sheer will power, he could somehow get them off of their stretchers, off of his hands.

'I can't have you stay here,' the man said, almost to himself. 'Any one of these men calling out, in their sleep even, and the game's up. The Jerries could be anywhere, we could be surrounded right now, and not know it.'

He stopped pacing.

'But you said the road was blocked?' Grandpa asked. 'For how long? I mean, how long until they clear it?'

'They? There—there is no 'they', pops,' he stammered. 'I'm it. I mean, we're in a fucking big hole right now.' He took off his helmet and ran his hand through his fair hair, his voice rising despite himself. 'I mean, somehow they just fucking slammed right through the middle of our guys, I guess. I don't get it. Hell, I hope we're holding onto it somewhere, at the edges, maybe, but not here, the line's completely gone. No one's supposed to be here, I mean, not us, not any more. There will be no 'they' coming—unless it's the Germans. And if they're coming . . .' his voice trailed off, as he replaced his helmet slowly.

Jo tried to think of what Queenie would do. She wouldn't have liked this rough soldier any more than Jo did, but Queenie could be so good at saying the right thing at the right time. Queenie could have bucked him up, bucked them all up with some cock-and-bull about how she was sure the enemy would pass to their south completely; or, if not, how she was confident they could manage nicely right where they were, with her and the doctor taking care of the wounded while the brave, outmanned captain protected them all.

She looked at the captain, his eyes now covered with his free hand, lost in thought, his rifle pointing impotently towards the ground. She tried to feel inside like Queenie would have felt; tried to cue the glorious background music of her mind, the way she used to be able to do. Jo could be indomitable, too. She could whip herself up into becoming indomitable, precisely because people like Queenie existed, would always exist in the United States of America and anywhere else in the world She sent Her citizens to defend freedom. She would prove that right was right—despite Dresden, don't even think of Dresden, Dresden couldn't really have happened—justice would reign. Jo might not live to see it herself, but this war was almost ended. And, in the end, goodness would prevail.

Although they ached, Jo drew back her tired shoulders and painfully straightened her spine, coming to attention, coming to life for the first time in a long time. The captain shook himself all over like a terrier, as if he had just made up his mind about something, and turned towards the flap.

'Captain,' Grandpa asked in passing, turning back towards one of the men on the cots. 'What blocked the road?'

'Hmm?' The man seemed genuinely confused for a moment, as if he had already explained a crucial point without it being comprehended. 'Oh, didn't I tell you? The medical convoy. They got strafed. We got there all right, in the end; but everyone was dead.'

'The men were all dead,' Jo corrected him, smiling nervously, walking towards him now, her stomach dropping, picturing the burning ambulances, upside down, piled up on the side of the obliterated road. But in her mind's eye, the nurses were still racing from fallen soldier to fallen soldier like they always had, like they always would, Queenie at their lead; her face covered in soot, her towel come loose and her dark hair messy around her face in the whipping wind, looking wild and beautiful and radiant in the red of the fires burning about her, calling out for the girls to rally round her and smiling. 'All the patients were lost. The drivers.'

The captain looked at Jo as if she were a little girl, a very stupid and tiresome girl who asked senseless questions of a man in a hurry. In his vacant eyes was something that could have been mistaken for pity, but was, in fact, a most profound sense of irritation. Only with great effort did he suppress the second word of his intended sentence; simply repeating, instead, the single word, 'Everyone.' Then he pushed aside the tent flap and stepped out into the night.

You've just read an excerpt from The Fire By Night.

ABOUT THE AUTHOR

Teresa Messineo spent seven years researching the history behind *The Fire By Night*, her first novel. A graduate of DeSales University, her varied interests include homeschooling her four children, volunteering with the underprivileged, medicine, swing dancing and competitive athletics. She lives near Philadelphia with her family.

IMPRINT: William Morrow
PRINT ISBN: 9780062459107

PRINT PRICE: $26.99
EBOOK ISBN: 9780062459121
EBOOK PRICE: $12.99
PUBLICATION DATE: 1/17/17
PUBLICITY CONTACT: Shelby Meizlik Shelby.Meizlik@harpercollins.com
RIGHTS CONTACT: Juliette Shapland Juliette.Shapland@harpercollins.com
Michele Corallo Michele.Corallo@harpercollins.com
EDITOR: Rachel Kahan
AGENT: Grainne Fox
AGENCY: C. Fletcher & Company LLC.

WE ARE UNPREPARED

A NOVEL

MEG LITTLE REILLY

SUMMARY

Ash and Pia, in their mid-30s, uproot themselves from Brooklyn to northeast Vermont seeking a more self-reliant lifestyle. Though Ash is well aware they are something of a hipster cliché, he looks forward to returning to his native state and a simpler life. But, after only a few months, paradise begins to vanish. Strange weather patterns emerge and the government cautiously predicts that a catastrophe could be coming. Ash and Pia begin to prepare along with the rest of the community, but a divide among the citizenry is mirrored in their own household. Ash supports the town's establishment in its disaster preparedness, but Pia falls in with radical "preppers" who want to move off the grid. When "The Storm" finally hits, it razes both external and internal landscapes, leaving everything—and everyone—permanently altered.

EXCERPT

Part One

I pine, I pine for my woodland home; I long for the mountain stream

That through the dark ravine flows on Till it finds the sun's bright beam.

I long to catch once more a breath Of my own pure mountain air,

And lay me down on the flowery turf In the dim old forest there.
*

O, for a gush of the wildwood strain That the birds sang to me then!

O, for an hour of the fresher life I knew in that haunted glen!

For my path is now in the stranger's land, And though I may love full well

Their grand old trees and their flowery meads, Yet I pine for thee, sweet dell.
*

I've sat in the homes of the proud and great, I've gazed on the artist's pride,

Yet never a pencil has painted thee, Thou rill of the mountain side.

And though bright and fair may be other lands, And as true their friends and free,

Yet my spirit will ever fondly turn, Green Mountain Home, to thee.

—*"Green Mountain Home" by Miss A.W. Sprague of Plymouth, Vermont. First published in 1860.*

Chapter One

Isolé—(French) / E-zo--LEE / adj.: isolate, remote, lonely. Isole—(English) / --so-le / n.: rural town in the Northeast

Kingdom of Vermont. Population: 6,481.

It would be narcissistic to assume that the earth conjured a storm simply to alter the course of my life. More likely, we'd been poisoning this world for years while ignoring the warning signs, and The Storm wasn't so much a cosmic intervention as it was a predictable response to our collectively reckless behavior. Either way, the resulting destruction—to North America and our orderly life in Isole—arrived so quickly that I swear we didn't see it coming.

Looking back, I realize how comforting those months leading up to The Storm had been as we focused on preparing for the disaster. News of the changing weather gave each of our lives a new clarity and direction. It didn't feel enjoyable at the time, but it was a big, concrete distraction in which to pour ourselves, even as other matters could have benefited from our attention. It was urgent, and living in a state of urgency can be invigorating. But the fear can be mistaken for purpose, which is even more dangerous than the threat itself.

Chapter Two

We were driving east on Route 15 when the world first learned of the coming storms. Pia and I had just met with a fertility specialist in Burlington and we were both staring straight ahead at the road as we digested the information we'd received there. I didn't want to see a doctor about having babies. That was for people who were old or sick or in a rush and we were none of those things. But it's true that we had sort of been trying on and off for a year, so with little persuasion, I agreed to the appointment. Conceiving a child had become Pia's obsession in the preceding months, and her determination trumped my ambivalence.

We sat completely still in our seats and stared at the empty road as we drove back toward our new home. I gripped the wheel at ten o'clock and two o'clock, focusing on the act of driving to avoid looking over at Pia, who I knew was crying silently. I could feel the steam from the fat tears that rolled down her smooth face. I wanted to comfort her, to make them stop, but I couldn't will myself to.

There had been soft, Celtic music playing in the waiting room of the Full Moon Fertility Center and amateurish oil paintings of naked women in various states of pregnancy hanging on the walls, all of which annoyed me immensely for their obviousness. Weeks earlier, blood had been drawn and samples had been submitted, and this was the day Doctor Tan-Face explained to us in a soothing voice that conceiving a child on our own was unlikely. Pia had a hormone imbalance that would require "assistance." It made Pia cry to hear this word, which made me almost as sad to see.

It was a hot September day in Vermont and everything that had been green was beginning to turn brown under the unrelenting sun. It was hotter and dryer than it should have been on September 20th. We passed roadside produce stands and fellow drivers occasionally, but were mostly alone for miles of farmland. Fireweed grew along the edges of the road and, if I squinted, I could see fluffy dandelion heads mingling with drying milkweeds in the fields. There was a group of grazing cows and a carload of children pointing excitedly at the lazy ladies. I was trying to conjure more sympathy for my wife as I took this all in. Species were propagating all around us but we needed *assistance*. I understood why this news was difficult to hear. Other couples had told us of the heartache of infertility and the shattering of a romantic fantasy for how this milestone is supposed to unfold. I wanted to feel that heartache with her, but any sadness was crowded out by an overwhelming sense of relief—relief that it was her faulty machinery and not mine, and mostly, relief that we had just been given the gift of more time. The doctor had explained that getting pregnant might take a little while, which is all I really wanted to hear him say—that I would have a little more time to live life like the young, happy thirty-five year old I believed myself to be.

The air blowing in from our open windows smelled like overheated livestock and corn that had passed its prime. I could picture the exact stage of transformation that the kernels on the mature stalks would be entering at that moment. The extreme heat had forced early harvests and they were already losing their plump, yellow corn complexions as the sugars dulled to starch. I knew those smells. I knew that the cut stalks were already so sharp that if you ran through them in your bare feet, they could slice right through the skin. These were passive memories, absorbed unknowingly in childhood and left dormant for the years I'd been away from Vermont. They surprised me in their specificity and sureness, awakened by the smallest triggers. It was as if a whole room in my brain had been locked for a long time, but when it finally reopened, every object was just as I had left it.

When the silent crying and focused driving got to be too much, I reached for the stereo dial on the dashboard of our aging Volvo, permanently set to Vermont Public Radio. It came on too loud, which was awkward at that moment. My hand rushed back to the knob, but as I started to turn it down, Pia grabbed my wrist and said, "Wait, Ash."

A somber, male NPR voice was explaining that the head of the National Oceanic and Atmospheric Administration had just briefed the President of the United States about the latest long-term storm forecast. At first it didn't sound all that serious. Big storms had already become the norm. Tornados, wildfires, floods, hurricanes—it seemed like some part of the country was always in a state of emergency. But the tone of the reporter's voice and the odd timing of the report suggested that there was something new here.

"What we know for sure," the reporter said, "is that, due to rapidly-rising sea surface temperatures in the Atlantic and Gulf of Mexico, we are now approaching a period of extreme weather events. NOAA is predicting as many as thirty named tropical storms and hurricanes in the coming months, along with likely heat waves and drought, and even severe blizzards. It's too early to know precisely when or what we're in for, but these water temperatures are unprecedented and the storms they trigger will almost certainly be record-breaking. These storms have the potential to be very, very disruptive."

He said *disruptive* with emphasis; we were expected to infer larger things from the restrained word.

"Jesus," I said out loud.

Pia had stopped crying. She was leaning in toward the dashboard, coaxing the news out of the speakers.

"How firm is this science?" a female interviewer asked the male voice, and I wished that we had heard the report from the beginning.

"Government scientists say the rising sea water temperatures and levels are reliable. They are less certain about how these variables will interact with other weather forces. Storm experts that I've spoken with say that there is a plausible worst-case-scenario that the government doesn't want to talk about just yet."

"And what's that?"

"If this warm air above the Atlantic collides with a colder pressure system from the west, they could create a sort of superstorm along the eastern seaboard, which could be positively devastating. But again, no government officials have made such a warning. All we know for sure right now is that we have several months of extreme weather events ahead. But I believe this is the first time the federal government has issued such an early and emphatic warning of this kind, so it must be dire."

The radio voices went on to discuss global ramifications of extreme weather—food scarcity, political unrest, war—but we had already drifted back into our own minds by then. Moments before, we were busy trying to create new life and now there uncertainty in the life before us. We didn't linger for long on the thought—our babies were as abstract then as the coming storms.

I turned right, toward our house, past the broken mailbox I kept meaning to replace and down the dirt path that served as our driveway. I loved everything about that house. I loved the way the overgrowth of sugar maples and yellow birch trees along the driveway created a sort of enchanted tunnel that spat you out steps from our expansive porch. I really loved the way the porch, crowded with potted plants and mismatched furniture, wrapped all the way around the faded yellow farmhouse. This was our dream home in our dream life and, though we had only been there for three months, it felt like we were always meant to live there. The yellow farmhouse was the realization of all the fantasies borne from our marriage. To be there, finally, was a victory.

There was a creek that ran through the backyard, threading all of our neighbors and hundreds of spring thaws together. Some of the people in the area kept their yards neatly manicured, but most were like us: they mowed now and then, but gave the wildflowers a wide berth and relished the sight of a deer or—even better—a brown bear, snacking on the ever encroaching blackberry bushes. This was where you lived if you wanted not to conquer nature, but to join it. This was the Northeast Kingdom of Vermont and there was nowhere else like it on earth.

I turned off the engine and looked over at Pia, whose expression had turned from sullen to intrigued. Her face had reassembled back to its baseline of beautiful. Pia was gorgeous. Her thick, wavy blond hair was twisted off over one shoulder, frizzing slightly in the unseasonable heat. She had bright green eyes protected by long lashes that were still wet with tears. She sat back and looked at me with one bare knee up on the car seat, short cut-off shorts nearly disappearing in that position. Her body and her utterly unselfconscious ownership of her body was an invitation—not just to me, but to the world. Pia was that enviable combination of beauty, self-possession, and grace that makes people want to be closer. She was magnetic. Not quite fit, but small and smooth in the most perfect ways. She attracted attention everywhere we went, male and female. Every head tilt and arm stretch seemed effortless, though I knew that they were choreographed for an imaginary camera that followed her around. As an artist, she'd achieved only middling success, but Pia was unmatched for the artfulness in which she inhabited her own skin.

"I think this is serious, Ash," Pia said. Her eyes were wide. "We all knew these storms were coming eventually, and now they're here—not that they would ever admit the *real* cause."

There had been no mention of global warming in the news report, but by then, no one needed our reluctant government to confirm what we knew to be true. Pia was reflexively defiant of all authority and she seemed to enjoy the vindication that this weather report was already providing. I reached a hand across the front seat to squeeze her knee, sensing that the mood in the car had shifted. We had been drawn out of our own anxious heads and were feeling unified now by our fear and fascination with the coming storms. A familiar wave of guilty relief washed over me. I suggested that we relax on the back porch with cold beers, which she did not object to.

Pia stretched out on a hammock on the porch, while I went inside to grab two Long Trail Ales from the fridge. The sun was low in the sky by then and our house was finally beginning to cool. Even though it was September, the temperature hadn't dropped below eighty-five during the day yet.

I held a wet beer against Pia's thigh, which made her squeal. She pulled me into the hammock with her, an unsteady arrangement, but I was happy to have her body pressed against mine after a particularly trying couple of days. She was a virtuoso of affection—both creative and infectious with her demonstration of love. After years together, I was still always grateful to receive it.

I ran a finger along the curve of her breast and she closed her eyes.

"We need to start planning," Pia said. "We need to start stocking up and fortifying the house and…getting seriously self-reliant."

We talked about self-reliance in those days like it was a state of higher consciousness. It was the explanation we gave for leaving our jobs in New York and starting a new life in Vermont. We wanted to grow things, and build things, preserve things, and pickle things. We wanted to play our own music and brew our own beer. This, we believed, was how one lives a *real* life. There was a pious promise in the notion of self-reliance—a promise that we would not only feel a deep sense of pride and moral superiority, but also that it would ensure eternal marital bliss. Some of this we were not wrong about: it was supremely satisfying to eat cucumbers that we had grown and sit on furniture we had made (two Adirondack chairs assembled from a kit, technically). Pia was taking a pottery class in those days and our house was filled with charmingly lopsided creamers and water pitchers with her initials carved into the underside, like a proud child's bounty from summer camp. I had taken a weekend-long seminar on beekeeping and the unopened bee materials that I ordered online were still stacked neatly against the house. When the news of The Storms broke, we were only three months into this real living adventure and we hadn't learned much at all yet.

Pia and I weren't alone in these aspirations. There were others like us around the country: young(ish) people, intent on living differently. In the aftermath of America's economic crisis, a burst housing bubble and an overheating earth, we were part of an unofficial movement-people who wanted to create a life that wasn't defined by a drive for more stuff. We wanted to spend less time at work and more time with each other. We were smug, sure, but I still believe we were basically right in our quest to find pleasure in simpler pursuits. It wasn't so much a rejection of our parents' choices as it was an admission that those choices weren't available to us. The world was different and we were adapting.

Isole, Vermont was an answer to those yearnings. It offered a delightful mix of hippies and rednecks, cohabitating in the picturesque valley between two small mountains. You only went there if you knew what you were looking for. There were old farm families and loggers who had been in Isole long enough to remember when it was pronounced in its traditional French EE-zo-LEE. But the economic engine of the region came from outside money by then—reclusive liberals with trust funds, self employed tech whizzes, and socially-responsible venture capitalists—all hiding out in a picturesque hamlet that was too far from a city to every be truly civilized.

I liked to think of myself as a native because I grew up in central Vermont, but the real locals knew us as outsiders. We had come from Brooklyn, where we spent the previous twelve years building successful and lucrative careers. Pia had worked in advertising and I was a partner at a graphic design firm. The firm was well established by the time I sold my portion of the business back to my colleagues, but I had been there in the early days, before we had an in-house gym and black tie holiday parties.

Pia and I fell in love with our Vermont farmhouse on vacation earlier that year. We had taken an extended spring weekend on Crystal Lake. It was too cold to swim, so we took long drives around the Northeast Kingdom, basking in the slowness and serenity. On the last day of our stay, we drove past a perfect yellow farmhouse on a slanted dirt road with a just posted For Sale sign out front. It was *our* sign, we decided. We had been waiting for it.

Years before, Pia and I had made a pact to live a different sort of life one day. We had only the vaguest plan to escape the city and remake ourselves, but we were sure the details of this plan would present themselves when it was time. So when we found the farmhouse, we recognized it as the natural extension of the dream we had created together. I sold my piece of the firm and stayed on as a long-distance consultant. Two months later, we were unpacking in Vermont. It was such a fast and easy process that we didn't have time to iron out all the wrinkles of our new life. Pia didn't have a new job lined up yet and we hadn't met a soul there.

It sounds reckless in the retelling, but that was an important part of its appeal. Pia was great at embracing the new and unpredictable, but I was far more cautious, so this leap to a new state also felt like a leap toward my wife. We were going to forge a new path together, armed only with years of shared daydreams about a country life.

The hammock rocked gently as the breeze picked up and I could smell the goldenrod that was being mowed at the farm upwind. Pia was still listing things that would need to be addressed before The Storms came: gutters, faulty wiring in the basement, a stuck bedroom window. I knew she was probably right; if this storm was for real then we did need to start preparing. But I stroked her hair and suggested that we spend the rest of the now-enjoyable Saturday relaxing. We could get to disaster preparations tomorrow.

"Hey dudes. What are you doing?" said a squeaky approaching voice.

It was our seven-year-old neighbor, August, whose dilapidated little house sat on the other side of a thick wall of trees and shrubs to the east. His place was invisible from our porch, but connected by a short, neat path that I had helped August clear to facilitate easy movement back and forth. I had met August on the first day of our arrival, when he walked through our open front door and began peppering us with questions. He seemed desperate for friends and bubbling with curiosity.

Since then, I'd seen him almost every day. He'd come over to kick a soccer ball back and forth or invite me to check out the new fort he'd built in the woods behind our homes. Pia thought August was sweet, but it was I who spent so much time with him. I wondered sometimes about the adults in his life who had left him so hungry for attention, but I didn't ask many questions, mainly because I didn't know what exactly to ask, but also because I enjoyed our time together and wanted to just be with him. And August was helpful. He'd spent his entire short life in those woods and he knew more about self-reliance and country living than Pia and I combined.

"What's up, buddy," I said, reaching a hand out for a sticky high-five.

As usual, August was barefoot, filthy, and smiling. There was burdock lodged in his curly auburn hair appeared to have taken hold days before.

August wanted to play frisbee so we hoisted our bodies out of the hammock and met him on the lawn. The mood had shifted and we were happy to play. That was the way things changed with Pia: she could be crying and sad, but the minute it was over, it was really over. Most of the time, this was a relief, though there were times when I knew we probably should have actually worked things through instead of just riding them out. But it was so much easier to just wait for storms to pass, and the highs were so high that we didn't want to look back at the lows once we had escaped them. We just drove forward, secure in the knowledge that we were in love and nothing was worth dwelling on. This unspoken arrangement required a willingness on my part to indulge every emotional whim that Pia wanted to follow. In return, she kept things uncomplicated and asked very few questions. Abiding by the rules of this dynamic felt intimate. It worked for us.

Pia dove theatrically as the frisbee left August's hands, which made him double over in laughter every time. I laughed along with them, but let my eyes wander to the group of flycatchers above. They were migrating south, no doubt, but they were several weeks late. They should have been in Central America by then. These were the details of nature that I never got wrong. I was as passionate about nature as Pia was about art, and I knew bird migratory patterns like the moles on my left arm. I assumed they were just as immovable. But the birds were confused and their travels had changed.

Our backyard was magnificent that day. The enormous sugar maples along the lawn's perimeter swayed cheerfully as the low sun illuminated their drying leaves. It would have been a perfect July day, were it not for the fact that it was late September and there was no shaking the feeling that everything was off. The leaves seemed to be skipping past their most brilliant orange-yellow-red phase and going straight to the browning at the end. We were playing frisbee in shorts for christ's sake. Weather was the primary topic of discussion in the Northeast Kingdom that summer—even more so than usual—because it was all so wrong. Everyone was nervous: the farmers, the maple sugarers, the people who relied on ski tourism, the ice fisherman and the hockey fans. Pia talked a lot about a global warming government cover-up, but I was the one in our household who truly mourned the changing Vermont climate. I had grown up there (technically, I grew up in Rutland, a sturdier, post-industrial town in central Vermont). Every milestone of my life was tied in some way to New England weather; and every romantic vision I had for our new life relied on the weather being right. Some part of me understood this to be unrealistic, but I wasn't ready to accept that.

When the sun finally disappeared and our toes started to chill in our flip-flops, we sent August home and Pia and I went inside to make dinner. I loved making dinner together. It was an activity that could lay the groundwork for hours of sexually charged companionship. It wasn't just sex—though that almost always came later—but also wine and storytelling and laughter and touching. Those nights always felt to me like scenes from a movie. I envisioned someone watching us through a window, not hearing exactly what we were saying, but being impressed by the ease and tenderness of our home life. It was the shade of domesticity that I liked marriage in.

Pia browned fat chunks of bacon in a pan that would soon be joined by split brussels sprouts and a drizzle of maple syrup, an addicting recipe she had acquired from the little girl who ran the farm stand down the road. These were the details we relished, but worked to seem cool about when we breathlessly relayed them to our friends back in Brooklyn. *We buy our sprouts from a farm girl down the road! That's where we get our eggs too—you have never eaten eggs until you've had just-laid eggs. I can't believe we ever bought our meat vacuum-sealed at the grocery store. Just-butchered and free range is the way to go. It's just the way life is here…* The narrative we'd created about our life in Vermont was almost as important as the experience itself.

I massaged salt and pepper into a local sirloin and carried it out the back screen door to place over high flames on the grill. Pia joined me minutes later, slipping a hand around my waste and lifting her pinot noir to my lips. I took a sip before leaning down to kiss her hard. I loved that I was almost a full head taller than her. Being tall and broad was my best physical feature. Without expending much effort on appearance, I projected the illusion of general fitness, even as my stomach softened slightly and my dark, groomed beard sprouted grays. I drew most of my confidence with women from my size, which worked fine for Pia who liked to be enveloped by someone larger than herself. On cue, she melted into my chest and then pushed me away, darting back inside to tend to her sautéing pans.

* * *

"I want to change the world," I once said to Pia during a marathon late night session of drinking, fooling around and philosophizing early in our courtship. We were on our second bottle of wine and both feeling drunk.

"No you don't," she laughed.

"I do!"

"No, people who want to change the world go on disaster relief missions in Haiti and deliver vaccines to babies in Africa. You just want to be outside and feel like less of a yuppie dick."

I considered this correction as I studied the pattern of the blanket beneath us. We were sitting on the floor in our tiny Brooklyn living room having a sort of indoor picnic.

"It's okay," Pia went on. "I'm the same. I'm too selfish to do something truly good, but I think choosing to live a life that doesn't make the world worse is okay too."

"Shit, you're right," I conceded. "So how do we not make the world worse?"

"Smaller ecological footprint, conscientious consumerism, freedom from prejudices, that sort of thing. It sounds trite but I don't think it is. You live a more thoughtful life than your parents did, and you teach your kids those values, and voila: the human race evolves. That's meaningful."

"I'd rather actually be a good person, but I guess you're right. Maybe that is meaningful," I agreed. "So let's make a pact to live that way. Somehow."

Pia stretched a hand toward me to formalize the agreement. "I love that. It's a deal."

We shook on it.

"I feel like a good person already," I said.

"Not good, just a not-bad person," she corrected.

We set our wine glasses aside and I dove toward her. She enveloped me with her legs and fell back.

Pia was a marvel to me in those early days—as witty and esoteric as she was sexy. It was just nice being together and we never wanted to stop.

Dinner was served on the dirty porch furniture, which looked perfect in the glow of a dozen tea lights that Pia had carefully arranged. We sat across from each other, drinking wine and discussing the superior origins and experiences of the dead animals before us. There would be no mention of her ovulation cycle or my quiet resistance to the project. This was a good night. After some discussion of the strange and beautiful sky, we eventually turned to the most obvious topic.

"So, what are we going to do, love?" Pia asked, more excited than scared. "These storms are just terrifying! We need a plan." I nodded. "We do need a plan. I can't imagine that our little landlocked state is in all that much danger, but I guess we should err on the side of caution and get this leaky old house sealed up. I assume that we'd stay here, even if a really big storm came, right?"

"Of course—we have to stay!" Pia said, gulping her wine. "This house is our baby. And where would we go anyhow? Certainly not to your parents' place. And certainly not to mine!"

I was surprised that she hadn't considered the possibility, but it's true that there wasn't really any reason to go to either of our parents' homes in the case of an emergency. We were adults and we were no less equipped to handle disaster than they were, though it felt like a level of adulthood we hadn't yet graduated to.

Pia's parents, both academics, lived in a tony Connecticut suburb outside of New York City, which is where they had raised their one beautiful child. They were aloof and opinionated, but they had always been kind enough to me. Pia spoke of them as if they were monsters. And maybe they were. I once assumed that she liked believing that hers had been a cruel childhood because it made her more interesting and tortured. But I was wrong about all that. Something had been missing from her childhood; there was a chaos inside of her that I couldn't account for.

I didn't like Pia's parents, but not for the reasons she provided. They offended a Yankee sensibility in me that valued industriousness and discipline. I couldn't understand what justified their haughtiness when, as far as I could tell, they hadn't left much of a mark on the world. It wasn't that their pretentions were unfamiliar to me—there was no shortage of artsy liberal affect in the corner of New England I grew up in. I just hated playing along with it. Pia's parents attended the symphony and followed culinary trends and read theater reviews, but they didn't create anything themselves and this bothered me. They seemed to believe that, by virtue of association with greatness, they too were great. They told us stories about so-and-so who just produced a one act play or wrote a book about his trek across Nepal as we nodded with appropriate awe. Visits with them required pretending that we weren't having cocktails with appreciators of great art, but with the artists themselves. All of this was made even more maddening by their undiluted disappointment at the lack of *formal* culture in our lives. That was their term for distinguishing the kind of culture that we enjoyed from the established arts of the aristocracy they believed themselves to be.

My family was less complicated in every way, a point that Pia liked to make when she was annoyed with me. My father was a lawyer at a local firm in Rutland, where I grew up with two sisters and a brother. I came second, which secured my rank as neither the most successful nor the most screwed-up of my siblings. My mom stayed at home and I believe Pia disapproved of this, but she never said so aloud. My parents volunteered at our schools and picked up trash on green-up days and supported local theater. Since moving to New York, I hadn't met anyone who cared about their community in the way my parents cared for their struggling town. I like my parents and, although my younger sister's kids and my brother's drug habits had commanded most of their attention in recent years, we were all okay. (My oldest sister lives in London with her wife. We had always gotten along well, though we've fallen out of touch in recent years.) This is what family looks like to me. It's not always joyful, but it's big and messy and kind of fun some of the time. I expected to have something similar one day, when I was ready.

"Yeah, we have to stay here no matter what," I agreed, pulling the collar on my sweater a little higher. It was cool outside now and so dark that I could barely see Pia's face floating above the candles.

She moved our bare plates aside and took a small notebook with a matching pen from the pocket of her bulky sweater. It was list time. Pia loved the idea of being a writer, someone who writes, so she was forever collecting pretty little notebooks to have on hand in case inspiration struck. But inspiration never stayed with her for more than a few minutes, so her notebooks were mostly used for frantic list-making, which struck much more frequently. She listed books she planned to read, organic foods she wanted to grow, yoga postures that would heal whatever was ailing her. Her lists were aspirational instructions for a life she wanted to live. They rarely materialized into much, but served a constructive role nonetheless, as if the mere act of putting her plans in writing set her on a path to self-improvement. I didn't object to the positivity of it all.

Pia had begun a shopping list of home supplies we would need for The Storms. She wrote: canned goods, multivitamins, water filtration system, solar blankets. It read more like a survival list for the apocalypse than a storm preparation plan. "Babe, I was thinking we would just, like, board up the windows and try to seal up the root cellar a bit," I said. "Do you really think we need all that?"

"It can't hurt to be prepared," Pia shrugged, still writing in the dark. "And if nothing comes of these storm predictions, then we'll have some extra supplies until the next time we need them. No harm done."

Her reasoning was sound, but there was an edge to her voice that surprised me. The coming storms excited her.

Pia came around to my side of the table and wrapped a wool blanket around both of our shoulders. It smelled like campfire from a previous summer outing. She put her arms around my chest for a quick squeeze and then turned back to her notebook. I listened to the leaves swaying with the wind and the din of summer insects that were somehow still abundant. Her hair fell all around us. I could smell the natural almond shampoo she had started using since adopting a more country approach to hygiene, which made her hair wilder than it used to be. Pia was getting charged with each new idea she recorded. I loved her like that: present and energized. I knew what my role was at those moments. I would be adoring and attentive, which I really was.

Pia pulled a knee up to her chest and I noticed a new drawing in ballpoint pen on her upper thigh. It was a tree with the face of an old man in its trunk. She must have done it that evening, mindlessly doodling in a moment of boredom. Our lives were filled with these small reminders of Pia's artistic gifts, washable and impermanent, but impressive. She had won awards in college for her oil paintings, and a prominent gallery in Manhattan offered to show her photography years before. But Pia lacked the discipline to carry out long-term projects and she changed mediums too often to be truly great with any of them. With focus, she could have earned a living doing the kind of art she loved.

"You're going to be great at this," Pia said.

"At what?"

"You know, bracing for these big weather events, finding industrious solutions to things, living without some of our old comforts. You like things a little difficult."

She was complimenting me, but teasing too. Since we'd started making real money, modern life was feeling a bit squishy for me. All morning espressos and personal trainers. I secretly feared that I was growing too attached to it all. A tiny alarm in the primal recesses of my brain had been going off, warning me to stay sharp and focused in case of future uncertainty. I never told Pia about this growing discomfort, but I should have guessed that she could sense it.

"Fingers crossed for frozen pipes," I smiled.

We stayed outside until nearly eleven, building our plan for The Storms and laughing—flirting even—as we huddled together in solidarity. When I finally convinced Pia that it was time to go to bed, she took my hand

and led me upstairs to our bedroom, where she instructed me to sit in a small antique chair to watch her slowly peel off each layer of her clothing.

It would have been comical on a less beautiful woman as she unbuttoned her oversized flannel shirt and pulled off fading green cotton underwear, but it wasn't. My physical response to Pia's naked body hadn't flagged in the years we'd been together. If anything, it had grown more intense as sex tapered off a little. When she was done undressing, she turned and walked her naked body to the bed to wait for me. Her ears and nose were still cold from the evening chill but the rest of her body was warm, hot even. I attempted restraint at first, but that didn't last, and what followed was the wild, forceful passion that we'd founded our relationship on years ago. Better even. We fucked like two people desperate to occupy one another. It was feral, afraid. Pia was alive, the weather was our common enemy, and I was relieved.

As she fell asleep beside me, my mind drifted back to our un-conceived baby and the news of The Storms. I wasn't ready for a baby, not then, but I loved Pia's desire for one because it was the embodiment of my favorite things about her: a hunger for new beginnings, adventure, and above all, optimism. Whether there was a place for optimism in the stormy new world we inhabited, I didn't know. And I wondered—for the first time in my life—whether this was still a world that babies wanted to be born into. And how could the answer to that question be anything other than an emphatic 'yes' if we are to go on living wholeheartedly? Is there a moment at which the human race should decide not to perpetuate itself, or will we keep going until the universe decides that for us and just wipes us out? The latter seemed more likely. So I wondered how the universe might kill off our species, whether it would be instantaneous and painless or cruelly slow. Perhaps it was already happening at a pace just slow enough to go undetected. Were we at a beginning or an end?

You've just read an excerpt from We Are Unprepared.

ABOUT THE AUTHOR

Meg Little Reilly is a former Treasury Spokesperson under President Obama, Deputy Communications Director for the Office of Management and Budget (OMB), communicator for the Environmental Defense Fund

(EDF) and producer for Vermont Public Radio. A native of Vermont, she is an UVM graduate with deep ties around the state. She currently lives in Boston with her husband Daniel and two daughters. For more information about the author, please visit her at http://www.meglittlereilly.com, www.facebook.com/meg.l.reilly or @MegLittleReilly.

IMPRINT: Mira Books
PRINT ISBN: 9780778319436
PRINT PRICE: $15.99
EBOOK ISBN: 9781460395882
EBOOK PRICE: $8.99
PUBLICATION DATE: 8/30/16
PUBLICITY CONTACT: Shara Alexander shara.alexander@harpercollins.com
RIGHTS CONTACT: Reka Rubin reka.rubin@harlequin.com
EDITOR: Kathy Sagan
AGENT: John Silbersack
AGENCY: Trident Media Group LLC

TERRITORIES SOLD:
UK, Australia, Poland

PROMOTIONAL INFORMATION:
Focus title at ALA Midwinter, ABA Winter Institute, BEA and ALA Annual; National galley distribution and press kit mailings; National media campaign, including print, broadcast and online outreach; Targeted trade and consumer advertising campaign; Library and independent bookseller outreach; Appearances at consumer book festivals; Online promotion, including social media and blogger outreach; Support through BookClubbish.com social media properties and newsletter; In-book advertising in selected Harlequin MIRA® imprint titles.

HELEN SEDGWICK

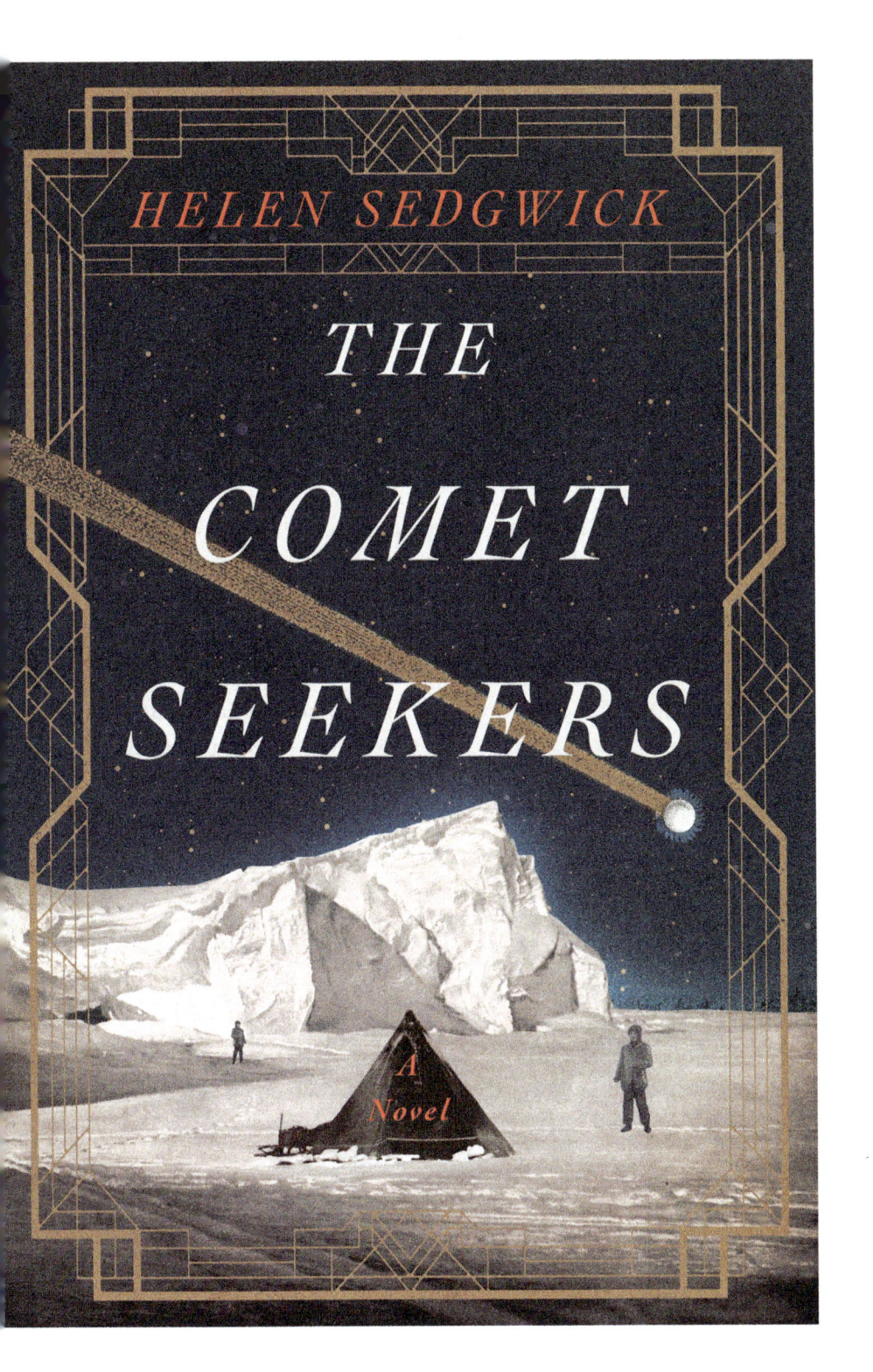

THE COMET SEEKERS

A Novel

SUMMARY

A magical, intoxicating debut novel, both intimate and epic, that intertwines the past, present, and future of two lovers bound by the passing of great comets overhead and a coterie of remarkable ancestors.

EXCERPT

Comet Giacobini, 2017

They arrive on the snow during the last endless day of summer. Forty-eight hours of light and then, they gather outside to watch their first sunset of the South. The ice shelf they're standing on is floating, slowly, towards the coast—will one day melt into the sea. There is nothing permanent about this never-ending white.

Róisín stamps her feet, watches the sky for the full twenty minutes of night, not that it ever gets dark. Dusk is the most she can hope for, this week at least; everything turning a golden red, the sun's rays like torchlight through the curved walls of a child's tent, the full moon opposite. It shines like a second sun but fainter, its reflected light a ghost of the star below the horizon.

During the day, some people run a marathon around the base—eight laps of the research station at minus ten degrees. Róisín joins them on their final lap. Her legs feel heavy; gulps of air chill her lungs. The winner is lying flat on the snow at the finish line. When he sees her looking he smiles up at her, says: You should try it.

Maybe next time, she says.

His name is François.

He holds his hand over his eyes, trying to shield the glare.

He looks so young.

One hour, forty minutes of darkness, and someone is behind her. Five days she has been here, five days she has searched the sky alone. Róisín turns around.

What are you looking for?

François is here, wanting to see what she's doing, to join in. She's not sure how she feels about that; she did not come here to make friends. Róisín thinks about telling him so, asking him to leave, but for some reason she decides to let him stay. Beside her, François looks at the sky and exhales.

There's a comet predicted, she says. It's going to be very bright. But it's too early. I mean, we're too soon.

Because it's not dark enough yet?

Yes. Well, that and other things.

It's beautiful, isn't it?

Above them, colours swirl like sea mist.

François stays where he is, doesn't ask any more questions. He doesn't take his eyes from the sky.

Róisín finds she has walked into the kitchen. She says she wants to help— it doesn't feel right with François in there on his own, cooking for sixteen, even though he's the chef. She offers to slice onions and retrieve diced meat from the freezer, watches his hands as he works. The smell is of roasting tomatoes and rosemary.

This was one of my favourites, he says, when I was a child.

Abbey Road is playing on the tape deck.

Róisín thinks of soft boiled eggs and soldiers. The sun is setting again.

Three hours, twenty minutes of darkness. The night is increasing by twenty minutes each day. It is building up to 21st March, when things will be perfectly balanced and there will be twelve hours of light and twelve hours of dark.

Every day, Róisín marks the calendar with a cross. Turning over the page—a photo of lights, traffic, people, noise, the cityscape a world away. She checks the footnote. It is Cape Town, and underneath Cape Town a day, three weeks away, is circled in blue.

She stands outside and listens through the muffled layer of her hood to the absolute silence of snow and ice dust and rock. Sometimes François comes outside to stand with her, but she never asks what they will be cooking the next day for dinner.

They hear on the radio that a group of sea lions have been spotted off the coast. The research team goes to investigate, Róisín and some of the others, taking cameras with long lenses, notebooks and food enough for two days. They're not far from the coast but it still feels like a hike from the base; four hours walk in snow boots, pulling the sleigh, is not easy. There was training for this job, a series of tests you had to pass: physical, survival, psychological.

As they approach the coast they can see kelp gulls circling; something must have died. On arrival they see that something has. One of the sea lions has been killed in a fight, over territory or perhaps a female. They take photographs, look for any tags from other research teams, keep their distance. The red of its blood seems like the most vivid, most deeply coloured thing Roisin has seen for years.

There is a building by the coast, a square, basic sort of place, where they can sleep, or at least rest, before making the hike home tomorrow. Lying down, Roisin turns to face the wall and cannot see the concrete two inches from her eyes in the dark.

She's alone. She's walking towards the dead sea lion even though she knows it's wrong; they are not allowed to get too close, not allowed to touch or interfere, but she sees the blood and has no choice—how did this happen? she asks the sea lion corpse, how did this happen? She tries to pick him up, but his skin is like whale blubber and she is repulsed.

She wakes, sick and longing, and full of guilt.

When they get back to the base she sees François in the kitchen. He turns, sees her; there is a look of wonder in his eyes that she wishes she understood, that she wants to share.

The door is only half-closed and Róisín's eyes only half shut when she hears a quiet tap tap at the window before sunrise. A rope has come lose from the sleigh they were using, snaking in the wind.

I heard it too, François whispers from the doorway, hardly making a sound. He is wearing thermal underwear and indoor boots, bobble hat and knitted gloves. She would have laughed, if her throat hadn't been so dry.

He lies next to her on the bed and together they listen to the whip of the rope on glass, through snow. As the light dawns, she pulls off his hat.

* * *

Sometimes, late at night, François writes to Severine, notepaper balanced on bent knees, head propped up on pillows. He describes the white, the snow, the sky so open he can see it curve around the Brunt ice shelf and meet the horizon in a swirl of frozen blue. He describes the Halley VI research station, each module standing self-sufficient on legs that keep it elevated above the floating ice, a strange caterpillar of research labs and sleeping quarters with a central red hub where they all meet to talk and wait for snowstorms to pass. As the days edge closer to winter the pages of his letter take on a chill. He asks her how she is, if the sun is warm in Bayeux.

He pulls the cover over his legs, rubs the scar on his thumb and looks down at red fading to silver; the two colours of this world.

I hope it's peaceful there, mama, he writes.

It is peaceful here, but I think a storm might be brewing.

What am I supposed to see? he asks, taking the binoculars from his eyes.

Róisín smiles.

Well, at this magnification, all you can make out is the comet's nucleus, which is the bright bit at the front…

He puts the binoculars back to his eyes, thinks about telling her he is not so young as she imagines.

…and the tail, which is the stream of dust and ice that gets blown out behind as it accelerates towards the sun.

So, it's ice?

Ice and rock and maybe some bits of molecules, you know, the interplanetary junk that gets picked up along the way.

It's not junk, he says, it's extraordinary.

You remind me of someone from a long time ago.

He turns to look at her; she hasn't mentioned her past before, and he doesn't know if he should ask her questions about it now.

I used to watch the comets when I was a child, he says, with my mother.

She was a scientist?

No, he laughs, no. She just loved them. Do you think it's strange to love something you don't understand?

Róisín shakes her head. Just human, she says.

Why is next Monday circled on the calendar?

The comet will be at its brightest.

Is that all?

He puts the binoculars down. His tone changes.

Róisín?

François leaves his room and goes in search of something to dull his restlessness. They are playing cards in the central hub; he lingers by the door then retreats back the way he came. He doesn't know why he's behaving like this. He has been knocked off balance; and worse, he didn't notice it happening.

When he looks back at his letter to Severine, the smudges of the words make it look as if he's been crying on the page. It doesn't matter. Of course it will not be sent, not any time soon—there is no airlifted postal service here. The next delivery is six months away. But even so, he describes the comet he has been watching, with Róisín, in the sky. I have seen its nucleus, he writes; I could make out its tail. It is a different colour to the stars, isn't that miraculous? I feel so close to home today, and so far away.

He folds his letter, written over weeks, and seals the envelope. Presses a first class stamp to his tongue. The taste lingers long after the letter has been safely stowed at the bottom of his case. He heads outside; he needs to sleep under the stars tonight.

* * *

Róisín opens the zip to François' tent slowly, not wanting to wake him if he is asleep. She's not sure what he's doing out here, but she saw the red tent in the starlight and knew that she had to join him.

Are you sleeping? she whispers.

Yes, he replies.

That's good, she smiles, though it's so dark she knows he won't be able to see that. I'll just talk, and you can sleep, she says, and we'll both feel better for it.

She talks about Liam, because she feels now that she has to speak about it, if she has any chance of letting it go.

And she suspects that François might have lost somebody too.

There is a gust of wind that makes the taught fabric of the tent resonate like a string; ripple with harmonics.

He closes his fingers around hers, but there is only a second of this closeness before she pulls away again.

I think I need to say goodbye, she says. I'm sorry.

He follows her outside as she leaves, but not back to the base—he has his own past to remember, or to forget. Instead he turns away and starts packing up the tent by the light of the morning stars, under the glow of the comet.

The next night François dreams there is a strange woman sitting on his bed, with a voice he knows but has never heard before.

So you found me, then, he says. I knew you were coming.

It's cold, she replies. You're on the wrong continent.

Could you take it easy on me, please? he says. I know why you're here.

He opens his eyes to an empty, watery room. He blinks; the water in his eyes clears for a second, and then returns.

He is surprised by the conviction of it—it is not logical, but undeniable nonetheless. He's been waiting for news even though the news couldn't reach him. He doesn't know what else he can do so he drinks, and cries, and lets his heart break because he knows—somehow he knows—that tonight, a world away, his mother has died.

Róisín hikes through the night, now and then stopping to take out her notebook from the side pocket of her jacket, mark with pencil where the comet is relative to the stars. She keeps walking until the base is no longer visible—she doesn't want any signs of humanity on the horizon. There is only one person she wants to see tonight. The wind is starting to get strong, biting at her skin even through her layers of protection—it is incredible, the way wind can do that. Soon it will be too dangerous to continue; she can see the swirls of ice ahead, where the wind is so strong it can lift the top layer of the ground.

Róisín chooses her spot carefully: a cave of sorts, an overhang of rock and ice that will provide some shelter from the wind. She looks up at the comet—still visible, still daring her on—then looks more precisely through her binoculars and marks it again on her map before starting to unpack the shelter.

Her highest marks in the Antarctic Survey were in the survival test. She has seen worse than this.

The shelter is red, bright red, the colour of something that can't be missed, should anyone look for it. Inside, by the light of the torch, everything is rosy and golden; tent torchlight is beautiful. The storm is getting louder though. She steps outside and is almost knocked off her feet, but she struggles to stand upright, facing the wind, and watches the comet on this, its brightest night. No storm will stop her.

Some say that comets seed life on lifeless planets. She finds that hard to believe. The comet is ice, it is burning with wind; wild, inhospitable, stunning. It is not unlike where she is standing. This is, perhaps, the closest a human being can get to travelling on a comet as it approaches perihelion. Clinging on for life.

The first time she wakes, she thinks something is trying to get inside; a big shape—a bear?—is pressing against her tent. It takes her a moment to realise it is the snow piling up outside, and that there are no bears here. Perhaps there is nothing here.

The next time she is back on soft, dandelioned grass; she is wearing pajamas and lying in the open air. Liam is beside her. No, this can't be right. There is no grass on the comet. Wait.

She finds the torch, turns on the light. It helps. She wonders if the sun will rise soon. Perhaps François will come in the morning and un-bury her from all this snow. Perhaps the snow itself will melt as they hurtle through space, towards the heat of the sun. Perhaps Liam will come home from wherever he wanted to go; he will have seen enough light, and she enough snow, and together they will lie on the farm grass and look up to the comets overhead and pretend like they don't need to breathe; and in secret, they will breathe.

Comet West, 1976

Róisín keeps looking out of the window as they eat their boiled eggs. Liam knows why; sundown is coming and she wants to be out before dark. Every night this week it has been the same; the comet was predicted, but still it hasn't arrived. There's only two days and a weekend left of the Easter holidays, and then she'll have to go home.

If he knew how, Liam would stop the time from moving forwards and stay in this week—this exact one—for all his life. He looks at the clock on the kitchen wall and Róisín looks at the dusk beyond the window, out to the red tent that is pitched up in the field.

The red tent was a present from his mum the year before she died. Liam knows it was from her because his dad would never have chosen something red, although it had both of their names on the label. His mum wore red; yellow and gold and red and purple, all the colours of the rainbow. She never seemed quite in the right place on their farm, so far from everywhere. Maybe that's why she left it so early. Inside the red tent, the light is different to anywhere else in the world; it is like being inside a balloon that is flying up into the sun.

Can I bring Bobby with me tonight?

Róisín rolls her eyes.

Liam's not really this young—he'll be seven later this year—and most nights he forgets about Bobby altogether, but if he's going to try to stay in this week forever, without time moving forwards, he'd quite like to keep Bobby with him.

Pandas don't live in tents.

Bobby does. He likes the red. Anyway, pandas don't live in Ireland either.

Róisín made Bobby stay in the house last night because of the risk of rain, although it didn't rain in the end and there was no comet either, so it was a bit of a wasted night. Liam thinks that maybe Bobby will be a good omen for them tonight.

If you like you can bring an omen too, he says.

I don't need one, Róisín zips up his coat by the back door and puts Bobby in his big coat pocket; I've got you.

While Liam arranges everything in the tent in the field, Róisín starts work on her maps. She's been drawing them every night. Maps of the nighttime sky, so that she can see how each thing moves, how near and far from each other they get. It was one of the first things she learnt to draw when she was little, and she still think it's the best. Why draw a square house with a triangular roof when you can draw the patterns in the stars? Liam thinks her maps look a bit like join-the-dots—that if he just knew how to read them properly something extraordinary would appear. Maybe the comet will help, like the code key he has in his colouring books. Yesterday he did a tractor.

Liam!

He puts Bobby in his sleeping bag and unzips the tent. The dark comes quickly; he's noticed that this past week.

I think it's come.

The comet?

Of course!

That's grand.

Róisín doesn't look at him the whole time; her eyes are fixed on the sky.

The comet is more like a blur really. Like someone has dropped a silver pen on a page of black paper and then smudged it with their thumb.

Is that it? Liam says. Why's it so small?

Because it's far away. But what you mean is why is it so faint. And that's because it's far away too, but it's moving towards us so it's going to get brighter.

When?

Maybe later tonight.

Are you sure?

Maybe tomorrow.

So what are we going to do tonight?

He's getting cold already, out here in the dark, what with it not even being Spring yet, not for a few weeks anyway.

Tonight we're going to watch it move, Róisín says, as she pulls her sleeping bag from inside the tent. If we lie here, we'll be able to see the sky all night long.

Liam crawls inside the tent. He's cold. He thinks that Róisín will follow him in, but he knows that's a stupid thing to think—she's never followed him anywhere. It's always the other way round.

He takes Bobby out of the sleeping bag, brushes away at the bits of grass on the floor of the tent and sits him up in the corner instead.

But it's not fun being in the tent on his own, even with Bobby, so he forces himself to count to one hundred and then he unzips the door again and looks out. Róisín is lying on her back in the sleeping bag.

He drags his sleeping bag out of the tent, lays it along the grass next to Róisín and wriggles inside.

I'm back, he says, although she doesn't reply and even if she did all she'd say is that he is stating the obvious. He always seems to be doing that.

Hold your breath and count, she says. If you count long enough, and hold your breath long enough, you'll be able to see it move. Because it's flying.

No it's not.

So it is. It's flying so fast and so far away it can change the whole sky in the time you can hold your breath for. It's the fastest thing in the solar system. You just have to hold on, and then you'll see.

Liam lies as still as he's ever been and watches, and waits, and holds on. The grass bristles against his skin, the night breeze blows his hair into his eyes but he doesn't move to brush it away. His face gets hotter the longer he goes without breathing, his lips purse into a tight wiggly line, eyes wide and gleaming, his hand grasping onto his cousin's.

Can you see it? she asks.

You breathed!

Liam lets out his breath, gasps in more nighttime air—it's the kind of air that smells of ice and fresh hay and pajamas.

Róisín's hand is clutching his, and they look at each other and breathe in unison, a big open-mouthed breath to sustain them for another thirty seconds, or sixty, as they turn their eyes back to the sky.

Nothing moves.

They both know what they want to be when they grow up. Liam is going to be a farmer like his dad and Róisín is going to move far away and become an astrophysicist. She knows the names of all the constellations, and the different shapes of the moon, and the order of the planets, and she knows when the comets are going to be in the sky. That's why she persuaded Liam to camp out in the field with her tonight, the night when it will be at its brightest. She stares up at the sky and then, still lying on the grass, holds the notebook high over her face and starts drawing.

What are you doing? He wants to understand.

Astronomy, she says. I'm mapping the sky. I have to mark where the comet is now in relation to the stars. So that we can see how far it moves. Otherwise we might forget.

It's *not* moving.

But it will. Have patience.

Liam rolls his eyes. This astronomy takes too long.

Look, she shows him her map. See those stars? I've marked them here. And the comet is in-between those two right now. See?

He nods, reluctantly.

You can go inside if you really want.

I don't want.

She tears off a blank sheet of paper and gives it to him, along with one of the spare pencils from her pencil case. She takes it with her everywhere, so she can always map the sky.

What should I draw?

Whatever you want to draw.

She always talks to him like this, as if she's the grown up, even though she's only two years older than he is.

He frowns in concentration; he's not going to ask her any more questions tonight. His pencil hovers over the page.

Liam falls asleep while the comet is still between the two stars overhead, buried deep into his sleeping bag with the zip done up to way over his head.

On the dew-damp grass in the early hours of the morning his drawing blends into indecipherable marks. The farm, the field, his house, the cows and sheep, his dad, the lack of his mum, and Róisín staring up at the sky: dots and lines that have been smudged out of context by a careless thumb until their meaning is lost.

You've just read an excerpt from The Comet Seekers.

ABOUT THE AUTHOR

Helen Sedgwick is a writer, editor, and former research physicist. She won a Scottish Book Trust New Writers Award and her writing has been published internationally and broadcast on BBC Radio 4. She has performed at the Edinburgh International Book Festival, the Edinburgh Fringe, and Glasgow's Aye Write. Having grown up in London, she now lives in the Scottish highlands with her partner, photographer Michael Gallacher.

IMPRINT: Harper
PRINT ISBN: 9780062448767
PRINT PRICE: $25.99
EBOOK ISBN: 9780062448781
EBOOK PRICE: $20.99
PUBLICATION DATE: 10/11/16
PUBLICITY CONTACT: Tina Andreadis Tina.Andreadis@harpercollins.com
EDITOR: Terry Karten
AGENT: Claudia Ballard
AGENCY: William Morris Endeavor

ONLY DAUGHTER

HOME CAN BE THE
MOST DANGEROUS
PLACE OF ALL

ANNA SNOEKSTRA

A NOVEL

SUMMARY

In 2003, sixteen-year-old Rebecca Winter disappeared. She'd been enjoying her teenage summer break: working at a fast food restaurant, crushing on an older boy and shoplifting with her best friend. Mysteriously ominous things began to happen—blood in the bed, periods of blackouts, a feeling of being watched—though Bec remained oblivious of what was to come. Eleven years later, she is replaced. A young woman, desperate after being arrested, claims to be the decade-missing Bec.

Soon the imposter is living Bec's life. Sleeping in her bed. Hugging her mother and father. Learning her best friends' names. Playing with her twin brothers. But Bec's welcoming family and enthusiastic friends are not quite as they seem. As the imposter dodges the detective investigating her case, she begins to delve into the life of the real Bec Winter—and soon realizes that whoever took Bec is still at large, and that she is in imminent danger.

EXCERPT

I've always been good at playing a part: the mysterious seductress for the sleazebag, the doe-eyed innocent for the protector. I had tried both on the security guard and neither seemed to be working.

I'd been so close. The supermarket doors had already slid open for me when his wide hand clamped on my shoulder. The main road was only fifteen paces away. A quiet street lined with yellow and orange leaved trees.

His grip tightened.

He brought me into the back office. A small cement box with no windows, barely big enough to fit the old filing cabinet, desk and printer. He took the bread roll, cheese, and apple out of my bag and laid them on the table between us. Seeing them spread out like that gave me a jolt of shame, but I tried my best to hold his eye. He said I wasn't going anywhere until I gave him some identification. Luckily, I had no wallet. Who needs a wallet when you don't have any money?

I attempted all my routines on him, letting tears flow when my insinuations fell flat. It wasn't my best performance; I couldn't stop looking at the bread. My stomach was beginning to cramp. I'd never felt hunger like this before.

I can hear him now, talking to the police on the other side of the locked door. I stare up at the notice board above the desk. This week's staff roster is there, alongside a memo about credit card procedures with a smiley face drawn on the bottom and a few photographs from a work night out.

I have never wanted to work in a supermarket. I've never wanted to work anywhere, but all of a sudden, I'm painfully jealous.

'Sorry to bother you with this. Little skank won't give me any ID.'

I wonder if he knows I can hear him.

'It's alright—we'll take it from here.' Another voice.

The door opens and two cops look in at me. It's a female and a male, both probably about my age. She has her dark hair pulled back in a neat ponytail. The guy is pasty and thin. I can tell straight away that he's going to be an asshole. They sit down on the other side of the table.

'My name is Constable Thompson and this is Constable Seirs. We understand that you were caught shoplifting from this store,' the male cop says, not even bothering to hide the boredom in his tone.

'No, actually, I wasn't,' I say, imitating my stepmom's perfect breeding. 'I was on my way to the register when he grabbed me. That man has a problem with women.'

They look at me doubtfully, their eyes sliding over my unwashed clothes and greasy hair. I wonder if I smell. My bruised and swollen face isn't doing me any favors. It was probably why I got caught in the first place.

'He was calling me foul names when he brought me back here,' I lower my voice, 'like *skank* and *whore*; disgusting. My father is a lawyer and I expect he'll want to sue for misconduct when I tell him what went on here today.'

They look at each other and I can immediately tell they don't buy it. I should have cried.

'Listen honey, it's going to be fine. Just give us your name and address. You'll be back home by the end of the day,' the girl-cop says.

She is my age and she's calling me pet names like I'm just a kid.

'The other option is that we book you now and take you back to the station. You'll have to wait in a cell while we sort out who you are. It will be a lot easier if you just give us your name now.'

They're trying to scare me and it's working, but not for the reason they think. Once they have my fingerprints it won't take them long to identify me. They'll find out what I did.

'I was so hungry,' I say, and the tremor in my tone isn't fake.

It's the look in their eyes that does it. A mix of pity and disgust. Like I'm worth nothing, just another stray for them to clean up. A memory slowly opens and I realize I know exactly how to get myself out of this.

The power of what I'm about to say is huge. It courses through my body like a shot of vodka, removing the tightness in my throat and sending tingles to the tips of my fingers. I don't feel helpless anymore; I know I can pull this off. Staring at her, then him, I let myself savor the moment. Watching them carefully to enjoy the exact instant their faces change.

'My name is Rebecca Winter. Eleven years ago, I was abducted.'

Chapter One

2014

I sit in an interview room with my face down, holding my coat tightly around myself. It's cold in here. I've been waiting for almost an hour, but I'm not worried. I imagine what a stir I've caused on the other side of that mirror. They're probably calling in the missing persons unit, looking up photographs of Rebecca and painstakingly comparing them to me. That should be enough to convince them; the likeness is uncanny.

I saw it months ago. I was wrapped up with Peter, a little bundle of warmth. Usually I got teary when I was hungover and just spent the day hiding in my room listening to sad music. It was different with him. We woke up at noon and sat on the couch all day eating pizza and smoking cigarettes until we started feeling better. That was back when I thought my parents' money didn't matter and all I needed was love.

We were watching some stupid show called *Wanted*. They were talking about a string of grisly murders at a place called Holden Valley Aged

Care in Melbourne and I started looking for the remote. Butchered grannies was definitely a mood killer. Just as I went to change the channel, the next story began and a photograph came up on the screen. She had my nose, my eyes, my copper-coloured hair. Even my freckles.

'Rebecca Winter finished her late shift at McDonald's, in the inner south Canberra suburb of Manuka, on the 17th of January 2003,' a man said in a dramatic voice over the photograph, 'but somewhere between her bus stop and home she disappeared, never to be seen again.'

'Holy shit, is that you?' Peter said.

The girl's parents appeared, saying their daughter had been missing for over a decade but they still had hope. The mother looked like she was about to cry. Another photograph: Rebecca Winter wearing a bright green dress, her arm slung around another teenage girl with blonde hair. For a foolish moment, I tried to remember if I had ever owned a dress like that.

A family portrait: The parents looking thirty years younger, two grinning brothers and Rebecca in the middle. Idyllic. They may as well have had a white picket fence in the background.

'Fuck, do you think that's your long lost twin or what?'

'Yeah, you wish!'

We'd started joking about Peter's gross twin fantasies and he forgot about it pretty soon. Nothing stuck around long in Peter's mind.

I try to remember every detail I can from the show. She was from Canberra, a teenager, maybe fifteen or sixteen at the time she want missing. In some ways, I was lucky the side of my face was bruised and swollen. It masked the subtle differences that distinguished us. I'll be well and truly gone by the time the bruising fades. I only need to buy myself enough time to get me out of the station, to the airport maybe.

For a moment, my mind wanders to what I would do after that. Call Dad? I hadn't spoken to him since I left. I had picked up a pay phone a few times, even punched in his mobile number. But then the sickening sound of soft weight crashing against metal would fill my head and I'd hang up with shaking hands. He wouldn't want to talk to me.

The door opens and the female cop peeks in and smiles at me.

'This won't take too much longer; can I get you something to eat?'

'Yes, please.'

The slight embarrassment in her voice, the way she looks at me and then quickly averts her eyes.

I had them.

She brings me a box of piping hot noodles from the takeaway next door. They're oily and a bit slimy, but I've never enjoyed a meal so much. Eventually, a detective comes into the room. He puts a file on the table and pulls out a chair. He looks brutish, with a thick neck and small eyes. I can tell by the way he sits down that my best chance with him is ego. He seems to be trying to take up as much space as possible, his arm resting on the chair next to him, his legs wide open. He smiles across the table.

'I'm sorry this is taking so long.'

'That's okay,' I say, wide eyes, small voice. I turn my face slightly, to make sure he's looking at the bruised side.

'We're going to bring you to the hospital soon, okay?'

'I'm not hurt, I just want to go home.'

'It's procedure. We've been calling your parents, but so far there's been no answer.'

I imagine the phone ringing in Rebecca Winter's empty house. That was probably for the best, her parents would just complicate things. The detective takes my silence as disappointment.

'Don't worry, I'm sure we'll get a hold of them soon. They'll need to come here to make the identification. Then you can go home together.'

That's the last thing I need, to be called out as a fraud in front of a room full of cops. My confidence starts to slip. I need to turn this around.

I speak into my lap, 'I want to go home more than anything.'

'I know, it won't be too much longer.' His voice is like a pat on the head, 'did you enjoy those?' He looks at the empty noodle box.

'They were really nice. Everyone has been so amazing,' I say, keeping with the timid victim act.

He opens the manila folder. It's Rebecca Winter's file. Interview time. My eyes scan the first page.

'Can you tell me your name?'

'Rebecca.' I keep my eyes down.

'And where have you been all this time Rebecca?' he says, leaning in to hear me.

'I don't know,' I whisper, 'I was so scared.'

'Was there anyone else there? Anyone else held with you?'

'No. Only me.'

He leans in closer, until his face is only inches from mine.

'You saved me,' I say, looking him right in the eyes. 'Thank you.'

I can see his chest swell. Canberra is only three hours from here. I just need to push a little harder. Now that he's feeling like the big man he won't be able to say no. It's my only chance to get out of here.

'Please, will you let me go home?'

'We really need to interview you and take you to the hospital to be examined, it's important.'

'Can we do that in Canberra?'

I let the tears start falling then. Men hate seeing girls cry, it makes them uncomfortable.

'You'll be transported back to Canberra soon, but there is a procedure we need to follow first, okay?'

'But you're the boss here, aren't you? If you say I can go they have to do what you say. I just want to see my mom.'

'Okay,' he says, jumping out of his seat, 'don't cry; let me see what I can do.'

He comes back to say he's worked it all out for me. I will be driven to Canberra by the cops who picked me up, and then the missing persons detective who worked on Rebecca Winter's case will take it from there. I nod and smile at him, looking up at him like he's my new hero.

I'll never reach Canberra. An airport would be easier, but I'm sure I can still get away from them somehow. Now that they see me as a victim, it won't be too hard.

As we walk out of the interview room, everyone turns to look at me. One woman has a receiver pressed to her ear.

'She's here now, just let me ask,' she puts the receiver against her chest and looks up at the detective. 'It's Mrs. Winter; we finally got a hold of her. She wants to talk to Rebecca. Is that okay?'

'Of course', the detective says, smiling at me.

The woman holds out the receiver. I look around, everyone has their heads bent but I can tell they are listening. I take the phone and hold it to my ear.

'Hello?'

'Becky, is that you?'

I open my mouth, needing to say something but I don't know what, but she keeps going.

'Oh honey, thank God. I can't believe it. Are you okay? They keep saying you aren't hurt, but I can't believe it. I love you so much. Are you alright?'

'I'm okay.'

'Stay where you are, your father and I coming to get you.'

Damn.

'We're just about to leave,' I say, in almost a whisper. I don't want her noticing my voice is all wrong.

'No, please, don't go anywhere. Stay where you're safe.'

'It'll be quicker this way, it's all sorted out.'

I can hear her swallowing, heavy and thick.

'We can be there really soon.' Her voice sounds strangled.

'I've got to go,' I say, and then looking around at all those pricked up ears I add, 'bye, Mom.'

I hear her sobbing as I hand the phone back.

The last glow of sunlight has disappeared and the sky is a pale grey. We've been driving for about an hour and the conversation has dried up. I can tell the cops are itching to ask me where I've been all this time, but they restrain themselves.

This is lucky really, because they would most likely have a better idea than I do where Rebecca Winter has spent the past decade.

Paul Kelly croons softly on the radio. Raindrops patter on the roof of the car and slide down the windows. I could fall asleep.

'Do you need me to turn the heater up?' Thomson asks, eyeing my coat.

'I'm okay,' I say.

The truth is I couldn't take my coat off, no matter that I was starting to feel a bit hot. I have a birthmark just below the crook of my elbow. A coffee-colored stain about the size of a twenty cent piece. I'd hated it as a kid. My mother always told me it was the mark left by an angel's kiss. It was one of the few memories I have of her. As I grew up I sort of started to like it, maybe because it made me think of her, or maybe just because it was so much a part of me. But it wasn't a part of Bec. I doubted that either of these idiots had looked closely enough at the missing persons file to see the word 'nil' under *birthmarks*, but it wasn't worth the risk.

I try to force myself to plan my escape. Instead, all I can think about is Rebecca's mom. The way she had said 'I love you' to me. It wasn't like when my Dad used to say it, when someone was watching or when he was trying to get me to be good. The way she had said it was so raw, so guttural, like it was coming from her core. This woman that we are zooming towards really did love me. Or, she loved who she thought I was. I wonder what she is doing right now. Calling her friends to tell them, washing sheets for me, dashing to the supermarket for extra food, worrying that she wouldn't sleep because she was so excited? I imagine what will happen when they call her to tell her that they lost me on the way. These two cops would probably get into a lot of trouble. I wouldn't mind that, but what about her? What about the cleanly made up bed waiting for me? The food in the fridge. All that love. It will just go to waste.

'I need to go to the bathroom,' I say, seeing a sign for a rest stop.

'Okay, honey. Are you sure you don't want to wait for a servo?'

'No.' I'm sick of being polite to them.

The car veers onto the dirt road and stops outside the brick toilet block. Next to it is an old barbeque and two picnic tables and behind that is solid bush land. If I get a decent head start, they won't be able to find me in there.

The female cop unclicks her seatbelt.

'I'm not a kid. I can take a piss by myself, thank you.'

I get out of the car, slamming the door behind me, not giving her a chance to argue. Raindrops fall onto my face, ice against my sweaty skin. It feels nice to be out of that sweltering car. I glance back before I walk into the toilet block. The headlights beam through the rain and behind the windscreen wipers I can see the cops talking and shifting in their seats.

The toilets are disgusting. The concrete floor is flooded and scrunched up wads of tissue float around like miniature icebergs. The place stinks of beer and vomit. A bottle of Carlton Draught rests next to the toilet and the rain beats against the tin roof. I imagine what my night tonight will be like, hiding in the rain. I'll have to wander until I reach a town, but then what? I'll be hungry again soon and I still don't have any money. The last week has been most horrible of my life. I'd had to pick up men in bars just to have somewhere to sleep and, one night, the worst one, I had no other option but to hide in a public toilet in a park. Jumping out of my skin at every noise. Imagining the worst. That night that felt like it would never end, like the light would never come. The toilet block looked a bit like this one.

For a moment, my resilience slips and I imagine the other alternative: the warm bed, the full stomach and the kisses on the forehead. It's enough.

The bottle breaks against the toilet seat easily. I pick a large shard. Squatting down in the cubicle, I hold my arm between my knees. I realize I've started to whimper, but there's no time now to be weak. One more minute and that cop will be checking on me. Pushing down on the brown blotch, the pain is shocking. There's more blood than I expected, but I don't stop. My flesh peels up, like the skin of a potato.

The lining of my jacket slips against the open wound as I pull it back on. I throw the gory evidence in the sanitary bin and wash the blood off my hands. My vision is beginning to blur and the oily noodles swirl in my stomach. I grip the sink and breathe steadily. I can do this.

The slam of a car door is followed by footsteps.

'Are you alright?' The female cop asks.

'I get a bit car sick,' I say, checking the sink for blood.

'Oh honey, we're almost there. Just tell us to pull over if you want to be sick.'

The rain is heavier now and the sky is a rich black. But the icy cold air helps to fight the nausea. I clamber into the back of the car and pull the door shut with my good arm. We veer back out onto the highway. I rest my throbbing arm up next to the headrests, afraid of the blood beginning to drip down to my wrist, and lean my head back against the window. I don't feel the sickness anymore, just a floating feeling. The even patter of the rain, the soft tones of the radio and the heat of the car lull me in to a near-sleep.

I'm not sure how long we've been driving in silence when they start talking.

'I think she's asleep.' The man's voice.

I hear the squeak of leather as the woman turns to look at me. I don't move.

'Looks like it. Must be tiring work being such a little bitch.'

'Where do you think she's been this whole time?'

'My guess? Ran off with some man, married probably. He must have gotten sick of her and given her the boot. I reckon he was rich, too, by the way she's been looking down her nose at everyone.'

'She said she was abducted.'

'I know. She's not acting like it though, is she?'

'Not really.'

'And she looks in pretty good nick, considering. If she was kidnapped, he must have been pretty fond of her, that's all I'm saying. What do you think?'

'I don't give a shit honestly,' he says. 'But I reckon there might be a commendation in it for us.'

'I don't know. Shouldn't she be in a hospital or something? I don't know if ass-hat was really meant to just let her leave when she clicked her fingers.'

'What is the protocol then? I know what we're meant to do when these kids go missing, but what about when they come back?'

'Fucked if I know. Must have been hung-over that day.'

They laugh, and then the car is quiet again.

'You know I've been wondering all day who it is she reminds me of,' the female cop says suddenly. 'It just hit me. It was this girl back in high school who told everyone she had a brain tumor; took a week off school for the operation. A bunch of us started a drive to raise money for her; I think we all thought she was going to die. She came back right as rain on Monday, though, and for a few hours she was the most popular girl in school. Then someone noticed that none of her hair was shaved, not even an inch. The whole thing was a crock of shit from start to finish.

'That girl, she looked at you just like our little princess back there looked at us when we met her. The way she takes you in, surveys you with that cold glint in her eyes like her head is going a million miles a minute trying to figure out the best way to fuck with you.'

After a while I stop listening to them talk. I remember I have to speak to the detective when I get to Canberra, but I feel too dizzy to try and plan my answers. The car pulls off the main road.

I wake to the jolt of the brakes and the light going on as the female cop opens her door.

'Wake up, little lady,' she says.

I try to sit, but my muscles feel like they're made of jelly.

I hear a new voice.

'You must be Constables Siers and Thompson. I'm Senior Inspector Andopolis. Thanks for pulling the overtime to bring her down.'

'No worries, Sir.'

'We better get started, I know her mother is over the moon, but I have a lot of questions for her first.'

I hear him pull the door next to me open.

'Rebecca, you can't imagine how pleased I am to see you,' he says. Then he kneels down beside me. 'Are you alright?'

I try to look at him but his face is swirling.

'Yes, I'm okay,' I mutter.

'Why is she so pale?' he calls sharply, 'what's happened to her?'

'She's fine, she just gets car sick,' the female cop says.

'Call an ambulance!' Andopolis snaps at her as he reaches over and undoes my seatbelt.

'Rebecca? Can you hear me? What's happened?'

'I hurt my arm when I was escaping,' I hear myself say. 'It's okay, just hurts a bit.'

He pulls my jacket to the side. There's dried blood all the way up to my collarbone. Seeing that makes my vision fade even more.

'You morons! You absolute fucking idiots!' His voice sounds far away now. I can't see the reaction from the cops; I can't see their faces paling. But I can imagine.

I smile as the last of my consciousness fades.

You've just read an excerpt from Only Daughter.

ABOUT THE AUTHOR

Anna Snoekstra was born in Canberra, Australia to two civil servants. At the age of eighteen she decided to avoid a full time job and a steady wage to move to Melbourne and become a writer. She studied creative writing and cinema at The University of Melbourne, followed by screenwriting at RMIT University. After finishing university, Anna wrote for independent films and fringe theatre, and directed music videos. During this time, she worked as a cheesemonger, a waitress, a barista, a nanny, a receptionist, a cinema attendant and a film reviewer. Anna now lives with her husband, cat and two housemates and works full time writing novels.

IMPRINT: Mira Books
PRINT ISBN: 9780778319443
PRINT PRICE: $15.99
EBOOK ISBN: 9781460395967
EBOOK PRICE: $7.99
PUBLICATION DATE: 9/27/16
PUBLICITY CONTACT: Emer Flounders emer.flounders@harpercollins.com
RIGHTS CONTACT: Reka Rubin reka.rubin@harlequin.com
EDITOR: Kerri Buckley
AGENT: MacKenzie Fraser-Bub
AGENCY: Fraser-Bub Literary

TERRITORIES SOLD:
Thailand, Korea, Turkey, China, Japan, Australia, Poland, Denmark, Finland, Germany, Holland, Norway, Sweden, United Kingdom, Spain

PROMOTIONAL INFORMATION:
Targeted trade and consumer advertising campaign; National galley distribution; Extensive library marketing; Book club and blogger outreach; Online promotion, including social media and book blogs; Support through Harlequin social media proper ties and newsletters; In-book advertising in selected MIRA® imprint titles; Featured title at www.MIRABooks.com.

PART THREE: NONFICTION

When in French

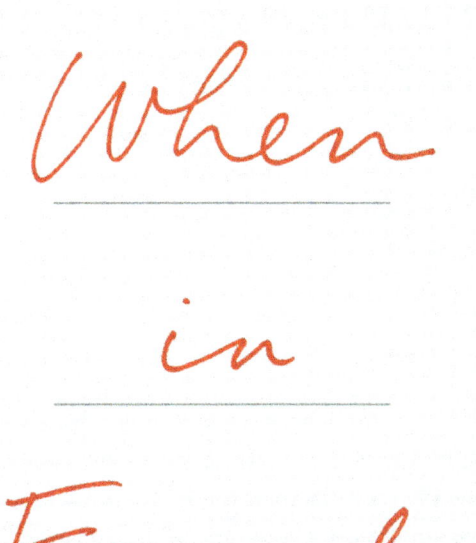

TITRE

LOVE *in a* SECOND LANGUAGE

Lauren Collins

AUTEUR

SUMMARY

When *New Yorker* staff writer Lauren Collins moves to Geneva, Switzerland, she decides to learn French—not just to be able to go about her day-to-day life, but in order to be closer to her French husband and his family. *When in French* is at once a hilarious and idiosyncratic memoir about the things we do for love, and an exploration across cultures and history into how we learn languages, and what they say about who we are.

EXCERPT

Chapter One

The Past Perfect

Le Plus-Que-Parfait

I hadn't wanted to live in Geneva. In fact, I had decisively wished not to, but there I was. Plastic ficuses flanked the entryway of the building. The corrugated brown carpet matched the matte brown fretwork of the elevator cage. The ground floor hosted the offices of a psychiatrist and those of an *iridologue*—a practitioner of a branch of alternative medicine that popularized when, in 1861, a Hungarian physician noticed similar streaks of color in the eyeballs of a broken-legged man and a broken-legged owl. Our apartment was one story up.

The bell rang. Newlywed and nearly speechless, I cracked open the door, a slab of oak with a beveled brass knob. Next to it, the landlord had installed a nameplate, giving the place the look less of a home than of a bilingual tax firm.

A man stood on the landing. He was dressed in black—T-shirt, pants, tool belt. A length of cord coiled around his left shoulder. In his right hand, he held a brush. Creosote darkened his face and arms, extending his sleeves to his fingernails and the underside of his palms. A red bandanna was tied around his neck. He actually wore a top hat. I hesitated before pushing the door open further, unsure whether I was up against a chimney sweep or some sort of Swiss strip-o-gram.

"*Bonjour*," I said, exhausting approximately half of my French vocabulary.

The man, remaining clothed, returned my greeting and began to explain why he was there. His words, though I couldn't understand them, jogged secondhand snatches of dialogue: per cantonal law, as the landlord had explained to my husband, who had transmitted the command to me, we had to have our fireplace cleaned once a year.

I led the chimney sweep to the living room. It was dominated by the fireplace, an antique thing in dark striated marble, with pot hooks and a pair of side ducts whose covers hinged open like lockets. Shifting his weight onto one leg with surprising grace, the chimney sweep leaned forward and stuck his head under the mantel. He poked around for a few minutes, letting out the occasional wheeze. Coming out of the arabesque, he turned to me and began, again, to speak.

On a musical level, whatever he was saying sounded cheerful, a scale-skittering ditty of *les* and *las*. Perhaps he was admiring the condition of the damper, or welcoming me to the neighborhood. He reached into his pocket, proffering a matchbook and a disc of cork. Then he disappeared back out the door.

Minutes went by as I examined his gifts. They seemed like props for a magic trick. More minutes passed. I launched into a version of rock, scissors, paper: since the cork couldn't conceivably do anything to the matches, then the matches must be meant to light the cork. Action was clearly required, but I feared potentially incinerating the chimney sweep, who, I guessed, was making some sort of inspection up on the roof.

Eventually he returned, chirping out some more instructions. I performed a repertoire of reassuring eyebrow raises and comprehending head nods. He scampered back up to the roof. I still had no idea, so I lit a match, held it to the cork, and tossed it behind the grate. The pile started smoking and hissing. After a few seconds, I lost my nerve and snuffed it out.

The chimney sweep resurfaced, less jolly. He had appointed an assistant who, it appeared, was actively thwarting his routine. This time he spoke in the supple, obvious tones one reserves for madwomen, especially those in possession of flammable objects. Reclaiming the half-charred piece of cork, he lit a fire and, potbelly jiggling, sprinted back up to the roof.

Finally, he returned and reported—I assume, since we used the fireplace without incident all that winter—that everything was in order.

"*Au revoir!*" I said, trying to regain his confidence, and my standing as chatelaine of this strange, drab domain. "Hello" and "good-bye" were a pair of bookends, propping up a vast library of blank volumes, void almanacs, novels full of sentiment I couldn't apprehend. It felt as though the instruction manual to living in Switzerland had been written in invisible ink.

I had moved to Geneva a month earlier to be with my husband, Olivier, who had moved there because his job required him to. My restaurant French was just passable. Drugstore French was a stretch. IKEA French was pretty much out of the question, meaning that, since Olivier, a native speaker, worked twice as many hours a week as Swiss stores were open, we went for months without things like lamps.

Olivier had already been living in Geneva for a year and a half. Meanwhile, I had remained in London, where we'd met. The commute was tolerable, then tiring. In the spring of 2013, as our wedding approached, it was becoming a drag. Finally, that June, a visa fiasco abruptly forced me to leave England. Memoirs of immigration, like memories of immigration, often begin with a sense of approach—the ship sailing into the harbor, the blurred countryside through the windows of a train. My arrival in Geneva, on British Airways, was a perfect anticlimax, the modern ache of displacement anesthetized amid blank corridors of orange liqueur and fountain pens.

When Lord Byron arrived in Switzerland for an extended holiday in May 1816—fleeing creditors, gossips, and his wife, from whom he had recently separated, after likely fathering a child with his half sister—his entourage included a valet, a footman, a personal physician, a monkey, and a peacock. That summer he wrote *The Prisoner of Chillon*, the tale of a sixteenth-century Genevan monk, most of whose family has been killed in battle or burned at the stake. "There were no stars, no earth, no time / No check, no change, no good, no crime," the poem reads. As a description of the local atmosphere, that seemed to me about right. Geneva was unlovely, but not hideous, as though no one had cared enough to do ugly with conviction. The city seemed suffused by complacency, as gray and costive as the clouds that hovered over Lac Léman.

The main attraction was a clock made of begonias. Transportation was by tram. At the Office Cantonal de la Population, I was given a "Practical

Guide to Living in Geneva," ostensibly a welcome booklet. "It is forbidden and not well looked upon to make too much noise in your apartment between 21:00 and 07:00," it read. "Also avoid talking too loudly, and shouting to call someone in public places." The booklet directed me to a web page, which listed further gradations of *bruit admissible* (acceptable noise) and *bruit excessif* (excessive noise). Vacuuming during the day was okay, but God help the voluptuary who ran the washing machine after work.

Geneva had long been a place of asylum, but its tradition of liberty in the religious and political realms had never given rise to a libertine scene. Even though nearly half of the population was foreign-born, the city remained resolutely uncosmopolitan, a tepid fondue of tea rooms, confectionaries, and storefronts selling things like hosiery and lutes. Every block had its *coiffeur*, just as every *coiffeur* had its lone patroness, getting her hair washed in the sink. It wasn't as though Genevans enjoyed the advantages of living in the countryside. Many of them, native and nouveau, had means. So why hadn't some son or daughter of the city, after traveling to New York or Paris or Beirut—to Dallas or Manchester—been inspired to open a place where the bread didn't come in a doily-lined wicker basket? Was there a dinkier phrase, in any language, than *métropole lémanique*?

After a month or so of heavy tramming, we decided to buy a car. We purchased insurance, which included coverage for theft, fire, natural disasters, and *dommages causé par les fouines*—damages caused by a type of local weasel. I traded in my American driver's license for a Swiss one. The process took seventeen minutes flat. One sodden afternoon not long after, we trammed over to the Citroën lot.

Alexandre, a customer service representative, greeted us. He smelled of cigarettes and was wearing a tie.

"So, *voici*," he said. (Switzerland had four official languages—German, French, Italian, and Romansh—and people tended to switch back and forth without warning, with varying degrees of success.) He led us to the car, a used gray hatchback parked outside the office on a covered ramp.

It was pouring, each drop of rain a suicide jumper, hurling itself onto the ramp's tin roof. We circled around the car, hoping to project a savvy vibe, as though any painted-over weasel damage would never get by us.

Olivier stopped on the car's left side and, because it seemed like the thing to do, opened the backseat door.

"You will soon have *les petits enfants*?" Alexandre said.

"Um, we just got married."

"*Ah, bon*? It was a Protestant or a Catholic ceremony?"

Our city hall wedding was an unimaginability for Alexandre. I was beginning to understand, only very slowly, that the city's conservatism was neither an accident of demographics nor an oversight but an enactment of its founding values by conscious design. In 1387, more than a hundred years before the Catholic Church began to loosen its prohibitions on usury, the bishop of Geneva signed a charter of liberties, granting the *genevois*, alone in Christendom, the privilege of lending money at interest. The elite became financiers. The aspirant became Swiss mercenaries. Famed for their ferocity with the halberd and the pike, they poured cash into the economy in an era when most of the world's population was getting paid in eggs.

The mentality had persisted: do your hell-raising—your eating in restaurants without doilies—abroad, and retreat to a place of imperturbable security. Voltaire wrote of Geneva, "There, one calculates, and never laughs." Stendhal, passing through seventy years later, concluded that the *genevois*, despite their wealth and worldly networks, were at heart a parochial people: "Their sweetest pleasure, when they are young, is to dream that one day they will be rich. Even when they indulge in some imprudence and give themselves to pleasure, the ones they choose are rustic and cheap: a walk, to the summit of some mountain where they drink milk." Monotony, then, was an economy. So that we could collectively accrue more capital, a curfew had been set.

Weekends were the worst. All of the shops closed at seven—except on Thursdays, when some of them closed at seven thirty—rendering Saturdays a dull frenzy of provisioning. Sundays were desolate, a relic of the Calvinist lockdown mentality that had sent the young Rousseau scrambling to Savoy. A relocation consultant furnished by Olivier's company said that there had been talk of easing the Sunday moratorium, but to no avail. "Approximately ninety-nine percent of Swiss people support it," he told us, sounding approximately one hundred percent like a Swiss person.

Geneva had its graces—the trams operated on an honor system; even the graffiti artists were mannerly, defacing the sides of statues that didn't face the street—but I took them as further proof that the city was second-rate. You could, of course, escape to any number of attractive places within driving range, and we passed many afternoons wandering the relatively bustling streets of Lyon. It seemed sad, though, that the main selling point of the place where we lived was its proximity to places where we'd rather live. And while the mountains that surrounded us were magnificent, the twenty-five or so times a year that we managed to take advantage of them didn't make up for the three hundred and forty times we didn't. On Sunday nights, after an outing, we'd return to our stockpiled supper and take out the recycling, casting bottles and cans into the maw of a public bin. This was our version of indulging in an impudence: you could get fined for recycling—*for* recycling, I had not missed a negative adverb—on the day of rest.

Behind its orderly facade—the apartment buildings with their sauerkraut paint jobs; the matrons in furs; the brutalist plazas; the allées of pollarded trees—Geneva was, if anything, faintly sinister. Its vaunted sense of discretion seemed a cover for dodginess, bourgeois respectability masking a sleazy milieu. What was going on in those clinics and *cabinets*? Whose money, obtained by what means, was stashed in the private banks? What was a "family office," anyhow?

One day I received an e-mail from the Intercontinental Hotel Genève, entitled "What You Didn't Know about Geneva." I did not know that the Intercontinental Hotel Genève "continues to cater to the likes of the Saudi Royal family and the ruling family of the United Arab Emirates," that the most expensive bottle of wine sold at auction was sold in Geneva (1947 Château Cheval Blanc, $304,375), that the most expensive diamond in the world was sold in Geneva (the Pink Star, a 59.6-carat oval-cut pink diamond, $83 million), or that Geneva "has witnessed numerous world records, such as the world's longest candy cane, measuring 51 feet long." I developed a theory I thought of as the Édouard Stern principle, after the French investment banker who was found dead in a penthouse apartment in Geneva—shot four times, wearing a flesh-colored latex catsuit, trussed. Read any truly tawdry news story, and Geneva will somehow play into it by the fifth paragraph. Balzac wrote that behind every great fortune lies a crime. In Switzerland, behind every crime seemed to lie a great fortune.

Around us Europe was reeling, but the stability of the Swiss franc, combined with the influx of people who sought to exploit it, made the city profoundly expensive. The stores were full of things we neither wanted nor could afford. I reacted by refusing to buy or do anything that I thought cost too much money, which was pretty much everything, and then complaining about my boredom. Geneva syndrome: becoming as tedious as your captor. The expanses of my calendar stretched as pristine as those of the Alps.

Olivier didn't love Geneva either, but he didn't experience it as an effacement. He said that it reminded him of a provincial French town in the 1980s—a setting and an epoch with which he was well acquainted, having grown up an hour outside Bordeaux during the Mitterrand years. His consolations were familiarities: reciting the call-and-response of francophone pleasantries with the women at the dry cleaners; reading *Le Canard enchaîné*, the French satirical newspaper, when it came out each Wednesday; watching the TV shows—many of them seemed to involve puppets—that he knew from home. He was living in a sitcom, with a laugh track and wacky neighbors. I was stranded in a silent film.

We had established our life together, in London, on more or less neutral ground: his continent, my language. It worked. Olivier was my guide to living outside of the behemoth of American culture; I was his guide to living inside the behemoth of English.

He had learned the language over the course of many years. When he was sixteen, his parents sent him to Saugerties, New York, for six weeks: a homestay with some acquaintances of the only American they knew, an English teacher in Bordeaux. Olivier landed at JFK, where a taxi picked him up. This was around the time of the Atlanta Olympic Games.

"What is the English for 'female athlete?'" he asked, wanting to be prepared to discuss current events.

" 'Bitch,'" the driver said.

They drove on toward Ulster County, Olivier straining for a glimpse of the famed Manhattan skyline. The patriarch of the host family was an arborist named Vern. Olivier remembers driving around Saugerties with Charlene, Vern's wife, and a friend of hers, who begged him over and over again to say "hamburger." He was mystified by the fact that Charlene called Vern "the Incredible Hunk."

Five years later Olivier found himself in England, a graduate student in mathematics. Unfortunately, his scholastic English—"Kevin is a blue-eyed boy" had been billed as a canonical phrase—had done little to prepare him for the realities of the language on the ground. "You've really improved," his roommate told him, six weeks into the term. "When you got here, you couldn't speak a word." At that point, Olivier had been studying English for half his life.

After England, he moved to California to study for a PhD, still barely able to cobble together a sentence. His debut as a teaching assistant for a freshman course in calculus was greeted by a mass defection. On the plus side, one day he looked out upon the residue of the crowd and noticed an attentive female student. She was wearing a T-shirt that read "Bonjour, Paris!"

By the time we met, Olivier had become not only a proficient English speaker but a sensitive, agile one. Upon moving to London in 2007, he'd had to take an English test to obtain his license as an amateur pilot. The examiner rated him "Expert": "Able to speak at length with a natural, effortless flow. Varies speech flow for stylistic effect, e.g. to emphasize a point. Uses appropriate discourse markers and connectors spontaneously." He was funny, quick, and colloquial. He wrote things like (before our third date), "Trying to think of an alternative to the bar-restaurant diptych, but maybe that's too ambitious." He said things like (riffing on a line from *Zoolander* as he pulled the car up, once again, to the right-hand curb), "I'm not an ambi-parker." I rarely gave any thought to the fact that English wasn't his native tongue.

One day, at the movies, Olivier approached the concession stand, taking out his wallet.

"A medium popcorn, a Sprite, and a Pepsi, please."

"Wait a second," I said. "Did you just specifically order a *Pepsi*?"

In a word, Olivier had been outed. Due to a traumatic experience at a drive-through in California, he confessed, he still didn't permit himself to pronounce the word "Coke" aloud. For me, it was a shocking discovery, akin to finding out that a peacock couldn't really fly. I felt extreme tenderness toward his vulnerability, mingled with wonderment at his ingenuity. I'd had no idea that he still, very occasionally, approached English in a defensive posture, feinting and dodging as he strutted along.

I only knew Olivier in his third language—he also spoke Spanish, the native language of his maternal grandparents, who had fled over the Pyrénées during the Spanish Civil War—but his powers of expression were one of the things that had made me fall in love with him. For all his rationality, he had a romantic streak, an attunement to the currents of feeling that run beneath the surface of words. Once he wrote me a letter—an inducement to what we might someday have together—in which every sentence began with "Maybe." Maybe he'd make me an omelet, he said, every day of my life.

We moved in together quickly. One night, we were watching a movie. I spilled a glass of water, and went to mop it up with some paper towels.

"They don't have very good capillarity," Olivier said.

"Huh?" I replied, continuing to dab at the puddle.

"Their capillarity isn't very good."

"What are you talking about? That's not even a word."

Olivier said nothing. A few days later, I noticed a piece of paper lying in the printer tray. It was a page from the Merriam-Webster online dictionary:

capillarity *noun* ka-pə-ˈler-ə-tē, -ˈla-rə-

1: the property or state of being capillary

2 : the action by which the surface of a liquid where it is in contact with a solid (as in a capillary tube) is elevated or depressed depending on the

relative attraction of the molecules of the liquid for each other and for those of the solid

Ink to a nib, my heart surged.

There was eloquence, too, in the way he expressed himself physically—a perfect grammar of balanced steps and filled glasses and fingertips on the back of my elbow, predicated on some quiet confidence that we were always already a compound subject. The first time we said good-bye, he put his hands around my waist and lifted me just half an inch off the ground: a kiss in commas. I was short; he was not much taller. We could look each other in the eye.

But despite the absence of any technical barrier to comprehension, we often had, in some weirdly basic sense, a hard time understanding each other. The critic George Steiner defined intimacy as "confident, quasi-immediate translation," a state of increasingly one-to-one correspondence in which "the external vulgate and the private mass of language grow more and more concordant." Translation, he explained, occurs both across and *inside* languages. You are performing a feat of interpretation anytime you attempt to communicate with someone who is not like you.

In addition to being French and American, Olivier and I were translating, to varying degrees, across a host of Steiner's categories: scientist/artist, atheist/believer, man/woman. It seemed sometimes as if generation was one of the few gaps across which we weren't attempting to stretch ourselves. I had been conditioned to believe in the importance of directness and sincerity, but Olivier valued a more disciplined self-presentation. If, to me, the definition of intimacy was letting it all hang out, to him that constituted a form of thoughtlessness. In the same way that Olivier liked it when I wore lipstick, or perfume—American men, in my experience, often claimed to prefer a more "natural" look—he trusted in a sort of emotional *maquillage*, in which people took a few minutes to compose their thoughts, rather than walking around, undone, in the affective equivalent of pajamas. For him, the success of *le couple*—a relationship, in French, was something you were, not something you were in—depended on restraint rather than uninhibitedness. Where I saw artifice, he saw artfulness.

Every couple struggles, to one extent or another, to communicate, but our differences, concealing one another like nesting dolls, inhibited our trust in one another in ways that we scarcely understood. Olivier was careful of what he said to the point of parsimony; I spent my words like an oligarch with a terminal disease. My memory was all moods and tones, while he had a transcriptionist's recall for the details of our exchanges. Our household spats, painfully often, degenerated into linguistic warfare.

"I'll clean the kitchen after I finish my dinner," I'd say. "First, I'm going to read my book."

"My dinner," he'd reply, in a babyish voice. "My book."

To him, the tendency of English speakers to use the possessive pronoun where none was strictly necessary sounded immature, stroppy even: my dinner, my book, my toy.

"Whatever, it's *my* language," I'd reply.

And why, he'd want to know later, had I said I'd clean the kitchen, when I'd only tidied it up? I'd reply that no native speaker—by which I meant no *normal person*—would ever make that distinction, feeling as though I were living with Andy Kaufman's Foreign Man. His literalism missed the point, in a way that was as maddening as it was easily mocked.

For better or for worse, there was something off about us, in the way that we homed in on each other's sentences, focusing too intently, as though we were listening to the radio with the volume down a notch too low. "You don't seem like a married couple," someone said, minutes after meeting us at a party. We fascinated each other and frustrated each other. We could go exhilaratingly fast, or excruciatingly slow, but we often had trouble finding a reliable intermediate setting, a conversational cruise control. We didn't possess that easy shorthand, encoding all manner of attitudes and assumptions, by which some people seem able, nearly telepathically, to make themselves mutually known.

In Geneva, my lack of French introduced an asymmetry. I needed Olivier to execute a task as basic as buying a train ticket. He was my translator, my navigator, my amanuensis, my taxi dispatcher, my schoolmaster, my patron, my critic. Like someone very young or very old, I was forced to depend on him almost completely. A few weeks after the chimney sweep's visit, the cable guy came: I dialed Olivier's number and surrendered the phone, quiescent as a traveler handing over his passport. I had always been the kind of person who bounded up to the maître d' at a restaurant, ready to wrangle for a table. Now, I hung back. I overpaid and under-asked—a tax on inarticulacy. I kept telling waiters that I was dead—*je suis finie*—when I meant to say that I had finished my salad.

I was lucky, I knew, privileged to be living in safety and comfort. Materially, my papers were in order. We had received a *livret de famille* from the French government, attesting that I was a member of the family of a European citizen. (The book, a sort of secular family bible, charged us to "assure together the moral and material direction of the family," and had space for the addition of twelve children.) My Swiss residency permit explained that I was entitled to reside in the country, with Olivier as my sponsor, under the auspices of *"regroupement familial."*

Emotionally, though, I was a displaced person. In leaving America and, then, leaving English, I had become a double exile or immigrant or ex-patriate or whatever I was. (The distinctions could seem vain—what was an "expat" but an immigrant who drinks at lunch?) I could go back, but I couldn't: Olivier had lived in the United States for seven years and was unwilling to repeat the experience, feeling he would never thrive in a professional culture dominated by extra-large men discussing college sports. I accepted this. Some of my friends were taken aback that a return to the States wasn't up for discussion, but I felt I didn't have much choice. I wasn't going to dragoon Olivier into an existence that he had tried, and disliked, and explicitly wanted to avoid. Besides, I enjoyed living in Europe. For me, the first move, the physical one, had been easy. The transition into another language, however, was proving unexpectedly wrenching. Even though I had been living abroad—happily; ecstatically, even—for three years, I felt newly untethered in Geneva, a ghost ship set sail from the shores of my mother tongue.

My state of mindlessness manifested itself in bizarre ways. I couldn't name the president of the country I lived in; I didn't know how to dial whatever the Swiss version was of 911. When I noticed that the grass medians in our neighborhood had grown shaggy with neglect, I momentarily thought, "I should call the city council," and then abandoned the thought: it seemed like scolding someone else's kids. Because I never checked the weather, I was often shivering or soaked. Every so often I would walk out the door and notice that the shops were shuttered and no one was wearing a suit. Olivier called these as "pop-up holidays"—Swiss observances of which we'd failed to get wind. Happy Saint Berthold's Day!

In Michel Butor's 1956 novel *Passing Time*, a French clerk is transferred to the fictitious English city of Bleston-on-Slee, a hellscape of fog and furnaces. "I had to struggle increasingly against the impression that all my efforts were foredoomed to failure, that I was going round and round a blank wall, that the doors were sham doors and the people dummies, the whole thing a hoax," the narrator says. Geneva felt similarly surreal. The city was a diorama, a failure of scale. Time seemed to unfurl vertically, as though, rather than moving through it, I was sinking down into it, like quicksand. I kept having a twinge in the upper right corner of my chest. It felt as though someone had pulled the cover too tight over a bed.

The gods punished their enemies by taking away their voices. Hera condemned Echo, the nymph whose stories so enchanted Zeus, to "prattle in a fainter tone, with mimic sounds, and accents not her own," forever repeating a few basic syllables. First God threw Adam and Eve out of the garden. Then he destroyed the Tower of Babel, casting humankind out of a linguistic paradise—where every object had a name and every name had an object and God was the word—in a kind of second fall. Language, as much as land, is a place. To be cut off from it is to be, in a sense, homeless.

Without language, my world diminished. One day I read about a study that demonstrated the importance of early exposure to language: in families on welfare, parents spoke about 600 words an hour to their children, while working-class parents spoke 1,200, and professional parents 2,100. By the time a child on welfare was three, he had heard 30 million fewer words than many of his peers, leaving him at an enduring disadvantage. I wondered how many fewer words I heard, read, and spoke each day in Geneva, deducting the conversations I couldn't overhear; the newspaper headlines I neglected to absorb; the pleasantries that I failed to utter, from which serendipitous encounters didn't occur.

The back of our apartment overlooked a paved courtyard, where more senior residents of the building parked their cars. We didn't have air-conditioning. Neither did anyone else. In the evening, when the weather was hot, people retracted the yellow and orange canvas awnings that shrouded their balconies, rolled up the metal shades that kept their homes dark as breadboxes, and flung open their windows, disengaging the triple perimeter of privacy that regimented Swiss domestic life. Pots clattered. Onions sizzled. A dozen conversations washed into our kitchen, the flotsam and jetsam of a summer night. There were blue screens, old songs, mean cats. Somebody was serving a cake.

It was a disorientingly intimate score. This wasn't the suburbs. Nor was it New York, or even London, where alarm clocks were the only sounds you ever heard. Family life, someone's else's plot, was drifting unbidden into our home. It slayed me—a reminder of all I wasn't taking part in, couldn't grasp, didn't know. Olivier took my melancholy as an affront. I was angry about being in Geneva, he calculated; he was the reason we were in Geneva; therefore, I was angry at him. He would get defensive. I would get loud. He would tell me to quiet down, citing the neighbors, a constituency with which I had no truck. I felt as though I were living behind the aural equivalent of a one-way mirror. I didn't think that anyone could hear my voice.

By linguists' best count, there are somewhere between 6,000 and 7,000 languages—almost as many as there are species of bird. Mandarin Chinese is the largest, with 848 million native speakers. Next is Spanish, with 415 million, followed by English, with 335 million. Ninety percent of the world's languages are each spoken by fewer than a hundred thousand people. According to UNESCO's *Atlas of the World's Languages in Danger*, eighteen of them—Apiaká, Bikya, Bishuo, Chaná, Dampelas, Diahói, Kaixána, Lae, Laua, Patwin, Pémono, Taushiro, Tinigua, Tolowa, Volow, Wintu-Nomlaki, Yahgan, and Yarawi—have only a single speaker left.

The existence of language, and the diversity of its forms, is one of humankind's primal mysteries. Herodotus reported that the pharaoh Psammetichus seized two newborn peasant children and gave them to a shepherd, commanding that no one was to speak a word within their earshot. He did this "because he wanted to hear what speech would first come from the children, when they were past the age of indistinct babbling." Two years passed. The children ran toward the shepherd, shouting something that sounded to him like *bekos*, the Phrygian word for bread. From this, the Egyptians concluded that the Phrygians were a more venerable race.

In the thirteen century, the Holy Roman emperor Frederick II performed a series of ghoulish experiments. According to the Franciscan monk Salimbene of Parma, he immured a live man in a cask, to see if his soul would escape. He plied two prisoners with food and drink, sending one to bed and the other out to hunt, and then had them disemboweled, to test which had better digested the feast. His research culminated with newborns, "bidding foster-mothers and nurses to suckle and bathe and wash the children, but in no wise to prattle or speak with them; for he would have learnt whether they would speak the Hebrew language (which had been the first), or Greek, or Latin, or Arabic, or perchance the tongue of their parents of whom they had been born. But he labored in vain, for the children could not live without clapping's of the hands, and gestures, and gladness of countenance, and blandishments." What happens when humans are prevented from acquiring language in the normal manner is impossible to know because it is unconscionable to facilitate—"the forbidden experiment."

Plato, Lucretius, Cicero, Voltaire, Rousseau, and Emerson all tried to explain, in one way or another, how languages evolved, and why there are so many of them. The question proved intractable enough that in 1865 the founders of the influential Société de Linguistique de Paris banned the discussion entirely, declaring, "The Society will accept no communication dealing with either the origin of language or the creation of a universal language." For much of the twentieth century the prohibition held, and the subject of the origin of language remained unfashionable and even taboo. Interest in language has resurged in recent years, alongside advances in brain imaging and cognitive science, but researchers—working in disciplines as diverse as primatology and neuropsychology—have yet to establish a definitive explanation of the origins and evolution of human speech. The linguists Morten Christensen and Simon Kirby have suggested that the mystery of language is likely "the hardest problem in science."

However people got to be scattered all over the earth, spouting mutually unintelligible tremulants and schwas and clicks, their ways of life are bound up in their languages. In addition to the various strangers with whom I couldn't interact in any but the most perfunctory of ways, there was Olivier's family, who now qualified by several thousand miles as my closest kin.

Olivier's brother Fabrice was thirty-two, an intensive care doctor in Paris. Their half brother, Hugo, was fifteen, a high-schooler near Bordeaux. They both spoke some English, but having to do so was an academic exercise, an exam around the dinner table that I hated to proctor. Their father, Jacques, a kind and raspy-voiced occupational doctor in Bordeaux, wrote beautifully—he'd studied English, along with German, in high school, and later taken an intensive course—but we had trouble understanding each other in conversation. I was unable to determine whether I considered Olivier's mother, Violeta, the ideal mother-in-law even though or because we were unable to sustain more than a five-second conversation in any language. A trained nurse, she worked as an administrator at a nursing home. She was the head of the local health care workers' union, and had recently led a strike in scrubs and three-inch heels. She and her second husband, Teddy, spoke no English whatsoever.

The first year that we were together, Violeta sent a package from Nespresso as a gift for Olivier. Because it was a surprise, she wrote to me, asking that I hide it away until his birthday.

The postman came. I signed for the parcel. As soon as he left, I proceeded to the computer, where I assured Violeta, quite elegantly, that I had taken delivery of the gift.

"*J'ai fait l'accouchement de la cafetière*," I typed, having checked and double-checked each word in my English-French dictionary.

Months went by before I learned that, by my account, I'd given birth to— as in, physically delivered, through the vagina—a coffee machine.

Grocery stores, as much as cathedrals or castles, reveal the essence of a place. In New York I'd shopped sparingly at the supermarket on my block—a cramped warren hawking concussed apples and a hundred kinds of milk. One day I'd bought for a rotisserie chicken. I'd taken it home and started shredding it to make a chicken salad. Halfway through,

I realized that there was a ballpoint pen sticking straight out of the breast—a galline Steve Martin with an arrow through the head. The next day, receipt in hand, I went back to the store and asked for a refund.

"Where's the chicken?" the cashier barked.

"I threw it away," I said. "It had a ballpoint pen in it."

The closest grocery store to our apartment in London was almost parodically civilized. A cooperatively owned chain, it sold bulbs and sponsored a choir. Nothing amused me more than shaving a few pence off the purchase of a pack of toilet paper with a discount card that read "Mrs. L Z Collins." I'd hand it over to an employee-shareholder in a candy-striped shirt and a quilted vest, who would deposit the toilet paper into a plastic bag emblazoned with a crest: "By Appointment to Her Majesty the Queen Grocer and Wine & Spirit Merchants." If the store made a show of a certain kind of Englishness, its shelves were pure British multiculturalism: preserved lemons, *gungo* peas, *mee goreng*, soba noodles, lapsang souchong smoked salmon. One November a "Thanksgiving" section appeared, featuring a mystifying array of maple syrup, dried mango chunks, and pickled beetroot.

As national rather than regional concerns, British supermarkets played an outsize role in public life. Every year, the launch of their competing Christmas puddings was attended by the sort of strangely consensual fanfare—everyone gets into it, even if it's silly—that Americans accord to each summer's blockbuster movies. The feedback loop of the food chain was tight: if a popular cookbook called for an obscure ingredient, the stores would quickly begin to carry it, a fact about which the newspapers would write, leading the cookbook to become even more popular, and the ingredient to materialize simultaneously in every British pantry. There was a coziness to the stores, amid their great convenience. Shopping in them always reminded me that London was a big city in a small country. From the £10 Dinner for Two deal at my supermarket—it included a starter or a pudding, a main course, a side dish, and an entire bottle of wine—I could extrapolate something about, and participate in, if I chose to, a typical middle-class British Friday night.

Food shopping in Geneva was a less idiosyncratic affair. For fruits and vegetables, I went often to the farmers' markets. They had nothing to do with yoga or gluten. They were just a cheaper place to buy better carrots. The selection, though, was limited. For everything else, there were the Swiss supermarkets—two chains distinguished, as far as I could tell, by the fact that one of them sold alcohol and the other didn't. I frequented the former, whose breakfasty theme colors made it seem like it was perpetually 7:00 a.m. Despite a few superficial points of contrast—you could find horse meat hanging alongside the chicken and the beef; the onions, taskingly, were the size of Ping-Pong balls—there wasn't much to distinguish the experience. Cruising the cold, clean aisles, I could have been in most any developed nation.

My nemesis there—my imaginary frenemy—was Betty Bossi, a fifty-eight-year-old busybody with pearl earrings and a shower cap of pin-curled hair. Betty Bossi was inescapable. There was nothing she didn't do, and nothing that she did appealingly: stuffed mushrooms, bean sprouts, Caesar salad, Greek salad, mixed salad, potato salad, lentil salad, red root salad, "dreams of escape" salad, guacamole, tzatziki sauce, mango slices, grated carrots, chicken curry, egg and spinach sandwiches, orange juice, pizza dough, pastry dough, goulash, tofu, dim sum, shrimp cocktail, bratwurst, stroganoff, gnocchi, riz Casimir (a Swiss concoction of rice, veal cutlets, pepperoni, pineapple, hot red peppers, cream, banana, and currants).

Who was she? Where did she come from? What kind of name was Betty Bossi? Her corporate biography revealed that she was the invention of a Zurich copywriter, who had conjured her in 1956 in flagrant imitation of Betty Crocker. "The first name Betty, fashionable in each of the country's three linguistic regions, was accepted straightaway by the publicity agency," it read. "Equally, her last name was widespread all over the country. Together, they sounded good and were easy to pronounce in all the linguistic regions."

Switzerland, like Britain, was a small country, but due to any number of historical and geographical factors—chief among them the fact that the population didn't share a common language—it didn't have a particularly cohesive culture. The political system was heavily decentralized. (Name a Swiss politician.) There was no film industry to speak of, no fashion, no music. (Name a Swiss movie.) With the exception of Roger Federer, who spent his down time in Dubai, there weren't really any public figures. (Name a Swiss celebrity.)

Swiss francophones looked to France for news and entertainment, while German speakers gravitated toward Germany, and Italian speakers to Italy. (Speakers of Romansh, which is said to be the closest descendant of spoken Latin, made up less than 1 percent of the population and almost always spoke another language.) Useful as it was, Switzerland's multilingualism rendered public life indistinct, a tuna surprise from the kitchen of Betty Bossi. The country was in Europe, but not of it. Its defining national attribute, neutrality, seemed at times to be a euphemism for a kind of self-interested disinterest. The morning after Russia announced that it was banning food products from the European Union, the front page of the local paper boasted "Russian Embargo Boosts Gruyère."

A few months later, it emerged that the supermarket chain that did not sell alcohol *was* selling mini coffee creamers whose lids featured portraits of Adolf Hitler. After a customer complained, a representative apologized for the error, saying, "I can't tell you how these labels got past our controls. Usually, the labels have pleasant images like trains, landscapes, and dogs—nothing polemic that can pose a problem." Betty Bossi as an icon; Hitler as a polemic. It was this bloodless quality that depressed me so much about Switzerland. My alienation stemmed less from a sense of being an outsider than it did from the feeling that there was nothing to be outside of.

The consolation prize of Geneva was the *grande boucherie*—a ninety-five-year-old emporium of shanks and shoulders and shins, aging woodcocks and unplucked capons, their feet the watery blue of a birthmark. The steaks were festooned with cherry tomatoes and sprigs of rosemary. The aproned butchers, surprisingly approachable for people of their level of expertise, would expound on the preparation of any dish. One day, craving steak tacos—Geneva's Mexican place only had pork ones, and a single order cost forty dollars—I convinced Olivier, who wasn't big on cooking, to chaperone me to the *boucherie*. I explained to him that I wanted to buy a *bavette de flanchet*, the closest thing I had been able to find to a flank steak, after Googling various permutations of "French" and "meat."

"Bonjour, monsieur," Olivier said. "On voudrait un flanchet, s'il vous plaît."

The butcher rifled around in the cold case, his fingers grazing hand-written placards: *rumsteak, entrecôte, tournedos, joue de boeuf. Ronde de gîte, paleron, faux-filet.*

"Malheureusement, je n'ai pas de flanchet aujourd'hui," he said. "En fait, on n'a généralement pas de flanchet."

"What?" I said.

"He doesn't have a flank steak."

The butcher reached into the case and pulled out a small, dark purse of beef.

"Je vous propose l'araignée. C'est bien savoureuse, comme le flanchet, mais plus tendre."

"What did he say?"

"He has an *araignée*."

"What is that?"

"No idea. *Araignée* means spider."

"Okay, take it."

"Bon, ça serait super."

The *araignée* is the muscle that sheaths the socket of a cow's hock bone, so called because of the strands of fat that crisscross its surface like a cobweb. In francophone Switzerland as in France, it is a humble but cherished cut. Different countries, I was surprised to learn, have different ways of dismantling a cow: an American butcher cuts straight across the carcass, sawing through bones when he meets them, but a French *boucher* follows the body's natural seams, extracting specific muscles. (American butchers are faster, but French butchers use more of the cow.) If you were to look at an American cow, in cross-section, it would be a perfectly geometric Mondrian. A French cow is a Kandinsky, all whorls and arcs. You can't get a porterhouse in Geneva, any more than you can get an *araignée* in New York: not because it doesn't translate, but because it doesn't exist.

A flank steak, I would have assumed, is a flank steak, no matter how you say it. We think of words as having one-to-one correspondences to objects, as though they were mere labels transposed onto irreducible phenomena. But even simple, concrete objects can differ according to the time, the place, and the language in which they are expressed. In Hebrew, "arm" and "hand" comprise a single word, *yad,* so that you can shake arms with a new acquaintance. In Hawaiian, meanwhile, *lima* encompasses "arm," "hand," and "finger."

In a famous experiment, linguists assembled a group of sixty containers and asked English, Spanish, and Mandarin speakers to identify them. What in English comprised nineteen jars, sixteen bottles, fifteen containers, five cans, three jugs, one tube, and one box, was, in Spanish, twenty-eight *frascos,* six *envases,* six *bidons,* three *aerosols,* three *botellas,* two *potes,* two *latas,* two *taros,* two *mamaderos,* and one *gotero, caja, talquera, taper, roceador,* and *pomo.* Mandarin speakers, meanwhile, identified forty *ping,* ten *guan,* five *tong,* four *he,* and a *guan.*

"The concepts we are trained to treat as distinct, the information our mother tongue continuously forces us to specify, the details it requires us to be attentive to, and the repeated associations it imposes on us—all these habits of speech can create habits of mind that affect more than merely the knowledge of language itself," the linguist Guy Deutscher has written. We don't call an arm an arm because it's an arm; it's an arm because we call it one. Language carves up the world into different morsels (a metaphor that a Russian speaker might refuse, as "carving," in Russian, can only be performed by an animate entity). It can fuse appendages and turn bottles into cans.

Almost as soon as I'd arrived in Geneva, I'd begun to feel the pull of French. Already, I was intrigued by the blend of rudeness and refinement, the tension between the everyday and the exalted, that characterized the little I knew of the language. "Having your cake and eating it too" was *Vouloir le beurre, l'argent, et le cul de la crémière* ("To want the butter, the money, and the ass of the dairywoman"). *Raplapla* meant "tired." A *frilleuse* was a woman who easily got cold. *La France profonde,* with its immemorial air, gave me chills in a way that "flyover country" didn't. I found it incredible that Olivier found it credible that the crash of Air France Flight 447 in 2009 could have been in some part attributable to a breakdown in the distinction between *vous* (the second person formal subject pronoun) and *tu* (the second person informal). Before the crash, the airline had promoted what was invariably referred to in the French press as an Anglo-Saxon-style management culture in which employees universally addressed each other as *tu*. The theory was that the policy had contributed to the creation of a power vacuum, in which no one could figure out who was supposed to be in charge.

French was the language of Racine, Flaubert, Proust, and *Paris Match*. It wasn't as if I were being forced to expend thousands of hours of my life in an attempt to acquire Bislama or Nordfriisk. Even if I had been, it would have been an interesting experiment, a way to try to differentiate between nature and nurture, circumstance and self. Learning the language would give me a *raison d'être* in Geneva, transforming it from a backwater into a hub of a kingdom I wanted to be a part of. I wasn't living in France, but I could live in French.

As long as I didn't speak French, I knew that a membrane, however delicate, would separate me from my family. I didn't mind being the comedy relative, birthing household appliances, but I sensed that the role might not become me for a lifetime. There were depths and shallows of intimacy I would never be able to navigate with a dual-language dictionary in hand. I didn't want to be irrelevant or obnoxious. More than anything, I feared being alienated from the children Olivier and I hoped one day to have—tiny half-francophones who would cross their sevens and blow raspberries when they were annoyed, saddled with a Borat of a mother, babbling away in a tongue I didn't understand. This would have been true in any language, but I sensed that it might be especially so in French, which in its orthodoxy seemed to exert particularly strong effects. "Do you want to see an Eskimo?" Saul Bellow wrote. "Turn to the *Encyclopédie Larousse*."

Our first New Year's in Switzerland, Jacques and Hugo decided to visit.

"They said they want to come in the morning," Olivier told me.

"Okay. When?"

"In the morning."

"No, but when?"

"In the morning!"

Olivier, I could see, was starting to get exasperated. So was I.

"What do you mean?" I said, a little too emphatically, as unable to reformulate my desire to know on which day of the week they would arrive as Olivier was to fathom another shade of meaning.

"What do you mean, 'What do I mean?' I meant exactly what I said."

"Well, what did you say, then?"

"I already said it."

"*What?*"

His voice grew low and a little bit sad.

"Talking to you in English," he said, "is like touching you with gloves."

You've just read an excerpt from When In French.

ABOUT THE AUTHOR

Lauren Collins began working at the *New Yorker* in 2003 and became a staff writer in 2008. Her subjects have included Michelle Obama, Donatella Versace, the graffiti artist Banksy, and the chef April Bloomfield. Since 2010, she has been based in Europe, covering stories from London, Paris, Copenhagen, and beyond. Her story on the *Daily Mail* was recently short-listed for the Feature Story of the Year by the *Foreign Press Association* in London.

IMPRINT: Penguin Press
PRINT ISBN: 9781594206443
PRINT PRICE: $27.00
EBOOK ISBN: 9780698191075
EBOOK PRICE: $13.99
PUBLICATION DATE: 9/13/16
PUBLICITY CONTACT: Sarah Hutson shutson@penguinrandomhouse.com
EDITOR: Ann Godoff
AGENT: Elyse Cheney
AGENCY: Elyse Cheney Literary Associates

New York Times Bestselling Author of
Broken Open

Marrow
A Love Story

Elizabeth Lesser

SUMMARY

From the author of *Broken Open*, a mesmerizing and courageous memoir: the story of two sisters uncovering the depth of their love through the life-and-death experience of a bone marrow transplant.

EXCERPT

Prelude

It starts on an August day, above Flathead Lake in Montana, just a few moments before heading out to a wedding I am to perform. Not that I have any right to marry people. "I'm a writer, not a minister," I told my young friends when they asked me to officiate. But they didn't care. I have known them both since they were children. Our lives are linked through my kids, who are their close friends, and their parents, who are my close friends, and through a tribe of other friends with many years behind us. And now we are all here, in Montana, to celebrate another link in the chain.

I am standing in the driveway of the house my family is renting, looking out at the enormous lake bordered in the distance by the jagged peaks of the Northern Rockies. As I wait for my husband and sons to join me, I take it all in: the sun illuminating the snowfields across the lake in Glacier National Park, the big sky, the grand expanses. It's a dramatic, impersonal landscape—the kind of place that takes my New England breath away.

My cell phone rings. I think of turning it off. I'm on vacation. It's a special day. My children are here, my closest friends. Who would I need to talk to? I check to see. A Vermont number. My sister. And so it starts:

"Liz? It's Maggie."

"Maggie?" I ask. Her voice is lower than usual. Dark. My heart jumps a beat. Maggie's voice is never dark. She is one of those people who seem to have descended from hummingbirds. She is tiny and light, and she never lands long enough for you to really know what's going on in her head. Always moving. Always chipper. Here. There. Gone. Back again.

"What's the matter?" I ask.

"I'm sick." That's all she says. A landscape bigger than Montana opens up between us. We both fall in.

"Sick? What kind of sick?"

"Cancer," she whispers. "I'm very sick."

Now it's her words that take my breath away. Finally I ask her what has happened and she tells me a jumbled tale of having weird symptoms, ignoring them, thinking they were one thing, and then finding out they were something quite different. Cancer. Lymphoma. The kind she will die from soon if she doesn't start treatment.

If anyone should not have to get cancer at this very moment, it is my little sister Maggie. After years of being married to the boy next door, the high school sweetheart, the man who has defined her, my sister is quite suddenly a single woman, unattached, on her own. A woman who created a storybook home is now homeless—housesitting here for one friend, and there for another. Her college-age children are like planets cut loose from gravity. Is it better for Maggie that our mother died recently and our father a few years previously? That she doesn't have to face their worry about her illness, their judgment about her failed marriage?

I feel something pulling at me from across the country, but even more so from deep within. As if there is a buried magnet in my body, quivering to the pull of my sister. What is the deepest part of the body? Is it the blood? The bone? The marrow of the bone? I don't even know what that means: the marrow of the bone. I will find out later.

Introduction

This book is a love story. It is primarily about the love between two sisters, but it is also about the kindness you must give to yourself if you are to truly love another. Love of self, love of other: two strands in the love braid. I have braided these strands together in all sorts of relationships, in varying degrees of grace and ineptitude. I've messed up in both directions: being self-centered, being a martyr; not knowing my own worth, not valuing the essential worth of the other. To love well is to get the balance right. It's the work of a lifetime. It's art. It's what this book is about.

When my sister's cancer recurred after seven years of remission; when we were told her only chance for survival was a bone marrow transplant; when test results confirmed I was a perfect marrow match; when we prepared ourselves, body and soul, to give and receive; when my marrow was harvested; when she received my stem cells that would become her blood cells; when we traveled together through the thickets of despair and hope; when she lived what she said was the best year of her life; when the cancer returned; when she faced the end; when she died; when all of this happened, I took up the strands of myself and braided them together with my sister's strands, and I finally got it right. Although "getting it right" sounds more tidy and final than love ever is. There is no ten-ways-to-get-it-right list when it comes to love. No exact formulas for when to be vulnerable and when to be strong, when to wait and when to pursue, when to relent and when to be a relentless love warrior. Rather, love is a mess, love is a dance, love is a miracle. Love is also stronger than death, but I'm only learning that now.

I must add here that there was another strand that my incredibly brave sister added to complete the love braid and, in doing so, inspired me to do the same. It is the secret strand, the one the philosopher Friedrich Nietzsche called "amor fati"—love of fate. Nietzsche described amor fati as the ability not to merely bear our fate but to love it. That's a tall order. To be human is to have the kind of fate that doles out all sorts of wondrous and horrible things. No one gets through life without big doses of confusion and angst, pain and loss. What's to love about that? And yet if you say yes to amor fati, if you practice loving the fullness of your fate, if you pick up the third strand of the love braid, you will thread ribbons of faith and gratitude and meaning through your life. Some will reject the idea of loving your fate as capitulation or naïvete; I say it's the way to wisdom and the key to love.

When I talk about love, I am not talking about romance. Romance is good. I like it a lot. It's fiery and fun. But it is merely one sliver of the love story. It's a mistake to reduce the whole ocean of love to a little flame of romance and then spend all of one's energy trying to keep that flame from burning out. In doing so, we give short shrift to the vast majority of our love relationships: parents, siblings, children, friends, colleagues, and, of course, mates after the initial passion has mellowed. Trying to sustain fairy-tale romance is a foolish quest. But you can sustain a different kind of love across a lifetime with a whole motley crew of people. It takes guts to love well, and it takes work to sustain important relationships, but I promise you, it is possible, and it's what our hearts are really longing for.

You may be thinking of dulled or bruised or ruined relationships in your life as you read this. You may be thinking, she doesn't know *my* sister, my brother, my ex, my kid, boss, friend, mate. And you may be right—it is not possible to heal or sustain every relationship. Sometimes we have to end things, or do the work of healing on our own. But I propose that most of our significant relationships can be mended, sweetened, enlarged. And I propose that deepening one relationship can unlock all sorts of goodness in your life—with other people, with your work, with your fate.

I propose this to you because my sister and I had a relationship comparable to most human relationships. We were imperfect people, with qualities that both supported and eroded our abilities to love. We were similar in some ways, yet also different enough to misunderstand each other, to judge each other, to reject each other. Sometimes we were close, and sometimes we were strangers. And like most people—and certainly like most siblings—we carted around with us bags of old stories and resentments and regrets. We dragged those bags from childhood into adulthood, into other relationships, into our work, into our families. We believed the stories in the bags—the tales we had heard about ourselves and told about each other. We had never unpacked those bags and showed each other what was in them.

Until we had to.

***

In the years between my sister's first cancer diagnosis and her last recurrence, she lived a remarkably full life. She re-created a home for herself and her new man; she rededicated her life to her children and her work and her art; she overcame several serious health crises; and she learned to manage the fear and pain that come with being a cancer survivor. Her life stabilized, as did our relationship and my own life. During that time I did what many writers spend their time doing: I started several books, but never finished them. With my first two published books, I had used my own life as the story line. But I was sick of talking about myself. So I decided to write a novel. That way, I could hide my story (and the stories of the poor people who have the misfortune of being related to me) behind created characters. But fiction is a different beast, and I couldn't wrestle a novel to completion. I started a fable and then a collection of essays, but nothing gelled.

The book I most wanted to write was about authenticity—the idea that beneath the chatter of the mind and the storms of the heart is a truer self, an essential self, a core, a soul. Call it what you like, but life has brought me to the point where I know that the striving and insecure ego is not the whole truth of who I am, or who you are. More and more, in glimpses caught through meditation and prayer, through acts of kindness and courage, and sometimes just by having a cup of coffee in the morning, a sip of wine with friends, I find myself quite suddenly in touch with a fullness of being that wakes me out of slumber. It's as if God is calling roll and I shoot up my hand, saying "Here!" This can happen at the oddest times. I'll be wheeling my cart through the grocery store or driving home after a long day at the office when grace descends and I am relieved of the illusion that I am merely a cranky, imperfect, overextended person. Instead, I sense a more dignified being hiding behind the assumed roles—a noble soul, riding faithfully through the human experience, related to everyone and everything, aware of the splendor at the heart of creation.

I wanted to write a book about *that* self—the soul self, the authentic self, the true self. I wanted to explore why we forget who we are, and how we can remember. I'd been thinking about this book for a long time, at least for as long as I have worked at Omega Institute, the retreat and conference center I cofounded in 1977, when I was still in my twenties. Through my work I have been exposed to a wide array of people—hundreds of thousands of workshop participants from all over the world, and the noted authors and artists, doctors and scientists, philosophers and spiritual teachers who come to Omega to help people heal and grow. It's been a good place for me to work because I'm an unapologetic voyeur. I've never doubted my purpose in life: It's to watch people. It's to ponder what the hell works here on Planet Earth and why it's so hard to put seemingly simple instructions for living into everyday actions—instructions like the Bible's "Love your neighbor as yourself" or Shakespeare's "This above all: to thine own self be true."

When you get down to it, the most widely accepted adages that have guided human beings across the ages all focus on the same ideas: to love the self, to give of the self, to be true to the self. But there's a problem with these guidelines: They presuppose you know what that self is. Someone forgot to mention the long process of uncovering the shining seed at the center of your identity. Being true to that self involves sifting through the layers of bad advice and unreasonable expectations of others. It requires seeing through your own delusions of grandeur or your fear of failure or your impostor syndrome or your conviction that there is something uniquely and obviously screwed up about your particular self.

My first job in life was being a midwife. I delivered enough babies to know that every one of us comes into this world in possession of a radiant, pure, good-to-the-core self. I witnessed this each time I touched the skin and looked into the eyes of a brand-new baby. I saw his self. I saw her soul. I sensed in each baby an essential self like no other self before it—a matchless, meaningful mash-up of biology, lineage, culture, and cosmic influences we can barely fathom.

And then we grow up, we become adults, and we spend so much of our time uncomfortable in our own skin—almost embarrassed at being human. We devalue and cover the original self, layer by layer, as we make our way through life. I wanted my next book to be a travel guide through the great journey of uncovering. "There is something in every one of you that waits and listens for the sound of the genuine in yourself," the civil rights leader Howard Thurman wrote. "That is the only true guide you will ever have." What better thing to write about than the act of listening for and then following *the only true guide you will ever have?*

But something was stopping me as I put fingertips to keyboard. Perhaps it was my ambivalence about much of the literature of "authenticity." There's a nagging narcissism to it. A book about being true to the self can read like a manual for joining a cult of one. Try to write about it and you're smack-dab in the middle of a perennial paradox: how knowledge of self, and love of self, and esteem of self go awry if they don't lead ultimately to understanding and respect and love of others.

And then there's the sticky question of "What is the self?" Is it merely a bundle of neural impulses held together by flesh and gravity for a tiny flash of time? And when the flash burns out, does our body turn to dust and our personal ego dissolve into the cosmic soup? Or is each one of us more substantial than that? Are we spiritual beings having a human experience? Does our soul continue once released from the confines of body and ego? And when, as human beings, we listen for guidance from our authentic core, is it really the eternal soul whose song we hear?

Even though I knew I would never definitively answer these questions (since no one ever has), I wanted to dive as deeply as I could into the mystery. The questions may have no firm answers, but the search for them brings us closer to the kind of life each of us yearns for. I may not be able to answer the big questions, but I do know a few things for sure: I know that people who have tasted the dignity and goodness of their own true nature are more likely to see and respect the dignity of others. I know that if I have an authentic self that is noble and sacred, then you have one too. This may sound like a no-brainer, but it's one of humanity's biggest stumbling blocks—this sense of me against the other. Instead of traveling side by side, helping each other as we fall and being inspired by each other as we rise, we defend ourselves; we attack; we try to go it alone. Instead of reveling in one another's shining authenticity, we compete, as if there is a limited amount of shine in the world, as if the only way to see the shining self is against the backdrop of a diminished other.

This became my most compelling reason to write about authenticity. To link up the liberation of the genuine self with the healing of our relationships and the mending of our human family. For all of the marvelous technological ways of connecting to each other, there's still so much loneliness, misunderstanding, and disconnection in the world. Connection is a basic human need. We want to be understood, seen, accepted, loved. We want to matter to each other. We want to relate, soul to soul.

And so I fumbled around, trying to craft a book that could shine a light on the path that leads to the authentic self, a self that defies description yet begs to be revealed. "One can't write directly about the soul," Virginia Woolf lamented in her diaries. "Looked at, it vanishes." Still, I wanted to look.

※※※

When I won the cosmic lottery and tested as a perfect match for my sister's bone marrow transplant, I did what I often do when I'm scared: I became an amateur researcher. I do not like to bury my head in the sand. Rather, I like to arm myself with knowledge, even if in the end the knowledge can become its own form of sand in which I bury myself. But in this case, the knowledge I acquired about bone marrow, stem cells, and the miracle of transplant became a bridge into one of the most significant experiences of my life. What I learned went way beyond biology. What my sister and I experienced was much more than a medical procedure.

My research revealed to me that bone marrow transplants are fraught with danger for the recipient. For months after the procedure my sister would face two life-threatening situations. First, her body might reject the stem cells that would be extracted from my bone marrow and transplanted into her bloodstream. And, second, my stem cells, once in my sister's body, might attack their new host. Rejection and attack. Both could kill her. The medical professionals were doing everything they could to ensure neither would happen. What if Maggie and I could help them? What if we left the clear sailing of the bone marrow transplant up to the doctors, and conducted a different kind of transplant? What if we met in the marrow of our souls and moved beyond our lifelong tendency to reject and attack each other?

People have said I was brave to undergo the bone marrow extraction. But I don't really think so—you'd have to be a miserable, crappy person to refuse the opportunity to save your sibling. But getting emotionally naked with my sister . . . *this* felt risky. To dig deep into never-expressed grievances, secret shame, behind-the-back stories, blame, and judgment wasn't something we had done before. But my sister's life hung in the balance. And so, over the course of a year, sometimes with the help of a guide but mostly on walks and over coffee, just the two of us, and sometimes with our other sisters, we opened our hearts, we left the past behind, and we walked together into a field of love.

What I learned from both transplants—the bone marrow transplant and the soul marrow transplant—is that the marrow of the bones and the marrow of the self are quite similar. Deep in the center of the bones are stem cells that can keep another person alive, perhaps not forever, but for a time and, in the case of my sister, for what she called the best year of her life. Deep in the center of the self are the soul cells of who you really are. Dig for them, believe in them, and offer them to another person, and you can heal each other's hearts and keep love alive forever.

Here's one more thing I learned. You don't have to wait for a life-and-death situation to offer the marrow of yourself to another person. We can all do it, we can do it now, and there's a chance that the life of our human family does indeed depend on it.

And this is how I finally came to write a book about authenticity and love.

Note to the Reader

Throughout the book you will find snippets from my sister's journals—"field notes," as she called them, from the varied layers of her life. Besides being a nurse, mother, farmer, baker, musician, and maple syrup producer, my Renaissance sister was also an artist and a writer. Her artwork evolved over the years into exceptional botanical pieces and prints that hang in people's homes all over the country. Her writing took the form of journals, hilarious letters and e-mails, illustrated children's books, and a memoir she dreamed of writing called *Lower Road*. She said there were enough things written about taking the higher road; she wanted to write about taking the lower road and finding higher ground the hard way. There was a long dirt road in her area with the actual name of Lower Road—a single lane that hugged a mountain and led into a hollow flanked on one side by marshes and ponds and on the other side by rusty trailers and old farmhouses. When she was a young visiting nurse, her work for the state of Vermont often took her to Lower Road. The book *Lower Road* was to be a chronicle of her relationship with her patients who lived there: the teenage mothers, the veterans with PTSD, the addicted, the abusive, the abused. The forgotten rural poor whom she cared for with a no-bullshit form of tenderness.

When Maggie's computer became her journal, she began emailing me entries: excerpts from the always changing *Lower Road*, field notes from the clinic she ran, funny stories about people she met at craft shows, joyful rants about her new home, about the wildness of the woods in springtime and the sweetness of the sugarhouse on dark cold nights when the maple sap ran. And when she got sick, her field notes came from the loneliness of her hospital bed and the window seat in her home. She wrote quickly, in run-on sentences, making up words, switching tenses all over the place. She never used capital letters and she bent grammar rules. She wrote like a hummingbird would write if it stayed still long enough to gather its thoughts and put them into words.

I had always planned to help Maggie craft a book out of her hummingbird words. She wanted me to, and that's why she sent me a whole mess of disorganized computer files. We began working on them when she was recovering from the transplant. But when her energy waned, I asked her how she would feel if I included some of her field notes in the book I was writing. I had been showing her early segments of my book, and she had a wistful appreciation for it—a sense of humor and also grief that she would not be around to see how it ended. Together we decided to include some of her words in my book, and so I scattered them throughout—a trail of Maggie's truth crisscrossing mine.

Part One

The Girls

You are born into your family and your family is born into you.
—Elizabeth Berg

Phone Bombs

When I was a kid, telephones were stationary objects. Most houses had one, or at the most two of them—one bolted onto the kitchen wall and the other on a bedside table, rarely used. When I became a teenager, my friends got phones in their rooms. Princess phones, they were called, usually pink, with push buttons instead of a dial, and a long cord so you could walk around or lie in bed and chat under the covers. The princess phone never made an appearance in my family's home. My sisters and I were barely allowed to talk on the phone at all. Why would we need one of our own?

Phones became omnipresent later on. First, cordless phones made their debut, and then of course came the cell phone. The cell phone changed everything. But before there were cell phones, what changed my relationship with the telephone was becoming a parent. Having children turned a benign object—the phone—into a time bomb. When it rang, I worried, and often my worst-case scenarios came true: a failed test, a bloody nose, a broken arm. One of my sons got suspended from middle school for giving away answers to an exam. During high school, another son was pulled over for speeding and the cop discovered pot in his pocket. I remember where I was when those calls came in.

Things I never thought would happen also traveled through the airwaves and into the phone like little bombs. *Ring!* My father died. *Ring!* Colleague quit. *Ring, ring!* Trade Towers blown to bits. And then there was the phone bomb from my sister at the wedding in Montana. On that day I learned to do something many people are born knowing and then spend years in therapy trying to unlearn: I went into denial. For a whole day. This was revolutionary for me, someone whose heart stays unreasonably open most of the time.

Like all of us, I have several characters living within me—there's my vigilant rational self who lives in my head, my wild emotional self lodged in my heart, and a deeper self that some call the soul. That deeper self is always there, wiser than worry, vaster than fear, quick to see through the eyes of love. But the rational self is a bossy guy that crowds out the soul on a regular basis. Sometimes the rational self is right on the money, but often it is small-minded and tyrannical and it leads me into a cul-de-sac of overthinking. And my emotional self can spin out of control like a crazed dervish, throwing off sparks of joy and wonder, anger and despair. Round and round, I follow my mind and my emotions. The human experience is dizzying if we can't find the still point in the midst of the turning.

The still point is there. It is always there. I know it. I have found it again and again, even within the most turbulent whirlwinds. It may take me a while, but at least now I know there is a still point, and that the storm will pass and the center will hold. When I am in the grips of too much thinking, too much feeling, when I am frightened or ashamed, judgmental or paranoid, self-righteous or jealous, I know to wait, I know to pray, I know to trust. And sometimes, when there's just too much noise—when my emotions whip up a storm, or my overactive mind chatters like a jackhammer—patience and prayer don't cut it. That's when it can be helpful to take a brief denial time-out.

Which is what I did in Montana after receiving the phone bomb from my sister. I locked up my emotional creature, turned off my repetitive mind, and went to the wedding without them. I mingled with the crowd; I oohed and aahed at the tent set in a wheat field under the big sky; I performed the ceremony as if I had done such a thing hundreds of times before. All the while, I kept the news of the phone bomb in some kind of top secret vault. Then, copying the behavior of partygoers throughout the ages, I downed several drinks at the reception so as to be able to make small talk and eat and dance. Denial! Where had you been all my life?

The next morning, I left the family behind and got on a plane. It was nearly empty. I had a row of seats all to myself—a good thing, because the minute I buckled the belt, my heart reopened on its own accord. I let the feelings come. I gave over the reins to my emotional self. She took off right away.

"Maggie's too young to die," I cried. "This is so unfair."

"There's no such thing as fair," rational self interrupted, making a predictable comeback.

"Well, it's terrible nonetheless." Now I was weeping. "She's in the middle of a divorce; she doesn't even have a home; her kids . . ."

Rational self was unmoved. "No such thing as terrible, either. It is what it is."

Emotional self and rational self went on like this for a while until I tired of their either/or banter. I closed my eyes, and noticed that my shoulders were up around my ears. I dropped them down, softened my whole body, and breathed my way toward the still point until I could hear the voice of my soul.

And there she was, telling me the truth: "Have faith," my soul said. "You'll see—your sister will grow from this; she'll rise to meet it. And you will too. You'll grieve and you'll learn, you'll rage and you'll worry, but through it all you will grow deeper and deeper into the truth of who you really are. You will, Maggie will, all who travel with her will uncover surprising treasures because of this path her soul has chosen." When soul speaks, there's really no arguing. Everyone else just shuts up and listens. The bigger story sparkles in the silence. What needs to be done is revealed. Mind and heart join hands and vow to work together.

For the rest of the plane ride I rested in the rare peace that the soul brings. It was as if I was being filled with fuel for the long journey ahead. I didn't know what would come. I didn't know how long a voyage I was embarking on. I didn't know that I would be brought all the way into the actual marrow of my bones, and deeper still into the holy marrow of my true self. I only knew to pray for the soul to be my guide.

The next day, driving from my home in New York to my sister in Vermont, worry and grief took over again. My heart filled with sadness. And not just for Maggie. Not just for the fearsome treatments she would have to go through and the unknown outcome and the ways in which nothing would ever again be the same for her. My heart also broke for us—for our family, for our story, for who we had always been and who I foolishly expected we would always be. "The girls," my heart whimpered, holding on tight to my three sisters, to the configuration of my childhood, to my known place in the world. I cried the words aloud: "The four girls."

"Oh, stop it," my mind snapped, sounding quite like my mother.

The Girls

I was born into a family of girls, the second of four daughters. My sisters and I were known as "the girls." Or just "girls," as in "Girls! Time for supper!" My mother yelled that line several thousand times over the years of mothering four daughters. We also heard this line a lot: "GIRLS. Stop bickering or I'll wallop you!" My father was famous for that one, threatening us with "wallops" as our family made its interminable car trips from New York to Vermont. My father's work as an advertising man who represented the ski industry took him—and therefore us—from his office in New York City to the mountains of Vermont all winter long. Why my parents insisted on bringing all four girls with them every weekend befuddles me to this day, but complain as we might, come Friday afternoon, we would cram ourselves into the station wagon for the four-hour drive north—vying for the window seats, cold and uncomfortable, tired and bored—until we finally fell asleep against each other.

Despite his threats, my father only came close to walloping one of us once, in all his years of being outnumbered and exasperated by "the girls." I cannot remember what drove him to attempt to deliver on his threat. I do remember, as do my sisters, the scene: Something I have done to provoke my father has caused him to chase me up the stairs of our house, swinging at my behind with my mother's purse. My sisters run after us, laughing. My mother stands at the bottom of the stairs, helplessly yelling, "Girls! Girls!" By the time my father catches up to me, he has lost his steam. He drops my mother's purse, throws up his hands, and, mumbling something about "the girls," stomps back down the stairs and escapes outside.

An advantage to having siblings is that the pressure is off any one child to live up to all the dreams of the parents. It's nearly impossible for one kid to do it all—to be well behaved *and* courageous, bookish *and* athletic, cooperative *and* original. And so siblings fill in for each other. But there's a disadvantage as well. Without advance agreement, siblings are assigned a role that can brand one for life. Show a tendency in one direction, and that becomes who you have to be all the time. This one's the saint, and that one's the rebel. This one will go far; that one will stay close. It can take a lifetime to escape the narrow boundaries of a fixed family identity.

This was certainly the case in my family. Where one of us was thin and athletic (my older sister), the other (me) was chubby and introspective. Where one excelled in school (me), another brought home bad grades (again, older sister). Where one stood up to our father's authority (me), my younger sisters were the quieter ones, the identified pleasers, intent on keeping the peace. And so we settled into those roles, hearing and telling stories about each other, branding ourselves and dragging those branded selves into the rest of our lives.

There were constant reminders—expressed or implied—of the characters we were to play on the family stage. My mother wouldn't allow me to take ballet lessons because I was not as "coordinated" as my sisters. She would drop off two of them at the little dance school taught by a teenager down the street, and then explain to me I couldn't go because my body was "anatomically incorrect" for ballet, but that shouldn't bother me because I was smart. She'd shame my older sister for her poor school habits, even as she giggled with her about my knock-knees and the way I looked in a bathing suit. Maggie, my younger sister, was the "good" one—the well-behaved girl, the one my mother could depend on. And our shy littlest sister was Daddy's favorite, overrun by her big sisters, forever locked into being the baby.

Like the pantheon of gods and goddesses in Greek mythology, siblings take on archetypal roles—roles that solidify one's sense of self long after childhood is over.

In our pantheon, I was the bossy one, the agitator—"the princess," they called me. Somehow I got it in my mind, even as a little girl, to challenge my father's power. It struck me as outrageous that in a family of women, my father got to call the shots. I wondered why my mother deferred to him even though she seemed more astute, and was certainly as educated and worldly. But these were the 1950s and '60s, and although my mother had graduated college with honors, my father established the family values, determined how we spent our time, and, when he was around, enforced what we did and didn't talk about.

The fact that we were four little girls didn't stop my father from including us in his adventurous activities, most of which were inspired by his time spent in the army, in the 10th Mountain Division—the ski troops—during World War II. It's not that he felt girls should have the same opportunities as boys. Rather, he didn't seem to notice we were girls. Or maybe he did and just preferred not to accept the fact that all of his offspring were female. We certainly were never asked if we wanted to join his regiment. It was just assumed.

In retrospect, I am grateful to my father for dragging us along on treks up New Hampshire's Mount Washington, with our heavy downhill skis strapped to our backs, or for insisting we trudge for miles to find a spot on a Long Island beach where we could escape the lifeguards and swim in the dangerous surf. We were never told we couldn't do something because of our gender. But all of us, including my mother, were ridiculed if we acted "like a girl." Small talk, gossip, worry, idleness, vanity—these were all signs of feminine weakness, according to my father, and if we demonstrated those behaviors, we risked his scorn. My mother metabolized and enforced the official policy: work hard, be strong, keep busy.

My parents were typical of many Americans raised in the "Greatest Generation." The Depression and the war molded their characters. They were vigorous, frugal, and civic-minded people who rarely complained. In their day, self-reflection was a waste of time and psychotherapy was for crazy people. And parenting? It was not yet a verb. People had children, fed and clothed them, sent them to school, made them do chores, and pretty much that was it. Sure, some parents took their kids to Little League or piano lessons, but mostly they left us alone. We played in our suburban neighborhood without adult supervision, helmets, or sunscreen. Rarely did my mother help us with homework, even though she was a high school English teacher who cared intensely about education. It was our task to excel, not hers.

My sisters and I spent an enormous amount of our childhood together, more so than many siblings. We competed not so much for our parents' approval, but more for each other's. We were constant and creative playmates, but we also were competitive and adversarial. As we grew up and became women, we grew further apart in some ways and stayed deeply connected in others. But always, just below the surface, unexplored and unexpressed, were those roles we had assumed in the family, those stories we had been told and believed, those conclusions we had come to about each other and ourselves.

You've just read an excerpt from Marrow.

ABOUT THE AUTHOR

Elizabeth Lesser is the *New York Times* bestselling author of *Broken Open* and the cofounder of the Omega Institute, an organization recognized internationally for its workshops and conferences focusing on health and healing, psychology and spirituality, and creativity and social change. Prior to her work at Omega, she was a midwife and childbirth educator. She attended Barnard College and San Francisco State University, and lives in the Hudson River Valley with her family.

IMPRINT: Harper Wave
PRINT ISBN: 9780062367631
PRINT PRICE: $25.99
EBOOK ISBN: 9780062367648
EBOOK PRICE: $20.99
PUBLICATION DATE: 9/20/16
PUBLICITY CONTACT: Victoria Comella Victoria.Comella@harpercollins.com
EDITOR: Karen Rinaldi
AGENT: Henry Dunow
AGENCY: Dunow, Carlson & Lerner Literary Agency

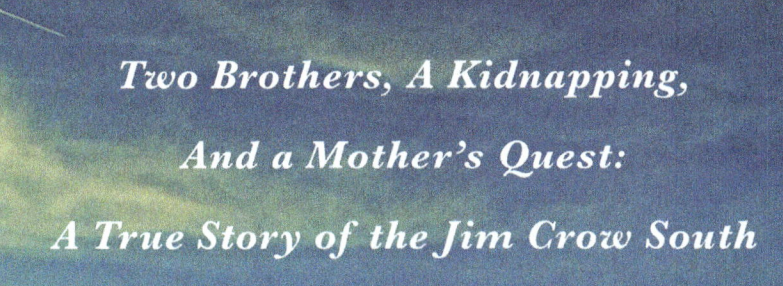

Two Brothers, A Kidnapping,
And a Mother's Quest:
A True Story of the Jim Crow South

TRUEVINE

BETH MACY

Author of the National Bestseller
FACTORY MAN

SUMMARY

The true story of two African-American brothers who were kidnapped and displayed as circus freaks, and whose mother endured a 28-year struggle to get them back. Through hundreds of interviews and decades of research, Beth Macy expertly explores a central and difficult question: Where were the brothers better off? On the world stage as stars or in poverty at home? *Truevine* is a compelling narrative rich in historical detail and rife with implications to race relations today.

EXCERPT

Prologue

'I Am the True Vine'

Their world was so blindingly white that the brothers had to squint to keep from crying. On a clear day, it hurt just to open their eyes. They blinked constantly, trying to make out the hazy objects in front of them, their brows furrowed and their eyes darting from side to side, trying to settle on a focal point. Their eyes were tinged with pink, their irises a watery pale blue.

Their skin was so delicate that it was possible, looking only at the backs of their hands, to mistake the young African-American brothers for the kind of white landed gentry who didn't have to eke out a living hoeing crabgrass from stony rows of tobacco or suckering the leaves from the stems.[i]

That was as true when they were old men as when they were little boys, back when a white man appeared in Truevine, Virginia, as their neighbors and relatives remembered it—that *very bad man*, they called him.

Back when everything they knew disappeared behind them in a cloud of red-clay dust.

The year was 1899, as the old people told the story, then and now; the place a sweltering tobacco farm in the Jim Crow South, a remote spot in the foothills of the Blue Ridge mountains where everyone they knew was either a former slave, or a child or grandchild of slaves. George and Willie Muse were just six and nine years old, but they worked a shift known by sharecroppers as "can see to can't see"—daylight to dark.[ii] *Can to can't,* for short.

Twenty miles away and 28 years earlier, a man born into slavery named Booker T. Washington had walked 400 miles from the mountains to the swampy plains, to get himself educated at Hampton Institute. "It was a whole race trying to go to school," he would write.[iii]

Forty miles in the other direction, another former slave named Lucy Addison had gotten herself educated at a Quaker college in Philadelphia. In 1886, Addison landed in the railroad boomtown of Roanoke, where she set up the city's first school for blacks in a two-story frame building with long benches and crude desks, using hand-me-down books from the city's white schools.[iv] She became such an icon of education that some elderly African Americans still have her faded portrait hanging on their walls, right next to the Rev. Martin Luther King Jr. and President Barack Obama. Addison inspired Ed Dudley, a dentist's son who would become President Truman's ambassador to Liberia. She taught future lawyer Oliver Hill, who would grow up to help overturn the separate-but-equal laws of the day in the landmark *Brown vs. Board of Education*.[v]

But such leaps were unheard of for black families in Truevine, where it would take decades before most learned to read and write.[vi] While Washington was on his way to fame and the founding of Tuskegee Institute, black children in Truevine were kept out of school when the harvest came in.

They had too much work to do.

Still, in this remote and tiny crossroads, where everyone knew everyone for generations back, George and Willie Muse were different. They were genetic anomalies: albinos born to black parents. Reared at a time when a black man could be jailed or even killed just for looking at a white woman—"reckless eyeballing," the charge was officially called—the Muse brothers were doubly cursed.

Their white skin burned at the first blush of sun, and their eyes watered constantly. They squinted so much that, even as children, they began to develop premature creases in their foreheads. So they looked down as they worked—they always looked down—heeding their mother's advice to never look toward the sun.

Harriett Muse was fiercely protective. She cloaked her boys in rags to keep their skin from blistering, and for the same reason she made them wear long sleeves when it was 100 degrees. When a vicious dog happened onto the tenant farm where they worked and lunged at little Willie, she chased it away with an iron skillet.[vii] She made the boys' favorite food, ashcakes, a simple cornbread baked over an open fire.

When it snowed she cobbled together a dessert called snow cream out of sugar, vanilla, eggs, and snow. When a rainbow appeared above the mountain ridges, she told them to take solace in it. "That's God's promise after the storm," she said.

She spoiled them as much as a poor sharecropper could, but George and Willie were expected to work, walking the rows of tobacco looking for bugs and picking cutworms off the leaves when they found them, squishing them between their fingers as they went.

The boys were squinting, as they usually were, when the bad man appeared. What a surprise the well-heeled stranger was in this hodgepodge of dirt roads, tobacco barns, and shacks, where tenants stuffed newspapers into holes in the walls to keep critters out, and the only dependable structure for miles was a white-frame meeting hall that doubled as a one-room school—a school the black community built by hand because the county provided a teacher but not a building for him to teach in.[viii]

The white man had arrived in the Virginia backwoods by horse and carriage. He cast a long shadow over the rows where the boys were crouched working. He went by the nickname "Candy," Willie Muse would later tell his family members, and he came from the Hollywood of that era: the circus.

At the turn of the last century, the height of circus popularity, bounty hunters scoured every nook and cranny of America's backwoods—and the world—looking for people they could transform into sideshow attractions: acts like Chang and Eng, the world's most famous conjoined twins, "discovered" by a British merchant in Siam (now Thailand) in 1829; or "The Wild Men of Borneo," as P.T. Barnum pitched a pair of dwarf brothers to audiences in 1880. . . though they actually hailed from a farm in Ohio.

Somehow the man had heard about the boys—maybe from a shopkeeper in nearby Rocky Mount, the county seat. Maybe a neighbor had seen the ads that circus showmen took out in newspapers and trade publications for "freak hunters," as they were called.[ix]

WANTED—To hear from the man that grows three feet in front of your eyes. . . . .Call DAN RICE, Sioux City, Iowa.[x]

Maybe even a member of their own family had given the boys up.

He found them working, alone and unsupervised, two snow-white field hands, no more than 70 pounds and four-feet tall, dressed in flour-sack clothes and turbans jerry-rigged out of rags and string. As he approached, stepping over the tobacco rows, the boys stood and nodded respectfully, as they'd been taught to do with white men.

When they removed their head coverings at his request, the man gasped. Their hair was kinky, and it was golden.

It was money in his pocket.

Harriett Muse had warned her sons about copperheads amid the tobacco rows, about wolves in the outlying fields. They knew about the perils of what scholars call peonage, the quasi-slavery state in which a man could be stripped to his waist, tied to a tree and lashed with a buggy whip—for the bold act of quitting one farmer's land to work for better wages down the road. They'd heard the adults talk about the lynch mob in nearby Rocky Mount in 1890, the year George was born, formed to rain vigilante justice down on five blacks accused of setting a fire that had destroyed much of the uptown. Two of the five were hung in the basement of the county jail before evidence surfaced, on appeal, that arson could not be proved.[xi]

"Before God I am as innocent of that charge as an angel," Bird Woods declared as a deputy slipped the noose around his neck. He spoke his truth even as his voice began to quake:

"I bear no malice in my heart towards any one, and my soul is going straight to heaven."[xii]

In 1893, the year of Willie's birth, a riot in nearby Roanoke erupted after a white produce vendor claimed that a black furnace worker, Thomas

Smith, had assaulted her near the city market. Before the next sunrise, two-dozen people were wounded and nine men were dead—including Smith, who was hung from a hickory tree, then shot, then dragged through the streets. As if that wasn't enough finality to the young furnace worker's life, the next morning they burned him on the banks of the Roanoke River while a crowd of 4,000 looked on, some clinging to pieces of the hanging rope they'd grabbed as mementos. The only evidence of linking Smith to the crime was the victim's vague description of her perpetrator: He was "tolerably black," she said, and wearing a slouch hat, a tilted wide-brimmed hat popular at the time.[xiii]

A Roanoke photo studio sold pictures of Smith hanging from a rope as a souvenir. It was the eighth known lynching in southwest Virginia that year.[xiv]

The region had always been a dangerous place to be black. But it had never occurred to Harriett that some far-off circus promoter would steal her boys, turn them into sideshow freaks, and, for decades, earn untold riches by enslaving them to his cause.

But by the end of that swelteringly hot day, Harriett later told people, she had felt it in her marrow—something had happened, and something was wrong. A white man in a carriage had been spotted roaming the area, she heard, and now George and Willie were gone.

In a dusty corner of Virginia's Piedmont, in a place named Truevine, for the only thing that gave Jim Crow-era blacks any semblance of hope at all—the biblical promise of a better life in the hereafter—Harriett Muse knew it for a fact. She'd already been robbed of dignified work, of monetary pay, of basic human rights, all because of the color of her skin.

Now someone had come along and taken the only thing she had left: her children.

For more than a century, that was the story Willie Muse and his relatives told. Their descendants had heard it, all of them, since the age of comprehension, then handed it down themselves, the way families do, stamping the memory with a kind of shared notarization. The story was practically seared into the Muse family DNA.

And, although it wasn't entirely accurate, not to the letter, the spirit of it certainly was.

The truth was actually far more surprising, and, as it usually is, far more tangled.

Part One

Chapter One: 'Sit Down and Shut Up'

The story seemed so crazy, many didn't believe it at first, black or white.

But for a century, it was whispered and handed down in the segregated black communities of Roanoke, the regional city hub about thirty miles away from Truevine. Worried parents would tell their children to stick together when they left home to see a circus, festival, or fair.

A retired African-American school principal recalls, at age 12, begging his mother to let him pick up odd jobs when a traveling circus visited town.[xv]

"They were hiring people to set up, but my Mom said no. She was really serious about it," he recalled.

The myth of the Muse kidnapping was so embedded in the local folklore that, long before he became a social science professor, Roanoke-born Reginald Shareef remembers thinking it was bunk when his mother said to him: "Be careful, or someone will snatch you up" just like what happened to the Muse brothers.

But eventually an adult took him aside and told him that a circus promoter really had forced them to become world-famous sideshow freaks, subjugating them for many years. And not only that, they had found their way back.

They were here. Now. Retired and hidden away in an attic of one of the houses on a segregated Roanoke city block, one of them living into the early aughts.

While adults relayed the story as a cautionary tale, kids teased each other about it. Nobody seemed to know for sure whether the Muses really lived in an attic—and the handed-down stories had key points of divergence—but the truth didn't stand in the way of a good story:

The brothers were Boo Radley twins. "The story had a mystery to it and a witchery in some people's minds," another retired educator told me. And some kids weren't sure whether it was the circus they should be afraid of—or the Muses.

In the 1960s, Shareef grew up in the same segregated neighborhood as the Muses; his grandmother lived two blocks away. He ran around with the great nephews of the Muse brothers. "They were a nice family, but the men were always getting into something," he recalled. "It's a wonder the women in that family didn't go crazy."

In 1996, Shareef published a pictorial history of Roanoke's black community and included a long-hidden photograph of the Muse brothers he'd found in the dusty archives of Roanoke's Harrison Museum of African American Culture. The caption he wrote contained errors—they weren't twins, and they weren't exactly toddlers when they were kidnapped—but the gist was correct: "Albino twins [George and Willie Muse] were stolen at age three and featured as 'freaks' for many years in the Ringling Brothers Circus."[xvi]

A Muse relative saw the photo in the book and called Shareef on the phone, demanding to know: Where'd you get that picture?

The family didn't like to talk about what had happened to their uncles—they'd all been taunted about it as kids.

"Your uncles eat raw meat!" classmates shouted at them on the playground.[xvii] Or, worse, curiosity seekers, blacks and whites, would show up on their front porch at all hours of the day and night, demanding to see them. Another albino relative, a niece, described that double curse of differentness rearing back on her. For years, she had a hard time leaving her house to go to the store.[xviii]

Not long after Shareef's book came out, George and Willie's great-niece Nancy Saunders went to the owner of that image, Frank Ewald, who ran Roanoke's premiere photo-finishing shop and gallery. A photo collector, Ewald had purchased the negatives of celebrated Roanoke street photographer George Davis, who'd taken the 1927 portrait of the brothers featured in Shareef's book. Ewald was in the process of launching a Davis photo exhibit when Nancy visited the gallery and politely said: Don't.

"She wasn't combative or threatening," Ewald recalled. "She just asked us not to exhibit them."

He didn't dare.

The first time painter and folk-art collector Brian Sieveking heard the story, he was an eight-year-old budding artist with a fascination for circus sideshows. He'd seen the Muses' picture at the Circus World Museum in Baraboo, Wisconsin, the original home of the Ringling Brothers Circus, and began drawing them in his sketchbooks next to other acts that struck his fancy, including Johnny Eck, "the Amazing Half-Boy"; and Chang and Eng, the original Siamese twins. "I got curious about the Muse brothers because you could easily understand the fat lady and the tall guy, but what exactly did these guys do?" recalled Sieveking, who is white, and now a 49-year-old art professor.[xix]

The summer he was twelve, his family moved from Cincinnati to a high-end subdivision outside Roanoke and enrolled him in a private school. He was lonely and bored, and took solace in a stack of decommissioned books for sale in a back room of the downtown library. There he stumbled upon a book called "You and Heredity," a quasi-scientific tome on genetics published in 1939.[xx] Proponents of the eugenics movement often used sideshows as propaganda about the dangers of miscegenation and of allowing the lower classes, especially those with genetic "flaws"—and most especially African Americans with such characteristics—to breed.

In a chapter titled "Structural Defects," Sieveking was stunned to find a photograph of an unnamed George and Willie Muse with a caption describing Roanoke as their hometown. His new town!

The hobby turned into obsession. A few summers later, he was working as a grocery store checkout clerk when the subject of the brothers came up in the break room. His coworkers were among the very few black people the teenaged Sieveking knew in Roanoke, which was, then and now, among the most housing-segregated cities in the South. They told him the Muse family lived "over in Rugby," a black neighborhood, where Willie Muse was approaching 100 and still very much alive.

Sieveking sent word that he'd like to interview Willie, as he had done, once, with Johnny Eck. He wanted to know more about their careers, and he'd become particularly interested in the 1944 Hartford Circus Fire, one of the worst fire disasters in American history (it killed 168 people). He would go on to paint a beautiful, haunting portrait of the fire—with the Muse brothers front and center. But he didn't get that interview.

"I wanted to ask Willie Muse about the fire," Sieveking recalled. "But I was told in no uncertain terms not to mess with Nancy," his primary caregiver and great-niece.

As a young journalist who'd arrived in Roanoke in 1989 to write feature stories for The Roanoke Times, it took two years before I mustered the nerve to mess with Nancy. A newspaper photographer had told me the bones of the kidnapping story, based on rumors he'd heard growing up in Roanoke. "It's the best story in town, but no one has been able to get it," he said.

By the time I poked my head into her tiny soul-food restaurant, with the idea of writing a story about her famous great-uncles, it was very clear that all personal details were going to be closely held, trickling out in dribs and drabs—and very much on Nancy Saunders's timeline. The first time I asked if I could interview her uncle Willie Muse, she pointed to a homemade sign on The Goody Shop wall. A customer had stenciled the words in black block letters on a white painted board and given it to her as a gift.

The sign said: "Sit down and shut up."

Willie was not now—nor would he ever be—available for comment. So, hoping to generate some goodwill for a future story on her uncles, I wrote a feature about her restaurant, a place where the menu never changes and isn't even written down. You're just supposed to know.

Legions of black Roanokers could already recite the daily specials I would eventually commit to memory: Tuesday is spaghetti or lasagna, except every other Tuesday, which is pork chops. Wednesday is fish and

Thursday country-fried steak. Friday is ribs, but you better come early because the ribs always sell out quickly. The line out front starts forming at noon, though lunch doesn't officially begin until 12:15 and not a minute before—and later if Nancy has to run home to check on Uncle Willie and finds him in the midst of a bad day. (His favorite special? Spaghetti Tuesday.)

For most of December, the place is closed so the Saunders women—Nancy and her mother Dot, cousin Louise and aunt Martha—can work on the hundreds of yeast rolls, cakes, and pies they make by advance special order for Christmas.

Among the other unwritten rules in the Goody Shop code: "Don't criticize, especially the fruitcake," I wrote. "When a novice Goody Shopper grimaced at the very mention of the jellied fruitstuff, Saunders snapped, 'I beg your pardon! You're getting ready to step on the wrong foot!'"[xxi] She pointed, again, to her sign.

She also kept a painted rock on top of her cash register, a gift from her preschooler nephew, whom she helped raise. She was not above picking it up—presumably in semi-jest—should a customer offend her.

When I returned for lunch, two days after my story ran—rib Fridays were my favorite—Nancy shook her finger at me, and it was clear I was not getting anything close to a pat on the back. Her mother, Dot, sat nearby peeling potatoes, watching "The Young & The Restless," and cringing at what she knew her daughter was about to say.

Nancy had been ready to send me packing the first time I walked in the restaurant and blithely inquired about her uncles, but soft-hearted Dot convinced her to let me stay and do the restaurant feature. A "Y&R" fan in my youth, I'd bonded quickly with Dot over the characters and was helping peel potatoes in her kitchen before the episode was over, much to Nancy's chagrin. (Victor Newman was a scoundrel, we both agreed.)

"You know what your story did?" Nancy barked. "It brought out a bunch of crazy white people, that's all!"

Paying customers, I might have added, but she was in no mood for backtalk. She walked past me without further comment. Uncle Willie's primary caregiver, she was leaving now to feed him and turn him in his bed, as she often did throughout the day, leaving the Goody Shop as many as five or six times a shift.

If Nancy Saunders had her way, her uncles' story would have stayed buried where she thought it belonged. The first time she heard it, she was just a child, and she found the whole tale embarrassing, and painfully raw. The year was 1961, and black and white people alike wanted to know: Were the light-skinned brothers black or white? Had they really been trapped in a cage and forced to eat raw meat?

These men deserved respect, Nancy knew. They did not deserve the gawkers who came by their house at all hours, banging on the front door.

By the time I came on the scene, no one talked about savages or circus freaks in front of Nancy, a sturdy woman with a no-frills Afro, graying at the temples, whose skin was nearly as white as the chef's coat she wore to work. She baked bread every bit as good as her great-grandmother Harriett's ashcakes—and she was every bit as fierce. Even Reg Shareef, who knew the family well, had never contemplated bringing the subject up.

"That is one exceptionally guarded family," he told me, advising baby steps. "You have to think of them as a tribe. They fall out with each other sometimes. But if you fall out with one of them, they will come roaring back at you like an army."

It was 10 more years before Nancy warmed up enough to let me co-write a newspaper series about her uncles, and only after Willie Muse's death in 2001. She didn't reveal much, though. She invited fellow reporter Jen McCaffery, photographer Josh Meltzer, and me inside the Muse brothers' house exactly once.

She made reference to a family Bible that we were not permitted to view, and for years after the series ran whenever I visited the restaurant she hinted that there was so much more to the story than we had found.

Our newspaper was the same one that had mocked her family's version of the kidnapping story decades before. It had looked the other way when city officials decimated two historic black neighborhoods in the name of mid-century progress, via urban renewal, or as the black community called it: "Negro removal." The newspaper cheered when the city knocked down hundreds of community homes and buildings, including the Muse family's Holiness church. It refused to print wedding announcements for black brides until the mid 1970s because, the white wealthy publisher reasoned, Roanoke had no black middle class.[xxii]

I myself had used a pair of pregnant black teens to illustrate a story about Roanoke's super-high teen pregnancy rate in 1993, a story that went viral before that Internet term existed and made the girls the object of ridicule, including by Rush Limbaugh. When the girls dropped out of school shortly after my story ran, it was devastating, including to me.

Words linger and words matter, I learned, and it's not possible to predict the fallout they can have on a subject's life.

It would take me 25 years, finally, to earn something *nearing* Nancy's trust; to convince her I wasn't one more candy peddler intent on exploiting her relatives for the color of their skin—or purely for my own financial benefit. As the literary critic Leslie Fiedler has put it: "[N]obody can write about Freaks without somehow exploiting them for his own ends."[xxiii]

Her uncles had come into her care in the 1960s, a situation Nancy considered her privilege as well as her duty, and her loyalty to them extended to everything from coordinating their retirement activities and doctor visits—restoring the love, respect and dignity that had been stolen from them as children—to holding their story close.

By 2008, she had begun, in her inimitably gruff (and usually funny and occasionally even sweet) way, to warm toward me. When I set out to write a 10-part series on caregiving for the elderly, Nancy was the first person I called for input.

"You gotta keep it real," she said, sharing names and numbers of people who would eventually become primary sources for that project. She periodically counseled me about other career and family stresses, advising me, "You can handle this. Listen, girl, if you can get back into Dot's kitchen, you can do anything."

When I hit a snag updating the story of the pregnant teens more than 20 years after my explosive first story, it seemed fate that Shannon Huff, now a 37-year-old mother of four, lived just around the corner from Nancy's northwest Roanoke ranch house. When some angry relatives tried to bully me into not running the story—physically threatening me and demanding a meeting with my newspaper bosses—Nancy reassured me, "You don't need their permission to do the story, just like you don't really need mine to write your book. Not *really* you don't."

And yet, months earlier, Nancy's permission is exactly what I sought. On the eve of publishing my first book, about a third-generation factory owner who had battled Chinese imports to save his company, I had given her a proof copy of "Factory Man," dog-earing a chapter on race relations I'd found particularly hard to navigate. It detailed decades of mistreatment of black furniture factory workers, miscegenation, and the sexual harassment of black domestic workers, who often resorted to wearing two girdles at the same time as a defense against their bosses' groping hands and outright rape.

"It's been that way down through history," Nancy said. "A friend of my mom's, she'd be vacuuming down the steps [on a housekeeping job], and the husband would be feeling her up from behind.

"My mom had to fill in for her one day. And so she told the man first thing, 'Don't make me open up your chest!' "

By which Dot Brown meant: with the tip of my knife.

Nancy and I had come a long way from the days of sit-down-and-shut-up.

Still, it was by no means a gimme when I called her in November 2013, asking for her blessing to pursue her uncles' story as a book. She was 64 at the time and recently retired, after closing the Goody Shop. I wanted her help delving into the family story as well as connecting with distant Muse relatives, including one albino Muse still living in Truevine.

"I'll think about it," Nancy said, and the message was clear: I was not to call back. She would call me.

More than six weeks later—oh, she enjoyed making me wait—she finally called. "I waited so I could give it to you as a present," she said.

It was Christmas morning, and Nancy had decided to let me write her uncles' story with her help and blessing. But on one condition:

"No matter what you find out or what your research turns up, you have to remember: In the end, they came out on top."

I knew the story's ending, I assured her. I'd already interviewed several people—nurses and doctors, neighbors and lawyers—all of whom described the late-life care she'd given her uncles as impeccable and extraordinary.

I was less certain about who had forced them into servitude in the first place, about their struggle to have their humanity acknowledged and their work compensated. How exactly, during the harsh years of Jim Crow, had they managed to escape?

Prologue

i Tobacco-growing in Virginia's piedmont of that era is outlined in Samuel C. Shelton's "The Culture and Management of Tobacco," The Southern Planter, April 1861, pp. 209-218.

ii Sharecropping life detailed in "The African-American as Sharecropper," by Tom Landenburg, at digitalhistory.uh.edu and also by Marshall Wingfield in Franklin County: A History (Berryville, Va.: Chesapeake Book Co., 1964).

iii Booker T. Washington, Up From Slavery (New York: Doubleday, Page & Co., 1907).

iv From an undated history of African-American schools in Roanoke, on file at the Harrison Museum of African American Culture, museum annex. The report also details a two-room building, "the earliest colored school" called Old Lick School, a one-room log building opened in 1872.

v "She Touched On Us To Eternity," by Beth Macy, The Roanoke Times, Feb. 5, 2006.

vi From 1870 Franklin County census figures culled in "Oh, Master," a six-volume set of local African-American history compiled and self-published by Audrey Dudley and Diane Hayes: Four of 33 blacks with the surname of Muse could read and write; three of twenty resident blacks with the surname Dickenson/Dickerson (Harriett's maiden name) could read and write.

vii Author interview, Nancy Saunders, June 2, 2014.

viii Author interview, A.J. Reeves, Sept. 15, 2014.

ix A typical ad from The Billboard: "WANTED—Freaks, Curiosities for Pit Show," seeking a "fat man, lady midget, glass blower, magician, anything suitable for high-class Pit Show," from Sept. 13, 1919.

x The Billboard, April 25, 1914.

xi The black-owned Richmond Planet opined that the case "tells in no uncertain tones the prejudiced conditions existing in that community, and makes one wish in vain for the resurrection of those human beings hanged for a crime which possibly they never committed," Dec. 20, 1890.

xii Daily Virginian, Aug. 23, 1890.

xiii "Race and Violence in Urbanizing Appalachia: The Roanoke Riot of 1893," by Rand Dotson, a chapter from Bruce Stewart's Blood In the Hills (Lexington, Ky.: The University Press of Kentucky, 2012). Also recounted in Susan Lebsock's A Murder in Virginia: Southern Justice on Trial (New York: Norton & Company, 2003).

xiv " 'And the Harvest of Blood Commenced,' " by Dwayne Yancey, The Roanoke Times, Sept. 20, 1993.

Chapter One

xv Author interview, Richard L. Chubb, Oct. 16, 2014.

xvi Photograph printed on p. 185 of The Roanoke Valley's African American Heritage: A Pictorial History (Virginia Beach: Donning Company Publishers, 1996).

xvii Ibid.

xviii Author interview, Louise Burrell, talking about her albino mother, Sept. 22, 2014.

xix Author interview, Brian Sieveking, Sept. 2, 2014.

xx From Amram Sheinfeld's You and Heredity (New York: Frederick A. Stokes Company, 1939), p. 147.

xxi "Made with love for 12 years now, customers have been coming back for The Goody Shop's Southern Cooking," by Beth Macy, Roanoke Times, Jan. 9, 1991.

xxii Author interview, Frosty Landon, then editorial page editor, Oct. 13, 2014.

xxiii Leslie Fiedler's Freaks: Myths and Images of the Secret Self (New York: Anchor Books, 1978), p. 171.

You've just read an excerpt from Truevine.

ABOUT THE AUTHOR

Beth Macy writes about outsiders and underdogs, and she is the author of the *New York Times* bestseller, *Factory Man*. Her work has appeared in national magazines and newspapers and *The Roanoke Times*, where her reporting has won more than a dozen national awards, including a Nieman Fellowship for Journalism at Harvard and the Lukas Prize from the Columbia School of Journalism. She lives in Roanoke, VA.

IMPRINT: Little, Brown and Company
PRINT ISBN: 9780316337540
PRINT PRICE: $28.00
EBOOK ISBN: 9780316337564
EBOOK PRICE: $14.99
PUBLICATION DATE: 10/18/16
EDITOR: John Parsley
AGENT: Peter McGuigan
AGENCY: Foundry Literary Media

PROMOTIONAL INFORMATION:
National media campaign, including television, print, radio, and online interviews; Digital marketing/publicity campaign, including features and reviews, specialized blog outreach, and downloadable excerpts; Social media campaign, including Facebook, Twitter, Instagram, Tumblr, Pinterest, and Goodreads.

UNLOCK YOUR PERSONAL
GENETIC CODE
TO EAT FOR YOUR GENES,
Lose Weight, and Reverse Aging

THE DNA RESTART

SHARON MOALEM, MD, PhD
NEW YORK TIMES BESTSELLING AUTHOR OF *SURVIVAL OF THE SICKEST*

SUMMARY

In *The DNA Restart*, Sharon Moalem, MD, PhD, provides a revolutionary step-by-step guide to the diet and lifestyle perfect for your individual genetic makeup. A physician, scientist, neurogeneticist and *New York Times* best-selling author, Dr. Moalem has spent the last two decades researching and formulating how to reset your own genetic code using five essential pillars: eat for your genes, reverse aging, eat umami, drink oolong tea and slow living. The DNA Restart Plan utilizes decades of in-depth scientific research into genetics, epigenetics nutrition and longevity to explain the pivotal role genes play in the journey to ideal weight and health status. Dr. Moalem's unique 28-day plan shows how to upgrade sleep, harness sensory awareness, and use exercise to reset your DNA; how to determine the right amount of protein, carbs and fats you need for your individual genetic makeup; and how to incorporate umami-rich recipes and oolong teas into your diet to genetically thrive. Delicious recipes with mix-and-match meal plans, inspiring testimonials and genetic self-tests round out this paradigm-shifting diet book.

EXCERPT

Part One
The DNA Restart 1st Pillar
Eat for Your Genes

The DNA Restart is a completely new way for you to view your genetic inheritance. The 1st Pillar, Eat for Your Genes, will help launch your 28-day DNA Restart plan to completely transform your relationship with food and, most important, your relationship with your genes.

But let's be up front: It's not going to be easy.

As I'm sure you've discovered for yourself, most people who've lost weight by dieting don't keep the weight off over the long term. As a physician and scientist, I know that most diets fail because of two important flaws. The first is simply a mind-numbing restrictive lack of a variety of food and meal choices, making it impossible to stick to the diet in the long term.

The second and most important reason is that, until now, there hasn't been a single diet that is designed with every single person on this planet in mind. Deep down, modesty aside, you know full well that you are not like anyone else. Nor have you ever been. What this means on a genetic level is that although you may be very similar to other people, there's absolutely no one else exactly like you in the entire universe.

Not even close.

Far from being benign, eating for someone else's genes can be deadly. Take Thomas, for example. During high school and college he both ran and swam competitively and had no problems keeping his weight in check. But later, when he became a busy father with two young kids at home and a demanding professional life that saw him traveling often, he found that he had little time left over for personal self-care like exercise. He rarely, if ever, donned his sneakers or found the time to hit the pool for an early morning swim. This lack of exercise combined with still eating the way he did in college left Thomas with an ever-increasing waistline. At the age of 47, Thomas now found himself the not-so-proud owner of a dreaded and bloated midlife beer belly.

After struggling to get into his business suit one morning, and being barely able to button his pants, Thomas decided on the spot that he'd had enough. It was time for him to make a change. He knew that if he didn't make some serious lifestyle modifications soon, he'd end up just like his two brothers, who both had diabetes and were in the early stages of heart disease.

With newfound motivation, Thomas was able to tap into the same dedication and physical persistence he had shown during his athletic youth and began to find his stride. With the help of a personal trainer, Thomas started off slowly at first. Within a year, he was back at the gym almost daily, both swimming and running six times a week. He also made significant dietary changes that included cutting out all cereal grains and substantially increasing his intake of protein. It took another year after that, but Thomas was now back at a level of physical performance he couldn't have dreamed of 2 years earlier. And one of the added benefits was that his love handles and dreaded beer belly were now a thing of the past. In their place was a peak athlete who now fixed his sights on qualifying for the Ironman World Championship competition in Hawaii just before his 50th birthday.

That's when Thomas's energy levels unexpectedly started to change. It was just barely perceptible in the beginning; his wife was the first to notice that he wasn't able to jump out of bed for his early morning swim with his usual vigor. This was followed by increasing feelings of fatigue no matter how much he slept. Within 6 months Thomas found himself completely and thoroughly physically exhausted without any good explanation. Maybe he was training too hard, or maybe his body just wasn't up for the challenge. When he found himself consistently unable to get up before his family for his early morning run, Thomas decided it was finally time to seek some medical help and made an appointment to see his doctor. After getting a clean bill of health from his physician, Thomas was at a loss for what to do next. Not having the energy to train any longer, he found himself becoming more and more depressed, his hopes of qualifying for the Ironman World Championship fading with each passing week.

What Thomas could not have known at the time was that his dietary changes were singularly responsible for his deteriorated health status. It was only after he took the leap of faith and did the DNA Restart that he discovered why he was feeling so ill. The reason was simple: No one, including his trainer who had recommended the high-protein diet in the first place, was thinking about Thomas's DNA. If they had, they would have discovered that by eating more protein in the form of red meat, Thomas was slowly but surely rusting to death.

The reason that Thomas became sick, as I was to discover and explain to him later, was not at all his fault. The answer was to be found in his genes. That's because Thomas unknowingly inherited versions of a gene called *HFE* that result in a condition called hereditary hemochromatosis.

People with this condition absorb way too much iron from their diets. In Thomas's case, the condition was made worse when he began to eat even more red meat, causing him to eventually literally rust from the inside out. All of that extra dietary iron builds up in the organs of people with hereditary hemochromatosis. Unchecked, this internal rusting can lead to things like cancer, heart disease, and diabetes. Thomas discovered the reason for his health deterioration through the DNA Restart, which gave him the knowledge to start eating for his genes. He also learned that his hemochromatosis wasn't the only reason his health was suffering. Through the DNA Restart genetic self-tests, he discovered that he actually had the genetic capacity to eat more carbohydrates. He has now significantly reduced his intake of red meat while reintroducing whole cereal grains and legumes, and the results speak for themselves. This increased carb allowance helped fuel his rigorous daily training program and road to recovery—a big surprise to both Thomas and his trainer. Thomas's energy levels are fully restored, and he let me know recently that he was able to not only qualify for but complete his first Ironman World Championship event. Not a small feat.

Up until now, there never has been a bespoke diet created and tailored for only your unique genetic needs. You have actually never once intentionally and methodically eaten for your genes.

That's about to change. I've created signature DNA Restart self-tests that are designed to hit upon the highest-yielding scientifically based results, and you can do these tests easily at home. And just like the multitude of DNA Restarters who have experienced the power of eating for their genes by employing the DNA Restart selftests, once you start eating for your genes, you'll never want to go back to eating genetically blind again.

Another added benefit of the DNA Restart self-tests is that you control what to do with the results. Most people are not aware that there is currently no universal US federal protection against genetic discrimination. This means that every time you subject yourself to a genetic test with a third party, there's no guarantee that your genetic information or results will remain private. The Genetic Information and Nondiscrimination Act (GINA) is limited in the types of protection it can provide you. Many people are shocked to find out that they may have absolutely no protection from genetic discrimination in matters of disability and life insurance. Some US states have been seeking to fill in the discrimination gaps left open by GINA, but there remains much work to be done. Please carefully consider this and keep it in mind when you consider any genetic testing done with a third party.

This is why I've created genetic self-tests that you can do at home without putting yourself at risk for future discrimination. Your genes belong to you, and your genetic information should not be available for others to access without your permission.

Chapter One
Why You Should Eat for Your Very Own Genes

The first and most important genetic self-test that I'm going to introduce you to is an incredibly powerful tool that will allow you to individualize your carbohydrate intake levels. The results of this first self-test will help you find out which one of three carbohydrate consumption categories you fall into.

Until recently it was assumed that we all inherited a copy of each gene, one from each parent. And that's why it was thought that you have two copies of every gene. Oh, how wrong we were. It turns out that some of us have a little more or less DNA than others. And far from being insignificant, the number of copies of genes you've inherited can have a tremendous impact on your life and health.

To get more nutritional horsepower out of your genome, for example, an ancestor of yours might have gifted you with multiple copies of a certain gene. Instead of the usual two copies of a gene, you may have inherited even a dozen copies or more. The technical term for this phenomenon is *copy number variation,* or CNV, and it seems that this has happened at many different times and places in our evolutionary history.[2] We all vary in the number of some of the genes that we have inherited—even within the same family.

Okay, so why should you care today how many copies of a gene you may have inherited from a specific ancestor thousands of years ago?

Because many of these variations in the number of specific genes you've inherited were passed on from your ancestors as an advantage when eating certain things for breakfast, lunch, or dinner. That dietary advantage for the specific nutritional environment would then be passed on and maintained down a specific genetic ancestral line. And as you're going to discover yourself, the copy number of certain genes you inherit plays a very important role in determining your optimal diet today. Using this information, you can follow an individualized diet that will help you get to and stay at your ideal weight, painlessly. And most importantly, it will do this while improving your overall health and increasing your genetic longevity. You'll gain all of these benefits simply because you understand your unique CNV when it comes to certain genes and how that should dictate your dietary choices. See why you should care?

That's why for the most part doing what others do when it comes to diet and lifestyle may be perfectly fine for them, but over a lifetime of bad genetic decision making, the consequences can even turn deadly for you.

Since the first complete draft of the human genome was published back in 2001, we are becoming more aware that the most striking and impactful genetic differences between us are actually found in genes that impact our diet. The way our bodies digest and use energy from the food we eat depends more upon what your recent genetic ancestors ate than we ever imagined. And these genetic differences can have an incredibly powerful influence on not just our basic nutritional needs but also on the amount of carbohydrates we can eat, down to the ability for us to either thrive or wilt upon consuming a large amount of protein.

To illustrate the importance of how genetic differences between people can affect what they should be eating, I have often asked my patients what type of fuel they use to power their cars. Here's why: Some makes and models require a high-grade gasoline while others can get by with the lowest and cheapest type around. Others even require a special type of fuel such as diesel or propane while some cars are now powered by electricity alone. When it comes to your car, you find out which type of fuel to use by consulting your vehicle's owner's manual.

Now you might think that we weren't born with a similar type of instructional manual. Or worse, you think or have been told that a manual like that might exist and that it would be applicable to *all* of us. In fact, what you have within you is incredibly more detailed and impressively individualized. I'm talking about a three-billion-letter genetic code that is full of individualized and unique wisdom that was collected and annotated over millennia *just for you*. Every nutritional adaptation that allowed your genetic ancestor to survive long enough to pass on that knowledge to his or her own children is in there—a veritable genetic tapestry gifted to you from every direct genetic ancestor you have ever had.

That tapestry when it's spread out is very, very large: about three billion genetic letters or nucleotides' worth making up your genome. And you actually have two genomes—one from your mother and one from your father, which is why you're not identical to either one. Within our genomes we also each have somewhere in the ballpark of 20,000 genes that do most of the genetic heavy lifting in our bodies. Nearly every single one of your trillion cells has an entire copy of your genome inside it.[3] That's how the folks on *CSI* were able to identify people with only a very small sample of hair or tissue.

Most of the knowledge within your own DNA is on genetic autopilot, requiring little conscious input from you as your cells use it on a moment-to-moment basis to keep you alive. But if you really want to start to eat for your genes, you're going to have to learn to speak their language. That's why I've devised a few crucial at-home self-tests in the DNA Restart that will help you start decoding your own unique genetic inheritance. This information is required so that you can eat for a better, longer, healthier life.

I've also included a few case studies of patients and colleagues to illustrate the power of what can happen when you finally start to eat for your own genes and stop eating for everyone else's. This is your life. Let's get you started on your way to eating for your genes.

Chapter Two
Why Some People Can Thrive on Carbs: The Saliva-Carb Connection

You may not pay much attention to your saliva, but it's a veritable cocktail of proteins and enzymes that have been fine-tuned to begin the process of digestion long before your food hits your belly. You can think of enzymes that are involved in digestion like kitchen appliances. Just like some people have kitchens without any appliances while other people have ones that are decked with the latest high-power culinary gadgets, we all differ in the types of genetic tools found in our saliva and that we have inherited to help us break down and digest our food.

Most people have an enzyme within their saliva called amylase, which, like a giant pair of shearing scissors, has the ability to cut apart big and bulky starch molecules into simpler sugars. That's the first step in making big threads of starch molecules available for the body to use easily as energy. And amylase is really good at cutting up starch. Don't believe me? If you're curious to see just how powerful amylase is, add your own saliva to a full jar of a starch-rich baby food like pureed bananas and put it back in the fridge. By the morning, the entire jar should be liquefied!

Some of us have supercharged saliva that's just waiting to cut apart the carbohydrates we eat by being packed full of amylase (saliva that's turbocharged can have up to 50 times more amylase). As it turns out, researchers were surprised to discover that we're not all endowed with the same amount of amylase in our saliva. Some people were actually found not to have any at all!

Remember what I told you about copy number variation? Well, you may or may not have inherited multiple copies of the gene your body uses to make the protein amylase, called *AMY1*. And the more copies of *AMY1* you've inherited from your parents, the more amylase you have in your saliva right now.

There are three things that really surprised researchers about the *AMY1* gene.

The first was that there's an incredible degree of variability when it comes to how many copies of *AMY1* people inherited. Some people have none, while others have as many as 20! That's copy number variation for you: If you have multiple copies of amylase, you are lucky enough to speedily burn through and digest a tremendous amount of starch while still only chewing your food.

Have no copies of *AMY1*? Well, your saliva will suffer for it because it will contain no amylase, making the task of breaking down carbohydrates metabolically daunting for your body.

Sometimes genetics can be that simple.

A similar genetic evolution is behind skin color: The darker your skin, the more your ancestors needed to be protected from the DNA-damaging radiation of the blaring overhead sun. And so it turns out, just like the color of your skin, the number of *AMY1* genes you've inherited is not random either.

It is actually highly dependent upon *where* your own unique genetic ancestors hail from. Okay, let me simplify all that: If you come from ancestors who relied heavily on starches, such as farmers growing and consuming cereal grains, you'll likely have been gifted with multiple copies of *AMY1* that can make tons of amylase in your saliva. If your recent genetic ancestors, on the other hand, were more into meat than potatoes, then the number of amylase genes you've inherited from them—not so much.

This is why one of the biggest genetic differences between you and your best friend will likely be in the genes that are in some way involved in the foods you should or should not be eating. Likewise, that's why the levels of amylase in your saliva will not be the same as someone else's with whom you may be sharing a meal. The more starch your ancestors ate in their daily diet over generations, the more copies of *AMY1* genes you've inherited. It's as simple as that. And these genetic differences and the duplicating of the *AMY1* in some of our ancestors I believe really kicked off with the domestication of grains in the last 10,000 years. There's good reason for this since a historical shift to a higher intake of carbohydrates through the consumption of cereal grains would be aided, as I'm about to show you, by having more copies of the amylase-producing *AMY1* gene.

If your ancestors switched to eating more cereal grains such as wheat and rice, you're much more likely to have inherited multiple copies of the *AMY1* gene with every generation. That's just the way genetics works. But you may be wondering: If it's useful to have multiple copies of *AMY1*, why didn't we all evolve to have them? The answer has to do with what I like to call biological home economics. Imagine that your genes are like employees who require a salary to work. The more copies of a gene you inherit, the more you will have to pay them to have them work for you. But if there's not much starch-digesting work to do because your ancestor is not spending his time eating bread and rice every day, then there's not much starch for the amylase from the *AMY1* gene to break down. So what then? The way biology works is that it would rather you not have to go and needlessly expand your genetic workforce with more copies of *AMY1* genes and instead save all of that biological energy to spend on other important physiological functions.

If all this wasn't enough for you to want to jump right in and find out how many copies of *AMY1* you might have inherited and how much amylase you correspondingly have in your own saliva, there's still one significant thing you need to know.

And here's the real kicker about amylase. You'd think that if you have saliva overflowing with amylase from additional copies of *AMY1*, then a carbohydrate meal would send you soaring into a sugar rush high because all that starch gets almost instantly converted to more sugars such as maltose (which is a disaccharide on its way to eventually becoming a simpler sugar like glucose). If that were the case, this would mean that people who have many copies of *AMY1* would not fare well eating a lot of carbohydrates because they'd be digesting starches much faster, which would send them barreling down a road to eventually higher risk for insulin resistance and obesity.

As it turns out, your body is more clever and interesting than anyone had ever imagined. As scientists from Monell Chemical Senses Center in Philadelphia together with colleagues from Rutgers University in New Brunswick, New Jersey, discovered to their surprise, the reverse actually happened: People with more amylase because of multiple copies of the *AMY1* gene had *lower* levels of glucose than people with fewer copies of *AMY1*, who had *higher* levels of glucose. On the surface, of course, this doesn't make much sense since people with more amylase are better and faster at digesting starches, which would mean that their glucose levels should be spiking.

But what they saw was the exact opposite.

Here's what made their experiment really clever: They also decided to measure the participants' insulin levels. Insulin is the hormone that helps shuttle glucose into cells so that they can use it for energy. And that's how the researchers got their answer. The people with more copies of *AMY1* were much quicker and more responsive to produce insulin in anticipation of the coming flood of sugars. So they were much better prepared—kind of like when Amazon hires more workers in anticipation of the yearly online holiday crush.

I believe that eating out of sync with our genes is the reason why some people are more prone to developing obesity and insulin resistance than others on a diet that's relatively high in starch/carbohydrates. In fact, research is now beginning to back this exact view as it's been found that people with the *lowest* copy number of the *AMY1* gene are actually much more likely to be obese.

When you take the long view—the one that biology loves to take—then this is completely in line with what you would expect. After all, when it comes to survival, having the ability to break down and deal with sugars released from eating a predominantly carbohydrate-based diet is a good thing for people who eat that kind of diet on a regular basis.

The lower the number of AMY1 genes (each one represented here as a black box) you've inherited from your parents, the more likely you are to be obese when eating a carb-heavy diet dominantly carbohydrate-based diet is a good thing for people who eat that kind of diet on a regular basis.

WHY SOME PEOPLE CAN THRIVE ON CARBS: THE SALIVA-CARB CONNECTION

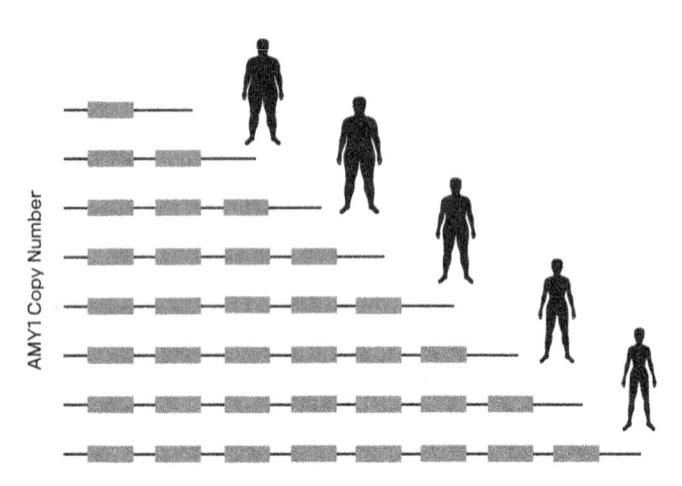

*The lower the number of **AMY1** genes (each one represented here as a black box) you've inherited from your parents, the more likely you are to be obese when eating a carb-heavy diet.*

The downside, of course, is when you didn't inherit many copies of the *AMY1* gene and still try to eat a lot of carbs. Very likely you will end up obese or diabetic or even both. So knowing how much amylase is in your saliva can be incredibly powerful to get you eating just the right amount of carbs. Yet be warned that no matter what genes you've inherited, if you're exposing yourself or your family to products that are needlessly loaded with carbs (think of the entire processed food sections of your local supermarket), your waistline will eventually become thoroughly ravaged no matter how many copies of *AMY1* you've inherited.

Honey is the one shining example of a simple carbohydrate sweetener that you are encouraged to enjoy on the DNA Restart. Filled to the brim with phytochemicals and antioxidants, honey was also the first antibiotic ointment used by your ancestors, who recognized its microbe-killing potential 4,000 years before the discovery of penicillin. I've spent many years looking for new microbe-killing compounds in different varieties of honey. Some of these honey-derived compounds, such as methyl syringate and methylglyoxal, have been shown to kill bacteria such as

Helicobacter pylori, which can cause duodenal ulcers and even gastric cancer. Honey has even been shown to kill antibiotic-resistant "superbug" bacteria such as methicillin-resistant *Staphylococcus aureus,* or MRSA. For all these reasons and more, you can have a maximum of 2 teaspoons of honey every day during your 28-day DNA Restart. When purchasing honey, look for some that hasn't been heated or filtered, and choose the one that appears the most viscous. If you don't mind a stronger taste, look for a darker-colored honey. As you'll see later as well, I've incorporated honey into some of the DNA Restart Recipes.

Unlike honey, processed sugars aren't just empty calories; they lack essential antioxidant and antimicrobial phytonutrients, which are crucial to sustain and nurture your body and DNA. That's why irrespective of your *AMY1* gene copy number, all processed sugars are banned on the DNA Restart.

No More Soft Drinks Ever
If you're looking to gain a lot of weight and make yourself insulin resistant at the same time, make sure to consume as many regular soft drinks as you can. One of the most common causes of obesity in my patients was from the overconsumption of liquid calories. What a waste! This phenomenon, of course, was not limited to my practice but has been chronicled as one of the leading vanguards in the obesity epidemic.

Obviously, drinking empty calories is not a good idea. And if you think you're doing yourself a really big favor by having a diet soda now and then, think again. As a society, we are consuming a convoy of tanker trucks full of artificial sweeteners every year. And we have absolutely no idea what the long-term health effects are of a lifetime of consuming this amount of sweeteners.

Or do we?

Studies are starting to trickle in that I and many of my scientific colleagues believe will turn into a flood of anything but sweet conclusions concerning the long-term health risks and consequences of consuming both sugar and artificially sweetened beverages, which also include coffee and tea. As for sugary drinks, by now it's fairly clear that consuming them in excess is in fact linked to developing Type 2 diabetes. But hold on a minute because this is where things get interesting.

℞ **DNA Restart Health Tip #1**
You are welcome to enjoy a maximum of 2 teaspoons of honey every day.
No processed sugar consumption allowed.

Honey is not just another form of sugar. It contains a very special combination of phytochemicals (which includes powerful antimicrobials and antioxidants) derived from all of the millions of flowers and trees honeybees needed to visit to make it. There are about 35,000 flowers in every teaspoon of honey!

Lost 15 pounds during my DNA Restart without even trying that hard! Finding out that my Carb Intake Category was Restricted kept me on track over the 28 days when planning my meals.

—Natalie, 39

If you happen to be following the advice of numerous health agencies and replacing your sugar-laden drinks with their diet equivalent, you probably think that these "diet" drinks are going to protect you from developing diabetes. Well, researchers at the University of Cambridge recently published findings from a study that addressed this very issue by following the habits of more than 25,000 people in the United Kingdom over a 4-year period. What they found was that even if you do replace sugar-sweetened drinks like soft drinks and tea and coffee with artificially sweetened ones, you still do not lower your overall risk of developing Type 2 diabetes. In fact, the only way to really lower your risk for developing Type 2 diabetes is to switch to drinking unsweetened coffee or tea or having good old plain water. Why this is the case is still not clear.

What I think is happening is that consuming artificial sweeteners is taxing your metabolic system. Just like your taste buds, your body is being fooled by a sweet taste that never materializes as sugar in any of its forms. It's as if your cells are getting ready for sex, with a lot of sweet foreplay, but no actual sugary fornication ever takes place. So over years of consumption, it's possible that your body stops listening to sweet hormonal signals from artificial sweeteners. After they've experienced so much rejection and disappointment, who can blame your cells for giving up and stubbornly becoming insulin resistant, the hallmark of Type 2 diabetes?

If you're truly keen on avoiding untold risks to your health, what alternatives do you really have? Maybe I'm a little more cautious than some health agencies out there. But why take part in this research, when you're totally free to opt out?

That's why on the DNA Restart you are expressly barred from the consumption of any artificial sweeteners. But I'm not just going to leave your active beverage life totally high and dry because Pillar 4 on the DNA Restart is all about a health-enhancing alternative drink that will change your waistline, microbiome, and much more.

You'd have to be hiding under a rock to not be aware of the dangers associated with things such as sugar-sweetened beverages like soft drinks, fruit juices, and even chocolate milk. So not surprisingly, none of those extraneous sugars are allowed on the DNA Restart. But don't even think about this now, as I'll be delving into what you can and cannot have on the DNA Restart in greater detail in the 2nd Pillar.

DNA Restart Health Tip #2
No sugar substitutes—whatsoever! Here's an easy list to watch out for.

1. Acesulfame K
2. Aspartame
3. Cyclamate
4. Neotame
5. Saccharine
6. Stevia
7. Sucralose
8. Sugar alcohols, such as xylitol

There are very good reasons for some of the vilification of having too many carbohydrates in our diets. Most of the carbs widely available today in their hyper-processed forms would be unrecognizable to *all* of our genetic ancestors, but they don't seem to be affecting all of us in the same ways. This is another important reason why you should be eating for your genes. Why should you be eating carbs like anyone else? It's time that you start eating carbs with your *AMY1* genes as your guide.

So let's get practical! What I've designed with the DNA Restart Cracker Self-Test is a way to finally eat the amount of carbohydrates that's in line with the number of *AMY1* genes you've inherited. The results from this self-test will place you in one of the three Carbohydrate Consumption Categories. After you complete the self-test, I will be giving you the individualized meal plans, including a few recipes and eating advice that will be tailored for your very own DNA Restart.

Let's get your carb intake aligned with your genes!

Chapter Three
The DNA Restart Cracker Self-Test
In this pillar, Eat for Your Genes, we're going to be unpacking key parts of your own genome at home with a few genetic self-tests, which I've designed just for you. The first genetic self-test will be the DNA Restart Cracker Self-Test. Results from this experiment will indicate how much amylase you have in your saliva and, through that result, about how many copies of the *AMY1* gene you've inherited from your parents.

What You'll Need for the DNA Restart Cracker Self-Test:
1. One saltine cracker (must be unsalted) or, if you're following a gluten-free diet, a dime-size piece of raw peeled potato

2. A timer

3. A pen or electronic device for your note taking

Dna Restart Cracker Self-Test: Let's Do It!
Get your cracker ready (or if you're gluten free, a dime-size piece of raw peeled potato) as well as a timer and something to take notes with. Make sure that your saltine cracker is unsalted, as the self-test requires it. Now break the cracker approximately in half, or if you're using a piece of raw potato, have it ready and place either one in front of you. The goal of the DNA Restart Cracker Self-Test is to find out which of the three carbohydrate consumption categories you fall into: Full, Moderate, or Restricted. You will get this information by the amount of time it takes for a change in taste to occur when you're chewing either the saltine cracker or potato. The longer you're chewing, the more likely the taste will change. If you never detect a change in taste, that's normal (and significant!), too. To

ensure that you get the most accurate results, you'll be running through the experiment three times and averaging the results.

Now get your timer out (most phones have at least one app for this function). Whenever you're ready, place the cracker or potato in your mouth and start timing and chewing. You'll need to pay really close attention now as the starch in the cracker or potato may already be starting to be digested by amylase in your saliva. If you feel yourself wanting to swallow, that's perfectly normal, but try to stop yourself. Try to imagine that you're simply chewing a piece of gum as you keep chewing.

As soon as you detect a change in taste or if you reach 30 seconds while timing, stop chewing, swallow, and note the time. Rerun the same self-test two more times. Now I want you to add up the three times and divide by three so that you can get to your DNA Restart Carbohydrate Consumption Category. Take your combined score and have a look at the following table to find your personal Carbohydrate Consumption Category.

The DNA Restart Cracker Self-Test:
Carbohydrate Consumption Categories

Time in Seconds for Taste Change	Carbohydrate Consumption Category
0–14	Full
Between 15–30	Moderate
More than 30	Restricted

It's important to note that this will be your guide for how much carbohydrate you should be having throughout your 28-day DNA Restart. From here you go to the Carbohydrate Consumption Estimate Guide, which will give you the specifics of your daily carb cost as a percentage and in grams.

The DNA Restart Carbohydrate Consumption Estimate Guide

Your Carbohydrate Consumption Category	Carbohydrate Intake* for Women in Grams	Carbohydrate Intake** for Men in Grams	Percentage of Carbohydrate Intake	Carb Cost Allowance in Points
Full	250	325	50%	13–16
Moderate	175	230	35%	9–12
Restricted	125	165	25%	5–8

*This is assuming an approximate average caloric intake of 2,000 kilocalories per day.
**This is assuming an approximate average caloric intake of 2,600 kilocalories per day.

Remember that these numbers are meant purely as an estimated guide, since your focus for the next 28 days will be to bring your life in line with your DNA and not to count calories. That being said, if you really want the weight to come off, you're going to have to be diligent regarding the amount and quality of food you eat. Today, we are all consuming more food than our DNA thrives on. Overeating literally stresses the body, which hurts our genes, saps our youth, and reduces our longevity. To make matters worse, our food has been stripped of essential phytonutrients and minerals, which used to nourish and strengthen our DNA. Pillars 1 through 5 of the DNA Restart have been designed to bring your life back in line with your genes.

Now if you're a visual type of person, I've also provided you with the pie charts below to give you the dietary breakdown for fats, proteins, and carbs.

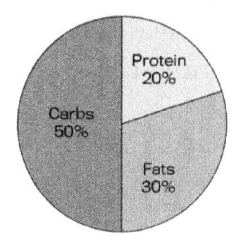

If your DNA Restart Carb Category is Full, you can have up to 50 percent of your calories coming from carbs, 20 percent from protein, and 30 percent from fats.

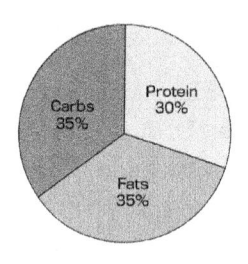

If your DNA Restart Carb Category is Moderate, you can have up to 35 percent of your calories coming from carbs, 30 percent from protein, and 35 percent from fats.

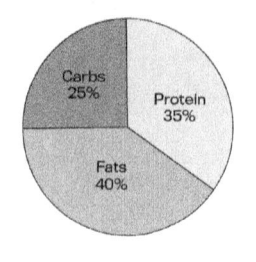

If your DNA Restart Carb Category came out to be Restricted, you can have up to 25 percent of your calories coming from carbs, 35 percent from protein, and 40 percent from fats.

☐ Protein ▦ Fats ■ Carbs

I've been struggling with Type 2 diabetes for more than 10 years. I got my diabetes under so much better control using the results from my DNA Restart Self-Tests and DNA Restart Carb Cost system guide. My doctor couldn't believe it and neither could I.
—Ryan, 64

I've also created a DNA Restart Carb Cost allowance guide so that you can effectively keep track and stay on top of your weekly carb dietary intake (see Chapter 43). The list I've provided has both common cereal grains and a few vegetables and their corresponding carb cost. The Carb Cost allowance system is meant to be a guide to get you to eat more in line with your DNA as per your results from your self-test; it is not meant to be a definitive list of all the food that may contain carbohydrates.

Here's how to calculate your weekly carb cost allowance:

1. Take the DNA Restart Cracker Self-Test on page 000.

2. Find your Carbohydrate Consumption Category from the results of your cracker self-test on page 000.

3. Your carb cost is like your weekly allowance for you to buy the carbs you need. Just make sure that you stay within your allowance budget for the week!

Carb Cost Allowance Breakdown:
Full Carbs: 13 to 16 points of carbs per week

Moderate Carbs: 9 to 12 points of carbs per week

Restricted Carbs: 5 to 8 points of carbs per week

Each recipe I've included in the back of the book will have modifications so that it can be enjoyed to the max by people in all three categories.

Chapter Four
What Happens When You Don't Eat for Your Genes?
Fiona was in her early thirties and desperately trying to get pregnant. She had never really thought seriously about starting a family, but all that changed for her when she met Will during her training in clinical psychology at the University of Pennsylvania. Most of the last decade and a half was devoted to working to complete her training, but now, as a newly

minted psychologist, she found a blossoming desire to have a child with Will, who had finished his law degree 2 years prior.

For the most part Fiona was always healthy, with the occasional bout of stomach pains that oscillated between loose stools and constipation that she attributed to the stress from the rigors of her program. And so they tried to conceive naturally at first, but with no success.

They often laughed at the irony that after many years of working so hard to avoid getting pregnant, now the tables had turned and they were doubling their efforts in their attempt to have a child. The first year was up, and with not even a small sign of a pregnancy in the making, they sought some medical advice from a local reproductive doctor. After making an appointment and going through the initial medical screening—a sperm count for Will and blood tests for both—they were scheduled to see the doctor and get the results.

The news for the most part was good. Their doctor said that all the tests came back normal, besides a little microcytic anemia and low ferritin on Fiona's part, which can be common in menstruating women of her age. She suggested that Fiona add an iron supplement to her diet or see a nutritionist they had on staff to get some nutritional advice. Other than that, there wasn't anything of real concern.

The doctor then discussed their options, including whether they still wanted to keep trying on their own. Perhaps they would increase their odds at a successful pregnancy by timing their sex with Fiona's ovulation. This sounded like the most reasonable option at the time for Fiona and Will. The doctor ended the visit with a gentle reminder that once some women reach their midthirties, their odds for a natural pregnancy start to decline precipitously. So they shouldn't spend too much time contemplating other options, as time wasn't on their side.

As her doctor had advised, Fiona made a follow-up appointment with the nutritionist on staff and spent more than an hour filling out a very exhaustive dietary questionnaire. She was happy to have seen the nutritionist because she actually confirmed that Fiona was eating a well-balanced diet. The only real suggestions were, given Fiona's anemia, to try to increase her dietary intake of iron and definitely increase her fiber consumption from whole cereal grains to help her become a little more regular.

Before they knew it, another year passed for Fiona and Will. They agreed that after trying for this long, they should return to the reproductive health clinic.

That's where I came in. Will e-mailed me that evening to see if I had any other suggestions or advice for them to maximize their chances of a successful pregnancy, and we scheduled a time to speak the next week. I first met him a few years prior when he was in New York City working at a small law firm. We spent a few minutes catching up, and then he let me know why he was calling. I mentioned to Will that there was some genetic testing they could consider, but for the most part their reproductive clinic had a great reputation, and the advice they were being given was medically sound. I asked Will a few more questions about Fiona's health. "You know, ever since she changed her diet, her anemia hasn't improved at all since the last time she checked, and she's been having much more stomach issues than I remember her having in the past. I thought that might be because of, you know, all the stress of trying to get pregnant."

I reflected quietly on everything Will had just shared with me for a moment before asking, "Will, does she eat gluten?"

"Yeah of course, she loves everything with gluten," replied Will.

This led to a lengthy conversation between us about the little-known silent symptom of celiac disease, and then some follow-up testing on Fiona, which conclusively proved that she was, in fact, fully gluten intolerant.

What's interesting is that with the rise in public awareness of celiac disease, many more people are aware of the havoc gluten can cause your gut if you have the disease, but they have no idea that it can cause serious fertility issues for those suffering without a proper diagnosis and subsequent dietary changes. Another little-known fact is that celiac disease can cause anemia, like it did for Fiona, which had nothing to do with the amount of iron she was getting in her diet but rather the intestinal changes that happened because of celiac. Without a diagnosis, there would just be no way of knowing that those daily iron supplements weren't actually being absorbed and used by her body.

The good news about Fiona and Will is that with the proper diagnosis of celiac disease, which included an intestinal biopsy, and the avoidance of all things gluten, it was possible to become fertile once again. And that's just what Fiona and Will happily discovered; they're now expecting their second child.

Classical cases of celiac disease are thought to have a genetic component. Most people with celiac disease have some type of shared Western European ancestry with two genes in particular, *HLA DQ-2* and *HLA DQ-8*, figuring as prime suspects. But not everyone with those or the multitude of other genes that have been implicated go on to develop celiac disease. There are screening tests for celiac disease—the most commonly available is the immunoglobulin A tissue transglutaminase, or tTG-IgA test—but for this type of testing to be meaningful, ironically, you must be eating lots of gluten.

The way to a diagnosis is usually from a tissue biopsy, where a piece of tissue is taken directly from a patient's small intestine, but as I said, you need to be eating gluten. Even with today's increased awareness of celiac disease, many people just like Fiona regrettably still go undiagnosed. Part of the reason may be the chameleon-like nature of the condition's symptoms, which can include everything from bloating to iron deficiency anemia, joint pain, fatigue, anxiety, and even infertility, like we saw with Fiona.

So you might be thinking by now that as part of the 28-day DNA Restart plan, I'm going to have you go gluten free.

The simple answer to that is no.

Though gluten is much maligned, and rightfully so in people with celiac disease, for the most part I believe that when gluten-tolerant people throw out all things "gluten," we are excluding a great source of nutrition from our daily dietary life (more on this in Pillar 2: Reverse Aging). This is especially true when you consider what I told you about the evolution of duplications of the amylase-producing gene, *AMY1*. There's no doubt some of us have definitely inherited genes that allow us today to safely and healthily eat more carbohydrates.

These carbohydrates can come from many sources—including whole cereal grains—some of which contain gluten. But not all cereal grains contain gluten. Rice, amaranth, and quinoa, for example, are naturally Gluten free. The most important question when it comes to gluten is why are so many people finding themselves sensitive today?

History Of Celiac Disease

Celiac disease is anything but a recent condition. That probably makes a lot of sense since experts believe it was more than 10,000 years ago that cereal crops such as barley and wheat were first domesticated. And that's a long time when it comes to diet and genetic adaptation. Many of the crops first grown in the area aptly referred to as the Fertile Crescent helped provide the caloric energy to fuel many of the world's great ancient civilizations, such as the Babylonian and Assyrian empires. This region spanned an incredibly large area in what is today modern Iraq, through to Israel, and all the way to the Nile delta, which is in modern day Egypt.

The first recorded case of celiac disease was described by a Greco-Roman physician named Aretaeus of Cappadocia, who lived about 1,800 years ago in what is now Turkey. Aretaeus named the condition *koiliakos*, a Greek word, meant to describe the abdominal suffering that his patients were feeling, and what millions of people since who suffer from celiac disease would unfortunately understand really well.

Today we consider celiac disease to be an autoimmune disease that is thought to affect around 1 percent of the world's population. Yet it took all the way until the 20th century for an actual celiac-gluten connection to be established. In 1950, Willem Dicke published his doctoral thesis describing how when afflicted patients were given strict diets, and stopped eating foods that contained gluten such as wheat and rye, their symptoms would improve.

We still do not fully understand why some people develop celiac disease. What we do know is that depending upon where your ancestors hail from—Western Europe seems to be a genetic hot spot—you might be at a higher risk for celiac disease. As I told Fiona, there are many genes that have been associated with celiac disease, with two genes in particular, *HLA DQ-2* and *HLA DQ-8,* as prime suspects. However, not everyone with these genes goes on to develop celiac disease, and it seems that there might be environmental factors that trigger the condition when a susceptible person is exposed to gluten.

In one of my previous books, *Survival of the Sickest*,[5] I described in great detail my theory that many common medical conditions are complicated "blessings." You may have inherited genes that predispose you to a condition such as high cholesterol, which offered your genetic ancestors some type of benefit or protection and allowed for their survival.

℞ DNA Restart Health Tip #3
Here's a list of cereal grains that contain gluten.

1. Barley	7. Oats (can be contaminated with gluten during processing)
2. Bulgur	
3. Farina	8. Rye
4. Farro	9. Semolina
5. Freekeh	10. Spelt
6. Kamut	11. Triticale
	12. Wheat

℞ DNA Restart Health Tip #4
Here's a list of grains that do not contain gluten.

1. Amaranth	6. Quinoa
2. Buckwheat	7. Rice
3. Fonio	8. Sorghum
4. Millet	9. Teff
5. Oats (gluten-free certified)	10. Wild rice

So, are there any benefits to having celiac disease? Actually, a theory has been proposed that Western Europeans are much more likely to get celiac disease because it made them anemic,[6] one of the complications of the condition. That may not make sense initially, but we now know definitively, with only rare exceptions, that all pathogenic bacteria are actually after your body's iron. This metal is the reason you get a fungal or bacterial infection in the first place. The more iron you have, the tastier a meal you would make in the eyes of pathogenic microbes (more on this later). This is why the better your body is at hiding its iron, the greater its ability to fight infections. I have spent the last 20 years investigating the biological and health implications of dietary metals, especially heavy metals like iron. Finally, after all those years, my research findings led me to discover a new antibiotic, the first in a new class of antibiotics that has been developed in more than 2 decades, that specifically targets "superbug" or resistant microbes like MRSA by interfering in the way they get and use iron. Since this discovery, I have stopped seeing patients and been devoting my time and energy to developing powerful clinical interventions that have the potential to improve the quality of millions of people's health and life.

So believe me, iron is a big deal: More than 50 million Europeans are thought to have died because of it due to the Bubonic Plague's many marches across Europe, beginning in the 14th century. Not everyone died, meaning some people survived. And it could very well be that the lack of iron, caused by celiac disease, would have helped play a small role to ensure the survival of some Western Europeans.

The Flip Side: When Gluten Isn't The Problem
Celiac disease is not the only example of a condition where your body may have a problem with wheat. Sneezing, sniffles, and headaches can be symptoms of hay fever, but they can also be caused by a wheat allergy. This is an example of when the body overreacts to something in the environment that is usually not harmful, in this case wheat, and tries to fight it off as if it's a foreign invader.

It's not known exactly how common wheat allergies are, but they're thought to be less common than celiac disease in America. The immunological quarrelsomeness that causes wheat allergies is the result of the body making an IgE antibody against proteins that are found in wheat, just like what happens when you have a pollen, dust, or mite allergy, and this reaction then drives all of the symptoms of the condition.

If you think that you may be suffering from a wheat allergy, it's really important that you see an allergist to get tested. If you are diagnosed with an allergy to wheat and not celiac disease, then you shouldn't limit yourself or your family to a gluten-free dietary existence. Why not be able to eat rye and other whole cereal grains that do not contain wheat?

But what about the multitudes of people who do not have the classical diagnosis of either celiac disease or a wheat allergy but obviously have real symptoms associated with eating gluten? The one recurring thing I've often heard from patients, friends, and family is that many of them who have real issues with gluten are being labeled as having *non-celiac gluten sensitivity*.

That doesn't surprise me given the many issues surrounding testing, especially the fact that you must be eating a lot of gluten weeks or even months prior to testing to test positive for celiac disease. Yet what was a small issue a few years ago has grown into an epidemic. And not everyone is happy with the label of non-celiac gluten sensitivity, or NCGS. Who wants to live with a label? People want actionable answers.

I've created a table to sort out some differences, including symptoms and causes, among celiac disease, wheat allergies, NCGS, and even irritable bowel syndrome (IBS).

Fortunately, there's been a lot more research trying to understand what's happening with people labeled with NCGS. There's now even a growing consensus that this large group of people is distinct from those who have celiac disease and wheat allergies. So if it's not celiac disease or a wheat allergy that's causing people so much dietary grief, what is the culprit behind our current dietary intolerance epidemic?

℞ *DNA Restart Health Tip #5*
Here's a list of common food allergens to watch out for.

1. Cereal grains—such as wheat
2. Eggs
3. Fish
4. Legumes—such as peanuts and soybeans
5. Seafood—such as clams, crabs, lobster, and shrimp
6. Seeds—such as poppy and sesame
7. Tree nuts—almonds, cashews, and walnuts

Differences among Celiac Disease, Wheat Allergy, Non-Celiac Gluten Sensitivity, and Irritable Bowel Syndrome

Type of Condition	What Are the Symptoms?	How to Diagnose?	How Common?	What's the Cause?
Celiac Disease	Bloating Stomach cramps	Blood test for immunoglobulin A tissue transglutaminase, or tTG-IgA test* intestinal biopsy	Most common in people with European ancestry. Thought to affect about 1 percent of people worldwide.	Autoimmune reaction to the exposure to gluten-containing foods in sensitive people.
Wheat Allergy	Skin rash/hives Stomach cramps Stuffy/runny nose Headaches Indigestion Anaphylaxis (rare)	Skin prick test Blood test for IgE antibody to wheat	Thought to affect 0.1 percent of people worldwide.	Allergy to wheat protein
Non-Celiac Gluten Sensitiviy (NCGS)	Bloating Stomach cramps Foggy mind Aphthous ulcers (canker sores)	Excluding celiac disease and wheat allergy A double-blind gluten challenge	Not known	Not known
Irritable Bowel Syndrome (IBS)	Stomach cramps/pain Bloating Gas Nausea Diarrhea and/or constipation Frequent bowel movements	No direct diagnostic testing available	As many as 20 percent of Americans report symptoms of IBS	Not known

1 As deep genetic sequencing revealed, even monozygotic, or "identical," twins do not always have the exact same DNA. That's without even accounting for a myriad of inherited and evolving epigenetic

2 You can learn more about the impact that CNVs can have on your health by reading one of my previous books, Inheritance: How our genes change our lives, and how our lives change our genes.

3 The only cells that don't have DNA are mature red blood cells. They actually got rid of their DNA to make more room so they could pack themselves full of more hemoglobin.

4 Aretaeus of Cappadocia is thought to have practiced medicine in both Alexandria and Rome. Besides

5 If you're interested to know more about why and how many of the common diseases affecting people today actually helped your ancestors survive, read Survival of the Sickest: A Medical Maverick Discovers Why We Need Disease.

6 Caused by a lack of iron.

You've just read an excerpt from The DNA Restart.

ABOUT THE AUTHOR

Sharon Moalem, MD, PhD, is an award-winning physician, scientist, inventor, and *New York Times* bestselling author whose books have been translated into more than 35 languages. He has been awarded more than 21 patents worldwide for his inventions in the fields of biotechnology and human health. His scientific work led to the discovery of a first-in-class member of a novel class of antibiotic compounds directed against multi-resistant or "superbug" microorganisms such as Methicillin-resistant Staphylococcus aureus (MRSA). Dr. Moalem has also cofounded three biotechnology companies and has served as an associate editor for the *Journal of Alzheimer's Disease*. Dr. Moalem and his research have been featured on the *Daily Show* with Jon Stewart, the *Today* show, the *New York Times, CNN, Good Morning America, O: The Oprah Magazine*, and *New Scientist*. He lives in New York City.

IMPRINT: Rodale
PRINT ISBN: 9781623366681
PRINT PRICE: US $26.99
EBOOK ISBN: 9781623366698
EBOOK PRICE: $21.50

PUBLICATION DATE: 9/6/16
PUBLICITY CONTACT: Yelena Gitlin Nesbit Yelena.Nesbit@rodale.com
RIGHTS CONTACT: Bob Niegowski Bob.Niegowski@rodale.com
EDITOR: Jennifer Levesque
AGENT: Richard Abate
AGENCY: 3 Arts Entertainment

TERRITORIES SOLD:
Rodale Inc, world rights

PROMOTIONAL INFORMATION:
National author publicity; National radio campaign; National print features and reviews; Online publicity and promotions; Advertising in Rodale magazines, preorder incentive campaign, Rodale Wellness online coverage, social media via author, Rodale Wellness and Rodale Books.

NEW YORK TIMES BESTSELLING AUTHOR

ANNE SEBBA

Les
PARISIENNES

HOW THE WOMEN of PARIS LIVED, LOVED
AND DIED UNDER NAZI OCCUPATION

SUMMARY

Paris in the 1940s was a place of fear, power, aggression, courage, deprivation, and secrets. During the occupation, the swastika flew from the Eiffel Tower and danger lurked on every corner. While Parisian men were either fighting at the front or captured and forced to work in German factories, the women of Paris were left behind where they would come face to face with the German conquerors on a daily basis, as waitresses, shop assistants, or wives and mothers, increasingly desperate to find food to feed their families as hunger became part of everyday life. When the Nazis and the puppet Vichy regime began rounding up Jews to ship east to concentration camps, the full horror of the war was brought home and the choice between collaboration and resistance became unavoidable. Sebba focuses on the role of women, many of whom faced life and death decisions every day. After the war ended, there would be a fierce settling of accounts between those who made peace with or, worse, helped the occupiers and those who fought the Nazis in any way they could.

EXCERPT

Prologue

Les Parisiennes

Paris, mid-July 2015, and the city is swelteringly hot. By July 19, thunder is in the air. I am sitting on a temporary stage, waiting for the rain, enraptured by an unremarkable woman in her late eighties telling a most remarkable story. Annette Krajcer is one of the few surviving victims of the most notorious roundup in French twentieth century history. When she was twelve she and her mother and sister were arrested by French police and taken in French buses to a sports stadium, the Vélodrome d'Hiver, along with 13,000 others including more than 4,000 children. After three days held in disgusting conditions with almost nothing to eat or drink and totally inadequate sanitary facilities, they were crammed into cattle cars and taken to another camp, Pithiviers, which was just a little better as they slept on straw-filled bunks and were given some meagre rations. But, after two weeks here, their mother was taken away and the sisters never saw her again. Abandoned, they were now taken back to Drancy, a holding camp in Paris. Most of the children who returned with them on this occasion did not survive much longer as they were now shipped to Auschwitz and gassed. But Annette and her sister Leah were, miraculously, saved. A cousin who worked as a secretary in the camp, saw their names on a list and managed to organise their liberation. They spent the next three years in hiding but at the end of the War were reunited with their father, who had been a prisoner of war working on a German farm in the Ardennes.

Today Annette is recounting those events to an audience of Parisian dignitaries, journalists and mostly elderly people. Her disturbing story is especially distressing because the mention of lists is a reminder of how the Jewish community itself was forced to compile names and addresses of its own members. She cannot, she says, pass a day without thinking of the other 4,000 children who did not have such useful cousins.

Also telling a story that oppressive morning is Séverine Darcque, a 33 year-old teacher who owes her existence to Pierrette Pauchard, a farmer's widow from Burgundy recently declared a Righteous Among Nations (the official term used by the state of Israel to describe non-Jews who risked their lives during the Holocaust to save Jews from extermination by the Nazis). Pierrette was among those French who put their own lives in danger to help Jews survive and Séverine's dramatic story shows how courageously many ordinary French people behaved. Pierrette saved at least five Jewish children who grew up alongside her own, one of whom was an abandoned 18-month-old baby named Colette Morgenbesser. Séverine is Colette's granddaughter but thinks of herself as a descendant of Pierrette too.

The stadium no longer exists but this ceremony is now held annually on a nearby site in the shadow of the Eiffel Tower following President Jacques Chirac's ground breaking 1995 speech when he officially recognised French culpability for the 1942 round up. The Vichy government, then headed by Pierre Laval, agreed to help the Nazi occupiers by delivering up all the foreign Jews, and their children born in France who were therefore French. The numbers of those who lived through the events being commemorated diminishes each year but some of their children now attend to honour their parents' memory. In less than an hour, the two women making formal addresses have revealed some of the myriad narratives which make up the complex patchwork of experiences in France during

Les Années Noires. In different ways they have both shown that 'the past' is not yet 'the past' in France. But above all they demonstrate how harshly the burden of decision so often fell on women, usually mothers, and how murky was the range of choices.

Echoes of the past continually resonate in modern day France, as what happened here during the 1940's has left scars of such impenetrable depth that many have not yet healed. There is still a fear among some that touching the scars may reopen them. Nearly eighty years after the conflict ended, I am frequently warned as I plan interviews and research for this book, to take into account that what to me is history is still the highly sensitive present for many; some people may not talk to me. Nowhere was this more evident than in modern day Vichy, the spa town which became Government headquarters after the Fall of France in 1940. The hotel which housed Marshall Pétain and many other government officials for four years now serves as the town's Tourist Information Office, yet the young staff working there when I visited were unable to confirm any details of life in the town in the 1940's, a period about which they apparently knew nothing. My request to see the plaque, located inside Vichy's opera house, which commemorates that it was there that on 10 July 1940 the National Assembly voted full power to Field Marshal Philippe Pétain, thus ending France's Third Republic, was turned down. Bizarrely, the plaque states that eighty members of the National Assembly voted to "affirm their attachment to the Republic, their love for freedom, and their faith in victory [over Germany]," not that 569 members did *not* affirm their attachment to the Third Republic. Indeed, they condemned it thus creating the Vichy regime, which governed the defeated country during the Occupation.

On one occasion in Paris I found myself caught up in a demonstration as thousands of French had chosen that day, Mother's Day in France, to protest the recent legalization of gay marriage. The events, bizarre in a modern nation renowned for its tolerance, resonated in a strange way for me as '*Journée de la Mère*' became a political matter of national importance for Vichy France. Pétain used such occasions to bolster the moral and cultural conservatism of his authoritarian regime, which glorified the family where the man was head, and the woman occupied a place on condition of being a mother. France's low birth rate had been a concern for many years and, ironically, one of many reasons for welcoming thousands of foreign Jews to France in previous decades had been to help counterbalance this. Under Pétain, teaching housekeeping, where girls had to learn how to make simple clothes, do laundry, bleaching, ironing, cookery, nutrition and other aspects of domestic hygiene for one hour minimum per week became obligatory in all *lycées* and *collèges* until the age of 18. * *La Loi du 18 Mars on L'enseignement ménager familial.* For alongside the World War was an attempt at a National Revolution, creating a society that would turn its back on republican values. The demonstration that I witnessed was largely peaceful, with the police estimating that about 150,000 people took part. But for me it was clear evidence of the persistence of the past in present day France. Even today there are significant financial advantages for mothers of three or more children.

During the last few years, several people I tried to talk to about their memories, or of how their family survived, simply refused to answer my emails or phone calls. Almost all who did agree and who had lived through what are often called 'The Dark Years,' began by telling me: "*Ah, c'est très compliqué...*" Very often, once we start speaking, it becomes clear that the choices they made during this decade had much to do with what happened to them or their parents during the previous conflict, World War One, or the War of 1914, as it is called here. Memories of that war were often 'cultivated,' preserved artefacts became relics as photos of battlefields and devastated towns acquired almost holy status and there remained deep seated mistrust of their German neighbour. Naughty French children in the twenties and thirties were often reprimanded with the refrain: 'if you don't behave, the *Boche* (offensive slang meaning a German soldier) will come and take you.'

But then, as the second war progressed, and Paris became a strangely empty city with few Frenchmen to be seen, other factors came into play. Many women in Paris responded positively to German men who were usually polite, often cultured and sometimes offered the only source of food. Many women, including intellectuals and resisters, played on their femininity to get what they wanted or needed sometimes using sex, sometimes being used for sex, and at all times concerned with their appearances and appearing fashionable. Melting cutlery in order to have a fashionable brooch, or buying leg paint to simulate stockings, occasionally took precedence over finding food.

I want to examine in the pages that follow what factors weighed most heavily on women, making them respond to the harsh and difficult circumstances in which they found themselves, in a particular way. M.R.D. Foot, historian of the SOE as well as soldier, was well aware of how many women, often young teenage girls, were heavily involved from the earliest days in helping men escape. "Evaders often found that they had to trust themselves entirely to women; and without the courage and devotion of its couriers and safe-house keepers, nearly all them women, no escape line could keep going at all," Foot wrote. (Stourton p78) Why did they choose to risk their young lives and their families? I will use the word choice - what choices they made - while recognising that not all of them had a real choice as defined by anyone living through the war years. For women, choice often meant more than simply how to live their own lives but how to protect their children and sometimes their elderly parents too. One interview was almost abruptly terminated when I asked the noted playwright, Jean-Claude Grumberg, if he could understand how his mother had made what I considered the unimaginably brave choice to pay a '*passeuse*', a woman who promised to take him and his slightly older brother to a place of greater safety in the south of France. As added protection, his mother was not allowed to know where the children were in case she was arrested and forced to reveal his information. Grumberg was silent at first and then stared at me disbelievingly.

'La choix, c'est contestable,' he replied eventually. Anyone who used the word choice in the context of the situation facing his mother could not have grasped the complexity of life for a Romanian-born Jewish woman in occupied Paris after 1942, a woman whose husband had been arrested, who could not speak fluent French, who was forbidden to move around freely or even, on a scorchingly hot day, to buy her Jewish children a drink in certain places at a certain time and was caring for a sick mother-in-law.

He repeated: "Choice? How can you ask me about choice?"

But I persisted, apologising for unintended offence, as choices, however heart-wrenching, were made by women, especially by women.

Sacha Josopivici, born in Egypt and travelling, she hoped, also to a place of greater safety with her child on false papers from Nice to La Bourboule while her husband was in Paris, had decided that "if the train was stopped and I was asked to account for myself I would most probably, despite my papers, say that I was Jewish. I felt that even though it would mean leaving you (her three-year-old son) with strangers, it was something I would have to do. There aren't many moments like that in life but I felt that this was one of them." In the event she did not have to make that choice. Other women, travelling on false papers, hid compromising documents in their children's bags. I have met those children and would not like to say the actions were without consequences.

"You were not given the choice," insists Jeannie, Vicomtesse de Clarens who, as Jeannie Rousseau, began resisting in 1939. "I don't even understand the question," she states with a rare clarity when asked, why did she risk her life? "It was a moral obligation to do what you are capable of doing. As a woman you could not join the army but you could use your brain. It was a must. How could you not do it?" (video interview with David Ignatius from Washington Spy Museum). And yet her clarion call to resist may have caused the deaths of others once they were prisoners of the Germans in work camps. Other women were brutally honest that there was a "taste for danger that drove us on… but above all it was the joy, the thrill of feeling useful, the camaraderie of battle in which all our weapons were born of love."(Ed Stourton p 192 quoting Dedée de Jongh)

And of course there were constantly lesser choices to be made. Was it collaborating to buy food on the black market if your children were thin, ill and vitamin deficient? Was sending your children to a cousin with a farm in the countryside acceptable? Was it a choice to walk out of a café or a restaurant if German soldiers walked in or was that deliberately courting danger as behaving disrespectfully could, as will become clear, have deathly consequences? Were those who made up lists and saved children of relatives before the children of strangers culpable? Or should one blame only those who forced them to create the lists in the first place?

I want the pages that follow to avoid black and white, good and evil, but instead to reveal constant moral ambiguity, like a kaleidoscope that can be turned in any number of ways to produce a different image. Such a multi-faceted image is far from grey. Was everyone who remained in Paris grinding the gears, pressing the buttons, stocking the shops and performing in theatres or nightclubs in some way complicit in the German adventure of keeping Paris alive and alight? The unreal situation of "occupation" is itself a perverting one, arguably more difficult morally than war. Of course there are fewer casualties, but fear, shame, anger and the terrible feeling of powerlessness together with the strong need to do something plus a complex and often heady mixture of hate and perhaps self-interest - not to speak of individual love affairs - confuse any straightforward response. I want to explore, with as little hindsight or judgment as I can muster - after all we British did not suffer occupation so what right have any of us to judge? - how I would have behaved, impossible of course since we were not put to the same test. One absolute: I think I would go to any length to save my children. A handful of women went to any length to save other people's children. But these are extremes and not all situations in the pages that follow are extremes offering absolute choices. It's the muddle of life that most of us engage in and which is so compelling for any writer or historian looking at France between 1939-1949, especially through the eyes of women. Turn the kaleidoscope one way and see women destroyed by the War; turn it the other, and find women whose lives were enhanced with new meaning and fulfilment.

When I began this book a male historian suggested I spend hours in the subterranean *Bibliotèque Nationale* reading the diaries of men like Hervé le Boterf and Jean Galtier Boissière. But, important though these may be, I have tried to find an alternative, often quieter and frequently lesser known set of voices. I have relied on interviews with women who lived through the events, of necessity as children, as well as diaries, letters, ration cards and memoirs of those no longer alive, both published and unpublished. I have watched intensely dramatic films, read hundreds of letters of denunciation, seen and touched hollow jewellery made with limited materials as well as cork or wooden-soled shoes, whose *clackety clack* provided the sound track to the Occupation. Some voices weave in and out of the story, occasionally in different locations, others disappear entirely from the narrative either through death or because they leave France entirely. It was always going to be hard finding women who admitted that they had worked for a German victory (although there are some) and so occasionally I have relied on a male account of a situation pertaining to women, or used historical records of women who betrayed.

It has been exciting and rewarding to discover that, unquestionably, women's influence and activities during these years were both considerably greater than might be expected from the public roles they were allowed to play in society at that time. Before 1939 women in French society were often invisible, without a vote and needing permission from husbands or fathers to work or own property. Yet women were actively using weapons in the resistance, hosting evaders on the run, delivering false identity papers as well as all the old familiar tasks of cooking shopping and caring for their homes. Women were now in charge, looking after the elderly as well as the children, duties which often prevented their own escape, and sometimes holding down a job as well. Shortages and lack of refrigeration forced women to queue, often for an average of four hours a day, to gather enough to feed the family they were being encouraged to bring into the world. Some women resorted to collaborating and some were straight forwardly victims but others were simply bystanders, caught in the crossfire, and it is their role that occasionally proved crucial.

One more thing: the word 'Parisienne' may summon up to many the image of a chic, slim woman who wears fashionably elegant clothes and is alluring to men. Undeniably, women in Paris used fashion to defy the occupier in a small way perhaps by adopting culottes to ride bicycles when the fuel ran out or by making ceramic tricolore buttons. Yet this is not a book about fashion even though fashion was important both to *les Parisiennes* themselves as well as the German occupiers. But, while admitting that the glamorous description fits some of the women in this book—women who wore designer suits while risking their lives to deliver vital information, women who believed that wearing an outrageously large hat was a form of resistance—I am giving it a wider meaning. Many typically Parisienne women found themselves, through necessity, living or subsisting outside Paris, while others in this story, while remaining in the city were not Parisienne in the accepted use of word. If I had been in any doubt about using the term to describe a woman not living in the city, but imprisoned in a camp, wearing rags, with sores on her skin, scars from lashings and unwashed hair, I felt justified when I learned that, instead of eating the ounce or so of fat she was given daily, she massaged it into her hands concluding that these needed preserving more than her stomach. That seemed to me the reasoning of a true Parisienne.

You've just read an excerpt from Les Parisiennes.

ABOUT THE AUTHOR

Anne Sebba is a biographer, lecturer, journalist and former Reuters foreign correspondent. She has written eight books, including acclaimed biographies of Jennie Churchill and Mother Theresa, as well as the *New York Times* bestseller *That Woman* about the life of Wallis Simpson. She is a member of the Society of Authors Executive Committee. www.annesebba.com.

IMPRINT: St. Martin's Press
PRINT ISBN: 9781250048592
PRINT PRICE: $27.99
EBOOK ISBN: 9781466849563
EBOOK PRICE: $14.99
PUBLICATION DATE: 10/18/16
PUBLICITY CONTACT: Dori Weintraub dori.weintraub@stmartins.com
RIGHTS CONTACT: Chris Scheina Chris.Scheina@macmillan.com
EDITOR: Charlie Spicer
AGENT: Clare Alexander
AGENCY: Aitken Alexander

TERRITORIES SOLD:
UK Rights: W&N
Translation Rights: Aitken Alexander Associates.

PROMOTIONAL INFORMATION:
We will be focused on reaching readers early and often via independent booksellers, online reading communities offering early reader reviews, academic and library channels, and blogs and organizational outlets. At publication, focus will be on national print, radio and online publicity.

During World War II, America's fledgling aeronautics industry hired black female mathematicians to fill a labor shortage. These "human computers" stayed on to work for NASA and make sure America won the Space Race. They fought for their country's future, and for their share of the American Dream. This is their untold story.

HIDDEN FIGURES

MARGOT LEE SHETTERLY

SUMMARY

The untold true story of the African-American female mathematicians at NASA who provided the calculations that helped fuel some of America's greatest achievements in space, told through the personal accounts of four women known as the "colored computers," set against the Jim Crow South and the civil rights movement.

EXCERPT

Preface

"Miss Land worked as a computer out at Langley," my father said, taking a right turn out of the parking lot of First Baptist Church in Hampton, Virginia.

My husband and I visited my parents just after Christmas in 2010, enjoying a few days away from our full-time life and work in Mexico. They squired us around town in their 20-year old green minivan, my father driving, my mother in the front passenger seat, Aran and I buckled in behind like siblings. My dad, gregarious as always, offered a stream of commentary that shifted fluidly from updates on the friends and neighbors we'd bumped into around town, to the weather forecast, to elaborate discourses on the physics underlying his latest research as a 66-year old doctoral student at Hampton University. He enjoyed touring my Maine born-and-raised husband through our neck of the woods, and refreshing my connection with local life and history in the process. During our time home, I spent afternoons with my mother catching matinees at the local cinema, while Aran tagged along with my father and his friends to Norfolk State University football games. We gorged on fried fish sandwiches at hole-in-the-wall joints near Buckroe Beach, visited the Hampton University museum's Native American art collection and haunted local antiques shops. As a callow 18-year old leaving for college, I'd seen my hometown as a mere launching pad for a life in worldlier locales, a place to be from rather than a place to be. But years and miles away from home could never attenuate the city's hold on my identity, and the more I explored places and people far from Hampton, the more my status as one if its daughters came to mean to me.

That day after church, we spent a long while catching up with the formidable Mrs. Land, who had been one of my favorite Sunday School teachers. Kathaleen Land, a retired NASA mathematician, still lived on her own well into her 90s and never missed a Sunday at church. We said our goodbyes to her, and clambered into the minivan, off to a family brunch. "A lot of the women around here, black and white, worked as computers," my father said, glancing at Aran in the rear view mirror but addressing us both. "Kathryn Peddrew, Vivian Adair, Sue Wilder…" he ticked off a few more names. "…And Katherine Johnson, who calculated the launch windows for the first astronauts."

The narrative triggered memories decades old, of spending a much-treasured day off from school at my father's office, at NASA's Langley Research Center. I rode shotgun in our 1970s Pontiac, my brother Ben and sister Lauren in the back as our father drove the twenty minutes from our house, straight over the Virgil Grissom Bridge, down Mercury Boulevard, to the road that led to the NASA gate. Daddy flashed his badge, and we sailed through to a campus of perfectly straight parallel streets lined from one end to the other by unremarkable two story red brick buildings. Only the giant hypersonic wind tunnel complex—a 100-foot ridged silver sphere presiding over four 60-foot smooth silver globes—offered visual evidence of entry into a real world version of the future.

Building 1236, my father's daily destination, contained a byzantine complex of government-grey cubicles, perfumed with the grown up smells of coffee and stale cigarette smoke. His engineering colleagues with their rumpled style and distracted manner seemed like exotic birds in a sanctuary. They gave us kids stacks of discarded 11 x 14 continuous form computer paper, printed on one side with cryptic arrays of numbers, the blank side a canvas for crayon masterpieces. Women occupied many of the cubicles; they answered phones and sat in front of typewriters, but also made hieroglyphic marks on transparent slides, and conferred with my father and other men in the office on the stacks of documents that littered their desks. That so many of them were African American, many of them my grandmother's age, struck me as simply a part of the natural order of things: growing up in Hampton, the face of science was brown like mine. My dad joined Langley in 1964 as an engineering intern and retired in 2004 an internationally respected climate scientist. Five of my father's seven siblings made their bones as engineers or technologists, and his best buddies—David Woods,

Elijah Kent, Weldon Staton—carved out successful engineering careers at Langley. Our next door neighbor taught physics at Hampton University. Our church abounded with mathematicians, supersonics experts held leadership positions in my mother's sorority and electrical engineers sat on the board of my parents' college alumni associations. The community certainly included black English professors, like my mother, as well as black doctors and dentists, black mechanics, janitors and contractors, black shoe repair owners, wedding planners, real estate agents and undertakers, several black lawyers and a handful of black Mary Kay salespeople. As a child, however, I knew so many African Americans working in science, math and engineering that I thought that's just what black folks did. Martin Luther King Jr. was a legend from a textbook; these people served as my role models and daily inspiration.

My father, growing up during segregation, experienced a different reality. "Become a physical education teacher," my grandfather said in 1962 to his 18-year-old son, who was hell-bent on studying electrical engineering at historically black Norfolk State College. In those days, a college educated African American with book smarts and common sense put their chips on a teaching job, or sought work at the post office. But my father, who built his first rocket in junior high metal shop class following the Sputnik launch in 1957, defied my grandfather, and plunged full steam ahead into engineering. Of course, my grandfather's fears weren't completely unfounded. As late as 1970, just 1% of America's engineers were black—a number that doubled to a whopping 2% by 1984. But the Federal Government did prove a more reliable source of employment for African Americans than the private sector: that same year, 8.4% of NASA's engineers were black.

NASA's African American employees learned to navigate their way through the space agency's engineering culture, and their successes in turn afforded their children previously unimaginable access to American society. Growing up with white friends and attending integrated schools, I took much of the groundwork they'd laid for granted. Every day I watched my father put on a suit and back out the driveway to make the 20 minute drive to Building 1236, demanding the best from himself, in order to give his best to the space program and to his family. Working at Langley, my father secured my family's place in the comfortable middle class, and

Langley became one of the anchors of our social life. Every summer, my siblings and I saved our allowances to buy tickets to ride ponies at the annual NASA carnival. Year after year, I confided my Christmas wish list to the NASA Santa at the Langley Children's Christmas party. For years, Ben, Lauren and my youngest sister Jocelyn, still a toddler, sat in the bleachers of the Langley Activities Building on Thursday nights, rooting for my dad and his "NBA" (NASA Basketball Association) team, The Stars. My Aunt Julia's husband Charles Foxx was the son of Ruth Bates Harris, a career civil servant and fierce advocate for the advancement of women and minorities; in 1974, NASA appointed her as its Deputy Assistant Administrator, the highest ranking woman at the agency. I was as much a product of NASA as the moon landing.

The National Advisory Committee on Aeronautics (NACA, NASA's predecessor agency) hired Jim Williams, its first African American engineer, in 1951. Even as guards mistook Williams for the janitor, and managers recovered from the shock that the University of Michigan grad they recruited sight unseen was a black man, Dorothy Vaughan, Mary Jackson and as many as 20 other black women were already using their manometers and 10-inch slide rules to parse wind tunnel data from research airplanes like the X-15. While my father learned the ropes in the early 1960s as an ambitious engineer-in-training, Katherine Johnson, more than a decade into her career as a mathematician, prepared the calculations that would land Neil Armstrong on the moon. I had known these women as community elders: enthusiastic Girl Scout leaders mentoring a younger generation of African American girls, stern, pantsuited figures organizing charity events, kindly Sunday School teachers harboring an infinite well of patience. They were my father's colleagues, my parents' friends.

Not until that Sunday drive home from church, with my husband beside me, did I ask myself: How did they get to Langley?

The spark of curiosity soon became an all-consuming fire. I peppered my father with questions about his early days at Langley, questions I'd never asked before. The following Sunday I interviewed Mrs. Land about the early days of Langley's computing pool, when part of her job responsibility was knowing which bathroom was earmarked for colored employees. Less than a week later I sat on the couch in Katherine Johnson's living room, sitting under a framed American flag that had been to the Moon, listening to a 93-year old with a memory sharper than mine recall segregated buses, years of teaching and raising a family, and working out the reentry angle for Alan Shepard's spaceflight. I scoured NASA archives and searched Ebay for vintage calculators like the ones the Computers used, listened to Christine Darden's stories of long years spent as a Data Analyst, waiting for the chance to prove herself as an engineer. Even as a professional in an integrated world, I had been the only black woman in enough drawing rooms and boardrooms to have an inkling of the chutzpah it took for an African American women in a segregated southern workplace to tell her bosses she was sure her calculations would put a man on the Moon. These women's trajectories set the stage for mine; immersing myself in their stories helped me understand my own.

Today, the hamlet which in 1962 dubbed itself "Spacetown USA" looks like any city in a modern and hyper-connected America. People of all races and nationalities mingle on Hampton's beaches and in its bus stations, the "Whites Only" signs of the past relegated to the local history museum and the memories of survivors of the Civil Rights revolution. Mercury Boulevard no longer conjures images of the eponymous mission that shot the first Americans beyond the atmosphere, and each day the memory of Virgil Grissom the man fades away from the bridge that bears his name. A downsized space program and decades of government cutbacks have hit the region hard; today, an ambitious college grad with a knack for numbers might set her sights on a gig at a Silicon Valley start-up, or make for one of the many technology firms that are conquering the NASDAQ from the Virginia suburbs outside of Washington DC.

But before a computer became an inanimate object, and before Mission Control landed in Houston; before Sputnik changed the course of history and before the NACA became NASA; before Brown v Board of Ed established that separate was in fact not equal, and before the poetry of Martin Luther King Jr's "I Have a Dream Speech" rang out over the steps of the Lincoln Memorial, the Colored Computers were helping America dominate aeronautics, space research and computer technology, carving out a place for themselves as female mathematicians who were also black, black mathematicians who were also female. For a group of bright and ambitious African American women, diligently prepared for a mathematical career and eager for a crack at the big leagues, Hampton, Virginia must have felt like the center of the universe.

Chapter One: A Door Opens

Melvin Butler, the Personnel Officer at the Langley Memorial Aeronautical Laboratory, had a problem, the scope and nature of which was made plain in a May 1943 telegram to the Civil Service's Chief of Field Operations. "This establishment has urgent need for approximately 100 Junior Physicists and Mathematicians, 100 Assistant Computers, 75 Minor Laboratory Apprentices, 125 Helper Trainees, 50 Stenographers and Typists," exclaimed the missive. Every morning at 7 AM, the bow-tied Butler and his staff sprang to life, dispatching the lab's station wagon to the local rail depot, the bus station and the ferry terminal to collect the men and women—so many women now, each day more women—who had made their way to the lonely finger of land on the Virginia coast. The shuttle conveyed the recruits to the door of the laboratory's Service Building, on the campus of Langley Field. Upstairs, Butler's staff whisked them through the first day stations: forms, photos, and the oath of office: *I will support and defend the Constitution of the United States against all enemies, foreign and domestic, so help me God.*

Thus installed, the newly-minted civil servants fanned out to take their places in one of the research facility's expanding inventory of buildings, each already as full as a pod ripe with peas. No sooner had Sherwood Butler, the laboratory's head of Procurement, laid the cornerstone on a new building before his brother Melvin set about filling it with new employees. Closets and hallways, stockrooms and shop floors stood in as makeshift offices. Someone came up with the bright idea of putting two desks head to head and jerryrigging the new pieces of furniture with a jumpseat, in order to squeeze three workers into space designed for two. In the four years since Hitler's troops overran Poland—since American interest and the European War converged into an all-consuming one—the laboratory's complement of 500 odd employees at the close of the decade had was on its way to 1,500. Yet, the great groaning war machine swallowed them whole, and remained hungry for more.

From his second floor office, Melvin Butler looked out upon the crescent-shaped airfield. Only the flow of civilian-clothed people distinguished the Army Air Corp's low brick buildings from those of the laboratory, the oldest outpost of the National Advisory Committee for Aeronautics. The two installations had grown up together, the air base devoted to the development of America's military air power capability, the laboratory a civilian agency charged with advancing the scientific understanding of aeronautics and disseminating their findings to the military and private industry. Since the beginning, the Army had allowed the laboratory to operate there on the campus of the airfield. The close relationship with the Army flyers served as a constant reminder to the engineers that every experiment they conducted had real world implications.

A cantilevered steel hangar glinted on sunny days, its shady and cavernous interior sheltering the machines and their minders from the elements. Men, sometimes individual, more often in groups of two or three, dressed in canvas jumpsuits, moved in trucks and jeeps from plane to plane, stopping to hover at this one or that like pollinating insects, checking them, filling them with gas, replacing parts, examining them, becoming one with them and taking off for the heavens. The music of airplane engines and propellers cycled through the various movements of takeoff, flight and landing, playing from before sunrise until dusk, each machine's sounds as unique to its minders as a baby's cry to its mother. Beneath the tenor notes of airplane engines played the bass roar of the laboratory's wind tunnels, turning their hurricanes-on-demand on to the planes—full-sized planes, model planes, plane parts.

Just two years prior, with the storm clouds gathering, President Roosevelt challenged the nation to produce 50,000 planes. It seemed an impossible task for a country tooled for just 3,000 of the flying machines. Now, America's aircraft industry was a production miracle, easily surpassing the mark by more than half. It was the largest industry in the world, the most productive, the most sophisticated, outproducing the Germans by more than three times and the Japanese by nearly five. The facts were clear to all belligerents: the final conquest would come from the sky. Victory through Air Power!

For the flyboys of the Air Corps, airplanes were mechanisms for transporting troops and supplies to combat zones, armed wings for pursuing enemies, sky-high launching pads for ship-sinking bombs. They reviewed their vehicles in an exhaustive preflight check-out before climbing into the sky; mechanics rolled up their sleeves and sharpened their eyes; a broken piston, an improperly locked shoulder harness, a faulty fuel tank light, could cost lives. But even before the plane responded to its pilot's knowing caress, its nature, its very DNA—from the shape of its wings to the cowling of its engine—had been manipulated, refined, massaged, deconstructed and recombined by the engineers next door.

Long before America's aircraft manufacturers placed one of their newly-conceived flying machines into production, the hands of the men who would fly it in the battlezones of World War II, before they began stamping them out by the hundreds in their manufacturing plants, they sent a working prototype to the Langley laboratory so that the design could be tested, refined and finalized. One of every three models already in production made its way to the lab for drag cleanup: The engineers parked the planes in the tunnels, making note of air-disturbing surfaces, bloated fuselages, uneven wing geometries. As prudent and thorough as the old family doctor, they examined every aspect of the air flowing over the plane, making careful note of the vital signs. NACA pilots, with an engineer riding shotgun, took the plane for a test flight. Did it roll unexpectedly? Did it stall? Was it hard to maneuver, resisting the pilot like a shopping cart with a bad wheel? The engineers subjected the airplanes to tests, capturing and analyzing the numbers, recommending improvements, some slight, others significant. Better engineering could save lives; even small improvements in speed and efficiency multiplied over millions of pilot miles added up to a difference that could tip the long term balance of the war in the Allies' favor.

"Victory through Air Power!" Henry Reid, Engineer-in-Charge of the Langley Laboratory, crooned to his employees, the shibboleth a reminder of the importance of the airplane to the war's outcome. "Victory through Air Power!" the NACA-ites repeated to each other, minding each decimal point, poring over differential equations and pressure distribution charts until eyes fatigued. In the battle of research, victory would be theirs.

Unless, of course, Melvin Butler failed to feed the three-shift, six-day a week operation with fresh minds. The engineers were one thing, but each engineer required the support of a number of others: craftsmen to build airplane models tested in the tunnels, mechanics to maintain the tunnels, and the nimble number crunchers to process the numerical deluge that issued from the research. Lift and drag, friction and flow....what was a plane but a bundle of physics? Physics, of course, meant math, and math meant mathematicians. And since the middle of the last decade, mathematicians had meant women. The first female computing pool, started in 1935, had caused an uproar among the men of the laboratory. How could a female mind prove fit for something so rigorous and precise as math? The very idea, investing $500 on a calculating machine so it could be used by a girl! But the girls had been good, very good—better at computing, in fact, than many of the engineers, the men themselves grudgingly admitted. With only a handful of girls winning the title "Mathematician"—a professional designation that put them on equal footing with entry-level male employees—the fact that most computers were designated as "subprofessionals" provided a boost to the laboratory's bottom line.

But now even the girls were harder to come by. Virginia Tucker, Langley's Head Computer, ran laps up and down the East Coast searching for coeds with even a modicum of analytical or mechanical skill, hoping for matriculating college students to fill the hundreds of open positions for computers, scientific aides, model makers, laboratory assistants, and yes, even mathematicians. She conscripted what seemed like entire classes of math graduates from her North Carolina alma mater, the Greenboro Colege for Women, and hunted at Virginia schools like Sweetbriar, in Lynchburg, and the State Teacher's College, in Farmville.

Melvin Butler leaned on the Civil Service and War Manpower Commission as hard as he could. He placed ads in the local newspaper ("Reduce your household duties! Women who are not afraid to roll up their sleeves and do jobs previously filled by men should call the Langley Memorial Aeronautical Laboratory), and made fervent pleas in the employee newsletter Air Scoop ("Are there members of your family or others you know who would like to play a part in gaining supremacy of the air? Have you friends of either sex who would like to do important work toward winning and shortening the war?"). The labor market was as exhausted as the war workers themselves.

A bright spot presented itself, in the form of another man's problem. A.

Philip Randolph, the head of the largest labor union in the country, demanded that Roosevelt open the lucrative war jobs to Negro applicants, threatening in the summer of 1941 to bring 100,000 Negroes to the nation's capital in protest should the president rebuff his demand. Roosevelt blinked. Who the hell is this guy Randolph? the president's aides fumed.

A tall, elegant black man with Shakespearean diction and the stare of an eagle, Asa Philip Randolph headed the 35,000 strong Brotherhood of Sleeping Car Porters, the largest black labor union in the country. The sleeping porters waited on customers in America's segregated passenger trains, their workday usually requiring the endurance of prejudice and humiliation, though the income of the job afforded them economic stability and social standing within the black community. Believing that civil rights were inextricably linked to economic rights, Randolph worked tirelessly for the inclusion of Negro Americans in the wealth of the country they had helped to build. Twenty years in the future, an elder Randolph would address the multitudes at another March on Washington, then concede the stage to a young, charismatic minister from Atlanta named Martin Luther King, Jr.

History would forever associate the black freedom movement with King's name, but as America oriented every aspect of its society toward war for the second time in thirty years, it was Randolph's long-term vision and the spectre of a march that never happened that pried open a door that had been closed like a bank vault since the end of Reconstruction. With two strokes of a pen—Executive Order 8802, ordering the desegregation of the defense industry, and Executive Order 9346, creating the Fair Employment Practices Committee to monitor the the task—Roosevelt primed the pump for a new source of labor to come into the tight production process.

Nearly two years after the showdown, as the laboratory's urgent missive reached the Civil Service, applications of qualified Negro female candidates began filtering in to the second floor of the Service Building, presenting themselves for consideration by the laboratory's Personnel staff. No photo advised as to the applicant's color—that had been stricken down the year before, as a part of anti discrimination measure. But the alma maters tipped the hand—West Virginia State University, Howard,

Arkansas AN&M, Hampton Institute just across town, Negro schools. Nothing in the applications indicated anything less than fitness for the job. If anything, they came with more experience that the white girls, with many years of teaching experience, on top of math or science degrees.

They would need a space for them all to sit together, Melvin Butler thought (surely they'd want that too...) Then they would have to appoint someone to head the new group, an experienced girl—white, obviously—someone whose disposition suited the sensitivity of the assignment. The Warehouse Building, a brand new space on the West Side, so new that it was still more wilderness than anything resembling a workplace, could be just the thing. His brother Sherwood's group had already moved there, as had some of the employees in the Personnel Department. With the drag cleanup tests happening around the clocks, the engineers would welcome the additional hands. So many of them were Northerners, agnostic on the racial issue, but devout when it came to mathematical talent.

Melvin Butler hailed from Portsmouth, just across the bay from Hampton. It required no imagination on his part to guess what some of his fellow Virginians would think of the idea of integrating Negro women into Langley's offices, the come-heres (as the Virginians called the newcomers to the state) and their strange ways be damned. They'd always had Negro employees in the lab—janitors, cafeteria workers, mechanic's assistants, groundskeepers. But Negroes who would be considered peers? A Jewish girl from New York, new to the lab, nearly ignited a scandal when she invited her Negro college roommate down to Hampton for a weekend visit. So Butler proceeded with discretion: no big announcement in the Daily Press, the local newspaper; no fanfare in Air Scoop, the laboratory's employee newsletter. But also with direction: nothing to herald the arrival of the Negro women to the laboratory, but nothing to derail their arrival either. Maybe he acted with the disposition of a white man progressive for his time or place, or maybe he was just a functionary carrying out his duty. Maybe he was both. State law—Virginia custom—kept him from truly progressive action, but maybe it gave him cover. Whatever his personal feelings on race, one thing was clear as the Virginia sky: Butler was a Langley man through and through, loyal to the laboratory, to its mission, to its worldview, and to its charge during the war. By nature—

and by mandate—he, and the rest of the NACA, were all about practical solutions.

So, too, was A. Philip Randolph. The leader's indefatigable activism, unrelenting pressure and superior organizing skills laid the foundation for what, in the 1960s, would come to be known as the Civil Rights Movement. But there was no way that Randolph, or the men at the Laboratory, or anyone else could have predicted that the chain of dominoes that sparked the hiring of a group of black female mathematicians at the Langley Memorial Aeronautical Laboratory would end at the moon. The seeds of the future, however, had already germinated, and would be nourished from the ferment of the present war that consumed all, and commanded all.

Still shrouded from view were the great aeronautical advances that would crush the notion that faster-than-sound flight was a physical impossibility, the electronic calculating devices that would amplify the power of science and technology to unthinkable dimensions, the millions of wartime women who would refuse to leave the American workplace and forever change the meaning of women's work, and the perseverance of America's Negro community, who would not be moved in their demands for full access to the founding ideals of their country. Most hidden of all, perhaps, was the knowledge that the black female mathematicians who walked into Langley in 1943 would find themselves at the intersections of all of those great transformations, their sharp minds and ambitions contributing to what America would consider one of its greatest victories.

In 1943, however, America existed in the urgent present, that span of time between the right now and the final victory they called the duration, the Space Race a phrase as meaningless as doggerel from a children's book, a computer still someone who wore a skirt. Responding to the needs of the here and now, Butler tipped the next domino, making a note to add another item to his brother Sherwood's seemingly endless requisition list: a metal bathroom sign, bearing the words "Colored Girls."

You've just read an excerpt from Hidden Figures.

ABOUT THE AUTHOR

Margot Lee Shetterly is a journalist and independent researcher currently developing The Human Computer Project, a collaboration with Macalester College American Studies professor Duchess Harris to create a digital archive of the stories of NASA's African-American Human Computers. In 2005, she founded *Inside México Magazine*, which became the most widely distributed English language publication in Mexico. She's been profiled in the *LA Times* and *Editor and Publisher*, among other publications. www.margotleeshetterly.com, Twitter: @margotshetterly.

IIMPRINT: William Morrow
PRINT ISBN: 9780062363596
PRINT PRICE: $27.99
EBOOK ISBN: 9780062363619
EBOOK PRICE: $14.99
PUBLICATION DATE: 9/6/16
PUBLICITY CONTACT: Shelby Meizlik Shelby.Meizlik@harpercollins.com
RIGHTS CONTACT: Mackenzie Brady mbrady@newleafliterary.com
EDITOR: Rachel Kahan
AGENT: Mackenzie Brady
AGENCY: New Leaf Literary

PROMOTIONAL INFORMATION:
National broadcast and print media campaign; 25-City radio satellite tour; Advertising in the SIBA Holiday Catalog; Cross-promotion with Fox 2000; Major reading group outreach, including reading group guide and features on Bookclubgirl.com and in the Book Club Girl newsletter; Early galley giveaways to consumers; Author video with outreach, including YouTube; Outreach to book bloggers; Library marketing; Academic marketing; Feature on HarperCollins Presents Podcast; Deep distribution of reader's edition.

Generation Chef

RISKING IT ALL *for a* NEW AMERICAN DREAM

KAREN STABINER

SUMMARY

Generation Chef takes readers inside what life is really like for the new generation of professional cooks. The heart of the narrative is the story of Jonah Miller, who, at age twenty-four, quits his job as a sous chef and attempts to fulfill a lifelong dream by opening the Basque restaurant Huertas in New York City, still the high-stakes center of the restaurant business. Journalist and food writer Karen Stabiner takes us through Huertas's roller-coaster first year while providing insight into the challenging world a young chef faces today—the intense financial pressures, the overcrowded field of aspiring cooks, and the impact of reviews and social media, which can dictate who survives. A fast-paced narrative filled with suspense, *Generation Chef* is a fascinating behind-the-scenes look at drive and passion in one of today's hottest professions.

EXCERPT

Chapter One

Opening Night

Jonah Miller bounded up the steep narrow stairs, each tread worn at the center from over a century of use, the only reminder that this place had ever been anything but his. In fifteen minutes, when the doors opened for the first time, it would be Huertas, a Spanish restaurant that had the 26-year-old chef almost $600,000 in debt before he sold his first beer—on paper, at least, as restaurant investors knew how bad the odds were of repayment, let alone profit, any time soon. Everything but the stairs was new, a practical compromise between the dream Jonah had carried in his head since he was sixteen and the realities of building codes and water lines and oven vents and his partners' input and, always, the budget. He had managed to erase the storefront's past as a pizza place that simply stopped paying rent and gave the keys back to the landlord, a Korean place that preceded it in failure, and, before all that, a vague something else. Now all he had to do was not fail as his predecessors had, in a business where it happened all the time.

Jonah was ten pounds lighter than usual on an already beanpole frame, skinny enough to catch his mother's attention and inspire his fiancé to make sure there was always take-out in the refrigerator for a late-night meal. His professional kitchen philosophy boiled down to "keep your head down and do the work," and he wasn't a screamer, like some chefs, so the stress of opening his first restaurant turned inward, instead, and eroded his appetite. He referred to the space that way, as his first restaurant, because there was no chance he'd stop at one.

At six foot two, he'd developed a slouch in deference to kitchen soffits that might want to knock him in the forehead or coworkers who preferred eye contact to staring at his chin. He was, he said, too tall to be a chef—which made him laugh, as he had never wanted to be anything else. The slump was part of an overall acknowledgement that cooking always came first. Jonah had gone to the same East Village barbershop for the last five years for a $15 adult version of a kid's buzz-cut, because it spared him having to make aesthetic decisions, or to engage in mindless conversation with someone who considered himself not a barber but a stylist. He had no tattoos, even though they were as ubiquitous as clogs in a restaurant kitchen. He wore anonymous dark cotton pants that were baggy enough to be comfortable on a 15-hour shift, and equally nondescript tee shirts and hoodies; no outlier colors or styles that required him to devote conscious thought to what he put on in the morning. His shoes were broken in and built for comfort.

What stood out was his new chef's shirt, blindingly white, its creased short sleeves not yet softened into shape by repeated washings. Jonah could have worn a more formal and more expensive double-breasted chef's coat, embroidered with "Huertas" and "Executive Chef Jonah Miller," but he chose the same shirt that the cooks and dishwasher and porter wore, and told them not to call him "Chef." Better to lead by example, he figured, than to insist on respect before he'd shown them what he could do. Hierarchy didn't mean anything. He was going to earn their admiration.

He took his place at the pass, a marble counter at the front of the narrow open kitchen and a particular source of pride—six old pieces of marble set into a steel frame, held in place with some adhesive, twelve-and-a-half square feet of work space for $200, the price of a single square foot if he'd insisted on a pristine new slab. He checked the inanimate objects that hadn't budged since the last time he looked, because he had to have something to do: A large Spanish ham on a metal skewer set into a wooden frame; little mismatched vintage dishes, one of Maldon salt and one of lemon wedges; a canister of tasting spoons; a metal spindle to hold completed order tickets; a jury-rigged rail that wouldn't last the week, to hold tickets that were still in play. He checked the fill level on his squirt bottle of olive oil, retied his long apron, and refolded and retucked a towel at exactly the right position on that apron tie, just behind his left arm. He walked back past the roast and sauté station and the fry station, peered inside the refrigerated drawers at the mixed greens and portioned proteins, and headed up to the wood-burning oven to survey the prep work of the one cook Jonah couldn't see. The oven had been there when he leased the space, and he wasn't about to spend money to move it, so they'd designed around the oven and ended up with a bathroom between it and the kitchen. Until everything was running smoothly, he'd shuttle back and forth to keep an eye on things. While he was up there, he reviewed the glass jars of citrus wedges that sat on the bar, to make sure that they looked good enough to suit him.

Jonah had played high school baseball, starting out as a pitcher until a chipped bone in his shoulder exiled him to shortstop and third base, and the pitcher's habit of miniscule last-minute adjustments—once the microscopic repositioning of fingers on the ball, now the equally fine placement of a knife on a cutting board—had stayed with him. It was a nice, familiar way to dissipate some of the tension.

If Jonah was right—and he had bet his professional future that he was—Huertas was exactly what a healthy range of people were looking for, from the East Village millennial crowd that cruised First Avenue to serious diners old enough to be their parents, to neighborhood residents looking for a regular haunt. He was going to serve them Basque food because he loved it and because it had newness going for it, as it was nowhere close to the saturation levels of Italian and Asian cuisines.

In the front room, where he expected the younger crowd to gather, he'd serve pintxos, little one-bite appetizers that would fly by on trays like dim sum, an endless array of impulse purchases served with Spanish beers and wines and traditional drinks like the kalimotxo, which was red wine and Coca-Cola. The pintxo list would lead off with the gilda, named for Rita Hayworth's character in the 1945 film "Gilda," a skewered white anchovy curved around a manzanilla green olive at one end and a guindilla pepper at the other. There would be some type of croqueta, jamon or mushroom or even fish, determined by what he had on hand, and a slice of bread topped with egg salad and a single shrimp—which might not sound as good as it tasted, but was going to look alluring enough to get people to take a chance. He could build a pintxo around a chunk of octopus or some homemade sausage; the point was to have a half dozen every day, and to change the list frequently, so that repeat customers had to start all over again once they got past the gilda.

He would offer conservas, tins of Spanish seafood, as Spain put its best seafood, its delicacies, into tins, and serve them with bread, condiments like aioli or lemon or pickled peppers, and homemade potato chips. There would be a few raciones, mid-sized plates, but for the most part the front room was a place to drink and snack and chat, either at the bar or at a table or standing up, which was what people did in Spain.

The dining room at the back was for what he called the menu del dia, four courses, pintxos through dessert, with choices for the egg course and entrée. Jonah planned to change some portion of it every week, at least, to keep people coming back for what qualified as a fine-dining bargain by New York City standards—a $52 fixed-price menu, with wine pairings for each course at $28.

His signature dining room dish was huevos rotos, or "broken eggs," which summed up what he was trying to do: Have fun with refined, reconsidered versions of Spanish classics. He'd tried the original at a Basque place in Madrid, a fried egg plopped on top of a batch of fried potatoes with a side of chorizo or chistorra sausage or jamon. Jonah's version had only the basic ingredients in common with the original. He used a hand-crank machine to spin an impaled russet into strands as slender as spaghetti, which he flash-fried, dressed with a chorizo vinaigrette, and topped with a sous vide egg and slivers of fresh scallions. As soon as the soft egg broke, it turned the vinaigrette into a richer sauce.

It was "carbonara with potatoes, like al dente pasta with chorizo Bolognese," he told the food writers who had already started to hover, because more of their readers understood Italian references than Spanish ones. It was also about a dime's worth of Idaho potatoes and a quarter's worth of chorizo, total cost per serving about two dollars for the egg course on the menu del dia. Jonah prided himself on his ability to wrangle food costs below the stiff 28 percent industry standard in New York City, which was lower than the national figure of 30 percent because other costs in the city were so high. He knew how to be frugal without sacrificing flavor or quality, and he'd already explained his philosophy to his sous chef, Jenni: "If there's something left over, use it." The chefs he'd worked for had taught him not to waste food, long before it became a politically-correct stance, so he repurposed things that a more wanton kitchen might discard, whether it was the duck breast trims that landed in the croquetas or cod skin that got turned into crispy chips he could use instead of a cracker as the base of a pintxo.

His version of migas, which meant "crumbs," was another mix of style and economy. In Spain, people made migas to use up old bread, toasting coarse breadcrumbs and mixing them with an egg or sausage and some greens. Jonah mixed his homemade crumbs with a sous vide egg and bent the rules from there—he planned to add whatever vegetables were in season along with whatever protein felt like a good match.

If he splurged, it was small-scale and with purpose. For the opening he indulged in an order of percebes, stubby little sheathed gooseneck barnacles that clung to the rocks in Galicia, in northern Spain, and were harvested by divers who had to cut them off with knives, still attached to the smaller rocks that sustained them—$20 a pound, probably twice that if he subtracted the weight of the rocks, but "a cool experience," said Jonah. "If you want to talk wild, this is wild." He steamed a small batch in water and white wine and showed the back-room servers how they worked, amid jokes about how they resembled little penises wearing little condoms; he snapped the soft part of the barnacle from its base, removed the sheath and ate what was inside, which was supposed to be an aphrodisiac, or at least that was the legend. It was a good story to tell about something people weren't going to find all over town. He planned to offer them to some of the back tables, but only if he had the time to go back there and eat one with the guests.

He had thought and rethought it all, endlessly, in the twenty months since he walked away from a sous chef job rather than bide his time waiting for a promotion to executive sous. He still had little idea what to expect. The big variable at Huertas was experience, or the lack of it. No one, not Jonah or his two general manager partners or his sous chef, had ever done their jobs before—each of them had leapfrogged over a step or two on the career trajectory to be here, skipped jobs that might have given them a more seasoned perspective. Jonah had been a sous chef for barely a year when he left Maialino, the Roman restaurant he had worked at since he graduated from NYU; he had never been an executive sous, never managed a kitchen team. Nate had been a beverage director at a popular group of barbecue restaurants within Danny Meyer's Union Square Hospitality Group, briefly, and Luke had been a host at the other end of the spectrum, at the elegant 40-year-old Le Cirque, but neither of them had ever run a front-of-house operation. Now they were general managers—and partners, as they'd each wagered a $10,000 investment on Jonah's ability to pull this off, in exchange for a small chunk of equity. His sous chef, Jenni, was a line cook only three years out of culinary school when he offered her the job. They had in common an impressive set of skills, given that their average age was 26, and an impatient ambition. Jonah reassured himself: The people who were opening Huertas were green but smart.

If they were a little insecure, it was a good thing, as they would be motivated to work that much harder. Luke had three servers with him in the dining room at the moment debating the proper seat-number rotation, which had plagued him for days. Identifying diners by number enabled servers to put each dish in front of the person who ordered it, and to avoid messy tableside queries like "Who has the duck?", but any system required consensus about how to number. Luke placed diner one in the southeast corner of a table and counted the rest clockwise, which left everyone confused about whether the two tables at the far side of the room should work the same way or be a mirror image of the others.

It wasn't an idle concern. In the worst-case scenario, the diner in seat three, who was allergic to shellfish, mistakenly got the plate intended for seat two, took a carefree bite, and ended the evening in the emergency room. As more people wandered in with an opinion, though, it became a lightning rod for anxiety. Nate listened just long enough to be exasperated, worried that he and Luke weren't exuding a suitably managerial air.

"We'll figure it out," he said, signaling that the conversation was over.

"For tonight it's the southeast corner for everyone." That resolved, he went back to his own way of coping with opening-night nerves, which involved never standing still. He checked the bar, he looked at the reservation list that was Luke's responsibility, he adjusted the music level up, and then circled back a moment later to adjust it down.

Jenni had nothing to do until an order came in, because her way of coping was to get ahead. She took pride in her exacting mis en place, the double row of small steel containers that held every seasoning and garnish and sauce she needed for the night's menu, a set-up worthy of a sous and an example to anyone who worked for her. It was almost enough to make her feel confident. She stepped over to review the line cooks' set-ups, and that helped, too. To bridge the rest of the gap between her experience and her new job, she chattered. She couldn't help it, and in between commenting on almost everything she apologized for doing so. No one seemed to mind, as her running commentary balanced out Jonah, who tended to get even quieter when he felt stressed.

The need to keep busy was contagious, so there was a flurry of nervous hygiene right before the doors opened. Jenni made sure that her long ponytail was tucked out of the way, even though it already was, and the line cook took notice and pulled her ponytail into an even more disciplined braid. Nate, whose downtown style involved a fitted dress shirt and narrow chinos with hems rolled to expose his ankle boots, darted into the bathroom to brush his teeth and then continued to prowl the space. Luke put on a sport coat and used his electric razor to eliminate any shadow that might have appeared since he shaved that morning.

Jonah watched a server make wipe towels, a precise ritual that seemed two-thirds necessity and one-third superstition. First she trimmed a small edge off a set of paper hand towels and then she moistened the slightly shorter towels so that they were neither too dry nor too drippy. Satisfied with the moisture content, she rolled them as tightly as possible and stacked them in a dish so that Jonah could wipe the rim of a plate before it went out. On opening night, this chore required an experienced front-of-house staffer, not some kid doing it for the first time. A properly rolled towel was a totem that said, This is a professional kitchen. A loose or uneven towel could be a sign that the whole place was about to unravel.

The last minutes before 5:30 were somehow very long and very short all at once, and Jonah had an extended moment, right before the first customers came in, when he let himself reflect on what was about to happen, unspooled the future like a kite on a breeze. Someday he'd split his time between Huertas and whatever came next—plural—with a system in place that enabled him to develop new concepts while his dependable kitchen staffs handled the day-to-day operations. Someday his restaurants would be an incubator for talented cooks who moved on to open their own places.

He dreamed of creating the kind of kitchens that people in the industry talked about with admiration—venerable ones like those at Danny Meyer's USHG, which owned Gramercy Tavern and Maialino, where Jonah had worked; kitchens run by chefs just a half-generation older than Jonah, like David Chang and April Bloomfield, who built empires on a radical redefinition of fine dining that questioned the need for tablecloths and distinct courses and even reservations; anyplace that the three principals of Major Food Group decided to open. The MFG trio were all in their thirties and in a seemingly fearless hurry, ready to reinvent their wildly popular first place, the 25-seat Torrisi Italian Specialties, even if it meant a radical change in the dinner menu and a tripling of its price. Torrisi catapulted them onto a rarified list of instant hits, and started a run of four restaurants in four years, with more on the way. The usually fickle opening crowds didn't move on from these places, unless it was to check out what the owners were doing next.

At the moment Jonah might be rolling trays of cod croquetas like some first-year line cook, but it was all in the service of his long-term plan. Some young chef with an irresistible menu was going to be the next phenomenon, and he had to believe he had as good a chance as any to be the one.

Nate broke the spell to give Jonah the latest news. Ryan Sutton, just named the lead New York City restaurant critic at eater.com after a stint at Bloomberg, had tweeted about Huertas' opening.

"That means he's coming," Nate told Jonah, assuming that a critic wouldn't bother mentioning a restaurant he intended to ignore.

He was hardly the only one paying attention. In the days leading up to the opening there had been announcements on Zagat, Tasting Table, Urban Daddy and Gothamist. On April 18, Huertas showed up as number ten on Grubstreet's weekly Power Rankings, New York magazine's list of the city's hottest restaurants—based on nothing but advance noise, as the restaurant wasn't yet open. The phone was ringing like mad, and a third of the opening night reservations were for people Jonah didn't know, "which would have been more if family and friends hadn't booked earlier." He'd had to post a sign on the front door on the final two nights of the five-night soft opening, a friends-and-family tryout, saying that Huertas was closed for a private party, because strangers who tracked openings came by hoping for an early glimpse.

It was exactly what Jonah had hoped for, despite the occasional twinge of anxiety about living up to the advance press, because the alternative was to be one of those chefs with a little neighborhood place nobody discovered for six months, if at all, and nobody reviewed, ever. He'd much rather get noticed.

Nate tried to achieve a similar enthusiasm, and failed. He was fixated on the fact that this was the first critic to weigh in.

"It would be nice," he muttered, "if somebody would let us open before they blew us up."

An hour into service, Jonah had already decided that the homemade potato chips for the boquerones plate needed more salt, that his homemade set-up for order tickets was a mess, and that the people at seats three and four at the bar should get their papas bravioli for free because they'd waited too long, which meant that the fryer wasn't hot enough. He rifled through the cooler drawer of micro-greens to replenish the small tray at the pass with the specific varieties he needed. In between orders he picked flecks of Superglue off his fingers. He'd successfully repaired the food processor earlier in the day, but now he couldn't feel the food.

He checked every plate that went out, even as he kept an eye on the big digital clock on the wall and waited for reinforcements to arrive. Jonah had set up an insurance policy for himself, three friends to help out at the start who had more experience than the rest of his kitchen staff, combined. He stopped holding his breath when the first one walked in at seven, after a day that had begun at 5:30 in the morning with a catered breakfast for 400. Dan shrugged off his exhaustion, carved out a little space for himself at the end of Jonah's pass, and began peeling lemons at warp speed, so that slivers of peel could be candied and used as a garnish for the rice pudding.

By eight the bar stools were full, people were standing at the counter across from the bar just as Jonah had imagined they would, the three booths across from the kitchen were full, and a steady stream of people walked by the kitchen on the way to the dining room. It was gratifying, but it was an illusion, and Jonah knew it. The opening crowd, most of it, was a fickle bunch that prized new over good, and a percentage of the bar crowd would likely never come back, because they were on their way to the next new place, loyal only to being current.

It was easy to spot them—funereal chic on the women, whose cut-out clothing had a mysterious chicken-and-egg relationship to their tattoos, and big shirts over little pants on the men. Silver studs on their shoes, belts and backpacks, and in their earlobes, unless they had a day job where it was acceptable to wear gauges, the earrings that opened a hole in the lobe. Anyone who was that committed to a look was not going to stick around to become a regular, because the whole point of their existence was to be wherever the next scene was.

The customers who walked past the kitchen to the dining room were older, probably more likely to settle in, potential regulars—and if this worked the way it was supposed to, regulars who came in more than once a week, because sometimes they opted for a lighter meal at the bar. But there would be attrition there, too, diners who decided they wanted more choice on the menu or less of something Jonah couldn't even speculate on.

There was no time to dwell, because the dominant noise, in Jonah's world, was the mechanical bleat of the little grey order printer that sat on the counter to his right. Jonah and Dan danced the experienced dance of cooks who'd worked the line in a crunch, somehow managing to do what they needed to do, fast, without colliding, and with an urgency that made everyone else try to stay out of their way rather than break up the pattern. Jonah reached up to a top shelf next to the combi-oven for a bag of almonds as Dan dipped out of his way and dove for a quart container of chocolate pieces from the cooler drawer. Without a word, they set out two little saucers of almonds and chocolate chunks for bar seats three and four, with the chef's compliments, a final apology for their late potatoes.

When the pace in the back room picked up, Dan silently stepped over next to Jonah and started plating cod entrees. This was how a kitchen was supposed to work, how Jonah hoped the Huertas kitchen would work once everyone got used to the rhythm and traffic patterns. Jonah had always loved working the hot line, and had nothing but admiration for the members of his special crew, Dan and two other friends—one an executive sous chef and one a sous—who had some free time between jobs and would arrive in mid-May and early June, respectively. "To be able to show up in the middle of service, help out, not be in the way, roll right in without even knowing what's on the menu is a unique talent," he said. In his kitchen, a great cook was the one who shut up and got the work done without taking up a lot of psychic space.

When Nate came over to ask how it was going, the question barely registered.

"Great," said Jonah, preoccupied with what was on the plate in front of him.

"Doesn't sound convincing."

Jonah shot him a distracted but managerial smile; he had to remember that people looked to him to set the tone. "It's great," he repeated, more loudly. "Dining room pacing's good."

The bar was moving a little too fast, but that was a good thing. The pintxo runner skidded toward the pass and asked for any pintxos at all, because he had a slew of new customers, including people who were drinking and eating in the middle of the front room, balancing their drinks and little plates in their hands because there was no space at the bar or the standing counter against the wall.

"Ten chorizo, eight shrimp, eight scallops," called Jonah over his shoulder, without stopping to turn around.

The final order of the night meant that housecleaning could begin, as much a daily ritual as the preparations that preceded service. Jonah wanted his kitchen as clean at the end of the day as it had been on the day they connected the kitchen appliances; it was a matter of self-respect as well as a smart habit, given the constant threat of a surprise city health inspection. Breaking down the kitchen was hardly a glamorous aspect of his job, not the kind of thing people saw when they watched food shows on television, and someday he'd graduate from having to participate. For now, he intended to work as hard as everyone else did—to establish a baseline standard that would survive when he took his two days off.

Food went into plastic pint or quart containers, the date and contents written on a piece of blue masking tape. Cheeses and ham and half-sheets of pintxos were covered with food-grade plastic wrap as tight as a trampoline. Cooks ran up and down the narrow stairs at an angle, one with a half-sheet held overhead, another carrying a hunk of cheese tucked close like a football, to store bigger items in the basement walk-in refrigerator. The bartenders decided whether the citrus wedges would last another day, stashed what could be stashed and wiped down every surface.

The dishwasher sprinted back and forth as though he were being timed on relay legs, darting from each cook's station to the sink at the rear of the kitchen and back again to return clean plates and platters and equipment to their rightful spot. He had informed Jonah during his job interview that he would only take a dishwashing job if there were a chance for him to move onto the line someday. In the meantime he made sure that his new boss saw how hardworking he was, no matter how menial the task.

Once the food was put away, the kitchen staff got on their hands and knees, or leaned hard against a cooking surface, or balanced on a counter to reach the exhaust fan, to soap down every surface. The smell of cleansers quickly smothered the smells of cheese and ham and wood-oven char, and after a half hour the space approximated a kitchen that had never been used. In the meantime the front-of-house staff, like any good dinner-party hosts, wiped tables, adjusted vases, and bused the last tables. Well after midnight, the last exhausted staffer left for home, or for a nearby bar to decompress.

Jonah slumped into a booth with Nate and Luke to try to make sense of what had just happened. They had sold so many pintxos that the servers had lost track of the numbers, which meant that they needed a better tally system right away. Runners were supposed to circulate with a tray until it was empty, and then come back to the pass to record who took what, but things had gotten too frantic, and they had forgotten how many they'd served and to whom, which meant that the restaurant lost sales. The dining room menu worked, though they all knew, without saying, that Dan's speed and efficiency had kept them from falling behind. The kitchen staff had tackled the nightly kitchen break-down with inappropriate good cheer, emptying and cleaning every drawer and cabinet and surface, something to be grateful for until the novelty wore off.

Jenni had found her rhythm and recovered from her opening-night jitters, and the cook at the wood-burning oven only burned her arm once. They'd used up all of the prepped ingredients except for a cup or two of pre-sliced potatoes, which Jonah took as a very good sign. The better his volume estimates, the fewer leftovers, the less money he threw away on unused product.

But before the partners went home, they had to address the missteps. They needed a "soignee" list to alert the staff to VIP customers and their preferences. They needed the food runners to keep an eye on the pass and grab hot plates as soon as they appeared, rather than wait to be called over. The bartender had to stay off his cell phone.

Most important, in terms of building a decent total check, they had to bus pintxo plates as soon as they were empty. If plates sat on the table, customers felt that they'd eaten enough. If they disappeared, customers stared at the empty space in front of them and were likelier to order from the next circulating tray.

They analyzed the particulars and listed the next day's tasks as though to compensate for a rising elation. It would be so easy to levitate—and after all, a small moment of celebration was called for, given how long they'd waited for this moment and how hard they'd worked. Jonah, who had worked at four previous openings as a line cook, was the most experienced member of the trio, in addition to being the majority owner. It seemed appropriate for him to provide a little happy context. This was, he told his partners, the smoothest opening he'd ever worked on, and he wasn't saying that because of any bias.

"I know stuff's going to go wrong, but I know we're going to fix it," he said. "And I think we're going to make money." He and Nate and Luke started to laugh, with relief as much as anything. He regaled them with a story a friend had just told him of a much bigger opening, twelve cooks to Huertas' four, 80 covers to tonight's 50, where the cooks had lost their synchronized rhythm and never got it back. "They went down in flames," was how the friend described it.

And Huertas hadn't. For all their inexperience, they'd pulled it off.

It was two in the morning before Jonah had a moment to himself, and more time until the adrenaline subsided and he could even think of sleep. He'd be back in the kitchen the next morning before ten to make his own stocks and prep for dinner. Eater.com was sending a photographer over at noon to shoot the restaurant's interior.

You've just read an excerpt from Generation Chef.

ABOUT THE AUTHOR

Karen Stabiner teaches the food writing course at Columbia University Graduate School of Journalism. She is a regular contributor to *The Wall Street Journal* and *The New York Times*, and is the author of multiple books, and in the food space the coauthor of the cookbooks *Family Table*, a collection of staff meal recipes and thirty stories of backstage life at Danny Meyer's Union Square Hospitality Group restaurants, and *The Valentino Cookbook* by Piero Selvaggio. Her essay and feature work has appeared in *Best Food Writing* anthologies, *The New York Times*, the *Los Angeles Times, Saveur, Travel & Leisure*, and *Gourmet*. She was an essay finalist for a James Beard Award.

IMPRINT: Avery
PRINT ISBN: 9781583335802
PRINT PRICE: $27.00
EBOOK ISBN: 9780698195806
EBOOK PRICE: $13.99
PUBLICATION DATE: 9/13/16
PUBLICITY CONTACT: Louisa Farrar lfarrar@penguinrandomhouse.com
EDITOR: Lucia Watson
AGENT: Eric Lupfer
AGENCY: William Morris Endeavor

DARLING DAYS

a memoir

iO TILLETT WRIGHT

SUMMARY

Unfolding in animated, crystalline prose, an emotionally raw, devastatingly powerful memoir of one young woman's extraordinary coming of age—a tale of gender and identity, freedom and addiction, rebellion and survival in the 1980s and 1990s, when punk, poverty, heroin, and art collided in the urban bohemia of New York's Lower East Side.

EXCERPT

January 8, 2016

Dear Ma,

Since my first conscious moments, you have been a gladiator to me—the fiercest example of a woman's power I could ever know.

We are some kind of twins, able to see each other in a room of closed eyes, able to hear each other in a world of silence, despite all the trauma layered into our story. You are the priestess at the head of my very small tribe.

Since I learned to use a phone and to this day, when our family wants to reach you, they do it through me. I am the whisperer, the only one who can ever locate you in the jungle of New York, because you will always call me back.

When no one could find you to break the news, it fell to me to tell you that your mother had died. The noise that came from you was animal pain. The realization that I would also one day lose you was so unbearable that I had to hang up.

For years, we were best friends. Long before the fights and the screaming and the law got involved.

Which is why I feel like I need to say a few things to you before you read this collection of stories intended to capture my life.

People often marvel at my having "turned out so normal." They ask how I'm not angry, how I'm not a fuck up, why I don't turn around and abuse people.

They say it's extraordinary that I've forgiven you.

I am hardly without effects. I am a vortex of damage. In my brief three decades, I have hurt people, betrayed trust, caused confusion and disappointment. I have sauntered around the shores of what some have called "an ocean of rage," avoiding what would eventually become a crippling anxiety.

It's taken thirty years for me to melt the sandstorm of emotions within myself into glass, but now that I have found acceptance, now that I have forged an understanding of happiness and built my own world, I finally grasp the beautiful gift that is the lens I possess. Through it, I can see that instead of a "mom," I have been given a moral compass.

Your solitude, your rigorous discipline in your body, the brilliant originality of your vision, as if your eyesight were replaced with a loop from another planet, these things are all gifts to me.

Your demons, the visitor that would seep into your eyeballs so many nights, clouding the kindness, turning your spit to poison; I do not begrudge you.

I bow in humbled respect at the feet of your loss, Ma.

Since I was a small child, you have recounted the story of Billy, your epic love, and his murder. Nothing has ever touched me or provoked as much empathy in my heart as that; the violence of your loss, so shortly before my arrival in this world. How could I have hated you?

I think, even as a tiny tot, I understood; Billy was taken from you, a tragedy without which I would never have existed, and thus, you were to be protected.

I've spent six years photographing 10,000 people who don't fit into what tradition demands they look like and who they should love. I have seen abhorrent, brutal rejections of children by their parents, and it has made me grateful.

People call me brave, for getting up on stages and being open with who I am, but I know no other way than to be proud of who I am, because of you.

I was given the most important gift two parents can give to their child: Your respect. My dignity.

So, whether or not you understood that I wanted a clean house, regular meals, and to know which version of you would come home at night; whether you grasped the inappropriate level of professional expectation you put on me as a child who just wanted to play; although your addictions ravaged our relationship for so many years—I understand.

I hope, now that we finally know where Billy was put to rest, that we can find a way to his remains, and close the gash that has defined you for three decades.

I will do everything I can to help you find peace, so you no longer have to medicate with flavored solvents and pharmaceutical hammers, so you are no longer the loneliest wolf.

Because of you, I know forgiveness.

Because of you, I know love.

Forever,

Your Bud

Part One

Heredity

"If it doesn't hurt like hell, it ain't worth a jack shit."—My Ma

Her

Chapter One

Babygirl's Gun

13 3rd Avenue, NYC, 1982

She said he gave her the little gun because it was classy and elegant, just like her. A feminine twist of metal and pearl. Lethal, just like her. She kept it under her pillow "in case."

Her bed was, is, and always will be under an open window, this one looking out onto 3rd Avenue. In 1981, her pillow filled a head/pistol sandwich, but she doesn't use a pillow now.

Then, she pulled her bleached blonde, bombshell locks into a ponytail when she slept, always with her man Billy. Under a pile of blankets in the winter or sweating naked in the summer, but always with her man.

The window gaped like a loyal simpleton, beaten by the sun, or drooling raindrops, but its mouth never closed. The window stayed open.

My mother's world was a riot of improvisations, everything in flux and nothing predictable except the open window and the radio on. Rhythm in the air. "Life! in the air" she'd say. It stays on. She would tape over the switch. Nobody fucks with Babygirl's radio.

Later, she would say that there was never a gun in the house. She would swear to this, like a mafia wife, blinded by passion or loyalty. Either way it wasn't completely true. There was a gun under her pillow. Whether or not he pulled it out before they shot him, nobody knows.

Them

Chapter Two

Birth

3rd Street between 2nd Ave and the Bowery, Late summer 1985

It was a full moon, the last night of August, 1985. My mother told my father to turn the video camera on because the baby was coming.

It was sticky hot outside, the kind of air you can feel. She waded uptown through warm pudding, to a swimming pool in Hell's Kitchen. Two weeks before, belly the size of a basketball, she had posed in a bikini at the Russian baths for a young photographer who told her that swimming was the best thing to loosen up her hips for birth. My mother had been swimming every day since.

Sounds travel differently in the summer. Horns are sharper, screams pierce, and cat calls work double time, trailing swinging booty shorts for blocks. In the mid 80's, street lights on Ninth Avenue winked on and off over sidewalks cluttered with garbage, the carts of fruit vendors, and the splayed bodies of crackheads, hugging the cement, sharp ribs laid bare in the heat.

Five lanes of headlights cut through the darkness, making Dick Tracy comic books out of countless shady instances, deals in doorways, pupils dilated from a thousand synthetic euphorias, uptown kids in Brooks Brothers and pearl earrings who thought Hell's Kitchen was coming "downtown" to cop. The beams backlit a fleet of musclebound tranny hookers, teetering back and forth on six inch heels between twenty dollar tricks. They carried box cutters in their garters in case tonight was the night some dumb motherfucker decided to let his Jesus guilt get the better of him after cumming on their miniskirt. At nearly six feet tall and broad in the shoulders, her eyes raw from the chlorine, Rhonna was perfectly camouflaged within the local wildlife.

They invented the word "Glamazon" for women like my mother. Grace Jones had the same severity and stature. Mix one part unicorn, three parts thunder storm, two parts wounded bull, and you'd have an approximation of the vibe my mother gives off. A wild tiger would be at a disadvantage in a fight. Bleached blonde hair sliced at her chin, eyes crystal blue. Her head is carved for the shoulder pad look, all bones and lines. Her face is anchored by a Greco-Roman nose that dives into crimson lips, full, and finely drawn, over ivories so impressive we call them her piano keys. Her muscles twist over her tiny bones like steel cables, and she leads with her chest like a native warrior, her hands made to grip a sword in battle.

The 70's and 80's were a primitive time in New York, a time of robbery, drugs, and rape, so a working model who favored mini-skirts and skin tight jeans had to be able to show her teeth. She learned to train a look on a man that could make him piss himself. She once carried a busted fluorescent tube through midtown and shook it in the face of street thugs like a jagged spear.

But that evening, my mother was slow moving, vulnerable, if ever fierce. She looked like a teenager carrying a backpack on her front, because little aside from her belly had grown during the pregnancy. Her hair was swept back, her skin clear and radiant, glowing the way pregnant women do, with a sharp nose and a head of blond curls like Alexander. Her bright red denim Daisy Dukes hadn't closed for weeks, so she wore them unzipped and rolled down. Maternity wear didn't enter her universe.

As she walked toward a Times Square teeming with 25 cent peep shows and twenty dollar hustlers waiting for daddy's to make their night, a vendor stepped out from under his awning and said, *"My god, I've never seen anything so beautiful!"*

My parents lived on a notorious block in their day; 3rd street, between second and third, an address that is innocuous now. The barnacled gore of used needles and crack pipes, the sludge of despondency, waste and murder, the freaky traces of poverty clawed into these crappy tenements, have long since been bleached out and washed away

My parents and their scene were there before the gleaming 7/11 and the thirty dollar brunch specials, lounging in their high-waisted jeans, collars turned up, hair teased out, blasting rap and jazz and no-wave from boom boxes. Before the East Village was referred to as "the NYU neighborhood," you had to use a pay phone to call your dealer, and you had to shout up to windows to be let in.

The Bowery Hotel, now a glamorous weekend landing pad for movie starlets, used to be a 24-hour gas station that served radioactive vindaloo on styrofoam plates to my mother in the middle of the night. Two mangy dogs roamed between the pumps, so dirty and caked with exhaust grease that one's fur had turned green, and the other one blue.

The street was no picnic at the turn of the previous century, when immigrants packed each apartment, six to a room. But by 1985, even with the city broke and in chaos, at the tail end of punk, and in the midst of a crack epidemic, Third Street stood out for the refinement of its violence, for its kaleidoscopic insanity.

Directly across the street from our building stood the largest men's shelter in New York, which had turned our block into a dumping ground for homeless people from all over the country, the abscessed injection point for the nation's addicted, vagrant, and mad, the Ellis Island of the criminally insane. America had been cutting loose it's mental patients for a decade, and blending them in with the detritus of society—the failed, the lost, the abandoned—and this toxic brew, refused at every back yard in the country, was being shipped in like barges of garbage, and unloaded onto our street, making it the festering point for every fuck up from as far away as Texas. The result was a low-key permanent riot.

My mother used to look out our window at the crowd, milling around like hyper-charged ants, and say:

"Look at 'em. America's undiagnosed misfits. They've got to self-medicate to survive, and all they got to work with is dope, crack, and Night-Train."

And many did not survive. At night there were so many homeless people sleeping shoulder-to-shoulder that you could hardly see the sidewalk. Occasionally, in the morning, an ambulance would come to take away a "late sleeper," leaving a grey silhouette in the concrete where the carcass had drained out.

On the corner opposite the gas station, the Salvation Army had set up a group home for delinquent boys, a half-way house for hopeless cases, which functioned like a prep-school for life across the street. Weekly, a police car would pull up onto the sidewalk and two officers would lead a youth out in handcuffs, nailed for robbing and raping a Japanese tourist in a stairwell somewhere.

To add to the stew, one avenue to the east, the infamous Hell's Angels had their east coast headquarters and clubhouse, and occasionally they would tear down the street, thirty to a posse, with no mufflers on their bikes, doing their best to get in a fight.

On the Fourth of July of every year, the Angels would blow up the block. A two-story American flag was strung from the north to the south side of the street, vibrating in the earsplitting waves of psychotic heavy metal blasting from stadium speakers jammed into the clubhouse windows. One year an M-80 exploded in a closed trash can and a triangle of galvanized shrapnel tore through the neck of a local Puerto Rican kid, killing him on the spot.

The police did what they could to stay outside of a four block radius from what they openly dubbed "the asshole of the universe." We called it home.

Three and a half months before her dip in Hell's Kitchen, in an apartment overlooking this miasma, my mother was up, at two in the morning, cooking herself something to eat. She had been working out feverishly for the last twelve weeks, trying to lose a stubborn little tire that had swelled around her waist. My father, staring at her in the darkness, saw her left hand draped protectively over her belly, and he knew immediately. It was pictured in a thousand frescos and altar pieces, this graceful and natural gesture of maternity.

"Rhonna, you're pregnant. We're having a baby."

Without context, this could seem like a sweet moment, a wonderful development in a relationship between two young lovers, perhaps looking forward to starting a family, or realizing some picket fence fantasy. Let me clear up that misunderstanding; my parents were just hot in the eighties. In fact, if we are going to grope around in the dark closet of existential responsibility, I blame the bathtub. A lot of relationships, and probably a lot of eighties babies can be traced back to the tenement tub.

Allow me to explain: when you walked into a one-bedroom, railroad apartment in an old tenement, you entered directly into the kitchen. Across from you were the stove and a refrigerator, and two inches from your right elbow was an iron bathtub, encased in white porcelain, a shorty, with little lion's paw feet, from the turn of the century, crafted for a little person. In our apartment, there was a dark bedroom to the left, and a sunny living room to the right.

People tend to underestimate the importance of a bathtub in the kitchen, in establishing the sexual tone of a Bohemian existence. It adds a whole new spice when friends take a bath while you are cooking dinner. Sensual mayhem.

Carrying an armful of records and a bottle of whiskey, my mother was all legs and skimpy outfits when she showed up on my father's doorstep. He had run into her before, once lying naked in a triangle of sunlight at the center of a cocktail party on the upper west side, and another time on the street, clutching everything she owned in two plastic bags. Freshly widowed, she was being ravaged by agonies beyond her control, and stalked by friends turned to suitors. Jailbirds who started hanging around after the mysterious murder of her husband by the police.

A week after their second encounter, my parents were both thrown out of a nightclub for drinking out of their own stash. Collared by a bouncer who knocked their heads together, they were tossed into the street. By this point, my father had seen all he needed to cast her as the unhinged and suicidal Ophelia in an avant-garde version of *Hamlet*, which he had been shooting for a few weeks.

At the apartment, "Hamlet" slept under a brown blanket in a corner of the living room amongst his paintings. He was a young friend of my father's who I would later know as Uncle Crispy—a wiry kid with a wild head of curls, whose long eyelashes beat down over big, soft brown eyes, and who talked shit with the raspy voice of a hustler. Crispy spent his time avoiding his duties as leading man, flirting with Rhonna, and darting out of the house.

She was up every night, howling old torch songs back into blasting speakers and swigging Johnny Walker in nothing but a china red skin-tight sweater. This perpetually naked tornado of energy and beauty living in his kitchen caused a great deal of excitement in my father's life. A great deal indeed. One thing leads to another, and they were rapidly entangled.

In truth, my father had never really seen her sleep. As a matter of fact, he can't recall ever seeing her lie down. Just getting her to sit was a feat, because she was the single most UP, energetic, physically active person he had ever encountered. Her exercise routines were particularly radical and savage, as was her diet, and her devotion was to staying lean, lithe, and skinny as hell.

In the few months leading up to this, she had been especially vigilant in her exertions, because she felt that she was putting on a little extra weight around the middle, and that wouldn't jive with the nightclub act she was rehearsing every day at a theater nearby. Her efforts had been unsuccessful in removing this bump, and so at two AM that night, as he watched her standing at the stove, shielding something deep within herself, he realized in a flash that she *was* protecting something, she was protecting me.

"*What the fuck are you talking about? I know my own body. I'm not pregnant, if I was pregnant, don't you think I'd be the first one to know?!*"

He insisted, pointing out the evidence, and finally she went out to an all-night pharmacy for a pregnancy test. Within a few hours, they were confronted with an unfathomable truth: they were going to have a baby.

The next morning, shouting and yelping, my father ran straight to the home of his old friend Francesco and his wife Alba, who had several kids. Alba, seeing that he was terrified, sat him down and in a perfectly relaxed, Italian way, said,

"*Sian, this is not something you plan. Babies come with the bread. Each* day, the bread is delivered, and one day it comes with a child. There is nothing to do but to accept it."

When he protested that he hadn't a clue how to care for an infant, she said,

"Don't worry. The child will teach you everything you need to know. The best teacher in the world is about to be born. They have a device called a scream, and they use it when anything is required. You will know exactly what to do, because the baby will TELL you."

My parents never had the intention of being a couple or building any kind of domestic life, but they made a pact: no matter what happened between them, they were going to care for the child, and failing that, they would at least make sure it was cared for. They explored all the options for a healthy birth, finally settling on a midwife, and even enrolling in breathing classes. My mother shelved the whiskey and focused her considerable energy on having the healthiest final trimester anyone has ever seen.

Which brings us back to that sweltering evening at the end of August. My father was standing on the corner of Third Street and the Bowery, talking to his friend Jean-Michel about his new fold-up bicycle. The mischievous young painter was wearing a full three piece tweed suit, sweating profusely, and my father was lecturing him about the dangers in such heat. Dismissing the mothering, Jean-Michel nodded over his shoulder, and said, "Maybe you should tend to your own garden."

Turning, Sian saw Rhonna coming through the traffic on their block. Carrying several bags, she was just slightly less concerned than usual with the cacophony around her, and she looked to be in pain. He rushed to her and, as he helped her upstairs she told him it was beginning.

"I need to swim."

By the time she returned from Hell's Kitchen that night, the gigantic moon was bursting from the sky. There was no question in her mind that the baby was coming. The scattered contractions confirmed as much.

My father picked up the phone and called the mid-wife that they had been training with. Both of them adverse to the concept of giving life surrounded by the dying, they had settled on the most natural birth possible, at home. The tiny, nun-like woman who they had contracted to help them was allegedly the best midwife in town.

Uptight and stroppy, she was someone who liked to play by the rules, so she and my parents had developed a mutual distaste for each other. Regardless, they had confidence in her, and now they were eager for her to come to the rescue. But their worst fears were realized: she told them that she couldn't make it. The full moon apparently had every mother in town popping out their progeny. She inquired about the frequency of the contractions, and when they told her they were few and far between, she said that in the morning, she would send another midwife, someone else.

"*Someone ELSE?!? WHO?!*"

My father was distraught, but my mother was cool. Splayed out naked on the hard wood floor, stretching and sweating, she let out a laugh. She heaved herself into the bathtub and said,

"*I couldn't give a fuck. I never liked that uptight bitch anyway.*"

Knees jammed into her teeth she looked into my father's terrified eyes and said, "*I'm happy she's busy.*"

They made it through the night without a birth, and in the morning my father went down and cleared himself a spot in the mayhem already underway to wait for "*someone else.*" He was wracked with worry, sure that they were going to be given a second-rate apprentice, some fool even less knowledgeable about childbirth than himself. They were headed for disaster.

Through the steaming heat and the crowds of human trash, he saw the shimmering mirage of a jewel. A tiny, elegant woman with a shock of silver hair in a yellow silk dhoti was making her way through the masses with the graceful strides of a prince. She was holding a piece of paper and checking it against addresses in doorways.

The second he saw her his breathing slowed. He sat up straight and watched her navigate the shit show. With perfect authority, she walked straight up to him and said, "*You must be Sian. I am Asoka, your midwife,*" and shooed him inside. She followed him up the stairs at a clip, firing questions at him in an Indo-British accent.

"Where is the mother? How often are the contractions? What are the nature of the contractions? Hurry, hurry, hurry."

She burst into the apartment and proclaimed:

"Yes, I am a replacement. We have never met before, and you are probably worried about my qualifications. Let me tell you, I have birthed 5,000 children with my bare hands, many of them at the foot of the Himalayan mountains. I know what I'm doing. Let me examine you. Get up! Why are you lying down?"

This is the nature of America, a place where immigrants who were doctors and master surgeons in their own countries come to find streets paved with gold, and end up driving taxis. By some idiotic bureaucratic oversight, my stunned parents had stumbled into the care of this wizard, who was not only first rate, but one of the most masterful midwives in the entire world. Someone who had birthed children under the most extreme conditions—from elevators to mud huts, from Bombay to Liverpool—that the United States didn't recognize as qualified for a birthing license. They could not have felt safer. They were delighted, in awe, in love.

Asoka put her hands on my mother's misshapen belly, and made a rather sober face. Feeling around, she had discovered that I was backwards, sitting spine to spine with my mother.

"Get up, get out of bed, grab a rag, and wash the floor! Like this."

Asoka dropped to her knees and began to demonstrate what she called "The Rock," a sweeping motion with the arms, dragging a rag back and forth across the floor, an activity that moved my mother's hips and was meant to reposition the baby correctly in the birth canal.

This was her philosophy. A woman giving birth is not sick. *You are as healthy as you will ever be. You are doing what you were designed to do, and your body is performing what it was put here to perform, and the last thing you will do is act ill. The BEST thing you can do is use your body, and generate as much activity as possible.* This was music to my mother's ears.

Having revolutionized their view of childbirth, and assuring them that there would be no delivery that night, Asoka went home to sleep. When she returned in the morning, she found my mother in a new state. She was in agony from more frequent contractions, and when Asoka examined her for the second time, naked on the wooden floor, she found that the baby had not yet turned. On top of that, my mother was dilating very slowly, so it was going to be a long haul.

After thirty hours they were all delirious. Rhonna's belly was deformed and stretched beyond anything she could imagine, and her formidable vocal chords were shredded from the screams.

At some point, with that much prolonged pain, your mind loosens, and your body takes over. Some ancient mechanism kicks in and puts you into autopilot. You have no control. Things are just happening inside of you.

Thirty-five hours in, my mother rolled up her eyes and checked out, leaving my father, nature, and Asoka Roy each with a hand on the reigns.

Asoka realized that if someone as powerful as my mother was unable to ride this out, they would need help. She looked into Sian's beleaguered face and said, "We are taking her to the hospital."

The little woman and the skinny boy carried Rhonna, screaming the whole way, down three flights of stairs. As they came to the shattered glass of the front door, my father looked out and saw the unimaginable: the gigantic men's shelter was having a fire drill. Seven hundred sweating bodies were teeming over the block, and pushing their way up his stoop. Seven hundred shirtless, Newport-smoking vagrants, shouting and hurling things, their voices like thunder, shaking the buildings.

Asoka squawked and he snapped to, pulling the door open. At that moment, her legs in my father's hands, finger nails digging into her midwife's arms, my mother let out a show-stopping scream.

A sea of men, the kind who carried knives in their teeth, went silent. Seven hundred faces turned toward the embattled trio. In awe of the most natural wonder, the sea parted. Hands came out to support them, and slowly, carefully, she was brought down the six concrete steps, bellowing from depths she didn't know she had. Someone brought a taxi from the corner, and they laid her into the back seat. Asoka with Rhonna, Sian in the front, they drove through the reverent crowd, and as they turned uptown on the Bowery the parting closed behind them and the roar erupted again.

The birthing room would be arranged according to my mother's requirements: lights out, music on—jazz, reggae, and blues. Asoka placed my exhausted, overwhelmed father at my mother's feet, and ordered him to hold her leg. She told him to soothe her, help her breathe. She elbowed away the doctors and nurses to ensure that my father was a central part of the arrival. 5,000 births and you learn to take no shit.

There was an enormous amount of pain and screaming. I crowned, but I wasn't going any further. Asoka gave my mother a little cut, and, suddenly, I arrived. I had come out backwards, covered in slime and blood, but I was a living, breathing little creature.

They put me on my mother's chest. My parents had made a point of not asking my gender, because they had no preference, it changed nothing for them, and they wanted the surprise.

Wrapped in blankets, breasts filled with so much milk they felt like cement, my mother looked down into the face of a tiny baby girl. To her, I looked like a mango. To my father, I looked like Winston Churchill crossed with a dried apple.

At that moment, both parents hovering over me, my tourmaline blue eyes popped open. Bang. Hello. Perhaps my infant intuition was trying to catch a glimpse of what would be a rare sight: the two of them together.

My father had been scribbling potential names on napkins for weeks. He was leaning toward a high and a low sound, a line and a disc, an on and an off, a moon and a demi goddess. Jupiter's moon, Io. The most volcanic object in the solar system. Now it was settled.

A few hours later, my Ma was ready to go. The doctors tried to convince her to stay the night, but Asoka had demolished their authority before going home to sleep, and Ma wanted to get the fuck out of there.

We went up to my grandparents' house and they took me out for a walk on my first night in this world, bundled up in blankets like a papoose.

Over the next few weeks, my parents took me to jazz clubs, and the theater, and to the dance floors at the Limelight and Danceteria. They put me right there on the table and let well-wishers come flocking. Rhonna was going to make sure she didn't raise a shy kid.

Us

Chapter Three

Fernando

Lower East Side, Summer 1989

Ma always says the day I was born was the hottest day New York has ever seen. Today she took that back.

"*Today,*" she says with a clenched jaw and eyes burning with furious excitement, "*is the hottest motherfucking day this town has ever had to melt through.*"

From where I am I can see the street steaming. Bodies all around me are nearly naked, glistening with sweat and glitter, writhing to blaring Samba music. I am at the front corner of a float, moving down Avenue C in the annual Brazilian Day Festival, which is a roaring parade of referee whistles, cow bells, and thunderous beats. As far as I can see, there are women in thongs and head-dresses, shirtless men in tiny shorts, and every variation of yellow and green, the colors of Brazil's national flag.

The sun crackles down on hundreds of smiling faces, including my friends Little Sean and Badu, who are hanging off the float with me. Everyone is dancing or singing or playing an instrument, sweating and dehydrated. Several people have climbed onto the back of our float in exhaustion and passed out.

My friends and our chariot are enclosed in a sea of samba school students dressed in all white, hitting giant drums in unison that hang from their waists. It's like an army band, only with a sexy South American sense of rhythm. You can hear the rumble coming from ten blocks away.

I am so slathered in SPF 70 that my headband keeps slipping down my face. It's hard for me to hold on to the edge of the float because my hands keep sliding off. Sean's mom's boyfriend built this monster of a rolling contraption out of a real boat. He put it on wheels, put a motor in it from a car he took apart, covered the whole thing with sheets and decorations and now, somehow, it's moving towards Houston Street. I'm sure it's going to fall apart any minute, so I hold on as tight to the edge as I can, swinging my hips to the music and sliding back and forth.

Ma is on the street in front of us, cutting a path down the Avenue with tight, hyperactive Samba steps, in a sparkling bathing suit hung with glittering tassel bits that shake back and forth with her waist, arms in the air. She dances alongside a fleet of women with bright cloth head-wraps and big, voluminous dresses called Bayanas. They're doing choreographed partner dances with men in tight pants and shirts with big, open collars who swing the women out so that their dresses sweep past them and curl back around.

I love this parade. I love the Brazilians. They have so much life. They love to dance, they love to sweat, they love music, and they love it LOUD. Ma is in ecstasy when she can dance freely like this with these people. I watch her move like an animal fulfilling nature's intentions, sweat pouring from her body.

A space parts between some of the drumming students, and a guy in a purple sequin suit appears on the other side of the crowd. He seems to be honing his focus on my Ma, and he is spinning toward her, kicking his legs, and waving his forearms. He is a damn good dancer this guy. Ma spots him and smiles in that demure way when she's willing to consider a dude, and he takes his opportunity.

Poppa moved out right around when my first tooth came in. They couldn't get along. They were never meant to. They couldn't share a life, much less a cramped space, so he found the nearest loft he could on the Bowery and moved out. Now I spend afternoons with him and his new girlfriend Rita. She's Brazilian too, and pregnant.

Ma and this dancer guy circle each other, dancing like it's their last day on earth, flailing wildly with every ounce of energy they have in them, ignoring the fact that the heat index probably broke an hour ago and even the sun is eager for the moon to take over.

His muscular shoulders are nearly popping the seams on the back of his sequin jacket. I can't even imagine how hot it must be inside there, but he doesn't take it off, he just keeps dancing.

He smiles at my Ma, flashing bright white teeth that contrast the darkness of his skin and the jet black of his hair. A gold chain glints on his broad chest, and every time he kicks his legs I notice the ferocity with which they snap back under him.

As we move further downtown, it gets hotter and hotter and people are starting to disintegrate in the swelter, but my Ma is getting more and more energy. Miraculously, so is purple sequins guy, and they are orbiting each other like burning fire planets, spinning faster, kicking higher, dipping lower.

The band members have started to peel off their shirts and are evaporating bottles of water over their steamy heads. Just when you'd think it was a lost cause though, the leader jumps back out in front of the troops and starts banging on a cowbell and dancing to his own beat, furiously blowing on his whistle. With his white t-shirt tied around his head, sweat pouring down his dark face, he starts bounding back and forth in front of the drummers, corralling them back into action. We hit a red light at First Avenue and he uses the pause to coordinate a unified commencement. Ma and suit guy are still dancing, watching the drummers merge back into each-other's rhythm. They are like the fuse that erupts the parade.

Everyone congregates back in the parking lot of the Cuando building when they're done, all fired up and yelling and still playing music, high off the energy of the crowd.

Cuando is a massive public school building that stretches across the better part of 2nd street, between 2nd Avenue and the Bowery. It has no electricity but lots of artists and junkies squat here.

Nilda and Virginia, two Puerto Rican ladies in their forties, are the matriarchs of the place, keeping the real nasty riff raff out, and a campfire going on the roof. They cook up rice and beans and homemade sofrito in a little cement penthouse, a mortar and pestle in one hand, and a can of Budweiser in the other.

We go up there and play the drums and soccer and throw balls around with abandon because the roof is enclosed by a huge, high black metal fence that bends in over us, so we can never lose the balls over the edge.

Because there's no electricity it gets gnarly at night in the hallways. When you have to take a piss, you just wander into one of the rooms and find a corner and let it go. Trying to find the bathroom could get you killed, tripping over a sleeping punk or musician and tumbling down the pitch black stairs.

The parking lot out front is a big, nasty mud pit with some plywood boards thrown down to make pathways for walking on. It's overflowing with the crowds from the parade, piles of drums, the start of a BBQ in a metal trash can, and the popping bottle sounds that signal the end of a long day.

The street is clogged with the makeshift floats, parked akimbo half on the sidewalk, coming in to dock and be dismantled once the sun goes down and everyone is drunk enough to give a fuck.

I am holding a piece of chicken, slathered in BBQ sauce, that Virginia gave me. Half the sauce is smeared across my face, and I am absolutely fine with that. Ma is discussing something with the Bayana ladies. Everyone has been preparing for the parade for weeks, building the floats and making the costumes, so we all know each other, and it's no surprise when purple sequin guy appears again at Ma's elbow.

He has a strong, fine jawbone, like a jaguar or a puma or something, and deep, dark caramel skin. A scar cuts across his forehead, which, I will later find out, he got from climbing barbed wire fences to pick pineapples straight from the tree in Brazil.

Flashing his blinding white teeth, he smiles, and says, *"Ey..."*

The Bayana lady looks at him and in her big, beautiful, rolling Brazilian accent says, *"Ohh Fernando. Honna, this is Fernando. Fernando, Honna,"* and moves away into the crowd to leave them to work fate. Fernando, smooth as chocolate, in a thick accent, says, *"Ey Honna. We go to another parade in Wash DC. Why don't you come?"*

She looks him straight in the eye, points to me with one lazy finger, and says, *"Hey Fernando, I got a tiny child right heres. We're not going to Washington, DC."*

The way they smile at each other is so loaded, and they are both still short of breath from their dance marathon, so their chests are heaving, but they only exchange a few more little pleasantries and he ambles away, resigned to her unattainability.

It's a year before they see each other again. We're walking up Broadway toward 14th street, and suddenly there he is, with some young buck Brazilian friend of his, taping signs to lampposts for house painting services. They catch sight of each other and that's it. She brings him home and he never leaves.

Over time I learn this: Fernando is from Belo Horizonte. He went to "Futbol" boot camp growing up, a place where they keep young men in a fenced-in encampment, training and training relentlessly, to become professional soccer players. He ended up playing for the national teams of Brazil, Portugal, and France, until the French stiffed him out of 25 Grand and he came to New York to be with his brothers. His legs are considered lethal weapons.

He told us that his uncle had shot his wife, in public, at a cafe in Brazil, and that the police turned their cheek to crimes of passion there. I watched my Ma react to that story, and later that night she said to me, *"Ah hell, I am never going to BRAHZIL!"*

But we knew then that he had the violent gene of jealousy. Ma told me Billy had it, too. That thing where something comes into people's eyes and they turn into an animal. Over on 12th street, in his new apartment, my father had already started fending off Rita's incinerating jealousy, her x-ray eyes that saw a thousand things that weren't there.

Fernando lives with us now. I like him a lot. He brings home pasta cooked in tomato oil, from the restaurant where he works in the kitchen. He takes me out on his shoulders when he goes selling shit, and he's teaching me the tricks of the trade—how to hustle people into spending more than they know they should on stuff they don't need, just by being charming. He's also teaching me how to be a master soccer player. We get along like gangbusters and from his shoulders I get a commanding view of the mercantile chaos of the midtown streets.

We all go to the beach together, and they make out while I build sand castles and make friends with the old people. We eat mangoes together and we dig the salt water. They are really in love, and I like that.

They created a Samba act together, Fernando and my Ma. At first it was a duet act, and then they expanded it to include other girls, in costumes and head-dresses, and then the musicians from the Samba school joined them, then eventually the Capoeiristas. The whole Carioca cachaça clatch. It was impressive and became a sensation for a little while. They'd do gigs at public schools during the day, and club shows at night.

Fernando's jealousy has been getting worse though. After one of the parties they came home in a cab and apparently he really threw a shit fit with one of the other girls there. It turned into a screaming match on the street, with him yelling nasty things at my Ma. When they exploded into the house, I was pretending to sleep but I listened to them tear into each other, him accusing her of all kinds of things I know she'd never do. My friend Badu was sleeping over, and eventually we got up and watched them yelling in the kitchen, until Fernando reared back and socked her square in the face.

I yelped, loud, but I couldn't move. I felt glued to the spot, but Badu ran straight for him and started wailing on his waist. Fernando, in the heat of the moment, kicked him in the shin and my tiny friend crumpled into a crying pile on the kitchen floor. That was a disaster, him kicking a little kid, and Fernando stormed out.

Then things changed, one night when I wasn't there. I was having a sleepover with my poppa and when I came back, something was different. Fernando wasn't warm anymore.

He started shouting Ma down in the street, saying mean things to sink her self-confidence. He got real insecure and started accusing her of more and more outlandish shit. She'd just grab my hand and keep walking, but I could see her holding back tears about it.

Ma worked out a signal with me that involved a hand behind her back. I was supposed to slip out and find the cops if she ever gave it.

One night, coming home from the beach, we see a cop car parked right outside our door, two officers in the front seat doing their paperwork by the light of the dashboard. It's a hot night, and the air between Fernando and my Ma is thick with heat and tension. Ma starts cooking when we get upstairs, but something lights Fernando's fuse. He starts yelling, his eyes like black fire, and when he hauls off and kicks a cabinet, denting the wooden door, Ma throws me the signal.

I take the stairs two at a time, almost tumbling down, throw open the heavy front door and wave the cops up.

"Hey! Hey! My Ma needs help! Come on!"

A lady cop and her fat partner come in and assess the situation; a burly man panting with aggression, a woman shielding her small child.

The lady cop says to my Ma, "What do you want to do with him?"

Heavy in the heart but looking Fernando straight in the face, Ma says, "Just get him outta here. There will be no violence around my little daughter, or myself."

So the cops drag him out, and we pack a suitcase with all his shit, including his passport, and drop it down in a neighbor's apartment so he doesn't have any excuse to come breaking the door down.

A few weeks later we're coming home late one night, just Ma and me. We went out to a bar and she had two glasses of wine for the first time in a real long time. As we're coming up to the building, she starts to cry. She's holding my hand and letting out these long, wailing, weeping sobs. It's disorienting to see my rock crumble. I don't know what to do.

We climb the steps to the building and suddenly she pulls back and puts her fist through the small square pane of glass in the thick metal door. It smashes on impact. This scares me. I have never seen my Ma get violent. When I look up into her eyes, she is gone, and there is a new creature there, eyes black with fire.

This sinister force will eventually creep into every crevice of our world, it will corrode our treasured bond, destroy my trust, and it will cripple my mother. The great equalizer, indiscriminate, brutal, and swift in its recruitment, I will watch as it nimbly swallows my fiercest protectors and leaves all of our lives forever stained.

You've just read an excerpt from Darling Days.

ABOUT THE AUTHOR

iO Tillett-Wright is an artist, activist, actor, speaker, and writer. Her artwork has been exhibited in New York and Tokyo and she has published three limited edition photography books. A featured contributor for the *New York Times' T Style Magazine*, her work has been featured in the *New York Times Magazine, New York Magazine, Brooklyn, Dossier, GQ, Elle, Bomb*, and *Huge*. iO will be the cohost (with Nev Schulman) of a new show on MTV. She lives in New York City.

IMPRINT: Ecco
PRINT ISBN: 9780062368201
PRINT PRICE: $26.99
EBOOK ISBN: 9780062368225
EBOOK PRICE: $21.99
PUBLICATION DATE: 9/27/16
PUBLICITY CONTACT: Sonya Cheuse Sonya.Cheuse@harpercollins.com
RIGHTS CONTACT: Michele Corallo Michele.Corallo@harpercollins.com
EDITOR: Daniel Halpern
AGENT: Bill Clegg
AGENCY: WME

Where Am I Now?

essays

🐧

"Growing up, I wanted to *be* Mara Wilson. WHERE AM I NOW? is a delight." **–Ilana Glazer, creator and star of BROAD CITY**

Mara Wilson

SUMMARY

For readers of Lena Dunham, Allie Brosh and Roxane Gay, this funny, poignant, daringly honest collection of personal essays introduces Mara Wilson—the former child actress best known for her starring roles in *Matilda* and *Mrs. Doubtfire*—as a brilliant new chronicler of the experience that is growing up young and female.

EXCERPT

Prologue

A few years ago, I found a video of myself on YouTube. It's from what I like to call my "sordid past" as a child actor. Like many moments in my childhood, I have no memory of it, but I do have a record.

I'm sitting next to Robin Williams, who is dressed and made up like a woman. We're on the set of *Mrs. Doubtfire*. The director is filming us so he can see what Robin's makeup looks like on camera, but I don't seem to know that. I am taking it very seriously.

"What's your name?" Robin says, affecting a slight Scottish brogue.

I look puzzled. *"Do I say my real name?"* I whisper to the girl beside me, an older girl with long dark hair. (This is Lisa Jakub, who is playing my big sister in *Doubtfire*. She will go on to become my honorary big sister in real life.)

"It doesn't matter," she whispers back.

"My name is Mara," I say to him, quietly. It's obvious, watching it now, that I'm not sure if I was supposed to say that. He tells me it's a beautiful name and that I'm wearing a beautiful dress, and asks me what I like to do. I shrug.

"We could make up stories. Do you like to make up stories?" he asks, trying again. Five-year-old me sits up a little straighter. He has said the magic word.

"Yeah, sometimes I like to make up stories," I say. When I was a little girl, there was nothing better to me than a story. I loved books, and I liked telling my own stories, too. I don't know exactly when I started telling them, but once I did, I never stopped. Sometimes I would even sing them. And these weren't just anecdotes or neat little fairy tales—they were more like epic poems, tales of adventure and morality to rival Virgil and Homer—at least in terms of length, if not quality. A shorter story could take all day, and one of my longer sagas lasted the entire summer between preschool and kindergarten. It got to the point where, whenever I said "I have a story," one of my brothers would cut me off, applauding and saying, "Oh, good story, good story!" before I'd even started.

Unaware that I have yet to learn about pacing, and that this story could potentially go on for days, Robin asks if I want to tell him one, so I go ahead, launching into a story about a bunny who went out into the woods when he should have waited for his parents to go with him. It's a morality tale, full of suspense and a man (or rabbit) versus nature motif, especially after the bunny is thrown from his raft into a raging river.

Robin nods along for the first minute, but as the story continues, he seems to be wondering how much longer it will go. Finally, I announce that the daddy bunny saved the baby bunny and lectured him, the mommy gave him medicine, and everyone had pie. The End. At that point, Robin lets out a low whistle, looks directly into the camera and says, "We'll be right back."

∗∗∗

I don't remember filming that video. I don't remember telling that story. Yet watching it as a twenty-something, I felt a remarkable sense of familiarity. If there's been a narrative theme in my life, it has been a need to find a narrative in everything. I found an audience as an actor, but even then, I spent all my time between shots sitting in my trailer, writing stories and screenplays. Adults would ask me if I wanted to continue being an actor when I grew up, and I would say, "Maybe, but I want to be a writer."

Age ten, writing when I should have been watching my sister.

From the time I broke up with Hollywood (more on that later) and moved to New York City, I've devoted myself to stories, as a playwright, oral storyteller, and host of my own storytelling show. And now, here I am, once again telling my stories to anyone who will listen. Mostly, my stories are about being young and a little out of place. It's how I've felt most of my life: I was born the first girl after three boys, the only Jewish kid in my class, the only girl I knew whose mother had died, the only neurotic in Southern California (or so it seemed), and the only child on film sets full of adults. I was always in someone else's world, and I always knew it. This, I've learned, is a far more common feeling than I once imagined.

But not everything about my experience has been universal. A few months after I found the video of Robin and me, it was taken down, apparently due to copyright infringement. I had to laugh. Most people have embarrassing videos of themselves as children. Few have theirs copyrighted by Twentieth Century Fox.

The Junior Anti-Sex League

My mother could not have picked a worse time to teach me about sex.

***

One night, when I was five years old, she turned on the TV to a special about sex education. Kids my brother Danny's age were holding bags of flour, calling them their "babies," and scrambling to find "babysitters" for them.

"Why are they doing that?" I said.

"They're learning about babies, how to take care of them, and how they're made," she said.

"Oh." I knew the last part: they were made in their mothers' bellies. I had seen my mother pregnant with my sister. But now the kids on the screen were in a classroom, and a teacher was talking to them about cells and body parts.

"What's she talking about?" I said.

"She's explaining sex to them."

I had heard that word before. I knew it was a loaded term, something grown-ups only said in whispers. "What is that?"

"It's how you make a baby," she said, and went on to describe the most absurd, unappealing process I could imagine.

She had always believed in telling children the truth, at least to the extent that they were capable of understanding. She was open about private parts and calling them by their real names. Her instincts about openness and honesty were right on, but still, I was horrified.

"You did that?" I blurted out. She nodded, and with a sickening feeling I counted up myself, my brothers and sister, and realized she must have done it *at least* five times.

"Any other questions?"

I had only one more. "When you did it, did you say 'Whoa'?" My mother had the best of intentions. She made it clear this was not something to be discussed in polite company, that it needed to be kept a secret. But I had a tendency to blurt out secrets. I have always been compulsively honest, and usually at the wrong time. Five months earlier I had ruined my father's birthday surprise party by asking, "You don't know about our cakes, right?"

Objectively speaking, sex seemed shockingly gross and ridiculous. But as the shock wore off, the world felt different. I could tell that sex was a Big Deal. It was something new and exciting, a secret grown-ups kept to themselves. Just knowing about it made me feel powerful. I had to tell someone.

And I had a big scene on the set of *Mrs. Doubtfire* the next day.

***

It was not my mother who had gotten me into acting. Not really. She was not a stage mother. But she was an actress: she had studied theater in college and never missed an opportunity to perform. My brothers and I went to Theodore Roosevelt Elementary School, and every year on Teddy Roosevelt's birthday, Teddy himself would come by, in person.

"...And I said, 'Don't you dare shoot that bear!' They made a little stuffed bear and named it after me, and that's why we call them teddy bears today!"

"Teddy" was only about five foot two, with D-cup breasts and a hat I had seen in my mother's closet, but her performance was convincing enough to make some of the kids ask, "Is that really him? I thought he was dead."

My mother disappeared into the role, morphing from a tiny woman into one of the most macho men who ever lived.

We lived in Burbank, in Southern California's San Fernando Valley, twenty minutes away from Hollywood. My mother always said of our hometown, "It's as if someone picked up a small city in the Midwest and plopped it down in the middle of Los Angeles." Burbank tried its hardest to stay quaint, but it was also home to Warner Brothers, NBC, and Disney Studios. The tentacles of the entertainment industry reached into everyone's lives. My father worked as an electronics engineer at CBS, NBC, and the local channel KTLA. Classmates came to school in cars with license plate frames reading "PART OF THE MAGIC: WALT DISNEY COMPANY," and my brothers would borrow movie screeners from friends with well-connected parents when we didn't want to wait for video. Given the omnipresence of the entertainment industry, getting into acting wasn't an unusual thing for a Burbank kid to do. Children all over the world do ridiculous, borderline dangerous things, and no one around them questions it, because it's ingrained in their culture. So it was with child acting in Southern California.

When I was a toddler, the oldest and most outgoing of my siblings, Danny, started trying out for commercials. He was cute and a quick study, booking a few TV ads, and even some small parts in movies. Watching my mother and Danny rehearse, I had an epiphany. What they did was like when I performed my stories at home, only better, because people *wanted* to see you perform! Shortly after my fifth birthday, I went right up to my mother and told her, "Mommy, I want to do what Danny does."

"No, you don't," she said.

They were already starting to feel burned out. She was relieved Danny had never become recognizably famous, and that he didn't want to be an actor when he grew up. He had been a confident, resilient kid, but the cycle of auditioning was getting to him. It would be worse with her anxious, oversensitive daughter.

"How about this," she said, when I kept asking to audition. "Your brothers and I are going to pretend to be the people at a commercial, okay? We'll tell you what to do and then tell you if you got the part."

Playing Polly Pockets on the set of one of my first commercials. I was not happy with what they did to my hair.

As always, I took playing pretend very seriously. I "acted" the lines about cereal or Barbies as well as I could, but every time my mother would say, "You were great, but you didn't get the part." And every time I would shrug.

"That's okay," I'd say. "I can just go on another one." For the first time in her life, my mother had no idea what to say.

I would follow Danny's example: get a few small roles, have fun with it, save some money for college, then give it up after a few years. I would never be famous. But after getting a few commercials, I was called in for a movie.

"So what would you think if your dad dressed up like a woman?" a man asked me, along with a few other girls who were auditioning. The other girls looked at the ground, murmuring, "I guess it would be funny." I burst out laughing and said, "I would be on the floor!"

I got called back. And then got called back again, and again. We were called to do a screen test in San Francisco, and before I knew it, I had the part. I was going to be in a movie.

But just because I'd gotten the part didn't mean I knew what I was doing. There was definitely a learning curve. For example, how was I supposed to know what to do if I had to go to the bathroom during the pool scene? (My mother and I eventually came up with a code so I wouldn't end up peeing on the lovely and handsome Pierce Brosnan.) How was I supposed to know that asking some of the crew members to "clap for me" was inappropriate? Everyone clapped for me when I sang in the Kindergarten Holiday concert. Why couldn't they do it here, too? My mother was, predictably, furious, pulling me aside and saying, "'Clap for me' is not acceptable!"

She and my father were determined not to let being in a movie go to my head. I always knew they loved me and they were proud, but they had to keep me grounded. If I said something like, "I'm the greatest!" my mother would be right there to bring me back down to earth.

"You're not the greatest," she said. "You're just an actor. You're just a kid."

***

The day after the sex talk, we were shooting a scene where we helped Sally Field choose a dress to wear to her birthday party. Her ex-husband, Robin Williams, has been denied custody of his kids, and to spend more time with them, he answers her ad for a housekeeper and nanny. Robin, dressed in full drag as an eccentric Scottish nanny named Mrs. Doubtfire, was supposed to come in, ask about the party, and realize he had a major conflict. Lisa Jakub would say her line, then I would say mine. But I wasn't focusing on the scene. I was bubbling with excitement, because I knew this *thing*, this big open secret, and I could not keep it in any longer.

My mother had stressed that sex was something that only happened when you were married, so when Virginia, one of the hair dressers, came over to touch up my bangs, I impulsively asked her, "Are you married?"

"Yes," she said.

"Oh," I said. "So you've *done it*, right?"

She looked surprised, then laughed, embarrassed. She didn't answer, and I felt unsatisfied. As soon as she walked away I announced in a singsong voice, "I KNOW ABOUT SE-EX! I KNOW ABOUT SE-EX!"

The whole crew was laughing, and I was giddy. They knew that *I knew* what they knew! I was triumphant, full of pure childish glee—until I saw my mother standing off to the side of the set. She was enraged. When my mother was angry, she was terrifying. She looked like Margaret Hamilton as the witch in *The Wizard of Oz*, or Emma Goldman's mug shot. How many times had she lectured me about behaving properly on the set? How many times in our conversation had she stressed that this was *not* something to talk about in public? How had I forgotten both of these things?

I immediately stopped singing, and with a sinking feeling I knew I had done something bad, and that I was going to be in deep trouble. Instantly, I felt humiliated, and worst of all, I knew I had brought it all on myself. I thought I might start crying. I wanted to apologize, tell my mother I would never do it again, anything to get that scary look off her face and rescue what was left of my pride.

I watched as Robin, in full Doubtfire drag, walked up to Chris, the director.

"Did you hear that Mara was asking Virginia about sex?" Robin said, and they both burst out laughing. They both had kids. They had both worked with kids. They knew what kids were like.

"You know, Mara," Chris said, turning to me, "if you want, you can tell Sally her dress is sexy."

I didn't dare. But I looked to my mother, and her face had softened a little. I was still going to get a lecture, but because they had been able to laugh it off, I had probably managed to avoid a spanking.

We always used to ask Chris Columbus when he'd discovered America. He would say "Around 1976."

I stayed awake that night, thinking of how badly I'd embarrassed myself. It was the first of many nights like that in my life. Did anyone else remember? What did they think of me? I had learned my lesson, and too well. Sex was powerful, something I needed to respect.

But if it was so secret and special, though, why did it suddenly seem to be everywhere?

***

There's a saying that if a child doesn't learn about sex from her parents, she'll learn about it on the street. I learned a good amount about it on one particular street: *Melrose Place.*

"You have an audition for a soap opera," my mother told me shortly after my sixth birthday, handing over my "sides," the script excerpt for the audition. "Your character's mother came from Russia, and her time here in America is almost up. She wants to stay here, though, so she gets married to a man named Matt, but he is actually gay."

"What does that mean?" I said.

"It means a man loves other men, not women. Or when women love women. It's just the way some people are."

"Oh, okay," I said. It seemed a little unusual, but not gross or disturbing. I thought of the girl at my preschool who had once told me she loved me and wanted to marry me. I had said "Sure" so as not to hurt her feelings.

"Two men can't *do it* like men and women do it, could they?" I asked my mother a while later, as an afterthought.

"Not like men and women, no," she said carefully, after a moment. "It wouldn't work."

Lucky them, I thought, not having to do any of that gross sex stuff.

***

I got the part. My mother laughed when she saw the call sheet: next to my name it said "(K)," for kid: I was going to be the only one on set.

At first, we would tape my episodes and watch them later, my parents fast-forwarding through the racier scenes. But eventually my mother relented and just let me watch the episodes in their entirety. She had a strange barometer for what was appropriate: she was upset when I watched *Hocus Pocus* at a friend's house, but took me to see *Four Weddings and a Funeral* in the theater. To be fair, she must have figured I wouldn't understand what was happening on *Melrose*—after all, I had thought the couple having sex in *Four Weddings* was just bouncing on a trampoline I couldn't see.

Melrose Place was the most terrifying show I had ever seen. People I knew and loved were playing characters who hurt one another in spectacularly detailed ways. Michael was driving drunk and doing it with three different women. Sydney was using drugs and doing it with three different men. Even Billy and Alison, the nice characters, were doing it, sometimes with each other, sometimes with other people. (Matt, my gay stepfather, didn't do anything bad, but that was because they weren't allowed to show two men kissing on TV.)

With my mother and Doug Savant on the set of Melrose Place.

I had always wondered what grown-ups got up to when they weren't with their kids, and now I knew. To me, *Melrose Place* was an exposé on the secret lives of grown-ups. A little exaggerated at times, maybe—probably in real life there were fewer fights ending in pools—but at its core, I believed it told the truth, and I was scandalized.

"I thought you were only allowed to do it if you were married!" I told my mother.

"I said you *should* only do it if you're married," she said.

But they did it anyway. "Should" meant nothing to them. There was only one conclusion I could make: children were clearly morally superior. Kids could be cruel, but it was simple and reflexive: you're in my way, so I'll push you; you said something I didn't like, so I'll call you stupid. But grown-up cruelty was premeditated, calculated, and clever. Kids, I believed, were virtuous because we didn't have that thing, that invisible, corrupting force that held all grown-ups in its sway: sex.

I wasn't sure if I trusted grown-ups anymore. I began to think they all had ulterior motives. When I started working on *Miracle on 34th Street* a few months later, there was a man on the set who bothered me: a warm, ebullient middle-aged man named Harry. He had a high voice, and he loved to joke with my mother. She would laugh and laugh, and I would worry, because I didn't see her like that with many people. Usually she was the funny one; the only person who really made her laugh was my father. Harry was in love with my mother, I decided, and I didn't trust him—especially not after the time I heard him tell my mother, "Darling, have I ever told you I *adore* you?" It never occurred to me that maybe Harry was not interested in my mother, or in women at all.

A lot of the grown-ups I knew in real life were nice. Most had kids themselves—so they'd *had* sex at one point, of course, but they weren't ruled by it. But others seemed obsessed with it.

When I was six, after I had just finished working on *Melrose Place,* I got sides for a creepy episode of *Picket Fences,* where a third-grade boy and girl hid in a closet to make out. The part was too old for me, anyway, but there was so much detail, just reading it made me uncomfortable. It was obviously written by a sex obsessed grown-up. They didn't kiss the way I had pecked my preschool boyfriend (which was only *after* we'd agreed to get married, and I still felt ashamed about it for years). They kissed deeply, like grown-ups in movies, and at one point the boy "started touching" the girl's chest. It felt wrong to me on several levels, and only seemed worse as I grew up.

People in Hollywood loved bringing kids into that grown-up world. They seemed to find it hilarious. Why else, when I was seven, would a journalist at the *French Kiss* premiere ask me if I knew what a French kiss was? Or the awful CBS News anchor who, on the red carpet at the premiere of *Nine Months,* asked me if I'd heard about Hugh Grant getting arrested.

"I, uh . . . Yes, I heard he was arrested." It was all over the news.

"So what's going on there, huh? What happened? What do you think?"

"I . . ." All I knew was that it had something to do with sex. Suddenly, I felt very small. I looked away, trying to see if I could find my mother. "I don't know."

At the Golden Globes that same year, I was interviewed for an entertainment show known for being a little risqué. The interviewer was a beautiful woman in a tight dress, with perfectly sculpted hair and eyebrows and an unplaceable accent.

"Zo, Mara," she said, "who do you sink iz ze sexiest man here tonight? John Travolta? Johnny Depp? Brad Pitt?" She raised her eyebrows suggestively at that last name. All I knew about Brad Pitt was that my mother thought he was overrated. Her celebrity crush was Anthony Hopkins.

I immediately felt annoyed. What kind of question was that? Who did this woman think I was? Leaning into the mic, I said, with uncharacteristic coolness, "I'm not like that."

Clearly, grown-ups didn't understand how kids thought about sex. To us, sex was gross or it was funny, nothing more. Sure, at every school there was always that one weird kid with his hands down his sweatpants, but surely he didn't understand the implications of what he was doing. Sex is nuanced, and nuance is beyond a kid's comprehension.

There were so many women at the Globes, all wearing so little. One wore a dress that draped loosely over her bust, and with only a glance, I could see her naked breasts.

"You know, Mom," I said, as my mother drove us to Burger King after the show, "the men looked great, but the women need to go home and get dressed!"

She laughed uproariously. "You're absolutely right."

There was only one conclusion to draw: the world was corrupt. Everyone was corrupted. People were showing off their nearly naked bodies, having sex for money, doing it with people whose last names they didn't even know. "Casual sex," they called it—I couldn't even imagine being a "casual kisser." I knew someday I was going to have to have sex (if only because I wanted to have kids), but until then, I was not going to let it get to me. I would never be the flirty, dirty, sex-obsessed kind of grown-up. The only thing more powerful than sex was refusing to let sex have power over you. I was against sex.

* * *

"I think it should be against the law to *do it* with someone you're not married to," I told my mother.

"You can't do that," she said. "You can't control people's lives and bodies like that."

I would do what I could. If it meant being Roosevelt Elementary's one-person Junior Anti-Sex League, I would do it. When Mark MacGregor learned that "banana" could be a euphemism for "penis" and started chasing girls around the schoolyard saying, "I'm the Banana Man!," I went to the adult on yard duty and said, very sternly, "This is not acceptable." After one of the boys I sometimes played with at recess blurted out "You're sexy!" I went straight to my teacher and said, "Carlos said a bad word about me." I spent a lot of time feeling scandalized, and I loved it. There is nothing more fun than being young and judgmental.

"Do you guys know what strippers are?" I asked some of the younger kids who, like me, sat on the bench talking and reading instead of playing during recess. Sets were a good place to pick up all kinds of interesting information.

"No," they said.

"Oh, it's awful," I said. "It's so gross. It's . . . No, I shouldn't tell you."

"No, tell us, tell us!"

"They're women who take their clothes off and dance around while men watch."

They were so bad and wrong, and I couldn't stop thinking about them.

A group of kids would cluster around me every recess to hear about the scourge of nude magazines and exotic dancers. And these were the good kids, the ones who never got "benched" during recess, who got stickers and plus marks on all their papers and ran for class president.

They were as appalled as I was, and as titillated. Sometimes we would even pretend we were fighting the owners of strip clubs and dirty magazines, making the world safe again for kids. The bad guy in my games and stories usually wasn't a guy at all, but a girl who did it with boys.

"Once upon a time, there was a girl—and she was a really bad girl—"

"How bad?"

"Well, she wasn't a virgin," I said.

***

While I might never have admitted it, I was afraid of sex. It was a force greater than anything I could imagine. If anyone other than me was talking about it, I couldn't handle it. My cousin once initiated a conversation about penises ("Aren't they so weird?"), and when I got home I felt so guilty I locked myself in the bathroom and cried. My mother insisted I let her in and demanded to know what was wrong.

"I can't tell you," I said.

"You have to tell your parents everything," she said, so firmly that I wondered if it was an official law.

"Today I talked about stuff I shouldn't have. . . ."

"Is that it?" She was so relieved she almost laughed.

The first time I heard a dirty joke, I nearly went catatonic. I was nine years old and playing with the daughter of one of my grown?up costars. When she asked if I wanted to hear a dirty joke, I assumed she was going to tell me the same punch line Paul Reubens (better known as Pee-wee Herman) had told me when we worked on *Matilda:* "A white horse fell in a mud puddle." ("You wanna hear a clean joke?" said Rhea Perlman, standing nearby. "They hosed him off.") Instead, she told me one involving a little boy, his grown-up teacher, and the punch line "That's not my finger." I had a full-on panic attack.

It was hard to accept that sex wasn't just something bad people did, and it obviously wasn't something just men did, either. Every time I looked at a pregnant woman, I knew what she had been up to a few months earlier. Even my beloved nanny, Shoshanna, had done it. She had come to L.A. with the intention of being an actress, but hadn't had much success breaking into film and TV. The only show she landed was a sleazy dating show, and in a moment of grown-up inconsistency, she'd decided to use our VCR to tape it. She tried to mute it every time they asked something that was "too old" for us, but I heard enough. When the host asked, "So have you ever gotten down to business on a kitchen floor?" I ran out of the room crying. What she had done was against my religion, my own pieced-together theology. Pre marital sex was a sin, and a big one, and big sins meant you wouldn't go to Heaven. What if the Christians were right and Hell really existed?

I worried for Shoshanna's soul until pop culture saved the day: I saw "Like a Virgin" on *Pop Up Video* and learned that more than 90 percent of women had premarital sex. They couldn't *all* be kept out of Heaven. That just seemed like a waste of otherwise perfectly good souls. Still, sex was dirty, and corrupting, and I was going to be one of the 10 percent who stayed pure.

**

Grown-ups said girls matured faster than boys, but even when middle school came I never got taller than the boys, like they said I would, and the boys I knew fully embraced sex long before girls would.

"Did you know," my friend Nicole had told me back in elementary school, "that when a boy thinks about a girl he likes, his *thing* gets hard?"

"Why does it do that?" I had said. What did thinking about girls have to do with it? The mind-body connection was beyond me. To those who grow up without a penis, boners are magic. But what boys did with them—even if I had only a vague idea what that was—was disgusting.

Boys were so careless. Boys with their willies, willy-nilly, shooting semen wherever they pleased. It was why I always wiped the seat carefully every time I used a unisex bathroom: I didn't want the last customer accidentally getting me pregnant.

Boys hit a certain age and became natural perverts. I'd heard they thought about sex every seven seconds, and also every time they touched their belts or put their hands in their pockets. All boys looked at porn. Even my sweet, smart brothers had their stash under the bathroom sink—I'd stumbled on it more than once while looking for the toilet paper. (Nerds to the very end, most of their stash was not magazines, but erotic stories printed off the Internet.) When I met my costar Cody on the set of *Thomas and the Magic Railroad*, I thought he was cute until he said: "Man, the porno mags here in the U.K. are nuts. Not like *Playboy*. *Playboy's* so boring. Here they show *everything*." I was disgusted, but not surprised.

Boys were awful, and I was embarrassed that I was starting to like them.

The summer before middle school had been an enlightening one. In June, when one of my summer camp crushes, Jake, finally took off the baseball cap he had been wearing the whole week and revealed his messy hair, I looked at him and the word "sexy" came to mind. *Don't think that*, I had scolded myself, but it was too late. By August, my world had changed. President Clinton was under fire for having an affair with an intern, the number one hit in the country was "Too Close" by Next, about a guy who gets an erection when a hot girl dances too close to him, and I had slow-danced with two boys at camp.

"Something happens after you turn eleven," I wrote in my diary a month after my eleventh birthday. "You start to like boys. *Really* like boys." I was ready to be boy-crazy. Unfortunately, I had no idea how to flirt. Usually, I behaved the same immature way the boys did, teasing them, mocking them, being aggressive. I had blown my chances with Jake from camp after pouring Pepsi in his hair. I knew it wasn't the way girls were supposed to flirt, but I didn't know what else to do. Boys liked pretty, nice girls, and I was awkward and angry. The last time I had a boy interested in me—besides fans, who didn't know me as a person, and Jacob Hirsch in third grade, who was probably just happy not to be the only Jewish kid in class—had been the aforementioned peck in preschool. Having kissed a boy then didn't seem like such a big deal anymore, and it certainly wasn't shameful. At least I had been able to get some attention.

Back at school, some of the girls were catching up with the boys.

A girl named Christina made out with a boy in front of the school, and Jeanette was dating a sixteen-year-old. T.S.S., I called them. The Slut Squad. I hated them, and made sure everyone knew it.

"Mara," asked my brother Danny, "what do they *do,* exactly?"

"Well, they . . ." They hadn't really done anything to me. Someone told me Christina had made a face at me once when my back was turned, but that was it. They just offended me, the way they strutted around, talking to boys like it was the most natural thing in the world. I didn't want to admit it, but I was jealous. I wanted a boyfriend. I wanted someone's sweaty hand in mine. I wanted to know what it was like to be kissed. French kissed.

At first I kept my urges secret. By eighth grade, though, something had changed. It seemed to happen to all of my friends simultaneously. Not only did we start to notice the physical changes, we embraced them: someone would make a dirty joke, and instead of feeling confused or disgusted, we felt *good*. It felt like a sugar high, but better. Hearts would race, palms would sweat, and bodies would tingle with an overwhelming feeling of anticipation. A wink from the right person, and I was on my own personal roller coaster.

That wasn't to say we actually had sex. For most of us, it was still abstract, even well into high school. For the most part, the people who did were "popular."

I had never been popular. I've heard that Dakota Fanning was homecoming queen and Blake Lively was senior class president, but fame never seemed to work in my favor. It could only be a substitute for good looks and coolness for so long. Kids I met at camp, on vacation, or at new schools would get excited and fawn over me for a day or two. ("So are you like a gazillionaire?" "Have you met Adam Sandler? He should write you into the Hanukkah song!") Then they'd get to know me, realize I was kind of a nerd, and decide I wasn't worth their attention. It usually happened around the time they saw my roller backpack.

***

Aside from a small group of school friends—all girls, except for Alex, my former preschool boyfriend, who later turned out to be gay—the only kids who really understood me were other child actors. At seven I had done a photo shoot for *Disney Adventures* on "Hollywood Kids," and I had never felt so felt accepted. Every one was like me, a little too smart for their age and a little too short, from sweet and pretty Lacey Chabert, to wry and witty Michael Fishman, to energetic and theatrical Adam Wylie, who would have been my make-out partner if I had taken that part in *Picket Fences.*

"You know what today was, Mom?" I said at the end of the day. "It was a pleasure." Except for when I accidentally elbowed Jonathan Taylor Thomas in the crotch.

If I ever got a boyfriend, I figured, he'd probably also be an actor. He probably wouldn't be, like, Disney star or *Malcolm in the Middle* famous, but at least he would understand my world.

✱✱✱

So it was fitting that my first real kiss—or kisses, but I'll get to that later—came on a whitewater rafting trip I went on with a bunch of other child stars. Nearly all the child actors I knew did charity work. Some were naturally sensitive and sought it out themselves, some had gotten perspective on their privilege from it to "ground" them. It was as much a social activity as it was an act of altruism. When I was finishing ninth grade, Patricia, who ran one of the charities, invited me and a couple of other kids on a weekend charity whitewater rafting trip. My parents wouldn't be there. I would be sharing a tent with Chelsea, a Burbank child actress whose sister had been on *Freaks and Geeks,* and a girl named Maxine, who didn't act, but liked charity work and loved hooking up with teen actors. My friends Tim, who had been in *Star Trek* and on *Malcolm in the Middle,* and Nicholas, who always seemed to play "that kid" in "that movie" everyone had heard of but had never seen, would be there. So would a slightly older and unbelievably cute teen actor named Greg, and four members of a boy band called Konniption.

When we arrived on a Friday afternoon, Patricia had the captains gave us a tutorial on how to raft. I listened to them, absently rubbing sunscreen onto my legs. Tim and Nicholas sat nearby.

"Enjoying the view?" I heard Nicholas say. Tim laughed, embarrassed. I followed his eye line and my breath caught in my chest. He had been staring at my legs.

No one had ever looked at me like that before. Not in a way I enjoyed, anyway. Freshman boys would stare at my breasts, and an eleventh grader had looked me up and down while I was wearing my halter?neck show choir dress. Those times, it seemed to happen in slow motion, making me feel both attractive and vulnerable. But this time, it felt unequivocally good. I liked Tim, definitely as a friend and maybe as more than a friend, and I liked feeling his eyes on me. I wanted more.

It was going to be an interesting weekend.

After the raft lessons, we were supposed to be spending time with the recipient kids, the ones we were supposed to be helping, the whole reason for the trip. We did hit it off with one of them, a boy named Darrell, who was our age, but most were much younger than us, and too shy. It was hard to relate.

"What are we supposed to do with them?" I asked Chelsea. She just shrugged. Her eyes were glued to Tim. We had already started to form a group, the three girls, the three boys, and Darrell.

"So which one do you like?" Chelsea whispered to me at breakfast the next morning. "I like Tim. Maxine likes Nicholas."

I thought both Tim and Greg were cute. Darrell was, too, with beautiful eyes, but he had a girlfriend, and even if he hadn't I wasn't sure about the ethics of flirting with a recipient kid. Greg was a little too cocky and a little too hot for his own good, but Chelsea had already staked her claim on Tim.

"Greg," I said.

It didn't matter. We all flirted with one another so much, I'm surprised we actually made it to the river at all.

"Should we tell them?" Chelsea asked when we got back to camp that afternoon, the three of us sitting around a picnic table.

"Tell them what?"

"That we like them." I looked to Maxine. She wasn't going to stop Chelsea, and neither, I realized, was I. At school I would have died if someone revealed a crush of mine, but here it didn't seem to matter.

"So guess what," Chelsea said when the boys came to join us. "We all have crushes on you."

"Maxine likes Nicholas," said Chelsea.

"Chelsea likes Tim," said Maxine. They both looked at me, and I shrugged, giving them the go-ahead.

"And Mara likes Greg," Chelsea added. Tim and Nicholas seemed flattered. Greg seemed unimpressed, giving me a lazy thumbs-up and saying, "Cool."

I knew I should have chosen Tim.

Everything was out in the open now. We climbed into a tent together to talk and cuddle. My legs were on Tim's leg, my arm around Nicholas, my hand in Chelsea's.

"You know," said Tim, "if this were happening anywhere else, I'd be like, 'Oh my God, a *girl* is lying on me,' but here it just feels like it's not a big deal." We all murmured in agreement. There was something special about this place. The grass under the tent might have been grass sod, but we were away from our parents and free to give in to our natural inclinations. Hormones were rushing like the river. It felt so grown up.

"It's like we're adults," I said.

"Yeah, totally," said Chelsea. "Hey, did you know there's a ride at Chuck E. Cheese's that can give a girl an orgasm?"

A round of Truth or Dare was inevitable, and from there we went on to Kill/Marry/Screw.

***

But soon we got tired of hypotheticals. We sent someone out to look for a bottle.

I don't know why we thought we'd never get caught. It wasn't as if our tent—right in the middle of the campsite—was soundproof, and we were loudly egging each other on the whole time, yelling "Kiss him!" "Kiss her!" while Greg blared "Hot in Herre" on repeat on a battery-powered radio he'd brought. The sun had set, and we were high on hormones. Poor Darrell sat watching while the rest of us started with cheek kisses, then mouths, and eventually started making out.

When we stumbled out of the tent for dinner, whispering and giggling, Patricia was standing there, her arms folded over her chest, waiting for us.

"We need to talk," she said, leading us off to a picnic table away from the main campsite. We were suddenly all very quiet. I had never seen Patricia angry. My heart was beating faster than it had all weekend, even faster than when I'd kissed Greg or pressed Tim to me and felt his heart against mine. This was a feeling I knew too well.

"Okay, guys," she said, in clipped tones, "I've been hearing a lot of 'Guess what the *stars* are doing right now!' It's one thing to do this on your own time, but doing it here makes us, as an organization, look bad, and you're making yourselves look bad. It's irresponsible and it's rude."

My eyes filled with tears.

"I'm sorry," I whispered, deeply ashamed.

"Are you going to tell our parents?" said Chelsea.

"It depends," she said. "If you guys straighten up and put some more effort into this—maybe wake up early to clean the campsite tomorrow—then we'll see."

Both Chelsea and I cried through dinner. We had known it wasn't right, but we had done it anyway. We woke up at six to scour the campsite and beg Patricia for forgiveness.

"You won't tell our parents, will you? Please? Mine will kill me."

She still didn't look happy, but she said, "I don't see any reason to." She had an organization to run, and bigger problems to address. I'd heard a rumor that Konniption had been smoking pot in their tent.

Chelsea and I were quiet as her parents drove us back to Burbank. On the ride home from Chelsea's house, my father told me, "You did a good thing this weekend, Mara," and I wanted to cry.

***

Once home, I shut myself in my room and flopped on the bed. All I had left was my guilt. It had all happened so fast. I would never even be able to remember who I had kissed first. Oh my god, I was a casual kisser. This wasn't how I was supposed to spend my weekend. This definitely wasn't how I was supposed to get my first kiss. Why had I done it?

But I knew why. Because it felt good. Because it was exciting. I had finally found something more fun than being judgmental.

I had always known my attitude toward sex would change, but I thought I'd always be able to control my impulses. I thought I could outsmart my instincts. If I were just bright enough and disciplined enough, I thought, I could outwit basic human biology. But I had felt it as much as everybody else there, if not more. In the end, every moralist is a hypocrite.

You've just read an excerpt from Where Am I Now?

ABOUT THE AUTHOR

Mara Wilson is a writer, playwright, actor, and storyteller perhaps best known as the little girl from *Mrs. Doubtfire, Miracle on 34th Street*, and *Matilda*. A graduate of NYU's Tisch School of the Arts, she regularly appears at live storytelling and comedy shows, including her own, *What Are You Afraid Of?*. Her writing can be found on *Jezebel, The Toast, McSweeney's, the Daily Beast*, and *Cracked.com*, and on her blog, MaraWilsonWritesStuff.com. A voice actor on the podcast *Welcome to Night Vale*, she will guest star on upcoming episodes of *Broad City* and *BoJack Horseman*. She lives in New York City.

IMPRINT: Penguin Books
PRINT ISBN: 9780143128229
PRINT PRICE: $16.00
EBOOK ISBN: 9780698407015
EBOOK PRICE: $11.99
PUBLICATION DATE: 9/13/16
PUBLICITY CONTACT: Rebecca Lang rlang@penguinrandomhouse.com
RIGHTS CONTACT: Sabila Khan skhan@penguinrandomhouse.com
EDITOR: Lindsey Schwoeri

AGENT: Alyssa Reuben
AGENCY: Paradigm Literary

PROMOTIONAL INFORMATION:
Author tour; National broadcast, radio and TV satellite tours; National review attention and Off-the-Book-Page features; Online/blog outreach; Cover reveal; ARCs; Online author chat; Book video; Social media outreach; Online advertising.

COPYRIGHT

Buzz Books 2016: Fall/Winter from Publishers Lunch. Copyright © 2016 by Cader Company Inc. All rights reserved.

Print edition ISBN 9780997396003

Excerpts used by permission of the following authors and publishers:

All Our Wrong Todays. Copyright © 2017 by Elan Mastai. Used by permission of Dutton, a division of Penguin Random House.

By Gaslight. Copyright © 2016 by Steven Price. Used by permission of Farrar, Straus and Giroux, a division of Macmillan.

A Change of Heart. Copyright © 2016 by Sonali Dev. Used by permission of Kensington Books.

Christina's World. Copyright © 2017 by Christina Baker Kline. Used by permission of William Morrow, a division of HarperCollins.

The Comet Seekers. Copyright © 2016 by Helen Sedgwick Limited. Used by permission of Harper, a division of HarperCollins.

Commonwealth. Copyright © 2016 by Ann Patchett. Used by permission of Harper, a division of HarperCollins.

The Couple Next Door. Copyright © 2016 by 1742145 Ontario Limited. Used by permission of Viking, a division of Penguin Random House.

Darling Days. Copyright © 2016 by iO Tillet-Wright. Used by permission of Ecco, a division of HarperCollins.

The DNA Restart. Copyright © 2016 by Sharon Moalem, MD, PhD. All rights reserved. Used by permission of Rodale.

Every Man a Menace. Copyright © 2016 by Patrick Hoffman. Used by permission of Atlantic Monthly Press, an imprint of Grove Atlantic.

The Fire By Night. Copyright © 2016 by Teresa Messineo. Used by permission of William Morrow, a division of HarperCollins.

Generation Chef. Copyright © 2016 by Karen Stabiner. Used by permission of Avery, a division of Penguin Random House.

A Gentleman in Moscow. Copyright © 2016 by Cetology, Inc. Used by permission of Viking, a division of Penguin Random House.

The Gentleman. Copyright © 2016 by Forrest Leo. Used by permission of Penguin Press, a division of Penguin Random House.

Hidden Figures. Copyright © 2016 by Margot Lee Shetterly. Used by permission of William Morrow, a division of HarperCollins.

History of Wolves. Copyright © 2017 by Emily Fridlund. Used by permission of Atlantic Monthly Press, an imprint of Grove Atlantic.

I Will Send Rain. Copyright © 2016 by Rae Meadows. Used by permission of Henry Holt and Company, a division of Macmillan.

Les Parisiennes. Copyright © 2016 by Anne Sebba. Used by permission of St. Martin's Press, a division of Macmillan.

Little Nothing. Copyright © 2016 by Marisa Silver. Used by permission of Blue Rider Press, a division of Penguin Random House.

Lucky Boy. Copyright © 2016 Shanthi Sekaran. Used by permission of Putnam, a division of Penguin Random House.

Marrow. Copyright © 2016 by Elizabeth Lesser. Used by permission of Harper Wave, a division of HarperCollins.

Mercury. Copyright © 2016 by Margot Livesey. Used by permission of Harper, a division of HarperCollins.

Mischling. Copyright © 2016 by Affinity Konar. Used by permission of Lee Boudreaux Books/ Little, Brown and Company, a division of Hachette Book Group.

The Mothers. Copyright © 2016 by Brit Bennett. Used by permission of Riverhead, a division of Penguin Random House.

News of the World. Copyright © 2016 by Paulette Jiles. Used by permission of William Morrow, a division of HarperCollins.

The Next. Copyright © 2016 by Stephanie Gangi. All rights reserved. Used by permission of St. Martin's Press, a division of Macmillan.

The Nix. Copyright © 2016 by Nathan Hill. Used by permission of Alfred A. Knopf, an imprint of The Knopf Doubleday Publishing Group, a division of Penguin Random House LLC.

No Witness But the Moon. Copyright © 2016 by Suzanne Chazin. Used by permission of Kensington Books.

The One Man. Copyright © 2016 by Andrew Gross. Used by permission of Minotaur, a division of Macmillan.

Only Daughter. Copyright © 2016 by Anna Elizabeth Snoekstra. Used by permission of Harlequin Mira.

The Orphan's Tale. Copyright © 2017 by Pam Jenoff. Used by permission of Harlequin Mira.

The Other Einstein. Copyright © 2016 by Marie Benedict. Used by permission of Sourcebooks Landmark.

The Terranauts. Copyright © 2016 T.C. Boyle. Used by permission of Ecco, a division of HarperCollins.

Things We Have In Common. Copyright © 2015 by Tasha Kavanagh. First published by Canongate Books, 2015. This edition published by Harlequin Mira, 2017. Used by permission of Harlequin Mira.

Today Will Be Different. Copyright © 2016 by Maria Semple. Used by permission of Little, Brown and Company, a division of Hachette Book Group.

Truevine. Copyright © 2016 by Beth Macy. Used by permission of Little, Brown and Company, a division of Hachette Book Group.

The Wangs vs. the World. Copyright © 2016 by Jade Chang. Used by permission of by permission of Houghton Mifflin Harcourt Publishing Company. All rights reserved.

We Are Unprepared. Copyright © 2016 by Margaret Reilly. Used by permission of Harlequin Mira.

When in French. Copyright © 2016 by Lauren Collins. Used by permission of Penguin Press, a division of Penguin Random House.

Where Am I Now? Copyright © 2016 by Mara Wilson. Used by permission of Penguin Books, a division of Penguin Random House.

The World is Reading

Imagine the Possibilities

PUBLISHERS

Tens of thousands of publishers worldwide trust Ingram to get their content into the hands of more readers worldwide. Everything under the sun a publisher needs to reach more readers and sell more books with speed and efficiency. All the most in-demand formats for more diverse revenue stream.

RETAILERS

Supply backed by speed. The faster you can meet demand the more likely you are to make repeat customers. Not only does Ingram have a huge selection of books, but we also have more distribution points across the globe for fast, reliable order fulfillment that keeps you happy and your customers happier.

EDUCATORS

From textbooks to digital courseware, Ingram connects educators, students, administrators, and researchers to the most relevant and innovative content in the world. With smarter services for academic institutions, Ingram's VitalSource spells success in today's quickly evolving educational environment.

LIBRARIES

The support libraries around the world need in their mission to offer patrons easy access to the right books, right when they want them. Our library services are built upon the belief that libraries are more than a depository for books, but critical community centers, where education and information thrive.

VISIT INGRAM AT BOOTH #929

www.ingramcontent.com/BEA

INGRAM.